THE PORTABLE
Matthew Arnold

EDITED BY

LIONEL TRILLING

PENGUIN BOOKS

Penguin Books Ltd, Harmondsworth,
Middlesex, England
Penguin Books, 625 Madison Avenue,
New York, New York 10022, U.S.A.
Penguin Books Australia Ltd, Ringwood,
Victoria, Australia
Penguin Books Canada Limited, 2801 John Street,
Markham, Ontario, Canada L3R 1B4
Penguin Books (N.Z.) Ltd, 182–190 Wairau Road,
Auckland 10, New Zealand

First published in the United States of America by
The Viking Press 1949
First published in Canada by
The Macmillan Company of Canada Limited 1949
Paperbound edition published 1951
Reprinted 1959, 1960, 1962, 1963, 1966 (three times),
1968, 1972, 1973
Published in Penguin Books 1980

LIBRARY OF CONGRESS CATALOGING IN PUBLICATION DATA
Arnold, Matthew, 1822–1888.
The portable Matthew Arnold.
Reprint of the 1949 ed. published by Viking Press,
New York, which was issued as no. 45 of the Viking
portable library.
Bibliography: p. 34.
I. Trilling, Lionel, 1905–1975. II. Title.
PR4021.T68 1980   821'.8   80-11582
ISBN 0 14 015.045 5

Printed in the United States of America by
Kingsport Press, Inc., Kingsport, Tennessee
Set in Caledonia

CONTENTS

v

CRITICISM

POLITICS

LETTERS

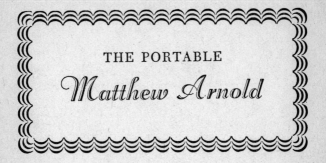

THE PORTABLE

Matthew Arnold

INTRODUCTION

OF THE literary men of the great English nineteenth century there are few who have stayed
quite so fresh, so immediate, and so relevant as Matthew
Arnold. It is not entirely easy to understand why this
should be so. For, as we usually judge power, Arnold is
not the most powerful of his contemporaries—he does
not make anything like, say, Carlyle's bold and dramatic
claim upon our attention. Nor does he hold his position
by reason of a massive and ranging body of work. His
poetical canon is relatively small; and of this canon it
must be said that some of its most ambitious items are
failures, and that, although almost every one of Arnold's
poems is in some way interesting, only a few are perfect
in their kind. Of his more extensive prose works, a considerable part—that which deals with religion—is likely
to be disregarded by modern readers, not because of its
subject but because of its way of dealing with its subject. His writing on literature and politics was carried
on in the free moments allowed him by his burdened
life as a civil servant, and the larger part of it consists
of occasional essays and lectures, forms which do not
easily establish their authority.

And then there is but little in Arnold's life story to
lend an extraneous interest to his work. He expressed
the wish that no biography of him be written. None has
been, and perhaps none can be, for the memorials of his

1

life, either by his own design or by that of his family, are sparse; his letters, with certain important exceptions, are not intimately revelatory; there are not many anecdotes about him in his maturity and those which do exist are pleasant but not especially pungent. The evidence of his poems and of certain of his letters seems to point to his having had an unhappy and significant love affair in his youth, but the Marguerite of his poems is no more to be identified than the Lucy of Wordsworth's. He very seldom uttered an autobiographical word, for he had, and declared, the intention of hiding his life. We know of great personal griefs most bravely borne; we know that, admiring gaiety, he was often sad; but we have no sense with him of the kind of tragic stress which marked the lives of so many of his contemporaries. It is true that if we are interested in him as a mind we can scarcely fail to see him as a person with unusual clearness, for nothing was ever reported of him personally that was at variance with the impression he makes in his writing. But our sense of him, though it may be firm, is never dramatic, never pointed up by anything in his conduct the least strange or unusual. A friend said in praise of Arnold that he had less personality than any man he had ever known: it was not our present sense of the word "personality" that Jowett intended—he meant that there was no impulse in Arnold to make any special claim for himself, or to call attention to himself, or to ask for any indulgence.

All this being so, the fact becomes the more striking that Arnold stands so solidly at the center of his age and is so important there, and, further, that he should be not merely a historically significant figure but a person whose living influence continues for so long a time after his age has become history. As a poet he reaches us not more powerfully but, we sometimes feel, more intimately than any other. As a critic he provided us with the essential terms for our debate in matters of taste and judgment. He established criticism as an intellectual discipline among the people of two nations and set its best tone. Wherever English-speaking people discuss literature as it does its work in the world, literature in its relation to the fate of man and nations, the name of Matthew Arnold appears, not always for agreement but always for reference. And where there is disagreement the generous-minded will in effect repeat what Gerard Manley Hopkins said in correction of Robert Bridges when the latter made a derogatory remark about Arnold: "I have more reason than you for disagreeing with him and thinking him very wrong, but nevertheless I am sure he is a rare genius and a great critic."

II

If we look for the reason of Arnold's continuing importance, we are not likely to find it in his talents alone, great as these are, but rather in the power of the tradition which he consciously undertook to continue and transmit. For our time, in England and America, Arnold is the great continuator and transmitter of the tradition of humanism.

The definitions of humanism are many, but let us here take it to be the attitude of those men who think it an advantage to live in society, and, at that, in a complex and highly developed society, and who believe that man fulfills his nature and reaches his proper stature in this circumstance. The personal virtues which humanism cherishes are intelligence, amenity, and tolerance; the particular courage it asks for is that which is exercised in the support of these virtues. The qualities of intelligence which it chiefly prizes are modulation and flexibility—it wants the mind to be, in the words of Montaigne which Arnold admired, *ondoyant et divers*.

The aspects of society that humanism most exalts are justice and continuity. That is why humanism is always being presented with a contradiction. For when it speaks of justice it holds that the human condition is absolute; yet when it speaks of continuity it implies that society is not absolute but pragmatic and even anomalous. Its intelligence dictates the removal of all that is anomalous; yet its ideal of social continuity is validated by its perception that the effort to destroy anomaly out of hand will probably bring new and even worse anomalies, the nature of man being what it is. "Let justice be done though the heavens fall" is balanced by awareness of the likelihood that after the heavens have fallen justice will not ever be done again. Hence the humanistic belief, often delusive, that society can change itself gradually by taking thought and revising sensibility. Hence too the humanistic valuation, possibly overvaluation, of discourse and letters.

For the elements of this tradition, wherever they were to be found, Matthew Arnold reached out with both hands—to Greece and Rome; to ancient India; to the Renaissance; to the *Éclaircissement* of France and the *Aufklärung* of Germany and to the continuation of these movements in contemporary Europe; to Plato, Aristotle, the *Bhagavad Gita*, Dante, Montaigne, Spinoza, Lessing, Goethe, Heine, Leopardi, Wordsworth, Emerson. For all the sophistication of his mind, he had what must seem to us an almost primitive belief in "wisdom." The written phrase that enshrined the discovered truth was almost magical to him. "Sayings" meant more to him than we can easily understand; he kept pocket diaries in which for each week he wrote down someone's formulated truth on which he—it is hard for us to understand this—meditated. It was as if he were obeying as literally as he might the commandment to fasten the truth upon the doorpost of his house and upon his hand and to set it as a frontlet between his eyes. Such was his belief in the power of thought, in the strength of the human continuity, in the possibility of the community of mind.

He had, we might say, a kind of passion for society. Yet beneath the social passion, giving meaning to what lay above, was the pain of a great loneliness. Indeed, Arnold's love of society and of the idea of social wholeness may be said to have sprung from his isolation. Strong as his social emotions were, he seems always to have been aware, often with great pain, of the sacrifices that are made to society. He knows that the social bonds, although they hold men safe, do not allow men easily to turn to look at themselves, let alone at each other; and although he knows that the self cannot develop without society, he knows too that the development comes at the cost of a painful pruning. In common with many men of the nineteenth-century generations, he had a sense of what is forced underground and into silence or unconsciousness.

> But often, in the world's most crowded streets,
> But often, in the din of strife,
> There rises an unspeakable desire
> After the knowledge of our buried life . . .

And again:

> Below the surface-stream, shallow and light,
> Of what we *say* we feel—below the stream,
> As light, of what we *think* we feel—there flows

With noiseless current strong, obscure and deep,
The central stream of what we feel indeed.

The sense of isolation, of isolation even from the true self, perhaps lies at the heart of the humanistic exaltation of society. Molière, after preaching social measure and amenity all his life, conceived the Misanthrope, and no insistence on social doctrine that Molière may make can convince us that he does not largely love this man who breaks the social concord to speak his mind, and it is exactly his author's love that makes Alceste's punishment so real. It was no academic theory, as people even of his own time were pleased to think, that dictated Arnold's devotion to the Greek tragic poets; rather was it their brilliant sense of the terror of loneliness. They were fascinated by the man who is set apart from other men by his fate or his own misguided will: Ajax or Oedipus or Philoctetes; or Achilles and Priam, each solitary under his doom, yet able for a moment to meet—the most terrible and most beautiful instant of community that literature has recorded—in the equal and courteous society of grief. And Arnold lived in an age when—it is one of the clichés of cultural history—man was becoming increasingly aware of loneliness. For the Romantic poets, who are the poets Arnold read in his boyhood and youth, the characteristic situation is that of the isolated individual who seeks to enter some communion. The isolation was felt to be not only social but also cosmic. The universe had undergone disruptive changes which the poets from Schiller through Leopardi to D. H. Lawrence have deplored, and in terms which do not much vary; science, they all tell us, has emptied the haunted air and demonstrated a universe in which man is a stranger. It is this double loneliness that makes Arnold's humanism, which was his response to isolation, so complete and so personally stamped.

Of the humanism that Arnold established for himself and tried to hand on to others, we must observe that it was active and not passive, that it was never a mere attitude, as humanism can indeed all too easily become —as for example when it sets itself up genteelly, as once it used to do, in the English departments of American universities. Arnold's humanism was never abstract, nor content with fighting a rearguard action. It carried its ark into battle and tested itself in the squabbles of the marketplace even while it said that squabbles and marketplaces did not encourage wisdom. It did what any idea must do, it looked to justification by results and took its chances. That is why Arnold must have for us something of the character of what we nowadays have taken to calling a "culture hero": that is, a man who gives himself in full submission and sacrifice to his historical moment in order to comprehend and control the elements which that moment brings. (As in tragic literature, as in general life, so in the life of intellect the heroic status does not depend upon the hero's material and effective success.)

III

This identification with a great tradition will perhaps account for Arnold's continuing interest, will explain why he, the least monumental of men, stands before us with a kind of monumental endurance and clearness. And yet anyone who has any sensitivity at all to the temper of our own time, and who yet undertakes to bring Arnold again to public notice at this moment, must experience at least one qualm of diffidence. If Arnold is established by his continuation and transmission of a great tradition, still we must see that our intellectual and emotional temper is now anything but cordial to humanism—has not, really, been cordial to humanism for some decades.

Humanism in modern Europe has long been identified with the bourgeoisie. Arnold himself made that identification in the sense that it was particularly to the middle class that he wanted to transmit the humanist tradition. He believed that the great intellectual work to be done in his time was with the middle class. This belief did not arise from any great admiration for this class, which, indeed, filled him with despair and which he treated mercilessly. But he thought that the middle class would take the leadership in the next great events of culture and politics and he wished to reform and enlighten it for the right performance of its historic role. The whole intention of Arnold's criticism was to increase the consciousness and imagination of this class, to give it a sense of the way the world goes and should go. Yet the middle class, where nowadays it exists at all—and on the continent of Europe it has probably ceased to exist in the historic sense—is not likely to respond to the humanist ideal. To be flexible and various in mind can scarcely be thought to be a present ideal of the democratic bourgeoisie. Tocqueville has set forth the reasons why democratic thought is not easily flexible and various, why, indeed, it is likely to become set and monolithic, and, in the end, stand in danger of being easily dominated. And even when the democratic bourgeoisie becomes dissatisfied with its own cultural condition, it is not nowadays inclined to make its protest in the name of humanism. For some decades now, that part of the middle class which protests has been losing its love of society, which, as it feels, has betrayed it. We have all in some degree become anarchistic. Sometimes the anarchism takes the form of admiration of or acquiescence in extreme forms of authoritarianism; a large part of the intellectual, liberal bourgeoisie no longer dislikes authoritarianism if only it is not called by its right name. More often our anarchism takes the more diffused form of disgust with the very idea of society. On the upper levels of our taste this disgust is expressed for us by Baudelaire, Rimbaud, Celine, and Kafka; on a lower level of taste by the details of our middle-grade fiction; and we can of course see the continuation of this taste for disgust in the popular and commercial art of our time. Disgust is expressed by violence, and it is to be noted of our intellectual temper that violence is a quality which is felt to have a peculiar intellectual sanction. Our preference, even as articulated by those who are most mild in their persons, is increasingly for the absolute and extreme, of which we feel violence to be the true sign. The gentlest of us will know that the tigers of wrath are to be preferred to the horses of instruction and will consider it an intellectual cowardice to take into account what happens to those who ride tigers. It is apposite that a book club which undertakes to protect its members from sordid novels should nevertheless advertise itself as not intending to purvey mere "sweetness and light," using the phrase which has come to be identified with Arnold and which has always been used as a stick with which to beat him, although indeed the phrase is not Arnold's at all but was borrowed by him from Jonathan Swift.

Swift is much in point here, for Swift had all the disgust and violence which we nowadays admire. They came to him, I believe, in a harder way than they come to our contemporary heroes of the spirit—his was a harder soul than theirs, more masculine, more resistant; he speaks from a larger, firmer, more specific experience of the world; he fought his madness and did not love it, feared it and did not make it a shamanistic distinction; he experienced disgust—no man more—but he cherished his indignation, thus affirming his sense of the attainable order of society, the loss of which had engendered his disgust, and he affirmed his connection with a type of humanity which, on the evidence of certain spirits of the past, he believed to be possible. All this makes Swift's expression of revulsion from human life and society far more worthy of notice than any recent expression of the same judgment. And what in effect is the reason for Swift's disgust with mankind, the reason he everywhere implies? Is it not the refusal of men to live by the virtues of humanism, to live reasonably in society, to seek order, to furnish themselves with, in Swift's own words, "the two noblest of things, sweetness and light"? The extremity of our own situation has led us to love extremity in ourselves, for men tend to adopt the nature of whatever overawes and oppresses them. But as Arnold says, "one gains nothing on the darkness by being . . . as incoherent as the darkness itself"—one gains nothing on the catastrophe by being as violent as the catastrophe itself. Arnold spoke quietly, and as if to his near equals, and without wrath: is it some deep ineradicable childishness in us, some recollection of the authenticity of the father's anger, that we prefer not to listen unless we are spoken to in wrath and that we do not believe what does not humiliate us?

IV

Matthew Arnold was born on December 24, 1822. At the time of his birth, his father Thomas Arnold was not yet famous; he was a young and unknown clergyman who lived in the little town of Laleham on the Thames and supported a growing family by receiving into his home young gentlemen whom he coached for entrance to the universities. Mary Penrose Arnold, Matthew's mother, was the daughter of a clerical family of some distinction.

Every family constructs a mythology of its talents and qualities and among the Arnolds it was accepted that Matthew derived his poetic gifts from his mother. She was of Cornish blood, and the people of Cornwall, being Celtic, are said to have a lively impulse to the life of the imagination. It needed—so the friends of the family felt—a strong poetical disposition from the mother to overcome the paternal strain, for the opinion was general that Thomas Arnold was the least poetical of men. The opinion was a just one only up to a point, for although it was true that Thomas Arnold was not hospitable to poetry and felt that it made too much of small things, yet his work as a historian is often marked by a high and sometimes subtle imagination.

From his mother too, Matthew seems to have inherited a certain affectation of manner, a touch of conscious elegance, which was always observed of him from youth through maturity. In 1851 Charlotte Brontë met the mother and son together and seems to have been troubled by them: "Mrs. Arnold . . . is a good and amiable woman, but the intellectual is not her forte, and she has no pretensions to power or completeness of character. . . . Those who have only seen Mrs. Arnold once will necessarily, I think, judge of her unfavorably; her manner on introduction disappointed me sensibly, as lacking that genuineness and simplicity one seemed to have a right to expect in the chosen life companion of Dr. Arnold. . . . It is observable that Matthew Arnold, the eldest son, and the author of the volume of poems . . . inherits his mother's defect. Striking and prepossessing in appearance, his manner displeases from its seeming foppery. I own it caused me at first to regard him with regretful surprise: the shade of Dr. Arnold seemed to me to frown on his young representative." In a letter of two years later Matthew Arnold remembers Charlotte Brontë as having a mind which "contains nothing but hunger, rebellion, and rage"—it could not have been a happy meeting. Yet Miss Brontë qualified her judgment in the same letter, for she spoke of the "real modesty" which "ere long . . . appeared under the assumed conceit," as well as what she calls the "genuine intellectual aspirations" and the "high educational acquirements"; and Arnold eventually made amends for his hard feelings by celebrating all the Brontës in his poem "Haworth Churchyard."

Arnold himself was aware of his "seeming foppery" and knew that it made difficulty for him. Writing of his bride to a friend who has not yet met her he says, "You'll like my Lucy; she has all my sweetness and none of my airs." The sweetness was his mother's too—she was a woman much loved and when her husband died at an early age his friends and pupils were devoted to Mrs. Arnold not merely for her husband's sake but for her own. Nor was Charlotte Brontë's estimate of her intelligence correct; Matthew's letters to her are as between intellectual equals and we have other attestations of her knowledge and good sense.

The fame of the son has now far surpassed that of the father, but Thomas Arnold was in his time one of the most notable men of England. We think of him now chiefly as the Headmaster of Rugby School, one of the best-remembered of educators, for good or bad the reformer and establisher of upper-class English schooling. But in the thirties of the last century, although his educational reforms were widely known, his reputation rested not so much on these as upon his social, historical, and religious writings. He was a man of bold and dramatic personality; he had great gifts of attraction and great powers of domination; his influence upon his pupils was so intense as sometimes to constitute a danger to their emotional and intellectual lives; from his associates of equal age, when he did not evoke hostility, he received a deep devotion; and his memory was a lively one long after he had died.

Nowadays we are likely to know Thomas Arnold almost wholly through Lytton Strachey's famous essay in *Eminent Victorians*. Strachey had a constitutional dislike of the effective character, particularly of the effective character in his own upper middle class, and he held the belief that inner contradictions of personality, or even normal complexity, constituted hypocrisy. Like so many members of his intellectual group, he is made uncomfortable by nothing so much as by a paternal figure, and Thomas Arnold was, above all else, a father. There is a degree of justification, therefore, in Strachey's making the headmastership of Rugby the center of the life of Thomas Arnold, who saw himself as the father-ruler, the lawgiver under God, of a boy-nation which he sought to elevate to self-government. This is indeed the paradigm of Thomas Arnold's political and historical thought, but he did not spend his life repeating the paradigm.

He was a man of great administrative gifts. Beyond his taking over the decayed Rugby School and making it the most orderly and influential school of his day, these talents never had full play. But he dreamed administration and thought of government as a holy art. At a time when the affairs of the Church were at the center of English political and intellectual life, he was a leader of English thought because he projected a close and vital connection between Church and State and a thorough reform of both. He was a historian of parts and passion, and he looked at the condition of England with the wisdom that history can sometimes give. Like his son after him he saw anarchy in the offing, England at the point of becoming prey to class conflict, the outcome of which he believed would be dictatorship. He saw, and was right in seeing, that the Church of England had lost influence with the large mass of people, that it had become aristocratic and exclusive and remote, quite unable to conceive and meet the new social conditions that had followed upon the Industrial Revolution. He projected a Church which should be truly national in the sense of including Protestant Christians of all sects, and which should take upon itself an ultimate social responsibility, seeing to the physical and intellectual as well as the spiritual and moral well-being of the people. His dream of a liberal and inclusive Church—"Broad Church" was the name by which it was usually called—which should occupy itself with so large a welfare brought him into conflict with the High Church party, which was Tory in politics, and particularly with that group of the High Church party which called itself Tractarian, the group led by Keble—Matthew's godfather and once Thomas Arnold's close friend—by Pusey, and by Newman. These men of the Oxford movement with their strong affinity with Patristic Christianity, with dogma, and even with Rome, rejected the social emphasis which Thomas Arnold insisted on and his joining the function of the Church with that of the State, which they feared the more because of the increasingly liberal and anti-ecclesiastical bias of the nation. In a day when religious matters were sure to be of immediate moment to all thinking people, the issues of politics and society were debated, and often brilliantly, in the context of religion. The terms of the debate, which are of course old in England, have left their mark on English social and political thought

up to the present day, and evidence of them is everywhere to be found in the writing of Thomas Arnold's
son.

v

Every man's biography is to be understood in relation
to his father, but from a father so strong, so decisive, so
successful, so fully a father as Thomas Arnold was, we
must expect a more than usual determination of the
son's life. And Mr. W. H. Auden, in an interesting sonnet, has spoken of Matthew Arnold's thrusting his poetic
gift into jail in order to prevent any contradiction of his
father's "holy final word." But before this happened—if
indeed it happened so—Matthew Arnold's response to
his father was an inverse one, as Charlotte Brontë saw.
He would not be earnest, he would not be serious in the
manner of the gifted model schoolboys with whom his
father's name was to be associated. Partly for discipli-
nary reasons, his father sent him for a year to his own
old strict school, Winchester, and there Matthew got
himself into trouble with his schoolmates by airily remarking to the headmaster in their hearing that he found
the work of his form quite light. When he came to
Rugby the following year he seems to have resisted the
notorious moral pressure of the place, although his close
friends were the notable boys who responded so entirely
to Dr. Arnold. Among these was Arthur Hugh Clough,
whose gifts and charm could not prevail against the
Rugby conscience which had been implanted in him and
which, working on a mind too sensitive and too literal, in
effect ruined his life.

The matter of his father's influence came to issue
when Matthew went to Oxford. There is no more engaging picture in all the personal history of English lit-

erature than that of the undergraduate Arnold. He was a strikingly handsome youth, with bold features and a fine head of hair of which he was to be vain up to his last years and which he then wore too long and anointed with French lotions. He was remarkable for his dress, which was likely to draw the judgment of foppishness. He liked to laugh, he liked to win laughter, and he was a great contriver of hoaxes. "We arrived here on Friday evening," runs the letter of a friend of his, "after sundry displays of the most consummate coolness on the part of our friend Matt, who pleasantly induced a belief into the passengers of the coach that I was a poor mad gentleman and he was my keeper." He read widely and without orthodoxy and he did not keep up his college work. When he joined a vacation reading party in 1844 he did his best to disrupt or to ignore it. "M. has gone out fishing when he ought properly to be working," Clough wrote to a friend, and there is another letter in which Clough touchingly complains of fatigue from unremitting work—he has been trying to make-pace for Arnold and has not dared to relax in the least for fear Arnold should stop entirely. The result was that, for all Arnold's admitted brilliance, he took his degree at Balliol with only second-class honors. His friends were disappointed but not surprised.

There was more than youthful high spirits in this conduct and his friends knew it. They were eventually to complain that Arnold was cold and remote; his irony and humor kept them at a distance and he seemed not to take them seriously. On at least one occasion Arnold felt it necessary to deny that he lacked affection for his friends. "I laugh too much and [my friends] make one's laughter mean too much," he said. Yet the truth is inescapable that Arnold, for all the actual warmth of his affection, did wish to keep his friends at a distance. The letters which he wrote to Clough say as much and give the reasons. Arnold was in process of becoming a poet—he was one already, for many of the poems of his first volume were written in one form or another in his Oxford days. He felt that the influence of his friends was harmful to his poetic powers. The friends were most intelligent and intellectual, most moral and most earnest. They were charged and overcharged with a sense of their duty in politics and religion and they nagged and worried their minds on all matters. Some were the products of Rugby, and the Rugby type was now distinguishable and well known at Oxford; others were simply decent responsible young men of the upper middle class with a sense of a part to play in the life of the nation. Arnold loved and respected them, but he had conceived that the poet does not live as they do, cannot possibly develop as a poet if he consents to the restless exercise of his intellect alone. He needs, rather, what Keats called in a famous phrase, "Negative Capability"—"that is, when a man is capable of being in uncertainties, mysteries, doubts, without any irritable reaching after fact and reason."

Arnold's letters to Clough, of which this volume contains a sizable selection, make one of the most interesting critical and psychological documents of the century as well as the best possible introduction to Arnold's life and poetry and thought. The young poet tries to explain to his earnest and intellectual friend—himself a poet in a modest and attractive way—that in poetry the surface is everything, that the poet thinks by means of images, that he cannot sustain, let alone accommodate in his poetry in a direct way, the restless intellectuality which characterizes modernity—this can only wear out his feelings and dry up in him the instinctual springs. He struggles to make clear to Clough that the poet does not express ideas but rather makes objects which by their shape and texture are meaningful enough, are ultimately meaningful, but which do not *contain* meaning as a box contains eggs. "You are a mere d——d depth hunter in poetry," he tells Clough when Clough is unable to find pleasure in Racine's *Phèdre,* presumably because he could find no ideas in it. But Arnold never could make Clough understand, and although we cannot quite say that it was a difference over aesthetics that attenuated their once-intimate friendship, still this aesthetic difference represented a crucial difference of personality and of response to the cultural situation that confronted them. Clough's search for certainty, his insistence upon an absolute and literal—and sometimes trifling—honesty ruined his career and, as Arnold felt, killed him. Arnold himself was fighting for his life as a poet and possibly for something more than that, and it is not extravagant to say that his dispute with Clough was in effect his dispute with his father. He was not dealing with ideas merely, but with his very heart. He knew that it was threatened by the intellectual and emotional temper of his age, and he fought, with fine intelligence, to save it. He himself was to believe that he had not succeeded. "I am past thirty," he writes to Clough, "and three parts iced over."

Arnold—it is most relevant to mention it here—grew up in the great shadow of Wordsworth, for Dr. Arnold had built a summer home at Fox How in Westmorland, which made the Arnolds near neighbors and eventually close friends of the Wordsworths. The old poet had been fond of Matthew and had followed his career with affectionate interest. In 1850 Wordsworth died and in the same year *The Prelude* appeared. No record exists of conversations between the old poet and the young, yet the matter that Arnold was debating with Clough was the very matter of Wordsworth's great poem, whose sub-

title is "The Growth of a Poet's Mind"; the drama of
The Prelude is the submission of Wordsworth's mind to
William Godwin's intellectualizing, the loss of his early
powers of imagination, the eventual recovery of these
powers by the revival of the instinctual life which is the
source of true knowledge. Arnold was to lose the poetic
powers of his youth, not wholly but in large part. But his
youthful struggle on their behalf was a great act and one
that is relevant to the spiritual situation of not his own
time alone.

VI

Arnold took his degree in 1844. In the following year
he recouped the second class by being elected a Fellow
of Oriel, a considerable honor and one in which Wordsworth, as we are told, took pleasure for his young friend.
In the interval he taught classics in the fifth form at
Rugby. His father had died suddenly in 1842, and
Rugby, under a new and inferior headmaster, depressed
him by its tone and routine and he writes of it irritably
and irreverently. As a master at his old school he maintained his college ways—there is an elaborate story of
his calling on a fellow master who was primly entertaining the strait-laced parents of a pupil; Arnold talked
dogs and horses like a sporting character until the parents were aghast at the moral tone of the Rugby masters
and in particular of Dr. Arnold's unregenerate son. Thus
the outward young man—but in 1846, during a visit to
France, he went to see the country described by George
Sand in her novels which he then passionately admired
and he wrote and asked permission to call at Nohant;
George Sand received him with kindness and simplicity;
Chopin "with his wonderful eyes" was of the company;
thirty years later, the year of her death, he learned from

John Morley, who had had it from Renan, that his hostess had said that her English visitor had reminded her of *"un Milton jeune et voyageant."*

In 1847 Arnold accepted the post of private secretary to Lord Lansdowne, a political peer, and for two years he touched the world of politics, power, and social distinction. In 1849 he published his first volume of verse, *The Strayed Reveller, and Other Poems;* a second volume appeared in 1852, *Empedocles on Etna and Other Poems.* Both were signed only with the initial A. and both were almost immediately withdrawn after publication and before more than a few copies had been sold. Despite the reticent signature, the authorship of the poems was scarcely a secret, but it was almost wholly a surprise, for the verse was not what had been expected of the young political secretary who was known for his good looks, his dandyism, and his airy manners. Seriousness of the severest kind marked these poems, and a deeply felt sadness. The two volumes were not well received by the press and on the whole they were not understood; their "difficulty" was often commented on. Readers with a special interest in poetry knew that this was a new and distinct voice; William Rossetti, for example, said as much in *The Germ,* but this was the response of the "little magazine" culture of the time. The more conventional and powerful press sensed chiefly the cultural subversiveness of Arnold's sadness and scolded him for not being at one with the energy and optimism of the age. The tone of this criticism was of the most provincial sort, often marked by a dull facetiousness—in the nineteenth century the respectable press of England was, in regard to literary criticism, very little better than that of the United States in the same period and very similar in tone. Arnold became the poet to be discovered by the "intellectuals"—they were then perhaps less remote from the general reader than they are now—and his reputation as a poet was of slow growth.

The *Empedocles* volume contains many poems which have reference to a love affair, an unhappy one, whose heroine bears or is given the name Marguerite; the tone of these poems suggests that they do not deal with a mere fiction but refer to an actual incident in Arnold's life. The nationality of the woman in question—she was French—and the place of meeting—Switzerland—are explicit; and her temperament and past, which provide the reason for the separation, are suggested quite precisely. A few sentences in the letters to Clough seem to support the factuality of the relationship, but beyond this there is no known evidence in its support. In 1851 Arnold married Frances Lucy Wightman, the daughter of Sir William Wightman, judge on the Queen's Bench.

The prospect of marriage made it necessary to find a means of support, which, at that time in England, was not an easy matter for a young writer of the upper middle class who, by reason of the sort of thing he wrote, could not hope to live by his pen; Arnold has for us the special interest of being one of the first of modern writers who undertook to maintain, by means extraneous to literature, both a literary career and a respectable life in the world. His chief, Lord Lansdowne, procured him a post in the Education Department as an inspector of schools. It was dreadful work for a poet, requiring long hours of travel, long days in overheated or drafty schools, solitary dinners at bad inns and hotels, long evenings in provincial hotel rooms reading examination papers. It took a great toll of his energies, leaving him but little impulse and but little time for poetical composition, yet he did not complain except as any man complains of a wearisome job. Some of his finest and most characteristic verse was written during the long period of his inspectorship, but the amount of it is all too small.

When Arnold took his post he had no interest whatever in popular education, but it was inevitable that his interest should grow. As his abilities became apparent to his superiors he was given increased responsibilities, notably the investigation of the educational practices of the Continent, and for this purpose he was sent on several missions. Eventually the problems of education took an important place in his thought and he became a leading authority on the subject. It is impossible not to regret the curtailment of his poetic life that Arnold's educational work brought about; yet it is equally impossible not to find a notable heroism and an antique propriety in a poet thus involving himself with the civic life.

In 1857 Arnold was elected to the Professorship of Poetry at Oxford. He was the first layman to occupy the chair and the first to lecture in English; hitherto the professors had always addressed their audiences in Latin. His inaugural lecture was "On the Modern Element in Literature," and it was with the modern element, although not always with modern literature, that he was henceforth to occupy himself in his utterances from the chair. He was elected for a second term in 1862. Within a few years his words were to reach far beyond his Oxford audiences; as a critic he very soon occupied a position of commanding influence first in England and then in America.

It is not hard to state the reasons for Arnold's success. He spoke about literature as a man to men, not as a scholar, not as a teacher, not really, for all his preoccupation with morality, as a preacher. His tone was firm and direct, but light; he was authoritative without bullying; and he was always clear. He spoke of literature as one who loved it and lived in it; but he spoke too as one who knew the world and lived in the world and believed that literature was connected in a complex multitude of ways with actual practical life. There is a famous phrase of Arnold's which, like so many of his phrases that caught the mind of his contemporary readers, has been much worried by the critics of our time: Arnold said that poetry—or literature in general—is a criticism of life, and the objection which is usually made is that poetry is so much more immediate and intense an experience than is suggested by the phrase, that it does so much more than criticize. But what Arnold meant is that literature—although it does indeed, in one of its activities, say specifically what is wrong with life—characteristically discharges its critical function by possessing in a high degree the qualities that we may properly look for in life but which we are likely to find there in all too small an amount—such qualities as coherence, energy, and brightness; and in its possession of these qualities literature stands as the mute measure of what life may be and is not. When Arnold speaks of Homer's "grand style," he has in mind, whether or not he says so, the mean style in which the British conduct their popular education; when he speaks of the simplicity of Homer's style he has in mind not only the clutter of contemporary poems but also, we must suppose, the clutter of contemporary life; and when he speaks of Homer's rapidity he has reference to what he elsewhere refers to as a middle class "drugged with business."

And so, without ever permitting his hearers or readers to lose sight of the true, essential nature of literature, without ever bending art to utility, he relates literature to actuality either as a symptom or as a condition. To be sure, he was not alone in making the relation, for the whole tendency of high criticism since early in the nineteenth century had been to put forward the social criterion of "adequacy" which Arnold invoked in his inaugural lecture and expounded in virtually all his critical essays, but no one had ever made the criterion quite so real, so direct and so simple, at the same time keeping it so wholly literary. The reader who first comes upon the great essay "The Function of Criticism at the Present Time" will be sure to wonder whether Arnold is speaking of literary criticism or of the criticism of politics and social theory, for his references are as frequent to political and social as to literary practice. And indeed when it came to the function of criticism Arnold did not distinguish; for him criticism had to do with the quality of life wherever manifested. This is the mark of the great critic. It is not surprising that Arnold should have advanced more and more into politics itself, into the theory of government. He does so as a poet and a literary critic, as one trained in the best possible way to judge the quality of life.

VII

From his professorship onward Arnold's life is much of a piece. His marriage seems to have been a happy one, but its happiness was three times shattered by terrible grief—his youngest son, Basil, died in January of 1868; his eldest, Thomas, an invalid from childhood, died in November of that year at the age of sixteen; in 1872 his second son Trevenen, called "Budge," died at eighteen. The great image of Sohrab sitting by his dead son was previsionary. Arnold bore these losses sternly; whatever his thoughts may have been, his words were for the grief of others, not for his own. He shared the feeling of Homer that the death of a young man was the most pathetic of happenings; no less did he hold in mind the other tragic feeling of the Greek poets, that it was the most fortunate thing. And quite apart from grief, his life was as sad as in his gay youth he expected it to be, for in his young manhood he had been much oppressed by the idea of the passing of youth and in his later years he never spoke other than bitterly in his verse of what the passing years bring. The note of the buried life and the lost way, of the ironies of the direction chosen, of the foiled, circuitous wanderer, is far too frequent, and too personal in its tone, to permit us not to suppose that he felt some part of himself was not being lived out. Yet his commitment to the duties of life and society was a large one; and his discipleship to Goethe was expressed in a sense of duty to his considerable powers of enjoyment. He could join Goethe in agreeing with Homer that our life is a kind of Hell, yet with Goethe he believed that it must be lived with as much pleasure as may be dragged from it.

Despite Arnold's increasing reputation and influence, his income was always limited. His salary from his educational post was relatively small and he began to look forward to retirement. The return from his books was not significant. In 1870, when his income from his writing was assessed at £1000 by the Income Tax Commissioners, "You see before you, gentlemen," he said to them, "what you have often heard of, *an unpopular author.*" The assessment was cut to £200 and Arnold said that he would have to write a great many articles to meet even this. The chairman bowed and said, "Then the public will have reason to be much obliged to us." In 1883 Gladstone offered him a pension of £250, presumably at the urging of John Morley; Arnold, after some hesitation, accepted it. Yet even with the pension, his income, after his salary should be reduced by his retirement, would not be sufficient for his family; for this reason and upon the encouragement of his friends, Henry James among them, he considered making a lecture tour of America.

The story of Arnold's visit to this country has been admirably told by Dr. Chilson Leonard, and it is a great pity that Dr. Leonard's account, a dissertation in manuscript in the Sterling Library at Yale, has not yet been published, for it makes a most illuminating summary of the condition of American culture at the time. America in the eighties was in some ways far more interested in intellectual matters than it is now. The curiosity about Arnold was not confined to a small group but was general; his reputation was high in the colleges and universities, but railway conductors read him with pleasure, and General Grant and P. T. Barnum were eager to hear him. Yet the American attitude toward Arnold was ambivalent, a compound of lively respect and quick suspicion. Americans were eager to learn from him; but then they feared that this great exponent of criticism would—criticize. In consequence, everything Arnold might say was likely to be heard with the exacerbated sensitivity of a self-defensive people. The differences between American and English manners made for misunderstanding. Not only the popular press but individuals who should have known better were quick to pass judgment on Arnold before he should judge America or them. The lack of "refinement" in his appearance—his complexion was high and he now had a certain stalwartness of port and his clothes fitted loosely—his tricks of speech, his accepting two cents in change when he had bought a newspaper, his having come to make money, his insufficient praise of Emerson, everything that might possibly be observed or guessed of him was fair game. But Arnold handled himself very well. He was simple and sweet-tempered and never let himself be rattled; and indeed there was, on the part of the Americans, always an overplus of courtesy, friendliness and admiration to reassure him. He toured all the Eastern seaboard (being in great demand among the colleges), a large part of the Middle West, and the upper South, and enjoyed himself enormously. He genuinely liked America. Many of the adverse judgments with which he had come prepared he very happily abandoned; but he never flattered and his comments in *Civilization in the United States* are precise and discriminating. He was accompanied on his tour by his wife and his daughter Lucy, and Lucy's marriage to an American gave him a sense of affectionate intimacy with the country. In 1886 he returned for a quiet visit to see his American grandchild.

The "quiet work" which he had celebrated in one of his earliest sonnets marked Arnold's last years. His remarkably good health was beginning to fail him a little, but he had always loved exercise and in 1885 he was still skating, in 1886 still swimming. He retired from his educational post in 1886 with many evidences of the affection which the teachers of his district felt for him. He continued to write for the magazines, most frequently on political subjects; it is to be noted that in his last years his liberalism became more rather than less adventurous. In 1888, on the 15th of April, he went to Liverpool to meet his daughter and granddaughter who were arriving from America; in his eagerness he leaped over a low fence and fell dead, his heart having failed.

VIII

Arnold's literary life is remarkable both for its diversity and for its coherence. Poetry, criticism, educational theory, politics, and religion: it is seldom that one man addresses himself to distinction in so many fields. Yet each of Arnold's activities has reference to the same dramatic event—to the struggle of a culture to stay spiritually alive. At each stage of his life a different preoccupation is dominant, although not exclusive, and each relates intimately to the others. The critical problems of his early maturity are implicit in the poetry of his youth. The standards upon which his literary criticism is based are at work in his writing on education; their reference has only to be widened for his political utterances; and his views of literature and politics give rise to his manner of dealing with the contemporary problems of religion.

This coherence of Arnold's career makes grateful the task of the editor who undertakes to present a generous selection of his work, for Arnold himself provides the shape of the book and to a large extent the principle of selection. This is not to say that I have not been subject to the usual editorial unhappiness at being forced by reason of space to omit certain poems and certain essays. Here, indeed, the coherence was a special difficulty; like any other writer, Arnold is not always at his best, but he is unfailingly relevant—always relevant at least to his purpose; and if one has an interest in that purpose one naturally feels that almost everything he said contributes to its clarity. But I have checked my inclusive impulses by keeping in mind the interests and best tastes of the general reader. It was to this person that Arnold himself always spoke and I think I have done right in permitting him still to do so, having it in mind that the general reader of now is somewhat changed from what he was in Arnold's day.

Over only one decision, a large one, did I find myself troubled by serious doubt. It will not be expected that I hesitated long over omitting any example of Arnold's writings on education, which are chiefly reports whose interest is now only historical. But I did feel a certain uneasiness over the decision to include none of his writings on religion. These were central to Arnold's life from 1870 to 1877 and they have, as I say, an intimate connection with his other work. They are frequently marked by verve and wit. And what they say is in a great tradition, for the theory that the Bible is essentially poetry, so to be read and understood, and that the utterances of the great poets are essentially religious, was stated first by Spinoza and subsequently by Coleridge. In Arnold's day it was a theory of great importance to those who wished to keep religion in what they thought to be its naturalistic essentials, purging it of all that was dogmatic, supernatural, or in conflict with science. To Tolstoy, for example, Arnold meant much; but then to us today Tolstoy as a religious thinker is himself not likely to mean much. It would be impossible for the student of Arnold, or of the nineteenth century, or of religion, to slight these works, yet they will scarcely be of interest to the general reader now. The religious, if they are generous, will see in Arnold a natural piety which is sometimes very moving; but they will be right to say that this is not religion. Even the nonreligious may exercise aesthetic judgment in matters of religion and indeed our age has given the unbelieving a sophisticated taste in religious literature; but the special force and pungency which they respond to in many religious and quasi-theological works they are not likely to find in Arnold's, which by very reason of their intention are relaxed and without an intensity of faith, although they do surely have a stubbornness of faith. Yet it would be wrong to exclude all representation of this aspect of Arnold's thought without recalling that it is of a piece with the rest of his effort; the intention of his religious work is to show the meaninglessness of all theological distinctions and, by the establishment of a kind of natural theology based on morality, to put an end to the dissidence and divergence of contemporary religious opinion and thus to advance the cause of social peace and order. But if one deals with theology at all one may precisely not use the standards of society; the ultimate nature of the universe does not yield to the criteria of reasonableness.

But society itself does yield to the criteria of reasonableness. It does not yield wholly but it yields largely. And the great continuing pertinence of Arnold derives from his sense of the extent and limits of this possibility. From his sense of the limits of the possibility comes the pathos of his poetry, or, at times, its stern and tragic tone—Sohrab lies dead, Thyrsis lies dead; the brave, the bright-minded, the gay, the energetic, do not easily survive in a world diseased and weary; the reason of the world will not organize itself for the preservation of courage, brightness, gaiety, and force. But from his sense of the extent of the possibility that reason may be made to prevail comes Arnold's hope, from which in turn derive his own courage, brightness, gaiety, and force, as much of these as can be kept in survival to do their work in a world that suspects them even while it craves them.

LIONEL TRILLING

CHRONOLOGY

1822 Matthew Arnold born December 24, at Laleham, the second child and eldest son of Thomas Arnold and Mary Penrose Arnold. His godfather was John Keble, who was to be one of the leaders of the Oxford Movement.

1828 Thomas Arnold appointed Headmaster of Rugby School.

1833 Thomas Arnold builds Fox How in Westmorland and Matthew is thus brought into living connection with a great tradition of English poetry—the Wordsworths were near neighbors and became close friends of the Arnolds, and William Wordsworth took an interest in young Matthew. The Arnold family divided its year between Fox How and Rugby.

1836 Matthew sent to his father's old school, Winchester, for a year.

1837 Makes tour of France with his parents. Enters Rugby. His close friends at the school were Arthur Hugh Clough, Thomas Hughes, who was later to become well known as a Christian Socialist and as the author of *Tom Brown at Rugby,* and Arthur Penrhyn Stanley, later Thomas Arnold's biographer, a historian of some eminence, and the Dean of Westminster Abbey.

1840 Wins Rugby Poetry Prize for his *Alaric at Rome,* which was printed by a local press, his first published work. In this schoolboy production can already be heard the particular note of quiet melancholy which was to be characteristic of Arnold's later verse. In the same year Arnold won a Balliol Scholarship.

1841 Visits France with his father and his brother Thomas. Enters Balliol College, Oxford. Balliol was then the center of the Oxford Movement, but, although Dr. Arnold was one of the principal antagonists of the Movement, Matthew was not concerned with it. Nevertheless he records the deep impression made upon him by Newman's sermons at St. Mary's.

1842 Wins a Hertford Scholarship. His father dies suddenly of heart disease at the age of forty-seven. (The disease seems to have been hereditary in the Arnold family. Possibly the knowledge of this accounts in part for the sadness of much of Matthew's verse. He himself was to die suddenly of heart failure.)

1843 Wins Newdigate Poetry Prize with *Cromwell.*

1844 Takes his degree, with only second-class honors in consequence of his refusal to read systematically.

1845 Teaches classics in the Fifth Form at Rugby. Elected to Fellowship at Oriel College.

1847 Becomes private secretary to Lord Lansdowne, who was active in politics. Tour on the Continent; visits George Sand, whose novels he had long admired.

1849 Publishes *The Strayed Reveller and Other Poems,* "by A." Withdraws the volume from publication. Appointed by Lord Lansdowne to an Inspectorship of schools.

1851 Marries Frances Lucy Wightman, daughter of Sir William Wightman, judge on the Queen's Bench.

1852 Publishes *Empedocles on Etna and Other Poems.* Withdraws it from circulation.

1853 Publishes *Poems.*

1855 Publishes *Poems, Second Series.* The volumes of 1853 and 1855 contain many of the poems of the volumes of 1849 and 1852.

1857 Elected Professor of Poetry at Oxford. He was the first nonclerical Professor of Poetry and the first to lecture in English. His inaugural lecture was "On the Modern Element in Literature." He was re-elected after his first term of five years. In later life he discouraged attempts to elect him yet again, feeling that younger men should be given the honor and opportunity of the chair.

1858 A mountain-climbing holiday in Switzerland. Publishes *Merope,* a drama in the classical form.

1859 Appointed Foreign Assistant Commissioner of the Duke of Newcastle's Commission to report on the condition of popular education in England. On his visit to Paris meets many of the leaders of French thought. Publishes a political pamphlet, *England and the Italian Question.*

1861 Delivers his Oxford Lectures, "On Translating Homer." Publishes the Report of his Commission, *The Popular Education of France;* the essay "Democracy" is his introduction to the volume.
Clough, the closest friend of Arnold's youth, dies.

1862 Begins to contribute essays on education and literature to the magazines.

1865 Publishes *Essays in Criticism.* Appointed Assistant Commissioner on the Schools Inquiry Commission to report on education in France, Germany, Switzerland, and Italy. Tour of Europe.

1867 Publishes *New Poems.* Publishes his lectures *On the Study of Celtic Literature,* delivered at Oxford in 1866.

1868 His infant son Basil dies in January; his eldest son Thomas, long an invalid, dies in November at the age of sixteen. Publishes *Schools and Universities of the Continent.*

1869 Publishes first collected edition of his poems. Publishes *Culture and Anarchy,* the theme of which was suggested by the enlargement of the franchise by the Reform Bill of 1867. The first chapter was his concluding lecture as Professor of Poetry.

1870 Publishes *St. Paul and Protestantism,* which had appeared the year before in the *Pall Mall Gazette.*

1871 Publishes *Friendship's Garland,* a series of humorous letters to the *Pall Mall Gazette* on English culture and politics.

1872 His son, William Trevenen, called "Budge," dies in February at the age of eighteen.

1873 Publishes *Literature and Dogma,* his most important work on religion.

1875 Publishes *God and the Bible,* a defense of *Literature and Dogma.*

1877 Publishes last essay on *Church and Religion*.

1879 Publishes *Mixed Essays*.

1882 Publishes *Irish Essays and Others*.

1883 Accepts from Gladstone a pension of £250 a year. Leaves for his lecture tour of America.

1885 Publishes the lectures he had delivered in America, *Discourses in America*.

1886 Visits Germany. Makes his second trip to America to visit his daughter, who had married an American and was soon to have a child. Retires from his Inspectorship of Schools in April, with many testimonies of the affection of the teachers in his district.

1888 Collects the essays for *Essays in Criticism, Second Series*, which appeared posthumously. On April 15 he died of heart failure in Liverpool where he had gone to meet his daughter on her arrival from America.

A NOTE ON BIBLIOGRAPHY

There is really no biography of Arnold in the usual sense of the word. Professor Louis Bonnerot's *Matthew Arnold, Poète* (Paris: Didier, 1947) bears the subtitle *Essai de Biographie Psychologique*. My own *Matthew Arnold* (New York: Norton, 1939; reissued by the Columbia University Press, 1949) I have characterized in its introduction as "a biography of Arnold's mind." Neither an essay in psychological biography nor a biography of a mind is, properly speaking, a biography; nevertheless the reader can derive from both books a reasonably full outline of Arnold's life, which he can supplement by *Letters of Matthew Arnold, 1848-1888*, edited by G. W. E. Russell (New York and London: Macmillan, 1895, 2 vols.), and, for certain important aspects of the early years, *The Letters of Matthew Arnold to Arthur*

Hugh Clough, edited by Howard Foster Lowry (London and New York: Oxford University Press, 1932); Dr. Lowry's introduction and notes are most informative. *The Notebooks of Matthew Arnold,* in an edition prepared by Dr. Lowry, will be published by the Oxford University Press not long after the publication of this present volume.

The best edition of Arnold's poems is that in the Oxford Standard Authors series. A completely new edition, prepared by Dr. Lowry and Professor Chauncey B. Tinker, will be published in 1949, to replace the older edition in the series. *The Poetry of Matthew Arnold: A Commentary,* by Tinker and Lowry (London and New York: Oxford University Press, 1940) is a helpful work.

Macmillan publishes Arnold's prose works, and both the Oxford Standard Authors series and Everyman's Library (Dutton) have handy volumes which include the first series of the *Essays in Criticism* and *On Translating Homer;* the Oxford volume includes several notable essays not reprinted by Arnold himself. The best edition of *Culture and Anarchy* is that prepared by J. Dover Wilson, the well-known Shakespeare scholar (Cambridge: Cambridge University Press, 1932).

Of critical essays on Arnold I can recommend the following:

John Dewey, "Arnold and Browning," in *Characters and Events* (New York: Holt, 1929), Vol. I.

T. S. Eliot, "Arnold and Pater," in *Selected Essays* (New York: Harcourt, Brace, 1932); and "Matthew Arnold" in *The Use of Poetry and the Use of Criticism* (Cambridge: Harvard University Press, 1932).

H. W. Garrod, *Poetry and the Criticism of Life* (New York and London: Oxford University Press, 1931).

R. H. Hutton, "The Poetry of Matthew Arnold," in *Essays in Literary Criticism* (London: Macmillan, 1888), 3rd edition; and "The Two Great Oxford Thinkers, Cardinal Newman and Matthew Arnold," in *Essays on Some of the Modern Guides of English Thought in Matters of Faith* (London: Macmillan, 1887).

F. R. Leavis, "Arnold as Critic," *Scrutiny*, December 1938, reprinted in *The Importance of Scrutiny*, edited by Eric Bentley (New York: George Stewart, 1948).

For a full bibliography of Arnold's work and of writing about Arnold up to 1934 see *Bibliographies of Twelve Victorian Authors* by T. G. Ehrsam, R. H. Deily, and R. M. Smith (New York: H. W. Wilson, 1936); for works written after 1934 Professor Bonnerot's list in the volume mentioned above is handy, although admittedly incomplete.

Poems

EDITOR'S NOTE

IT IS not hard to identify the elements which go to make the success of Arnold's most strikingly successful poems. One is Arnold's command of a music which, though limited in variety, is very beautiful. It is a music perhaps not wholly in accord with our contemporary notions of what the music of poetry should be, but its charm is nonetheless available to us. The other element is Arnold's bold dramatic way of using great objects, often great geographical or topographical objects, in relation to which the subjective states of the poem organize themselves and seem themselves to acquire an objective actuality. Such objects are, in "Dover Beach," the beach, the Channel, the cliffs, the coast of France, the Aegean, and then suddenly, beneath the hotel window, the astonishing appearance of the "ignorant armies"; or in "The Scholar Gipsy" the fresh, clear, seventeenth-century Thames, the Mediterranean, the impatient young sea captain at the tiller of his galley; or in "Sohrab and Rustum" the father sitting motionless—we believe it will be forever—by his dead son, then the whole course of the great river Oxus, to the regard of which the reader's mind is therapeutically wrenched.

There is also a class of Arnold's poems which are less striking in their particular kind of success but which are nevertheless delightful and impressive. In these poems the elements I have spoken of are at work at a lesser intensity, but they are certainly present, and to them we owe the pleasure of, say, Callicles's songs in "Empedocles on Etna," or of the darkly eloquent "To a Gipsy Child by the Sea-shore."

But Arnold wrote a good many poems in which his power of imagery plays very little part and in which the characteristic lyric note gives way to, at best, a kind of recitative, or, at worst, to something uneuphonious or even of false quality (for Arnold's ear could fail drastically). These poems, we may suppose, suffer from an excess or a misapplication of Arnold's theories about plainness and directness of diction, and it is difficult to find in them any of what are usually accounted the elements of specifically poetical effectiveness. Yet when we have made our aesthetic judgment, the fact remains—and it is, after all, an aesthetic fact—that poems like "Courage" or "Self-Dependence" or "Stanzas from the Grande Chartreuse" are moving and memorable. Arnold is thus in a certain sense a unique poet—in the sense that many of his poems succeed with us out of all proportion to their specifically poetic success. For with him we do more than tolerate the dryness of tone into which he occasionally falls, or his reliance upon statement rather than upon the translation of emotion or idea into music and image: we come to have an affection for what are usually accounted faults, to think of them as being the marks of the directness of Arnold's communication with us.

From among Arnold's long poems it was inevitable that I should choose "Empedocles on Etna," which is certainly one of the central documents of the cultural situation of Arnold's period. The whole of "Sohrab and Rustum" does, I think, still make claims on our interest, but I have had room for only the grand conclusion. This and some fine bitter lines rescued from "Tristam and Iseult" are the only passages given in excerpt. I have tried to resist the traditional estimates of which of Arnold's shorter poems are most characteristic and important and have chosen only those which to my own taste seemed the most interesting.

THE STRAYED REVELLER

The portico of Circe's Palace. Evening.

PERSONS

A Youth
Circe
Ulysses

THE YOUTH

Faster, faster,
O Circe, Goddess,
Let the wild, thronging train,
The bright procession
Of eddying forms,
Sweep through my soul!
Thou standest, smiling
Down on me; thy right arm,
Lean'd up against the column there,
Props thy soft cheek;
Thy left holds, hanging loosely,
The deep cup, ivy-cinctur'd,
I held but now.

Is it then evening
So soon? I see, the night dews,
Cluster'd in thick beads, dim
The agate brooch-stones
On thy white shoulder.
The cool night-wind, too,
Blows through the portico,
Stirs thy hair, Goddess,
Waves thy white robe.

CIRCE

Whence art thou, sleeper?

THE YOUTH

When the white dawn first
Through the rough fir-planks
Of my hut, by the chestnuts,
Up at the valley-head,
Came breaking, Goddess,
I sprang up, I threw round me
My dappled fawn-skin:
Passing out, from the wet turf,
Where they lay, by the hut door,
I snatch'd up my vine-crown, my fir-staff,
All drench'd in dew:
Came swift down to join
The rout early gather'd
In the town, round the temple,
Iacchus' white fane
On yonder hill.

Quick I pass'd, following
The wood-cutters' cart-track
Down the dark valley;—I saw
On my left, through the beeches,
Thy palace, Goddess,
Smokeless, empty:
Trembling, I enter'd; beheld
The court all silent,
The lions sleeping;
On the altar, this bowl.
I drank, Goddess—
And sunk down here, sleeping,
On the steps of thy portico.

CIRCE

Foolish boy! Why tremblest thou?
Thou lovest it, then, my wine?
Wouldst more of it? See, how glows,
Through the delicate flush'd marble,
The red creaming liquor,
Strown with dark seeds!
Drink, then! I chide thee not,
Deny thee not my bowl.
Come, stretch forth thy hand, then—so,—
Drink, drink again!

THE YOUTH

Thanks, gracious One!
Ah, the sweet fumes again!
More soft, ah me!
More subtle-winding
Than Pan's flute-music.
Faint—faint! Ah me!
Again the sweet sleep.

CIRCE

Hist! Thou—within there!
Come forth, Ulysses!
Art tired with hunting?
While we range the woodland,
See what the day brings.

ULYSSES

Ever new magic!
Hast thou then lur'd hither,
Wonderful Goddess, by thy art,
The young, languid-ey'd Ampelus,
Iacchus' darling—

Or some youth belov'd of Pan,
Of Pan and the Nymphs?
That he sits, bending downward
His white, delicate neck
To the ivy-wreath'd marge
Of thy cup:——the bright, glancing vine-leaves
That crown his hair,
Falling forwards, mingling
With the dark ivy-plants,
His fawn-skin, half untied,
Smear'd with red wine-stains? Who is he,
That he sits, overweigh'd
By fumes of wine and sleep,
So late, in thy portico?
What youth, Goddess,——what guest
Of Gods or mortals?

CIRCE

Hist! he wakes!
I lur'd him not hither, Ulysses.
Nay, ask him!

THE YOUTH

Who speaks? Ah! Who comes forth
To thy side, Goddess, from within?
How shall I name him?
This spare, dark-featur'd,
Quick-ey'd stranger?
Ah! and I see too
His sailor's bonnet,
His short coat, travel-tarnish'd,
With one arm bare.——
Art thou not he, whom fame
This long time rumours
The favour'd guest of Circe, brought by the waves?

Art thou he, stranger?
The wise Ulysses,
Laertes' son?

ULYSSES

I am Ulysses.
And thou, too, sleeper?
Thy voice is sweet.
It may be thou hast follow'd
Through the islands some divine bard,
By age taught many things,
Age and the Muses;
And heard him delighting
The chiefs and people
In the banquet, and learn'd his songs,
Of Gods and Heroes,
Of war and arts,
And peopled cities
Inland, or built
By the grey sea.—If so, then hail!
I honour and welcome thee.

THE YOUTH

The Gods are happy.
They turn on all sides
Their shining eyes:
And see, below them,
The Earth, and men.

They see Tiresias
Sitting, staff in hand,
On the warm, grassy
Asopus' bank:
His robe drawn over
His old, sightless head:

Revolving inly
The doom of Thebes.

They see the Centaurs
In the upper glens
Of Pelion, in the streams,
Where red-berried ashes fringe
The clear-brown shallow pools;
With streaming flanks, and heads
Rear'd proudly, snuffing
The mountain wind.

They see the Indian
Drifting, knife in hand,
His frail boat moor'd to
A floating isle thick matted
With large-leav'd, low-creeping melon-plants,
And the dark cucumber.
He reaps, and stows them,
Drifting—drifting:—round him,
Round his green harvest-plot,
Flow the cool lake-waves:
The mountains ring them.

They see the Scythian
On the wide Stepp, unharnessing
His wheel'd house at noon.
He tethers his beast down, and makes his meal,
Mares' milk, and bread
Bak'd on the embers:—all around
The boundless waving grass-plains stretch, thick-starr'd
With saffron and the yellow hollyhock
And flag-leav'd iris flowers.
Sitting in his cart

He makes his meal: before him, for long miles,
Alive with bright green lizards,
And the springing bustard fowl,
The track, a straight black line,
Furrows the rich soil: here and there
Clusters of lonely mounds
Topp'd with rough-hewn,
Grey, rain-blear'd statues, overpeer
The sunny Waste.

They see the Ferry
On the broad, clay-laden
Lone Chorasmian stream: thereon
With snort and strain,
Two horses, strongly swimming, tow
The ferry-boat, with woven ropes
To either bow
Firm-harness'd by the mane:—a Chief,
With shout and shaken spear
Stands at the prow, and guides them: but astern,
The cowering Merchants, in long robes,
Sit pale beside their wealth
Of silk-bales and of balsam-drops,
Of gold and ivory,
Of turquoise-earth and amethyst,
Jasper and chalcedony,
And milk-barr'd onyx stones.
The loaded boat swings groaning
In the yellow eddies.
The Gods behold them.

They see the Heroes
Sitting in the dark ship
On the foamless, long-heaving,

Violet sea:
At sunset nearing
The Happy Islands.

These things, Ulysses,
The wise Bards also
Behold and sing.
But oh, what labour!
O Prince, what pain!

They too can see
Tiresias:—but the Gods,
Who give them vision,
Added this law:
That they should bear too
His groping blindness,
His dark foreboding,
His scorn'd white hairs;
Bear Hera's anger
Through a life lengthen'd
To seven ages.

They see the Centaurs
On Pelion:—then they feel,
They too, the maddening wine
Swell their large veins to bursting: in wild pain
They feel the biting spears
Of the grim Lapithae, and Theseus, drive,
Drive crashing through their bones: they feel
High on a jutting rock in the red stream
Alcmena's dreadful son
Ply his bow:—such a price
The Gods exact for song;
To become what we sing.

They see the Indian
On his mountain lake:—but squalls
Make their skiff reel, and worms
In the unkind spring have gnaw'd
Their melon-harvest to the heart: They see
The Scythian:—but long frosts
Parch them in winter-time on the bare Stepp,
Till they too fade like grass: they crawl
Like shadows forth in spring.

They see the Merchants
On the Oxus' stream:—but care
Must visit first them too, and make them pale.
Whether, through whirling sand,
A cloud of desert robber-horse has burst
Upon their caravan: or greedy kings,
In the wall'd cities the way passes through,
Crush'd them with tolls: or fever-airs,
On some great river's marge,
Mown them down, far from home.

They see the Heroes
Near harbour:—but they share
Their lives, and former violent toil, in Thebes,
Seven-gated Thebes, or Troy:
Or where the echoing oars
Of Argo, first,
Startled the unknown Sea.

The old Silenus
Came, lolling in the sunshine,
From the dewy forest coverts,
This way, at noon.
Sitting by me, while his Fauns

Down at the water side
Sprinkled and smooth'd
His drooping garland,
He told me these things.

But I, Ulysses,
Sitting on the warm steps,
Looking over the valley,
All day long, have seen,
Without pain, without labour,
Sometimes a wild-hair'd Maenad;
Sometimes a Faun with torches;
And sometimes, for a moment,
Passing through the dark stems
Flowing-rob'd—the belov'd,
The desir'd, the divine,
Belov'd Iacchus.

Ah cool night-wind, tremulous stars!
Ah glimmering water—
Fitful earth-murmur—
Dreaming woods!
Ah golden-hair'd, strangely-smiling Goddess,
And thou, prov'd, much enduring,
Wave-toss'd Wanderer!
Who can stand still?
Ye fade, ye swim, ye waver before me.
The cup again!

Faster, faster,
O Circe, Goddess,
Let the wild thronging train,
The bright procession
Of eddying forms,
Sweep through my soul!

○

TO A FRIEND

Who prop, thou ask'st, in these bad days, my mind?
He much, the old man, who, clearest-soul'd of men,
Saw The Wide Prospect,[1] and the Asian Fen,
And Tmolus' hill, and Smyrna's bay, though blind.
Much he, whose friendship I not long since won,
That halting slave, who in Nicopolis
Taught Arrian, when Vespasian's brutal son
Clear'd Rome of what most sham'd him. But be his
My special thanks, whose even-balanc'd soul,
From first youth tested up to extreme old age,
Business could not make dull, nor Passion wild:
Who saw life steadily, and saw it whole:
The mellow glory of the Attic stage;
Singer of sweet Colonus, and its child.

○

SHAKESPEARE

Others abide our question. Thou art free.
We ask and ask: Thou smilest and art still,
Out-topping knowledge. For the loftiest hill
That to the stars uncrowns his majesty,
Planting his steadfast footsteps in the sea,
Making the Heaven of Heavens his dwelling-place,
Spares but the cloudy border of his base
To the foil'd searching of mortality:
And thou, who didst the stars and sunbeams know,

[1] Εὐρώπη [Europe].

Self-school'd, self-scann'd, self-honour'd, self-secure,
Didst walk on Earth unguess'd at. Better so!
All pains the immortal spirit must endure,
   All weakness that impairs, all griefs that bow,
   Find their sole voice in that victorious brow.

❍

WRITTEN IN BUTLER'S SERMONS

Affections, Instincts, Principles, and Powers,
Impulse and Reason, Freedom and Control—
So men, unravelling God's harmonious whole,
Rend in a thousand shreds this life of ours.
Vain labour! Deep and broad, where none may see,
Spring the foundations of the shadowy throne
Where man's one Nature, queen-like, sits alone,
Centred in a majestic unity;
And rays her powers, like sister islands, seen
Linking their coral arms under the sea:
Or cluster'd peaks, with plunging gulfs between
Spann'd by aërial arches, all of gold;
Whereo'er the chariot wheels of Life are roll'd
In cloudy circles, to eternity.

❍

TO AN INDEPENDENT PREACHER

WHO PREACHED THAT WE SHOULD BE "IN HARMONY WITH NATURE"

"In harmony with Nature?" Restless fool,
Who with such heat dost preach what were to thee,
When true, the last impossibility;
To be like Nature strong, like Nature cool:—

Know, man hath all which Nature hath, but more,
And in that *more* lie all his hopes of good.
Nature is cruel; man is sick of blood:
Nature is stubborn; man would fain adore:
Nature is fickle; man hath need of rest:
Nature forgives no debt, and fears no grave;
Man would be mild, and with safe conscience blest.
Man must begin, know this, where Nature ends;
Nature and man can never be fast friends.
Fool, if thou canst not pass her, rest her slave!

○

TO A REPUBLICAN FRIEND, 1848

God knows it, I am with you. If to prize
Those virtues, priz'd and practis'd by too few,
But priz'd, but lov'd, but eminent in you,
Man's fundamental life: if to despise
The barren optimistic sophistries
Of comfortable moles, whom what they do
Teaches the limit of the just and true—
And for such doing have no need of eyes:
If sadness at the long heart-wasting show
Wherein earth's great ones are disquieted:
If thoughts, not idle, while before me flow
The armies of the homeless and unfed:—
    If these are yours, if this is what you are,
    Then am I yours, and what you feel, I share.

○

TO A REPUBLICAN FRIEND, 1848,
CONTINUED

Yet, when I muse on what life is, I seem
Rather to patience prompted, than that proud
Prospect of hope which France proclaims so loud,
France, fam'd in all great arts, in none supreme.
Seeing this Vale, this Earth, whereon we dream,
Is on all sides o'ershadow'd by the high
Uno'erleap'd Mountains of Necessity,
Sparing us narrower margin than we deem.
Nor will that day dawn at a human nod,
When, bursting through the network superpos'd
By selfish occupation—plot and plan,
Lust, avarice, envy—liberated man,
All difference with his fellow man compos'd,
Shall be left standing face to face with God.

○

RELIGIOUS ISOLATION

TO THE SAME

Children (as such forgive them) have I known,
Ever in their own eager pastime bent
To make the incurious bystander, intent
On his own swarming thoughts, an interest own;
Too fearful or too fond to play alone.
Do thou, whom light in thine own inmost soul
(Not less thy boast) illuminates, control
Wishes unworthy of a man full-grown.

What though the holy secret which moulds thee
Moulds not the solid Earth? though never Winds
Have whisper'd it to the complaining Sea,
Nature's great law, and law of all men's minds?
    To its own impulse every creature stirs:
    Live by thy light, and Earth will live by hers.

TO A GIPSY CHILD BY THE SEA-SHORE

DOUGLAS, ISLE OF MAN

Who taught this pleading to unpractis'd eyes?
Who hid such import in an infant's gloom?
Who lent thee, child, this meditative guise?
What clouds thy forehead, and fore-dates thy doom?

Lo! sails that gleam a moment and are gone;
The swinging waters, and the cluster'd pier.
Not idly Earth and Ocean labour on,
Nor idly do these sea-birds hover near.

But thou, whom superfluity of joy
Wafts not from thine own thoughts, nor longings vain,
Nor weariness, the full-fed soul's annoy;
Remaining in thy hunger and thy pain:

Thou, drugging pain by patience; half averse
From thine own mother's breast, that knows not thee;
With eyes that sought thine eyes thou didst converse,
And that soul-searching vision fell on me.

Glooms that go deep as thine I have not known:
Moods of fantastic sadness, nothing worth.

Thy sorrow and thy calmness are thine own:
Glooms that enhance and glorify this earth.

What mood wears like complexion to thy woe?—
His, who in mountain glens, at noon of day,
Sits rapt, and hears the battle break below?—
Ah! thine was not the shelter, but the fray.

What exile's, changing bitter thoughts with glad?
What seraph's, in some alien planet born?—
No exile's dream was ever half so sad,
Nor any angel's sorrow so forlorn.

Is the calm thine of stoic souls, who weigh
Life well, and find it wanting, nor deplore:
But in disdainful silence turn away,
Stand mute, self-centred, stern, and dream no more?

Or do I wait, to hear some grey-hair'd king
Unravel all his many-colour'd lore:
Whose mind hath known all arts of governing,
Mus'd much, lov'd life a little, loath'd it more?

Down the pale cheek long lines of shadow slope,
Which years, and curious thought, and suffering give—
Thou hast foreknown the vanity of hope,
Foreseen thy harvest—yet proceed'st to live.

O meek anticipant of that sure pain
Whose sureness grey-hair'd scholars hardly learn!
What wonder shall time breed, to swell thy strain?
What heavens, what earth, what suns shalt thou discern?

Ere the long night, whose stillness brooks no star,
Match that funereal aspect with her pall,

I think, thou wilt have fathom'd life too far,
Have known too much—or else forgotten all.

The Guide of our dark steps a triple veil
Betwixt our senses and our sorrow keeps:
Hath sown with cloudless passages the tale
Of grief, and eas'd us with a thousand sleeps.

Ah! not the nectarous poppy lovers use,
Not daily labour's dull, Lethaean spring,
Oblivion in lost angels can infuse
Of the soil'd glory, and the trailing wing;

And though thou glean, what strenuous gleaners may,
In the throng'd fields where winning comes by strife;
And though the just sun gild, as all men pray,
Some reaches of thy storm-vext stream of life;

Though that blank sunshine blind thee: though the cloud
That sever'd the world's march and thine, is gone:
Though ease dulls grace, and Wisdom be too proud
To halve a lodging that was all her own:

Once, ere the day decline, thou shalt discern,
Oh once, ere night, in thy success, thy chain.
Ere the long evening close, thou shalt return,
And wear this majesty of grief again.

○

THE FORSAKEN MERMAN

Come, dear children, let us away;
Down and away below.
Now my brothers call from the bay;

Now the great winds shorewards blow;
Now the salt tides seawards flow;
Now the wild white horses play,
Champ and chafe and toss in the spray.
Children dear, let us away.
This way, this way.

Call her once before you go.
Call once yet.
In a voice that she will know:
"Margaret! Margaret!"
Children's voices should be dear
(Call once more) to a mother's ear:
Children's voices, wild with pain.
Surely she will come again.
Call her once and come away.
This way, this way.
"Mother dear, we cannot stay."
The wild white horses foam and fret.
Margaret! Margaret!

Come, dear children, come away down.
Call no more.
One last look at the white-wall'd town,
And the little grey church on the windy shore.
Then come down.
She will not come though you call all day.
Come away, come away.

Children dear, was it yesterday
We heard the sweet bells over the bay?
In the caverns where we lay,
Through the surf and through the swell,
The far-off sound of a silver bell?
Sand-strewn caverns, cool and deep,

Where the winds are all asleep;
Where the spent lights quiver and gleam;
Where the salt weed sways in the stream;
Where the sea-beasts rang'd all round
Feed in the ooze of their pasture-ground;
Where the sea-snakes coil and twine,
Dry their mail and bask in the brine;
Where great whales come sailing by,
Sail and sail, with unshut eye,
Round the world for ever and aye?
When did music come this way?
Children dear, was it yesterday?

Children dear, was it yesterday
(Call yet once) that she went away?
Once she sate with you and me,
On a red gold throne in the heart of the sea,
And the youngest sate on her knee.
She comb'd its bright hair, and she tended it well,
When down swung the sound of the far-off bell.
She sigh'd, she look'd up through the clear green sea.
She said; "I must go, for my kinsfolk pray
In the little grey church on the shore to-day.
'Twill be Easter-time in the world—ah me!
And I lose my poor soul, Merman, here with thee."
I said; "Go up, dear heart, through the waves;
Say thy prayer, and come back to the kind sea-caves."
She smil'd, she went up through the surf in the bay.
Children dear, was it yesterday?

Children dear, were we long alone?
"The sea grows stormy, the little ones moan.
Long prayers," I said, "in the world they say.
Come," I said, and we rose through the surf in the bay.
We went up the beach, by the sandy down

Where the sea-stocks bloom, to the white-wall'd town.
Through the narrow pav'd streets, where all was still,
To the little grey church on the windy hill.
From the church came a murmur of folk at their prayers,
But we stood without in the cold blowing airs.
We climb'd on the graves, on the stones, worn with rains.
And we gaz'd up the aisle through the small leaded
          panes.
She sate by the pillar; we saw her clear:
"Margaret, hist! come quick, we are here.
Dear heart," I said, "we are long alone.
The sea grows stormy, the little ones moan."
But, ah, she gave me never a look,
For her eyes were seal'd to the holy book.
"Loud prays the priest; shut stands the door."
Come away, children, call no more.
Come away, come down, call no more.

  Down, down, down.
Down to the depths of the sea.
She sits at her wheel in the humming town,
Singing most joyfully.
Hark, what she sings; "O joy, O joy,
For the humming street, and the child with its toy.
For the priest, and the bell, and the holy well.
For the wheel where I spun,
And the blessed light of the sun."
And so she sings her fill,
Singing most joyfully,
Till the shuttle falls from her hand,
And the whizzing wheel stands still.
She steals to the window, and looks at the sand;
And over the sand at the sea;
And her eyes are set in a stare;
And anon there breaks a sigh,

And anon there drops a tear,
From a sorrow-clouded eye,
And a heart sorrow-laden,
A long, long sigh,
For the cold strange eyes of a little Mermaiden,
And the gleam of her golden hair.

Come away, away children.
Come children, come down.
The hoarse wind blows colder;
Lights shine in the town.
She will start from her slumber
When gusts shake the door;
She will hear the winds howling,
Will hear the waves roar.
We shall see, while above us
The waves roar and whirl,
A ceiling of amber,
A pavement of pearl.
Singing, "Here came a mortal,
But faithless was she.
And alone dwell for ever
The kings of the sea."

But, children, at midnight,
When soft the winds blow;
When clear falls the moonlight;
When spring-tides are low:
When sweet airs come seaward
From heaths starr'd with broom;
And high rocks throw mildly
On the blanch'd sands a gloom:
Up the still, glistening beaches,
Up the creeks we will hie;
Over banks of bright seaweed

The ebb-tide leaves dry.
We will gaze, from the sand-hills,
At the white, sleeping town;
At the church on the hill-side—
     And then come back down.
Singing, "There dwells a lov'd one,
But cruel is she.
She left lonely for ever
The kings of the sea."

O

IN UTRUMQUE PARATUS

If, in the silent mind of One all-pure,
     At first imagin'd lay
The sacred world; and by procession sure
From those still deeps, in form and colour drest,
Seasons alternating, and night and day,
The long-mus'd thought to north south east and west
     Took then its all-seen way:

O waking on a world which thus-wise springs!
     Whether it needs thee count
Betwixt thy waking and the birth of things
Ages or hours: O waking on Life's stream!
By lonely pureness to the all-pure Fount
(Only by this thou canst) the colour'd dream
     Of Life remount.

Thin, thin the pleasant human noises grow;
     And faint the city gleams;
Rare the lone pastoral huts: marvel not thou!
The solemn peaks but to the stars are known,
But to the stars, and the cold lunar beams:

Alone the sun arises, and alone
    Spring the great streams.

But, if the wild unfather'd mass no birth
    In divine seats hath known:
In the blank, echoing solitude, if Earth,
Rocking her obscure body to and fro,
Ceases not from all time to heave and groan,
Unfruitful oft, and, at her happiest throe,
    Forms, what she forms, alone:

O seeming sole to awake, thy sun-bath'd head
    Piercing the solemn cloud
Round thy still dreaming brother-world outspread!
O man, whom Earth, thy long-vext mother, bare
Not without joy; so radiant, so endow'd—
(Such happy issue crown'd her painful care)
    Be not too proud!

O when most self-exalted most alone,
    Chief dreamer, own thy dream!
Thy brother-world stirs at thy feet unknown;
Who hath a monarch's hath no brother's part;
Yet doth thine inmost soul with yearning teem.
O what a spasm shakes the dreamer's heart—
    "I too but seem!"

EMPEDOCLES ON ETNA

A DRAMATIC POEM

PERSONS

Empedocles.
Pausanias, a physician.
Callicles, a young harp-player.

The Scene of the Poem is on Mount Etna; at first in the forest region, afterwards on the summit of the mountain.

ACT I, SCENE I: *A Pass in the forest region of Etna. Morning.*

CALLICLES

(*Alone, resting on a rock by the path*)

The mules, I think, will not be here this hour.
They feel the cool wet turf under their feet
By the stream-side, after the dusty lanes
In which they have toil'd all night from Catana,
And scarcely will they budge a yard. O Pan!
How gracious is the mountain at this hour!
A thousand times have I been here alone
Or with the revellers from the mountain towns,
But never on so fair a morn;—the sun
Is shining on the brilliant mountain crests,

And on the highest pines: but further down
Here in the valley is in shade; the sward
Is dark, and on the stream the mist still hangs;
One sees one's foot-prints crush'd in the wet grass,
One's breath curls in the air; and on these pines
That climb from the stream's edge, the long grey tufts,
Which the goats love, are jewell'd thick with dew.
Here will I stay till the slow litter comes.
I have my harp too—that is well.—Apollo!
What mortal could be sick or sorry here?
I know not in what mind Empedocles,
Whose mules I follow'd, may be coming up,
But if, as most men say, he is half mad
With exile, and with brooding on his wrongs,
Pausanias, his sage friend, who mounts with him,
Could scarce have lighted on a lovelier cure.
The mules must be below, far down. I hear
Their tinkling bells, mix'd with the song of birds,
Rise faintly to me—now it stops!—Who's here?
Pausanias! and on foot? alone?

PAUSANIAS

              And thou, then?
I left thee supping with Peisianax,
With thy head full of wine, and thy hair crown'd,
Touching thy harp as the whim came on thee,
And prais'd and spoil'd by master and by guests
Almost as much as the new dancing girl.
Why hast thou follow'd us?

CALLICLES

            The night was hot,
And the feast past its prime; so we slipp'd out,
Some of us, to the portico to breathe;—
Peisianax, thou know'st, drinks late;—and then,

As I was lifting my soil'd garland off,
I saw the mules and litter in the court,
And in the litter sate Empedocles;
Thou, too, wert with him. Straightway I sped home;
I saddled my white mule, and all night long
Through the cool lovely country follow'd you,
Pass'd you a little since as morning dawn'd,
And have this hour sate by the torrent here,
Till the slow mules should climb in sight again.
And now?

PAUSANIAS

                And now, back to the town with speed!
Crouch in the wood first, till the mules have pass'd;
They do but halt, they will be here anon.
Thou must be viewless to Empedocles;
Save mine, he must not meet a human eye.
One of his moods is on him that thou know'st.
I think, thou would'st not vex him.

CALLICLES

                        No—and yet
I would fain stay and help thee tend him; once
He knew me well, and would oft notice me.
And still, I know not how, he draws me to him,
And I could watch him with his proud sad face,
His flowing locks and gold-encircled brow
And kingly gait, for ever; such a spell
In his severe looks, such a majesty
As drew of old the people after him,
In Agrigentum and Olympia,
When his star reign'd, before his banishment,
Is potent still on me in his decline.
But oh, Pausanias, he is changed of late!
There is a settled trouble in his air

Admits no momentary brightening now;
And when he comes among his friends at feasts,
'Tis as an orphan among prosperous boys.
Thou know'st of old he loved this harp of mine,
When first he sojourn'd with Peisianax;
He is now always moody, and I fear him.
But I would serve him, soothe him, if I could,
Dared one but try.

PAUSANIAS

    Thou wert a kind child ever.
He loves thee, but he must not see thee now.
Thou hast indeed a rare touch on thy harp,
He loves that in thee, too; there was a time
(But that is pass'd) he would have paid thy strain
With music to have drawn the stars from heaven.
He has his harp and laurel with him still,
But he has laid the use of music by,
And all which might relax his settled gloom.
Yet thou may'st try thy playing if thou wilt,
But thou must keep unseen; follow us on,
But at a distance; in these solitudes,
In this clear mountain air, a voice will rise,
Though from afar, distinctly; it may soothe him.
Play when we halt, and, when the evening comes
And I must leave him (for his pleasure is
To be left musing these soft nights alone
In the high unfrequented mountain spots),
Then watch him, for he ranges swift and far,
Sometimes to Etna's top, and to the cone;
But hide thee in the rocks a great way down,
And try thy noblest strains, my Callicles,
With the sweet night to help thy harmony.
Thou wilt earn my thanks sure, and perhaps his.

CALLICLES

More than a day and night, Pausanias,
Of this fair summer weather, on these hills,
Would I bestow to help Empedocles.
That needs no thanks; one is far better here
Than in the broiling city in these heats.
But tell me, how hast thou persuaded him
In this his present fierce, man-hating mood,
To bring thee out with him alone on Etna?

PAUSANIAS

Thou hast heard all men speaking of Pantheia,
The woman who at Agrigentum lay
Thirty long days in a cold trance of death,
And whom Empedocles call'd back to life.
Thou art too young to note it, but his power
Swells with the swelling evil of this time,
And holds men mute to see where it will rise.
He could stay swift diseases in old days,
Chain madmen by the music of his lyre,
Cleanse to sweet airs the breath of poisonous streams,
And in the mountain chinks inter the winds.
This he could do of old; but now, since all
Clouds and grows daily worse in Sicily,
Since broils tear us in twain, since this new swarm
Of sophists has got empire in our schools
Where he was paramount, since he is banish'd,
And lives a lonely man in triple gloom,
He grasps the very reins of life and death.
I ask'd him of Pantheia yesterday,
When we were gather'd with Peisianax,
And he made answer, I should come at night
On Etna here, and be alone with him,
And he would tell me, as his old, tried friend,

Who still was faithful, what might profit me;
That is, the secret of this miracle.

CALLICLES

Bah! Thou a doctor? Thou art superstitious.
Simple Pausanias, 'twas no miracle!
Pantheia, for I know her kinsmen well,
Was subject to these trances from a girl.
Empedocles would say so, did he deign;
But he still lets the people, whom he scorns,
Gape and cry wizard at him, if they list.
But thou, thou art no company for him;
Thou art as cross, as soured as himself.
Thou hast some wrong from thine own citizens,
And then thy friend is banish'd, and on that,
Straightway thou fallest to arraign the times,
As if the sky was impious not to fall.
The sophists are no enemies of his;
I hear, Gorgias, their chief, speaks nobly of him,
As of his gifted master and once friend.
He is too scornful, too high-wrought, too bitter.
'Tis not the times, 'tis not the sophists vex him;
There is some root of suffering in himself,
Some secret and unfollow'd vein of woe,
Which makes the time look black and sad to him.
Pester him not in this his sombre mood
With questionings about an idle tale,
But lead him through the lovely mountain paths,
And keep his mind from preying on itself,
And talk to him of things at hand and common,
Not miracles; thou art a learned man,
But credulous of fables as a girl.

PAUSANIAS

And thou, a boy whose tongue outruns his knowledge,

And on whose lightness blame is thrown away.
Enough of this! I see the litter wind
Up by the torrent-side, under the pines.
I must rejoin Empedocles. Do thou
Crouch in the brush-wood till the mules have pass'd;
Then play thy kind part well. Farewell till night!

SCENE II: *Noon. A Glen on the highest skirts
of the woody region of Etna.*

PAUSANIAS

The noon is hot; when we have cross'd the stream
We shall have left the woody tract, and come
Upon the open shoulder of the hill.
See how the giant spires of yellow bloom
Of the sun-loving gentian, in the heat,
Are shining on those naked slopes like flame!
Let us rest here; and now, Empedocles,
Pantheia's history.

A harp-note below is heard.

EMPEDOCLES

                    Hark! what sound was that
Rose from below? If it were possible,
And we were not so far from human haunt,
I should have said that some one touch'd a harp.
Hark! there again!

PAUSANIAS

                    'Tis the boy Callicles,
The sweetest harp-player in Catana,
He is for ever coming on these hills,
In summer, to all country festivals,
With a gay revelling band; he breaks from them

Sometimes, and wanders far among the glens.
But heed him not, he will not mount to us;
I spoke with him this morning. Once more, therefore,
Instruct me of Pantheia's story, Master,
As I have pray'd thee.

EMPEDOCLES

That? and to what end?

PAUSANIAS

It is enough that all men speak of it.
But I will also say, that when the Gods
Visit us as they do with sign and plague,
To know those spells of time that stay their hand
Were to live free from terror.

EMPEDOCLES

Spells? Mistrust them.
Mind is the spell which governs earth and heaven.
Man has a mind with which to plan his safety;
Know that, and help thyself.

PAUSANIAS

But thy own words?
"The wit and counsel of man was never clear,
Troubles confuse the little wit he has."
Mind is a light which the Gods mock us with,
To lead those false who trust it.

The harp sounds again.

EMPEDOCLES

Hist! once more!
Listen, Pausanias!—Aye, 'tis Callicles!
I know those notes among a thousand. Hark!

CALLICLES

Sings unseen, from below.

The track winds down to the clear stream,
To cross the sparkling shallows; there
The cattle love to gather, on their way
To the high mountain pastures, and to stay,
Till the rough cow-herds drive them past,
Knee-deep in the cool ford; for 'tis the last
Of all the woody, high, well-water'd dells
On Etna; and the beam
Of noon is broken there by chestnut boughs
Down its steep verdant sides; the air
Is freshen'd by the leaping stream, which throws
Eternal showers of spray on the moss'd roots
Of trees, and veins of turf, and long dark shoots
Of ivy-plants, and fragrant hanging bells
Of hyacinths, and on late anemonies,
That muffle its wet banks; but glade,
And stream, and sward, and chestnut trees,
End here; Etna beyond, in the broad glare
Of the hot noon, without a shade,
Slope behind slope, up to the peak, lies bare;
The peak, round which the white clouds play.

In such a glen, on such a day,
On Pelion, on the grassy ground,
Chiron, the aged Centaur, lay,
The young Achilles standing by.
The Centaur taught him to explore
The mountains; where the glens are dry,
And the tired Centaurs come to rest,
And where the soaking springs abound,
And the straight ashes grow for spears,
And where the hill-goats come to feed,

And the sea-eagles build their nest.
He show'd him Phthia far away,
And said: O boy, I taught this lore
To Peleus, in long distant years!
He told him of the Gods, the stars,
The tides;—and then of mortal wars,
And of the life which heroes lead
Before they reach the Elysian place
And rest in the immortal mead;
And all the wisdom of his race.

The music below ceases, and Empedocles speaks, accompanying himself in a solemn manner on his harp.

EMPEDOCLES

The out-spread world to span
A cord the Gods first slung,
And then the soul of man
There, like a mirror, hung,
And bade the winds through space impel the gusty toy.

Hither and thither spins
The wind-borne mirroring soul,
A thousand glimpses wins,
And never sees a whole;
Looks once, and drives elsewhere, and leaves its last
    employ.

The Gods laugh in their sleeve
To watch man doubt and fear,
Who knows not what to believe
Since he sees nothing clear,
And dares stamp nothing false where he finds nothing
    sure.

Is this, Pausanias, so?
And can our souls not strive,
But with the winds must go,
And hurry where they drive?
Is Fate indeed so strong, man's strength indeed so poor?

I will not judge! that man,
Howbeit, I judge as lost,
Whose mind allows a plan
Which would degrade it most;
And he treats doubt the best who tries to see least ill.

Be not, then, fear's blind slave!
Thou art my friend; to thee,
All knowledge that I have,
All skill I wield, are free;
Ask not the latest news of the last miracle,

Ask not what days and nights
In trance Pantheia lay,
But ask how thou such sights
May'st see without dismay;
Ask what most helps when known, thou son of Anchitus!

What? hate, and awe, and shame
Fill thee to see our world;
Thou feelest thy soul's frame
Shaken and rudely hurl'd.
What? life and time go hard with thee too, as with us;

Thy citizens, 'tis said,
Envy thee and oppress,
Thy goodness no men aid,

All strive to make it less;
Tyranny, pride, and lust fill Sicily's abodes;

Heaven is with earth at strife,
Signs make thy soul afraid,
The dead return to life,
Rivers are dried, winds stay'd;
Scarce can one think in calm, so threatening are the
      Gods;

And we feel, day and night,
The burden of ourselves—
Well, then, the wiser wight
In his own bosom delves,
And asks what ails him so, and gets what cure he can.

The sophist sneers: Fool, take
Thy pleasure, right or wrong!
The pious wail: Forsake
A world these sophists throng!
Be neither saint nor sophist-led, but be a man.

These hundred doctors try
To preach thee to their school.
We have the truth! they cry.
And yet their oracle,
Trumpet it as they will, is but the same as thine.

Once read thy own breast right,
And thou hast done with fears!
Man gets no other light,
Search he a thousand years.
Sink in thyself! there ask what ails thee, at that shrine!

What makes thee struggle and rave?
Why are men ill at ease?—

'Tis that the lot they have
Fails their own will to please;
For man would make no murmuring, were his will
      obey'd.

And why is it, that still
Man with his lot thus fights?—
'Tis that he makes this *will*
The measure of his *rights*,
And believes Nature outraged if his will's gainsaid.

Couldst thou, Pausanias, learn
How deep a fault is this!
Couldst thou once discern
Thou hast no *right* to bliss,
No title from the Gods to welfare and repose;

Then thou wouldst look less mazed
Whene'er from bliss debarr'd,
Nor think the Gods were crazed
When thy own lot went hard.
But we are all the same—the fools of our own woes!

For, from the first faint morn
Of life, the thirst for bliss
Deep in man's heart is born;
And, sceptic as he is,
He fails not to judge clear if this be quench'd or no.

Nor is that thirst to blame!
Man errs not that he deems
His welfare his true aim,
He errs because he dreams
The world does but exist that welfare to bestow.

We mortals are no kings
For each of whom to sway

A new-made world up-springs
    Meant merely for his play;
No, we are strangers here; the world is from of old.

    In vain our pent wills fret,
    And would the world subdue.
    Limits we did not set
    Condition all we do;
Born into life we are, and life must be our mould.

    Born into life—man grows
    Forth from his parents' stem,
    And blends their bloods, as those
    Of theirs are blent in them;
So each new man strikes root into a far fore-time.

    Born into life—we bring
    A bias with us here,
    And, when here, each new thing
    Affects us we come near;
To tunes we did not call our being must keep chime.

    Born into life—in vain,
    Opinions, those or these,
    Unalter'd to retain
    The obstinate mind decrees;
Experience, like a sea, soaks all-effacing in.

    Born into life—who lists
    May what is false hold dear,
    And for himself make mists
    Through which to see less clear;
The world is what it is, for all our dust and din.

    Born into life—'tis we,
    And not the world, are new.

Our cry for bliss, our plea,
Others have urged it too;
Our wants have all been felt, our errors made before.

No eye could be too sound
To observe a world so vast,
No patience too profound
To sort what's here amass'd;
How man may here best live no care too great to explore.

But we—as some rude guest
Would change, where'er he roam,
The manners there profess'd
To those he brings from home—
We mark not the world's course, but would have *it* take
    ours.

The world's course proves the terms
On which man wins content;
Reason the proof confirms;
We spurn it, and invent
A false course for the world, and for ourselves, false
    powers.

Riches we wish to get,
Yet remain spendthrifts still;
We would have health, and yet
Still use our bodies ill;
Bafflers of our own prayers, from youth to life's last
    scenes.

We would have inward peace,
Yet will not look within;
We would have misery cease,
Yet will not cease from sin;
We want all pleasant ends, but will use no harsh means;

We do not what we ought,
What we ought not, we do,
And lean upon the thought
That chance will bring us through;
But our own acts, for good or ill, are mightier powers.

Yet, even when man forsakes
All sin,—is just, is pure,
Abandons all which makes
His welfare insecure—
Other existences there are, that clash with ours.

Like us, the lightning fires
Love to have scope and play;
The stream, like us, desires
An unimpeded way;
Like us, the Libyan wind delights to roam at large.

Streams will not curb their pride
The just man not to entomb,
Nor lightnings go aside
To leave his virtues room;
Nor is that wind less rough which blows a good man's
      barge.

Nature, with equal mind,
Sees all her sons at play;
Sees man control the wind,
The wind sweep man away;
Allows the proudly-riding and the founder'd bark.

And, lastly, though of ours
No weakness spoil our lot,
Though the non-human powers

    Of Nature harm us not,
The ill-deeds of other men make often *our* life dark.

    What were the wise man's plan?—
    Through this sharp, toil-set life,
    To fight as best he can,
    And win what's won by strife.
But we an easier way to cheat our pains have found.

    Scratch'd by a fall, with moans
    As children of weak age
    Lend life to the dumb stones
    Whereon to vent their rage,
And bend their little fists, and rate the senseless ground;

    So, loath to suffer mute,
    We, peopling the void air,
    Make Gods to whom to impute
    The ills we ought to bear;
With God and Fate to rail at, suffering easily.

    Yet grant—as sense long miss'd
    Things that are now perceiv'd,
    And much may still exist
    Which is not yet believ'd—
Grant that the world were full of Gods we cannot see;

    All things the world which fill
    Of but one stuff are spun,
    That we who rail are still,
    With what we rail at, one;
One with the o'er-labour'd Power that through the
    breadth and length

    Of earth, and air, and sea,
    In men, and plants, and stones,

Hath toil perpetually,
And struggles, pants, and moans;
Fain would do all things well, but sometimes fails in
strength.

And patiently exact
This universal God
Alike to any act
Proceeds at any nod,
And quietly declaims the cursings of himself.

This is not what man hates,
Yet he can curse but this.
Harsh Gods and hostile Fates
Are dreams! this only *is;*
Is everywhere; sustains the wise, the foolish elf.

Nor only, in the intent
To attach blame elsewhere,
Do we at will invent
Stern Powers who make their care
To embitter human life, malignant Deities;

But, next, we would reverse
The scheme ourselves have spun,
And what we made to curse
We now would lean upon,
And feign kind Gods who perfect what man vainly tries.

Look, the world tempts our eye,
And we would know it all!
We map the starry sky,
We mine this earthen ball,
We measure the sea-tides, we number the sea-sands;

We scrutinize the dates
Of long-past human things,
The bounds of effac'd states,
The lines of deceas'd kings;
We search out dead men's words, and works of dead
men's hands;

We shut our eyes, and muse
How our own minds are made,
What springs of thought they use,
How righten'd, how betray'd;
And spend our wit to name what most employ unnam'd;

But still, as we proceed,
The mass swells more and more
Of volumes yet to read,
Of secrets yet to explore.
Our hair grows grey, our eyes are dimm'd, our heat is
tamed.

We rest our faculties,
And thus address the Gods:
"True science if there is,
It stays in your abodes;
Man's measures cannot mete the immeasurable All;

"You only can take in
The world's immense design,
Our desperate search was sin,
Which henceforth we resign,
Sure only that *your* mind sees all things which befall!"

Fools! that in man's brief term
He cannot all things view,

Affords no ground to affirm
That there are Gods who do!
Nor does being weary prove that he has where to rest!

Again: our youthful blood
Claims rapture as its right;
The world, a rolling flood
Of newness and delight,
Draws in the enamour'd gazer to its shining breast;

Pleasure to our hot grasp
Gives flowers after flowers,
With passionate warmth we clasp
Hand after hand in ours;
Nor do we soon perceive how fast our youth is spent.

At once our eyes grow clear;
We see in blank dismay
Year posting after year,
Sense after sense decay;
Our shivering heart is mined by secret discontent;

Yet still, in spite of truth,
In spite of hopes entomb'd,
That longing of our youth
Burns ever unconsum'd,
Still hungrier for delight as delights grow more rare.

We pause; we hush our heart,
And then address the Gods:
"The world hath fail'd to impart
The joy our youth forbodes,
Fail'd to fill up the void which in our breasts we bear.

"Changeful till now, we still
Look'd on to something new;

Let us, with changeless will,
Henceforth look on to you,
To find with you the joy we in vain *here* require!"

Fools! that so often here
Happiness mock'd our prayer,
I think, might make us fear
A like event elsewhere!
Make us, not fly to dreams, but moderate desire!

And yet, for those who know
Themselves, who wisely take
Their way through life, and bow
To what they cannot break,
Why should I say that life need yield but *moderate* bliss?

Shall we, with temper spoil'd,
Health sapp'd by living ill,
And judgement all embroil'd
By sadness and self-will,
Shall *we* judge what for man is not true bliss or is?

Is it so small a thing
To have enjoy'd the sun,
To have lived light in the spring,
To have loved, to have thought, to have done;
To have advanc'd true friends, and beat down baffling
foes;

That we must feign a bliss
Of doubtful future date,
And, while we dream on this,
Lose all our present state,
And relegate to worlds yet distant our repose?

Not much, I know, you prize
What pleasures may be had,
Who look on life with eyes
Estrang'd, like mine, and sad;
And yet the village churl feels the truth more than you,

Who's loath to leave this life
Which to him little yields;
His hard-task'd sunburnt wife,
His often-labour'd fields,
The boors with whom he talk'd, the country spots he
knew.

But thou, because thou hear'st
Men scoff at Heaven and Fate,
Because the Gods thou fear'st
Fail to make blest thy state,
Tremblest, and wilt not dare to trust the joys there are.

I say: Fear not! Life still
Leaves human effort scope.
But, since life teems with ill,
Nurse no extravagant hope;
Because thou must not dream, thou need'st not then de-
spair!

*A long pause. At the end of it the notes of a harp below
are again heard, and Callicles sings.*

CALLICLES

Far, far from here,
The Adriatic breaks in a warm bay
Among the green Illyrian hills; and there
The sunshine in the happy glens is fair,
And by the sea, and in the brakes.

The grass is cool, the sea-side air
Buoyant and fresh, the mountain flowers
As virginal and sweet as ours.
And there, they say, two bright and aged snakes,
Who once were Cadmus and Harmonia,
Bask in the glens or on the warm sea-shore,
In breathless quiet, after all their ills.
Nor do they see their country, nor the place
Where the Sphinx lived among the frowning hills,
Nor the unhappy palace of their race,
Nor Thebes, nor the Ismenus, any more.

There those two live, far in the Illyrian brakes.
They had stay'd long enough to see,
In Thebes, the billow of calamity
Over their own dear children roll'd,
Curse upon curse, pang upon pang,
For years, they sitting helpless in their home,
A grey old man and woman; yet of old
The Gods had to their marriage come,
And at the banquet all the Muses sang.

Therefore they did not end their days
In sight of blood; but were rapt, far away,
To where the west wind plays,
And murmurs of the Adriatic come
To those untrodden mountain lawns; and there
Placed safely in changed forms, the Pair
Wholly forget their first sad life, and home,
And all that Theban woe, and stray
For ever through the glens, placid and dumb.

EMPEDOCLES

That was my harp-player again!—where is he?
Down by the stream?

PAUSANIAS

Yes, Master, in the wood.

EMPEDOCLES

He ever loved the Theban story well!
But the day wears. Go now, Pausanias,
For I must be alone. Leave me one mule;
Take down with thee the rest to Catana.
And for young Callicles, thank him from me;
Tell him I never fail'd to love his lyre:
But he must follow me no more to-night.

PAUSANIAS

Thou wilt return to-morrow to the city?

EMPEDOCLES

Either to-morrow or some other day,
In the sure revolutions of the world,
Good friend, I shall revisit Catana.
I have seen many cities in my time
Till my eyes ache with the long spectacle,
And I shall doubtless see them all again;
Thou know'st me for a wanderer from of old.
Meanwhile, stay me not now. Farewell, Pausanias!

He departs on his way up the mountain.

PAUSANIAS (*alone*)

I dare not urge him further; he must go.
But he is strangely wrought!—I will speed back
And bring Peisianax to him from the city;
His counsel could once soothe him. But, Apollo!
How his brow lighten'd as the music rose!
Callicles must wait here, and play to him;

I saw him through the chestnuts far below,
Just since, down at the stream.—Ho! Callicles!

He descends, calling.

Act II: *Evening. The Summit of Etna.*

EMPEDOCLES

            Alone!—
On this charr'd, blacken'd, melancholy waste,
Crown'd by the awful peak, Etna's great mouth,
Round which the sullen vapour rolls—alone!
Pausanias is far hence, and that is well,
For I must henceforth speak no more with man.
He has his lesson too, and that debt's paid;
And the good, learned, friendly, quiet man,
May bravelier front his life, and in himself
Find henceforth energy and heart; but I,
The weary man, the banish'd citizen—
Whose banishment is not his greatest ill,
Whose weariness no energy can reach,
And for whose hurt courage is not the cure—
What should I do with life and living more?

No, thou art come too late, Empedocles!
And the world hath the day, and must break thee,
Not thou the world. With men thou canst not live,
Their thoughts, their ways, their wishes, are not thine;
And being lonely thou art miserable,
For something has impair'd thy spirit's strength,
And dried its self-sufficing fount of joy.
Thou canst not live with men nor with thyself—
Oh sage! oh sage!—Take then the one way left;
And turn thee to the elements, thy friends,
Thy well-tried friends, thy willing ministers,

And say:—Ye servants, hear Empedocles,
Who asks this final service at your hands!
Before the sophist brood hath overlaid
The last spark of man's consciousness with words—
Ere quite the being of man, ere quite the world
Be disarray'd of their divinity—
Before the soul lose all her solemn joys,
And awe be dead, and hope impossible,
And the soul's deep eternal night come on,
Receive me, hide me, quench me, take me home!

*He advances to the edge of the crater. Smoke and fire
break forth with a loud noise, and Callicles is heard
below singing.*

CALLICLES

The lyre's voice is lovely everywhere!
In the court of Gods, in the city of men,
And in the lonely rock-strewn mountain glen,
In the still mountain air.

Only to Typho it sounds hatefully!
To Typho only, the rebel o'erthrown,
Through whose heart Etna drives her roots of stone,
To imbed them in the sea.

Wherefore dost thou groan so loud?
Wherefore do thy nostrils flash,
Through the dark night, suddenly,
Typho, such red jets of flame?—
Is thy tortur'd heart still proud?
Is thy fire-scath'd arm still rash?
Still alert thy stone-crush'd frame?
Doth thy fierce soul still deplore
The ancient rout by the Cilician hills,
And that curst treachery on the Mount of Gore?

Do thy bloodshot eyes still see
The fight that crown'd thy ills,
Thy last defeat in this Sicilian sea?
Hast thou sworn, in thy sad lair,
Where erst the strong sea-currents suck'd thee down,
Never to cease to writhe, and try to sleep,
Letting the sea-stream wander through thy hair?
That thy groans, like thunder deep,
Begin to roll, and almost drown
The sweet notes, whose lulling spell
Gods and the race of mortals love so well,
When through thy caves thou hearest music swell?

But an awful pleasure bland
Spreading o'er the Thunderer's face,
When the sound climbs near his seat,
The Olympian council sees;
As he lets his lax right hand,
Which the lightnings doth embrace,
Sink upon his mighty knees.
And the eagle, at the beck
Of the appeasing gracious harmony,
Droops all his sheeny, brown, deep-feather'd neck,
Nestling nearer to Jove's feet;
While o'er his sovereign eye
The curtains of the blue films slowly meet,
And the white Olympus peaks
Rosily brighten, and the sooth'd Gods smile
At one another from their golden chairs,
And no one round the charmèd circle speaks.
Only the loved Hebe bears
The cup about, whose draughts beguile
Pain and care, with a dark store
Of fresh-pull'd violets wreath'd and nodding o'er;
And her flush'd feet glow on the marble floor.

EMPEDOCLES

He fables, yet speaks truth.
The brave impetuous heart yields everywhere
To the subtle, contriving head;
Great qualities are trodden down,
And littleness united
Is become invincible.

These rumblings are not Typho's groans, I know!
These angry smoke-bursts
Are not the passionate breath
Of the mountain-crush'd, tortur'd, intractable Titan king!
But over all the world
What suffering is there not seen
Of plainness oppress'd by cunning,
As the well-counsell'd Zeus oppress'd
The self-helping son of earth!
What anguish of greatness
Rail'd and hunted from the world,
Because its simplicity rebukes
This envious, miserable age!
I am weary of it!—
Lie there, ye ensigns
Of my unloved pre-eminence
In an age like this!
Among a people of children,
Who throng'd me in their cities,
Who worshipp'd me in their houses,
And ask'd, not wisdom,
But drugs to charm with,
But spells to mutter—
All the fool's-armoury of magic!—Lie there,
My golden circlet!
My purple robe!

CALLICLES (*from below*)

As the sky-brightening south-wind clears the day,
And makes the mass'd clouds roll,
The music of the lyre blows away
The clouds that wrap the soul.

Oh, that Fate had let me see
That triumph of the sweet persuasive lyre!
That famous, final victory
When jealous Pan with Marsyas did conspire!

When, from far Parnassus' side,
Young Apollo, all the pride
Of the Phrygian flutes to tame,
To the Phrygian highlands came!
Where the long green reed-beds sway
In the rippled waters grey
Of that solitary lake
Where Maeander's springs are born;
Where the ridg'd pine-wooded roots
Of Messogis westward break,
Mounting westward, high and higher.
There was held the famous strife;
There the Phrygian brought his flutes,
And Apollo brought his lyre;
And, when now the westering sun-
Touch'd the hills, the strife was done,
And the attentive Muses said:
"Marsyas! thou art vanquishèd."
Then Apollo's minister
Hang'd upon a branching fir
Marsyas, that unhappy Faun,
And began to whet his knife.
But the Maenads, who were there,

Left their friend, and with robes flowing
In the wind, and loose dark hair
O'er their polish'd bosoms blowing,
Each her ribbon'd tambourine
Flinging on the mountain sod,
With a lovely frighten'd mien
Came about the youthful God.
But he turn'd his beauteous face
Haughtily another way,
From the grassy sun-warm'd place,
Where in proud repose he lay,
With one arm over his head,
Watching how the whetting sped.

But aloof, on the lake strand,
Did the young Olympus stand,
Weeping at his master's end;
For the Faun had been his friend.
For he taught him how to sing,
And he taught him flute-playing.
Many a morning had they gone
To the glimmering mountain lakes,
And had torn up by the roots
The tall crested water-reeds
With long plumes, and soft brown seeds,
And had carved them into flutes,
Sitting on a tabled stone
Where the shoreward ripple breaks.
And he taught him how to please
The red-snooded Phrygian girls,
Whom the summer evening sees
Flashing in the dance's whirls
Underneath the starlit trees
In the mountain villages.
Therefore now Olympus stands,

At his master's piteous cries
Pressing fast with both his hands
His white garment to his eyes,
Not to see Apollo's scorn;
Ah, poor Faun, poor Faun! ah, poor Faun!

EMPEDOCLES

And lie thou there,
My laurel bough!
Scornful Apollo's ensign, lie thou there!
Though thou hast been my shade in the world's heat—
Though I have loved thee, lived in honouring thee—
Yet lie thou there,
My laurel bough!

I am weary of thee!
I am weary of the solitude
Where he who bears thee must abide!
Of the rocks of Parnassus,
Of the gorge of Delphi,
Of the moonlit peaks, and the caves.
Thou guardest them, Apollo!
Over the grave of the slain Pytho,
Though young, intolerably severe;
Thou keepest aloof the profane,
But the solitude oppresses thy votary!
The jars of men reach him not in thy valley—
But can life reach him?
Thou fencest him from the multitude—
Who will fence him from himself?
He hears nothing but the cry of the torrents
And the beating of his own heart.
The air is thin, the veins swell—
The temples tighten and throb there—
Air! air!

Take thy bough; set me free from my solitude!
I have been enough alone!

Where shall thy votary fly then? back to men?—
But they will gladly welcome him once more,
And help him to unbend his too tense thought,
And rid him of the presence of himself,
And keep their friendly chatter at his ear,
And haunt him, till the absence from himself,
That other torment, grow unbearable;
And he will fly to solitude again,
And he will find its air too keen for him,
And so change back; and many thousand times
Be miserably bandied to and fro
Like a sea-wave, betwixt the world and thee,
Thou young, implacable God! and only death
Shall cut his oscillations short, and so
Bring him to poise. There is no other way.

And yet what days were those, Parmenides!
When we were young, when we could number friends
In all the Italian cities like ourselves,
When with elated hearts we join'd your train,
Ye Sun-born Virgins! on the road of truth.
Then we could still enjoy, then neither thought
Nor outward things were clos'd and dead to us,
But we receiv'd the shock of mighty thoughts
On simple minds with a pure natural joy;
And if the sacred load oppress'd our brain,
We had the power to feel the pressure eased,
The brow unbound, the thoughts flow free again,
In the delightful commerce of the world.
We had not lost our balance then, nor grown
Thought's slaves, and dead to every natural joy!

The smallest thing could give us pleasure then!
The sports of the country people,
A flute-note from the woods,
Sunset over the sea;
Seed-time and harvest,
The reapers in the corn,
The vinedresser in his vineyard,
The village-girl at her wheel!

Fullness of life and power of feeling, ye
Are for the happy, for the souls at ease,
Who dwell on a firm basis of content!—
But he, who has outliv'd his prosperous days,
But he, whose youth fell on a different world
From that on which his exiled age is thrown,
Whose mind was fed on other food, was train'd
By other rules than are in vogue to-day,
Whose habit of thought is fix'd, who will not change,
But in a world he loves not must subsist
In ceaseless opposition, be the guard
Of his own breast, fetter'd to what he guards,
That the world win no mastery over him;
Who has no friend, no fellow left, not one;
Who has no minute's breathing space allow'd
To nurse his dwindling faculty of joy—
Joy and the outward world must die to him,
As they are dead to me!

A long pause, during which Empedocles remains motionless, plunged in thought. The night deepens. He moves forward and gazes round him, and proceeds:

And you, ye stars,
Who slowly begin to marshal,
As of old, in the fields of heaven,
Your distant, melancholy lines!

Have *you*, too, survived yourselves?
Are *you*, too, what I fear to become?
You, too, once lived!
You too moved joyfully
Among august companions
In an older world, peopled by Gods,
In a mightier order,
The radiant, rejoicing, intelligent Sons of Heaven!
But now, you kindle
Your lonely, cold-shining lights,
Unwilling lingerers
In the heavenly wilderness,
For a younger, ignoble world;
And renew, by necessity,
Night after night your courses,
In echoing unnear'd silence,
Above a race you know not.
Uncaring and undelighted,
Without friend and without home;
Weary like us, though not
Weary with our weariness.

No, no, ye stars! there is no death with you,
No languor, no decay! Languor and death,
They are with me, not you! ye are alive!
Ye and the pure dark ether where ye ride
Brilliant above me! And thou, fiery world,
That sapp'st the vitals of this terrible mount
Upon whose charr'd and quaking crust I stand,
Thou, too, brimmest with life!—the sea of cloud
That heaves its white and billowy vapours up
To moat this isle of ashes from the world,
Lives!—and that other fainter sea, far down,
O'er whose lit floor a road of moonbeams leads
To Etna's Liparëan sister-fires

And the long dusky line of Italy—
That mild and luminous floor of waters lives,
With held-in joy swelling its heart!—I only,
Whose spring of hope is dried, whose spirit has fail'd—
I, who have not, like these, in solitude
Maintain'd courage and force, and in myself
Nursed an immortal vigour—I alone
Am dead to life and joy; therefore I read
In all things my own deadness.

A long silence. He continues:

Oh that I could glow like this mountain!
Oh that my heart bounded with the swell of the sea!
Oh that my soul were full of light as the stars!
Oh that it brooded over the world like the air!

But no, this heart will glow no more! thou art
A living man no more, Empedocles!
Nothing but a devouring flame of thought—
But a naked, eternally restless mind!

After a pause:

To the elements it came from
Everything will return.
Our bodies to earth,
Our blood to water,
Heat to fire,
Breath to air.
They were well born, they will be well entomb'd!
But mind? . . .

And we might gladly share the fruitful stir
Down in our mother earth's miraculous womb!
Well might it be
With what roll'd of us in the stormy main!

We might have joy, blent with the all-bathing air,
Or with the nimble radiant life of fire!

But mind—but thought—
If these have been the master part of us—
Where will *they* find their parent element?
What will receive *them*, who will call *them* home?
But we shall still be in them, and they in us,
And we shall be the strangers of the world,
And they will be our lords, as they are now;
And keep us prisoners of our consciousness,
And never let us clasp and feel the All
But through their forms, and modes, and stifling veils.
And we shall be unsatisfied as now,
And we shall feel the agony of thirst,
The ineffable longing for the life of life
Baffled for ever: and still thought and mind
Will hurry us with them on their homeless march,
Over the unallied unopening earth,
Over the unrecognizing sea; while air
Will blow us fiercely back to sea and earth,
And fire repel us from its living waves.
And then we shall unwillingly return
Back to this meadow of calamity,
This uncongenial place, this human life;
And in our individual human state
Go through the sad probation all again,
To see if we will poise our life at last,
To see if we will now at last be true
To our own only true, deep-buried selves,
Being one with which we are one with the whole world;
Or whether we will once more fall away
Into some bondage of the flesh or mind,
Some slough of sense, or some fantastic maze
Forg'd by the imperious lonely thinking-power.

And each succeeding age in which we are born
Will have more peril for us than the last;
Will goad our senses with a sharper spur,
Will fret our minds to an intenser play,
Will make ourselves harder to be discern'd.
And we shall struggle awhile, gasp and rebel;
And we shall fly for refuge to past times,
Their soul of unworn youth, their breath of greatness;
And the reality will pluck us back,
Knead us in its hot hand, and change our nature.
And we shall feel our powers of effort flag,
And rally them for one last fight, and fail;
And we shall sink in the impossible strife,
And be astray for ever.

Slave of sense

I have in no wise been; but slave of thought?—
    And who can say:—I have been always free,
Lived ever in the light of my own soul?—
I cannot! I have lived in wrath and gloom,
Fierce, disputatious, ever at war with man,
Far from my own soul, far from warmth and light.
But I have not grown easy in these bonds—
But I have not denied what bonds these were!
Yea, I take myself to witness,
That I have loved no darkness,
Sophisticated no truth,
Nursed no delusion,
Allow'd no fear!

And therefore, O ye elements, I know—
Ye know it too—it hath been granted me
Not to die wholly, not to be all enslav'd.
I feel it in this hour! The numbing cloud
Mounts off my soul; I feel it, I breathe free!

Is it but for a moment?
Ah! boil up, ye vapours!
Leap and roar, thou sea of fire!
My soul glows to meet you.
Ere it flag, ere the mists
Of despondency and gloom
Rush over it again,
Receive me! Save me!

He plunges into the crater.

CALLICLES (*from below*)

Through the black, rushing smoke-bursts,
Thick breaks the red flame;
All Etna heaves fiercely
Her forest-cloth'd frame.

Not here, O Apollo!
Are haunts meet for thee.
But, where Helicon breaks down
In cliff to the sea,

Where the moon-silver'd inlets
Send far their light voice
Up the still vale of Thisbe,
O speed, and rejoice!

On the sward at the cliff-top
Lie strewn the white flocks;
On the cliff-side the pigeons
Roost deep in the rocks.

In the moonlight the shepherds,
Soft lull'd by the rills,

Lie wrapt in their blankets,
Asleep on the hills.

—What forms are these coming
So white through the gloom?
What garments out-glistening
The gold-flower'd broom?

What sweet-breathing presence
Out-perfumes the thyme?
What voices enrapture
The night's balmy prime?—

'Tis Apollo comes leading
His choir, the Nine.
—The leader is fairest,
But all are divine.

They are lost in the hollows!
They stream up again!
What seeks on this mountain
The glorified train?—

They bathe on this mountain,
In the spring by their road;
Then on to Olympus,
Their endless abode!

—Whose praise do they mention?
Of what is it told?—
What will be for ever;
What was from of old.

First hymn they the Father
Of all things; and then

The rest of immortals,
The action of men.

The day in his hotness,
The strife with the palm;
The night in her silence,
The stars in their calm.

○

EXCUSE

I too have suffer'd: yet I know
She is not cold, though she seems so:
She is not cold, she is not light;
But our ignoble souls lack might.

She smiles and smiles, and will not sigh,
While we for hopeless passion die;
Yet she could love, those eyes declare,
Were but men nobler than they are.

Eagerly once her gracious ken
Was turn'd upon the sons of men.
But light the serious visage grew—
She look'd, and smiled, and saw them through.

Our petty souls, our strutting wits,
Our labour'd puny passion-fits—
Ah, may she scorn them still, till we
Scorn them as bitterly as she!

Yet oh, that Fate would let her see
One of some worthier race than we;

One for whose sake she once might prove
How deeply she who scorns can love.

His eyes be like the starry lights—
His voice like sounds of summer nights—
In all his lovely mien let pierce
The magic of the universe.

And she to him will reach her hand,
And gazing in his eyes will stand,
And know her friend, and weep for glee,
And cry—*Long, long I've look'd for thee.*—

Then will she weep—with smiles, till then,
Coldly she mocks the sons of men.
Till then her lovely eyes maintain
Their gay, unwavering, deep disdain.

◯

INDIFFERENCE

I must not say that thou wert true,
Yet let me say that thou wert fair.
And they that lovely face who view,
They will not ask if truth be there.

Truth—what is truth? Two bleeding hearts
Wounded by men, by Fortune tried,
Outwearied with their lonely parts,
Vow to beat henceforth side by side.

The world to them was stern and drear;
Their lot was but to weep and moan.

Ah, let them keep their faith sincere,
For neither could subsist alone!

But souls whom some benignant breath
Has charm'd at birth from gloom and care,
These ask no love—these plight no faith,
For they are happy as they are.

The world to them may homage make,
And garlands for their forehead weave.
And what the world can give, they take:
But they bring more than they receive.

They smile upon the world: their ears
To one demand alone are coy.
They will not give us love and tears—
They bring us light, and warmth, and joy.

It was not love that heav'd thy breast,
Fair child! it was the bliss within.
Adieu! and say that one, at least,
Was just to what he did not win.

○

LONGING

Come to me in my dreams, and then
By day I shall be well again.
For then the night will more than pay
The hopeless longing of the day.

Come, as thou cam'st a thousand times,
A messenger from radiant climes,

And smile on thy new world, and be
As kind to others as to me.

Or, as thou never cam'st in sooth,
Come now, and let me dream it truth.
And part my hair, and kiss my brow,
And say—*My love! why sufferest thou?*

Come to me in my dreams, and then
By day I shall be well again.
For then the night will more than pay
The hopeless longing of the day.

○

THE LAKE

Again I see my bliss at hand;
The town, the lake are here.
My Marguerite smiles upon the strand
Unalter'd with the year.

I know that graceful figure fair,
That cheek of languid hue;
I know that soft enkerchief'd hair,
And those sweet eyes of blue.

Again I spring to make my choice;
Again in tones of ire
I hear a God's tremendous voice—
"Be counsell'd, and retire!"

Ye guiding Powers, who join and part,
What would ye have with me?
Ah, warn some more ambitious heart,
And let the peaceful be!

◯

PARTING

Ye storm-winds of Autumn
Who rush by, who shake
The window, and ruffle
The gleam-lighted lake;
Who cross to the hill-side
Thin-sprinkled with farms,
Where the high woods strip sadly
Their yellowing arms;—
   Ye are bound for the mountains—
Ah, with you let me go
Where your cold distant barrier,
The vast range of snow,
Through the loose clouds lifts dimly
Its white peaks in air—
How deep is their stillness!
Ah! would I were there!

But on the stairs what voice is this I hear,
Buoyant as morning, and as morning clear?
Say, has some wet bird-haunted English lawn
Lent it the music of its trees at dawn?
Or was it from some sun-fleck'd mountain-brook
That the sweet voice its upland clearness took?
    Ah! it comes nearer—
    Sweet notes, this way!

Hark! fast by the window
The rushing winds go,
To the ice-cumber'd gorges,
The vast seas of snow.

There the torrents drive upward
Their rock-strangled hum,
There the avalanche thunders
The hoarse torrent dumb.
—I come, O ye mountains!
Ye torrents, I come!

But who is this, by the half-open'd door,
Whose figure casts a shadow on the floor?
The sweet blue eyes—the soft, ash-colour'd hair—
The cheeks that still their gentle paleness wear—
The lovely lips, with their arch smile, that tells
The unconquer'd joy in which her spirit dwells—
          Ah! they bend nearer—
          Sweet lips, this way!

Hark! the wind rushes past us—
Ah! with that let me go
To the clear waning hill-side
Unspotted by snow,
There to watch, o'er the sunk vale,
The frore mountain wall,
Where the nich'd snow-bed sprays down
Its powdery fall.
There its dusky blue clusters
The aconite spreads;
There the pines slope, the cloud-strips
Hung soft in their heads.
No life but, at moments,
The mountain-bee's hum.
—I come, O ye mountains!
Ye pine-woods, I come!

Forgive me! forgive me!
   Ah, Marguerite, fain

Would these arms reach to clasp thee:—
　　But see! 'tis in vain.

In the void air towards thee
　　My strain'd arms are cast.
But a sea rolls between us—
　　Our different past.

To the lips, ah! of others,
　　Those lips have been prest,
And others, ere I was,
　　Were clasp'd to that breast;

Far, far from each other
　　Our spirits have grown.
And what heart knows another?
　　Ah! who knows his own?

Blow, ye winds! lift me with you!
　　I come to the wild.
Fold closely, O Nature!
　　Thine arms round thy child.

To thee only God granted
　　A heart ever new:
To all always open;
　　To all always true.

Ah, calm me! restore me!
　　And dry up my tears
On thy high mountain platforms,
　　Where Morn first appears,

Where the white mists, for ever,
　　Are spread and upfurl'd;

In the stir of the forces
        Whence issued the world.

○

ABSENCE

In this fair stranger's eyes of grey
Thine eyes, my love, I see.
I shudder: for the passing day
Had borne me far from thee.

This is the curse of life: that not
A nobler calmer train
Of wiser thoughts and feelings blot
Our passions from our brain;

But each day brings its petty dust
Our soon-chok'd souls to fill,
And we forget because we must,
And not because we will.

I struggle towards the light; and ye,
Once-long'd-for storms of love!
If with the light ye cannot be,
I bear that ye remove.

I struggle towards the light; but oh,
While yet the night is chill,
Upon Time's barren, stormy flow,
Stay with me, Marguerite, still!

○

DESTINY

Why each is striving, from of old,
To love more deeply than he can?
Still would be true, yet still grows cold?
—Ask of the Powers that sport with man!

They yok'd in him, for endless strife,
A heart of ice, a soul of fire;
And hurl'd him on the Field of Life,
An aimless unallay'd Desire.

○

TO MARGUERITE
IN RETURNING A VOLUME
OF THE LETTERS OF ORTIS

Yes: in the sea of life enisl'd,
With echoing straits between us thrown,
Dotting the shoreless watery wild,
We mortal millions live *alone*.
  The islands feel the enclasping flow,
And then their endless bounds they know.

But when the moon their hollows lights
And they are swept by balms of spring,
And in their glens, on starry nights,
The nightingales divinely sing;
And lovely notes, from shore to shore,
Across the sounds and channels pour;

Oh then a longing like despair
Is to their farthest caverns sent;
For surely once, they feel, we were
Parts of a single continent.
Now round us spreads the watery plain—
Oh might our marges meet again!

Who order'd, that their longing's fire
Should be, as soon as kindled, cool'd?
Who renders vain their deep desire?—
    A God, a God their severance rul'd;
And bade betwixt their shores to be
The unplumb'd, salt, estranging sea.

◑

HUMAN LIFE

What mortal, when he saw,
Life's voyage done, his heavenly Friend,
Could ever yet dare tell him fearlessly:
"I have kept uninfring'd my nature's law;
The inly-written chart thou gavest me
To guide me, I have steer'd by to the end"?

Ah! let us make no claim
On life's incognizable sea
To too exact a steering of our way!
Let us not fret and fear to miss our aim
If some fair coast has lured us to make stay,
Or some friend hail'd us to keep company!

Aye, we would each fain drive
At random, and not steer by rule!

Weakness! and worse, weakness bestow'd in vain!
Winds from our side the unsuiting consort rive,
We rush by coasts where we had lief remain;
Man cannot, though he would, live chance's fool.

No! as the foaming swathe
Of torn-up water, on the main,
Falls heavily away with long-drawn roar
On either side the black deep-furrow'd path
Cut by an onward-labouring vessel's prore,
And never touches the ship-side again;

Even so we leave behind,
As, charter'd by some unknown Powers,
We stem across the sea of life by night,
The joys which were not for our use design'd,
The friends to whom we had no natural right,
The homes that were not destined to be ours.

☉

SELF-DECEPTION

Say, what blinds us, that we claim the glory
Of possessing powers not our share?—
Since man woke on earth, he knows his story,
But, before we woke on earth, we were.

Long, long since, undower'd yet, our spirit
Roam'd, ere birth, the treasuries of God:
Saw the gifts, the powers it might inherit;
Ask'd an outfit for its earthly road.

Then, as now, this tremulous, eager Being
Strain'd, and long'd, and grasp'd each gift it saw.

Then, as now, a Power beyond our seeing
Stav'd us back, and gave our choice the law.

   Ah, whose hand that day through heaven guided
Man's blank spirit, since it was not we?
Ah, who sway'd our choice, and who decided
What our gifts, and what our wants should be?

   For, alas! he left us each retaining
Shreds of gifts which he refus'd in full.
Still these waste us with their hopeless straining—
Still the attempt to use them proves them null.

   And on earth we wander, groping, reeling;
Powers stir in us, stir and disappear.
Ah, and he, who placed our master-feeling,
Fail'd to place our master-feeling clear.

   We but dream we have our wish'd-for powers.
Ends we seek we never shall attain.
Ah, *some* power exists there, which is ours?
Some end is there, we indeed may gain?

○

LINES WRITTEN BY A DEATH-BED

   Yes, now the longing is o'erpast,
   Which, dogg'd by fear and fought by shame,
   Shook her weak bosom day and night,
   Consum'd her beauty like a flame,
   And dimm'd it like the desert blast.
   And though the curtains hide her face,
   Yet were it lifted to the light
   The sweet expression of her brow

Would charm the gazer, till his thought
Eras'd the ravages of time,
Fill'd up the hollow cheek, and brought
A freshness back as of her prime—
So healing is her quiet now.
So perfectly the lines express
A placid, settled loveliness;
Her youngest rival's freshest grace.

But ah, though peace indeed is here,
And ease from shame, and rest from fear;
Though nothing can dismarble now
The smoothness of that limpid brow;
Yet is a calm like this, in truth,
The crowning end of life and youth?
And when this boon rewards the dead,
Are all debts paid, has all been said?
And is the heart of youth so light,
Its step so firm, its eye so bright,
Because on its hot brow there blows
A wind of promise and repose
From the far grave, to which it goes?
Because it has the hope to come,
One day, to harbour in the tomb?
Ah no, the bliss youth dreams is one
For daylight, for the cheerful sun,
For feeling nerves and living breath—
Youth dreams a bliss on this side death.
It dreams a rest, if not more deep,
More grateful than this marble sleep.
It hears a voice within it tell—
"Calm's not life's crown, though calm is well."
'Tis all perhaps which man acquires:
But 'tis not what our youth desires.

○

From TRISTRAM AND ISEULT

Dear saints, it is not sorrow, as I hear,
Not suffering, that shuts up eye and ear
To all which has delighted them before,
And lets us be what we were once no more.
No: we may suffer deeply, yet retain
Power to be mov'd and sooth'd, for all our pain.
By what of old pleas'd us, and will again.
No: 'tis the gradual furnace of the world,
In whose hot air our spirits are upcurl'd
Until they crumble, or else grow like steel—
Which kills in us the bloom, the youth, the spring—
Which leaves the fierce necessity to feel,
But takes away the power—this can avail,
By drying up our joy in everything,
To make our former pleasures all seem stale.
This, or some tyrannous single thought, some fit
Of passion, which subdues our souls to it,
Till for its sake alone we live and move—
Call it ambition, or remorse, or love—
This too can change us wholly, and make seem
All that we did before, shadow and dream.

○

MEMORIAL VERSES

APRIL, 1850

Goethe in Weimar sleeps, and Greece,
Long since, saw Byron's struggle cease.
But one such death remain'd to come.

The last poetic voice is dumb.
What shall be said o'er Wordsworth's tomb?

When Byron's eyes were shut in death,
We bow'd our head and held our breath.
He taught us little: but our soul
Had *felt* him like the thunder's roll.
With shivering heart the strife we saw
Of Passion with Eternal Law;
And yet with reverential awe
We watch'd the fount of fiery life
Which serv'd for that Titanic strife.

When Goethe's death was told, we said—
Sunk, then, is Europe's sagest head.
Physician of the Iron Age,
Goethe has done his pilgrimage.
He took the suffering human race,
He read each wound, each weakness clear—
And struck his finger on the place
And said—*Thou ailest here, and here.*—
He look'd on Europe's dying hour
Of fitful dream and feverish power;
His eye plung'd down the weltering strife,
The turmoil of expiring life;
He said—*The end is everywhere:*
Art still has truth, take refuge there.
And he was happy, if to know
Causes of things, and far below
His feet to see the lurid flow
Of terror, and insane distress,
And headlong fate, be happiness.

And Wordsworth!—Ah, pale Ghosts, rejoice!
For never has such soothing voice

Been to your shadowy world convey'd,
Since erst, at morn, some wandering shade
Heard the clear song of Orpheus come
Through Hades, and the mournful gloom.
Wordsworth has gone from us—and ye,
Ah, may ye feel his voice as we.
He too upon a wintry clime
Had fallen—on this iron time
Of doubts, disputes, distractions, fears.
He found us when the age had bound
Our souls in its benumbing round;
He spoke, and loos'd our heart in tears.
He laid us as we lay at birth
On the cool flowery lap of earth;
Smiles broke from us and we had ease.
The hills were round us, and the breeze
Went o'er the sun-lit fields again:
Our foreheads felt the wind and rain.
Our youth return'd: for there was shed
On spirits that had long been dead,
Spirits dried up and closely-furl'd,
The freshness of the early world.

   Ah, since dark days still bring to light
Man's prudence and man's fiery might,
Time may restore us in his course
Goethe's sage mind and Byron's force:
But where will Europe's latter hour
Again find Wordsworth's healing power?
Others will teach us how to dare,
And against fear our breast to steel:
Others will strengthen us to bear—
But who, ah who, will make us feel?
The cloud of mortal destiny,

Others will front it fearlessly—
But who, like him, will put it by?

Keep fresh the grass upon his grave,
O Rotha! with thy living wave.
Sing him thy best! for few or none
Hears thy voice right, now he is gone.

○

COURAGE

True, we must tame our rebel will:
True, we must bow to Nature's law:
Must bear in silence many an ill;
Must learn to wait, renounce, withdraw.

Yet now, when boldest wills give place,
When Fate and Circumstance are strong,
And in their rush the human race
Are swept, like huddling sheep, along;

Those sterner spirits let me prize,
Who, though the tendence of the whole
They less than us might recognize,
Kept, more than us, their strength of soul.

Yes, be the second Cato prais'd!
Not that he took the course to die—
But that, when 'gainst himself he rais'd
His arm, he rais'd it dauntlessly.

And, Byron! let us dare admire,
If not thy fierce and turbid song,

Yet that, in anguish, doubt, desire,
Thy fiery courage still was strong.

The sun that on thy tossing pain
Did with such cold derision shine,
He crush'd thee not with his disdain—
    He had his glow, and thou hadst thine.

Our bane, disguise it as we may,
Is weakness, is a faltering course.
Oh that past times could give our day,
Join'd to its clearness, of their force!

◌

SELF-DEPENDENCE

Weary of myself, and sick of asking
What I am, and what I ought to be,
At the vessel's prow I stand, which bears me
Forwards, forwards, o'er the starlit sea.

And a look of passionate desire
O'er the sea and to the stars I send:
"Ye who from my childhood up have calm'd me,
Calm me, ah, compose me to the end.

"Ah, once more," I cried, "ye Stars, ye Waters,
On my heart your mighty charm renew:
Still, still let me, as I gaze upon you,
Feel my soul becoming vast like you."

From the intense, clear, star-sown vault of heaven,
Over the lit sea's unquiet way,

In the rustling night-air came the answer—
"Wouldst thou *be* as these are? *Live* as they.

"Unaffrighted by the silence round them,
Undistracted by the sights they see,
These demand not that the things without them
Yield them love, amusement, sympathy.

"And with joy the stars perform their shining,
And the sea its long moon-silver'd roll.
For alone they live, nor pine with noting
All the fever of some differing soul.

"Bounded by themselves, and unobservant
In what state God's other works may be,
In their own tasks all their powers pouring,
These attain the mighty life you see."

———————

O air-born Voice! long since, severely clear,
A cry like thine in my own heart I hear.
"Resolve to be thyself: and know, that he
Who finds himself, loses his misery."

◑

A SUMMER NIGHT

In the deserted moon-blanch'd street
How lonely rings the echo of my feet!
Those windows, which I gaze at, frown,
Silent and white, unopening down,
Repellent as the world:—but see!
A break between the housetops shows

The moon, and, lost behind her, fading dim
Into the dewy dark obscurity
Down at the far horizon's rim,
　　Doth a whole tract of heaven disclose.

　　And to my mind the thought
Is on a sudden brought
Of a past night, and a far different scene.
Headlands stood out into the moon-lit deep
As clearly as at noon;
The spring-tide's brimming flow
Heav'd dazzlingly between;
Houses with long white sweep
Girdled the glistening bay:
Behind, through the soft air,
The blue haze-cradled mountains spread away.
　　That night was far more fair;
But the same restless pacings to and fro,
And the same vainly-throbbing heart was there,
And the same bright calm moon.
　　And the calm moonlight seems to say—
Hast thou then still the old unquiet breast
That neither deadens into rest
Nor ever feels the fiery glow
That whirls the spirit from itself away,
But fluctuates to and fro
Never by passion quite possess'd
And never quite benumb'd by the world's sway?—
And I, I know not if to pray
Still to be what I am, or yield, and be
Like all the other men I see.

For most men in a brazen prison live,
Where in the sun's hot eye,
With heads bent o'er their toil, they languidly

Their lives to some unmeaning taskwork give,
Dreaming of naught beyond their prison wall.
And as, year after year,
Fresh products of their barren labour fall
From their tired hands, and rest
Never yet comes more near,
Gloom settles slowly down over their breast.
And while they try to stem
The waves of mournful thought by which they are prest,
Death in their prison reaches them
Unfreed, having seen nothing, still unblest.

And the rest, a few,
Escape their prison, and depart
On the wide Ocean of Life anew.
There the freed prisoner, where'er his heart
Listeth, will sail;
Nor does he know how there prevail,
Despotic on life's sea,
Trade-winds that cross it from eternity.
Awhile he holds some false way, undebarr'd
By thwarting signs, and braves
The freshening wind and blackening waves.
And then the tempest strikes him, and between
The lightning bursts is seen
Only a driving wreck,
And the pale Master on his spar-strewn deck
With anguish'd face and flying hair
Grasping the rudder hard,
Still bent to make some port he knows not where,
Still standing for some false impossible shore.
And sterner comes the roar
Of sea and wind, and through the deepening gloom
Fainter and fainter wreck and helmsman loom,
And he too disappears, and comes no more.

Is there no life, but these alone?
Madman or slave, must man be one?

Plainness and clearness without shadow of stain!
Clearness divine!
Ye Heavens, whose pure dark regions have no sign
Of languor, though so calm, and though so great
Are yet untroubled and unpassionate:
Who though so noble share in the world's toil,
And though so task'd keep free from dust and soil:
I will not say that your mild deeps retain
A tinge, it may be, of their silent pain
Who have long'd deeply once, and long'd in vain;
But I wall rather say that you remain
A world above man's head, to let him see
How boundless might his soul's horizons be,
How vast, yet of what clear transparency.
How it were good to sink there, and breathe free.
How fair a lot to fill
Is left to each man still.

◑

THE BURIED LIFE

Light flows our war of mocking words, and yet,
Behold, with tears my eyes are wet.
I feel a nameless sadness o'er me roll.
    Yes, yes, we know that we can jest,
We know, we know that we can smile;
But there's a something in this breast
To which thy light words bring no rest,
And thy gay smiles no anodyne.
    Give me thy hand, and hush awhile,

And turn those limpid eyes on mine,
And let me read there, love, thy inmost soul.

Alas, is even Love too weak
To unlock the heart, and let it speak?
Are even lovers powerless to reveal
To one another what indeed they feel?
I knew the mass of men conceal'd
Their thoughts, for fear that if reveal'd
They would by other men be met
With blank indifference, or with blame reprov'd:
I knew they liv'd and mov'd
Trick'd in disguises, alien to the rest
Of men, and alien to themselves—and yet
The same heart beats in every human breast.

But we, my love—does a like spell benumb
Our hearts—our voices?—must we too be dumb?

Ah, well for us, if even we,
Even for a moment, can get free
Our heart, and have our lips unchain'd:
For that which seals them hath been deep ordain'd.

Fate, which foresaw
How frivolous a baby man would be,
By what distractions he would be possess'd,
How he would pour himself in every strife,
And well-nigh change his own identity;
That it might keep from his capricious play
His genuine self, and force him to obey,
Even in his own despite, his being's law,
Bade through the deep recesses of our breast
The unregarded River of our Life
Pursue with indiscernible flow its way;

And that we should not see
The buried stream, and seem to be
Eddying about in blind uncertainty,
Though driving on with it eternally.

   But often, in the world's most crowded streets,
But often, in the din of strife,
There rises an unspeakable desire
After the knowledge of our buried life,
A thirst to spend our fire and restless force
In tracking out our true, original course;
A longing to inquire
Into the mystery of this heart that beats
So wild, so deep in us, to know
Whence our thoughts come and where they go.
And many a man in his own breast then delves,
But deep enough, alas, none ever mines:
And we have been on many thousand lines,
And we have shown on each talent and power,
But hardly have we, for one little hour,
Been on our own line, have we been ourselves;
Hardly had skill to utter one of all
The nameless feelings that course through our breast,
But they course on for ever unexpress'd.
And long we try in vain to speak and act
Our hidden self, and what we say and do
Is eloquent, is well—but 'tis not true:
   And then we will no more be rack'd
With inward striving, and demand
Of all the thousand nothings of the hour
Their stupefying power;
Ah yes, and they benumb us at our call:
Yet still, from time to time, vague and forlorn,
From the soul's subterranean depth upborne
As from an infinitely distant land,

Come airs, and floating echoes, and convey
A melancholy into all our day.

    Only—but this is rare—
When a belovèd hand is laid in ours,
When, jaded with the rush and glare
Of the interminable hours,
Our eyes can in another's eyes read clear,
When our world-deafen'd ear
Is by the tones of a lov'd voice caress'd,—
    A bolt is shot back somewhere in our breast
And a lost pulse of feeling stirs again:
The eye sinks inward, and the heart lies plain,
And what we mean, we say, and what we would, we
    know.
A man becomes aware of his life's flow,
And hears its winding murmur, and he sees
The meadows where it glides, the sun, the breeze.

    And there arrives a lull in the hot race
Wherein he doth for ever chase
That flying and elusive shadow, Rest.
An air of coolness plays upon his face,
And an unwonted calm pervades his breast.
    And then he thinks he knows
The Hills where his life rose,
And the Sea where it goes.

◯

A FAREWELL

My horse's feet beside the lake,
Where sweet the unbroken moonbeams lay,
Sent echoes through the night to wake
Each glistening strand, each heath-fring'd bay.

The poplar avenue was pass'd,
 And the roof'd bridge that spans the stream.
Up the steep street I hurried fast,
Led by thy taper's starlike beam.

I came; I saw thee rise:—the blood
Came flushing to thy languid cheek.
Lock'd in each other's arms we stood,
In tears, with hearts too full to speak.

Days flew: ah, soon I could discern
A trouble in thine alter'd air.
Thy hand lay languidly in mine—
Thy cheek was grave, thy speech grew rare.

I blame thee not:—this heart, I know,
To be long lov'd was never fram'd;
For something in its depths doth glow
Too strange, too restless, too untam'd.

And women—things that live and move
Min'd by the fever of the soul—
They seek to find in those they love
Stern strength, and promise of control.

They ask not kindness, gentle ways;
These they themselves have tried and known:
They ask a soul that never sways
With the blind gusts which shake their own.

I too have felt the load I bore
In a too strong emotion's sway;
I too have wish'd, no woman more,
This starting, feverish heart away:

I too have long'd for trenchant force
And will like a dividing spear;
Have prais'd the keen, unscrupulous course,
Which knows no doubt, which feels no fear.

But in the world I learnt, what there
Thou too wilt surely one day prove,
That will, that energy, though rare,
Are yet far, far less rare than love.

Go then! till Time and Fate impress
This truth on thee, be mine no more!
They will: for thou, I feel, no less
Than I, wert destin'd to this lore.

We school our manners, act our parts:
But He, who sees us through and through,
Knows that the bent of both our hearts
Was to be gentle, tranquil, true.

And though we wear out life, alas,
Distracted as a homeless wind,
In beating where we must not pass,
In seeking what we shall not find;

Yet we shall one day gain, life past,
Clear prospect o'er our being's whole;
Shall see ourselves, and learn at last
Our true affinities of soul.

We shall not then deny a course
To every thought the mass ignore;
We shall not then call hardness force,
Nor lightness wisdom any more.

Then, in the eternal Father's smile,
Our sooth'd, encourag'd souls will dare
To *seem* as free from pride and guile,
As good, as generous, as they *are*.

Then we shall know our friends: though much
Will have been lost—the help in strife;
The thousand sweet still joys of such
As hand in hand face earthly life;—

Though these be lost, there will be yet
A sympathy august and pure;
Ennobled by a vast regret,
And by contrition seal'd thrice sure.

And we, whose ways were unlike here,
May then more neighbouring courses ply;
May to each other be brought near,
And greet across infinity.

How sweet, unreach'd by earthly jars,
My sister! to behold with thee
The hush among the shining stars,
The calm upon the moonlit sea.

How sweet to feel, on the boon air,
All our unquiet pulses cease;
To feel that nothing can impair
The gentleness, the thirst for peace—

The gentleness too rudely hurl'd
On this wild earth of hate and fear:
The thirst for peace a raving world
Would never let us satiate here.

LINES
WRITTEN IN KENSINGTON GARDENS

In this lone open glade I lie,
Screen'd by deep boughs on either hand;
And at its head, to stay the eye,
Those black-crown'd, red-boled pine-trees stand.

Birds here make song, each bird has his,
Across the girdling city's hum.
How green under the boughs it is!
How thick the tremulous sheep-cries come!

Sometimes a child will cross the glade
To take his nurse his broken toy;
Sometimes a thrush flit overhead
Deep in her unknown day's employ.

Here at my feet what wonders pass,
What endless, active life is here!
What blowing daisies, fragrant grass!
An air-stirr'd forest, fresh and clear.

Scarce fresher is the mountain sod
Where the tired angler lies, stretch'd out,
And, eased of basket and of rod,
Counts his day's spoil, the spotted trout.

In the huge world which roars hard by
Be others happy, if they can!
But in my helpless cradle I
Was breathed on by the rural Pan.

I, on men's impious uproar hurl'd,
Think often, as I hear them rave,
That peace has left the upper world,
And now keeps only in the grave.

Yet here is peace for ever new!
When I, who watch them, am away,
Still all things in this glade go through
The changes of their quiet day.

Then to their happy rest they pass;
The flowers close, the birds are fed,
The night comes down upon the grass,
The child sleeps warmly in his bed.

Calm soul of all things! make it mine
To feel, amid the city's jar,
That there abides a peace of thine,
Man did not make, and cannot mar!

The will to neither strive nor cry,
The power to feel with others give!
Calm, calm me more! nor let me die
Before I have begun to live.

MORALITY

We cannot kindle when we will
The fire that in the heart resides,
The spirit bloweth and is still,
In mystery our soul abides:
    But tasks in hours of insight will'd
Can be through hours of gloom fulfill'd.

With aching hands and bleeding feet
We dig and heap, lay stone on stone;
We bear the burden and the heat
Of the long day, and wish 'twere done.
   Not till the hours of light return
All we have built do we discern.

Then, when the clouds are off the soul,
When thou dost bask in Nature's eye,
Ask, how *she* view'd thy self-control,
Thy struggling task'd morality.
   Nature, whose free, light, cheerful air,
Oft made thee, in thy gloom, despair.

And she, whose censure thou dost dread,
Whose eye thou wert afraid to seek,
See, on her face a glow is spread,
A strong emotion on her cheek.
   "Ah child," she cries, "that strife divine—
Whence was it, for it is not mine?

"There is no effort on *my* brow—
I do not strive, I do not weep.
I rush with the swift spheres, and glow
In joy, and, when I will, I sleep.—
   Yet that severe, that earnest air,
I saw, I felt it once—but where?

"I knew not yet the gauge of Time,
Nor wore the manacles of Space.
I felt it in some other clime—
I saw it in some other place.
   —'Twas when the heavenly house I trod,
And lay upon the breast of God."

◯

From SOHRAB AND RUSTUM [1]

And, with a grave mild voice, Sohrab replied:—
"Desire not that, my father; thou must live.
For some are born to do great deeds, and live,
As some are born to be obscur'd, and die.
Do thou the deeds I die too young to do,
And reap a second glory in thine age.
Thou art my father, and thy gain is mine.
But come: thou seest this great host of men
Which follow me; I pray thee, slay not these:
Let me entreat for them: what have they done?
They follow'd me, my hope, my fame, my star.
Let them all cross the Oxus back in peace.
But me thou must bear hence, not send with them,

---

[1] It is impossible, for reasons of space, to include the whole of
"Sohrab and Rustum," but the conclusion of the poem, and most
especially the famous passage on the course of the River Oxus, may
not be omitted from any selection of Arnold's verse.

Rustum is the Persian epic hero; Sohrab is his son by a princess
whom he had loved in early youth. Sohrab knows the identity of
his father and longs to find him, but Rustum does not even know
that he has a son. When they meet in single combat between the
Persian and the Tartar armies, Rustum as the champion of the former,
Sohrab as the champion of the latter, Rustum fights under an assumed name. Yet Sohrab suspects that his antagonist is the great
Rustum and begs him to say so; Rustum, for his part, is drawn to
the youth and urges him to retire from an unequal contest. But
Sohrab will not withdraw and Rustum will not disclose his identity.
They fight, and at the climax of the combat Rustum cries aloud his
name to terrify his enemy; Sohrab, not terrified but astonished, lowers
his shield and is exposed to Rustum's spear, which pierces his side.
Dying, he threatens the revenge his father Rustum will take. When
Rustum denies that he ever had a son, Sohrab shows the family in-
signia of Rustum pricked on his arm. The proof is indisputable and
the father and son at last know each other. In his grief and despair
Rustum wishes for his own death.—L. T.

But carry me with thee to Seistan,
And place me on a bed, and mourn for me,
Thou, and the snow-hair'd Zal, and all thy friends.
And thou must lay me in that lovely earth,
And heap a stately mound above my bones,
And plant a far-seen pillar over all:
That so the passing horseman on the waste
May see my tomb a great way off, and say—
Sohrab, the mighty Rustum's son, lies there,
Whom his great father did in ignorance kill—
And I be not forgotten in my grave."
    And, with a mournful voice, Rustum replied:—
"Fear not; as thou hast said, Sohrab, my son,
So shall it be: for I will burn my tents,
And quit the host, and bear thee hence with me,
And carry thee away to Seistan,
And place thee on a bed, and mourn for thee,
With the snow-headed Zal, and all my friends
And I will lay thee in that lovely earth,
And heap a stately mound above thy bones,
And plant a far-seen pillar over all:
And men shall not forget thee in thy grave.
And I will spare thy host: yea, let them go:
Let them all cross the Oxus back in peace.
What should I do with slaying any more?
For would that all whom I have ever slain
Might be once more alive; my bitterest foes,
And they who were call'd champions in their time,
And through whose death I won that fame I have;
And I were nothing but a common man,
A poor, mean soldier, and without renown,
So thou mightest live too, my Son, my Son!
Or rather would that I, even I myself,
Might now be lying on this bloody sand,
Near death, and by an ignorant stroke of thine,

Not thou of mine; and I might die, not thou;
And I, not thou, be borne to Seistan;
And Zal might weep above my grave, not thine;
And say—*O son, I weep thee not too sore,*
For willingly, I know, thou met'st thine end.—
But now in blood and battles was my youth,
And full of blood and battles is my age;
And I shall never end this life of blood."

Then, at the point of death, Sohrab replied:—
"A life of blood indeed, thou dreadful Man!
But thou shalt yet have peace; only not now:
Not yet: but thou shalt have it on that day,
When thou shalt sail in a high-masted Ship,
Thou and the other peers of Kai-Khosroo,
Returning home over the salt blue sea,
From laying thy dear Master in his grave."

And Rustum gaz'd on Sohrab's face, and said:—
"Soon be that day, my Son, and deep that sea!
Till then, if Fate so wills, let me endure."

He spoke; and Sohrab smil'd on him, and took
The spear, and drew it from his side, and eas'd
His wound's imperious anguish: but the blood
Came welling from the open gash, and life
Flow'd with the stream: all down his cold white side
The crimson torrent ran, dim now, and soil'd,
Like the soil'd tissue of white violets
Left, freshly gather'd, on their native bank,
By romping children, whom their nurses call
From the hot fields at noon: his head droop'd low,
His limbs grew slack; motionless, white, he lay—
White, with eyes closed; only when heavy gasps,
Deep, heavy gasps, quivering through all his frame,
Convuls'd him back to life, he open'd them,
And fix'd them feebly on his father's face:
Till now all strength was ebb'd, and from his limbs

Unwillingly the spirit fled away,
Regretting the warm mansion which it left,
And youth and bloom, and this delightful world.
  So, on the bloody sand, Sohrab lay dead.
And the great Rustum drew his horseman's cloak
Down o'er his face, and sate by his dead son.
As those black granite pillars, once high-rear'd
By Jemshid in Persepolis, to bear
His house, now, mid their broken flights of steps,
Lie prone, enormous, down the mountain side—
So in the sand lay Rustum by his son.
  And night came down over the solemn waste,
And the two gazing hosts, and that sole pair,
And darken'd all; and a cold fog, with night,
Crept from the Oxus. Soon a hum arose,
As of a great assembly loos'd, and fires
Began to twinkle through the fog: for now
Both armies mov'd to camp, and took their meal:
The Persians took it on the open sands
Southward; the Tartars by the river marge:
And Rustum and his son were left alone.
  But the majestic River floated on,
Out of the mist and hum of that low land,
Into the frosty starlight, and there mov'd,
Rejoicing, through the hush'd Chorasmian waste,
Under the solitary moon: he flow'd
Right for the Polar Star, past Orgunjè,
Brimming, and bright, and large: then sands begin
To hem his watery march, and dam his streams,
And split his currents; that for many a league
The shorn and parcell'd Oxus strains along
Through beds of sand and matted rushy isles—
Oxus, forgetting the bright speed he had
In his high mountain cradle in Pamere,
A foil'd circuitous wanderer:—till at last

The long'd-for dash of waves is heard, and wide
His luminous home of waters opens, bright
And tranquil, from whose floor the new-bath'd stars
Emerge, and shine upon the Aral Sea.

○

PHILOMELA

Hark! ah, the Nightingale!
The tawny-throated!
Hark! from that moonlit cedar what a burst!
What triumph! hark—what pain!

O Wanderer from a Grecian shore,
Still, after many years, in distant lands,
Still nourishing in thy bewilder'd brain
That wild, unquench'd, deep-sunken, old-world pain—
    Say, will it never heal?
And can this fragrant lawn
With its cool trees, and night,
And the sweet, tranquil Thames,
And moonshine, and the dew,
To thy rack'd heart and brain
    Afford no balm?

    Dost thou to-night behold
Here, through the moonlight on this English grass,
The unfriendly palace in the Thracian wild?
    Dost thou again peruse
With hot cheeks and sear'd eyes
The too clear web, and thy dumb Sister's shame?
    Dost thou once more assay
Thy flight, and feel come over thee,
Poor Fugitive, the feathery change

Once more, and once more seem to make resound
With love and hate, triumph and agony,
Lone Daulis, and the high Cephissian vale?
    Listen, Eugenia—
How thick the bursts come crowding through the leaves!
    Again—thou hearest!
Eternal Passion!
Eternal Pain!

REQUIESCAT

Strew on her roses, roses,
    And never a spray of yew.
In quiet she reposes:
    Ah! would that I did too.

Her mirth the world required:
    She bath'd it in smiles of glee.
But her heart was tired, tired,
    And now they let her be.

Her life was turning, turning,
    In mazes of heat and sound.
But for peace her soul was yearning,
    And now peace laps her round.

Her cabin'd, ample Spirit,
    It flutter'd and fail'd for breath.
To-night it doth inherit
    The vasty Hall of Death.

◯

THE SCHOLAR GIPSY [1]

Go, for they call you, Shepherd, from the hill;
  Go, Shepherd, and untie the wattled cotes:
    No longer leave thy wistful flock unfed,
  Nor let thy bawling fellows rack their throats,
    Nor the cropp'd grasses shoot another head.
      But when the fields are still,
  And the tired men and dogs all gone to rest,
    And only the white sheep are sometimes seen
    Cross and recross the strips of moon-blanch'd green;
      Come, Shepherd, and again renew the quest.

Here, where the reaper was at work of late,
  In this high field's dark corner, where he leaves
    His coat, his basket, and his earthen cruise,
  And in the sun all morning binds the sheaves,
    Then here, at noon, comes back his stores to use;
      Here will I sit and wait,

[1] There was very lately a lad in the University of Oxford, who
was by his poverty forced to leave his studies there; and at last to
join himself to a company of vagabond gipsies. Among these extravagant people, by the insinuating subtilty of his carriage, he quickly got
so much of their love and esteem as that they discovered to him their
mystery. After he had been a pretty while well exercised in the trade,
there chanced to ride by a couple of scholars, who had formerly been
of his acquaintance. They quickly spied out their old friend among
the gipsies; and he gave them an account of the necessity which
drove him to that kind of life, and told them that the people he
went with were not such impostors as they were taken for, but that
they had a traditional kind of learning among them, and could do
wonders by the power of imagination, their fancy binding that of
others: that himself had learned much of their art, and when he had
compassed the whole secret, he intended, he said, to leave their company, and give the world an account of what he had learned.—GLAN-
VIL's Vanity of Dogmatizing, 1661. (Arnold's note.)

While to my ear from uplands far away
    The bleating of the folded flocks is borne,
    With distant cries of reapers in the corn—
      All the live murmur of a summer's day.

Screen'd is this nook o'er the high, half-reap'd field,
    And here till sun-down, Shepherd, will I be.
      Through the thick corn the scarlet poppies peep,
    And round green roots and yellowing stalks I see
      Pale blue convolvulus in tendrils creep:
        And air-swept lindens yield
Their scent, and rustle down their perfum'd showers
    Of bloom on the bent grass where I am laid,
    And bower me from the August sun with shade;
      And the eye travels down to Oxford's towers:

And near me on the grass lies Glanvil's book—
    Come, let me read the oft-read tale again,
      The story of that Oxford scholar poor
    Of pregnant parts and quick inventive brain,
      Who, tir'd of knocking at Preferment's door,
        One summer morn forsook
His friends, and went to learn the Gipsy lore,
    And roam'd the world with that wild brotherhood,
    And came, as most men deem'd, to little good,
      But came to Oxford and his friends no more.

But once, years after, in the country lanes,
    Two scholars whom at college erst he knew
      Met him, and of his way of life inquir'd.
Whereat he answer'd, that the Gipsy crew,
      His mates, had arts to rule as they desir'd
        The workings of men's brains;
And they can bind them to what thoughts they will:
    "And I," he said, "the secret of their art,

When fully learn'd, will to the world impart:
  But it needs heaven-sent moments for this skill."

This said, he left them, and return'd no more,
  But rumours hung about the country side
    That the lost Scholar long was seen to stray,
  Seen by rare glimpses, pensive and tongue-tied,
    In hat of antique shape, and cloak of grey,
      The same the Gipsies wore.
  Shepherds had met him on the Hurst in spring;
    At some lone alehouse in the Berkshire moors,
    On the warm ingle bench, the smock-frock'd boors
      Had found him seated at their entering,

But, mid their drink and clatter, he would fly:
  And I myself seem half to know thy looks,
    And put the shepherds, Wanderer, on thy trace;
  And boys who in lone wheatfields scare the rooks
    I ask if thou hast pass'd their quiet place;
      Or in my boat I lie
  Moor'd to the cool bank in the summer heats,
    Mid wide grass meadows which the sunshine fills,
    And watch the warm green-muffled Cumner hills,
      And wonder if thou haunt'st their shy retreats.

For most, I know, thou lov'st retired ground.
  Thee, at the ferry, Oxford riders blithe,
    Returning home on summer nights, have met
  Crossing the stripling Thames at Bab-lock-hithe,
    Trailing in the cool stream thy fingers wet,
      As the slow punt swings round:
  And leaning backwards in a pensive dream,
    And fostering in thy lap a heap of flowers
    Pluck'd in shy fields and distant Wychwood bowers,
      And thine eyes resting on the moonlit stream:

And then they land, and thou art seen no more.
   Maidens who from the distant hamlets come
     To dance around the Fyfield elm in May,
   Oft through the darkening fields have seen thee roam,
     Or cross a stile into the public way.
       Oft thou hast given them store
   Of flowers—the frail-leaf'd, white anemone—
     Dark bluebells drench'd with dews of summer
        eves—
     And purple orchises with spotted leaves—
      But none has words she can report of thee.

And, above Godstow Bridge, when hay-time's here
   In June, and many a scythe in sunshine flames,
     Men who through those wide fields of breezy grass
   Where black-wing'd swallows haunt the glittering
        Thames,
     To bathe in the abandon'd lasher pass,
      Have often pass'd thee near
   Sitting upon the river bank o'ergrown:
     Mark'd thy outlandish garb, thy figure spare,
     Thy dark vague eyes, and soft abstracted air;
      But, when they came from bathing, thou wert
       gone.

At some lone homestead in the Cumner hills,
   Where at her open door the housewife darns,
     Thou hast been seen, or hanging on a gate
   To watch the threshers in the mossy barns.
     Children, who early range these slopes and late
      For cresses from the rills,
   Have known thee watching, all an April day,
     The springing pastures and the feeding kine;

And mark'd thee, when the stars come out and
     shine,
     Through the long dewy grass move slow away.

In Autumn, on the skirts of Bagley wood,
     Where most the Gipsies by the turf-edg'd way
         Pitch their smok'd tents, and every bush you see
     With scarlet patches tagg'd and shreds of grey,
         Above the forest ground call'd Thessaly—
         The blackbird picking food
     Sees thee, nor stops his meal, nor fears at all;
         So often has he known thee past him stray
         Rapt, twirling in thy hand a wither'd spray,
         And waiting for the spark from Heaven to fall.

And once, in winter, on the causeway chill
     Where home through flooded fields foot-travellers go,
         Have I not pass'd thee on the wooden bridge
     Wrapt in thy cloak and battling with the snow,
         Thy face towards Hinksey and its wintry ridge?
         And thou hast climb'd the hill
     And gain'd the white brow of the Cumner range,
         Turn'd once to watch, while thick the snowflakes
         fall,
         The line of festal light in Christ-Church hall—
         Then sought thy straw in some sequester'd
         grange.

But what—I dream! Two hundred years are flown
     Since first thy story ran through Oxford halls,
         And the grave Glanvil did the tale inscribe
     That thou wert wander'd from the studious walls
         To learn strange arts, and join a Gipsy tribe:
         And thou from earth art gone
     Long since, and in some quiet churchyard laid;

Some country nook, where o'er thy unknown grave
  Tall grasses and white flowering nettles wave—
    Under a dark red-fruited yew-tree's shade.

—No, no, thou hast not felt the lapse of hours.
  For what wears out the life of mortal men?
    'Tis that from change to change their being rolls:
    'Tis that repeated shocks, again, again,
      Exhaust the energy of strongest souls,
        And numb the elastic powers.
  Till having us'd our nerves with bliss and teen,
    And tir'd upon a thousand schemes our wit,
    To the just-pausing Genius we remit
      Our worn-out life, and are—what we have been.

Thou hast not liv'd, why should'st thou perish, so?
  Thou hadst *one* aim, *one* business, *one* desire:
    Else wert thou long since number'd with the
          dead—
    Else hadst thou spent, like other men, thy fire.
      The generations of thy peers are fled,
        And we ourselves shall go;
  But thou possessest an immortal lot,
    And we imagine thee exempt from age
    And living as thou liv'st on Glanvil's page,
      Because thou hadst—what we, alas, have not!

For early didst thou leave the world, with powers
  Fresh, undiverted to the world without,
    Firm to their mark, not spent on other things;
  Free from the sick fatigue, the languid doubt,
    Which much to have tried, in much been baffled,
          brings.
      O Life unlike to ours!
  Who fluctuate idly without term or scope,

Of whom each strives, nor knows for what he
    strives,
And each half lives a hundred different lives;
    Who wait like thee, but not, like thee, in hope.

Thou waitest for the spark from Heaven: and we,
    Vague half-believers of our casual creeds,
      Who never deeply felt, nor clearly will'd,
Whose insight never has borne fruit in deeds,
      Whose weak resolves never have been fulfill'd;
        For whom each year we see
    Breeds new beginnings, disappointments new;
      Who hesitate and falter life away,
        And lose to-morrow the ground won to-day—
      Ah, do not we, Wanderer, await it too?

Yes, we await it, but it still delays,
    And then we suffer; and amongst us One,
      Who most has suffer'd, takes dejectedly
His seat upon the intellectual throne;
      And all his store of sad experience he
        Lays bare of wretched days;
    Tells us his misery's birth and growth and signs,
      And how the dying spark of hope was fed,
      And how the breast was sooth'd, and how the head,
      And all his hourly varied anodynes.

This for our wisest: and we others pine,
    And wish the long unhappy dream would end,
      And waive all claim to bliss, and try to bear,
With close-lipp'd Patience for our only friend,
      Sad Patience, too near neighbour to Despair:
        But none has hope like thine.
    Thou through the fields and through the woods dost
      stray,

Roaming the country side, a truant boy,
Nursing thy project in unclouded joy,
  And every doubt long blown by time away.

O born in days when wits were fresh and clear,
  And life ran gaily as the sparkling Thames;
    Before this strange disease of modern life,
  With its sick hurry, its divided aims,
    Its heads o'ertax'd, its palsied hearts, was rife—
      Fly hence, our contact fear!
Still fly, plunge deeper in the bowering wood!
    Averse, as Dido did with gesture stern
    From her false friend's approach in Hades turn,
      Wave us away, and keep thy solitude.

Still nursing the unconquerable hope,
  Still clutching the inviolable shade,
    With a free onward impulse brushing through,
  By night, the silver'd branches of the glade—
    Far on the forest skirts, where none pursue,
      On some mild pastoral slope
Emerge, and resting on the moonlit pales,
    Freshen thy flowers, as in former years,
    With dew, or listen with enchanted ears,
      From the dark dingles, to the nightingales.

But fly our paths, our feverish contact fly!
  For strong the infection of our mental strife,
    Which, though it gives no bliss, yet spoils for rest;
  And we should win thee from thy own fair life,
    Like us distracted, and like us unblest.
      Soon, soon thy cheer would die,
Thy hopes grow timorous, and unfix'd thy powers,
    And thy clear aims be cross and shifting made:
    And then thy glad perennial youth would fade,
      Fade, and grow old at last, and die like ours.

Then fly our greetings, fly our speech and smiles!
  —As some grave Tyrian trader, from the sea,
    Descried at sunrise an emerging prow
Lifting the cool-hair'd creepers stealthily,
    The fringes of a southward-facing brow
      Among the Aegean isles;
  And saw the merry Grecian coaster come,
    Freighted with amber grapes, and Chian wine,
    Green bursting figs, and tunnies steep'd in brine;
    And knew the intruders on his ancient home,

The young light-hearted Masters of the waves;
  And snatch'd his rudder, and shook out more sail,
    And day and night held on indignantly
O'er the blue Midland waters with the gale,
    Betwixt the Syrtes and soft Sicily,
      To where the Atlantic raves
  Outside the Western Straits, and unbent sails
    There, where down cloudy cliffs, through sheets of
        foam,
    Shy traffickers, the dark Iberians come;
    And on the beach undid his corded bales.

◯

STANZAS
FROM THE GRANDE CHARTREUSE

Through Alpine meadows soft-suffused
With rain, where thick the crocus blows,
Past the dark forges long disused,
The mule-track from Saint Laurent goes.
The bridge is cross'd, and slow we ride,
Through forest, up the mountain-side.

The autumnal evening darkens round,
The wind is up, and drives the rain;
While hark! far down, with strangled sound
Doth the Dead Guiers' stream complain,
Where that wet smoke among the woods
Over his boiling cauldron broods.

Swift rush the spectral vapours white
Past limestone scars with ragged pines,
Showing—then blotting from our sight.
Halt! through the cloud-drift something shines!
High in the valley, wet and drear,
The huts of Courrerie appear.

Strike leftward! cries our guide; and higher
Mounts up the stony forest-way.
At last the encircling trees retire;
Look! through the showery twilight grey
What pointed roofs are these advance?
A palace of the Kings of France?

Approach, for what we seek is here.
Alight and sparely sup and wait
For rest in this outbuilding near;
Then cross the sward and reach that gate;
Knock; pass the wicket! Thou art come
To the Carthusians' world-famed home.

The silent courts, where night and day
Into their stone-carved basins cold
The splashing icy fountains play,
The humid corridors behold,
Where ghostlike in the deepening night
Cowl'd forms brush by in gleaming white.

The chapel, where no organ's peal
Invests the stern and naked prayer.
With penitential cries they kneel
And wrestle; rising then, with bare
And white uplifted faces stand,
Passing the Host from hand to hand;

Each takes; and then his visage wan
Is buried in his cowl once more.
The cells—the suffering Son of Man
Upon the wall! the knee-worn floor!
And, where they sleep, that wooden bed,
Which shall their coffin be, when dead.

The library, where tract and tome
Not to feed priestly pride are there,
To hymn the conquering march of Rome,
Nor yet to amuse, as ours are;
They paint of souls the inner strife,
Their drops of blood, their death in life.

The garden, overgrown—yet mild
Those fragrant herbs are flowering there!
Strong children of the Alpine wild
Whose culture is the brethren's care;
Of human tasks their only one,
And cheerful works beneath the sun.

Those halls too, destined to contain
Each its own pilgrim host of old,
From England, Germany, or Spain—
All are before me! I behold
The House, the Brotherhood austere!
And what am I, that I am here?

For rigorous teachers seized my youth,
And purged its faith, and trimm'd its fire,
Show'd me the high white star of Truth,
There bade me gaze, and there aspire;
Even now their whispers pierce the gloom:
What dost thou in this living tomb?

Forgive me, masters of the mind!
At whose behest I long ago
So much unlearnt, so much resign'd!
I come not here to be your foe.
I seek these anchorites, not in ruth,
To curse and to deny your truth;

Not as their friend or child I speak!
But as on some far northern strand,
Thinking of his own Gods, a Greek
In pity and mournful awe might stand
Before some fallen Runic stone—
For both were faiths, and both are gone.

Wandering between two worlds, one dead,
The other powerless to be born,
With nowhere yet to rest my head,
Like these, on earth I wait forlorn.
Their faith, my tears, the world deride;
I come to shed them at their side.

Oh, hide me in your gloom profound,
Ye solemn seats of holy pain!
Take me, cowl'd forms, and fence me round,
Till I possess my soul again!
Till free my thoughts before me roll,
Not chafed by hourly false control.

For the world cries your faith is now
But a dead time's exploded dream;
My melancholy, sciolists say,
Is a pass'd mode, an outworn theme—
As if the world had ever had
A faith, or sciolists been sad.

Ah, if it *be* pass'd, take away,
At least, the restlessness—the pain!
Be man henceforth no more a prey
To these out-dated stings again!
The nobleness of grief is gone—
Ah, leave us not the fret alone!

But, if you cannot give us ease,
Last of the race of them who grieve
Here leave us to die out with these
Last of the people who believe!
Silent, while years engrave the brow;
Silent—the best are silent now.

Achilles ponders in his tent,
The kings of modern thought are dumb;
Silent they are, though not content,
And wait to see the future come.
They have the grief men had of yore,
But they contend and cry no more.

Our fathers water'd with their tears
This sea of time whereon we sail;
Their voices were in all men's ears
Who pass'd within their puissant hail.
Still the same Ocean round us raves,
But we stand mute and watch the waves.

For what avail'd it, all the noise
And outcry of the former men?
Say, have their sons obtain'd more joys?
Say, is life lighter now than then?
The sufferers died, they left their pain;
The pangs which tortured them remain.

What helps it now, that Byron bore,
With haughty scorn which mock'd the smart,
Through Europe to the Aetolian shore
The pageant of his bleeding heart?
That thousands counted every groan,
And Europe made his woe her own?

What boots it, Shelley! that the breeze
Carried thy lovely wail away,
Musical through Italian trees
That fringe thy soft blue Spezzian bay?
Inheritors of thy distress
Have restless hearts one throb the less?

Or are we easier, to have read,
O Obermann! the sad, stern page,
Which tells us how thou hidd'st thy head
From the fierce tempest of thine age
In the lone brakes of Fontainebleau,
Or chalets near the Alpine snow?

Ye slumber in your silent grave!
The world, which for an idle day
Grace to your mood of sadness gave,
Long since hath flung her weeds away.
The eternal trifler breaks your spell;
But we—we learnt your lore too well!

There may, perhaps, yet dawn an age,
More fortunate, alas! than we,
Which without hardness will be sage,
And gay without frivolity.
Sons of the world, oh, haste those years;
But, till they rise, allow our tears!

Allow them! We admire with awe
The exulting thunder of your race;
You give the universe your law,
You triumph over time and space.
Your pride of life, your tireless powers,
We mark them, but they are not ours.

We are like children rear'd in shade
Beneath some old-world abbey wall
Forgotten in a forest-glade
And secret from the eyes of all;
Deep, deep the greenwood round them waves,
Their abbey, and its close of graves.

But where the road runs near the stream,
Oft through the trees they catch a glance
Of passing troops in the sun's beam—
Pennon, and plume, and flashing lance!
Forth to the world those soldiers fare,
To life, to cities, and to war.

And through the woods, another way,
Faint bugle-notes from far are borne,
Where hunters gather, staghounds bay,
Round some old forest-lodge at morn;
Gay dames are there in sylvan green,
Laughter and cries—those notes between!

The banners flashing through the trees
Make their blood dance and chain their eyes;
That bugle-music on the breeze
Arrests them with a charm'd surprise.
Banner by turns and bugle woo:
Ye shy recluses, follow too!

O children, what do ye reply?—
"Action and pleasure, will ye roam
Through these secluded dells to cry
And call us? but too late ye come!
Too late for us your call ye blow
Whose bent was taken long ago.

"Long since we pace this shadow'd nave;
We watch those yellow tapers shine,
Emblems of hope over the grave,
In the high altar's depth divine;
The organ carries to our ear
Its accents of another sphere.

"Fenced early in this cloistral round
Of reverie, of shade, of prayer,
How should we grow in other ground?
How should we flower in foreign air?
Pass, banners, pass, and bugles, cease!
And leave our desert to its peace!"

TO MARGUERITE

We were apart: yet, day by day,
I bade my heart more constant be;
I bade it keep the world away,

And grow a home for only thee:
Nor fear'd but thy love likewise grew,
Like mine, each day more tried, more true.

The fault was grave: I might have known,
What far too soon, alas, I learn'd—
The heart can bind itself alone,
And faith is often unreturn'd.—
   Self-sway'd our feelings ebb and swell:
Thou lov'st no more: Farewell! Farewell!

Farewell! and thou, thou lonely heart,
Which never yet without remorse
Even for a moment did'st depart
From thy remote and spherèd course
To haunt the place where passions reign,
Back to thy solitude again!

Back, with the conscious thrill of shame
Which Luna felt, that summer night,
Flash through her pure immortal frame,
When she forsook the starry height
To hang over Endymion's sleep
Upon the pine-grown Latmian steep;—

Yet she, chaste Queen, had never prov'd
How vain a thing is mortal love,
Wandering in Heaven, far remov'd.
But thou hast long had place to prove
This truth—to prove, and make thine own:
   Thou hast been, shalt be, art, alone.

Or, if not quite alone, yet they
Which touch thee are unmating things—
Ocean, and Clouds, and Night, and Day;

line continuity.

Lorn Autumns and triumphant Springs;
And life, and others' joy and pain,
And love, if love, of happier men.

Of happier men—for they, at least,
Have *dream'd* two human hearts might blend
In one, and were through faith releas'd
From isolation without end
Prolong'd, nor knew, although not less
Alone than thou, their loneliness.

fatalism.

THYRSIS

A MONODY

*To commemorate the author's friend, Arthur Hugh
Clough, who died at Florence, 1861*

> Thus yesterday, to-day, to-morrow come,
> They hustle one another and they pass;
> But all our hustling morrows only make
> The smooth to-day of God.
> > *From* LUCRETIUS, *an unpublished Tragedy.*

How changed is here each spot man makes or fills!
In the two Hinkseys nothing keeps the same;
The village-street its haunted mansion lacks,
And from the sign is gone Sibylla's name,
And from the roofs the twisted chimney-stacks;
Are ye too changed, ye hills?
See, 'tis no foot of unfamiliar men
To-night from Oxford up your pathway strays
Here came I often, often, in old days;
Thyrsis and I; we still had Thyrsis then.

Runs it not here, the track by Childsworth Farm,
    Up past the wood, to where the elm-tree crowns
        The hill behind whose ridge the sunset flames?
The signal-elm, that looks on Ilsley Downs,
        The Vale, the three lone weirs, the youthful
            Thames?—
            This winter-eve is warm,
    Humid the air; leafless, yet soft as spring,
        The tender purple spray on copse and briers;
        And that sweet City with her dreaming spires,
    She needs not June for beauty's heightening,

Lovely all times she lies, lovely to-night!
    Only, methinks, some loss of habit's power
        Befalls me wandering through this upland dim;
    Once pass'd I blindfold here, at any hour,
        Now seldom come I, since I came with him.
            That single elm-tree bright
    Against the west—I miss it! is it gone?
        We prized it dearly; while it stood, we said,
        Our friend, the Scholar-Gipsy, was not dead;
    While the tree lived, he in these fields lived on.

Too rare, too rare, grow now my visits here!
    But once I knew each field, each flower, each stick;
        And with the country-folk acquaintance made
    By barn in threshing-time, by new-built rick.
        Here, too, our shepherd-pipes we first assay'd.
            Ah me! this many a year
    My pipe is lost, my shepherd's-holiday!
        Needs must I lose them, needs with heavy heart
        Into the world and wave of men depart;
    But Thyrsis of his own will went away.

It irk'd him to be here, he could not rest.
  He loved each simple joy the country yields,
    He loved his mates; but yet he could not keep,
For that a shadow lower'd on the fields,
    Here with the shepherds and the silly sheep.
        Some life of men unblest
  He knew, which made him droop, and fill'd his head.
    He went; his piping took a troubled sound
    Of storms that rage outside our happy ground;
He could not wait their passing, he is dead!

So, some tempestuous morn in early June,
  When the year's primal burst of bloom is o'er,
    Before the roses and the longest day—
When garden-walks, and all the grassy floor,
    With blossoms, red and white, of fallen May,
        And chestnut-flowers are strewn—
So have I heard the cuckoo's parting cry,
    From the wet field, through the vext garden-trees,
    Come with the volleying rain and tossing breeze:
The bloom is gone, and with the bloom go I.

Too quick despairer, wherefore wilt thou go?
  Soon will the high Midsummer pomps come on,
    Soon will the musk carnations break and swell,
Soon shall we have gold-dusted snapdragon,
    Sweet-William with its homely cottage-smell,
        And stocks in fragrant blow;
Roses that down the alleys shine afar,
    And open, jasmine-muffled lattices,
    And groups under the dreaming garden-trees,
And the full moon, and the white evening-star.

He hearkens not! light comer, he is flown!
  What matters it? next year he will return,

And we shall have him in the sweet spring-days,
  With whitening hedges, and uncrumpling fern,
    And blue-bells trembling by the forest-ways,
      And scent of hay new-mown.
But Thyrsis never more we swains shall see!
    See him come back, and cut a smoother reed,
    And blow a strain the world at last shall heed—
For Time, not Corydon, hath conquer'd thee.

Alack, for Corydon no rival now!—
  But when Sicilian shepherds lost a mate,
    Some good survivor with his flute would go,
  Piping a ditty sad for Bion's fate,
      And cross the unpermitted ferry's flow,
        And relax Pluto's brow,
And make leap up with joy the beauteous head
    Of Proserpine, among whose crownèd hair
    Are flowers, first open'd on Sicilian air,
And flute his friend, like Orpheus, from the dead.

O easy access to the hearer's grace
  When Dorian shepherds sang to Proserpine!
    For she herself had trod Sicilian fields,
  She knew the Dorian water's gush divine,
      She knew each lily white which Enna yields,
        Each rose with blushing face;
  She loved the Dorian pipe, the Dorian strain.
    But ah, of our poor Thames she never heard!
    Her foot the Cumner cowslips never stirr'd!
And we should tease her with our plaint in vain.

Well! wind-dispers'd and vain the words will be,
  Yet, Thyrsis, let me give my grief its hour
    In the old haunt, and find our tree-topp'd hill!
Who, if not I, for questing here hath power?

I know the wood which hides the daffodil,
  I know the Fyfield tree,
I know what white, what purple fritillaries
  The grassy harvest of the river-fields,
  Above by Ensham, down by Sandford, yields,
And what sedg'd brooks are Thames's tributaries;

I know these slopes; who knows them if not I?—
  But many a dingle on the loved hill-side,
    With thorns once studded, old, white-blossom'd
      trees,
  Where thick the cowslips grew, and, far descried,
    High tower'd the spikes of purple orchises,
      Hath since our day put by
  The coronals of that forgotten time.
    Down each green bank hath gone the ploughboy's
      team,
    And only in the hidden brookside gleam
  Primroses, orphans of the flowery prime.

Where is the girl, who, by the boatman's door,
  Above the locks, above the boating throng,
    Unmoor'd our skiff, when, through the Wytham
      flats,
  Red loosestrife and blond meadow-sweet among,
    And darting swallows, and light water-gnats,
      We track'd the shy Thames shore?
  Where are the mowers, who, as the tiny swell
    Of our boat passing heav'd the river-grass,
    Stood with suspended scythe to see us pass?—
  They all are gone, and thou art gone as well.

Yes, thou art gone! and round me too the night
  In ever-nearing circle weaves her shade.
    I see her veil draw soft across the day,

I feel her slowly chilling breath invade
  The cheek grown thin, the brown hair sprent with
          grey;
    I feel her finger light
Laid pausefully upon life's headlong train;
  The foot less prompt to meet the morning dew,
  The heart less bounding at emotion new,
And hope, once crush'd, less quick to spring again.

And long the way appears, which seem'd so short
  To the unpractis'd eye of sanguine youth;
    And high the mountain-tops, in cloudy air,
The mountain-tops where is the throne of Truth,
    Tops in life's morning-sun so bright and bare!
        Unbreachable the fort
Of the long-batter'd world uplifts its wall.
    And strange and vain the earthly turmoil grows,
    And near and real the charm of thy repose,
And night as welcome as a friend would fall.

But hush! the upland hath a sudden loss
  Of quiet;—Look! adown the dusk hill-side,
    A troop of Oxford hunters going home,
As in old days, jovial and talking, ride!
    From hunting with the Berkshire hounds they
          come—
        Quick, let me fly, and cross
Into yon further field!—'Tis done; and see,
    Back'd by the sunset, which doth glorify
    The orange and pale violet evening-sky,
Bare on its lonely ridge, the Tree! the Tree!

I take the omen! Eve lets down her veil,
  The white fog creeps from bush to bush about,
    The west unflushes, the high stars grow bright,

And in the scatter'd farms the lights come out.
    I cannot reach the Signal-Tree to-night,
        Yet, happy omen, hail!
Hear it from thy broad lucent Arno vale
      (For there thine earth-forgetting eyelids keep
      The morningless and unawakening sleep
Under the flowery oleanders pale),

Hear it, O Thyrsis, still our Tree is there!—
    Ah, vain! These English fields, this upland dim,
      These brambles pale with mist engarlanded,
That lone, sky-pointing tree, are not for him.
      To a boon southern country he is fled,
        And now in happier air,
Wandering with the great Mother's train divine
      (And purer or more subtle soul than thee,
      I trow, the mighty Mother doth not see!)
Within a folding of the Apennine,

Thou hearest the immortal strains of old.
    Putting his sickle to the perilous grain
      In the hot cornfield of the Phrygian king,
For thee the Lityerses song again
      Young Daphnis with his silver voice doth sing;
        Sings his Sicilian fold,
His sheep, his hapless love, his blinded eyes;
      And how a call celestial round him rang
      And heavenward from the fountain-brink he
        sprang,
And all the marvel of the golden skies.

There thou art gone, and me thou leavest here
    Sole in these fields; yet will I not despair;
      Despair I will not, while I yet descry
    'Neath the soft canopy of English air

That lonely Tree against the western sky.
  Still, still these slopes, 'tis clear,
Our Gipsy-Scholar haunts, outliving thee!
  Fields where soft sheep from cages pull the hay,
  Woods with anemonies in flower till May,
Know him a wanderer still; then why not me?

A fugitive and gracious light he seeks,
  Shy to illumine; and I seek it too.
    This does not come with houses or with gold,
  With place, with honour, and a flattering crew;
    'Tis not in the world's market bought and sold.
      But the smooth-slipping weeks
  Drop by, and leave its seeker still untired;
    Out of the heed of mortals he is gone,
    He wends unfollow'd, he must house alone;
  Yet on he fares, by his own heart inspired.

Thou too, O Thyrsis, on like quest wert bound,
  Thou wanderedst with me for a little hour;
    Men gave thee nothing, but this happy quest,
  If men esteem'd thee feeble, gave thee power,
    If men procured thee trouble, gave thee rest.
      And this rude Cumner ground,
  Its fir-topped Hurst, its farms, its quiet fields,
    Here cam'st thou in thy jocund youthful time,
    Here was thine height of strength, thy golden
        prime;
  And still the haunt beloved a virtue yields.

What though the music of thy rustic flute
  Kept not for long its happy, country tone,
    Lost it too soon, and learnt a stormy note
  Of men contention-tost, of men who groan,

Which task'd thy pipe too sore, and tired thy
    throat—
    It fail'd, and thou wast mute;
Yet hadst thou alway visions of our light,
  And long with men of care thou couldst not stay,
  And soon thy foot resumed its wandering way,
Left human haunt, and on alone till night.

Too rare, too rare, grow now my visits here!
  'Mid city-noise, not, as with thee of yore,
    Thyrsis, in reach of sheep-bells is my home!
Then through the great town's harsh, heart-wearying
    roar,
  Let in thy voice a whisper often come,
    To chase fatigue and fear:
Why faintest thou? I wander'd till I died.
  Roam on! the light we sought is shining still.
  Dost thou ask proof? Our Tree yet crowns the hill,
Our Scholar travels yet the loved hillside.

○

EPIGRAPH TO *NEW POEMS*, 1867

Though the Muse be gone away,
Though she move not earth to-day,
Souls, erewhile who caught her word,
Ah! still harp on what they heard.

○

DOVER BEACH

The sea is calm to-night,
The tide is full, the moon lies fair
Upon the Straits;—on the French coast, the light

Gleams, and is gone; the cliffs of England stand,
Glimmering and vast, out in the tranquil bay.
Come to the window, sweet is the night air!
Only, from the long line of spray
Where the ebb meets the moon-blanch'd sand,
Listen! you hear the grating roar
Of pebbles which the waves suck back, and fling,
At their return, up the high strand,
Begin, and cease, and then again begin,
With tremulous cadence slow, and bring
The eternal note of sadness in.

Sophocles long ago
Heard it on the Aegaean, and it brought
Into his mind the turbid ebb and flow
Of human misery; we
Find also in the sound a thought,
Hearing it by this distant northern sea.

The sea of faith
Was once, too, at the full, and round earth's shore
Lay like the folds of a bright girdle furl'd;
But now I only hear
Its melancholy, long, withdrawing roar,
Retreating to the breath
Of the night-wind down the vast edges drear
And naked shingles of the world.

Ah, love, let us be true
To one another! for the world, which seems
To lie before us like a land of dreams,
So various, so beautiful, so new,
Hath really neither joy, nor love, nor light,
Nor certitude, nor peace, nor help for pain;

And we are here as on a darkling plain
Swept with confused alarms of struggle and flight,
Where ignorant armies clash by night.

FRAGMENT OF CHORUS
OF A *DEJANEIRA*

O frivolous mind of man,
Light ignorance, and hurrying, unsure thoughts,
Though man bewails you not,
How I bewail you!

Little in your prosperity
Do you seek counsel of the Gods.
Proud, ignorant, self-adored, you live alone.
In profound silence stern
Among their savage gorges and cold springs
Unvisited remain
The great oracular shrines.

Thither in your adversity
Do you betake yourselves for light,
But strangely misinterpret all you hear.
For you will not put on
New hearts with the inquirer's holy robe,
And purged, considerate minds.

And him on whom, at the end
Of toil and dolour untold,
The Gods have said that repose
At last shall descend undisturb'd,
Him you expect to behold

In an easy old age, in a happy home;
No end but this you praise.

But him, on whom, in the prime
Of life, with vigour undimm'd,
With unspent mind, and a soul
Unworn, undebased, undecay'd,
Mournfully grating, the gates
Of the city of death have forever closed—
Him, I count *him*, well-starr'd.

○

EARLY DEATH AND FAME

For him who must see many years,
I praise the life which slips away
Out of the light and mutely; which avoids
Fame, and her less fair followers, envy, strife,
Stupid detraction, jealousy, cabal,
Insincere praises; which descends
The quiet mossy track to age.

But, when immature death
Beckons too early the guest
From the half-tried banquet of life,
Young, in the bloom of his days;
Leaves no leisure to press,
Slow and surely, the sweets
Of a tranquil life in the shade;
Fuller for him be the hours!
Give him emotion, though pain!
Let him live, let him feel: *I have lived!*
Heap up his moments with life,
Triple his pulses with fame!

YOUTH AND CALM

'Tis death! and peace, indeed, is here,
And ease from shame, and rest from fear.
There's nothing can dismarble now
The smoothness of that limpid brow.
But is a calm like this, in truth,
The crowning end of life and youth,
And when this boon rewards the dead,
Are all debts paid, has all been said?
And is the heart of youth so light,
Its step so firm, its eye so bright,
Because on its hot brow there blows
A wind of promise and repose
From the far grave, to which it goes;
Because it has the hope to come,
One day, to harbour in the tomb?
Ah no, the bliss youth dreams is one
For daylight, for the cheerful sun,
For feeling nerves and living breath—
Youth dreams a bliss on this side death!
It dreams a rest, if not more deep,
More grateful than this marble sleep.
It hears a voice within it tell:
Calm's not life's crown, though calm is well.
'Tis all perhaps which man acquires,
But 'tis not what our youth desires.

○

GROWING OLD

What is it to grow old?
Is it to lose the glory of the form,
The lustre of the eye?
Is it for beauty to forgo her wreath?
Yes, but not this alone.

Is it to feel our strength—
Not our bloom only, but our strength—decay?
Is it to feel each limb
Grow stiffer, every function less exact,
Each nerve more weakly strung?

Yes, this, and more! but not,
Ah, 'tis not what in youth we dream'd 'twould be!
'Tis not to have our life
Mellow'd and soften'd as with sunset glow,
A golden day's decline!

'Tis not to see the world
As from a height, with rapt prophetic eyes,
And heart profoundly stirr'd;
And weep, and feel the fullness of the past,
The years that are no more!

It is to spend long days
And not once feel that we were ever young.
It is to add, immured
In the hot prison of the present, month
To month with weary pain.

It is to suffer this,
And feel but half, and feebly, what we feel.
Deep in our hidden heart
Festers the dull remembrance of a change,
But no emotion—none.

It is—last stage of all—
When we are frozen up within, and quite
The phantom of ourselves,
To hear the world applaud the hollow ghost
Which blamed the living man.

○

THE PROGRESS OF POESY

A VARIATION

Youth rambles on life's arid mount,
And strikes the rock, and finds the vein,
And brings the water from the fount,
The fount which shall not flow again.

The man mature with labour chops
For the bright stream a channel grand,
And sees not that the sacred drops
Ran off and vanish'd out of hand.

And then the old man totters nigh
And feebly rakes among the stones.
The mount is mute, the channel dry;
And down he lays his weary bones.

○

THE LAST WORD

Creep into thy narrow bed,
Creep, and let no more be said!
Vain thy onset! all stands fast;
Thou thyself must break at last.

Let the long contention cease!
Geese are swans, and swans are geese.
Let them have it how they will!
Thou art tired; best be still!

They out-talk'd thee, hiss'd thee, tore thee.
Better men fared thus before thee;
Fired their ringing shot and pass'd,
Hotly charged—and broke at last.

Charge once more, then, and be dumb!
Let the victors, when they come,
When the forts of folly fall,
Find thy body by the wall.

○

RUGBY CHAPEL
NOVEMBER, 1857

Coldly, sadly descends
The autumn evening. The Field
Strewn with its dank yellow drifts
Of wither'd leaves, and the elms,

Fade into dimness apace,
Silent;—hardly a shout
From a few boys late at their play!
The lights come out in the street,
In the school-room windows; but cold,
Solemn, unlighted, austere,
Through the gathering darkness, arise
The Chapel walls, in whose bound
Thou, my father! art laid.

There thou dost lie, in the gloom
Of the autumn evening. But ah!
That word, *gloom,* to my mind
Brings thee back in the light
Of thy radiant vigour again!
In the gloom of November we pass'd
Days not of gloom at thy side;
Seasons impair'd not the ray
Of thine even cheerfulness clear.
Such thou wast; and I stand
In the autumn evening, and think
Of bygone autumns with thee.

Fifteen years have gone round
Since thou arosest to tread,
In the summer morning, the road
Of death, at a call unforeseen,
Sudden. For fifteen years,
We who till then in thy shade
Rested as under the boughs
Of a mighty oak, have endured
Sunshine and rain as we might,
Bare, unshaded, alone,
Lacking the shelter of thee.

O strong soul, by what shore
Tarriest thou now? For that force,
Surely, has not been left vain!
Somewhere, surely, afar,
In the sounding labour-house vast
Of being, is practised that strength,
Zealous, beneficent, firm!

Yes, in some far-shining sphere,
Conscious or not of the past,
Still thou performest the word
Of the Spirit in whom thou dost live,
Prompt, unwearied, as here!
Still thou upraisest with zeal
The humble good from the ground,
Sternly repressest the bad.
Still, like a trumpet, dost rouse
Those who with half-open eyes
Tread the border-land dim
'Twixt vice and virtue; reviv'st,
Succourest;—this was thy work,
This was thy life upon earth.

What is the course of the life
Of mortal men on the earth?—
Most men eddy about
Here and there—eat and drink,
Chatter and love and hate,
Gather and squander, are raised
Aloft, are hurl'd in the dust,
Striving blindly, achieving
Nothing; and, then they die—
Perish; and no one asks
Who or what they have been,

More than he asks what waves
In the moonlit solitudes mild
Of the midmost Ocean, have swell'd,
Foam'd for a moment, and gone.

And there are some, whom a thirst
Ardent, unquenchable, fires,
Not with the crowd to be spent,
Not without aim to go round
In an eddy of purposeless dust,
Effort unmeaning and vain.
Ah yes, some of us strive
Not without action to die
Fruitless, but something to snatch
From dull oblivion, nor all
Glut the devouring grave!
We, we have chosen our path—
Path to a clear-purposed goal,
Path of advance! but it leads
A long, steep journey, through sunk
Gorges, o'er mountains in snow!
Cheerful, with friends, we set forth;
Then, on the height, comes the storm!
Thunder crashes from rock
To rock, the cataracts reply;
Lightnings dazzle our eyes;
Roaring torrents have breach'd
The track, the stream-bed descends
In the place where the wayfarer once
Planted his footstep—the spray
Boils o'er its borders; aloft,
The unseen snow-beds dislodge
Their hanging ruin;—alas,
Havoc is made in our train!
Friends who set forth at our side

Falter, are lost in the storm!
We, we only, are left!
With frowning foreheads, with lips
Sternly compress'd, we strain on,
On—and at nightfall, at last,
Come to the end of our way,
To the lonely inn 'mid the rocks;
Where the gaunt and taciturn Host
Stands on the threshold, the wind
Shaking his thin white hairs—
Holds his lantern to scan
Our storm-beat figures, and asks:
Whom in our party we bring?
Whom we have left in the snow?
Sadly we answer: We bring
Only ourselves; we lost
Sight of the rest in the storm.
Hardly ourselves we fought through,
Stripp'd, without friends, as we are.
Friends, companions, and train
The avalanche swept from our side.

But thou would'st not *alone*
Be saved, my father! *alone*
Conquer and come to thy goal,
Leaving the rest in the wild.
We were weary, and we
Fearful, and we, in our march,
Fain to drop down and to die.
Still thou turnedst, and still
Beckonedst the trembler, and still
Gavest the weary thy hand!
If, in the paths of the world,
Stones might have wounded thy feet,

Toil or dejection have tried
Thy spirit, of that we saw
Nothing! to us thou wert still
Cheerful, and helpful, and firm.
Therefore to thee it was given
Many to save with thyself;
And, at the end of thy day,
O faithful shepherd! to come,
Bringing thy sheep in thy hand.

And through thee I believe
In the noble and great who are gone;
Pure souls honour'd and blest
By former ages, who else—
Such, so soulless, so poor,
Is the race of men whom I see—
Seem'd but a dream of the heart,
Seem'd but a cry of desire.
Yes! I believe that there lived
Others like thee in the past,
Not like the men of the crowd
Who all round me to-day
Bluster or cringe, and make life
Hideous, and arid, and vile;
But souls temper'd with fire,
Fervent, heroic, and good,
Helpers and friends of mankind.

Servants of God!—or sons
Shall I not call you? because
Not as servants ye knew
Your Father's innermost mind,
His, who unwillingly sees
One of his little ones lost—

Yours is the praise, if mankind
Hath not as yet in its march
Fainted, and fallen, and died!

See! in the rocks of the world
Marches the host of mankind,
A feeble, wavering line.
Where are they tending?—A God
Marshall'd them, gave them their goal.—
Ah, but the way is so long!
Years they have been in the wild!
Sore thirst plagues them; the rocks,
Rising all round, overawe.
Factions divide them; their host
Threatens to break, to dissolve.
Ah, keep, keep them combined!
Else, of the myriads who fill
That army, not one shall arrive!
Sole they shall stray; in the rocks
Labour for ever in vain,
Die one by one in the waste.

Then, in such hour of need
Of your fainting, dispirited race,
Ye, like angels, appear,
Radiant with ardour divine.
Beacons of hope, ye appear!
Languor is not in your heart,
Weakness is not in your word,
Weariness not on your brow.
Ye alight in our van; at your voice,
Panic, despair, flee away.
Ye move through the ranks, recall
The stragglers, refresh the outworn,
Praise, re-inspire the brave.

Order, courage, return.
Eyes rekindling, and prayers,
Follow your steps as ye go.
Ye fill up the gaps in our files,
Strengthen the wavering line,
Stablish, continue our march,
On, to the bound of the waste,
On, to the City of God.

Criticism

EDITOR'S NOTE

OUR CONTEMPORARY literary criticism, in all its various schools, is continuous with the literary criticism of the Romantic Movement. For it was the Romantic critics of Germany who established the assumption on which every serious contemporary critic works—the assumption of the transcendent importance of literature as an agent, or at the least as an indication, of the health of individuals and society. Preceding cultural epochs had certainly not represented literature as without importance, but the value and function of literature had never before been so grandiosely and so specifically stated as it was by Lessing, the Schlegels, and Schiller. It was their view of literature that prevailed with Wordsworth and Coleridge, who passed it on to Shelley and Keats. Matthew Arnold may be thought of as the writer who, in the English tradition of criticism, serves as the bridge from the great periods of Romanticism to the present.

Arnold struck the characteristic note of his critical thought in the Preface to the 1853 edition of his poems. In that remarkable essay, he undertook to explain why he had suppressed his long dramatic poem, "Empedocles on Etna." He quotes Schiller as saying that all art is dedicated to joy, and then remarks the strange human ability to find joy in the literary representation of terrible calamitous events—in tragedy, he says, "the more tragic the situation, the deeper becomes the enjoyment; and the situation is more tragic in proportion as it becomes more terrible." But, he goes on, modern practice and theory have evolved a kind of representation of calamitous situations which is unlike tragedy in that "the suffering finds no vent in action." In these representations "a continuous state of mental distress is prolonged, unrelieved by incident, hope, or resistance" and "there is everything to be endured, nothing to be done." In such representations there is, Arnold says, "inevitably something morbid," and because "Empedocles on Etna" fell into this class he withdrew it. And in his Inaugural Address, "On the Modern Element in Literature," Arnold reserves the word "adequate" for that literature which, while it truthfully represents the calamitous conditions of life, gives us at the same time the sense of the mental and emotional energy with which calamity may be met.

No critic is ever right in the sense that he says all that may be said about an art, or in the sense that what he does say about an art cannot, by one example or another, be shown to be incomplete. We properly judge a critic's virtue not by his freedom from error but by the nature of the mistakes he does make, for he makes them, if he is worth reading, because he has in mind something beside his perceptions about art in itself—he has in mind the demands he makes upon life; and those critics are most to be trusted who allow these demands, in all their particularity, to be detected by their readers. There is never any doubt about what Arnold demands of life—energy, fineness, and scope in the individual and in society. At the behest of his sense of life—of life as it was at his own moment of history—he no doubt overvalued certain qualities of literature and undervalued others. But his mistakes are in the open, and so are the lively principles by which he made them. To enjoy Arnold as a critic it is not necessary to agree with his particular literary judgments, not with any of them. It is only necessary to be aware of the generosity and commitment of his enterprise.

PREFACE TO *POEMS,*

EDITION OF 1853

IN TWO small volumes of Poems, published anony-
mously, one in 1849, the other in 1852, many of the
Poems which compose the present volume have already
appeared. The rest are now published for the first time.

I have, in the present collection, omitted the Poem
from which the volume published in 1852 took its
title. I have done so, not because the subject of it was
a Sicilian Greek born between two and three thousand
years ago, although many persons would think this a
sufficient reason. Neither have I done so because I had,
in my own opinion, failed in the delineation which I
intended to effect. I intended to delineate the feelings
of one of the last of the Greek religious philosophers, one
of the family of Orpheus and Musaeus, having survived
his fellows, living on into a time when the habits of Greek
thought and feeling had begun fast to change, character to dwindle, the influence of the Sophists to prevail.
Into the feelings of a man so situated there entered much
that we are accustomed to consider as exclusively modern; how much, the fragments of Empedocles himself
which remain to us are sufficient at least to indicate.
What those who are familiar only with the great monuments of early Greek genius suppose to be its exclusive
characteristics, have disappeared; the calm, the cheerfulness, the disinterested objectivity have disappeared:
the dialogue of the mind with itself has commenced;

modern problems have presented themselves; we hear already the doubts, we witness the discouragement, of Hamlet and of Faust.

The representation of such a man's feelings must be interesting, if consistently drawn. We all naturally take pleasure, says Aristotle, in any imitation or representation whatever: this is the basis of our love of Poetry: and we take pleasure in them, he adds, because all knowledge is naturally agreeable to us; not to the philosopher only, but to mankind at large. Every representation therefore which is consistently drawn may be supposed to be interesting, inasmuch as it gratifies this natural interest in knowledge of all kinds. What is *not* interesting, is that which does not add to our knowledge of any kind; that which is vaguely conceived and loosely drawn; a representation which is general, indeterminate, and faint, instead of being particular, precise, and firm.

Any accurate representation may therefore be expected to be interesting; but, if the representation be a poetical one, more than this is demanded. It is demanded, not only that it shall interest, but also that it shall inspirit and rejoice the reader: that it shall convey a charm, and infuse delight. For the Muses, as Hesiod says, were born that they might be "a forgetfulness of evils, and a truce from cares": and it is not enough that the Poet should add to the knowledge of men, it is required of him also that he should add to their happiness. "All Art," says Schiller, "is dedicated to Joy, and there is no higher and no more serious problem, than how to make men happy. The right Art is that alone, which creates the highest enjoyment."

A poetical work, therefore, is not yet justified when it has been shown to be an accurate, and therefore interesting representation; it has to be shown also that it is a representation from which men can derive enjoy-

ment. In presence of the most tragic circumstances, represented in a work of Art, the feeling of enjoyment, as
is well known, may still subsist: the representation of
the most utter calamity, of the liveliest anguish, is not
sufficient to destroy it: the more tragic the situation,
the deeper becomes the enjoyment; and the situation
is more tragic in proportion as it becomes more terrible.

What then are the situations, from the representation
of which, though accurate, no poetical enjoyment can
be derived? They are those in which the suffering finds
no vent in action; in which a continuous state of mental
distress is prolonged, unrelieved by incident, hope, or
resistance; in which there is everything to be endured,
nothing to be done. In such situations there is inevitably
something morbid, in the description of them something
monotonous. When they occur in actual life, they are
painful, not tragic; the representation of them in poetry
is painful also.

To this class of situations, poetically faulty as it
appears to me, that of Empedocles, as I have endeavoured to represent him, belongs; and I have therefore
excluded the Poem from the present collection.

And why, it may be asked, have I entered into this
explanation respecting a matter so unimportant as the
admission or exclusion of the Poem in question? I have
done so, because I was anxious to avow that the sole
reason for its exclusion was that which has been stated
above; and that it has not been excluded in deference
to the opinion which many critics of the present day
appear to entertain against subjects chosen from distant
times and countries: against the choice, in short, of any
subjects but modern ones.

"The Poet," it is said,[1] and by an intelligent critic,

[1] In *The Spectator* of April 2nd, 1853. The words quoted were
not used with reference to poems of mine. (*Arnold's note.*)

"the Poet who would really fix the public attention must leave the exhausted past, and draw his subjects from matters of present import, and *therefore* both of interest and novelty."

Now this view I believe to be completely false. It is worth examining, inasmuch as it is a fair sample of a class of critical dicta everywhere current at the present day, having a philosophical form and air, but no real basis in fact; and which are calculated to vitiate the judgment of readers of poetry, while they exert, so far as they are adopted, a misleading influence on the practice of those who write it.

What are the eternal objects of Poetry, among all nations and at all times? They are actions; human actions; possessing an inherent interest in themselves, and which are to be communicated in an interesting manner by the art of the Poet. Vainly will the latter imagine that he has everything in his own power; that he can make an intrinsically inferior action equally delightful with a more excellent one by his treatment of it; he may indeed compel us to admire his skill, but his work will possess, within itself, an incurable defect.

The Poet, then, has in the first place to select an excellent action; and what actions are the most excellent? Those, certainly, which most powerfully appeal to the great primary human affections: to those elementary feelings which subsist permanently in the race, and which are independent of time. These feelings are permanent and the same; that which interests them is permanent and the same also. The modernness or antiquity of an action, therefore, has nothing to do with its fitness for poetical representation; this depends upon its inherent qualities. To the elementary part of our nature, to our passions, that which is great and passionate is eternally interesting; and interesting solely in proportion to its greatness and to its passion. A great human action of a thousand years ago is more interesting to it than a smaller human action of to-day, even though upon the representation of this last the most consummate skill may have been expended, and though it has the advantage of appealing by its modern language, familiar manners, and contemporary allusions, to all our transient feelings and interests. These, however, have no right to demand of a poetical work that it shall satisfy them; their claims are to be directed elsewhere. Poetical works belong to the domain of our permanent passions: let them interest these, and the voice of all subordinate claims upon them is at once silenced.

Achilles, Prometheus, Clytemnestra, Dido—what modern poem presents personages as interesting, even to us moderns, as these personages of an "exhausted past"? We have the domestic epic dealing with the details of modern life which pass daily under our eyes; we have poems representing modern personages in contact with the problems of modern life, moral, intellectual, and social; these works have been produced by poets the most distinguished of their nation and time; yet I fearlessly assert that *Hermann and Dorothea, Childe Harold,* "Jocelyn," *The Excursion,* leave the reader cold in comparison with the effect produced upon him by the latter books of the *Iliad,* by the *Orestea,* or by the episode of Dido. And why is this? Simply because in the three latter cases the action is greater, the personages nobler, the situations more intense: and this is the true basis of the interest in a poetical work, and this alone.

It may be urged, however, that past actions may be interesting in themselves, but that they are not to be adopted by the modern Poet, because it is impossible for him to have them clearly present to his own mind, and he cannot therefore feel them deeply, nor represent them forcibly. But this is not necessarily the case. The externals of a past action, indeed, he cannot know with the precision of a contemporary; but his business is with its essentials. The outward man of Oedipus or of Macbeth, the houses in which they lived, the ceremonies of their courts, he cannot accurately figure to himself; but neither do they essentially concern him. His business is with their inward man; with their feelings and behaviour in certain tragic situations, which engage their passions as men; these have in them nothing local and casual; they are as accessible to the modern Poet as to a contemporary.

The date of an action, then, signifies nothing: the action itself, its selection and construction, this is what is all-important. This the Greeks understood far more clearly than we do. The radical difference between their poetical theory and ours consists, as it appears to me, in this: that, with them, the poetical character of the action in itself, and the conduct of it, was the first consideration; with us, attention is fixed mainly on the value of the separate thoughts and images which occur in the treatment of an action. They regarded the whole; we regard the parts. With them, the action predominated over the expression of it; with us, the expression predominates over the action. Not that they failed in expression, or were inattentive to it; on the contrary, they are the highest models of expression, the unapproached masters of the *grand style*: but their expression is so excellent because it is so admirably kept in its right degree of prominence; because it is so simple and so well subordinated; because it draws its force directly from the pregnancy of the matter which it conveys. For what reason was the Greek tragic poet confined to so limited a range of subjects? Because there are so few actions which unite in themselves, in the highest degree, the conditions of excellence: and it was not thought that on any but an excellent subject could an excellent Poem be constructed. A few actions, therefore, eminently adapted for tragedy, maintained almost exclusive possession of the Greek tragic stage; their significance appeared inexhaustible; they were as permanent problems, perpetually offered to the genius of every fresh poet. This too is the reason of what appears to us moderns a certain baldness of expression in Greek tragedy; of the triviality with which we often reproach the remarks of the chorus, where it takes part in the dialogue: that the action itself, the situation of Orestes, or Merope, or Alcmaeon, was to stand the central point of interest, unforgotten, absorbing, principal; that no accessories were for a moment to distract the spectator's attention from this; that the tone of the parts was to be perpetually kept down, in order not to impair the grandiose effect of the whole. The terrible old mythic story on which the drama was founded stood, before he entered the theatre, traced in its bare outlines upon the spectator's mind; it stood in his memory, as a group of statuary, faintly seen, at the end of a long and dark vista: then came the Poet, embodying outlines, developing situations, not a word wasted, not a sentiment capriciously thrown in: stroke upon stroke, the drama proceeded: the light deepened upon the group; more and more it revealed itself to the rivetted gaze of the spectator: until at last, when the final words were spoken, it stood before him in broad sunlight, a model of immortal beauty.

This was what a Greek critic demanded; this was what a Greek poet endeavoured to effect. It signified nothing to what time an action belonged; we do not find that the *Persae* occupied a particularly high rank among the dramas of Aeschylus, because it represented a matter of contemporary interest: this was not what a cultivated Athenian required; he required that the permanent elements of his nature should be moved; and dramas of which the action, though taken from a long-distant mythic time, yet was calculated to accomplish this in a higher degree than that of the *Persae*, stood higher in his estimation accordingly. The Greeks felt, no doubt, with their exquisite sagacity of taste, that an action of present times was too near them, too much mixed up with what was accidental and passing, to form a sufficiently grand, detached, and self-subsistent object for a tragic poem: such objects belonged to the domain of the comic poet, and of the lighter kinds of poetry. For the more serious kinds, for *pragmatic* poetry, to use an excellent expression of Polybius, they were more difficult and severe in the range of subjects which they permitted. Their theory and practice alike, the admirable treatise of Aristotle, and the unrivalled works of their poets, exclaim with a thousand tongues— "All depends upon the subject; choose a fitting action, penetrate yourself with the feeling of its situations; this done, everything else will follow."

But for all kinds of poetry alike there was one point on which they were rigidly exacting; the adaptability of the subject to the kind of poetry selected, and the careful construction of the poem.

How different a way of thinking from this is ours! We can hardly at the present day understand what Menander meant, when he told a man who inquired as to the progress of his comedy that he had finished it, not having yet written a single line, because he had constructed the action of it in his mind. A modern critic would have assured him that the merit of his piece depended on the brilliant things which arose under his pen as he went along. We have poems which seem to exist merely for the sake of single lines and passages; not for the sake of producing any total-impression. We have critics who seem to direct their attention merely to detached expressions, to the language about the action, not to the action itself. I verily think that the majority of them do not in their hearts believe that there is such a thing as a total-impression to be derived from a poem at all, or to be demanded from a poet; they think the term a commonplace of metaphysical criticism. They will permit the Poet to select any action he pleases, and to suffer that action to go as it will, provided he gratifies them with occasional bursts of fine writing, and with a shower of isolated thoughts and images. That is, they permit him to leave their poetical sense ungratified, provided that he gratifies their rhetorical sense and their curiosity. Of his neglecting to gratify these, there is little danger; he needs rather to be warned against the danger of attempting to gratify these alone; he needs rather to be perpetually reminded to prefer his action to everything else; so to treat this, as to permit its inherent excellences to develop themselves, without interruption from the intrusion of his personal peculiarities: most fortunate, when he most entirely succeeds in effacing himself, and in enabling a noble action to subsist as it did in nature.

But the modern critic not only permits a false practice; he absolutely prescribes false aims.—"A true allegory of the state of one's own mind in a representative history," the Poet is told, "is perhaps the highest thing that one can attempt in the way of poetry."—And accordingly he attempts it. An allegory of the state of one's own mind, the highest problem of an art which imitates actions! No assuredly, it is not, it never can be so: no great poetical work has ever been produced with such an aim. Faust itself, in which something of the kind is attempted, wonderful passages as it contains, and in spite of the unsurpassed beauty of the scenes which relate to Margaret, Faust itself, judged as a whole, and judged strictly as a poetical work, is defective: its illustrious author, the greatest poet of modern times, the greatest critic of all times, would have been the first to acknowledge it; he only defended his work, indeed, by asserting it to be "something incommensurable."

The confusion of the present times is great, the multitude of voices counselling different things bewildering, the number of existing works capable of attracting a young writer's attention and of becoming his models, immense: what he wants is a hand to guide him through the confusion, a voice to prescribe to him the aim which he should keep in view, and to explain to him that the value of the literary works which offer themselves to his attention is relative to their power of helping him forward on his road towards this aim. Such a guide the English writer at the present day will nowhere find. Failing this, all that can be looked for, all indeed that can be desired, is, that his attention should be fixed on excellent models; that he may reproduce, at any rate, something of their excellence, by penetrating himself with their works and by catching their spirit, if he cannot be taught to produce what is excellent independently.

Foremost among these models for the English writer stands Shakespeare: a name the greatest perhaps of all poetical names; a name never to be mentioned without reverence. I will venture, however, to express a doubt, whether the influence of his works, excellent and fruitful for the readers of poetry, for the great majority, has been of unmixed advantage to the writers of it. Shakespeare indeed chose excellent subjects; the world could afford no better than Macbeth, or Romeo and Juliet, or Othello:

he had no theory respecting the necessity of choosing subjects of present import, or the paramount interest attaching to allegories of the state of one's own mind; like all great poets, he knew well what constituted a poetical action; like them, wherever he found such an action, he took it; like them, too, he found his best in past times. But to these general characteristics of all great poets he added a special one of his own; a gift, namely, of happy, abundant, and ingenious expression, eminent and unrivalled: so eminent as irresistibly to strike the attention first in him, and even to throw into comparative shade his other excellences as a poet. Here has been the mischief. These other excellences were his fundamental excellences *as a poet*; what distinguishes the artist from the mere amateur, says Goethe, is *Architectonicè* in the highest sense; that power of execution, which creates, forms, and constitutes: not the profoundness of single thoughts, not the richness of imagery, not the abundance of illustration. But these attractive accessories of a poetical work being more easily seized than the spirit of the whole, and these accessories being possessed by Shakespeare in an unequalled degree, a young writer having recourse to Shakespeare as his model runs great risk of being vanquished and absorbed by them, and, in consequence, of reproducing, according to the measure of his power, these, and these alone. Of this preponderating quality of Shakespeare's genius, accordingly, almost the whole of modern English poetry has, it appears to me, felt the influence. To the exclusive attention on the part of his imitators to this it is in a great degree owing, that of the majority of modern poetical works the details alone are valuable, the composition worthless. In reading them one is perpetually reminded of that terrible sentence on a modern French poet—*il dit tout ce qu'il veut, mais malheureusement il n'a rien à dire.*

Let me give an instance of what I mean. I will take it from the works of the very chief among those who seem to have been formed in the school of Shakespeare: of one whose exquisite genius and pathetic death render him for ever interesting. I will take the poem of "Isabella, or the Pot of Basil," by Keats. I choose this rather than the "Endymion," because the latter work (which a modern critic has classed with *The Faerie Queene!*), although undoubtedly there blows through it the breath of genius, is yet as a whole so utterly incoherent, as not strictly to merit the name of a poem at all. The poem of "Isabella," then, is a perfect treasure-house of graceful and felicitous words and images: almost in every stanza there occurs one of those vivid and picturesque turns of expression, by which the object is made to flash upon the eye of the mind, and which thrill the reader with a sudden delight. This one short poem contains, perhaps, a greater number of happy single expressions which one could quote than all the extant tragedies of Sophocles. But the action, the story? The action in itself is an excellent one; but so feebly is it conceived by the Poet, so loosely constructed, that the effect produced by it, in and for itself, is absolutely null. Let the reader, after he has finished the poem of Keats, turn to the same story in the *Decameron:* he will then feel how pregnant and interesting the same action has become in the hands of a great artist, who above all things delineates his object; who subordinates expression to that which it is designed to express.

I have said that the imitators of Shakespeare, fixing their attention on his wonderful gift of expression, have directed their imitation to this, neglecting his other excellences. These excellences, the fundamental excellences of poetical art, Shakespeare no doubt possessed them—possessed many of them in a splendid degree; but it may perhaps be doubted whether even he himself did not sometimes give scope to his faculty of expression to the prejudice of a higher poetical duty. For we must never forget that Shakespeare is the great poet he is from his skill in discerning and firmly conceiving an excellent action, from his power of intensely feeling a situation, of intimately associating himself with a character; not from his gift of expression, which rather even leads him astray, degenerating sometimes into a fondness for curiosity of expression, into an irritability of fancy, which seems to make it impossible for him to say a thing plainly, even when the press of the action demands the very directest language, or its level character the very simplest. Mr. Hallam, than whom it is impossible to find a saner and more judicious critic, has had the courage (for at the present day it needs courage) to remark, how extremely and faultily difficult Shakespeare's language often is. It is so: you may find main scenes in some of his greatest tragedies, *King Lear* for instance, where the language is so artificial, so curiously tortured, and so difficult, that every speech has to be read two or three times before its meaning can be comprehended. This over-curiousness of expression is indeed but the excessive employment of a wonderful gift—of the power of saying a thing in a happier way than any other man; nevertheless, it is carried so far that one understands what M. Guizot meant, when he said that Shakespeare appears in his language to have tried all styles except that of simplicity. He has not the severe and scrupulous self-restraint of the ancients, partly no doubt, because he had a far less cultivated and exacting audience: he has indeed a far wider range than they had, a far richer fertility of thought; in this respect he rises above them: in his strong conception of his subject, in the genuine way in which he is penetrated with it, he resembles them, and is unlike the moderns: but in the accurate limitation of it, the conscientious rejection of superfluities, the simple and rigorous development of it from the first line of his work to the last, he falls below them, and comes nearer to the moderns. In his chief works, besides what he has of his own, he has the elementary soundness of the ancients; he has their important action and their large and broad manner: but he has not their purity of method. He is therefore a less safe model; for what he has of his own is personal, and inseparable from his own rich nature; it may be imitated and exaggerated, it cannot be learned or applied as an art; he is above all suggestive; more valuable, therefore, to young writers as men than as artists. But clearness of arrangement, rigour of development, simplicity of style—these may to a certain extent be learned: and these may, I am convinced, be learned best from the ancients, who although infinitely less suggestive than Shakespeare, are thus, to the artist, more instructive.

What, then, it will be asked, are the ancients to be our sole models? the ancients with their comparatively narrow range of experience, and their widely different circumstances? Not, certainly, that which is narrow in the ancients, nor that in which we can no longer sympathize. An action like the action of the *Antigone* of Sophocles, which turns upon the conflict between the heroine's duty to her brother's corpse and that to the laws of her country, is no longer one in which it is possible that we should feel a deep interest. I am speaking too, it will be remembered, not of the best sources of intellectual stimulus for the general reader, but of the best models of instruction for the individual writer. This last may certainly learn of the ancients, better than anywhere else, three things which it is vitally important for him to know:—the all-importance of the choice of a subject; the necessity of accurate construction; and the subordinate character of expression. He will learn from them how unspeakably superior is the effect of the one moral impression left by a great action treated as a whole, to the effect produced by the most striking single thought or by the happiest image. As he penetrates into the spirit of the great classical works, as he becomes gradually aware of their intense significance, their noble simplicity, and their calm pathos, he will be convinced that it is this effect, unity and profoundness of moral impression, at which the ancient Poets aimed; that it is this which constitutes the grandeur of their works, and which makes them immortal. He will desire to direct his own efforts towards producing the same effect. Above all, he will deliver himself from the jargon of modern criticism, and escape the danger of producing poetical works conceived in the spirit of the passing time, and which partake of its transitoriness.

The present age makes great claims upon us: we owe it service, it will not be satisfied without our admiration. I know not how it is, but their commerce with the ancients appears to me to produce, in those who constantly practise it, a steadying and composing effect upon their judgment, not of literary works only, but of men and events in general. They are like persons who have had a very weighty and impressive experience: they are more truly than others under the empire of facts, and more independent of the language current among those with whom they live. They wish neither to applaud nor to revile their age: they wish to know what it is, what it can give them, and whether this is what they want. What they want, they know very well; they want to educe and cultivate what is best and noblest in themselves: they know, too, that this is no easy task—χαλεπὸν, as Pittacus said, χαλεπὸν ἐσθλὸν ἔμμεναι—and they ask themselves sincerely whether their age and its literature can assist them in the attempt. If they are endeavouring to practise any art, they remember the plain and simple proceedings of the old artists, who attained their grand results by penetrating themselves with some noble and significant action, not by inflating themselves with a belief in the preeminent importance and greatness of their own times. They do not talk of their mission, nor of interpreting their age, nor of the coming Poet; all this, they know, is the mere delirium of vanity; their business is not to praise their age, but to afford to the men who live in it the highest pleasure which they are capable of feeling. If asked to afford this by means of subjects drawn from the age itself, they ask what special fitness the present age has for supplying them: they are told that it is an era of progress, an age commissioned to carry out the great ideas of industrial development and social amelioration. They reply that with all this they can do nothing; that the elements they need for the exercise of their art are great actions, calculated powerfully and delightfully to affect what is permanent in the human soul; that so far as the present age can supply such actions, they will gladly make use of them; but that an age wanting in moral grandeur can with difficulty supply such, and an age of spiritual discomfort with difficulty be powerfully and delightfully affected by them.

A host of voices will indignantly rejoin that the present age is inferior to the past neither in moral grandeur nor in spiritual health. He who possesses the discipline I speak of will content himself with remembering the judgments passed upon the present age, in this respect, by the two men, the one of strongest head, the other of widest culture, whom it has produced; by Goethe and by Niebuhr. It will be sufficient for him that he knows the opinions held by these two great men respecting the present age and its literature; and that he feels assured in his own mind that their aims and demands upon life were such as he would wish, at any rate, his own to be; and their judgment as to what is impeding and disabling such as he may safely follow. He will not, however, maintain a hostile attitude towards the false pretensions of his age; he will content himself with not being overwhelmed by them. He will esteem himself fortunate if he can succeed in banishing from his mind all feelings of contradiction, and irritation, and impatience; in order to delight himself with the contemplation of some noble action of a heroic time, and to enable others, through his representation of it, to delight in it also.

I am far indeed from making any claim, for myself, that I possess this discipline; or for the following Poems, that they breathe its spirit. But I say, that in the sincere endeavour to learn and practise, amid the bewildering confusion of our times, what is sound and true in poetical art, I seemed to myself to find the only sure guidance, the only solid footing, among the ancients. They, at any rate, knew what they wanted in Art, and we do not. It is this uncertainty which is disheartening, and not hostile criticism. How often have I felt this when reading words of disparagement or of cavil: that it is the uncertainty as to what is really to be aimed at which makes our difficulty, not the dissatisfaction of the critic, who himself suffers from the same uncertainty. *Non me tua fervida terrent Dicta: Dii me terrent, et Jupiter hostis.*

Two kinds of *dilettanti*, says Goethe, there are in poetry: he who neglects the indispensable mechanical part, and thinks he has done enough if he shows spirituality and feeling; and he who seeks to arrive at poetry merely by mechanism, in which he can acquire an artisan's readiness, and is without soul and matter. And he adds, that the first does most harm to Art, and the last to himself. If we must be *dilettanti*: if it is im-

possible for us, under the circumstances amidst which
we live, to think clearly, to feel nobly, and to delineate
firmly: if we cannot attain to the mastery of the great
artists—let us, at least, have so much respect for our
Art as to prefer it to ourselves: let us not bewilder our
successors: let us transmit to them the practice of Poetry,
with its boundaries and wholesome regulative laws,
under which excellent works may again, perhaps, at
some future time, be produced, not yet fallen into oblivion through our neglect, not yet condemned and can-
celled by the influence of their eternal enemy, Caprice.

○

ADVERTISEMENT TO THE
SECOND EDITION OF *POEMS*

○

I HAVE allowed the Preface to the former edition of
these Poems to stand almost without change, because
I still believe it to be, in the main, true. I must not, however, be supposed insensible to the force of much that
has been alleged against portions of it, or unaware that
it contains many things incompletely stated, many things
which need limitation. It leaves, too, untouched the
question, how far, and in what manner, the opinions
there expressed respecting the choice of subjects apply
to lyric poetry; that region of the poetical field which is
chiefly cultivated at present. But neither have I time
now to supply these deficiencies, nor is this the proper

place for attempting it: on one or two points alone I wish to offer, in the briefest possible way, some explanation.

An objection has been ably urged to the classing together, as subjects equally belonging to a past time, Oedipus and Macbeth. And it is no doubt true that to Shakespeare, standing on the verge of the middle ages, the epoch of Macbeth was more familiar than that of Oedipus. But I was speaking of actions as they presented themselves to us moderns: and it will hardly be said that the European mind, since Voltaire, has much more affinity with the times of Macbeth than with those of Oedipus. As moderns, it seems to me, we have no longer any direct affinity with the circumstances and feelings of either; as individuals, we are attracted towards this or that personage, we have a capacity for imagining him, irrespective of his times, solely according to a law of personal sympathy; and those subjects for which we feel this personal attraction most strongly, we may hope to treat successfully. Alcestis or Joan of Arc, Charlemagne or Agamemnon—one of these is not really nearer to us now than another; each can be made present only by an act of poetic imagination: but this man's imagination has an affinity for one of them, and that man's for another.

It has been said that I wish to limit the Poet in his choice of subjects to the period of Greek and Roman antiquity: but it is not so: I only counsel him to choose for his subjects great actions, without regarding to what time they belong. Nor do I deny that the poetic faculty can and does manifest itself in treating the most trifling action, the most hopeless subject. But it is a pity that power should be wasted; and that the Poet should be compelled to impart interest and force to his subject, instead of receiving them from it, and thereby doubling his impressiveness. There is, it has been excellently said, an immortal strength in the stories of great actions: the most gifted poet, then, may well be glad to supplement with it that mortal weakness, which, in presence of the vast spectacle of life and the world, he must for ever feel to be his individual portion.

Again, with respect to the study of the classical writers of antiquity: it has been said that we should emulate rather than imitate them. I make no objection: all I say is, let us study them. They can help to cure us of what is, it seems to me, the great vice of our intellect, manifesting itself in our incredible vagaries in literature, in art, in religion, in morals; namely, that it is *fantastic,* and wants *sanity.* Sanity—that is the great virtue of the ancient literature: the want of that is the great defect of the modern, in spite of all its variety and power. It is impossible to read carefully the great ancients, without losing something of our caprice and eccentricity; and to emulate them we must at least read them.

○

ON TRANSLATING HOMER

FIRST LECTURE

○

IT HAS more than once been suggested to me that I should translate Homer. That is a task for which I have neither the time nor the courage; but the suggestion led me to regard yet more closely a poet whom I had al-

ready long studied, and for one or two years the works of
Homer were seldom out of my hands. The study of classical literature is probably on the decline; but, whatever
may be the fate of this study in general, it is certain that,
as instruction spreads and the number of readers increases, attention will be more and more directed to the
poetry of Homer, not indeed as part of a classical course,
but as the most important poetical monument existing.
Even within the last ten years two fresh translations of the
Iliad have appeared in England: one by a man of great
ability and genuine learning, Professor Newman; the
other by Mr. Wright, the conscientious and painstaking
translator of Dante. It may safely be asserted that neither of these works will take rank as the standard translation of Homer; that the task of rendering him will still
be attempted by other translators. It may perhaps be
possible to render to these some service, to save them
some loss of labour, by pointing out rocks on which their
predecessors have split, and the right objects on which
a translator of Homer should fix his attention.

It is disputed what aim a translator should propose
to himself in dealing with his original. Even this preliminary is not yet settled. On one side it is said that the
translation ought to be such "that the reader should, if
possible, forget that it is a translation at all, and be lulled
into the illusion that he is reading an original work,—
something original" (if the translation be in English),
"from an English hand." The real original is in this case,
it is said, "taken as a basis on which to rear a poem that
shall affect our countrymen as the original may be conceived to have affected its natural hearers." On the other
hand, Mr. Newman, who states the foregoing doctrine
only to condemn it, declares that he "aims at precisely
the opposite: to retain every peculiarity of the original,
so far as he is able, *with the greater care the more for-*

eign it may happen to be"; so that it may "never be forgotten that he is imitating, and imitating in a different material." The translator's "first duty," says Mr. Newman, "is a historical one, to be *faithful*." Probably both sides would agree that the translator's "first duty is to be faithful"; but the question at issue between them is, in what faithfulness consists.

My one object is to give practical advice to a translator; and I shall not the least concern myself with theories of translation as such. But I advise the tranlator not to try "to rear on the basis of the *Iliad,* a poem that shall affect our countrymen as the original may be conceived to have affected its natural hearers"; and for this simple reason, that we cannot possibly tell *how* the *Iliad* "affected its natural hearers." It is probably meant merely that he should try to affect Englishmen powerfully, as Homer affected Greeks powerfully; but this direction is not enough, and can give no real guidance. For all great poets affect their hearers powerfully, but the effect of one poet is one thing, that of another poet another thing: it is our translator's business to reproduce the effect of Homer, and the most powerful emotion of the unlearned English reader can never assure him whether he has *re*produced this, or whether he has produced something else. So, again, he may follow Mr. Newman's directions, he may try to be "faithful," he may "retain every peculiarity of his original"; but who is to assure him, who is to assure Mr. Newman himself, that, when he has done this, he has done that for which Mr. Newman enjoins this to be done, "adhered closely to Homer's manner and habit of thought"? Evidently the translator needs some more practical directions than these. No one can tell him how Homer affected the Greeks; but there are those who can tell him how Homer affects *them*. These are scholars; who possess, at the same time with knowledge of

Greek, adequate poetical taste and feeling. No translation will seem to them of much worth compared with
the original; but they alone can say whether the translation produces more or less the same effect upon them
as the original. They are the only competent tribunal in
this matter: the Greeks are dead; the unlearned Englishman has not the data for judging; and no man can safely
confide in his own single judgment of his own work. Let
not the translator, then, trust to his notions of what the
ancient Greeks would have thought of him; he will lose
himself in the vague. Let him not trust to what the ordinary English reader thinks of him; he will be taking the
blind for his guide. Let him not trust to his own judgment of his own work; he may be misled by individual
caprices. Let him ask how his work affects those who
both know Greek and can appreciate poetry; whether to
read it gives the Provost of Eton, or Professor Thompson
at Cambridge, or Professor Jowett here in Oxford, at all
the same feeling which to read the original gives them. I
consider that when Bentley said of Pope's translation,
"It was a pretty poem, but must not be called Homer,"
the work, in spite of all its power and attractiveness, was
judged.

'Ως ἂν ὁ φρόνιμος ὁρίσειεν,—"as the judicious would
determine,"—that is a test to which every one professes
himself willing to submit his works. Unhappily, in most
cases, no two persons agree as to who "the judicious"
are. In the present case, the ambiguity is removed: I
suppose the translator at one with me as to the tribunal
to which alone he should look for judgment; and he has
thus obtained a practical test by which to estimate the
real success of his work. How is he to proceed, in order
that his work, tried by this test, may be found most successful?

First of all, there are certain negative counsels which

I will give him. Homer has occupied men's minds so much, such a literature has arisen about him, that every one who approaches him should resolve strictly to limit himself to that which may directly serve the object for which he approaches him. I advise the translator to have nothing to do with the questions, whether Homer ever existed; whether the poet of the *Iliad* be one or many; whether the *Iliad* be one poem or an *Achilleis* and an *Iliad* stuck together; whether the Christian doctrine of the Atonement is shadowed forth in the Homeric mythology; whether the Goddess Latona in any way prefigures the Virgin Mary, and so on. These are questions which have been discussed with learning, with ingenuity, nay, with genius; but they have two inconveniences, —one general for all who approach them, one particular for the translator. The general inconvenience is that there really exist no data for determining them. The particular inconvenience is that their solution by the translator, even were it possible, could be of no benefit to his translation.

I advise him, again, not to trouble himself with constructing a special vocabulary for his use in translation; with excluding a certain class of English words, and with confining himself to another class, in obedience to any theory about the peculiar qualities of Homer's style. Mr. Newman says that "the entire dialect of Homer being essentially archaic, that of a translator ought to be as much Saxo-Norman as possible, and owe as little as possible to the elements thrown into our language by classical learning." Mr. Newman is unfortunate in the observance of his own theory; for I continually find in his translation words of Latin origin, which seem to me quite alien to the simplicity of Homer,—"responsive," for instance, which is a favourite word of Mr. Newman, to represent the Homeric ἀμειβόμενος:

Great Hector of the motley helm thus spake to her *responsive*.
But thus *responsively* to him spake god-like Alexander.

And the word "celestial," again, in the grand address of
Zeus to the horses of Achilles,

You, who are born *celestial*, from Eld and Death exempted!

seems to me in that place exactly to jar upon the feeling
as too bookish. But, apart from the question of Mr. Newman's fidelity to his own theory, such a theory seems to
me both dangerous for a translator and false in itself.
Dangerous for a translator; because, wherever one finds
such a theory announced (and one finds it pretty often),
it is generally followed by an explosion of pedantry; and
pedantry is of all things in the world the most un-
Homeric. False in itself; because, in fact, we owe to the
Latin element in our language most of that very rapidity
and clear decisiveness by which it is contradistinguished
from the German, and in sympathy with the languages
of Greece and Rome: so that to limit an English translator of Homer to words of Saxon origin is to deprive
him of one of his special advantages for translating
Homer. In Voss's well-known translation of Homer, it
is precisely the qualities of his German language itself,
something heavy and trailing both in the structure of its
sentences and in the words of which it is composed,
which prevent his translation, in spite of the hexameters,
in spite of the fidelity, from creating in us the impression
created by the Greek. Mr. Newman's prescription, if followed, would just strip the English translator of the advantage which he has over Voss.

The frame of mind in which we approach an author
influences our correctness of appreciation of him; and
Homer should be approached by a translator in the
simplest frame of mind possible. Modern sentiment tries

to make the ancient not less than the modern world its
own; but against modern sentiment in its applications
to Homer the translator, if he would feel Homer truly—
and unless he feels him truly, how can he render him
truly?—cannot be too much on his guard. For example:
the writer of an interesting article on English translations of Homer, in the last number of the *National Review*, quotes, I see, with admiration, a criticism of Mr.
Ruskin on the use of the epithet φυσίζοος, "life-giving,"
in that beautiful passage in the third book of the *Iliad*,
which follows Helen's mention of her brothers Castor
and Pollux as alive, though they were in truth dead:

> ὣς φάτο · τοὺς δ' ἤδη κατέχεν φυσίζοος αἶα
> ἐν Λακεδαίμονι αὖθι, φίλῃ ἐν πατρίδι γαίῃ.[1]

"The poet," says Mr. Ruskin, "has to speak of the earth
in sadness; but he will not let that sadness affect or
change his thought of it. No; though Castor and Pollux
be dead, yet the earth is our mother still,—fruitful, life-
giving." This is a just specimen of that sort of application of modern sentiment to the ancients, against which
a student, who wishes to feel the ancients truly, cannot
too resolutely defend himself. It reminds one, as, alas!
so much of Mr. Ruskin's writing reminds one, of those
words of the most delicate of living critics: "Comme
tout genre de composition a son écueil particulier, *celui
du genre romanesque, c'est le faux*." The reader may
feel moved as he reads it; but it is not the less an example of "le faux" in criticism; it is false. It is not true, as
to that particular passage, that Homer called the earth
φυσίζοος, because, "though he had to speak of the earth
in sadness, he would not let that sadness change or
affect his thought of it," but consoled himself by considering that "the earth is our mother still,—fruitful, life-

---

[1] *Iliad*, iii, 243. (Arnold's note.)

giving." It is not true, as a matter of general criticism, that this kind of sentimentality, eminently modern, inspires Homer at all. "From Homer and Polygnotus I every day learn more clearly," says Goethe, "that in our life here above ground we have, properly speaking, to enact Hell:" [1]—if the student must absolutely have a keynote to the *Iliad,* let him take this of Goethe, and see what he can do with it; it will not, at any rate, like the tender 'pantheism of Mr. Ruskin, falsify for him the whole strain of Homer.

These are negative counsels; I come to the positive. When I say, the translator of Homer should above all be penetrated by a sense of four qualities of his author;— that he is eminently rapid; that he is eminently plain and direct, both in the evolution of his thought and in the expression of it, that is, both in his syntax and in his words; that he is eminently plain and direct in the substance of his thought, that is, in his matter and ideas; and, finally that he is eminently noble;—I probably seem to be saying what is too general to be of much service to anybody. Yet it is strictly true that, for want of duly penetrating themselves with the first-named quality of Homer, his rapidity, Cowper and Mr. Wright have failed in rendering him; that, for want of duly appreciating the second-named quality, his plainness and directness of style and diction, Pope and Mr. Sotheby have failed in rendering him; that for want of appreciating the third, his plainness and directness of ideas, Chapman has failed in rendering him; while for want of appreciating the fourth, his nobleness, Mr. Newman, who has clearly seen some of the faults of his predecessors, has yet failed more conspicuously than any of them.

Coleridge says, in his strange language, speaking of

[1] *Briefwechsel zwischen Schiller und Goethe,* vi, 230. (*Arnold's note.*)

the union of the human soul with the divine essence, that this takes place

> Whene'er the mist, which stands 'twixt God and thee,
> Defecates to a pure transparency;

and so, too, it may be said of that union of the translator with his original, which alone can produce a good translation, that it takes place when the mist which stands between them—the mist of alien modes of thinking, speaking, and feeling on the translator's part—"defecates to a pure transparency," and disappears. But between Cowper and Homer—(Mr. Wright repeats in the main Cowper's manner, as Mr. Sotheby repeats Pope's manner, and neither Mr. Wright's translation nor Mr. Sotheby's has, I must be forgiven for saying, any proper reason for existing)—between Cowper and Homer there is interposed the mist of Cowper's elaborate Miltonic manner, entirely alien to the flowing rapidity of Homer; between Pope and Homer there is interposed the mist of Pope's literary artificial manner, entirely alien to the plain naturalness of Homer's manner; between Chapman and Homer there is interposed the mist of the fancifulness of the Elizabethan age, entirely alien to the plain directness of Homer's thought and feeling; while between Mr. Newman and Homer is interposed a cloud of more than Egyptian thickness,—namely, a manner, in Mr. Newman's version, eminently ignoble, while Homer's manner is eminently noble.

I do not despair of making all these propositions clear to a student who approaches Homer with a free mind. First, Homer is eminently rapid, and to this rapidity the elaborate movement of Miltonic blank verse is alien. The reputation of Cowper, that most interesting man and excellent poet, does not depend on his translation of Homer; and in his preface to the second edition, he him-

self tells us that he felt,—he had too much poetical taste
not to feel,—on returning to his own version after six
or seven years, "more dissatisfied with it himself than
the most difficult to be pleased of all his judges." And he
was dissatisfied with it for the right reason,—that "it
seemed to him deficient *in the grace of ease.*" Yet he
seems to have originally misconceived the manner of
Homer so much, that it is no wonder he rendered him
amiss. "The similitude of Milton's manner to that of
Homer is such," he says, "that no person familiar with
both can read either without being reminded of the
other; and it is in those breaks and pauses to which the
numbers of the English poet are so much indebted, both
for their dignity and variety, that he chiefly copies the
Grecian." It would be more true to say: "The unlikeness
of Milton's manner to that of Homer is such, that no
person familiar with both can read either without being
struck with his difference from the other; and it is in his
breaks and pauses that the English poet is most unlike
the Grecian."

The inversion and pregnant conciseness of Milton or
Dante are, doubtless, most impressive qualities of style;
but they are the very opposites of the directness and
flowingness of Homer, which he keeps alike in passages
of the simplest narrative, and in those of the deepest
emotion. Not only, for example, are these lines of Cowper un-Homeric:

> So numerous seemed those fires the banks between
> Of Xanthus, blazing, and the fleet of Greece
> In prospect all of Troy;

where the position of the word "blazing" gives an
entirely un-Homeric movement to this simple passage,
describing the fires of the Trojan camp outside of Troy;
but the following lines, in that very highly-wrought

passage where the horse of Achilles answers his master's reproaches for having left Patroclus on the field of battle, are equally un-Homeric:

> For not through sloth or tardiness on us
> Aught chargeable, have Ilium's sons thine arms
> Stript from Patroclus' shoulders; but a God
> Matchless in battle, offspring of bright-haired
> Latona, him contending in the van
> Slew, for the glory of the chief of Troy.

Here even the first inversion, "have Ilium's sons thine arms Stript from Patroclus' shoulders," gives the reader a sense of a movement not Homeric; and the second inversion, "a God him contending in the van Slew," gives this sense ten times stronger. Instead of moving on without check, as in reading the original, the reader twice finds himself, in reading the translation, brought up and checked. Homer moves with the same simplicity and rapidity in the highly-wrought as in the simple passage.

It is in vain that Cowper insists on his fidelity: "my chief boast is that I have adhered closely to my original:"—"the matter found in me, whether the reader like it or not, is found also in Homer; and the matter not found in me, how much soever the reader may admire it, is found only in Mr. Pope." To suppose that it is *fidelity* to an original to give its matter, unless you at the same time give its manner; or, rather, to suppose that you can really give its matter at all, unless you can give its manner, is just the mistake of our pre-Raphaelite school of painters, who do not understand that the peculiar effect of nature resides in the whole and not in the parts. So the peculiar effect of a poet resides in his manner and movement, not in his words taken separately. It is well known how conscientiously literal is Cowper in his translation of Homer. It is well known how extravagantly free is Pope.

> So let it be!
> Portents and prodigies are lost on me:

that is Pope's rendering of the words,

Ξάνθε, τί μοι θάνατον μαντεύεαι; οὐδέ τί σε χρή·[1]

> Xanthus, why prophesiest thou my death to me? thou needest
> not at all:

yet, on the whole, Pope's translation of the *Iliad* is more
Homeric than Cowper's, for it is more rapid.

Pope's movement, however, though rapid, is not of the
same kind as Homer's; and here I come to the real objection to rhyme in a translation of Homer. It is commonly said that rhyme is to be abandoned in a translation of Homer, because "the exigences of rhyme," to
quote Mr. Newman, "positively forbid faithfulness"; because "a just translation of any ancient poet in rhyme,"
to quote Cowper, "is impossible." This, however, is
merely an accidental objection to rhyme. If this were all,
it might be supposed, that if rhymes were more abundant, Homer could be adequately translated in rhyme.
But this is not so; there is a deeper, a substantial objection to rhyme in a translation of Homer. It is, that rhyme
inevitably tends to pair lines which in the original are
independent, and thus the movement of the poem is
changed. In these lines of Chapman, for instance, from
Sarpedon's speech to Glaucus, in the twelfth book of the
Iliad:

> O friend, if keeping back
> Would keep back age from us, and death, and that we might
>   not wrack
> In this life's human sea at all, but that deferring now
> We shunned death ever,—nor would I half this vain valor
>   show,
> Nor glorify a folly so, to wish thee to advance;

[1] *Iliad*, xix, 420. (*Arnold's note.*)

But since we *must* go, though not here, and that besides the
  chance
Proposed now, there are infinite fates,

etc. Here the necessity of making the line,

Nor glorify a folly so, to wish thee to advance,

rhyme with the line which follows it, entirely changes
and spoils the movement of the passage.

οὔτε κεν αὐτὸς ἐνὶ πρώτοισι μαχοίμην,
οὔτε κε σὲ στέλλοιμι μάχην ἐς κυδιάνειραν [1]

Neither would I myself go forth to fight with the foremost,
Nor would I urge thee on to enter the glorious battle,

says Homer; there he stops, and begins an opposed
movement:

νῦν δ'—ἔμπης γὰρ Κῆρες ἐφεστᾶσιν θανάτοιο—

But—for a thousand fates of death stand close to us always—

This line, in which Homer wishes to go away with the
most marked rapidity from the line before, Chapman is
forced, by the necessity of rhyming, intimately to con-
nect with the line before.

But since we *must* go, though not here, and that besides the
  chance—

The moment the word *chance* strikes our ear, we are
irresistibly carried back to *advance* and to the whole
previous line, which, according to Homer's own feeling,
we ought to have left behind us entirely, and to be moving farther and farther away from.

Rhyme certainly, by intensifying antithesis, can in-
tensify separation, and this is precisely what Pope does;
but this balanced rhetorical antithesis, though very effective, is entirely un-Homeric. And this is what I mean by
saying that Pope fails to render Homer, because he does
not render his plainness and directness of style and dic-

[1] *Iliad*, xii, 324. (Arnold's note.)

tion. Where Homer marks separation by moving away, Pope marks it by antithesis. No passage could show this better than the passage I have just quoted, on which I will pause for a moment.

Robert Wood, whose *Essay on the Genius of Homer* is mentioned by Goethe as one of the books which fell into his hands when his powers were first developing themselves, and strongly interested him, relates of this passage a striking story. He says that in 1762, at the end of the Seven Years' War, being then Under-Secretary of State, he was directed to wait upon the President of the Council, Lord Granville, a few days before he died, with the preliminary articles of the Treaty of Paris. "I found him," he continues, "so languid, that I proposed postponing my business for another time; but he insisted that I should stay, saying, it could not prolong his life to neglect his duty; and repeating the following passage out of Sarpedon's speech, he dwelled with particular emphasis on the third line, which recalled to his mind the distinguishing part he had taken in public affairs:

ὦ πέπον, εἰ μὲν γὰρ πόλεμον περὶ τόνδε φυγόντε,
αἰεὶ δὴ μέλλοιμεν ἀγήρω τ᾽ ἀθανάτω ετ
ἔσσεσθ᾽, οὔτε κεν αὐτὸς ἐνὶ πρώτοισι μαχοίμην,[1]
οὔτε κε σὲ στέλλοιμι μάχην ἐς κυδιάνειραν·
νῦν δ᾽—ἔμπης γὰρ Κῆρες ἐφεστᾶσιν θανάτοιο
μυρίαι, ἃς οὐκ ἔστι φυγεῖν βροτόν οὐδ᾽ ὑπαλύξαι—
ἴομεν.[2]

[1] These are the words on which Lord Granville "dwelled with particular emphasis." (*Arnold's note.*)

[2] [This is William Cullen Bryant's rendering of Sarpedon's speech:
            O my friend, if we,
Leaving this war, could flee from age and death,
I should not here be fighting in the van,
Nor would I send thee to the glorious war,
But now, since many are the modes of death
Impending o'er us, which no man can hope
To shun, let us press on and give renown
To other men, or win it for ourselves!]

His Lordship repeated the last word several times with a calm and determinate resignation; and, after a serious pause of some minutes, he desired to hear the Treaty read, to which he listened with great attention, and recovered spirits enough to declare the approbation of a dying statesman (I use his own words) 'on the most glorious war, and most honourable peace, this nation ever saw.'" [1]

I quote this story, first, because it is interesting as exhibiting the English aristocracy at its very height of culture, lofty spirit, and greatness, towards the middle of the last century. I quote it, secondly, because it seems to me to illustrate Goethe's saying which I mentioned, that our life, in Homer's view of it, represents a conflict and a hell; and it brings out, too, what there is tonic and fortifying in this doctrine. I quote it, lastly, because it shows that the passage is just one of those in translating which Pope will be at his best, a passage of strong emotion and oratorical movement, not of simple narrative or description.

Pope translates the passage thus:

> Could all our care elude the gloomy grave
> Which claims no less the fearful than the brave,
> For lust of fame I should not vainly dare
> In fighting fields, nor urge thy soul to war:
> But since, alas! ignoble age must come,
> Disease, and death's inexorable doom;
> The life which others pay, let us bestow,
> And give to fame what we to nature owe.

Nothing could better exhibit Pope's prodigious talent, and nothing, too, could be better in its own way. But, as Bentley said, "You must not call it Homer." One

---

[1] Robert Wood, *Essay on the Original Genius and Writings of Homer*, London, 1775, p. vii. (*Arnold's note.*)

feels that Homer's thought has passed through a literary
and rhetorical crucible, and come out highly intellectualised; come out in a form which strongly impresses
us, indeed, but which no longer impresses us in the
same way as when it was uttered by Homer. The antithesis of the last two lines—

> The life which others pay, let us bestow,
> And give to fame what we to nature owe—

is excellent, and is just suited to Pope's heroic couplet;
but neither the antithesis itself, nor the couplet which
conveys it, is suited to the feeling or to the movement
of the Homeric ἴομεν.

A literary and intellectualised language is, however,
in its own way well suited to grand matters; and Pope,
with a language of this kind and his own admirable
talent, comes off well enough as long as he has passion,
or oratory, or a great crisis to deal with. Even here, as
I have been pointing out, he does not render Homer;
but he and his style are in themselves strong. It is when
he comes to level passages, passages of narrative or
description, that he and his style are sorely tried, and
prove themselves weak. A perfectly plain direct style
can of course convey the simplest matter as naturally
as the grandest; indeed, it must be harder for it, one
would say, to convey a grand matter worthily and nobly,
than to convey a common matter, as alone such a matter
should be conveyed, plainly and simply. But the style
of Rasselas is incomparably better fitted to describe a
sage philosophising than a soldier lighting his campfire.
The style of Pope is not the style of Rasselas; but it is
equally a literary style, equally unfitted to describe a
simple matter with the plain naturalness of Homer.

Every one knows the passage at the end of the eighth
book of the *Iliad*, where the fires of the Trojan encamp-

ment are likened to the stars. It is very far from my wish to hold Pope up to ridicule, so I shall not quote the commencement of the passage, which in the original is of great and celebrated beauty, and in translating which Pope has been singularly and notoriously fortunate. But the latter part of the passage, where Homer leaves the stars, and comes to the Trojan fires, treats of the plainest, most matter-of-fact subject possible, and deals with this, as Homer always deals with every subject, in the plainest and most straightforward style. "So many in number, between the ships and the streams of Xanthus, shone forth in front of Troy the fires kindled by the Trojans. There were kindled a thousand fires in the plain; and by each one there sat fifty men in the light of the blazing fire. And the horses, munching white barley and rye, and standing by the chariots, waiting for the bright-throned Morning." [1]

In Pope's translation, this plain story becomes the following:

> So many flames before proud Ilion blaze,
> And brighten glimmering Xanthus with their rays;
> The long reflections of the distant fires
> Gleam on the walls, and tremble on the spires.
> A thousand piles the dusky horrors gild,
> And shoot a shady lustre o'er the field.
> Full fifty guards each flaming pile attend,
> Whose umbered arms, by fits, thick flashes send;
> Loud neigh the coursers o'er their heaps of corn,
> And ardent warriors wait the rising morn.

It is for passages of this sort, which, after all, form the bulk of a narrative poem, that Pope's style is so bad. In elevated passages he is powerful, as Homer is power-

---

[1] *Iliad*, viii, 560. (*Arnold's note.*)

ful, though not in the same way; but in plain narrative, where Homer is still powerful and delightful, Pope, by the inherent fault of his style, is ineffective and out of taste. Wordsworth says somewhere, that wherever Virgil seems to have composed "with his eye on the object," Dryden fails to render him. Homer invariably composes "with his eye on the object," whether the object be a moral or a material one: Pope composes with his eye on his style, into which he translates his object, whatever it is. That, therefore, which Homer conveys to us immediately, Pope conveys to us through a medium. He aims at turning Homer's sentiments pointedly and rhetorically; at investing Homer's description with ornament and dignity. A sentiment may be changed by being put into a pointed and oratorical form, yet may still be very effective in that form; but a description, the moment it takes its eyes off that which it is to describe, and begins to think of ornamenting itself, is worthless.

Therefore, I say, the translator of Homer should penetrate himself with a sense of the plainness and directness of Homer's style; of the simplicity with which Homer's thought is evolved and expressed. He has Pope's fate before his eyes, to show him what a divorce may be created even between the most gifted translator and Homer by an artificial evolution of thought and a literary cast of style.

Chapman's style is not artificial and literary like Pope's, nor his movement elaborate and self-retarding like the Miltonic movement of Cowper. He is plainspoken, fresh, vigorous, and, to a certain degree, rapid; and all these are Homeric qualities. I cannot say that I think the movement of his fourteen-syllable line, which has been so much commended, Homeric; but on this point I shall have more to say by and by, when I come to speak of Mr. Newman's metrical exploits. But it is not distinctly anti-Homeric, like the movement of Milton's blank verse; and it has a rapidity of its own. Chapman's diction, too, is generally good, that is, appropriate to Homer; above all, the syntactical character of his style is appropriate. With these merits, what prevents his translation from being a satisfactory version of Homer? Is it merely the want of literal faithfulness to his original, imposed upon him, it is said, by the exigences of rhyme? Has this celebrated version, which has so many advantages, no other and deeper defect than that? Its author is a poet, and a poet, too, of the Elizabethan age; the golden age of English literature as it is called, and on the whole truly called; for, whatever be the defects of Elizabethan literature (and they are great), we have no development of our literature to compare with it for vigour and richness. This age, too, showed what it could do in translating, by producing a master-piece, its version of the Bible.

Chapman's translation has often been praised as eminently Homeric. Keats's fine sonnet in its honour every one knows; but Keats could not read the original, and therefore could not really judge the translation. Coleridge, in praising Chapman's version, says at the same time, "It will give you small idea of Homer." But the grave authority of Mr. Hallam pronounces this translation to be "often exceedingly Homeric"; and its latest editor boldly declares that by what, with a deplorable style, he calls "his own innative Homeric genius," Chapman "has thoroughly identified himself with Homer"; and that "we pardon him even for his digressions, for they are such as we feel Homer himself would have written."

I confess that I can never read twenty lines of Chapman's version without recurring to Bentley's cry, "This is not Homer!" and that from a deeper cause than any unfaithfulness occasioned by the fetters of rhyme.

I said that there were four things which eminently distinguished Homer, and with a sense of which Homer's translator should penetrate himself as fully as possible. One of these four things was, the plainness and directness of Homer's ideas. I have just been speaking of the plainness and directness of his style; but the plainness and directness of the contents of his style, of his ideas themselves, is not less remarkable. But as eminently as Homer is plain, so eminently is the Elizabethan literature in general, and Chapman in particular, fanciful. Steeped in humours and fantasticality up to its very lips, the Elizabethan age, newly arrived at the free use of the human faculties after their long term of bondage, and delighting to exercise them freely, suffers from its own extravagance in this first exercise of them, can hardly bring itself to see an object quietly or to describe it temperately. Happily, in the translation of the Bible, the sacred character of their original inspired the translators with such respect that they did not dare to give the rein to their own fancies in dealing with it. But, in dealing with works of profane literature, in dealing with poetical works above all, which highly stimulated them, one may say that the minds of the Elizabethan translators were *too* active; that they could not forbear importing so much of their own, and this of a most peculiar and Elizabethan character, into their original, that they effaced the character of the original itself.

Take merely the opening pages to Chapman's translation, the introductory verses, and the dedications. You will find:

An Anagram of the name of our Dread Prince,
My most gracious and sacred Mæcenas,

Henry, Prince of Wales,
Our Sunn, Heyr, Peace, Life,—

Henry, son of James the First, to whom the work is dedicated. Then comes an address,

To the sacred Fountain of Princes,
Sole Empress of Beauty and Virtue, Anne, Queen
Of England, [etc.]

All the Middle Age, with its grotesqueness, its conceits, its irrationality, is still in these opening pages; they by themselves are sufficient to indicate to us what a gulf divides Chapman from the "clearest-souled" of poets, from Homer; almost as great a gulf as that which divides him from Voltaire. Pope has been sneered at for saying that Chapman writes "somewhat as one might imagine Homer himself to have written before he arrived at years of discretion." But the remark is excellent: Homer expresses himself like a man of adult reason, Chapman like a man whose reason has not yet cleared itself. For instance, if Homer had had to say of a poet, that he hoped his merit was now about to be fully established in the opinion of good judges, he was as incapable of saying this as Chapman says it,—"Though truth in her very nakedness sits in so deep a pit, that from Gades to Aurora, and Ganges, few eyes can sound her, I hope yet those few here will so discover and confirm that the date being out of her darkness in this morning of our poet, he shall now gird his temples with the sun,"—I say, Homer was as incapable of saying this in that manner, as Voltaire himself would have been. Homer, indeed, has actually an affinity with Voltaire in the unrivalled clearness and straightforwardness of his thinking; in the way in which he keeps to one thought at a time, and puts that thought forth in its complete natural plainness, instead of being led away from it by some fancy striking him in connection with it, and being beguiled to wander off with this fancy till his original thought, in its natural reality, knows him no more. What could better show us how gifted a race was this Greek race? The same member of it has not only the power of profoundly touching that natural heart of humanity which it is Voltaire's weakness that he cannot reach, but can also address the understanding with all Voltaire's admirable simplicity and rationality.

My limits will not allow me to do more than shortly illustrate, from Chapman's version of the *Iliad,* what I mean when I speak of this vital difference between Homer and an Elizabethan poet in the quality of their thought; between the plain simplicity of the thought of the one, and the curious complexity of the thought of the other. As in Pope's case, I carefully abstain from choosing passages for the express purpose of making Chapman appear ridiculous; Chapman, like Pope, merits in himself all respect, though he too, like Pope, fails to render Homer.

In that tonic speech of Sarpedon, of which I have said so much, Homer, you may remember, has:

εἰ μὲν γὰρ πόλεμον περὶ τόνδε φυγόντε
αἰεὶ δὴ μέλλοιμεν ἀγήρω τ᾽ ἀθανάτω τε
ἔσσεσθ᾽,—

> if indeed, but once *this* battle avoided,
We were for ever to live without growing old, and immortal.

Chapman cannot be satisfied with this, but must add a fancy to it:

> if keeping back
Would keep back age from us, and death, and *that we might
not wrack
In this life's human sea at all;*

and so on. Again; in another passage which I have before quoted, where Zeus says to the horses of Peleus,

τί σφῶϊ δόμεν Πηλῆϊ ἄνακτι
θνητῷ; ὑμεῖς δ' ἐστὸν ἀγήρω τ' ἀθανάτω τε[1]

Why gave we you to royal Peleus, to a mortal? but ye are
without old age, and immortal.

Chapman sophisticates this into:

Why gave we you t' a mortal king, when immortality
And *incapacity of age so dignifies your states?*

Again; in the speech of Achilles to his horses, where
Achilles, according to Homer, says simply, "Take heed
that ye bring your master safe back to the host of the
Danaans, in some other sort than the last time, when
the battle is ended," Chapman sophisticates this into:

*When with blood, for this day's fast observed, revenge shall
    yield
Our heart satiety,* bring us off.

In Hector's famous speech, again, at his parting from
Andromache, Homer makes him say: "Nor does my own
heart so bid me" (to keep safe behind the walls), "since
I have learned to be staunch always, and to fight among
the foremost of the Trojans, busy on behalf of my
father's great glory, and my own." [2] In Chapman's hands
this becomes:

                    The spirit I first did breathe
Did never teach me that; much less, since the contempt of
    death
Was settled in me, *and my mind knew what a worthy was,*

---

[1] *Iliad*, xvii, 443. (Arnold's note.)
[2] *Iliad*, vi, 444. (Arnold's note.)

Whose office is to lead in fight, and give no danger pass
Without improvement. In this fire must Hector's trial shine:
Here must his country, father, friends, be in him made divine.

You see how ingeniously Homer's plain thought is *tormented*, as the French would say, here. Homer goes on: "For well I know this in my mind and in my heart, the day will be, when sacred Troy shall perish":

ἔσσεται ἦμαρ, ὅτ' ἄν ποτ' ὀλώλῃ Ἴλιος ἱρή.

Chapman makes this:

And such a *stormy* day shall come, in mind and soul I know
When sacred Troy *shall shed her towers, for tears of over-*
    throw.

I might go on for ever, but I could not give you a better illustration than this last, of what I mean by saying that the Elizabethan poet fails to render Homer because he cannot forbear to interpose a play of thought between his object and its expression. Chapman translates his object into Elizabethan, as Pope translates it into the Augustan of Queen Anne; both convey it to us through a medium. Homer, on the other hand, sees his object and conveys it to us immediately.

And yet, in spite of this perfect plainness and directness of Homer's style, in spite of this perfect plainness and directness of his ideas, he is eminently *noble;* he works as entirely in the grand style, he is as grandiose, as Phidias, or Dante, or Michael Angelo. This is what makes his translators despair. "To give relief," says Cowper, "to prosaic subjects" (such as dressing, eating, drinking, harnessing, travelling, going to bed), that is to treat such subjects nobly, in the grand style, "without seeming unreasonably tumid, is extremely difficult." It *is* difficult, but Homer has done it. Homer is precisely the incomparable poet he is, because he has done it. His translator must not be tumid, must not be artificial, must not be literary; true: but then also he must not be commonplace, must not be ignoble. I have shown you how translators of Homer fail by wanting rapidity, by wanting simplicity of style, by wanting plainness of thought: in a second lecture I will show you how a translator fails by wanting nobility.

○

PREFACE TO
ESSAYS IN CRITICISM

SECOND EDITION, 1869

○

SEVERAL of the Essays which are here collected and reprinted had the good or the bad fortune to be much criticised at the time of their first appearance. I am not now going to inflict upon the reader a reply to those criticisms; for one or two explanations which are desirable, I shall elsewhere, perhaps, be able some day to find an opportunity; but, indeed, it is not in my nature,—some of my critics would rather say, not in my power,—to dispute on behalf of any opinion, even my own, very obstinately. To try and approach truth on one side after another, not to strive or cry, nor to persist in pressing forward, on any one side, with violence and self-will,—it is only thus, it seems to me, that mortals may hope to gain any vision of the mysterious Goddess, whom we shall never see except in outline, but only thus even in outline. He who will do nothing but fight impetuously towards her on his own, one, favourite, particular line, is inevitably destined to run his head into the folds of the black robe in which she is wrapped.

So it is not to reply to my critics that I write this preface, but to prevent a misunderstanding, of which certain phrases that some of them use make me apprehensive. Mr. Wright, one of the many translators of Homer, has published a Letter to the Dean of Canterbury, complaining of some remarks of mine, uttered now a long while ago, on his version of the *Iliad*. One cannot be always studying one's own works, and I was really under the impression, till I saw Mr. Wright's complaint, that I had spoken of him with all respect. The reader may judge of my astonishment, therefore, at finding, from Mr. Wright's pamphlet, that I had "declared with much solemnity that there is not any proper reason for his existing." That I never said; but, on looking back at my Lectures on translating Homer, I find that I did say, not that Mr. Wright, but that Mr. Wright's version of the *Iliad*, repeating in the main the merits and defects of Cowper's version, as Mr. Sotheby's repeated those of Pope's version, had, if I might be pardoned for saying so, no proper reason for existing. Elsewhere I expressly spoke of the merit of his version; but I confess that the phrase, qualified as I have shown, about its want of a proper reason for existing, I used. Well, the phrase had, perhaps, too much vivacity; we have all of us a right to exist, we and our works; an unpopular author should be the last person to call in question this right. So I gladly withdraw the offending phrase, and I am sorry for having used it; Mr. Wright, however, would perhaps be more indulgent to my vivacity, if he considered that we are none of us likely to be lively much longer. My vivacity is but the last sparkle of flame before we are all in the dark, the last glimpse of colour before we all go into drab,—the drab of the earnest, prosaic, practical, austerely literal future. Yes, the world will soon be the Philistines'! and then, with every voice, not of thunder, silenced, and the whole earth filled and ennobled every morning by the magnificent roaring of the young lions of the *Daily Telegraph,* we shall all yawn in one another's faces with the dismallest, the most unimpeachable gravity.

But I return to my design in writing this Preface. That design was, after apologising to Mr. Wright for my vivacity of five years ago, to beg him and others to let me bear my own burdens, without saddling the great and famous University, to which I have the honour to belong, with any portion of them. What I mean to deprecate is such phrases as, "his professorial assault," "his assertions issued *ex cathedra,*" "the sanction of his name as the representative of poetry," and so on. Proud as I am of my connection with the University of Oxford, I can truly say, that knowing how unpopular a task one is undertaking when one tries to pull out a few more stops in that powerful but at present somewhat narrow-toned organ, the modern Englishman, I have always sought to stand by myself, and to compromise others as little as possible. Besides this, my native modesty is such, that I have always been shy of assuming the honourable style of Professor, because this is a title I share with so many distinguished men,—Professor Pepper, Professor Anderson, Professor Frickel, and others,—who adorn it, I feel, much more than I do.

However, it is not merely out of modesty that I prefer to stand alone, and to concentrate on myself, as a plain citizen of the republic of letters, and not as an office-bearer in a hierarchy, the whole responsibility for all I write; it is much more out of genuine devotion to the University of Oxford, for which I feel, and always must feel, the fondest, the most reverential attachment. In an epoch of dissolution and transformation, such as that on which we are now entered, habits, ties, and associations are inevitably broken up, the action of individuals becomes more distinct, the shortcomings, errors, heats, disputes, which necessarily attend individual action, are brought into greater prominence. Who would not gladly keep clear, from all these passing clouds, an august institution which was there before they arose, and which will be there when they have blown over?

It is true, the *Saturday Review* maintains that our epoch of transformation is finished; that we have found our philosophy; that the British nation has searched all anchorages for the spirit, and has finally anchored itself, in the fulness of perfected knowledge, on Benthamism. This idea at first made a great impression on me; not only because it is so consoling in itself, but also because it explained a phenomenon which in the summer of last year had, I confess, a good deal troubled me. At that time my avocations led me to travel almost daily on one of the Great Eastern Lines,—the Woodford Branch. Every one knows that the murderer, Müller, perpetrated his detestable act on the North London Railway, close by. The English middle class, of which I am myself a feeble unit, travel on the Woodford Branch in large numbers. Well, the demoralisation of our class,—the class which (the newspapers are constantly saying it, so I may repeat it without vanity) has done all the great things which have ever been done in England,—the demoralisation, I say, of our class, caused by the Bow tragedy, was something bewildering. Myself a transcenden-

talist (as the *Saturday Review* knows), I escaped the
infection; and, day after day, I used to ply my agitated
fellow-travellers with all the consolations which my transcendentalism would naturally suggest to me. I reminded
them how Caesar refused to take precautions against as-
sassination, because life was not worth having at the
price of an ignoble solicitude for it. I reminded them
what insignificant atoms we all are in the life of the
world. "Suppose the worst to happen," I said, addressing
a portly jeweller from Cheapside; "suppose even yourself
to be the victim; *il n'y a pas d'homme nécessaire.* We
should miss you for a day or two upon the Woodford
Branch; but the great mundane movement would still go
on, the gravel walks of your villa would still be rolled,
dividends would still be paid at the Bank, omnibuses
would still run, there would still be the old crush at the
corner of Fenchurch Street." All was of no avail. Nothing could moderate, in the bosom of the great English
middle class, their passionate, absorbing, almost blood-
thirsty clinging to life. At the moment I thought this
over-concern a little unworthy; but the *Saturday Review*
suggests a touching explanation of it. What I took for the
ignoble clinging to life of a comfortable worldling, was,
perhaps, only the ardent longing of a faithful Bentham-
ite, traversing an age still dimmed by the last mists of
transcendentalism, to be spared long enough to see his
religion in the full and final blaze of its triumph. This
respectable man, whom I imagined to be going up to
London to serve his shop, or to buy shares, or to attend
an Exeter Hall meeting, or to assist at the deliberations
of the Marylebone Vestry, was, perhaps, in real truth, on
a pious pilgrimage, to obtain from Mr. Bentham's execu-
tors a sacred bone of his great, dissected master.

And yet, after all, I cannot but think that the *Saturday*

Review has here, for once, fallen a victim to an idea,—
a beautiful but deluding idea,—and that the British nation has not yet, so entirely as the reviewer seems to
imagine, found the last word of its philosophy. No, we
are all seekers still! seekers often make mistakes, and I
wish mine to redound to my own discredit only, and not
to touch Oxford. Beautiful city! so venerable, so lovely,
so unravaged by the fierce intellectual life of our century
so serene!

There are our young barbarians all at play!

And yet, steeped in sentiment as she lies, spreading her
gardens to the moonlight, and whispering from her towers the last enchantments of the Middle Age, who will
deny that Oxford, by her ineffable charm, keeps ever
calling us nearer to the true goal of all of us, to the ideal,
to perfection,—to beauty, in a word, which is only truth
seen from another side?—nearer, perhaps, than all the
science of Tübingen. Adorable dreamer, whose heart has
been so romantic! who hast given thyself so prodigally,
given thyself to sides and to heroes not mine, only never
to the Philistines! home of lost causes, and forsaken beliefs, and unpopular names, and impossible loyalties!
what example could ever so inspire us to keep down the
Philistine in ourselves, what teacher could ever so save
us from that bondage to which we are all prone, that
bondage which Goethe, in those incomparable lines on
the death of Schiller, makes it his friend's highest praise
(and nobly did Schiller deserve the praise) to have left
miles out of sight behind him;—the bondage of *"was uns
alle bändigt,* DAS GEMEINE!" She will forgive me, even
if I have unwittingly drawn upon her a shot or two
aimed at her unworthy son; for she is generous, and the
cause in which I fight is, after all, hers. Apparitions of a

day, what is our puny warfare against the Philistines, compared with the warfare which this queen of romance has been waging against them for centuries, and will wage after we are gone?

○

THE FUNCTION OF CRITICISM AT THE PRESENT TIME

○

MANY objections have been made to a proposition which, in some remarks of mine on translating Homer, I ventured to put forth; a proposition about criticism, and its importance at the present day. I said: "Of the literature of France and Germany, as of the intellect of Europe in general, the main effort, for now many years, has been a critical effort; the endeavour, in all branches of knowledge, theology, philosophy, history, art, science, to see the object as in itself it really is." I added, that owing to the operation in English literature of certain causes, "almost the last thing for which one would come to English literature is just that very thing which now Europe most desires,—criticism"; and that the power and value of English literature was thereby impaired. More than one rejoinder declared that the importance I here assigned to criticism was excessive, and asserted the inherent superiority of the creative effort of the human spirit over its critical effort. And the other day, having been led by a Mr. Shairp's excellent notice of Wordsworth[1] to turn again to his biography, I found, in the words of this great man, whom I, for one, must always listen to with the profoundest respect, a sentence passed on the critic's business, which seems to justify every possible disparagement of it. Wordsworth says in one of his letters:

"The writers in these publications" (the Reviews), "while they prosecute their inglorious employment, cannot be supposed to be in a state of mind very favourable for being affected by the finer influences of a thing so pure as genuine poetry."

And a trustworthy reporter of his conversation quotes a more elaborate judgment to the same effect:

"Wordsworth holds the critical power very low, infinitely lower than the inventive; and he said to-day that if the quantity of time consumed in writing critiques on the works of others were given to original composition, of whatever kind it might be, it would be much better employed; it would make a man find out sooner his own level, and it would do infinitely less mischief. A false or malicious criticism may do much injury to the minds of others; a stupid invention, either in prose or verse, is quite harmless."

It is almost too much to expect of poor human nature, that a man capable of producing some effect in one line of literature, should, for the greater good of society, vol-

---

[1] I cannot help thinking that a practice, common in England during the last century, and still followed in France, of printing a notice of this kind,—a notice by a competent critic,—to serve as an introduction to an eminent author's works, might be revived among us with advantage. To introduce all succeeding editions of Wordsworth, Mr. Shairp's notice might, it seems to me, excellently serve; it is written from the point of view of an admirer, nay, of a disciple, and that is right; but then the disciple must be also, as in this case he is, a critic, a man of letters, not, as too often happens, some relation or friend with no qualification for his task except affection for his author. (Arnold's note.)

untarily doom himself to impotence and obscurity in another. Still less is this to be expected from men addicted to the composition of the "false or malicious criticism" of which Wordsworth speaks. However, everybody would admit that a false or malicious criticism had better never have been written. Everybody, too, would be willing to admit, as a general proposition, that the critical faculty is lower than the inventive. But is it true that criticism is really, in itself, a baneful and injurious employment; is it true that all time given to writing critiques on the works of others would be much better employed if it were given to original composition, of whatever kind this may be? Is it true that Johnson had better have gone on producing more *Irenes* instead of writing his *Lives of the Poets*; is it certain that Wordsworth himself was better employed in making his Ecclesiastical Sonnets than when he made his celebrated Preface so full of criticism, and criticism of the works of others? Wordsworth was himself a great critic, and it is to be sincerely regretted that he has not left us more criticism; Goethe was one of the greatest of critics, and we may sincerely congratulate ourselves that he has left us so much criticism. Without wasting time over the exaggeration which Wordsworth's judgment on criticism clearly contains, or over an attempt to trace the causes,—not difficult, I think, to be traced,—which may have led Wordsworth to this exaggeration, a critic may with advantage seize an occasion for trying his own conscience, and for asking himself of what real service, at any given moment, the practice of criticism either is or may be made to his own mind and spirit, and to the minds and spirits of others.

The critical power is of lower rank than the creative. True; but in assenting to this proposition, one or two things are to be kept in mind. It is undeniable that the exercise of a creative power, that a free creative activity, is the highest function of man; it is proved to be so by man's finding in it his true happiness. But it is undeniable, also, that men may have the sense of exercising this free creative activity in other ways than in producing great works of literature or art; if it were not so, all but a very few men would be shut out from the true happiness of all men. They may have it in well-doing, they may have it in learning, they may have it even in criticising. This is one thing to be kept in mind. Another is, that the exercise of the creative power in the production of great works of literature or art, however high this exercise of it may rank, is not at all epochs and under all conditions possible; and that therefore labour may be vainly spent in attempting it, which might with more fruit be used in preparing for it, in rendering it possible. This creative power works with elements, with materials; what if it has not those materials, those elements, ready for its use? In that case it must surely wait till they are ready. Now, in literature,—I will limit myself to literature, for it is about literature that the question arises,— the elements with which the creative power works are ideas; the best ideas on every matter which literature touches, current at the time. At any rate we may lay it down as certain that in modern literature no manifestation of the creative power not working with these can be very important or fruitful. And I say *current* at the time, not merely accessible at the time; for creative literary genius does not principally show itself in discovering new ideas, that is rather the business of the philosopher. The grand work of literary genius is a work of synthesis and exposition, not of analysis and discovery; its gift lies in the faculty of being happily inspired by a certain intellectual and spiritual atmosphere, by a certain order of ideas, when it finds itself in them; of dealing divinely with these ideas, presenting them in the most effective and attractive combinations,—making beautiful works with them, in short. But it must have the atmosphere, it must find itself amidst the order of ideas, in order to work freely; and these it is not so easy to command. This is why great creative epochs in literature are so rare, this is why there is so much that is unsatisfactory in the productions of many men of real genius; because, for the creation of a master-work of literature two powers must concur, the power of the man and the power of the moment, and the man is not enough without the moment; the creative power has, for its happy exercise, appointed elements, and those elements are not in its own control.

Nay, they are more within the control of the critical power. It is the business of the critical power, as I said in the words already quoted, "in all branches of knowledge, theology, philosophy, history, art, science, to see the object as in itself it really is." Thus it tends, at last, to make an intellectual situation of which the creative power can profitably avail itself. It tends to establish an order of ideas, if not absolutely true, yet true by comparison with that which it displaces; to make the best ideas prevail. Presently these new ideas reach society, the touch of truth is the touch of life, and there is a stir and growth everywhere; out of this stir and growth come the creative epochs of literature.

Or, to narrow our range, and quit these considerations of the general march of genius and of society,—considerations which are apt to become too abstract and impalpable,—every one can see that a poet, for instance, ought to know life and the world before dealing with them in poetry; and life and the world being in modern times very complex things, the creation of a modern poet, to be worth much, implies a great critical effort behind it; else it must be a comparatively poor, barren, and short-lived affair. This is why Byron's poetry had so little endurance in it, and Goethe's so much; both Byron and Goethe had a great productive power, but Goethe's was nourished by a great critical effort providing the true materials for it, and Byron's was not; Goethe knew life and the world, the poet's necessary subjects, much more comprehensively and thoroughly than Byron. He knew a great deal more of them, and he knew them much more as they really are.

It has long seemed to me that the burst of creative activity in our literature, through the first quarter of this century, had about it in fact something premature; and that from this cause its productions are doomed, most of them, in spite of the sanguine hopes which accompanied and do still accompany them, to prove hardly more lasting than the productions of far less splendid epochs. And this prematureness comes from its having proceeded without having its proper data, without sufficient materials to work with. In other words, the English poetry of the first quarter of this century, with plenty of energy, plenty of creative force, did not know enough. This makes Byron so empty of matter, Shelley so incoherent, Wordsworth even, profound as he is, yet so wanting in completeness and variety. Wordsworth cared little for books, and disparaged Goethe. I admire Wordsworth, as he is, so much that I cannot wish him different; and it is vain, no doubt, to imagine such a man different from what he is, to suppose that he *could* have been different. But surely the one thing wanting to make Wordsworth an even greater poet than he is,—his thought richer, and his influence of wider application,—was that he should have read more books, among them, no doubt, those of that Goethe whom he disparaged without reading him.

But to speak of books and reading may easily lead to a misunderstanding here. It was not really books and reading that lacked to our poetry at this epoch: Shelley had plenty of reading, Coleridge had immense reading. Pindar and Sophocles,—as we all say so glibly, and often with so little discernment of the real import of what we are saying,—had not many books; Shakespeare was no deep reader. True; but in the Greece of Pindar and Sophocles, in the England of Shakespeare, the poet lived in a current of ideas in the highest degree animating and nourishing to the creative power; society was, in the fullest measure, permeated by fresh thought, intelligent and alive. And this state of things is the true basis for the creative power's exercise, in this it finds its data, its materials, truly ready for its hand; all the books and reading in the world are only valuable as they are helps to this. Even when this does not actually exist, books and reading may enable a man to construct a kind of semblance of it in his own mind, a world of knowledge and intelligence in which he may live and work. This is by no means an equivalent to the artist for the nationally diffused life and thought of the epochs of Sophocles or Shakespeare; but, besides that it may be a means of preparation for such epochs, it does really constitute, if many share in it, a quickening and sustaining atmosphere of great value. Such an atmosphere the many-sided learning and the long and widely combined critical effort of Germany formed for Goethe, when he lived and worked. There was no national glow of life and thought there as in the Athens of Pericles or the England of Elizabeth. That was the poet's weakness. But there was a sort of equivalent for it in the complete culture and unfettered thinking of a large body of Germans. That was his strength. In the England of the first quarter of this century there was neither a national glow of life and thought, such as we had in the age of Elizabeth, nor yet a culture and a force of learning and criticism such as were to be found in Germany. Therefore the creative power of poetry wanted, for success in the highest sense, materials and a basis; a thorough interpretation of the world was necessarily denied to it.

At first sight it seems strange that out of the immense stir of the French Revolution and its age should not have come a crop of works of genius equal to that which came out of the stir of the great productive time of Greece, or out of that of the Renascence, with its powerful episode the Reformation. But the truth is that the stir of the French Revolution took a character which essentially distinguished it from such movements as these. These were, in the main, disinterestedly intellectual and spiritual movements; movements in which the human spirit looked for its satisfaction in itself and in the increased play of its own activity. The French Revolution took a political, practical character. The movement, which went on in France under the old *régime,* from 1700 to 1789, was far more really akin than that of the Revolution itself to the movement of the Renascence; the France of Voltaire and Rousseau told far more powerfully upon the mind of Europe than the France of the Revolution. Goethe reproached this last expressly with having "thrown quiet culture back." Nay, and the true key to how much in our Byron, even in our Wordsworth, is this!—that they had their source in a great movement of feeling, not in a great movement of mind. The French Revolution, however,—that object of so much blind love and so much blind hatred,—found undoubtedly its motive-power in the intelligence of men, and not in their practical sense; this is what distinguishes it from the English Revolution of Charles the First's time. This is what makes it a more spiritual event than our Revolution, an event of much more powerful and world-wide interest, though practically less successful; it appeals to an order of ideas which are universal, certain, perma-

nent. 1789 asked of a thing, Is it rational? 1642 asked of
a thing, Is it legal? or, when it went furthest, Is it according to conscience? This is the English fashion, a fashion to be treated, within its own sphere, with the highest
respect; for its success, within its own sphere, has been
prodigious. But what is law in one place is not law in
another; what is law here to-day is not law even here
to-morrow; and as for conscience, what is binding on one
man's conscience is not binding on another's. The old
woman who threw her stool at the head of the surpliced
minister in St. Giles's Church at Edinburgh obeyed an
impulse to which millions of the human race may be permitted to remain strangers. But the prescriptions of reason are absolute, unchanging, of universal validity; *to
count by tens is the easiest way of counting*—that is a
proposition of which every one, from here to the Antip-
odes, feels the force; at least I should say so if we did
not live in a country where it is not impossible that any
morning we may find a letter in the *Times* declaring that
a decimal coinage is an absurdity. That a whole nation
should have been penetrated with an enthusiasm for
pure reason, and with an ardent zeal for making its
prescriptions triumph, is a very remarkable thing, when
we consider how little of mind, or anything so worthy
and quickening as mind, comes into the motives which
alone, in general, impel great masses of men. In spite of
the extravagant direction given to this enthusiasm, in
spite of the crimes and follies in which it lost itself, the
French Revolution derives from the force, truth, and
universality of the ideas which it took for its law, and
from the passion with which it could inspire a multitude
for these ideas, a unique and still living power; it is,—it
will probably long remain,—the greatest, the most animating event in history. And as no sincere passion for
the things of the mind, even though it turn out in many

respects an unfortunate passion, is ever quite thrown away and quite barren of good, France has reaped from hers one fruit—the natural and legitimate fruit though not precisely the grand fruit she expected: she is the country in Europe where *the people* is most alive.

But the mania for giving an immediate political and practical application to all these fine ideas of the reason was fatal. Here an Englishman is in his element: on this theme we can all go on for hours. And all we are in the habit of saying on it has undoubtedly a great deal of truth. Ideas cannot be too much prized in and for themselves, cannot be too much lived with; but to transport them abruptly into the world of politics and practice, violently to revolutionise this world to their bidding,—that is quite another thing. There is the world of ideas and there is the world of practice; the French are often for suppressing the one and the English the other; but neither is to be suppressed. A member of the House of Commons said to me the other day: "That a thing is an anomaly, I consider to be no objection to it whatever." I venture to think he was wrong; that a thing is an anomaly *is* an objection to it, but absolutely and in the sphere of ideas: it is not necessarily, under such and such circumstances, or at such and such a moment, an objection to it in the sphere of politics and practice. Joubert has said beautifully: *"C'est la force et le droit qui règlent toutes choses dans le monde; la force en attendant le droit."* (Force and right are the governors of this world; force till right is ready.) *Force till right is ready*; and till right is ready, force, the existing order of things, is justified, is the legitimate ruler. But right is something moral, and implies inward recognition, free assent of the will; we are not ready for right,—*right*, so far as we are concerned, *is not ready*,—until we have attained this sense of seeing it and willing it. The way in which for

us it may change and transform force, the existing order
of things, and become, in its turn, the legitimate ruler
of the world, should depend on the way in which, when
our time comes, we see it and will it. Therefore for
other people enamoured of their own newly discerned
right, to attempt to impose it upon us as ours, and violently to substitute their right for our force, is an act of
tyranny, and to be resisted. It sets at nought the second
great half of our maxim, *force till right is ready*. This
was the grand error of the French Revolution; and its
movement of ideas, by quitting the intellectual sphere
and rushing furiously into the political sphere, ran, indeed, a prodigious and memorable course, but produced
no such intellectual fruit as the movement of ideas of
the Renascence, and created, in opposition to itself, what
I may call an *epoch of concentration*. The great force of
that epoch of concentration was England; and the great
voice of that epoch of concentration was Burke. It is the
fashion to treat Burke's writings on the French Revolution as superannuated and conquered by the event; as
the eloquent but unphilosophical tirades of bigotry and
prejudice. I will not deny that they are often disfigured
by the violence and passion of the moment, and that in
some directions Burke's view was bounded, and his observation therefore at fault. But on the whole, and for
those who can make the needful corrections, what distinguishes these writings is their profound, permanent,
fruitful, philosophical truth. They contain the true philosophy of an epoch of concentration, dissipate the
heavy atmosphere which its own nature is apt to engender round it, and make its resistance rational instead of
mechanical.

But Burke is so great because, almost alone in England, he brings thought to bear upon politics, he satu-
rates politics with thought. It is his accident that his

ideas were at the service of an epoch of concentration, not of an epoch of expansion; it is his characteristic that he so lived by ideas, and had such a source of them welling up within him, that he could float even an epoch of concentration and English Tory politics with them. It does not hurt him that Dr. Price and the Liberals were enraged with him; it does not even hurt him that George the Third and the Tories were enchanted with him. His greatness is that he lived in a world which neither English Liberalism nor English Toryism is apt to enter;— the world of ideas, not the world of catchwords and party habits. So far is it from being really true of him that he "to party gave up what was meant for mankind," that at the very end of his fierce struggle with the French Revolution, after all his invectives against its false pretensions, hollowness, and madness, with his sincere convictions of its mischievousness, he can close a memorandum on the best means of combating it, some of the last pages he ever wrote,—the *Thoughts on French Affairs,* in December 1791,—with these striking words:—

"The evil is stated, in my opinion, as it exists. The remedy must be where power, wisdom, and information, I hope, are more united with good intentions than they can be with me. I have done with this subject, I believe, for ever. It has given me many anxious moments for the last two years. *If a great change is to be made in human affairs, the minds of men will be fitted to it; the general opinions and feelings will draw that way. Every fear, every hope will forward it; and then they who persist in opposing this mighty current in human affairs, will appear rather to resist the decrees of Providence itself, than the mere designs of men. They will not be resolute and firm, but perverse and obstinate.*"

That return of Burke upon himself has always seemed to me one of the finest things in English literature, or in-

deed in any literature. That is what I call living by ideas:
when one side of a question has long had your earnest
support, when all your feelings are engaged, when you
hear all round you no language but one, when your party
talks this language like a steam-engine and can imagine
no other,—still to be able to think, still to be irresistibly
carried, if so it be, by the current of thought to the opposite side of the question, and, like Balaam, to be unable to speak anything *but what the Lord has put in your
mouth.* I know nothing more striking, and I must add
that I know nothing more un-English.

For the Englishman in general is like my friend the
Member of Parliament, and believes, point-blank, that
for a thing to be an anomaly is absolutely no objection
to it whatever. He is like the Lord Auckland of Burke's
day, who, in a memorandum on the French Revolution,
talks of certain "miscreants, assuming the name of philosophers, who have presumed themselves capable of
establishing a new system of society." The Englishman
has been called a political animal, and he values what
is political and practical so much that ideas easily become objects of dislike in his eyes, and thinkers, "miscreants," because ideas and thinkers have rashly med-
dled with politics and practice. This would be all very
well if the dislike and neglect confined themselves to
ideas transported out of their own sphere, and meddling rashly with practice; but they are inevitably extended to ideas as such, and to the whole life of intelligence; practice is everything, a free play of the mind is
nothing. The notion of the free play of the mind upon
all subjects being a pleasure in itself, being an object of
desire, being an essential provider of elements without
which a nation's spirit, whatever compensations it may
have for them, must, in the long run, die of inanition,
hardly enters into an Englishman's thoughts. It is notice-

able that the word *curiosity,* which in other languages is used in a good sense, to mean, as a high and fine quality of man's nature, just this disinterested love of a free play of the mind on all subjects, for its own sake,—it is noticeable, I say, that this word has in our language no sense of the kind, no sense but a rather bad and disparaging one. But criticism, real criticism, is essentially the exercise of this very quality. It obeys an instinct prompting it to try to know the best that is known and thought in the world, irrespectively of practice, politics, and everything of the kind; and to value knowledge and thought as they approach this best, without the intrusion of any other considerations whatever. This is an instinct for which there is, I think, little original sympathy in the practical English nature, and what there was of it has undergone a long benumbing period of blight and suppression in the epoch of concentration which followed the French Revolution.

But epochs of concentration cannot well endure for ever; epochs of expansion, in the due course of things, follow them. Such an epoch of expansion seems to be opening in this country. In the first place all danger of a hostile forcible pressure of foreign ideas upon our practice has long disappeared; like the traveller in the fable, therefore, we begin to wear our cloak a little more loosely. Then, with a long peace, the ideas of Europe steal gradually and amicably in, and mingle, though in infinitesimally small quantities at a time, with our own notions. Then, too, in spite of all that is said about the absorbing and brutalising influence of our passionate material progress, it seems to me indisputable that this progress is likely, though not certain, to lead in the end to an apparition of intellectual life; and that man, after he has made himself perfectly comfortable and has now to determine what to do with himself next, may begin to remember that he has a mind, and that the mind may be made the source of great pleasure. I grant it is mainly the privilege of faith, at present, to discern this end to our railways, our business, and our fortune-making; but we shall see if, here as elsewhere, faith is not in the end the true prophet. Our ease, our travelling, and our unbounded liberty to hold just as hard and securely as we please to the practice to which our notions have given birth, all tend to beget an inclination to deal a little more freely with these notions themselves, to canvass them a little, to penetrate a little into their real nature. Flutterings of curiosity, in the foreign sense of the word, appear amongst us, and it is in these that criticism must look to find its account. Criticism first; a time of true creative activity, perhaps,—which, as I have said, must inevitably be preceded amongst us by a time of criticism,—hereafter, when criticism has done its work.

It is of the last importance that English criticism should clearly discern what rule for its course, in order to avail itself of the field now opening to it, and to produce fruit for the future, it ought to take. The rule may be summed up in one word,—*disinterestedness*. And how is criticism to show disinterestedness? By keeping aloof from what is called "the practical view of things"; by resolutely following the law of its own nature, which is to be a free play of the mind on all subjects which it touches. By steadily refusing to lend itself to any of those ulterior, political, practical considerations about ideas, which plenty of people will be sure to attach to them, which perhaps ought often to be attached to them, which in this country at any rate are certain to be attached to them quite sufficiently, but which criticism has really nothing to do with. Its business is, as I have said, simply to know the best that is known and thought in the world, and by in its turn making this known, to create a current of true and fresh ideas. Its business is to do this with inflexible honesty, with due ability; but its business is to do no more, and to leave alone all questions of practical consequences and applications, questions which will never fail to have due prominence given to them. Else criticism, besides being really false to its own nature, merely continues in the old rut which it has hitherto followed in this country, and will certainly miss the chance now given to it. For what is at present the bane of criticism in this country? It is that practical considerations cling to it and stifle it. It subserves interests not its own. Our organs of criticism are organs of men and parties having practical ends to serve, and with them those practical ends are the first thing and the play of mind the second; so much play of mind as is compatible with the prosecution of those practical ends is all that is wanted. An organ like the *Revue des Deux Mondes,* having for its main function to understand and utter the best that is known and thought in the world, existing, it may be said, as just an organ for a free play of the mind, we have not. But we have the *Edinburgh Review,* existing as an organ of the old Whigs, and for as much play of mind as may suit its being that; we have the *Quarterly Review,* existing as an organ of the Tories, and for as much play of mind as may suit its being that; we have the *British Quarterly Review,* existing as an organ of the political Dissenters, and for as much play of mind as may suit its being that; we have the *Times,* existing as an organ of the common, satisfied, well-to-do Englishman, and for as much play of mind as may suit its being that. And so on through all the various fractions, political and religious, of our society; every fraction has, as such, its organ of criticism, but the notion of combining all fractions in the common pleasure of a free disinterested play of mind meets with no favour.

Directly this play of mind wants to have more scope, and to forget the pressure of practical considerations a little, it is checked, it is made to feel the chain. We saw this the other day in the extinction, so much to be regretted, of the *Home and Foreign Review*. Perhaps in no organ of criticism in this country was there so much knowledge, so much play of mind; but these could not save it. The *Dublin Review* subordinates play of mind to the practical business of English and Irish Catholicism, and lives. It must needs be that men should act in sects and parties, that each of these sects and parties should have its organ, and should make this organ subserve the interests of its action; but it would be well, too, that there should be a criticism, not the minister of these interests, not their enemy, but absolutely and entirely independent of them. No other criticism will ever attain any real authority or make any real way towards its end,—the creating a current of true and fresh ideas.

It is because criticism has so little kept in the pure intellectual sphere, has so little detached itself from practice, has been so directly polemical and controversial, that it has so ill accomplished, in this country, its best spiritual work; which is to keep man from a self-satisfaction which is retarding and vulgarising, to lead him towards perfection, by making his mind dwell upon what is excellent in itself, and the absolute beauty and fitness of things. A polemical practical criticism makes men blind even to the ideal imperfection of their practice, makes them willingly assert its ideal perfection, in order the better to secure it against attack; and clearly this is narrowing and baneful for them. If they were reassured on the practical side, speculative considerations of ideal perfection they might be brought to entertain, and their spiritual horizon would thus gradually widen. Sir Charles Adderley says to the Warwickshire farmers:

"Talk of the improvement of breed! Why, the race we ourselves represent, the men and women, the old Anglo-Saxon race, are the best breed in the whole world. . . . The absence of a too enervating climate, too unclouded skies, and a too luxurious nature, has produced so vigorous a race of people, and has rendered us so superior to all the world."

Mr. Roebuck says to the Sheffield cutlers:

"I look around me and ask what is the state of England? Is not property safe? Is not every man able to say what he likes? Can you not walk from one end of England to the other in perfect security? I ask you whether, the world over or in past history, there is anything like it? Nothing. I pray that our unrivalled happiness may last."

Now obviously there is a peril for poor human nature in words and thoughts of such exuberant self-satisfaction, until we find ourselves safe in the streets of the Celestial City.

> *Das wenige verschwindet leicht dem Blicke*
> *Der vorwärts sieht, wie viel noch übrig bleibt—*

says Goethe; "the little that is done seems nothing when we look forward and see how much we have yet to do." Clearly this is a better line of reflection for weak humanity, so long as it remains on this earthly field of labour and trial.

But neither Sir Charles Adderley nor Mr. Roebuck is by nature inaccessible to considerations of this sort. They only lose sight of them owing to the controversial life we all lead, and the practical form which all speculation takes with us. They have in view opponents whose aim

is not ideal, but practical; and in their zeal to uphold
their own practice against these innovators, they go so
far as even to attribute to this practice an ideal perfection. Somebody has been wanting to introduce a six-
pound franchise, or to abolish church-rates, or to collect
agricultural statistics by force, or to diminish local self-
government. How natural, in reply to such proposals,
very likely improper or ill-timed, to go a little beyond
the mark and to say stoutly, "Such a race of people as
we stand, so superior to all the world! The old Anglo-
Saxon race, the best breed in the whole world! I pray
that our unrivalled happiness may last! I ask you
whether, the world over or in past history, there is anything like it?" And so long as criticism answers this
dithyramb by insisting that the old Anglo-Saxon race
would be still more superior to all others if it had no
church-rates, or that our unrivalled happiness would last
yet longer with a six-pound franchise, so long will the
strain, "The best breed in the whole world!" swell louder
and louder, everything ideal and refining will be lost out
of sight, and both the assailed and their critics will remain in a sphere, to say the truth, perfectly unvital, a
sphere in which spiritual progression is impossible. But
let criticism leave church-rates and the franchise alone,
and in the most candid spirit, without a single lurking
thought of practical innovation, confront with our dithyramb this paragraph on which I stumbled in a newspaper immediately after reading Mr. Roebuck:

"A shocking child murder has just been committed at
Nottingham. A girl named Wragg left the workhouse
there on Saturday morning with her young illegitimate
child. The child was soon afterwards found dead on
Mapperly Hills, having been strangled. Wragg is in
custody."

Nothing but that; but, in juxtaposition with the ab-

solute eulogies of Sir Charles Adderley and Mr. Roebuck, how eloquent, how suggestive are those few lines!
"Our old Anglo-Saxon breed, the best in the whole
world!"—how much that is harsh and ill-favoured there
is in this best! *Wragg!* If we are to talk of ideal perfection, of "the best in the whole world," has any one re-
flected what a touch of grossness in our race, what an
original short-coming in the more delicate spiritual perceptions, is shown by the natural growth amongst us of
such hideous names,—Higginbottom, Stiggins, Bugg! In
Ionia and Attica they were luckier in this respect than
"the best race in the world"; by the Ilissus there was no
Wragg, poor thing! And "our unrivalled happiness";—
what an element of grimness, bareness, and hideousness
mixes with it and blurs it; the workhouse, the dismal
Mapperly Hills,—how dismal those who have seen them
will remember;—the gloom, the smoke, the cold, the
strangled illegitimate child! "I ask you whether, the
world over or in past history, there is anything like it?"
Perhaps not, one is inclined to answer; but at any rate,
in that case, the world is very much to be pitied. And
the final touch,—short, bleak and inhuman: *Wragg is in
custody.* The sex lost in the confusion of our unrivalled
happiness; or (shall I say?) the superfluous Christian
name lopped off by the straightforward vigour of our
old Anglo-Saxon breed! There is profit for the spirit in
such contrasts as this; criticism serves the cause of perfection by establishing them. By eluding sterile conflict,
by refusing to remain in the sphere where alone narrow
and relative conceptions have any worth and validity,
criticism may diminish its momentary importance, but
only in this way has it a chance of gaining admittance
for those wider and more perfect conceptions to which
all its duty is really owed. Mr. Roebuck will have a poor
opinion of an adversary who replies to his defiant songs

of triumph only by murmuring under his breath, *Wragg is in custody*; but in no other way will these songs of triumph be induced gradually to moderate themselves, to get rid of what in them is excessive and offensive, and to fall into a softer and truer key.

It will be said that it is a very subtle and indirect action which I am thus prescribing for criticism, and that, by embracing in this manner the Indian virtue of detachment and abandoning the sphere of practical life, it condemns itself to a slow and obscure work. Slow and obscure it may be, but it is the only proper work of criticism. The mass of mankind will never have any ardent zeal for seeing things as they are; very inadequate ideas will always satisfy them. On these inadequate ideas reposes, and must repose, the general practice of the world. That is as much as saying that whoever sets himself to see things as they are will find himself one of a very small circle; but it is only by this small circle resolutely doing its own work that adequate ideas will ever get current at all. The rush and roar of practical life will always have a dizzying and attracting effect upon the most collected spectator, and tend to draw him into its vortex; most of all will this be the case where that life is so powerful as it is in England. But it is only by remaining collected, and refusing to lend himself to the point of view of the practical man, that the critic can do the practical man any service; and it is only by the greatest sincerity in pursuing his own course, and by at last convincing even the practical man of his sincerity, that he can escape misunderstandings which perpetually threaten him.

For the practical man is not apt for fine distinctions, and yet in these distinctions truth and the highest culture greatly find their account. But it is not easy to lead a practical man,—unless you reassure him as to your

practical intentions, you have no chance of leading him,
—to see that a thing which he has always been used to
look at from one side only, which he greatly values, and
which, looked at from that side, quite deserves, perhaps,
all the prizing and admiring which he bestows upon it,
—that this thing, looked at from another side, may appear much less beneficent and beautiful, and yet retain
all its claims to our practical allegiance. Where shall we
find language innocent enough, how shall we make the
spotless purity of our intentions evident enough, to enable us to say to the political Englishman that the British
Constitution itself, which, seen from the practical side,
looks such a magnificent organ of progress and virtue,
seen from the speculative side,—with its compromises,
its love of facts, its horror of theory, its studied avoidance of clear thoughts,—that, seen from this side, our
august Constitution sometimes looks,—forgive me,
shade of Lord Somers!—a colossal machine for the man-
ufacture of Philistines? How is Cobbett to say this and
not be misunderstood, blackened as he is with the smoke
of a lifelong conflict in the field of political practice? how
is Mr. Carlyle to say it and not be misunderstood, after
his furious raid into this field with his *Latter-day Pam-
phlets*? how is Mr. Ruskin, after his pugnacious political
economy? I say, the critic must keep out of the region of
immediate practice in the political, social, humanitarian
sphere if he wants to make a beginning for that more
free speculative treatment of things, which may perhaps
one day make its benefits felt even in this sphere, but in
a natural and thence irresistible manner.

Do what he will, however, the critic will still remain
exposed to frequent misunderstandings, and nowhere
so much as in this country. For here people are particularly indisposed even to comprehend that without this
free disinterested treatment of things, truth and the

highest culture are out of the question. So immersed are they in practical life, so accustomed to take all their notions from this life and its processes, that they are apt to think that truth and culture themselves can be reached by the processes of this life, and that it is an impertinent singularity to think of reaching them in any other. "We are all *terræ filii*," cries their eloquent advocate; "all Philistines together. Away with the notion of proceeding by any other course than the course dear to the Philistines; let us have a social movement, let us organise and combine a party to pursue truth and new thought, let us call it *the liberal party*, and let us all stick to each other, and back each other up. Let us have no nonsense about independent criticism, and intellectual delicacy, and the few and the many. Don't let us trouble ourselves about foreign thought; we shall invent the whole thing for ourselves as we go along. If one of us speaks well, applaud him; if one of us speaks ill, applaud him too; we are all in the same movement, we are all liberals, we are all in pursuit of truth." In this way the pursuit of truth becomes really a social, practical, pleasurable affair, almost requiring a chairman, a secretary, and advertisements; with the excitement of an occasional scandal, with a little resistance to give the happy sense of difficulty overcome; but, in general, plenty of bustle and very little thought. To act is so easy, as Goethe says; to think is so hard! It is true that the critic has many temptations to go with the stream, to make one of the party movement, one of these *terræ filii*; it seems ungracious to refuse to be a *terræ filius* when so many excellent people are; but the critic's duty is to refuse, or, if resistance is vain, at least to cry with Obermann: *Périssons en résistant.*

How serious a matter it is to try and resist, I had ample opportunity of experiencing when I ventured some time ago to criticise the celebrated first volume of Bishop Colenso.[1] The echoes of the storm which was then raised I still, from time to time, hear grumbling round me. That storm arose out of a misunderstanding almost inevitable. It is a result of no little culture to attain to a clear perception that science and religion are two wholly different things. The multitude will for ever confuse them; but happily that is of no great real importance, for while the multitude imagines itself to live by its false science, it does really live by its true religion. Dr. Colenso, however, in his first volume did all he could to strengthen the confusion, and to make it dangerous. He did this with the best intentions, I freely admit, and with the most candid ignorance that this was the natural effect of what he was doing; but, says Joubert, "Ignorance, which in matters of morals extenuates the crime, is itself, in intellectual matters, a crime of the first order." I criticised Bishop Colenso's speculative confusion. Immediately there was a cry raised: "What is this? here is a liberal attacking a liberal. Do not you belong to the movement? are you not a friend of truth? Is not Bishop Colenso in pursuit of truth? then speak with proper respect of his book. Dr. Stanley is another friend of truth, and you speak with proper respect of his book; why make these invidious differences? both books are excellent, admirable, liberal; Bishop Colenso's perhaps the

---

[1] So sincere is my dislike to all personal attack and controversy, that I abstain from reprinting, at this distance of time from the occasion which called them forth, the essays in which I criticised Dr. Colenso's book; I feel bound, however, after all that has passed, to make here a final declaration, of my sincere impenitence for having published them. Nay, I cannot forbear repeating yet once more, for his benefit and that of his readers, this sentence from my original remarks upon him. *There is truth of science and truth of religion; truth of science does not become truth of religion till it is made religious.* And I will add: Let us have all the science there is from the men of science; from the men of religion let us have religion. (Arnold's note.)

most so, because it is the boldest, and will have the best practical consequences for the liberal cause. Do you want to encourage to the attack of a brother liberal his, and your, and our implacable enemies, the *Church and State Review* or the *Record*,—the High Church rhinoceros and the Evangelical hyaena? Be silent, therefore; or rather speak, speak as loud as ever you can! and go into ecstasies over the eighty and odd pigeons."

But criticism cannot follow this coarse and indiscriminate method. It is unfortunately possible for a man in pursuit of truth to write a book which reposes upon a false conception. Even the practical consequences of a book are to genuine criticism no recommendation of it, if the book is, in the highest sense, blundering. I see that a lady who herself, too, is in pursuit of truth, and who writes with great ability, but a little too much, perhaps, under the influence of the practical spirit of the English liberal movement, classes Bishop Colenso's book and M. Renan's together, in her survey of the religious state of Europe, as facts of the same order, works, both of them, of "great importance"; "great ability, power, and skill"; Bishop Colenso's, perhaps, the most powerful; at least, Miss Cobbe gives special expression to her gratitude that to Bishop Colenso "has been given the strength to grasp, and the courage to teach, truths of such deep import." In the same way, more than one popular writer has compared him to Luther. Now it is just this kind of false estimate which the critical spirit is, it seems to me, bound to resist. It is really the strongest possible proof of the low ebb at which, in England, the critical spirit is, that while the critical hit in the religious literature of Germany is Dr. Strauss's book, in that of France M. Renan's book, the book of Bishop Colenso is the critical hit in the religious literature of England. Bishop Colenso's book reposes on a total misconception of the essential elements of the religious problem, as that problem is now presented for solution. To criticism, therefore, which seeks to have the best that is known and thought on this problem, it is, however well meant, of no importance whatever. M. Renan's book attempts a new synthesis of the elements furnished to us by the Four Gospels. It attempts, in my opinion, a synthesis, perhaps premature, perhaps impossible, certainly not successful. Up to the present time, at any rate, we must acquiesce in Fleury's sentence on such recastings of the Gospel story: *Quiconque s'imagine la pouvoir mieux écrire, ne l'entend pas.* M. Renan had himself passed by anticipation a like sentence on his own work, when he said: "If a new presentation of the character of Jesus were offered to me, I would not have it; its very clearness would be, in my opinion, the best proof of its insufficiency." His friends may with perfect justice rejoin that at the sight of the Holy Land, and of the actual scene of the Gospelstory, all the current of M. Renan's thoughts may have naturally changed, and a new casting of that story irresistibly suggested itself to him; and that this is just a case for applying Cicero's maxim: Change of mind is not inconsistency—*nemo doctus unquam mutationem consilii inconstantiam dixit esse.* Nevertheless, for criticism, M. Renan's first thought must still be the truer one, as long as his new casting so fails more fully to commend itself, more fully (to use Coleridge's happy phrase about the Bible) to *find* us. Still M. Renan's attempt is, for criticism, of the most real interest and importance, since, with all its difficulty, a fresh synthesis of the New Testament *data*—not a making war on them, in Voltaire's fashion, not a leaving them out of mind, in the world's fashion, but the putting a new construction upon them, the taking them from under the old, traditional, conventional point of view and placing them under a new one,

—is the very essence of the religious problem, as now presented; and only by efforts in this direction can it receive a solution.

Again, in the same spirit in which she judges Bishop Colenso, Miss Cobbe, like so many earnest liberals of our practical race, both here and in America, herself sets vigorously about a positive reconstruction of religion, about making a religion of the future out of hand, or at least setting about making it. We must not rest, she and they are always thinking and saying, in negative criticism, we must be creative and constructive; hence we have such works as her recent *Religious Duty,* and works still more considerable, perhaps, by others, which will be in every one's mind. These works often have much ability; they often spring out of sincere convictions, and a sincere wish to do good; and they sometimes, perhaps, do good. Their fault is (if I may be permitted to say so) one which they have in common with the British College of Health, in the New Road. Every one knows the British College of Health; it is that building with the lion and the statue of the Goddess Hygeia before it; at least I am sure about the lion, though I am not absolutely certain about the Goddess Hygeia. This building does credit, perhaps, to the resources of Dr. Morrison and his disciples; but it falls a good deal short of one's idea of what a British College of Health ought to be. In England, where we hate public interference and love individual enterprise, we have a whole crop of places like the British College of Health; the grand name without the grand thing. Unluckily, creditable to individual enterprise as they are, they tend to impair our taste by making us forget what more grandiose, noble, or beautiful character properly belongs to a public institution. The same may be said of the religions of the future of Miss Cobbe and others. Creditable, like the

British College of Health, to the resources of their authors, they yet tend to make us forget what more grandiose, noble, or beautiful character properly belongs to religious constructions. The historic religions, with all their faults, have had this; it certainly belongs to the religious sentiment, when it truly flowers, to have this; and we impoverish our spirit if we allow a religion of the future without it. What then is the duty of criticism here? To take the practical point of view, to applaud the liberal movement and all its works,—its New Road religions of the future into the bargain,—for their general utility's sake? By no means; but to be perpetually dissatisfied with these works, while they perpetually fall short of a high and perfect ideal.

For criticism, these are elementary laws; but they never can be popular, and in this country they have been very little followed, and one meets with immense obstacles in following them. That is a reason for asserting them again and again. Criticism must maintain its independence of the practical spirit and its aims. Even with well-meant efforts of the practical spirit it must express dissatisfaction, if in the sphere of the ideal they seem impoverishing and limiting. It must not hurry on to the goal because of its practical importance. It must be patient, and know how to wait; and flexible, and know how to attach itself to things and how to withdraw from them. It must be apt to study and praise elements that for the fulness of spiritual perfection are wanted, even though they belong to a power which in the practical sphere may be maleficent. It must be apt to discern the spiritual shortcomings or illusions of powers that in the practical sphere may be beneficent. And this without any notion of favouring or injuring, in the practical sphere, one power or the other; without any notion of playing off, in this sphere, one power against the other.

When one looks, for instance, at the English Divorce Court,—an institution which perhaps has its practical conveniences, but which in the ideal sphere is so hideous; an institution which neither makes divorce impossible nor makes it decent, which allows a man to get rid of his wife, or a wife of her husband, but makes them drag one another first, for the public edification, through a mire of unutterable infamy,—when one looks at this charming institution, I say, with its crowded trials, its newspaper reports, and its money compensations, this institution in which the gross unregenerate British Philistine has indeed stamped an image of himself,—one may be permitted to find the marriage theory of Catholicism refreshing and elevating. Or when Protestantism, in virtue of its supposed rational and intellectual origin, gives the law to criticism too magisterially, criticism may and must remind it that its pretensions, in this respect, are illusive and do it harm; that the Reformation was a moral rather than an intellectual event; that Luther's theory of grace no more exactly reflects the mind of the spirit than Bossuet's philosophy of history reflects it; and that there is no more antecedent probability of the Bishop of Durham's stock of ideas being agreeable to perfect reason than of Pope Pius the Ninth's. But criticism will not on that account forget the achievements of Protestantism in the practical and moral sphere; nor that, even in the intellectual sphere, Protestantism, though in a blind and stumbling manner, carried forward the Renascence, while Catholicism threw itself violently across its path.

I lately heard a man of thought and energy contrasting the want of ardour and movement which he now found amongst young men in this country with what he remembered in his own youth, twenty years ago. "What reformers we were then!" he exclaimed; "What a zeal we had! how we canvassed every institution in Church and State, and were prepared to remodel them all on first principles!" He was inclined to regret, as a spiritual flagging, the lull which he saw. I am disposed rather to regard it as a pause in which the turn to a new mode of spiritual progress is being accomplished. Everything was long seen, by the young and ardent amongst us, in inseparable connection with politics and practical life. We have pretty well exhausted the benefits of seeing things in this connection, we have got all that can be got by so seeing them. Let us try a more disinterested mode of seeing them; let us betake ourselves more to the serener life of the mind and spirit. This life, too, may have its excesses and dangers; but they are not for us at present. Let us think of quietly enlarging our stock of true and fresh ideas, and not, as soon as we get an idea or half an idea, be running out with it into the street, and trying to make it rule there. Our ideas will, in the end, shape the world all the better for maturing a little. Perhaps in fifty years' time it will in the English House of Commons be an objection to an institution that it is an anomaly, and my friend the Member of Parliament will shudder in his grave. But let us in the meanwhile rather endeavour that in twenty years' time it may, in English literature, be an objection to a proposition that it is absurd. That will be a change so vast, that the imagination almost fails to grasp it. *Ab integro sæclorum nascitur ordo.*

If I have insisted so much on the course which criticism must take where politics and religion are concerned, it is because, where these burning matters are in question, it is most likely to go astray. I have wished, above all, to insist on the attitude which criticism should adopt towards things in general; on its right tone and temper of mind. But then comes another question as to the subject-matter which literary criticisms should most seek. Here, in general, its course is determined for it by the idea which is the law of its being; the idea of a disinterested endeavour to learn and propagate the best that is known and thought in the world, and thus to establish a current of fresh and true ideas. By the very nature of things, as England is not all the world, much of the best that is known and thought in the world cannot be of English growth, must be foreign; by the nature of things, again, it is just this that we are least likely to know, while English thought is streaming in upon us from all sides, and takes excellent care that we shall not be ignorant of its existence. The English critic of literature, therefore, must dwell much on foreign thought, and with particular heed on any part of it, which, while significant and fruitful in itself, is for any reason specially likely to escape him. Again, judging is often spoken of as the critic's one business, and so in some sense it is; but the judgment which almost insensibly forms itself in a fair and clear mind, along with fresh knowledge, is the valuable one; and thus knowledge, and ever fresh knowledge, must be the critic's great concern for himself. And it is by communicating fresh knowledge, and letting his own judgment pass along with it,—but insensibly, and in the second place, not the first, as a sort of companion and clue, not as an abstract lawgiver,—that the critic will generally do most good to his readers. Sometimes, no doubt, for the sake of establishing an author's place in literature, and his relation to a central standard (and if this is not done, how are we to get at our *best in the world?*) criticism may have to deal with a subject-matter so familiar that fresh knowledge is out of the question, and then it must be all judgment; an enunciation and detailed application of principles. Here the great safeguard is never to let oneself become abstract, always to retain an intimate and lively consciousness of the truth of what one is saying, and, the moment this fails us, to be sure that something is wrong. Still under all circumstances, this mere judgment and application of principles is, in itself, not the most satisfactory work to the critic; like mathematics, it is tautological, and cannot well give us, like fresh learning, the sense of creative activity.

But stop, some one will say; all this talk is of no practical use to us whatever; this criticism of yours is not what we have in our minds when we speak of criticism; when we speak of critics and criticism, we mean critics and criticism of the current English literature of the day; when you offer to tell criticism its function, it is to this criticism that we expect you to address yourself. I am sorry for it, for I am afraid I must disappoint these expectations. I am bound by my own definition of criticism: *a disinterested endeavour to learn and propagate the best that is known and thought in the world.* How much of current English literature comes into this "best that is known and thought in the world"? Not very much I fear; certainly less, at this moment, than of the current literature of France or Germany. Well, then, am I to alter my definition of criticism, in order to meet the requirements of a number of practising English critics, who, after all, are free in their choice of a business? That would be making criticism lend itself just to one of those alien practical considerations, which, I have said, are so fatal to it. One may say, indeed, to those who have to deal with the mass—so much better disregarded—of current English literature, that they may at all events endeavour, in dealing with this, to try it, so far as they can, by the standard of the best that is known and thought in the world; one may say, that to get anywhere near this standard, every critic should try and possess one great literature, at least, besides his own; and the more unlike his own, the better. But, after all, the criticism I am really concerned with,—the criticism which alone can much help us for the future, the criticism which, throughout Europe, is at the present day meant, when so much stress is laid on the importance of criticism and the critical spirit,—is a criticism which regards Europe as being, for intellectual and spiritual purposes, one great confederation, bound to a joint action and working to a common result; and whose members have, for their proper outfit, a knowledge of Greek, Roman, and Eastern antiquity, and of one another. Special, local, and temporary advantages being put out of account, that modern nation will in the intellectual and spiritual sphere make most progress, which most thoroughly carries out this program. And what is that but saying that we too, all of us, as individuals, the more thoroughly we carry it out, shall make the more progress?

There is so much inviting us!—what are we to take? what will nourish us in growth towards perfection? That is the question which, with the immense field of life and of literature lying before him, the critic has to answer; for himself first, and afterwards for others. In this idea of the critic's business the essays brought together in the following pages have had their origin; in this idea, widely different as are their subjects, they have, perhaps, their unity.

I conclude with what I said at the beginning: to have the sense of creative activity is the great happiness and the great proof of being alive, and it is not denied to criticism to have it; but then criticism must be sincere, simple, flexible, ardent, ever widening its knowledge. Then it may have, in no contemptible measure, a joyful sense of creative activity; a sense which a man of insight and conscience will prefer to what he might derive from a poor, starved, fragmentary, inadequate creation. And at some epochs no other creation is possible.

Still, in full measure, the sense of creative activity belongs only to genuine creation; in literature we must never forget that. But what true man of letters ever can forget it? It is no such common matter for a gifted nature to come into possession of a current of true and living ideas, and to produce amidst the inspiration of them, that we are likely to underrate it. The epochs of Æschylus and Shakespeare make us feel their pre-eminence. In an epoch like those is, no doubt, the true life of literature; there is the promised land, towards which criticism can only beckon. That promised land it will not be ours to enter, and we shall die in the wilderness: but to have desired to enter it, to have saluted it from afar, is already, perhaps, the best distinction among contemporaries; it will certainly be the best title to esteem with posterity.

◌

THE LITERARY INFLUENCE
OF ACADEMIES

◌

IT IS impossible to put down a book like the history of the French Academy, by Pellisson and D'Olivet, which M. Charles Livet has lately re-edited, without being led to reflect upon the absence, in our own country, of any institution like the French Academy, upon the probable causes of this absence, and upon its results. A thousand voices will be ready to tell us that this absence is a signal mark of our national superiority; that it is in great part owing to this absence that the exhilarating words of Lord Macaulay, lately given to the world by his very clever nephew, Mr. Trevelyan, are so profoundly true: "It may safely be said that the literature now extant in the English language is of far greater value than all the literature which three hundred years ago was extant in all the languages of the world together." I daresay this is so; only, remembering Spinoza's maxim that the two great banes of humanity are self-conceit and the laziness coming from self-conceit, I think it may do us good, instead of resting in our pre-eminence with perfect security, to look a little more closely why this is so, and whether it is so without any limitations.

But first of all I must give a very few words to the outward history of the French Academy. About the year 1629, seven or eight persons in Paris, fond of literature, formed themselves into a sort of little club to meet at one another's houses and discuss literary matters. Their meetings got talked of, and Cardinal Richelieu, then minister and all-powerful, heard of them. He himself had a noble passion for letters, and for all fine culture; he was interested by what he heard of the nascent society. Himself a man in the grand style, if ever man was, he had the insight to perceive what a potent instrument of the grand style was here to his hand. It was the beginning of a great century for France, the seventeenth; men's minds were working, the French language was forming. Richelieu sent to ask the members of the new society whether they would be willing to become a body with a public character holding regular meetings. Not without a little hesitation,—for apparently they found themselves very well as they were, and these seven or eight gentlemen of a social and literary turn were not perfectly at their ease as to what the great and terrible minister could want with them,—they consented. The favours of a man like Richelieu are not easily refused, whether they are honestly meant or no; but, this favour of Richelieu's was meant quite honestly. The Parliament, however, had its doubts of this. The Parliament had none of Richelieu's enthusiasm about letters and culture; it was jealous of the apparition of a new public body in the State; above all, of a body called into existence by Richelieu. The King's letters-patent, establishing and authorising the new society, were granted early in 1635; but, by the old constitution of France, these letters-patent required the verification of the Parliament. It was two years and a half—towards the autumn of 1637— before the Parliament would give it; and it then gave it only after pressing solicitations, and earnest assurances of the innocent intentions of the young Academy. Jocose people said that this society with its mission to purify and embellish the language, filled with terror a body of lawyers like the French Parliament, the stronghold of barbarous jargon and of chicane.

This improvement of the language was in truth the declared grand aim for the operations of the Academy. Its statutes of foundation, approved by Richelieu before the royal edict establishing it was issued, say expressly: "The Academy's principal function shall be to work with all the care and all the diligence possible at giving sure rules to our language, and rendering it pure, eloquent, and capable of treating the arts and sciences." This zeal for making a nation's great instrument of thought,—its language,—correct and worthy, is undoubtedly a sign full of promise,—a weighty earnest of future power. It is said that Richelieu had it in his mind that French should succeed Latin in its general ascendency, as Latin had succeeded Greek; if it was so, even this wish has to some extent been fulfilled. But, at any rate, the *ethical* influences of style in language,—its close relations, so often pointed out, with character,—are most important. Richelieu, a man of high culture, and, at the same time, of great character, felt them profoundly; and that he should have sought to regularise, strengthen, and perpetuate them by an institution for perfecting language, is alone a striking proof of his governing spirit and of his genius.

This was not all he had in his mind, however. The new Academy, now enlarged to a body of forty members, and meant to contain all the chief literary men of France, was to be a *literary tribunal*. The works of its members were to be brought before it previous to publication, were to be criticised by it, and finally, if it saw fit, to be published with its declared approbation. The works of other writers, not members of the Academy, might also, at the request of these writers themselves, be passed under the Academy's review. Besides this, in essays and discussions the Academy examined and judged works already published, whether by living or dead authors, and literary matters in general. The celebrated opinion on Corneille's *Cid*, delivered in 1637 by the Academy at Richelieu's urgent request, when this poem, which strongly occupied public attention, had been attacked by M. de Scudéry, shows how fully Richelieu designed his new creation to do duty as a supreme court of literature, and how early it in fact began to exercise this function. One[1] who had known Richelieu declared, after the Cardinal's death, that he had projected a yet greater institution than the Academy, a sort of grand European college of art, science, and literature, a Prytaneum, where the chief authors of all Europe should be gathered together in one central home, there to live

[1] La Mesnardière. (*Arnold's note.*)

in security, leisure, and honour;—that was a dream which will not bear to be pulled about too roughly. But the project of forming a high court of letters for France was no dream; Richelieu in great measure fulfilled it. This is what the Academy, by its idea, really is; this is what it has always tended to become; this is what it has, from time to time, really been; by being, or tending to be this, far more than even by what it has done for the language, it is of such importance in France. To give the law, the tone to literature, and that tone a high one, is its business. "Richelieu meant it," says M. Sainte-Beuve, "to be a *haut jury*,"—a jury the most choice and author-itative that could be found on all important literary mat-ters in question before the public; to be, as it in fact be-came in the latter half of the eighteenth century, "a sovereign organ of opinion." "The duty of the Academy is," says M. Renan, "*maintenir la délicatesse de l'esprit français*"—to keep the fine quality of the French spirit unimpaired; it represents a kind of "*maîtrise en fait de bon ton*"—the authority of a recognised master in mat-ters of tone and taste. "All ages," says M. Renan again, "have had their inferior literature; but the great danger of our time is that this inferior literature tends more and more to get the upper place. No one has the same advan-tage as the Academy for fighting against this mischief"; the Academy, which, as he says elsewhere, has even spe-cial facilities for "creating a form of intellectual culture *which shall impose itself on all around*." M. Sainte-Beuve and M. Renan are, both of them, very keen-sighted critics; and they show it signally by seizing and putting so prominently forward this character of the French Academy.

Such an effort to set up a recognised authority, im-posing on us a high standard in matters of intellect and taste, has many enemies in human nature. We all of us like to go our own way, and not to be forced out of the atmosphere of commonplace habitual to most of us;— *"was uns alle bändigt,"* says Goethe, *"das Gemeine."* We like to be suffered to lie comfortably in the old straw of our habits, especially of our intellectual habits, even though this straw may not be very clean and fine. But if the effort to limit this freedom of our lower nature finds, as it does and must find, enemies in human nature, it finds also auxiliaries in it. Out of the four great parts, says Cicero, of the *honestum,* or good, which forms the matter on which *officium,* or human duty, finds employment, one is the fixing of a *modus* and an *ordo,* a measure and an order, to fashion and wholesomely constrain our action, in order to lift it above the level it keeps if left to itself, and to bring it nearer to perfection. Man alone of living creatures, he says, goes feeling after *"quid sit ordo, quid sit quod deceat, in factis dictisque qui* modus"—the discovery of an *order,* a law of *good taste,* a *measure* for his words and actions. Other creatures submissively follow the law of their nature; man alone has an impulse leading him to set up some other law to control the bent of his nature.

This holds good, of course, as to moral matters, as well as intellectual matters: and it is of moral matters that we are generally thinking when we affirm it. But it holds good as to intellectual matters too. Now, probably, M. Sainte-Beuve had not these words of Cicero in his mind when he made, about the French nation, the assertion I am going to quote; but, for all that, the assertion leans for support, one may say, upon the truth conveyed in those words of Cicero, and wonderfully illustrates and confirms them. "In France," says M. Sainte-Beuve, "the first consideration for us is not whether we are amused and pleased by a work of art or mind, nor is it whether we are touched by it. What we seek above all to learn is, whether *we were right* in being amused with it, and in applauding it, and in being moved by it." Those are very remarkable words, and they are, I believe, in the main quite true. A Frenchman has, to a considerable degree, what one may call a conscience in intellectual matters; he has an active belief that there is a right and a wrong in them, that he is bound to honour and obey the right, that he is disgraced by cleaving to the wrong. All the world has, or professes to have, this conscience in moral matters. The word *conscience* has become almost confined, in popular use, to the moral sphere, because this lively susceptibility of feeling is, in the moral sphere, so far more common than in the intellectual sphere; the livelier, in the moral sphere, this susceptibility is, the greater becomes a man's readiness to admit a high standard of action, an ideal authoritatively correcting his everyday moral habits; here, such willing admission of authority is due to sensitiveness of conscience. And a like deference to a standard higher than one's own habitual standard in intellectual matters, a like respectful recognition of a superior ideal, is caused, in the intellectual sphere, by sensitiveness of intelligence. Those whose intelligence is quickest, openest, most sensitive, are readiest with this deference; those whose intelligence is less delicate and sensitive are less disposed to it. Well, now we are on the road to see why the French have their Academy and we have nothing of the kind.

What are the essential characteristics of the spirit of our nation? Not, certainly, an open and clear mind, not a quick and flexible intelligence. Our greatest admirers would not claim for us that we have these in a pre-eminent degree; they might say that we had more of them than our detractors gave us credit for; but they would not assert them to be our essential characteristics.

They would rather allege, as our chief spiritual characteristics, energy and honesty; and, if we are judged fa-
vourably and positively, not invidiously and negatively,
our chief characteristics are no doubt, these:—energy
and honesty, not an open and clear mind, not a quick
and flexible intelligence. Openness of mind and flexibility of intelligence were very signal characteristics of the
Athenian people in ancient times; everybody will feel
that. Openness of mind and flexibility of intelligence are
remarkable characteristics of the French people in modern times; at any rate, they strikingly characterise them
as compared with us; I think everybody, or almost everybody, will feel that. I will not now ask what more the
Athenian or the French spirit has than this, nor what
shortcomings either of them may have as a set-off against
this; all I want now to point out is that they have this,
and that we have it in a much lesser degree. Let me remark, however, that not only in the moral sphere, but
also in the intellectual and spiritual sphere, energy and
honesty are most important and fruitful qualities; that,
for instance, of what we call genius energy is the most
essential part. So, by assigning to a nation energy and
honesty as its chief spiritual characteristics,—by refusing to it, as at all eminent characteristics, openness of
mind and flexibility of intelligence,—we do not by any
means, as some people might at first suppose, relegate its
importance and its power of manifesting itself with
effect from the intellectual to the moral sphere. We only
indicate its probable special line of successful activity in
the intellectual sphere, and, it is true, certain imperfections and failings to which, in this sphere, it will always
be subject. Genius is mainly an affair of energy, and
poetry is mainly an affair of genius; therefore a nation
whose spirit is characterised by energy may well be eminent in poetry;—and we have Shakespeare. Again, the

highest reach of science is, one may say, an inventive power, a faculty of divination, akin to the highest power exercised in poetry; therefore, a nation whose spirit is characterised by energy may well be eminent in science; —and we have Newton. Shakespeare and Newton: in the intellectual sphere there can be no higher names. And what that energy, which is the life of genius, above everything demands and insists upon, is freedom; entire independence of all authority, prescription, and routine, —the fullest room to expand as it will. Therefore, a nation whose chief spiritual characteristic is energy, will not be very apt to set up, in intellectual matters, a fixed standard, an authority, like an academy. By this it certainly escapes certain real inconveniences and dangers, and it can, at the same time, as we have seen, reach undeniably splendid heights in poetry and science. On the other hand, some of the requisites of intellectual work are specially the affair of quickness of mind and flexibility of intelligence. The form, the method of evolution, the precision, the proportions, the relations of the parts to the whole, in an intellectual work, depend mainly upon them. And these are the elements of an intellectual work which are really most communicable from it, which can most be learned and adopted from it, which have, therefore, the greatest effect upon the intellectual performance of others. Even in poetry, these requisites are very important; and the poetry of a nation, not eminent for the gifts on which they depend, will, more or less, suffer by this shortcoming. In poetry, however, they are, after all, secondary, and energy is the first thing; but in prose they are of first-rate importance. In its prose literature, therefore, and in the routine of intellectual work generally, a nation with no particular gifts for these will not be so successful. These are what, as I have said, can to a certain degree be learned and appropriated, while the free activity of genius cannot. Academies consecrate and maintain them, and, therefore, a nation with an eminent turn for them naturally establishes academies. So far as routine and authority tend to embarrass energy and inventive genius, academies may be said to be obstructive to energy and inventive genius, and, to this extent, to the human spirit's general advance. But then this evil is so much compensated by the propagation, on a large scale, of the mental aptitudes and demands which an open mind and a flexible intelligence naturally engender, genius itself, in the long run, so greatly finds its account in this propagation, and bodies like the French Academy have such power for promoting it, that the general advance of the human spirit is perhaps, on the whole, rather furthered than impeded by their existence.

How much greater is our nation in poetry than prose! how much better, in general, do the productions of its spirit show in the qualities of genius than in the qualities of intelligence! One may constantly remark this in the work of individuals; how much more striking, in general, does any Englishman,—of some vigour of mind, but by no means a poet,—seem in his verse than in his prose! His verse partly suffers from his not being really a poet, partly, no doubt, from the very same defects which impair his prose, and he cannot express himself with thorough success in it. But how much more powerful a personage does he appear in it, by dint of feeling, and of originality and movement of ideas, than when he is writing prose! With a Frenchman of like stamp, it is just the reverse: set him to write poetry, he is limited, artificial, and impotent; set him to write prose, he is free, natural, and effective. The power of French literature is in its prose-writers, the power of English literature is in its poets. Nay, many of the celebrated French poets depend wholly for their fame upon the qualities of intelligence which they exhibit,—qualities which are the distinctive support of prose; many of the celebrated English prose-writers depend wholly for their fame upon the qualities of genius and imagination which they exhibit, —qualities which are the distinctive support of poetry. But, as I have said, the qualities of genius are less transferable than the qualities of intelligence; less can be immediately learned and appropriated from their product; they are less direct and stringent intellectual agencies, though they may be more beautiful and divine. Shakespeare and our great Elizabethan group were certainly more gifted writers than Corneille and his group; but what was the sequel to this great literature, this literature of genius, as we may call it, stretching from Marlowe to Milton? What did it lead up to in English literature? To our provincial and second-rate literature of the eighteenth century. What, on the other hand, was the sequel to the literature of the French "great century," to this literature of intelligence, as, by comparison with our Elizabethan literature, we may call it; what did it lead up to? To the French literature of the eighteenth century, one of the most powerful and pervasive intellectual agencies that have ever existed,—the greatest European force of the eighteenth century. In science, again, we had Newton, a genius of the very highest order, a type of genius in science, if ever there was one. On the continent, as a sort of counterpart to Newton, there was Leibnitz; a man, it seems to me (though on these matters I speak under correction), of much less creative energy of genius, much less power of divination than Newton, but rather a man of admirable intelligence, a type of intelligence in science, if ever there was one. Well, and what did they each directly lead up to in science? What was the intellectual generation that sprang from each of them? I only repeat what the men of science have themselves pointed out. The man of genius was continued by the English analysts of the eighteenth century, comparatively powerless and obscure followers of the renowned master; the man of intelligence was continued by successors like Bernouilli, Euler, Lagrange, and Laplace, the greatest names in modern mathematics.

What I want the reader to see is, that the question as to the utility of academies to the intellectual life of a nation is not settled when we say, for instance: "Oh, we have never had an academy, and yet we have, confessedly, a very great literature." It still remains to be asked: "What sort of a great literature? a literature great in the special qualities of genius, or great in the special qualities of intelligence?" If in the former, it is by no means sure that either our literature, or the general intellectual life of our nation, has got already, without academies, all that academies can give. Both the one and the other may very well be somewhat wanting in those qualities of intelligence, out of a lively sense for which a body like the French Academy, as I have said, springs, and which such a body does a great deal to spread and confirm. Our literature, in spite of the genius manifested in it, may fall short in form, method, precision, proportions, arrangement,—all of them, I have said, things where intelligence proper comes in. It may be comparatively weak in prose, that branch of literature where intelligence proper is, so to speak, all in all. In this branch it may show many grave faults to which the want of a quick flexible intelligence, and of the strict standard which such an intelligence tends to impose, makes it liable; it may be full of haphazard, crudeness, provincialism, eccentricity, violence, blundering. It may be a less stringent and effective intellectual agency, both upon our own nation and upon the world at large, than other literatures which show less genius, perhaps, but more intelligence.

The right conclusion certainly is that we should try, so far as we can, to make up our shortcomings; and that to this end, instead of always fixing our thoughts upon the points in which our literature, and our intellectual life generally, are strong, we should, from time to time, fix them upon those in which they are weak, and so learn to perceive clearly what we have to amend. What is our second great spiritual characteristic,—our honesty,— good for, if it is not good for this? But it will,—I am sure it will,—more and more, as time goes on, be found good for this. ·

Well, then, an institution like the French Academy, —an institution owing its existence to a national bent towards the things of the mind, towards culture, towards clearness, correctness and propriety in thinking and speaking, and, in its turn, promoting this bent,—sets standards in a number of directions, and creates, in all these directions, a force of educated opinion, checking and rebuking those who fall below these standards, or who set them at nought. Educated opinion exists here as in France; but in France the Academy serves as a sort of centre and rallying-point to it, and gives it a force which it has not got here. Why is all the *journeyman-work* of literature, as I may call it, so much worse done here than it is in France? I do not wish to hurt anyone's feelings; but surely this is so. Think of the difference between our books of reference and those of the French, between our biographical dictionaries (to take a striking instance) and theirs; think of the difference between the translations of the classics turned out for Mr. Bohn's library and those turned out for M. Nisard's collection! As a general rule, hardly any one amongst us, who knows French and German well, would use an English book of reference when he could get a French or German one; or would look at an English prose translation of an ancient author when he could get a French or German one. It is not that there do not exist in England, as in France, a number of people perfectly well able to discern what is good, in these things, from what is bad, and preferring what is good; but they are isolated, they form no powerful body of opinion, they are not strong enough to set a standard, up to which even the journeyman-work of literature must be brought, if it is to be vendible. Ignorance and charlatanism in work of this kind are always trying to pass off their wares as excellent, and to cry down criticism as the voice of an insignificant, overfastidious minority; they easily persuade the multitude that this is so when the minority is scattered about as it is here, not so easily when it is banded together as in the French Academy. So, again, with freaks in dealing with language; certainly all such freaks tend to impair the power and beauty of language; and how far more common they are with us than with the French! To take a very familiar instance. Every one has noticed the way in which the *Times* chooses to spell the word "diocese"; it always spells it "dioce*ss*" [1] deriving it, I suppose, from *Zeus* and *census*. The *Journal des Débats* might just as well write "diocess" instead of "diocèse," but imagine the *Journal des Débats* doing so! Imagine an educated Frenchman indulging himself in an orthographical antic of this sort, in face of the grave respect with which the Academy and its dictionary invest the French language! Some people will say these are little things; they are not; they are of bad example. They tend to spread the baneful notion that there is no such thing as a high correct standard in intellectual matters; that every one may as

[1] The *Times* has now (1868) abandoned this spelling and adopted the ordinary one. (*Arnold's note.*)

well take his own way; they are at variance with the severe discipline necessary for all real culture; they confirm us in habits of wilfulness and eccentricity, which hurt our minds, and damage our credit with serious people. The late Mr. Donaldson was certainly a man of great ability, and I, who am not an Orientalist, do not pretend to judge his *Jashar*: but let the reader observe the form which a foreign Orientalist's judgment of it naturally takes. M. Renan calls it a *tentative malheureuse,* a failure, in short; this it may be, or it may not be; I am no judge. But he goes on: "It is astonishing that a recent article" (in a French periodical, he means) "should have brought forward as the last word of German exegesis a work like this, composed by a doctor of the University of Cambridge, and universally condemned by German critics." You see what he means to imply: an extravagance of this sort could never have come from Germany, where there is a great force of critical opinion controlling a learned man's vagaries, and keeping him straight; it comes from the native home of intellectual eccentricity of all kinds,[1]—from England— from a doctor of the University of Cambridge:—and I daresay he would not expect much better things from a doctor of the University of Oxford. Again, after speaking of what Germany and France have done for the history of Mahomet: "America and England," M. Renan goes on, "have also occupied themselves with Mahomet." He mentions Washington Irving's *Life of Mahomet,* which does not, he says, evince much of an historical sense, a *sentiment historique fort élevé*; "but," he proceeds, "this book shows a real progress, when one thinks that in 1829

[1] A critic declares I am wrong in saying that M. Renan's language implies this. I still think that there is a shade, a *nuance* of expression, in M. Renan's language, which does imply this; but I confess, the only person who can really settle such a question is M. Renan himself. (Arnold's note.)

Mr. Charles Forster published two thick volumes, which enchanted the English *révérends,* to make out that Mahomet was the little horn of the he-goat that figures in the eighth chapter of Daniel, and that the Pope was the great horn. Mr. Forster founded on this ingenious parallel a whole philosophy of history, according to which the Pope represented the Western corruption of Christianity, and Mahomet the Eastern; thence the striking resemblances between Mahometanism and Popery." And in a note M. Renan adds: "This is the same Mr. Charles Forster who is the author of a mystification about the Sinaitic inscriptions, in which he declares he finds the primitive language." As much as to say: "It is an Englishman, be surprised at no extravagance." If these innuendoes had no ground, and were made in hatred and malice, they would not be worth a moment's attention; but they come from a grave Orientalist, on his own subject, and they point to a real fact;—the absence, in this country, of any force of educated literary and scientific opinion, making aberrations like those of the author of *The One Primeval Language* out of the question. Not only the author of such aberrations, often a very clever man, suffers by the want of check, by the not being kept straight, and spends force in vain on a false road, which, under better discipline, he might have used with profit on a true one; but all his adherents, both "reverends" and others, suffer too, and the general rate of information and judgment is in this way kept low.

In a production which we have all been reading lately, a production stamped throughout with a literary quality very rare in this country, and of which I shall have a word to say presently—*urbanity*; in this production, the work of a man never to be named by any son of Oxford without sympathy, a man who alone in Oxford of his generation, alone of many generations, conveyed to us in his genius that same charm, that same ineffable sentiment which this exquisite place itself conveys,—I mean Dr. Newman,—an expression is frequently used which is more common in theological than literary language, but which seems to me fitted to be of general service; the *note* of so and so, the note of catholicity, the note of antiquity, the note of sanctity, and so on. Adopting this expressive word, I say that in the bulk of the intellectual work of a nation which has no centre, no intellectual metropolis like an academy, like M. Sainte-Beuve's "sovereign organ of opinion," like M. Renan's "recognised authority in matters of tone and taste,"—there is observable a *note of provinciality*. Now to get rid of provinciality is a certain stage of culture; a stage the positive result of which we must not make of too much importance, but which is, nevertheless, indispensable; for it brings us on to the platform where alone the best and highest intellectual work can be said fairly to begin. Work done after men have reached this platform is *classical*; and that is the only work which, in the long run, can stand. All the *scoriæ* in the work of men of great genius who have not lived on this platform are due to their not having lived on it. Genius raises them to it by moments, and the portions of their work which are immortal are done at these moments; but more of it would have been immortal if they had not reached this platform at moments only, if they had had the culture which makes men live there.

The less a literature has felt the influence of a supposed centre of correct information, correct judgment, correct taste, the more we shall find in it this note of provinciality. I have shown the note of provinciality as caused by remoteness from a centre of correct information. Of course the note of provinciality from the want

of a centre of correct taste is still more visible, and it
is also still more common. For here great—even the
greatest—powers of mind most fail a man. Great powers
of mind will make him inform himself thoroughly, great
powers of mind will make him think profoundly, even
with ignorance and platitude all round him; but not
even great powers of mind will keep his taste and style
perfectly sound and sure, if he is left too much to himself, with no "sovereign organ of opinion" in these matters near him. Even men like Jeremy Taylor and Burke
suffer here. Take this passage from Taylor's funeral sermon on Lady Carbery:

"So have I seen a river, deep and smooth, passing with
a still foot and a sober face, and paying to the *fiscus,* the
great exchequer of the sea, a tribute large and full; and
hard by it a little brook, skipping and making a noise upon
its unequal and neighbour bottom; and after all its talking and bragged motion, it paid to its common audit
no more than the revenues of a little cloud or a contemptible vessel: so have I sometimes compared the
issues of her religion to the solemnities and famed out-
sides of another's piety."

That passage has been much admired, and, indeed,
the genius in it is undeniable. I should say, for my part,
that genius, the ruling divinity of poetry, had been too
busy in it, and intelligence, the ruling divinity of prose,
not busy enough. But can any one, with the best models
of style in his head, help feeling the note of provinciality
there, the want of simplicity, the want of measure, the
want of just the qualities that make prose classical? If
he does not feel what I mean, let him place beside the
passage of Taylor this passage from the Panegyric of
St. Paul, by Taylor's contemporary, Bossuet:

*"Il ira, cet ignorant dans l'art de bien dire, avec cette
locution rude, avec cette phrase qui sent l'étranger, il ira*

en cette Grèce polie, la mère des philosophes et des orateurs; et malgré la résistance du monde, il y établira plus d'Eglises que Platon n'y a gagné de disciples par cette éloquence qu'on a crue divine."

There we have prose without the note of provinciality —classical prose, prose of the centre.

Or take Burke, our greatest English prose-writer, as I think; take expressions like this:

"Blindfold themselves, like bulls that shut their eyes when they push, they drive, by the point of their bayonets, their slaves, blindfolded, indeed, no worse than their lords, to take their fictions for currencies, and to swallow down paper pills by thirty-four millions sterling at a dose."

Or this:

"They used it" (the royal name) "as a sort of navelstring, to nourish their unnatural offspring from the bowels of royalty itself. Now that the monster can purvey for its own subsistence, it will only carry the mark about it, as a token of its having torn the womb it came from."

Or this:

"Without one natural pang, he" (Rousseau) "casts away, as a sort of offal and excrement, the spawn of his disgustful amours, and sends his children to the hospital of foundlings."

Or this:

"I confess I never liked this continual talk of resistance and revolution, or the practice of making the extreme medicine of the constitution its daily bread. It renders the habit of society dangerously valetudinary; it is taking periodical doses of mercury sublimate, and swallowing down repeated provocatives of cantharides to our love of liberty."

I say that is extravagant prose; prose too much suf-

fered to indulge its caprices; prose at too great a distance
from the centre of good taste; prose, in short, with the
note of provinciality. People may reply, it is rich and imaginative; yes, that is just it, it is *Asiatic* prose, as the
ancient critics would have said; prose somewhat barbarously rich and over-loaded. But the true prose is Attic
prose.

Well, but Addison's prose is Attic prose. Where, then,
it may be asked, is the note of provinciality in Addison?
I answer, in the commonplace of his ideas.[1] This is a
matter worth remarking. Addison claims to take leading
rank as a moralist. To do that, you must have ideas of
the first order on your subject—the best ideas, at any
rate, attainable in your time—as well as be able to express them in a perfectly sound and sure style. Else you
show your distance from the centre of ideas by your
matter; you are provincial by your matter, though you
may not be provincial by your style. It is comparatively
a small matter to express oneself well, if one will be
content with not expressing much, with expressing only
trite ideas; the problem is to express new and profound
ideas in a perfectly sound and classical style. He is the
true classic, in every age, who does that. Now Addison
has not, on his subject of morals, the force of ideas of
the moralists of the first class—the classical moralists;

[1] A critic says this is paradoxical, and urges that many second-rate
French academicians have uttered the most commonplace ideas possible; but Addison is not a second-rate man. He is a man of the order,
I will not say of Pascal, but at any rate of La Bruyère and Vauvenargues; why does he not equal them? I say because of the medium
in which he finds himself, the atmosphere in which he lives and
works; an atmosphere which tells unfavourably, or rather *tends* to tell
unfavourably (for that is the truer way of putting it) either upon
style or else upon ideas; tends to make even a man of great ability
either a Mr. Carlyle or else a Lord Macaulay.

It is to be observed, however, that Lord Macaulay's style has in
its turn suffered by his failure in ideas, and this cannot be said of
Addison's. (*Arnold's note.*)

he has not the best ideas attainable in or about his time, and which were, so to speak, in the air then, to be seized by the finest spirits; he is not to be compared for power, searchingness, or delicacy of thought to Pascal or La Bruyère or Vauvenargues; he is rather on a level, in this respect, with a man like Marmontel; therefore, I say, he has the note of provinciality as a moralist; he is provincial by his matter, though not by his style.

To illustrate what I mean by an example. Addison, writing as a moralist on fixedness in religious faith, says:

"Those who delight in reading books of controversy do very seldom arrive at a fixed and settled habit of faith. The doubt which was laid revives again, and shows itself in new difficulties; and that generally for this reason,—because the mind, which is perpetually tossed in controversies and disputes, is apt to forget the reasons which had once set it at rest, and to be disquieted with any former perplexity when it appears in a new shape, or is started by a different hand."

It may be said, that is classical English, perfect in lucidity, measure, and propriety. I make no objection; but, in my turn, I say that the idea expressed is perfectly trite and barren, and that it is a note of provinciality in Addison, in a man whom a nation puts forward as one of its great moralists, to have no profounder and more striking idea to produce on this great subject. Compare, on the same subject, these words of a moralist really of the first order, really at the centre by his ideas,—Joubert:

"L'expérience de beaucoup d'opinions donne à l'esprit beaucoup de flexibilité et l'affermit dans celles qu'il croit les meilleures."

With what a flash of light that touches the subject! how it sets us thinking! what a genuine contribution to moral science it is!

In short, where there is no centre like an academy,

if you have genius and powerful ideas, you are apt not to have the best style going; if you have precision of style and not a genius, you are apt not to have the best ideas going.

The provincial spirit, again, exaggerates the value of its ideas for want of a high standard at hand by which to try them. Or rather, for want of such a standard, it gives one idea too much prominence at the expense of others; it orders its ideas amiss; it is hurried away by fancies; it likes and dislikes too passionately, too exclusively. Its admiration weeps hysterical tears, and its disapprobation foams at the mouth. So we get the *eruptive* and the *aggressive* manner in literature; the former prevails most in our criticism, the latter in our newspapers. For, not having the lucidity of a large and centrally placed intelligence, the provincial spirit has not its graciousness; it does not persuade, it makes war; it has not urbanity, the tone of the city, of the centre, the tone which always aims at a spiritual and intellectual effect, and not excluding the use of banter, never disjoins banter itself from politeness, from felicity. But the provincial tone is more violent, and seems to aim rather at an effect upon the blood and senses than upon the spirit and intellect; it loves hard hitting rather than persuading. The newspaper, with its party spirit, its thorough-goingness, its resolute avoidance of shades and distinctions, its short, highly charged, heavy-shotted articles, its style so unlike that style *lenis minimeque pertinax*—easy and not too violently insisting,—which the ancients so much admired, is its true literature; the provincial spirit likes in the newspaper just what makes the newspaper such bad food for it,—just what made Goethe say, when he was pressed hard about the immorality of Byron's poems, that, after all, they were not so immoral as the newspapers. The French talk of the *brutalité des jour-*

naux anglais. What strikes them comes from the necessary inherent tendencies of newspaper-writing not being
checked in England by any centre of intelligent and ur-
bane spirit, but rather stimulated by coming in contact
with a provincial spirit. Even a newspaper like the *Saturday Review,* that old friend of all of us, a newspaper
expressly aiming at an immunity from the common
newspaper-spirit, aiming at being a sort of organ of
reason,—and, by thus aiming, it merits great gratitude
and has done great good,—even the *Saturday Review,*
replying to some foreign criticism on our precautions
against invasion, falls into a strain of this kind:

"To do this" (to take these precautions) "seems to
us eminently worthy of a great nation, and to talk of it
as unworthy of a great nation, seems to us eminently
worthy of a great fool."

There is what the French mean when they talk of
the *brutalité des journaux anglais;* there is a style certainly as far removed from urbanity as possible,—a style
with what I call the note of provinciality. And the same
note may not unfrequently be observed even in the ideas
of this newspaper, full as it is of thought and cleverness:
certain ideas allowed to become fixed ideas, to prevail
too absolutely. I will not speak of the immediate present, but, to go a little while back, it had the critic who
so disliked the Emperor of the French; it had the critic
who so disliked the subject of my present remarks—
academies; it had the critic who was so fond of the German element in our nation, and, indeed, everywhere;
who ground his teeth if one said *Charlemagne* instead of
Charles the Great, and, in short, saw all things in Teu-
tonism, as Malebranche saw all things in God. Certainly
any one may fairly find faults in the Emperor Napoleon
or in academies, and merit in the German element; but
it is a note of the provincial spirit not to hold ideas of

this kind a little more easily, to be so devoured by them, to suffer them to become crotchets.

In England there needs a miracle of genius like Shakespeare's to produce balance of mind, and a miracle of intellectual delicacy like Dr. Newman's to produce urbanity of style. How prevalent all round us is the want of balance of mind and urbanity of style! How much, doubtless, it is to be found in ourselves,—in each of us! but, as human nature is constituted, every one can see it clearest in his contemporaries. There, above all, we should consider it, because they and we are exposed to the same influences; and it is in the best of one's contemporaries that it is most worth considering, because one then most feels the harm it does, when one sees what they would be without it. Think of the difference between Mr. Ruskin exercising his genius, and Mr. Ruskin exercising his intelligence; consider the truth and beauty of this:

"Go out, in the spring-time, among the meadows that slope from the shores of the Swiss lakes to the roots of their lower mountains. There, mingled with the taller gentians and the white narcissus, the grass grows deep and free; and as you follow the winding mountain paths, beneath arching boughs all veiled and dim with blossom, —paths that for ever droop and rise over the green banks and mounds sweeping down in scented undulation, steep to the blue water, studded here and there with new-mown heaps, filling all the air with fainter sweetness,—look up towards the higher hills, where the waves of everlasting green roll silently into their long inlets among the shadows of the pines. . . ."

There is what the genius, the feeling, the temperament in Mr. Ruskin, the original and incommunicable part, has to do with; and how exquisite it is! All the critic could possibly suggest, in the way of objection, would be, perhaps, that Mr. Ruskin is there trying to make prose do more than it can perfectly do; that what he is there attempting he will never, except in poetry, be able to accomplish to his own entire satisfaction: but he accomplishes so much that the critic may well hesitate to suggest even this. Place beside this charming passage another,—a passage about Shakespeare's names, where the intelligence and judgment of Mr. Ruskin, the acquired, trained, communicable part in him, are brought into play,—and see the difference:

"Of Shakespeare's names I will afterwards speak at more length; they are curiously—often barbarously— mixed out of various traditions and languages. Three of the clearest in meaning have been already noticed. Desdemona—'δυσδαιμονία,' *miserable fortune*—is also plain enough. Othello is, I believe, 'the careful'; all the calamity of the tragedy arising from the single flaw and error in his magnificently collected strength. Ophelia, 'serviceableness,' the true, lost wife of Hamlet, is marked as having a Greek name by that of her brother, Laertes; and its signification is once exquisitely alluded to in that brother's last word of her, where her gentle preciousness is opposed to the uselessness of the churlish clergy:—'A *ministering* angel shall my sister be, when thou liest howling.' Hamlet is, I believe, connected in some way with 'homely,' the entire event of the tragedy turning on betrayal of home duty. Hermione (ἔρμα), 'pillar-like' (ἥ εἶδος ἔχε χρυσῆς Ἀφρδίη); Titania (τιτήνη), 'the queen'; Benedick and Beatrice, 'blessed and blessing'; Valentine and Proteus, 'enduring or strong' (*valens*), and 'changeful.' Iago and Iachimo have evidently the same root—probably the Spanish Iago, Jacob, 'the supplanter.'

Now, really, what a piece of extravagance all that is! I will not say that the meaning of Shakespeare's names

(I put aside the question as to the correctness of Mr. Ruskin's etymologies) has no effect at all, may be entirely lost sight of; but to give it that degree of prominence is to throw the reins to one's whim, to forget all moderation and proportion, to lose the balance of one's mind altogether. It is to show in one's criticism, to the highest excess, the note of provinciality.

Again, there is Mr. Palgrave, certainly endowed with a very fine critical tact: his *Golden Treasury* abundantly proves it. The plan of arrangement which he devised for that work, the mode in which he followed his plan out, nay, one might even say, merely the juxtaposition, in pursuance of it, of two such pieces as those of Wordsworth and Shelley which form the 285th and 286th in his collection, show a delicacy of feeling in these matters which is quite indisputable and very rare. And his notes are full of remarks which show it too. All the more striking, conjoined with so much justness of perception, are certain freaks and violences in Mr. Palgrave's criticism, mainly imputable, I think, to the critic's isolated position in this country, to his feeling himself too much left to take his own way, too much without any central authority representing high culture and sound judgment, by which he may be, on the one hand, confirmed as against the ignorant, on the other, held in respect when he himself is inclined to take liberties. I mean such things as this note on Milton's line,

The great Emathian conqueror bade spare . . .

"When Thebes was destroyed, Alexander ordered the house of Pindar to be spared. *He was as incapable of appreciating the poet as Louis XIV of appreciating Racine; but even the narrow and barbarian mind of Alexander could understand the advantage of a showy act of homage to poetry."* A note like that I call a freak or a violence; if this disparaging view of Alexander and Louis XIV, so unlike the current view, is wrong,—if the current view is, after all, the truer one of them,—the note is a freak. But, even if its disparaging view is right, the note is a violence; for abandoning the true mode of intellectual action—persuasion, the instilment of conviction,—it simply astounds and irritates the hearer by contradicting without a word of proof or preparation, his fixed and familiar notions; and this is mere violence. In either case, the fitness, the measure, the centrality, which is the soul of all good criticism, is lost, and the note of provinciality shows itself.

Thus, in the famous *Handbook*, marks of a fine power of perception are everywhere discernible, but so, too, are marks of the want of sure balance, of the check and support afforded by knowing one speaks before good and severe judges. When Mr. Palgrave dislikes a thing, he feels no pressure constraining him either to try his dislike closely or to express it moderately; he does not mince matters, he gives his dislike all its own way; both his judgment and his style would gain if he were under more restraint. "The style which has filled London with the dead monotony of Gower or Harley Streets, or the pale commonplace of Belgravia, Tyburnia, and Kensington; which has pierced Paris and Madrid with the feeble frivolities of the Rue Rivoli and the Strada de Toledo." He dislikes the architecture of the Rue Rivoli, and he puts it on a level with the architecture of Belgravia and Gower Street; he lumps them all together in one condemnation, he loses sight of the shade, the distinction, which is everything here; the distinction, namely, that the architecture of the Rue Rivoli expresses show, splendour, pleasure,—unworthy things, perhaps, to express alone and for their own sakes, but it expresses them;

whereas the architecture of Gower Street and Belgravia merely expresses the impotence of the architect to express anything. Then, as to style: "sculpture which stands in a contrast with Woolner hardly more shameful than diverting." . . . "passing from Davy or Faraday to the art of the mountebank or the science of the spirit-rapper." . . . "it is the old, old story with Marochetti, the frog trying to blow himself out to bull dimensions. He may puff and be puffed, but he will never do it." We all remember that shower of amenities on poor M. Marochetti. Now, here Mr. Palgrave himself enables us to form a contrast which lets us see just what the presence of an academy does for style; for he quotes a criticism by M. Gustave Planche on this very M. Marochetti. M. Gustave Planche was a critic of the very first order, a man of strong opinions, which he expressed with severity; he, too, condemns M. Marochetti's work, and Mr. Palgrave calls him as a witness to back what he has himself said; certainly Mr. Palgrave's translation will not exaggerate M. Planche's urbanity in dealing with M. Marochetti, but, even in this translation, see the difference in sobriety, in measure, between the critic writing in Paris and the critic writing in London:

"These conditions are so elementary, that I am at a perfect loss to comprehend how M. Marochetti has neglected them. There are soldiers here like the leaden playthings of the nursery: it is almost impossible to guess whether there is a body beneath the dress. We have here no question of style, not even of grammar; it is nothing beyond mere matter of the alphabet of art. To break these conditions is the same as to be ignorant of spelling."

That is really more formidable criticism than Mr. Palgrave's, and yet in how perfectly temperate a style! M. Planche's advantage is, that he feels himself to be speaking before competent judges, that there is a force of cultivated opinion for him to appeal to. Therefore, he must not be extravagant, and he need not storm; he must satisfy the reason and taste,—that is his business. Mr. Palgrave, on the other hand, feels himself to be speaking before a promiscuous multitude, with the few good judges so scattered through it as to be powerless; therefore, he has no calm confidence and no self-control; he relies on the strength of his lungs; he knows that big words impose on the mob, and that, even if he is outrageous, most of his audience are apt to be a great deal more so.[1]

Again, the first two volumes of Mr. Kinglake's *Invasion of the Crimea* were certainly among the most successful and renowned English books of our time. Their style was one of the most renowned things about them, and yet how conspicuous a fault in Mr. Kinglake's style is this overcharge of which I have been speaking! Mr. James Gordon Bennett, of the *New York Herald,* says, I believe, that the highest achievement of the human intellect is what he calls "a good editorial." This is not quite so; but, if it were so, on what a height would these two volumes by Mr. Kinglake stand! I have already spoken of the Attic and the Asiatic styles; besides these, there is the Corinthian style. That is the style for "a good editorial," and Mr. Kinglake has really reached perfection in it. It has not the warm glow, blithe movement, and soft pliancy of life, as the Attic style has; it has not the over-heavy richness and encumbered gait of the Asiatic style; it has glitter without warmth, rapidity without ease, effectiveness without charm. Its characteristic is, that it has no *soul;* all it exists for, is to get

[1] When I wrote this I had before me the first edition of Mr. Palgrave's *Handbook.* I am bound to say that in the second edition much strong language has been expunged, and what remains, softened. (Arnold's note.)

its ends, to make its points, to damage its adversaries,
to be admired, to triumph. A style so bent on effect at
the expense of soul, simplicity, and delicacy; a style so
little studious of the charm of the great models; so far
from classic truth and grace, must surely be said to have
the note of provinciality. Yet Mr. Kinglake's talent is a
really eminent one, and so in harmony with our intellectual habits and tendencies, that, to the great bulk of
English people, the faults of his style seem its merits;
all the more needful that criticism should not be dazzled
by them.

We must not compare a man of Mr. Kinglake's literary
talent with French writers like M. de Bazancourt. We
must compare him with M. Thiers. And what a superiority in style has M. Thiers from being formed in a good
school, with severe traditions, wholesome restraining
influences! Even in this age of Mr. James Gordon Bennett, his style has nothing Corinthian about it, its lightness and brightness make it almost Attic. It is not quite
Attic, however; it has not the infallible sureness of Attic
taste. Sometimes his head gets a little hot with the fumes
of patriotism, and then he crosses the line, he loses perfect measure, he declaims, he raises a momentary smile.
France condemned "à être l'effroi du monde *dont elle
pourrait être l'amour*,"—Cæsar, whose exquisite simplicity M. Thiers so much admires, would not have
written like that. There is, if I may be allowed to say so,
the slightest possible touch of fatuity in such language,
—of that failure in good sense which comes from too
warm a self-satisfaction. But compare this language
with Mr. Kinglake's Marshal St. Arnaud—"dismissed
from the presence" of Lord Raglan or Lord Stratford,
"cowed and pressed down" under their "stern reproofs,"
or under "the majesty of the great Elchi's Canning brow
and tight, merciless lips!" The failure in good sense and

good taste there reaches far beyond what the French mean by *fatuity*; they would call it by another word, a word expressing blank defect of intelligence, a word for which we have no exact equivalent in English,—*bête*. It is the difference between a venial, momentary, good-tempered excess, in a man of the world, of an amiable and social weakness,—vanity; and a serious, settled, fierce, narrow, provincial misconception of the whole relative value of one's own things and the things of others. So baneful to the style of even the cleverest man may be the total want of checks.

In all I have said, I do not pretend that the examples given prove my rule as to the influence of academies; they only illustrate it. Examples in plenty might very likely be found to set against them; the truth of the rule depends, no doubt, on whether the balance of all the examples is in its favour or not; but actually to strike this balance is always out of the question. Here, as everywhere else, the rule, the idea, if true, commends itself to the judicious, and then the examples make it clearer still to them. This is the real use of examples, and this alone is the purpose which I have meant mine to serve. There is also another side to the whole question, —as to the limiting and prejudicial operation which academies may have; but this side of the question it rather behoves the French, not us, to study.

The reader will ask for some practical conclusion about the establishment of an Academy in this country, and perhaps I shall hardly give him the one he expects. But nations have their own modes of acting, and these modes are not easily changed; they are even consecrated, when great things have been done in them. When a literature has produced Shakespeare and Milton, when it has even produced Barrow and Burke, it cannot well abandon its traditions; it can hardly begin, at this late time of day, with an institution like the French Academy. I think academies with a limited, special, scientific scope, in the various lines of intellectual work,—academies like that of Berlin, for instance,—we with time may, and probably shall, establish. And no doubt they will do good; no doubt the presence of such influential centres of correct information will tend to raise the standard amongst us for what I have called the *journeyman-work* of literature, and to free us from the scandal of such biographical dictionaries as Chalmers's, or such translations as a recent one of Spinoza, or perhaps, such philological freaks as Mr. Forster's about the one primeval language. But an academy quite like the French Academy, a sovereign organ of the highest literary opinion, a recognised authority in matters of intellectual tone and taste, we shall hardly have, and perhaps we ought not to wish to have it. But then every one amongst us with any turn for literature will do well to remember to what shortcomings and excesses, which such an academy tends to correct, we are liable; and the more liable, of course, for not having it. He will do well constantly to try himself in respect of these, steadily to widen his culture, severely to check in himself the provincial spirit; and he will do this the better the more he keeps in mind that all mere glorification by ourselves of ourselves, or our literature, in the strain of what, at the beginning of these remarks, I quoted from Lord Macaulay, is both vulgar, and, besides being vulgar, retarding.

○

THE STUDY OF POETRY

○

"THE FUTURE of poetry is immense, because in poetry, where it is worthy of its high destinies, our race, as time goes on, will find an ever surer and surer stay. There is not a creed which is not shaken, not an accredited dogma which is not shown to be questionable, not a received tradition which does not threaten to dissolve. Our religion has materialised itself in the fact, in the supposed fact; it has attached its emotion to the fact, and now the fact is failing it. But for poetry the idea is everything; the rest is a world of illusion, of divine illusion. Poetry attaches its emotion to the idea; the idea *is* the fact. The strongest part of our religion to-day is its unconscious poetry."

Let me be permitted to quote these words of my own, as uttering the thought which should, in my opinion, go with us and govern us in all our study of poetry. In the present work it is the course of one great contributory stream to the world-river of poetry that we are invited to follow. We are here invited to trace the stream of English poetry. But whether we set ourselves, as here, to follow only one of the several streams that make the mighty river of poetry, or whether we seek to know them all, our governing thought should be the same. We should conceive of poetry worthily, and more highly than it has been the custom to conceive of it. We should conceive of it as capable of higher uses, and called to higher destinies, than those which in general men have assigned to it hitherto. More and more mankind will discover that we have to turn to poetry to interpret life for us, to console us, to sustain us. Without poetry, our science will appear incomplete; and most of what now passes with us for religion and philosophy will be replaced by poetry. Science, I say, will appear incomplete without it. For finely and truly does Wordsworth call poetry "the impassioned expression which is in the countenance of all science"; and what is a countenance without its expression? Again, Wordsworth finely and truly calls poetry "the breath and finer spirit of all knowledge": our religion, parading evidences such as those on which the popular mind relies now; our philosophy, pluming itself on its reasonings about causation and finite and infinite being; what are they but the shadows and dreams and false shows of knowledge? The day will come when we shall wonder at ourselves for having trusted to them, for having taken them seriously; and the more we perceive their hollowness, the more we shall prize "the breath and finer spirit of knowledge" offered to us by poetry.

But if we conceive thus highly of the destinies of poetry, we must also set our standard for poetry high, since poetry, to be capable of fulfilling such high destinies, must be poetry of a high order of excellence. We must accustom ourselves to a high standard and to a strict judgment. Sainte-Beuve relates that Napoleon one day said, when somebody was spoken of in his presence as a charlatan: "Charlatan as much as you please; but where is there *not* charlatanism?"—"Yes," answers Sainte-Beuve, "in politics, in the art of governing mankind, that is perhaps true. But in the order of thought, in art, the glory, the eternal honour is that charlatanism shall find no entrance; herein lies the inviolableness of that noble portion of man's being." It is admirably said, and let us hold fast to it. In poetry, which is thought and art in one, it is the glory, the eternal honour, that charlatanism shall find no entrance; that this noble sphere be kept inviolate and inviolable. Charlatanism is for confusing or obliterating the distinctions between excellent and inferior, sound and unsound or only half-sound, true and untrue or only half-true. It is charlatanism, conscious or unconscious, whenever we confuse or obliterate these. And in poetry, more than anywhere else, it is unpermissible to confuse or obliterate them. For in poetry the distinction between excellent and inferior, sound and unsound or only half-sound, true and untrue or only half-true, is of paramount importance. It is of paramount importance because of the high destinies of poetry. In poetry, as a criticism of life under the conditions fixed for such a criticism by the laws of poetic truth and poetic beauty, the spirit of our race will find, we have said, as time goes on and as other helps fail, its consolation and stay. But the consolation and stay will be of power in proportion to the power of the criticism of life. And the criticism of life will be of power in proportion as the poetry conveying it is excellent rather than inferior, sound rather than unsound or half-sound, true rather than untrue or half-true.

The best poetry is what we want; the best poetry will be found to have a power of forming, sustaining, and delighting us, as nothing else can. A clearer, deeper sense of the best in poetry, and of the strength and joy to be drawn from it, is the most precious benefit which we can gather from a poetical collection such as the present. And yet in the very nature and conduct of such a collection there is inevitably something which tends to obscure in us the consciousness of what our benefit should be, and to distract us from the pursuit of it. We should therefore steadily set it before our minds at the outset, and should compel ourselves to revert constantly to the thought of it as we proceed.

Yes; constantly in reading poetry, a sense for the best, the really excellent, and of the strength and joy to be drawn from it, should be present in our minds and should govern our estimate of what we read. But this real estimate, the only true one, is liable to be superseded, if we are not watchful, by two other kinds of estimate, the historic estimate and the personal estimate, both of which are fallacious. A poet or a poem may count to us historically, they may count to us on grounds personal to ourselves, and they may count to us really. They may count to us historically. The course of development of a nation's language, thought, and poetry, is profoundly interesting; and by regarding a poet's work as a stage in this course of development we may easily bring ourselves to make it of more importance as poetry than in itself it really is, we may come to use a language of quite exaggerated praise in criticising it; in short, to over-rate it. So arises in our poetic judgments the fallacy caused by the estimate which we may call historic. Then, again, a poet or a poem may count to us on grounds personal to ourselves. Our personal affinities, likings, and circumstances, have great power to sway our estimate of this or that poet's work, and to make us attach more importance to it as poetry than in itself it really possesses, because to us it is, or has been, of high importance. Here also we over-rate the object of our interest, and apply to it a language of praise which is quite exaggerated. And thus we get the source of a second fallacy in our poetic judgments—the fallacy caused by an estimate which we may call personal.

Both fallacies are natural. It is evident how naturally

the study of the history and development of a poetry
may incline a man to pause over reputations and works
once conspicuous but now obscure, and to quarrel with
a careless public for skipping, in obedience to mere tradition and habit, from one famous name or work in its
national poetry to another, ignorant of what it misses,
and of the reason for keeping what it keeps, and of the
whole process of growth in its poetry. The French have
become diligent students of their own early poetry,
which they long neglected; the study makes many of
them dissatisfied with their so-called classical poetry, the
court-tragedy of the seventeenth century, a poetry which
Pellisson long ago reproached with its want of the true
poetic stamp, with its *politesse stérile et rampante,* but
which nevertheless has reigned in France as absolutely
as if it had been the perfection of classical poetry indeed. The dissatisfaction is natural; yet a lively and accomplished critic, M. Charles d'Héricault, the editor of
Clément Marot, goes too far when he says that "the
cloud of glory playing round a classic is a mist as dangerous to the future of a literature as it is intolerable
for the purposes of history." "It hinders," he goes on,
"it hinders us from seeing more than one single point,
the culminating and exceptional point; the summary,
fictitious and arbitrary, of a thought and of a work. It
substitutes a halo for a physiognomy, it puts a statue
where there was once a man, and hiding from us all
trace of the labour, the attempts, the weaknesses, the
failures, it claims not study but veneration; it does not
show us how the thing is done, it imposes upon us a
model. Above all, for the historian this creation of classic
personages is inadmissible; for it withdraws the poet
from his time, from his proper life, it breaks historical relationships, it blinds criticism by conventional admiration, and renders the investigation of literary origins un-

acceptable. It gives us a human personage no longer, but a God seated immovable amidst His perfect work, like Jupiter on Olympus; and hardly will it be possible for the young student, to whom such work is exhibited at such a distance from him, to believe that it did not issue ready made from that divine head."

All this is brilliantly and tellingly said, but we must plead for a distinction. Everything depends on the reality of a poet's classic character. If he is a dubious classic, let us sift him; if he is a false classic, let us explode him. But if he is a real classic, if his work belongs to the class of the very best (for this is the true and right meaning of the word *classic, classical*), then the great thing for us is to feel and enjoy his work as deeply as ever we can, and to appreciate the wide difference between it and all work which has not the same high character. This is what is salutary, this is what is formative; this is the great benefit to be got from the study of poetry. Everything which interferes with it, which hinders it, is injurious. True, we must read our classic with open eyes, and not with eyes blinded with superstition; we must perceive when his work comes short, when it drops out of the class of the very best, and we must rate it, in such cases, at its proper value. But the use of this negative criticism is not in itself, it is entirely in its enabling us to have a clearer sense and a deeper enjoyment of what is truly excellent. To trace the labour, the attempts, the weaknesses, the failures of a genuine classic, to acquaint oneself with his time and his life and his historical relationships, is mere literary dilettantism unless it has that clear sense and deeper enjoyment for its end. It may be said that the more we know about a classic the better we shall enjoy him; and, if we lived as long as Methuselah and had all of us heads of perfect clearness and wills of perfect steadfastness, this might be true in fact as it is plausible in theory. But the case here is much the same as the case with the Greek and Latin studies of our schoolboys. The elaborate philological groundwork which we require them to lay is in theory an admirable preparation for appreciating the Greek and Latin authors worthily. The more thoroughly we lay the groundwork, the better we shall be able, it may be said, to enjoy the authors. True, if time were not so short, and schoolboys' wits not so soon tired and their power of attention exhausted; only, as it is, the elaborate philological preparation goes on, but the authors are little known and less enjoyed. So with the investigator of "historic origins" in poetry. He ought to enjoy the true classic all the better for his investigations; he often is distracted from the enjoyment of the best, and with the less good he overbusies himself, and is prone to over-rate it in proportion to the trouble which it has cost him.

The idea of tracing historic origins and historical relationships cannot be absent from a compilation like the present. And naturally the poets to be exhibited in it will be assigned to those persons for exhibition who are known to prize them highly, rather than to those who have no special inclination towards them. Moreover the very occupation with an author, and the business of exhibiting him, disposes us to affirm and amplify his importance. In the present work, therefore, we are sure of frequent temptation to adopt the historic estimate, or the personal estimate, and to forget the real estimate; which latter, nevertheless, we must employ if we are to make poetry yield us its full benefit. So high is that benefit, the benefit of clearly feeling and of deeply enjoying the really excellent, the truly classic in poetry, that we do well, I say, to set it fixedly before our minds as our object in studying poets and poetry, and to make the desire of attaining it the one principle to which, as the *Imitation* says, whatever we may read or come to know, we always return. *Cum multa legeris et cognoveris, ad unum semper oportet redire principium.*

The historic estimate is likely in especial to affect our judgment and our language when we are dealing with ancient poets; the personal estimate when we are dealing with poets our contemporaries, or at any rate modern. The exaggerations due to the historic estimate are not in themselves, perhaps, of very much gravity. Their report hardly enters the general ear; probably they do not always impose even on the literary men who adopt them. But they lead to a dangerous abuse of language. So we hear Cædmon, amongst our own poets, compared to Milton. I have already noticed the enthusiasm of one accomplished French critic for "historic origins." Another eminent French critic, M. Vitet, comments upon that famous document of the early poetry of his nation, the *Chanson de Roland*. It is indeed a most interesting document. The *joculator* or *jongleur* Taillefer, who was with William the Conqueror's army at Hastings, marched before the Norman troops, so said the tradition, singing "of Charlemagne and of Roland and of Oliver, and of the vassals who died at Roncevaux"; and it is suggested that in the *Chanson de Roland* by one Turoldus or Théroulde, a poem preserved in a manuscript of the twelfth century in the Bodleian Library at Oxford, we have certainly the matter, perhaps even some of the words, of the chant which Taillefer sang. The poem has vigour and freshness; it is not without pathos. But M. Vitet is not satisfied with seeing in it a document of some poetic value, and of very high historic and linguistic value; he sees in it a grand and beautiful work, a monument of epic genius. In its general design he finds the grandiose conception, in its details he finds the constant

union of simplicity with greatness, which are the marks,
he truly says, of the genuine epic, and distinguish it
from the artificial epic of literary ages. One thinks of
Homer; this is the sort of praise which is given to
Homer, and justly given. Higher praise there cannot well
be, and it is the praise due to epic poetry of the highest
order only, and to no other. Let us try, then, the *Chanson de Roland* at its best. Roland, mortally wounded,
lays himself down under a pine-tree, with his face
turned towards Spain and the enemy—

> De plusurs choses à remembrer li prist,
> De tantes teres cume li bers cunquist,
> De dulce France, des humes de sun lign,
> De Charlemagne sun seignor ki l'nurrit.[1]

That is primitive work, I repeat, with an undeniable
poetic quality of its own. It deserves such praise, and
such praise is sufficient for it. But now turn to Homer—

> Ὥς φάτο· τοὺς δ᾽ ἤδη κατέχεν φυσίζοος αἶα
> ἐν Λακεδαίμονι αὖθι, φίλῃ ἐν πατρίδι γαίῃ.[2]

We are here in another world, another order of poetry
altogether; here is rightly due such supreme praise as
that which M. Vitet gives to the *Chanson de Roland*.
If our words are to have any meaning, if our judgments
are to have any solidity, we must not heap that supreme
praise upon poetry of an order immeasurably inferior.

Indeed there can be no more useful help for discovering what poetry belongs to the class of the truly excel-

---

[1] "Then began he to call many things to remembrance,—all the
lands which his valour conquered, and pleasant France, and the men
of his lineage, and Charlemagne his liege lord who nourished him."
—*Chanson de Roland*, iii, 939-42. (Arnold's note.)

[2] So said she; they long since in Earth's soft arms were reposing,
There, in their own dear land, their fatherland, Lacedæmon.
Iliad, iii, 243, 244 (translated by Dr. Hawtrey).
(Arnold's note.)

lent, and can therefore do us most good, than to have always in one's mind lines and expressions of the great masters, and to apply them as a touchstone to other poetry. Of course we are not to require this other poetry to resemble them; it may be very dissimilar. But if we have any tact we shall find them, when we have lodged them well in our minds, an infallible touchstone for detecting the presence or absence of high poetic quality, and also the degree of this quality, in all other poetry which we may place beside them. Short passages, even single lines, will serve our turn quite sufficiently. Take the two lines which I have just quoted from Homer, the poet's comment on Helen's mention of her brothers;—or take his

> Ἄ δειλώ, τί σφῶϊ δόμεν Πηλῆϊ ἄνακτι
> θνητᾷ; ὑμεῖς δ' ἐστὸν ἀγήρω τ' ἀθανάτω τε.
> ἤ ἵνα δυστήνοισι μετ' ἀνδράσιν ἄλγε ἔχητον;[1]

the address of Zeus to the horses of Peleus;—or take finally his

> Καὶ σέ, γέρον, τὸ πρὶν μὲν ἀκούομεν ὄλβιον εἶναι·[2]

the words of Achilles to Priam, a suppliant before him. Take that incomparable line and a half of Dante, Ugolino's tremendous words—

> Io no piangeva; sì dentro impietrai.
> Piangevan elli . . .[3]

take the lovely words of Beatrice to Virgil—

> Io son fatta da Dio, sua mercè, tale,

---

[1] Ah, unhappy pair, why gave we you to King Peleus, to a mortal? but ye are without old age, and immortal. Was it that with men born to misery ye might have sorrow?—*Iliad*, xvii, 443-45. (*Arnold's note.*)

[2] "Nay, and thou too, old man, in former days wast, as we hear, happy."—*Iliad*, xxiv, 543. (*Arnold's note.*)

[3] "I wailed not, so of stone grew I within;—they wailed."—*Inferno*, xxxiii, 39, 40. (*Arnold's note.*)

Che la vostra miseria non mi tange,
Nè fiamma d'esto incendio non m'assale . . .[1]

take the simple, but perfect, single line—

In la sua volontade è nostra pace.[2]

Take of Shakespeare a line or two of Henry the Fourth's
expostulation with sleep—

Wilt thou upon the high and giddy mast
Seal up the ship-boy's eyes, and rock his brains
In cradle of the rude imperious surge . . .

and take, as well, Hamlet's dying request to Horatio—

If thou didst ever hold me in thy heart,
Absent thee from felicity awhile,
And in this harsh world draw thy breath in pain
To tell my story . . .

Take of Milton that Miltonic passage—

Darken'd so, yet shone
Above them all the archangel; but his face
Deep scars of thunder had intrench'd, and care
Sat on his faded cheek . . .

add two such lines as—

And courage never to submit or yield
And what is else not to be overcome . . .

and finish with the exquisite close to the loss of Proserpine, the loss

. . . which cost Ceres all that pain
To seek her through the world.

[1] "Of such sort hath God, thanked be His mercy, made me, that
your misery toucheth me not, neither doth the flame of this fire
strike me."—*Inferno*, ii, 91-93. (*Arnold's note.*)
[2] "In His will is our peace."—*Paradiso*, iii, 85. (*Arnold's note.*)

These few lines, if we have tact and can use them, are enough even of themselves to keep clear and sound our judgments about poetry, to save us from fallacious estimates of it, to conduct us to a real estimate.

The specimens I have quoted differ widely from one another, but they have in common this: the possession of the very highest poetical quality. If we are thoroughly penetrated by their power, we shall find that we have acquired a sense enabling us, whatever poetry may be laid before us, to feel the degree in which a high poetical quality is present or wanting there. Critics give themselves great labour to draw out what in the abstract constitutes the characters of a high quality of poetry. It is much better simply to have recourse to concrete examples;—to take specimens of poetry of the high, the very highest quality, and to say: The characters of a high quality of poetry are what is expressed *there*. They are far better recognised by being felt in the verse of the master, than by being perused in the prose of the critic. Nevertheless if we are urgently pressed to give some critical account of them, we may safely, perhaps, venture on laying down, not indeed how and why the characters arise, but where and in what they arise. They are in the matter and substance of the poetry, and they are in its manner and style. Both of these, the substance and matter on the one hand, the style and manner on the other, have a mark, an accent, of high beauty, worth, and power. But if we are asked to define this mark and accent in the abstract, our answer must be: No, for we should thereby be darkening the question, not clearing it. The mark and accent are as given by the substance and matter of that poetry, by the style and manner of that poetry, and of all other poetry which is akin to it in quality.

Only one thing we may add as to the substance and

matter of poetry, guiding ourselves by Aristotle's profound observation that the superiority of poetry over history consists in its possessing a higher truth and a higher seriousness (φιλοσοφώτερον καὶ σπουδαιότερον). Let us add, therefore, to what we have said, this: that the substance and matter of the best poetry acquire their special character from possessing, in an eminent degree, truth and seriousness. We may add yet further, what is in itself evident, that to the style and manner of the best poetry their special character, their accent, is given by their diction, and, even yet more, by their movement. And though we distinguish between the two characters, the two accents, of superiority, yet they are nevertheless vitally connected one with the other. The superior character of truth and seriousness, in the matter and substance of the best poetry, is inseparable from the superiority of diction and movement marking its style and manner. The two superiorities are closely related, and are in steadfast proportion one to the other. So far as high poetic truth and seriousness are wanting to a poet's matter and substance, so far also, we may be sure, will a high poetic stamp of diction and movement be wanting to his style and manner. In proportion as this high stamp of diction and movement, again, is absent from a poet's style and manner, we shall find, also, that high poetic truth and seriousness are absent from his substance and matter.

So stated, these are but dry generalities; their whole force lies in their application. And I could wish every student of poetry to make the application of them for himself. Made by himself, the application would impress itself upon his mind far more deeply than made by me. Neither will my limits allow me to make any full application of the generalities above propounded; but in the hope of bringing out, at any rate, some significance in them, and of establishing an important principle more firmly by their means, I will, in the space which remains to me, follow rapidly from the commencement the course of our English poetry with them in my view.

Once more I return to the early poetry of France, with which our own poetry, in its origins, is indissolubly connected. In the twelfth and thirteenth centuries, that seed-time of all modern language and literature, the poetry of France had a clear predominance in Europe. Of the two divisions of that poetry, its productions in the *langue d'oil* and its productions in the *langue d'oc,* the poetry of the *langue d'oc,* of southern France, of the troubadours, is of importance because of its effect on Italian literature;—the first literature of modern Europe to strike the true and grand note, and to bring forth, as in Dante and Petrarch it brought forth, classics. But the predominance of French poetry in Europe, during the twelfth and thirteenth centuries, is due to its poetry of the *langue d'oil,* the poetry of northern France and of the tongue which is now the French language. In the twelfth century the bloom of this romance-poetry was earlier and stronger in England, at the court of our Anglo-Norman kings, than in France itself. But it was a bloom of French poetry; and as our native poetry formed itself, it formed itself out of this. The romance-poems which took possession of the heart and imagination of Europe in the twelfth and thirteenth centuries are French; "they are," as Southey justly says, "the pride of French literature, nor have we anything which can be placed in competition with them." Themes were supplied from all quarters; but the romance-setting which was common to them all, and which gained the ear of Europe, was French. This constituted for the French poetry, literature, and language, at the height of the Middle Age, an unchallenged predominance. The Italian

Brunetto Latini, the master of Dante, wrote his *Treasure* in French because, he says, *"la parleure en est plus délitable et plus commune à toutes gens."* In the same century, the thirteenth, the French romance-writer, Christian of Troyes, formulates the claims, in chivalry and letters, of France, his native country, as follows:

> Or vous ert par ce livre apris,
> Que Gresse ot de chevalerie
> Le premier los et de clergie;
> Puis vint chevalerie à Rome,
> Et de la clergie la some,
> Qui ore est en France venue.
> Diex doinst qu'ele i soit retenue,
> Et que li lius li abelisse
> Tant que de France n'isse
> L'onor qui s'i est arestée!

Now by this book you will learn that first Greece had the renown for chivalry and letters; then chivalry and the primacy in letters passed to Rome, and now it is come to France. God grant it may be kept there; and that the place may please it so well, that the honour which has come to make stay in France may never depart thence!

Yet it is now all gone, this French romance-poetry, of which the weight of substance and the power of style are not unfairly represented by this extract from Christian of Troyes. Only by means of the historic estimate can we persuade ourselves now to think that any of it is of poetical importance.

But in the fourteenth century there comes an Englishman nourished on this poetry, taught his trade by this poetry, getting words, rhyme, metre from this poetry; for even of that stanza which the Italians used, and which Chaucer derived immediately from the Italians, the basis and suggestion was probably given in France.

Chaucer (I have already named him) fascinated his contemporaries, but so too did Christian of Troyes and Wolfram of Eschenbach. Chaucer's power of fascination, however, is enduring; his poetical importance does not need the assistance of the historic estimate; it is real. He is a genuine source of joy and strength, which is flowing still for us and will flow always. He will be read, as time goes on, far more generally than he is read now. His language is a cause of difficulty for us; but so also, and I think in quite as great a degree, is the language of Burns. In Chaucer's case, as in that of Burns, it is a difficulty to be unhesitatingly accepted and overcome.

If we ask ourselves wherein consists the immense superiority of Chaucer's poetry over the romance-poetry— why it is that in passing from this to Chaucer we suddenly feel ourselves to be in another world, we shall find that his superiority is both in the substance of his poetry and in the style of his poetry. His superiority in substance is given by his large, free, simple, clear yet kindly view of human life,—so unlike the total want, in the romance-poets, of all intelligent command of it. Chaucer has not their helplessness; he has gained the power to survey the world from a central, a truly human point of view. We have only to call to mind the Prologue to *The Canterbury Tales*. The right comment upon it is Dryden's: "It is sufficient to say, according to the proverb, that *here is God's plenty*." And again: "He is a perpetual fountain of good sense." It is by a large, free, sound representation of things, that poetry, this high criticism of life, has truth of substance; and Chaucer's poetry has truth of substance.

Of his style and manner, if we think first of the romance-poetry and then of Chaucer's divine liquidness of diction, his divine fluidity of movement, it is difficult to

speak temperately. They are irresistible, and justify all
the rapture with which his successors speak of his "gold
dew-drops of speech." Johnson misses the point entirely
when he finds fault with Dryden for ascribing to Chaucer the first refinement of our numbers, and says that
Gower also can show smooth numbers and easy rhymes.
The refinement of our numbers means something far
more than this. A nation may have versifiers with smooth
numbers and easy rhymes, and yet may have no real
poetry at all. Chaucer is the father of our splendid English poetry; he is our "well of English undefiled," because by the lovely charm of his diction, the lovely
charm of his movement, he makes an epoch and founds
a tradition. In Spenser, Shakespeare, Milton, Keats, we
can follow the tradition of the liquid diction, the fluid
movement, of Chaucer; at one time it is his liquid diction
of which in these poets we feel the virtue, and at another
time it is his fluid movement. And the virtue is irresistible.

Bounded as is my space, I must yet find room for
an example of Chaucer's virtue, as I have given examples to show the virtue of the great classics. I feel disposed to say that a single line is enough to show the
charm of Chaucer's verse; that merely one line like
this—

O martyr souded [1] in virginitee!

has a virtue of manner and movement such as we shall
not find in all the verse of romance-poetry;—but this is
saying nothing. The virtue is such as we shall not find,
perhaps, in all English poetry, outside the poets whom
I have named as the special inheritors of Chaucer's tradition. A single line, however, is too little if we have not

[1] The French *soudé*; soldered, fixed fast. (*Arnold's note.*)

the strain of Chaucer's verse well in our memory; let us take a stanza. It is from *The Prioress's Tale,* the story of the Christian child murdered in a Jewry—

> My throte is cut unto my nekke-bone
> Saidè this child, and as by way of kinde
> I should have deyd, yea, longè time agone;
> But Jesu Christ, as ye in bookès finde,
> Will that his glory last and be in minde,
> And for the worship of his mother dere
> Yet may I sing *O Alma* loud and clere.

Wordsworth has modernised this Tale, and to feel how delicate and evanescent is the charm of verse, we have only to read Wordsworth's first three lines of this stanza after Chaucer's—

> My throat is cut unto the bone, I trow,
> Said this young child, and by the law of kind
> I should have died, yea, many hours ago.

The charm is departed. It is often said that the power of liquidness and fluidity in Chaucer's verse was dependent upon a free, a licentious dealing with language, such as is now impossible; upon a liberty, such as Burns too enjoyed, of making words like *neck, bird,* into a dissyllable by adding to them, and words like *cause, rhyme,* into a dissyllable by sounding the *e* mute. It is true that Chaucer's fluidity is conjoined with this liberty, and is admirably served by it; but we ought not to say that it was dependent upon it. It was dependent upon his talent. Other poets with a like liberty do not attain to the fluidity of Chaucer; Burns himself does not attain to it. Poets, again, who have a talent akin to Chaucer's, such as Shakespeare or Keats, have known how to attain to his fluidity without the like liberty.

And yet Chaucer is not one of the great classics. His poetry transcends and effaces, easily and without effort,

all the romance-poetry of Catholic Christendom; it transcends and effaces all the English poetry contemporary
with it, it transcends and effaces all the English poetry
subsequent to it down to the age of Elizabeth. Of such
avail is poetic truth of substance, in its natural and
necessary union with poetic truth of style. And yet, I
say, Chaucer is not one of the great classics. He has not
their accent. What is wanting to him is suggested by the
mere mention of the name of the first great classic of
Christendom, the immortal poet who died eighty years
before Chaucer,—Dante. The accent of such verse as

In la sua volontade è nostra pace . . .

is altogether beyond Chaucer's reach; we praise him,
but we feel that this accent is out of the question for
him. It may be said that it was necessarily out of the
reach of any poet in the England of that stage of growth.
Possibly; but we are to adopt a real, not a historic, estimate of poetry. However we may account for its absence, something is wanting, then, to the poetry of
Chaucer, which poetry must have before it can be
placed in the glorious class of the best. And there is no
doubt what that something is. It is the σπουδαιότης, the
high and excellent seriousness, which Aristotle assigns as
one of the grand virtues of poetry. The substance of
Chaucer's poetry, his view of things and his criticism of
life, has largeness, freedom, shrewdness, benignity; but
it has not this high seriousness. Homer's criticism of life
has it, Dante's has it, Shakespeare's has it. It is this
chiefly which gives to our spirits what they can rest
upon; and with the increasing demands of our modern
ages upon poetry, this virtue of giving us what we can
rest upon will be more and more highly esteemed. A
voice from the slums of Paris, fifty or sixty years after
Chaucer, the voice of poor Villon out of his life of riot

and crime, has at its happy moments (as, for instance, in the last stanza of "La Belle Heaulmière" [1]) more of this important poetic virtue of seriousness than all the productions of Chaucer. But its apparition in Villon, and in men like Villon, is fitful; the greatness of the great poets, the power of their criticism of life, is that their virtue is sustained.

To our praise, therefore, of Chaucer as a poet there must be this limitation; he lacks the high seriousness of the great classics, and therewith an important part of their virtue. Still, the main fact for us to bear in mind about Chaucer is his sterling value according to that real estimate which we firmly adopt for all poets. He has poetic truth of substance, though he has not high poetic seriousness, and corresponding to his truth of substance he has an exquisite virtue of style and manner. With him is born our real poetry.

For my present purpose I need not dwell on our Elizabethan poetry, or on the continuation and close of this poetry in Milton. We all of us profess to be agreed in the estimate of this poetry; we all of us recognise it as great poetry, our greatest, and Shakespeare and Milton

---

[1] The name *Heaulmière* is said to be derived from a headdress (helm) worn as a mark by courtesans. In Villon's ballad, a poor old creature of this class laments her days of youth and beauty. The last stanza of the ballad runs thus—

> Ainsi le bon temps regretons
> Entre nous, pauvres vieilles sottes,
> Assises bas, à croppetons,
> Tout en ung tas comme pelottes;
> A petit feu de chenevottes
> Tost allumées, tost estainctes.
> Et jadis fusmes si mignottes!
> Ainsi en prend à maintz et maintes.

Thus amongst ourselves we regret the good time, poor silly old things, low-seated on our heels, all in a heap like so many balls; by a little fire of hemp-stalks, soon lighted, soon spent. And once we were such darlings! So fares it with many and many a one. (*Arnold's note.*)

as our poetical classics. The real estimate, here, has universal currency. With the next age of our poetry divergency and difficulty begin. An historic estimate of that poetry has established itself; and the question is, whether it will be found to coincide with the real estimate.

The age of Dryden, together with our whole eighteenth century which followed it, sincerely believed itself to have produced poetical classics of its own, and even to have made advance, in poetry, beyond all its predecessors. Dryden regards as not seriously disputable the opinion "that the sweetness of English verse was never understood or practised by our fathers." Cowley could see nothing at all in Chaucer's poetry. Dryden heartily admired it, and, as we have seen, praised its matter admirably; but of its exquisite manner and movement all he can find to say is that "there is the rude sweetness of a Scotch tune in it, which is natural and pleasing, though not perfect." Addison, wishing to praise Chaucer's numbers, compares them with Dryden's own. And all through the eighteenth century, and down even into our own times, the stereotyped phrase of approbation for good verse found in our early poetry has been, that it even approached the verse of Dryden, Addison, Pope, and Johnson.

Are Dryden and Pope poetical classics? Is the historic estimate, which represents them as such, and which has been so long established that it cannot easily give way, the real estimate? Wordsworth and Coleridge, as is well known, denied it; but the authority of Wordsworth and Coleridge does not weigh much with the young generation, and there are many signs to show that the eighteenth century and its judgments are coming into favour again. Are the favourite poets of the eighteenth century classics?

It is impossible within my present limits to discuss the question fully. And what man of letters would not shrink from seeming to dispose dictatorially of the claims of two men who are, at any rate, such masters in letters as Dryden and Pope; two men of such admirable talent, both of them, and one of them, Dryden, a man, on all sides, of such energetic and genial power? And yet, if we are to gain the full benefit from poetry, we must have the real estimate of it. I cast about for some mode of arriving, in the present case, at such an estimate without offence. And perhaps the best way is to begin, as it is easy to begin, with cordial praise.

When we find Chapman, the Elizabethan translator of Homer, expressing himself in his preface thus: "Though truth in her very nakedness sits in so deep a pit, that from Gades to Aurora and Ganges few eyes can sound her, I hope yet those few here will so discover and confirm that, the date being out of her darkness in this morning of our poet, he shall now gird his temples with the sun,"—we pronounce that such a prose is intolerable. When we find Milton writing: "And long it was not after, when I was confirmed in this opinion, that he, who would not be frustrate of his hope to write well hereafter in laudable things, ought himself to be a true poem,"—we pronounce that such a prose has its own grandeur, but that it is obsolete and inconvenient. But when we find Dryden telling us: "What Virgil wrote in the vigour of his age, in plenty and at ease, I have undertaken to translate in my declining years; struggling with wants, oppressed with sickness, curbed in my genius, liable to be misconstrued in all I write,"—then we exclaim that here at last we have the true English prose, a prose such as we would all gladly use if we only knew how. Yet Dryden was Milton's contemporary.

But after the Restoration the time had come when

our nation felt the imperious need of a fit prose. So, too, the time had likewise come when our nation felt the imperious need of freeing itself from the absorbing pre-occupation which religion in the Puritan age had exercised. It was impossible that this freedom should be brought about without some negative excess, without some neglect and impairment of the religious life of the soul; and the spiritual history of the eighteenth century shows us that the freedom was not achieved without them. Still, the freedom was achieved; the preoccupation, an undoubtedly baneful and retarding one if it had continued, was got rid of. And as with religion amongst us at that period, so it was also with letters. A fit prose was a necessity; but it was impossible that a fit prose should establish itself amongst us without some touch of frost to the imaginative life of the soul. The needful qualities for a fit prose are regularity, uniformity, precision, balance. The men of letters, whose destiny it may be to bring their nation to the attainment of a fit prose, must of necessity, whether they work in prose or in verse, give a predominating, an almost exclusive attention to the qualities of regularity, uniformity, precision, balance. But an almost exclusive attention to these qualities involves some repression and silencing of poetry.

We are to regard Dryden as the puissant and glorious founder, Pope as the splendid high priest, of our age of prose and reason, of our excellent and indispensable eighteenth century. For the purposes of their mission and destiny their poetry, like their prose, is admirable. Do you ask me whether Dryden's verse, take it almost where you will, is not good?

> A milk-white Hind, immortal and unchanged,
> Fed on the lawns and in the forest ranged.

I answer: Admirable for the purposes of the inaugurator

of an age of prose and reason. Do you ask me whether Pope's verse, take it almost where you will, is not good?

> To Hounslow Heath I point, and Banstead Down;
> Thence comes your mutton, and these chicks my own.

I answer: Admirable for the purposes of the high priest of an age of prose and reason. But do you ask me whether such verse proceeds from men with an adequate poetic criticism of life, from men whose criticism of life has a high seriousness, or even, without that high seriousness, has poetic largeness, freedom, insight, benignity? Do you ask me whether the application of ideas to life in the verse of these men, often a powerful application, no doubt, is a powerful *poetic* application? Do you ask me whether the poetry of these men has either the matter or the inseparable manner of such an adequate poetic criticism; whether it has the accent of

> Absent thee from felicity awhile . . .

or of

> And what is else not to be overcome . . .

or of

> O martyr souded in virginitee!

I answer: It has not and cannot have them; it is the poetry of the builders of an age of prose and reason. Though they may write in verse, though they may in a certain sense be masters of the art of versification, Dryden and Pope are not classics of our poetry, they are classics of our prose.

Gray is our poetical classic of that literature and age; the position of Gray is singular, and demands a word of notice here. He has not the volume or the power of poets who, coming in times more favourable, have attained to an independent criticism of life. But he lived with the great poets, he lived, above all, with the Greeks, through perpetually studying and enjoying them; and he caught their poetic point of view for regarding life, caught their poetic manner. The point of view and the manner are not self-sprung in him, he caught them of others; and he had not the free and abundant use of them. But whereas Addison and Pope never had the use of them, Gray had the use of them at times. He is the scantiest and frailest of classics in our poetry, but he is a classic.

And now, after Gray, we are met, as we draw towards the end of the eighteenth century, we are met by the great name of Burns. We enter now on times where the personal estimate of poets begins to be rife, and where the real estimate of them is not reached without difficulty. But in spite of the disturbing pressures of personal partiality, of national partiality, let us try to reach a real estimate of the poetry of Burns.

By his English poetry Burns in general belongs to the eighteenth century, and has little importance for us.

> Mark ruffian Violence, distain'd with crimes,
> Rousing elate in these degenerate times;
> View unsuspecting Innocence a prey,
> As guileful Fraud points out the erring way;
> While subtle Litigation's pliant tongue
> The life-blood equal sucks of Right and Wrong!

Evidently this is not the real Burns, or his name and fame would have disappeared long ago. Nor is Clarinda's love-poet, Sylvander, the real Burns either. But he tells us himself: "These English songs gravel me to death. I have not the command of the language that I have of my native tongue. In fact, I think that my ideas are more barren in English than in Scotch. I have been at 'Duncan Gray' to dress it in English, but all I can do is desperately stupid." We English turn naturally, in Burns, to the poems in our own language, because we can read them easily; but in those poems we have not the real Burns.

The real Burns is of course in his Scotch poems. Let us boldly say that of much of this poetry, a poetry dealing perpetually with Scotch drink, Scotch religion, and Scotch manners, a Scotchman's estimate is apt to be personal. A Scotchman is used to this world of Scotch drink, Scotch religion, and Scotch manners; he has a tenderness for it; he meets its poet half way. In this tender mood he reads pieces like the "Holy Fair" or "Halloween." But this world of Scotch drink, Scotch religion, and Scotch manners is against a poet, not for him, when it is not a partial countryman who reads him; for in itself it is not a beautiful world, and no one can deny that it is of advantage to a poet to deal with a beautiful world. Burns's world of Scotch drink, Scotch religion, and Scotch manners, is often a harsh, a sordid, a repulsive world; even the world of his "Cotter's Saturday Night" is not a beautiful world. No doubt a poet's criticism of life may have such truth and power that it triumphs over its world and delights us. Burns may triumph over his world, often he does triumph over his world, but let us observe how and where. Burns is the first case we have had where the bias of the personal estimate tends to mislead; let us look at him closely, he can bear it.

Many of his admirers will tell us that we have Burns, convivial, genuine, delightful, here—

> Leeze me on drink! it gies us mair
>   Than either school or college;
> It kindles wit, it waukens lair,
>   It pangs us fou o' knowledge.
> Be 't whisky gill or penny wheep

> Or ony stronger potion,
> It never fails, on drinking deep,
> To kittle up our notion
> By night or day.

There is a great deal of that sort of thing in Burns, and it is unsatisfactory, not because it is bacchanalian poetry, but because it has not that accent of sincerity which bacchanalian poetry, to do it justice, very often has. There is something in it of bravado, something which makes us feel that we have not the man speaking to us with his real voice; something, therefore, poetically unsound.

With still more confidence will his admirers tell us that we have the genuine Burns, the great poet, when his strain asserts the independence, equality, dignity, of men, as in the famous song "For a' that and a' that"—

> A prince can mak' a belted knight,
> A marquis, duke, and a' that;
> But an honest man's aboon his might,
> Guid faith he mauna fa' that!
> For a' that, and a' that,
> Their dignities, and a' that,
> The pith o' sense, and pride o' worth,
> Are higher rank than a' that.

Here they find his grand, genuine touches; and still more, when this puissant genius, who so often set morality at defiance, falls moralising—

> The sacred lowe o' weel-placed love
> Luxuriantly indulge it;
> But never tempt th' illicit rove,
> Tho' naething should divulge it.
> I waive the quantum o' the sin,
> The hazard o' concealing,
> But och! it hardens a' within,
> And petrifies the feeling.

Or in a higher strain—

> Who made the heart, 'tis He alone
>   Decidedly can try us;
> He knows each chord, its various tone;
>   Each spring, its various bias.
> Then at the balance let's be mute,
>   We never can adjust it;
> What's *done* we partly may compute,
>   But know not what's resisted.

Or in a better strain yet, a strain, his admirers will say, unsurpassable—

> To make a happy fire-side clime
>   To weans and wife,
> That's the true pathos and sublime
>   Of human life.

There is a criticism of life for you, the admirers of Burns will say to us; there is the application of ideas to life! There is, undoubtedly. The doctrine of the last-quoted lines coincides almost exactly with what was the aim and end, Xenophon tells us, of all the teaching of Socrates. And the application is a powerful one; made by a man of vigorous understanding, and (need I say?) a master of language.

But for supreme poetical success more is required than the powerful application of ideas to life; it must be an application under the conditions fixed by the laws of poetic truth and poetic beauty. Those laws fix as an essential condition, in the poet's treatment of such matters as are here in question, high seriousness;—the high seriousness which comes from absolute sincerity. The accent of high seriousness, born of absolute sincerity, is what gives to such verse as

> In la sua volontade è nostra pace . . .

to such criticism of life as Dante's, its power. Is this accent felt in the passages which I have been quoting from Burns? Surely not; surely, if our sense is quick, we must perceive that we have not in those passages a voice from the very inmost soul of the genuine Burns; he is not speaking to us from these depths, he is more or less preaching. And the compensation for admiring such passages less, from missing the perfect poetic accent in them, will be that we shall admire more the poetry where that accent is found.

No; Burns, like Chaucer, comes short of the high seriousness of the great classics, and the virtue of matter and manner which goes with that high seriousness is wanting to his work. At moments he touches it in a profound and passionate melancholy, as in those four immortal lines taken by Byron as a motto for *The Bride of Abydos*, but which have in them a depth of poetic quality such as resides in no verse of Byron's own—

> Had we never loved sae kindly,
> Had we never loved sae blindly,
> Never met, or never parted,
> We had ne'er been broken-hearted.

But a whole poem of that quality Burns cannot make; the rest, in the "Farewell to Nancy," is verbiage.

We arrive best at the real estimate of Burns, I think, by conceiving his work as having truth of matter and truth of manner, but not the accent or the poetic virtue of the highest masters. His genuine criticism of life, when the sheer poet in him speaks, is ironic; it is not—

> Thou Power Supreme, whose mighty scheme
> These woes of mine fulfil,
> Here firm I rest, they must be best
> Because they are Thy will!

It is far rather: "Whistle owre the lave o't!" Yet we may say of him as of Chaucer, that of life and the world, as they come before him, his view is large, free, shrewd, benignant,—truly poetic, therefore; and his manner of rendering what he sees is to match. But we must note, at the same time, his great difference from Chaucer. The freedom of Chaucer is heightened, in Burns, by a fiery, reckless energy; the benignity of Chaucer deepens, in Burns, into an overwhelming sense of the pathos of things;—of the pathos of human nature, the pathos, also, of non-human nature. Instead of the fluidity of Chaucer's manner, the manner of Burns has spring, bounding swiftness. Burns is by far the greater force, though he has perhaps less charm. The world of Chaucer is fairer, richer, more significant than that of Burns; but when the largeness and freedom of Burns get full sweep, as in *Tam o' Shanter,* or still more in that puissant and splendid production, *The Jolly Beggars,* his world may be what it will, his poetic genius triumphs over it. In the world of *The Jolly Beggars* there is more than hideousness and squalor, there is bestiality; yet the piece is a superb poetic success. It has a breadth, truth, and power which make the famous scene in Auerbach's Cellar, of Goethe's *Faust,* seem artificial and tame beside it, and which are only matched by Shakespeare and Aristophanes.

Here, where his largeness and freedom serve him so admirably, and also in those poems and songs where to shrewdness he adds infinite archness and wit, and to benignity infinite pathos, where his manner is flawless, and a perfect poetic whole is the result,—in things like the address to the mouse whose home he had ruined, in things like "Duncan Gray," "Tam Glen," "Whistle and I'll come to you my Lad," "Auld Lang Syne" (this list might be made much longer),—here we have the genuine

Burns, of whom the real estimate must be high indeed. Not a classic, nor with the excellent σπουδαιότης of the great classics, nor with a verse rising to a criticism of life and a virtue like theirs; but a poet with thorough truth of substance and an answering truth of style, giving us a poetry sound to the core. We all of us have a leaning towards the pathetic, and may be inclined perhaps to prize Burns most for his touches of piercing, sometimes almost intolerable, pathos; for verse like—

> We twa hae paidl't i' the burn
>   From mornin' sun till dine;
> But seas between us braid hae roar'd
>   Sin auld lang syne . . .

where he is as lovely as he is sound. But perhaps it is by the perfection of soundness of his lighter and archer masterpieces that he is poetically most wholesome for us. For the votary misled by a personal estimate of Shelley, as so many of us have been, are, and will be,— of that beautiful spirit building his many-coloured haze of words and images

> Pinnacled dim in the intense inane—

no contact can be wholesomer than the contact with Burns at his archest and soundest. Side by side with the

> On the brink of the night and the morning
>   My coursers are wont to respire,
> But the Earth has just whispered a warning
>   That their flight must be swifter than fire . . .

of *Prometheus Unbound,* how salutary, how very salutary, to place this from "Tam Glen"—

> My minnie does constantly deave me
>   And bids me beware o' young men;
> They flatter, she says, to deceive me;
>   But wha can think sae o' Tam Glen?

But we enter on burning ground as we approach the poetry of times so near to us—poetry like that of Byron, Shelley, and Wordsworth—of which the estimates are so often not only personal, but personal with passion. For my purpose, it is enough to have taken the single case of Burns, the first poet we come to of whose work the estimate formed is evidently apt to be personal, and to have suggested how we may proceed, using the poetry of the great classics as a sort of touchstone, to correct this estimate, as we had previously corrected by the same means the historic estimate where we met with it. A collection like the present, with its succession of celebrated names and celebrated poems, offers a good opportunity to us for resolutely endeavouring to make our estimates of poetry real. I have sought to point out a method which will help us in making them so, and to exhibit it in use so far as to put any one who likes in a way of applying it for himself.

At any rate the end to which the method and the estimate are designed to lead, and from leading to which, if they do lead to it, they get their whole value,—the benefit of being able clearly to feel and deeply to enjoy the best, the truly classic, in poetry,—is an end, let me say it once more at parting, of supreme importance. We are often told that an era is opening in which we are to see multitudes of a common sort of readers, and masses of a common sort of literature; that such readers do not want and could not relish anything better than such literature, and that to provide it is becoming a vast and profitable industry. Even if good literature entirely lost currency with the world, it would still be abundantly worth while to continue to enjoy it by oneself. But it never will lose currency with the world, in spite of momentary appearances; it never will lose supremacy. Currency and supremacy are insured to it, not indeed by the world's delicate and conscious choice, but by something far deeper,—by the instinct of self-preservation in humanity.

◎

WORDSWORTH

◎

I REMEMBER hearing Lord Macaulay say, after Wordsworth's death, when subscriptions were being collected to found a memorial of him, that ten years earlier more money could have been raised in Cambridge alone, to do honour to Wordsworth, than was now raised all through the country. Lord Macaulay had, as we know, his own heightened and telling way of putting things, and we must always make allowance for it. But probably it is true that Wordsworth has never, either before or since, been so accepted and popular, so established in possession of the minds of all who profess to care for poetry, as he was between the years 1830 and 1840, and at Cambridge. From the very first, no doubt, he had his believers and witnesses. But I have myself heard him declare that, for he knew not how many years, his poetry had never brought him in enough to buy his shoe-strings. The poetry-reading public was very slow to recognise him, and was very easily drawn away from him. Scott effaced him with this public, Byron effaced him.

The death of Byron seemed, however, to make an opening for Wordsworth. Scott, who had for some time

ceased to produce poetry himself, and stood before the
public as a great novelist; Scott, too genuine himself not
to feel the profound genuineness of Wordsworth, and
with an instinctive recognition of his firm hold on nature
and of his local truth, always admired him sincerely, and
praised him generously. The influence of Coleridge upon
young men of ability was then powerful, and was still
gathering strength; this influence told entirely in favour
of Wordsworth's poetry. Cambridge was a place where
Coleridge's influence had great action, and where
Wordsworth's poetry, therefore, flourished especially.
But even amongst the general public its sale grew large,
the eminence of its author was widely recognised, and
Rydal Mount became an object of pilgrimage. I remember Wordsworth relating how one of the pilgrims, a
clergyman, asked him if he had ever written anything
besides the *Guide to the Lakes*. Yes, he answered mod-
estly, he had written verses. Not every pilgrim was a
reader, but the vogue was established, and the stream of
pilgrims came.

Mr. Tennyson's decisive appearance dates from 1842.
One cannot say that he effaced Wordsworth as Scott and
Byron had effaced him. The poetry of Wordsworth had
been so long before the public, the suffrage of good
judges was so steady and so strong in its favour, that by
1842 the verdict of posterity, one may almost say, had
been already pronounced, and Wordsworth's English
fame was secure. But the vogue, the ear and applause
of the great body of poetry-readers, never quite thoroughly perhaps his, he gradually lost more and more,
and Mr. Tennyson gained them. Mr. Tennyson drew to
himself, and away from Wordsworth, the poetry-reading
public, and the new generations. Even in 1850, when
Wordsworth died, this diminution of popularity was

visible, and occasioned the remark of Lord Macaulay which I quoted at starting.

The diminution has continued. The influence of Coleridge has waned, and Wordsworth's poetry can no longer draw succour from this ally. The poetry has not, however, wanted eulogists; and it may be said to have brought its eulogists luck, for almost every one who has praised Wordsworth's poetry has praised it well. But the public has remained cold, or, at least, undetermined. Even the abundance of Mr. Palgrave's fine and skilfully chosen specimens of Wordsworth, in the *Golden Treasury,* surprised many readers, and gave offence to not a few. To tenth-rate critics and compilers, for whom any violent shock to the public taste would be a temerity not to be risked, it is still quite permissible to speak of Wordsworth's poetry, not only with ignorance, but with impertinence. On the Continent he is almost unknown.

I cannot think, then, that Wordsworth has, up to this time, at all obtained his deserts. "Glory," said M. Renan the other day, "glory after all is the thing which has the best chance of not being altogether vanity." Wordsworth was a homely man, and himself would certainly never have thought of talking of glory as that which, after all, has the best chance of not being altogether vanity. Yet we may well allow that few things are less vain than *real* glory. Let us conceive of the whole group of civilised nations as being, for intellectual and spiritual purposes, one great confederation, bound to a joint action and working towards a common result; a confederation whose members have a due knowledge both of the past, out of which they all proceed, and of one another. This was the ideal of Goethe, and it is an ideal which will impose itself upon the thoughts of our modern societies more and more. Then to be recognised by the verdict of such a confederation as a master, or even as a seriously and eminently worthy workman, in one's own line of intellectual or spiritual activity, is indeed glory; a glory which it would be difficult to rate too highly. For what could be more beneficent, more salutary? The world is forwarded by having its attention fixed on the best things; and here is a tribunal, free from all suspicion of national and provincial partiality, putting a stamp on the best things, and recommending them for general honour and acceptance. A nation, again, is furthered by recognition of its real gifts and successes; it is encouraged to develop them further. And here is an honest verdict, telling us which of our supposed successes are really, in the judgment of the great impartial world, and not in our own private judgment only, successes, and which are not.

It is so easy to feel pride and satisfaction in one's own things, so hard to make sure that one is right in feeling it! We have a great empire. But so had Nebuchadnezzar. We extol the "unrivalled happiness" of our national civilisation. But then comes a candid friend, and remarks that our upper class is materialised, our middle class vulgarised, and our lower class brutalised. We are proud of our painting, our music. But we find that in the judgment of other people our painting is questionable, and our music non-existent. We are proud of our men of science. And here it turns out that the world is with us; we find that in the judgment of other people, too, Newton among the dead, and Mr. Darwin among the living, hold as high a place as they hold in our national opinion.

Finally, we are proud of our poets and poetry. Now poetry is nothing less than the most perfect speech of man, that in which he comes nearest to being able to utter the truth. It is no small thing, therefore, to succeed eminently in poetry. And so much is required for duly estimating success here, that about poetry it is perhaps hardest to arrive at a sure general verdict, and takes longest. Meanwhile, our own conviction of the superiority of our national poets is not decisive, is almost certain to be mingled, as we see constantly in English eulogy of Shakespeare, with much of provincial infatuation. And we know what was the opinion current amongst our neighbours the French—people of taste, acuteness, and quick literary tact—not a hundred years ago, about our great poets. The old *Biographie Universelle* notices the pretension of the English to a place for their poets among the chief poets of the world, and says that this is a pretension which to no one but an Englishman can ever seem admissible. And the scornful, disparaging things said by foreigners about Shakespeare and Milton, and about our national over-estimate of them, have been often quoted, and will be in every one's remembrance.

A great change has taken place, and Shakespeare is now generally recognised, even in France, as one of the greatest of poets. Yes, some anti-Gallican cynic will say, the French rank him with Corneille and with Victor Hugo! But let me have the pleasure of quoting a sentence about Shakespeare, which I met with by accident not long ago in the *Correspondant*, a French review which not a dozen English people, I suppose, look at. The writer is praising Shakespeare's prose. With Shakespeare, he says, "prose comes in whenever the subject, being more familiar, is unsuited to the majestic English iambic." And he goes on: "Shakespeare is the king of poetic rhythm and style, as well as the king of the realm of thought; along with his dazzling prose, Shakespeare has succeeded in giving us the most varied, the most harmonious verse which has ever sounded upon the human ear since the verse of the Greeks." M. Henry Cochin, the writer of this sentence, deserves our gratitude for it; it would not be easy to praise Shakespeare, in a single sentence, more justly. And when a foreigner and a Frenchman writes thus of Shakespeare, and when Goethe says of Milton, in whom there was so much to repel Goethe rather than to attract him, that "nothing has been ever done so entirely in the sense of the Greeks as *Samson Agonistes*," and that "Milton is in very truth a poet whom we must treat with all reverence," then we understand what constitutes a European recognition of poets and poetry as contradistinguished from a merely national recognition, and that in favour both of Milton and of Shakespeare the judgment of the high court of appeal has finally gone.

I come back to M. Renan's praise of glory, from which I started. Yes, real glory is a most serious thing, glory authenticated by the Amphictyonic Court of final appeal, definitive glory. And even for poets and poetry, long and difficult as may be the process of arriving at the right award, the right award comes at last, the definitive glory rests where it is deserved. Every establishment of such a real glory is good and wholesome for mankind at large, good and wholesome for the nation which produced the poet crowned with it. To the poet himself it can seldom do harm; for he, poor man, is in his grave, probably, long before his glory crowns him.

Wordsworth has been in his grave for some thirty years, and certainly his lovers and admirers cannot flatter themselves that this great and steady light of glory as yet shines over him. He is not fully recognised at home; he is not recognised at all abroad. Yet I firmly believe that the poetical performance of Wordsworth is, after that of Shakespeare and Milton, of which all the world now recognises the worth, undoubtedly the most considerable in our language from the Elizabethan age to the present time. Chaucer is anterior; and on other grounds, too, he cannot well be brought into the comparison. But taking the roll of our chief poetical names, besides Shakespeare and Milton, from the age of Elizabeth downwards, and going through it,—Spenser, Dryden, Pope, Gray, Goldsmith, Cowper, Burns, Coleridge, Scott, Campbell, Moore, Byron, Shelley, Keats (I mention those only who are dead),—I think it certain that Wordsworth's name deserves to stand, and will finally stand, above them all. Several of the poets named have gifts and excellences which Wordsworth has not. But taking the performance of each as a whole, I say that Wordsworth seems to me to have left a body of poetical work superior in power, in interest, in the qualities which give enduring freshness, to that which any one of the others has left.

But this is not enough to say. I think it certain, further, that if we take the chief poetical names of the Continent since the death of Molière, and, omitting Goethe, confront the remaining names with that of Wordsworth, the result is the same. Let us take Klopstock, Lessing, Schiller, Uhland, Rückert, and Heine for Germany; Filicaia, Alfieri, Manzoni, and Leopardi for Italy; Racine, Boileau, Voltaire, André Chenier, Béranger, Lamartine, Musset, M. Victor Hugo (he has been so long celebrated that although he still lives I may be permitted to name him) for France. Several of these, again, have evidently gifts and excellences to which Wordsworth can make no pretension. But in real poetical achievement it seems to me indubitable that to Wordsworth, here again, belongs the palm. It seems to me that Wordsworth has left behind him a body of poetical work which wears, and will wear, better on the whole than the performance of any one of these personages, so far more brilliant and celebrated, most of them, than the homely poet of Rydal. Wordsworth's performance in poetry is on the whole, in power, in interest, in the qualities which give enduring freshness, superior to theirs.

This is a high claim to make for Wordsworth. But if it is a just claim, if Wordsworth's place among the poets who have appeared in the last two or three centuries is after Shakespeare, Molière, Milton, Goethe, indeed, but before all the rest, then in time Wordsworth will have his due. We shall recognise him in his place, as we recognise Shakespeare and Milton; and not only we ourselves shall recognise him, but he will be recognised by Europe also. Meanwhile, those who recognise him already may do well, perhaps, to ask themselves whether there are not in the case of Wordsworth certain special obstacles which hinder or delay his due recognition by others, and whether these obstacles are not in some measure removable.

The Excursion and *The Prelude,* his poems of greatest bulk, are by no means Wordsworth's best work. His best work is in his shorter pieces, and many indeed are there of these which are of first-rate excellence. But in his seven volumes the pieces of high merit are mingled with a mass of pieces very inferior to them; so inferior to them that it seems wonderful how the same poet should have produced both. Shakespeare frequently has lines and passages in a strain quite false, and which are entirely unworthy of him. But one can imagine his smiling if one could meet him in the Elysian Fields and tell him so; smiling and replying that he knew it perfectly well himself, and what did it matter? But with Wordsworth the case is different. Work altogether inferior, work quite uninspired, flat and dull, is produced by him with evident unconsciousness of its defects, and he presents it to us with the same faith and seriousness as his best work. Now a drama or an epic fill the mind, and one does not look beyond them; but in a collection of short pieces the

impression made by one piece requires to be continued
and sustained by the piece following. In reading Wordsworth the impression made by one of his fine pieces is
too often dulled and spoiled by a very inferior piece
coming after it.

Wordsworth composed verses during a space of some
sixty years; and it is no exaggeration to say that within
one single decade of those years, between 1798 and
1808, almost all his really first-rate work was produced.
A mass of inferior work remains, work done before and
after this golden prime, imbedding the first-rate work
and clogging it, obstructing our approach to it, chilling,
not unfrequently, the high-wrought mood with which we
leave it. To be recognised far and wide as a great poet,
to be possible and receivable as a classic, Wordsworth
needs to be relieved of a great deal of the poetical baggage which now encumbers him. To administer this relief is indispensable, unless he is to continue to be a poet
for the few only,—a poet valued far below his real worth
by the world.

There is another thing. Wordsworth classified his
poems not according to any commonly received plan of
arrangement, but according to a scheme of mental physiology. He has poems of the fancy, poems of the imagination, poems of sentiment and reflection, and so on. His
categories are ingenious but far-fetched, and the result
of his employment of them is unsatisfactory. Poems are
separated one from another which possess a kinship of
subject or of treatment far more vital and deep than the
supposed unity of mental origin, which was Wordsworth's reason for joining them with others.

The tact of the Greeks in matters of this kind was infallible. We may rely upon it that we shall not improve
upon the classification adopted by the Greeks for kinds
of poetry; that their categories of epic, dramatic, lyric,

and so forth, have a natural propriety, and should be adhered to. It may sometimes seem doubtful to which of two categories a poem belongs; whether this or that poem is to be called, for instance, narrative or lyric, lyric or elegiac. But there is to be found in every good poem a strain, a predominant note, which determines the poem as belonging to one of these kinds rather than the other; and here is the best proof of the value of the classification, and of the advantage of adhering to it. Wordsworth's poems will never produce their due effect until they are freed from their present artificial arrangement, and grouped more naturally.

Disengaged from the quantity of inferior work which now obscures them, the best poems of Wordsworth, I hear many people say, would indeed stand out in great beauty, but they would prove to be very few in number, scarcely more than half a dozen. I maintain, on the other hand, that what strikes me with admiration, what establishes in my opinion Wordsworth's superiority, is the great and ample body of powerful work which remains to him, even after all his inferior work has been cleared away. He gives us so much to rest upon, so much which communicates his spirit and engages ours!

This is of very great importance. If it were a comparison of single pieces, or of three or four pieces, by each poet, I do not say that Wordsworth would stand decisively above Gray, or Burns, or Coleridge, or Keats, or Manzoni, or Heine. It is in his ampler body of powerful work that I find his superiority. His good work itself, his work which counts, is not all of it, of course, of equal value. Some kinds of poetry are in themselves lower kinds than others. The ballad kind is a lower kind; the didactic kind, still more, is a lower kind. Poetry of this latter sort counts, too, sometimes, by its biographical interest partly, not by its poetical interest pure and simple; but then this can only be when the poet producing it has the power and importance of Wordsworth, a power and importance which he assuredly did not establish by such didactic poetry alone. Altogether, it is, I say, by the great body of powerful and significant work which remains to him, after every reduction and deduction has been made, that Wordsworth's superiority is proved.

To exhibit this body of Wordsworth's best work, to clear away obstructions from around it, and to let it speak for itself, is what every lover of Wordsworth should desire. Until this has been done, Wordsworth, whom we, to whom he is dear, all of us know and feel to be so great a poet, has not had a fair chance before the world. When once it has been done, he will make his way best, not by our advocacy of him, but by his own worth and power. We may safely leave him to make his way thus, we who believe that a superior worth and power in poetry finds in mankind a sense responsive to it and disposed at last to recognise it. Yet at the outset, before he has been duly known and recognised, we may do Wordsworth a service, perhaps, by indicating in what his superior power and worth will be found to consist, and in what it will not.

Long ago, in speaking of Homer, I said that the noble and profound application of ideas to life is the most essential part of poetic greatness. I said that a great poet receives his distinctive character of superiority from his application, under the conditions immutably fixed by the laws of poetic beauty and poetic truth, from his application, I say, to his subject, whatever it may be, of the ideas

On man, on nature, and on human life,

which he has acquired for himself. The line quoted is Wordsworth's own; and his superiority arises from his powerful use, in his best pieces, his powerful application to his subject, of ideas "on man, on nature, and on human life."

Voltaire, with his signal acuteness, most truly remarked that "no nation has treated in poetry moral ideas with more energy and depth than the English nation." And he adds: "There, it seems to me, is the great merit of the English poets." Voltaire does not mean, by "treating in poetry moral ideas," the composing moral and didactic poems;—that brings us but a very little way in poetry. He means just the same thing as was meant when I spoke above "of the noble and profound application of ideas to life"; and he means the application of these ideas under the conditions fixed for us by the laws of poetic beauty and poetic truth. If it is said that to call these ideas *moral* ideas is to introduce a strong and injurious limitation, I answer that it is to do nothing of the kind, because moral ideas are really so main a part of human life. The question, *how to live,* is itself a moral idea; and it is the question which most interests every man, and with which, in some way or other, he is perpetually occupied. A large sense is of course to be given to the term *moral.* Whatever bears upon the question, "how to live," comes under it.

> Nor love thy life, nor hate; but, what thou liv'st,
> Live well; how long or short, permit to heaven.

In those fine lines Milton utters, as every one at once perceives, a moral idea. Yes, but so too, when Keats consoles the forward-bending lover on the Grecian Urn, the lover arrested and presented in immortal relief by the sculptor's hand before he can kiss, with the line,

> Forever wilt thou love, and she be fair—

he utters a moral idea. When Shakespeare says, that

> We are such stuff
> As dreams are made of, and our little life
> Is rounded with a sleep,

he utters a moral idea.

Voltaire was right in thinking that the energetic and profound treatment of moral ideas, in this large sense, is what distinguishes the English poetry. He sincerely meant praise, not dispraise or hint of limitation; and they err who suppose that poetic limitation is a necessary consequence of the fact, the fact being granted as Voltaire states it. If what distinguishes the greatest poets is their powerful and profound application of ideas to life, which surely no good critic will deny, then to prefix to the term ideas here the term moral makes hardly any difference, because human life itself is in so preponderating a degree moral.

It is important, therefore, to hold fast to this: that poetry is at bottom a criticism of life; that the greatness of a poet lies in his powerful and beautiful application of ideas to life,—to the question: How to live. Morals are often treated in a narrow and false fashion; they are bound up with systems of thought and belief which have had their day; they are fallen into the hands of pedants and professional dealers; they grow tiresome to some of us. We find attraction, at times, even in a poetry of revolt against them; in a poetry which might take for its motto Omar Khayyam's words: "Let us make up in the tavern for the time which we have wasted in the mosque." Or we find attractions in a poetry indifferent to them; in a poetry where the contents may be what they will, but where the form is studied and exquisite. We delude ourselves in either case; and the best cure for our delusion is to let our minds rest upon that great and inexhaustible word *life*, until we learn to enter into its meaning. A poetry of revolt against moral ideas is a poetry of revolt against *life*; a poetry of indifference towards moral ideas is a poetry of indifference towards *life*.

Epictetus had a happy figure for things like the play of the senses, or literary form and finish, or argumentative ingenuity, in comparison with "the best and master thing" for us, as he called it, the concern, how to live. Some people were afraid of them, he said, or they disliked and undervalued them. Such people were wrong; they were unthankful or cowardly. But the things might also be over-prized, and treated as final when they are not. They bear to life the relation which inns bear to home. "As if a man, journeying home, and finding a nice inn on the road, and liking it, were to stay for ever at the inn! Man, thou hast forgotten thine object; thy journey was not *to* this, but *through* this. 'But this inn is taking.' And how many other inns, too, are taking, and how many fields and meadows! but as places of passage merely. You have an object, which is this: to get home, to do your duty to your family, friends, and fellow-countrymen, to attain inward freedom, serenity, happiness, contentment. Style takes your fancy, arguing takes your fancy, and you forget your home and want to make your abode with them and to stay with them, on the plea that they are taking. Who denies that they are taking? but as places of passage, as inns. And when I say this, you suppose me to be attacking the care for style, the care for argument. I am not; I attack the resting in them, the not looking to the end which is beyond them."

Now, when we come across a poet like Théophile Gautier, we have a poet who has taken up his abode at an inn, and never got farther. There may be inducements to this or that one of us, at this or that moment, to find delight in him, to cleave to him; but after all, we do not change the truth about him,—we only stay ourselves in his inn along with him. And when we come across a poet like Wordsworth, who sings

> Of truth, of grandeur, beauty, love and hope.
> And melancholy fear subdued by faith,
> Of blessed consolations in distress,
> Of moral strength and intellectual power,
> Of joy in widest commonalty spread—

then we have a poet intent on "the best and master thing," and who prosecutes his journey home. We say, for brevity's sake, that he deals with *life*, because he deals with that in which life really consists. This is what Voltaire means to praise in the English poets,—this dealing with what is really life. But always it is the mark of the greatest poets that they deal with it; and to say that the English poets are remarkable for dealing with it, is only another way of saying, what is true, that in poetry the English genius has especially shown its power.

Wordsworth deals with it, and his greatness lies in his dealing with it so powerfully. I have named a number of celebrated poets above all of whom he, in my opinion, deserves to be placed. He is to be placed above poets like Voltaire, Dryden, Pope, Lessing, Schiller, because these famous personages, with a thousand gifts and merits, never, or scarcely ever, attain the distinctive accent and utterance of the high and genuine poets—

> Quique pii vates et Phœbo digna locuti,

at all. Burns, Keats, Heine, not to speak of others in our list, have this accent;—who can doubt it? And at the same time they have treasures of humour, felicity, passion, for which in Wordsworth we shall look in vain. Where, then, is Wordsworth's superiority? It is here; he deals with more of *life* than they do; he deals with *life*, as a whole, more powerfully.

No Wordsworthian will doubt this. Nay, the fervent Wordsworthian will add, as Mr. Leslie Stephen does, that Wordsworth's poetry is precious because his philosophy is sound; that his "ethical system is as distinctive and capable of exposition as Bishop Butler's"; that his poetry is informed by ideas which "fall spontaneously into a scientific system of thought." But we must be on our guard against the Wordsworthians, if we want to secure for Wordsworth his due rank as a poet. The Wordsworthians are apt to praise him for the wrong things, and to lay far too much stress upon what they call his philosophy. His poetry is the reality, his philosophy,—so far, at least, as it may put on the form and habit of "a scientific system of thought," and the more that it puts them on,—is illusion. Perhaps we shall one day learn to make this proposition general, and to say: Poetry is the reality, philosophy the illusion. But in Wordsworth's case, at any rate, we cannot do him justice until we dismiss his formal philosophy.

The Excursion abounds with philosophy, and therefore *The Excursion* is to the Wordsworthian what it never can be to the disinterested lover of poetry,—a satisfactory work. "Duty exists," says Wordsworth, in *The Excursion*; and then he proceeds thus—

> . . . Immutably survive,
> For our support, the measures and the forms,
> Which an abstract Intelligence supplies,
> Whose kingdom is, where time and space are not.

And the Wordsworthian is delighted, and thinks that here is a sweet union of philosophy and poetry. But the disinterested lover of poetry will feel that the lines carry us really not a step farther than the proposition which they would interpret; that they are a tissue of elevated but abstract verbiage, alien to the very nature of poetry.

Or let us come direct to the centre of Wordsworth's philosophy, as "an ethical system, as distinctive and capable of systematical exposition as Bishop Butler's"—

> . . . One adequate support
> For the calamities of mortal life
> Exists, one only;—an assured belief
> That the procession of our fate, howe'er
> Sad or disturbed, is ordered by a Being
> Of infinite benevolence and power;
> Whose everlasting purposes embrace
> All accidents, converting them to good.

That is doctrine such as we hear in church too, religious and philosophic doctrine; and the attached Wordsworthian loves passages of such doctrine, and brings them forward in proof of his poet's excellence. But however true the doctrine may be, it has, as here presented, none of the characters of *poetic* truth, the kind of truth which we require from a poet, and in which Wordsworth is really strong.

Even the "intimations" of the famous "Ode," those corner-stones of the supposed philosophic system of Wordsworth,—the idea of the high instincts and affections coming out in childhood, testifying of a divine home recently left, and fading away as our life proceeds, —this idea, of undeniable beauty as a play of fancy, has itself not the character of poetic truth of the best kind; it has no real solidity. The instinct of delight in Nature and her beauty had no doubt extraordinary strength in Wordsworth himself as a child. But to say that universally this instinct is mighty in childhood, and tends to die away afterwards, is to say what is extremely doubtful. In many people, perhaps with the majority of educated persons, the love of nature is nearly imperceptible at ten years old, but strong and operative at thirty. In general we may say of these high instincts of early childhood, the base of the alleged systematic philosophy of Wordsworth, what Thucydides says of the early achievements of the Greek race: "It is impossible to speak with certainty of what is so remote; but from all that we can really investigate, I should say that they were no very great things."

Finally, the "scientific system of thought" in Wordsworth gives us at last such poetry as this, which the devout Wordsworthian accepts—

> O for the coming of that glorious time
> When, prizing knowledge as her noblest wealth
> And best protection, this Imperial Realm,
> While she exacts allegiance, shall admit
> An obligation, on her part, to *teach*
> Them who are born to serve her and obey;
> Binding herself by statute to secure,
> For all the children whom her soil maintains,
> The rudiments of letters, and inform
> The mind with moral and religious truth.

Wordsworth calls Voltaire dull, and surely the production of these un-Voltairian lines must have been imposed on him as a judgment! One can hear them being quoted at a Social Science Congress; one can call up the whole scene. A great room in one of our dismal provincial towns; dusty air and jaded afternoon daylight; benches full of men with bald heads and women in spectacles; an orator lifting up his face from a manuscript written within and without to declaim these lines of Wordsworth; and in the soul of any poor child of nature who may have wandered in thither, an unutterable sense of lamentation, and mourning, and woe!

"But turn we," as Wordsworth says, "from these bold,

bad men," the haunters of Social Science Congresses. And let us be on our guard, too, against the exhibitors and extollers of a "scientific system of thought" in Wordsworth's poetry. The poetry will never be seen aright while they thus exhibit it. The cause of its greatness is simple, and may be told quite simply. Wordsworth's poetry is great because of the extraordinary power with which Wordsworth feels the joy offered to us in nature, the joy offered to us in the simple primary affections and duties; and because of the extraordinary power with which, in case after case, he shows us this joy, and renders it so as to make us share it.

The source of joy from which he thus draws is the truest and most unfailing source of joy accessible to man. It is also accessible universally. Wordsworth brings us word, therefore, according to his own strong and characteristic line, he brings us word

Of joy in widest commonalty spread.

Here is an immense advantage for a poet. Wordsworth tells of what all seek, and tells of it at its truest and best source, and yet a source where all may go and draw for it.

Nevertheless, we are not to suppose that everything is precious which Wordsworth, standing even at this perennial and beautiful source, may give us. Wordsworthians are apt to talk as if it must be. They will speak with the same reverence of "The Sailor's Mother," for example, as of "Lucy Gray." They do their master harm by such lack of discrimination. "Lucy Gray" is a beautiful success; "The Sailor's Mother" is a failure. To give aright what he wishes to give, to interpret and render successfully, is not always within Wordsworth's own command. It is within no poet's command; here is the part of the

Muse, the inspiration, the God, the "not ourselves." In Wordsworth's case, the accident, for so it may almost be called, of inspiration, is of peculiar importance. No poet, perhaps, is so evidently filled with a new and sacred energy when the inspiration is upon him; no poet, when it fails him, is so left "weak as is a breaking wave." I remember hearing him say that "Goethe's poetry was not inevitable enough." The remark is striking and true; no line in Goethe, as Goethe said himself, but its maker knew well how it came there. Wordsworth is right, Goethe's poetry is not inevitable; not inevitable enough. But Wordsworth's poetry, when he is at his best, is inevitable, as inevitable as Nature herself. It might seem that Nature not only gave him the matter for his poem, but wrote his poem for him. He has no style. He was too conversant with Milton not to catch at times his master's manner, and he has fine Miltonic lines; but he has no assured poetic style of his own, like Milton. When he seeks to have a style he falls into ponderosity and pomposity. In *The Excursion* we have his style, as an artistic product of his own creation; and although Jeffrey completely failed to recognise Wordsworth's real greatness, he was yet not wrong in saying of *The Excursion*, as a work of poetic style: "This will never do." And yet magical as is that power, which Wordsworth has not, of assured and possessed poetic style, he has something which is an equivalent for it.

Every one who has any sense for these things feels the subtle turn, the heightening, which is given to a poet's verse by his genius for style. We can feel it in the

> After life's fitful fever, he sleeps well—

of Shakespeare; in the

> . . . though fall'n on evil days,
> On evil days though fall'n, and evil tongues—

of Milton. It is the incomparable charm of Milton's
power of poetic style which gives such worth to *Paradise
Regained,* and makes a great poem of a work in which
Milton's imagination does not soar high. Wordsworth has
in constant possession, and at command, no style of this
kind; but he had too poetic a nature, and had read the
great poets too well, not to catch, as I have already remarked, something of it occasionally. We find it not only
in his Miltonic lines; we find it in such a phrase as this,
where the manner is his own, not Milton's—

> . . . the fierce confederate storm
> Of sorrow barricadoed evermore
> Within the walls of cities;

although even here, perhaps, the power of style, which
is undeniable, is more properly that of eloquent prose
than the subtle heightening and change wrought by
genuine poetic style. It is style, again, and the elevation
given by style, which chiefly makes the effectiveness
of "Laodameia." Still the right sort of verse to choose
from Wordsworth, if we are to seize his true and most
characteristic form of expression, is a line like this from
"Michael"—

> And never lifted up a single stone.

There is nothing subtle in it, no heightening, no study
of poetic style, strictly so called, at all; yet it is expression of the highest and most truly expressive kind.

Wordsworth owed much to Burns, and a style of perfect plainness, relying for effect solely on the weight
and force of that which with entire fidelity it utters,
Burns could show him.

> The poor inhabitant below
> Was quick to learn and wise to know,
> And keenly felt the friendly glow

> And softer flame;
> But thoughtless follies laid him low
> And stain'd his name.

Every one will be conscious of a likeness here to Wordsworth; and if Wordsworth did great things with this nobly plain manner, we must remember, what indeed he himself would always have been forward to acknowledge, that Burns used it before him.

Still Wordsworth's use of it has something unique and unmatchable. Nature herself seems, I say, to take the pen out of his hand, and to write for him with her own bare, sheer, penetrating power. This arises from two causes; from the profound sincereness with which Wordsworth feels his subject, and also from the profoundly sincere and natural character of his subject itself. He can and will treat such a subject with nothing but the most plain, first-hand, almost austere naturalness. His expression may often be called bald, as, for instance, in the poem of "Resolution and Independence"; but it is bald as the bare mountain tops are bald, with a baldness which is full of grandeur.

Wherever we meet with the successful balance, in Wordsworth, of profound truth of subject with profound truth of execution, he is unique. His best poems are those which most perfectly exhibit this balance. I have a warm admiration for "Laodameia" and for the great "Ode"; but if I am to tell the very truth, I find "Laodameia" not wholly free from something artificial, and the great "Ode" not wholly free from something declamatory. If I had to pick out poems of a kind most perfectly to show Wordsworth's unique power, I should rather choose poems such as "Michael," "The Fountain," "The Highland Reaper." And poems with the peculiar and unique beauty which distinguishes these, Wordsworth produced in considerable number; besides very many other poems of which the worth, although not so rare as the worth of these, is still exceedingly high.

On the whole, then, as I said at the beginning, not only is Wordsworth eminent by reason of the goodness of his best work, but he is eminent also by reason of the great body of good work which he has left to us. With the ancients I will not compare him. In many respects the ancients are far above us, and yet there is something that we demand which they can never give. Leaving the ancients, let us come to the poets and poetry of Christendom. Dante, Shakespeare, Molière, Milton, Goethe, are altogether larger and more splendid luminaries in the poetical heaven than Wordsworth. But I know not where else, among the moderns, we are to find his superiors.

To disengage the poems which show his power, and to present them to the English-speaking public and to the world, is the object of this volume. I by no means say that it contains all which in Wordsworth's poems is interesting. Except in the case of "Margaret," a story composed separately from the rest of *The Excursion*, and which belongs to a different part of England, I have not ventured on detaching portions of poems, or on giving any piece otherwise than as Wordsworth himself gave it. But under the conditions imposed by this reserve, the volume contains, I think, everything, or nearly everything, which may best serve him with the majority of lovers of poetry, nothing which may disserve him.

I have spoken lightly of Wordsworthians; and if we are to get Wordsworth recognised by the public and by the world, we must recommend him not in the spirit of a clique, but in the spirit of disinterested lovers of poetry. But I am a Wordsworthian myself. I can read with pleasure and edification "Peter Bell," and the whole

series of *Ecclesiastical Sonnets,* and the address to Mr.
Wilkinson's spade, and even the "Thanksgiving Ode";—
everything of Wordsworth, I think, except "Vaudracour
and Julia." It is not for nothing that one has been brought
up in the veneration of a man so truly worthy of homage;
that one has seen him and heard him, lived in his neigh-
bourhood, and been familiar with his country. No
Wordsworthian has a tenderer affection for this pure and
sage master than I, or is less really offended by his
defects. But Wordsworth is something more than the
pure and sage master of a small band of devoted followers, and we ought not to rest satisfied until he is
seen to be what he is. He is one of the very chief glories
of English Poetry; and by nothing is England so glorious
as by her poetry. Let us lay aside every weight which
hinders our getting him recognised as this, and let our
one study be to bring to pass, as widely as possible and
as truly as possible, his own word concerning his poems:
"They will co-operate with the benign tendencies in
human nature and society, and will, in their degree, be
efficacious in making men wiser, better, and happier."

○

BYRON

○

WHEN at last I held in my hand the volume of
poems which I had chosen from Wordsworth, and
began to turn over its pages, there arose in me almost
immediately the desire to see beside it, as a companion
volume, a like collection of the best poetry of Byron.

Alone amongst our poets of the earlier part of this century, Byron and Wordsworth not only furnish material enough for a volume of this kind, but also, as it seems to me, they both of them gain considerably by being thus exhibited. There are poems of Coleridge and of Keats equal, if not superior, to anything of Byron or Wordsworth; but a dozen pages or two will contain them, and the remaining poetry is of a quality much inferior. Scott never, I think, rises as a poet to the level of Byron and Wordsworth at all. On the other hand, he never falls below his own usual level very far; and by a volume of selections from him, therefore, his effectiveness is not increased. As to Shelley there will be more question; and indeed Mr. Stopford Brooke, whose accomplishments, eloquence, and love of poetry we must all recognise and admire, has actually given us Shelley in such a volume. But for my own part I cannot think that Shelley's poetry, except by snatches and fragments, has the value of the good work of Wordsworth and Byron; or that it is possible for even Mr. Stopford Brooke to make up a volume of selections from him which, for real substance, power, and worth, can at all take rank with a like volume from Byron or Wordsworth.

Shelley knew quite well the difference between the achievement of such a poet as Byron and his own. He praises Byron too unreservedly, but he sincerely felt, and he was right in feeling, that Byron was a greater poetical power than himself. As a man, Shelley is at a number of points immeasurably Byron's superior; he is a beautiful and enchanting spirit, whose vision, when we call it up, has far more loveliness, more charm for our soul, than the vision of Byron. But all the personal charm of Shelley cannot hinder us from at last discovering in his poetry the incurable want, in general, of a sound subject-matter, and the incurable fault, in consequence, of unsubstantiality. Those who extol him as the poet of clouds, the poet of sunsets, are only saying that he did not, in fact, lay upon the poet's right subject-matter; and in honest truth, with all his charm of soul and spirit, and with all his gift of musical diction and movement, he never, or hardly ever, did. Except, as I have said, for a few short things and single stanzas, his original poetry is less satisfactory than his translations, for in these the subject-matter was found for him. Nay, I doubt whether his delightful Essays and Letters, which deserve to be far more read than they are now, will not resist the wear and tear of time better, and finally come to stand higher, than his poetry.

There remain to be considered Byron and Words-worth. That Wordsworth affords good material for a volume of selections, and that he gains by having his poetry thus presented, is an old belief of mine which led me lately to make up a volume of poems chosen out of Wordsworth, and to bring it before the public. By its kind reception of the volume, the public seems to show itself a partaker in my belief. Now Byron also supplies plenty of material for a like volume, and he too gains, I think, by being so presented. Mr. Swinburne urges, indeed, that "Byron, who rarely wrote anything either worthless or faultless, can only be judged or appreciated in the mass; the greatest of his works was his whole work taken together." It is quite true that Byron rarely wrote anything either worthless or faultless; it is quite true also that in the appreciation of Byron's power a sense of the amount and variety of his work, defective though much of his work is, enters justly into our estimate. But although there may be little in Byron's poetry which can be pronounced either worthless or fault-less, there are portions of it which are far higher in worth and far more free from fault than others. And although, again, the abundance and variety of his production is undoubtedly a proof of his power, yet I question whether by reading everything which he gives us we are so likely to acquire an admiring sense even of his variety and abundance, as by reading what he gives us at his happier moments. Varied and abundant he amply proves himself even by this taken alone. Receive him absolutely without omission or compression, follow his whole outpouring stanza by stanza and line by line from the very commencement to the very end, and he is capable of being tiresome.

Byron has told us himself that *The Giaour* "is but a string of passages." He has made full confession of his own negligence. "No one," says he, "has done more through negligence to corrupt the language." This accusation brought by himself against his poems is not just; but when he goes on to say of them, that "their faults, whatever they may be, are those of negligence and not of labour," he says what is perfectly true. "*Lara*," he declares, "I wrote while undressing after coming home from balls and masquerades, in the year of revelry, 1814. The *Bride* was written in four, *The Corsair* in ten days." He calls this "a humiliating confession, as it proves my own want of judgment in publishing, and the public's in reading, things which cannot have stamina for permanence." Again he does his poems injustice; the producer of such poems could not but publish them, the public could not but read them. Nor could Byron have produced his work in any other fashion; his poetic work could not have first grown and matured in his own mind, and then come forth as an organic whole; Byron had not enough of the artist in him for this, nor enough of self-command. He wrote, as he truly tells us, to relieve himself, and he went on writing because he found the relief become indispensable. But it was inevitable that works so produced should be, in general, "a string of passages," poured out, as he describes them, with rapidity and excitement, and with new passages constantly suggesting themselves, and added while his work was going through the press. It is evident that we have here neither deliberate scientific construction, nor yet the instinctive artistic creation of poetic wholes; and that to take passages from work produced as Byron's was is a very different thing from taking passages out of the *Oedipus* or *The Tempest,* and deprives the poetry far less of its advantage.

Nay, it gives advantage to the poetry, instead of depriving it of any. Byron, I said, has not a great artist's profound and patient skill in combining an action or in developing a character,—a skill which we must watch and follow if we are to do justice to it. But he has a wonderful power of vividly conceiving a single incident, a single situation; of throwing himself upon it, grasping it as if it were real and he saw and felt it, and of making us see and feel it too. *The Giaour* is, as he truly called it, "a string of passages," not a work moving by a deep internal law of development to a necessary end; and our total impression from it cannot but receive from this, its inherent defect, a certain dimness and indistinctness. But the incidents of the journey and death of Hassan, in that poem, are conceived and presented with a vividness not to be surpassed; and our impression from them is correspondingly clear and powerful. In *Lara*, again, there is no adequate development either of the character of the chief personage or of the action of the poem; our total impression from the work is a confused one. Yet such an incident as the disposal of the slain Ezzelin's body passes before our eyes as if we actually saw it. And in the same way as these bursts of incident, bursts of sentiment also, living and vigorous, often occur in the midst of poems which must be admitted to be but weakly conceived and loosely combined wholes. Byron cannot but be a gainer by having attention concentrated upon what is vivid, powerful, effective in his work, and withdrawn from what is not so.

Byron, I say, cannot but be a gainer by this, just as Wordsworth is a gainer by a like proceeding. I esteem Wordsworth's poetry so highly, and the world, in my opinion, has done it such scant justice, that I could not rest satisfied until I had fulfilled, on Wordsworth's behalf, a long-cherished desire;—had disengaged, to the best of my power, his good work from the inferior work joined with it, and had placed before the public the body of his good work by itself. To the poetry of Byron the world has ardently paid homage; full justice from his contemporaries, perhaps even more than justice, his torrent of poetry received. His poetry was admired, adored, "with all its imperfections on its head,"—in spite of negligence, in spite of diffuseness, in spite of repetitions, in spite of whatever faults it possessed. His name is still great and brilliant. Nevertheless the hour of irresistible vogue has passed away for him; even for Byron it could not but pass away. The time has come for him, as it comes for all poets, when he must take his real and permanent place, no longer depending upon the vogue of his own day and upon the enthusiasm of his contemporaries. Whatever we may think of him, we shall not be subjugated by him as they were; for, as he cannot be for us what he was for them, we cannot admire him so hotly and indiscriminately as they. His faults of negligence, of diffuseness, of repetition, his faults of whatever kind, we shall abundantly feel and unsparingly criticise; the mere interval of time between us and him makes disillusion of this kind inevitable. But how then will Byron stand, if we relieve him too, so far as we can, of the encumbrance of his inferior and weakest work, and if we bring before us his best and strongest work in one body together? That is the question which I, who can even remember the latter years of Byron's vogue, and have myself felt the expiring wave of that mighty influence, but who certainly also regard him, and have long regarded him, without illusion, cannot but ask myself, cannot but seek to answer. The present volume is an attempt to provide adequate data for answering it.

Byron has been over-praised, no doubt. "Byron is one of our French superstitions," says M. Edmond Scherer; but where has Byron not been a superstition? He pays now the penalty of this exaggerated worship. "Alone among the English poets his contemporaries, Byron," said M. Taine, *atteint à la cîme,*—gets to the top of the poetic mountain." But the idol that M. Taine had thus adored M. Scherer is almost for burning. "In Byron," he declares, "there is a remarkable inability ever to lift himself into the region of real poetic art,— art impersonal and disinterested,—at all. He has fecundity, eloquence, wit, but even these qualities themselves are confined within somewhat narrow limits. He has treated hardly any subject but one,—himself; now the man, in Byron, is of a nature even less sincere than the poet. This beautiful and blighted being is at bottom a coxcomb. He posed all his life long."

Our poet could not well meet with more severe and unsympathetic criticism. However, the praise often given to Byron has been so exaggerated as to provoke, perhaps, a reaction in which he is unduly disparaged. "As various in composition as Shakespeare himself, Lord Byron has embraced," says Sir Walter Scott, "every topic of human life, and sounded every string on the divine harp, from its slightest to its most powerful and

heart-astounding tones." It is not surprising that some
one with a cool head should retaliate, on such provoca-
tion as this, by saying: "He has treated hardly any
subject but one, *himself*." "In the very grand and tremendous drama of *Cain*," says Scott, "Lord Byron has
certainly matched Milton on his own ground." And Lord
Byron has done all this, Scott adds, "while managing
his pen with the careless and negligent ease of a man of
quality." Alas, "managing his pen with the careless and
negligent ease of a man of quality," Byron wrote in his
Cain—

> Souls that dare look the Omnipotent tyrant in
> His everlasting face, and tell him that
> His evil is not good;

or he wrote—

> . . . And *thou* would'st go on aspiring
> To the great double Mysteries! the *two Principles!* [1]

One has only to repeat to oneself a line from *Paradise
Lost* in order to feel the difference.

Sainte-Beuve, speaking of that exquisite master of
language, the Italian poet Leopardi, remarks how often
we see the alliance, singular though it may at first sight
appear, of the poetical genius with the genius for scholarship and philology. Dante and Milton are instances
which will occur to every one's mind. Byron is so negligent in his poetical style, he is often, to say the truth,
so slovenly, slipshod, and infelicitous, he is so little
haunted by the true artist's fine passion for the correct
use and consummate management of words, that he
may be described as having for this artistic gift the insensibility of the barbarian;—which is perhaps only
another and a less flattering way of saying, with Scott,
that he "manages his pen with the careless and negli-

[1] The italics are in the original. (*Arnold's note.*)

gent ease of a man of quality." Just of a piece with the rhythm of

> Dare you await the event of a few minutes'
> Deliberation?

or of

> All shall be void—
> Destroy'd!

is the diction of

> Which now is painful to these eyes,
> Which have not seen the sun to rise;

or of

> . . . there let him lay!

or of the famous passage beginning

> He who hath bent him o'er the dead;

with those trailing relatives, that crying grammatical solecism, that inextricable anacolouthon! To class the work of the author of such things with the work of the authors of such verse as

> In the dark backward and abysm of time—

or as

> Presenting Thebes, or Pelops' line,
> Or the tale of Troy divine—

is ridiculous. Shakespeare and Milton, with their secret of consummate felicity in diction and movement, are of another and an altogether higher order from Byron, nay, for that matter, from Wordsworth also; from the author of such verse as

> Sol hath dropt into his harbour—

or (if Mr. Ruskin pleases) as

> Parching summer hath no warrant—

as from the author of

> All shall be void—
> Destroy'd!

With a poetical gift and a poetical performance of the very highest order, the slovenliness and tunelessness of much of Byron's production, the pompousness and ponderousness of much of Wordsworth's are incompatible. Let us admit this to the full.

Moreover, while we are hearkening to M. Scherer, and going along with him in his fault-finding, let us admit, too, that the man in Byron is in many respects as unsatisfactory as the poet. And, putting aside all direct moral criticism of him,—with which we need not concern ourselves here,—we shall find that he is unsatisfactory in the same way. Some of Byron's most crying faults as a man,—his vulgarity, his affectation,—are really akin to the faults of commonness, of want of art, in his workmanship as a poet. The ideal nature for the poet and artist is that of the finely touched and finely gifted man, the εὐφυής of the Greeks; now, Byron's nature was in substance not that of the εὐφυής at all, but rather, as I have said, of the barbarian. The want of fine perception which made it possible for him to formulate either the comparison between himself and Rousseau, or his reason for getting Lord Delawarr excused from a "licking" at Harrow, is exactly what made possible for him also his terrible dealings in, *An ye wool; I have redde thee; Sunburn me; Oons, and it is excellent well.* It is exactly, again, what made possible for him his precious dictum that Pope is a Greek temple, and a string of other criticisms of the like force; it is exactly, in fine, what deteriorated the quality of his poetic production. If we think of a good representative of that finely touched and exquisitely gifted nature which is the ideal nature for the poet and artist,—if we think of Raphael, for instance, who truly is εὐφυής just as Byron is not,—we shall bring into clearer light the connection in Byron between the faults of the man and the faults of the poet. With Raphael's character Byron's sins of vulgarity and false criticism would have been impossible, just as with Raphael's art Byron's sins of common and bad workmanship.

Yes, all this is true, but it is not the whole truth about Byron nevertheless; very far from it. The severe criticism of M. Scherer by no means gives us the whole truth about Byron, and we have not yet got it in what has been added to that criticism here. The negative part of the true criticism of him we perhaps have; the positive part, by far the more important, we have not. Byron's admirers appeal eagerly to foreign testimonies in his favour. Some of these testimonies do not much move me; but one testimony there is among them which will always carry, with me at any rate, very great weight,— the testimony of Goethe. Goethe's sayings about Byron were uttered, it must however be remembered, at the height of Byron's vogue, when that puissant and splendid personality was exercising its full power of attraction. In Goethe's own household there was an atmosphere of glowing Byron-worship; his daughter-in-law was a passionate admirer of Byron, nay, she enjoyed and prized his poetry, as did Tieck and so many others in Germany at that time, much above the poetry of Goethe himself. Instead of being irritated and rendered jealous by this, a nature like Goethe's was inevitably led by it to heighten, not lower, the note of his praise. The Time-Spirit, or *Zeit-Geist,* he would himself have said, was working just then for Byron. This working of the *Zeit-Geist* in his favour was an advantage added to By-

ron's other advantages, an advantage of which he had
a right to get the benefit. This is what Goethe would
have thought and said to himself; and so he would have
been led even to heighten somewhat his estimate of
Byron, and to accentuate the emphasis of praise. Goethe
speaking of Byron at that moment was not and could
not be quite the same cool critic as Goethe speaking of
Dante, or Molière, or Milton. This, I say, we ought to
remember in reading Goethe's judgments on Byron and
his poetry. Still, if we are careful to bear this in mind,
and if we quote Goethe's praise correctly,—which is
not always done by those who in this country quote it,
—and if we add to it that great and due qualification
added to it by Goethe himself,—which so far as I have
seen has never yet been done by his quoters in this country at all,—then we shall have a judgment on Byron,
which comes, I think, very near to the truth, and which
may well command our adherence.

In his judicious and interesting *Life of Byron*, Professor Nichol quotes Goethe as saying that Byron "is undoubtedly to be regarded as the greatest genius of our
century." What Goethe did really say was "the greatest
talent," not "the greatest *genius*." The difference is important, because, while talent gives the notion of power
in a man's performance, genius gives rather the notion
of felicity and perfection in it; and this divine gift of
consummate felicity by no means, as we have seen, belongs to Byron and to his poetry. Goethe said that
Byron "must unquestionably be regarded as the greatest
talent of the century." [1] He said of him moreover: "The
English may think of Byron what they please, but it is
certain that they can point to no poet who is his like.

[1] "Der ohne Frage als das grösste Talent des Jahrhunderts an-
zusehen ist." (*Arnold's note.*)

He is different from all the rest, and in the main greater." Here, again, Professor Nichol translates: "They can show no (living) poet who is to be compared to him";—inserting the word *living*, I suppose, to prevent its being thought that Goethe would have ranked Byron, as a poet, above Shakespeare and Milton. But Goethe did not use, or, I think, mean to imply, any limitation such as is added by Professor Nichol. Goethe said simply, and he meant to say, "*no* poet." Only the words which follow[1] ought not, I think, to be rendered, "who is to be compared to him," that is to say, "*who is his equal as a poet.*" They mean rather, "who may properly be compared with him," "*who is his parallel.*" And when Goethe said that Byron was "in the main greater" than all the rest of the English poets, he was not so much thinking of the strict rank, as poetry, of Byron's production; he was thinking of that wonderful personality of Byron which so enters into his poetry, and which Goethe called "a personality such, for its eminence, as has never been yet, and such as is not likely to come again." He was thinking of that "daring, dash, and grandiosity," [2] of Byron, which are indeed so splendid; and which were, so Goethe maintained, of a character to do good, because "everything great is formative," and what is thus formative does us good.

The faults which went with this greatness, and which impaired Byron's poetical work, Goethe saw very well. He saw the constant state of warfare and combat, the "negative and polemical working," which makes Byron's poetry a poetry in which we can so little find rest; he saw the *Hang zum Unbegrenzten,* the straining after the

---

[1] "Der ihm zu vergleichen wäre." (Arnold's note.)

[2] "Byron's Kühnheit, Keckheit und Grandiosität, ist das nicht alles bildend?—Alles Grosse bildet, sobald wir es gewahr werden." (Arnold's note.)

unlimited, which made it impossible for Byron to produce poetic wholes such as *The Tempest* or *Lear*; he saw the *zu viel Empirie*, the promiscuous adoption of all the matter offered to the poet by life, just as it was offered, without thought or patience for the mysterious transmutation to be operated on this matter by poetic form. But in a sentence which I cannot, as I say, remember to have yet seen quoted in any English criticism of Byron, Goethe lays his finger on the cause of all these defects in Byron, and on his real source of weakness both as a man and as a poet. "The moment he reflects, he is a child," says Goethe; *"sobald er reflektiert ist er ein Kind."*

Now if we take the two parts of Goethe's criticism of Byron, the favourable and the unfavourable, and put them together, we shall have, I think, the truth. On the one hand, a splendid and puissant personality—a personality "in eminence such as has never been yet, and is not likely to come again"; of which the like, therefore, is not to be found among the poets of our nation, by which Byron "is different from all the rest, and in the main greater." Byron is, moreover, "the greatest talent of our century." On the other hand, this splendid personality and unmatched talent, this unique Byron, "is quite too much in the dark about himself";[1] nay, "the moment he begins to reflect, he is a child." There we have, I think, Byron complete; and in estimating him and ranking him we have to strike a balance between the gain which accrues to his poetry, as compared with the productions of other poets, from his superiority, and the loss which accrues to it from his defects.

A balance of this kind has to be struck in the case of all poets except the few supreme masters in whom a profound criticism of life exhibits itself in indissoluble

[1] "Gar zu dunkel über sich selbst." (*Arnold's note.*)

connection with the laws of poetic truth and beauty. I have seen it said that I allege poetry to have for its characteristic this: that it is a criticism of life; and that I make it to be thereby distinguished from prose, which is something else. So far from it, that when I first used this expression, *a criticism of life,* now many years ago, it was to literature in general that I applied it, and not to poetry in especial. "The end and aim of all literature," I said, "is, if one considers it attentively, nothing but that: *a criticism of life.*" And so it surely is; the main end and aim of all our utterance, whether in prose or in verse, is surely a criticism of life. We are not brought much on our way, I admit, towards an adequate definition of poetry as distinguished from prose by that truth; still a truth it is, and poetry can never prosper if it is forgotten. In poetry, however, the criticism of life has to be made conformably to the laws of poetic truth and poetic beauty. Truth and seriousness of substance and matter, felicity and perfection of diction and manner, as these are exhibited in the best poets, are what constitute a criticism of life made in conformity with the laws of poetic truth and poetic beauty; and it is by knowing and feeling the work of those poets, that we learn to recognise the fulfilment and non-fulfilment of such conditions.

The moment, however, that we leave the small band of the very best poets, the true classics, and deal with poets of the next rank, we shall find that perfect truth and seriousness of matter, in close alliance with perfect truth and felicity of manner, is the rule no longer. We have now to take what we can get, to forego something here, to admit compensation for it there; to strike a balance, and to see how our poets stand in respect to one another when that balance has been struck. Let us observe how this is so.

We will take three poets, among the most considerable of our century: Leopardi, Byron, Wordsworth. Giacomo Leopardi was ten years younger than Byron, and he died thirteen years after him; both of them, therefore, died young—Byron at the age of thirty-six, Leopardi at the age of thirty-nine. Both of them were of noble birth, both of them suffered from physical defect, both of them were in revolt against the established facts and beliefs of their age; but here the likeness between them ends. The stricken poet of Recanati had no country, for an Italy in his day did not exist; he had no audience, no celebrity. The volume of his poems, published in the very year of Byron's death, hardly sold, I suppose, its tens, while the volumes of Byron's poetry were selling their tens of thousands. And yet Leopardi has the very qualities which we have found wanting to Byron; he has the sense for form and style, the passion for just expression, the sure and firm touch of the true artist. Nay, more, he has a grave fulness of knowledge, an insight into the real bearings of the questions which as a sceptical poet he raises, a power of seizing the real point, a lucidity, with which the author of *Cain* has nothing to compare. I can hardly imagine Leopardi reading the

> . . . And *thou* would'st go on aspiring
> To the great double Mysteries! the *two Principles!*

or following Byron in his theological controversy with Dr. Kennedy, without having his features overspread by a calm and fine smile, and remarking of his brilliant contemporary, as Goethe did, that "the moment he begins to reflect, he is a child." But indeed whoever wishes to feel the full superiority of Leopardi over Byron in philosophic thought, and in the expression of it, has only to

read one paragraph of one poem, the paragraph of *La Ginestra,* beginning

> Sovente in queste piagge,

and ending

> Non so se il riso o la pietà prevale.

In like manner, Leopardi is at many points the poetic superior of Wordsworth too. He has a far wider culture than Wordsworth, more mental lucidity, more freedom from illusions as to the real character of the established fact and of reigning conventions; above all, this Italian, with his pure and sure touch, with his fineness of perception, is far more of the artist. Such a piece of pompous dulness as

> O for the coming of that glorious time,

and all the rest of it, or such lumbering verse as Mr. Ruskin's enemy,

> Parching summer hath no warrant—

would have been as impossible to Leopardi as to Dante. Where, then, is Wordsworth's superiority? for the worth of what he has given us in poetry I hold to be greater, on the whole, than the worth of what Leopardi has given us. It is in Wordsworth's sound and profound sense

> Of joy in widest commonalty spread;

whereas Leopardi remains with his thoughts ever fixed upon the *essenza insanabile,* upon the *acerbo, indegno mistero delle cose.* It is in the power with which Wordsworth feels the resources of joy offered to us in nature, offered to us in the primary human affections and duties, and in the power with which, in his moments of inspiration, he renders this joy, and makes us, too, feel it; a

force greater than himself seeming to lift him and to prompt his tongue, so that he speaks in a style far above any style of which he has the constant command, and with a truth far beyond any philosophic truth of which he has the conscious and assured possession. Neither Leopardi nor Wordsworth are of the same order with the great poets who made such verse as

> Τλητὸν γὰρ Μοῖραι θυμὸν θέσαν ἀνθρώποισιν·

or as

> In la sua volontade è nostra pace;

or as

> . . . Men must endure
> Their going hence, even as their coming hither;
> Ripeness is all.

But as compared with Leopardi, Wordsworth, though at many points less lucid, though far less a master of style, far less of an artist, gains so much by his criticism of life being, in certain matters of profound importance, healthful and true, whereas Leopardi's pessimism is not, that the value of Wordsworth's poetry, on the whole, stands higher for us than that of Leopardi's, as it stands higher for us, I think, than that of any modern poetry except Goethe's.

Byron's poetic value is also greater, on the whole, than Leopardi's; and his superiority turns in the same way upon the surpassing worth of something which he had and was, after all deduction has been made for his shortcomings. We talk of Byron's *personality*, "a personality in eminence such as has never been yet, and is not likely to come again"; and we say that by this personality Byron is "different from all the rest of English poets, and in the main greater." But can we not be a little

more circumstantial, and name that in which the wonderful power of this personality consisted? We can; with the instinct of a poet Mr. Swinburne has seized upon it and named it for us. The power of Byron's personality lies in "the splendid and imperishable excellence which covers all his offences and outweighs all his defects: *the excellence of sincerity and strength.*"

Byron found our nation, after its long and victorious struggle with revolutionary France, fixed in a system of established facts and dominant ideas which revolted him. The mental bondage of the most powerful part of our nation, of its strong middle class, to a narrow and false system of this kind, is what we call British Philistinism. That bondage is unbroken to this hour, but in Byron's time it was even far more deep and dark than it is now. Byron was an aristocrat, and it is not difficult for an aristocrat to look on the prejudices and habits of the British Philistine with scepticism and disdain. Plenty of young men of his own class Byron met at Almack's or at Lady Jersey's, who regarded the established facts and reigning beliefs of the England of that day with as little reverence as he did. But these men, disbelievers in British Philistinism in private, entered English public life, the most conventional in the world, and at once they saluted with respect the habits and ideas of British Philistinism as if they were a part of the order of creation, and as if in public no sane man would think of warring against them. With Byron it was different. What he called the *cant* of the great middle part of the English nation, what we call its Philistinism, revolted him; but the cant of his own class, deferring to this Philistinism and profiting by it, while they disbelieved in it, revolted him even more. "Come what may," are his own words, "I will never flatter the million's canting in any shape." His class in general, on the other hand, shrugged their

shoulders at this cant, laughed at it, pandered to it, and ruled by it. The falsehood, cynicism, insolence, misgovernment, oppression, with their consequent unfailing crop of human misery, which were produced by this state of things, roused Byron to irreconcilable revolt and battle. They made him indignant, they infuriated him; they were so strong, so defiant, so maleficent,—and yet he felt that they were doomed. "You have seen every trampler down in turn," he comforts himself with saying, "from Buonaparte to the simplest individuals." The old order, as after 1815 it stood victorious, with its ignorance and misery below, its cant, selfishness, and cynicism above, was at home and abroad equally hateful to him. "I have simplified my politics," he writes, "into an utter detestation of all existing governments." And again: "Give me a republic. The king-times are fast finishing; there will be blood shed like water and tears like mist, but the peoples will conquer in the end. I shall not live to see it, but I foresee it."

Byron himself gave the preference, he tells us, to politicians and doers, far above writers and singers. But the politics of his own day and of his own class,—even of the Liberals of his own class,—were impossible for him. Nature had not formed him for a Liberal peer, proper to move the Address in the House of Lords, to pay compliments to the energy and self-reliance of British middle-class Liberalism, and to adapt his politics to suit it. Unfitted for such politics, he threw himself upon poetry as his organ; and in poetry his topics were not Queen Mab, and the Witch of Atlas, and the Sensitive Plant—they were the upholders of the old order, George the Third and Lord Castlereagh and the Duke of Wellington and Southey, and they were the canters and tramplers of the great world, and they were his enemies and himself.

Such was Byron's personality, by which "he is different from all the rest of English poets, and in the main greater." But he posed all his life, says M. Scherer. Let us distinguish. There is the Byron who posed, there is the Byron with his affectations and silliness, the Byron whose weakness Lady Blessington, with a woman's acuteness, so admirably seized: "His great defect is flippancy and a total want of self-possession." But when this theatrical and easily criticised personage betook himself to poetry, and when he had fairly warmed to his work, then he became another man; then the theatrical personage passed away; then a higher power took possession of him and filled him; then at last came forth into light that true and puissant personality, with its direct strokes, its ever-welling force, its satire, its energy, and its agony. This is the real Byron; whoever stops at the theatrical preludings does not know him. And this real Byron may well be superior to the stricken Leopardi, he may well be declared "different from all the rest of English poets, and in the main greater," in so far as it is true of him, as M. Taine well says, that "all other souls, in comparison with his, seem inert"; in so far as it is true of him that with superb, exhaustless energy, he maintained, as Professor Nichol well says, "the struggle that keeps alive, if it does not save, the soul"; in so far, finally, as he deserves (and he does deserve) the noble praise of him which I have already quoted from Mr. Swinburne; the praise for "the splendid and imperishable excellence which covers all his offences and outweighs all his defects: *the excellence of sincerity and strength*."

True, as a man, Byron could not manage himself, could not guide his ways aright, but was all astray. True, he has no light, cannot lead us from the past to the future; "the moment he reflects, he is a child." The way out of the false state of things which enraged him he

did not see,—the slow and laborious way upward; he
had not the patience, knowledge, self-discipline, virtue,
requisite for seeing it. True, also, as a poet, he has no
fine and exact sense for word and structure and rhythm;
he has not the artist's nature and gifts. Yet a personality
of Byron's force counts for so much in life, and a rhetorician of Byron's force counts for so much in literature!
But it would be most unjust to label Byron, as M.
Scherer is disposed to label him, as a rhetorician only.
Along with his astounding power and passion he had a
strong and deep sense for what is beautiful in nature,
and for what is beautiful in human action and suffering.
When he warms to his work, when he is inspired, Nature
herself seems to take the pen from him as she took it
from Wordsworth, and to write for him as she wrote for
Wordsworth, though in a different fashion, with her own
penetrating simplicity. Goethe has well observed of
Byron, that when he is at his happiest his representation
of things is as easy and real as if he were improvising. It
is so; and his verse then exhibits quite another and a
higher quality from the rhetorical quality,—admirable
as this also in its own kind of merit is,—of such verse as

> Minions of splendour shrinking from distress,

and of so much more verse of Byron's of that stamp.
Nature, I say, takes the pen for him; and then, assured
master of a true poetic style though he is not, any more
than Wordsworth, yet as from Wordsworth at his best
there will come such verse as

> Will no one tell me what she sings?

so from Byron, too, at his best, there will come such
verse as

> He heard it, but he heeded not; his eyes
> Were with his heart, and that was far away.

Of verse of this high quality, Byron has much; of verse of a quality lower than this, of a quality rather rhetorical than truly poetic, yet still of extraordinary power and merit, he has still more. To separate, from the mass of poetry which Byron poured forth, all this higher portion, so superior to the mass, and still so considerable in quantity, and to present it in one body by itself, is to do a service, I believe, to Byron's reputation, and to the poetic glory of our country.

Such a service I have in the present volume attempted to perform. To Byron, after all the tributes which have been paid to him, here is yet one tribute more—

> Among thy mightier offerings here are mine!

not a tribute of boundless homage certainly, but sincere; a tribute which consists not in covering the poet with eloquent eulogy of our own, but in letting him, at his best and greatest, speak for himself. Surely the critic who does most for his author is the critic who gains readers for his author himself, not for any lucubrations on his author;—gains more readers for him, and enables those readers to read him with more admiration.

And in spite of his prodigious vogue, Byron has never yet, perhaps, had the serious admiration which he deserves. Society read him and talked about him, as it reads and talks about "Endymion" today; and with the same sort of result. It looked in Byron's glass as it looks in Lord Beaconsfield's, and sees, or fancies that it sees, its own face there; and then it goes its way, and straightway forgets what manner of man it saw. Even of his passionate admirers, how many never got beyond the theatrical Byron, from whom they caught the fashion of deranging their hair, or of knotting their neck-handkerchief, or of leaving their shirt-collar unbuttoned; how few profoundly felt his vital influence, the influence of his spendid and imperishable excellence of sincerity and strength!

His own aristocratic class, whose cynical make-believe drove him to fury; the great middle class, on whose impregnable Philistinism he shattered himself to pieces,—how little have either of these felt Byron's vital influence! As the inevitable break-up of the old order comes, as the English middle class slowly awakens from its intellectual sleep of two centuries, as our actual present world, to which this sleep has condemned us, shows itself more clearly,—our world of an aristocracy materialised and null, a middle class purblind and hideous, a lower class crude and brutal,—we shall turn our eyes again, and to more purpose, upon this passionate and dauntless soldier of a forlorn hope, who, ignorant of the future and unconsoled by its promises, nevertheless waged against the conservation of the old impossible world so fiery battle; waged it till he fell,—waged it with such splendid and imperishable excellence of sincerity and strength.

Wordsworth's value is of another kind. Wordsworth has an insight into permanent sources of joy and consolation for mankind which Byron has not; his poetry gives us more which we may rest upon than Byron's,—more which we can rest upon now, and which men may rest upon always. I place Wordsworth's poetry, therefore, above Byron's on the whole, although in some points he was greatly Byron's inferior, and although Byron's poetry will always, probably, find more readers than Wordsworth's, and will give pleasure more easily. But these two, Wordsworth and Byron, stand, it seems to me, first and pre-eminent in actual performance, a glorious pair, among the English poets of this century. Keats had probably, indeed, a more consummate poetic gift than either of them; but he died having produced too little and being as yet too immature to rival them. I for my part can never even think of equalling with them any other of their contemporaries;—either Coleridge, poet and philosopher wrecked in a mist of opium; or Shelley, beautiful and ineffectual angel, beating in the void his luminous wings in vain. Wordsworth and Byron stand out by themselves. When the year 1900 is turned, and our nation comes to recount her poetic glories in the century which has then just ended, the first names with her will be these.

○

SHELLEY

○

NOWADAYS all things appear in print sooner or later; but I have heard from a lady who knew Mrs. Shelley a story of her which, so far as I know, has not appeared in print hitherto. Mrs. Shelley was choosing a school for her son, and asked the advice of this lady, who gave for advice—to use her own words to me— "Just the sort of banality, you know, one does come out with: Oh, send him somewhere where they will teach him to think for himself!" I have had far too long a training as a school inspector to presume to call an utterance of this kind a *banality*; however, it is not on this advice that I now wish to lay stress, but upon Mrs. Shelley's reply to it. Mrs. Shelley answered: "Teach him to think for himself? Oh, my God, teach him rather to think like other people!"

To the lips of many and many a reader of Professor

Dowden's volumes a cry of this sort will surely rise, called forth by Shelley's life as there delineated. I have read those volumes with the deepest interest, but I regret their publication, and am surprised, I confess, that Shelley's family should have desired or assisted it. For my own part, at any rate, I would gladly have been left with the impression, the ineffaceable impression, made upon me by Mrs. Shelley's first edition of her husband's collected poems. Medwin and Hogg and Trelawny had done little to change the impression made by those four delightful volumes of the original edition of 1839. The text of the poems has in some places been mended since; but Shelley is not a classic, whose various readings are to be noted with earnest attention. The charm of the poems flowed in upon us from that edition and the charm of the character. Mrs. Shelley had done her work admirably; her introductions to the poems of each year, with Shelley's prefaces and passages from his letters, supplied the very picture of Shelley to be desired. Somewhat idealised by tender regret and exalted memory Mrs. Shelley's representation no doubt was. But without sharing her conviction that Shelley's character, impartially judged, "would stand in fairer and brighter light than that of any contemporary," we learned from her to know the soul of affection, of "gentle and cordial goodness," of eagerness and ardour for human happiness, which was in this rare spirit—so mere a monster unto many. Mrs. Shelley said in her general preface to her husband's poems: "I abstain from any remark on the occurrences of his private life, except inasmuch as the passions which they engendered inspired his poetry; this is not the time to relate the truth." I for my part could wish, I repeat, that that time had never come.

But come it has, and Professor Dowden has given us the *Life of Percy Bysshe Shelley* in two very thick vol-

umes. If the work was to be done, Professor Dowden has
indeed done it thoroughly. One or two things in his biography of Shelley I could wish different, even waiving
the question whether it was desirable to relate in full
the occurrences of Shelley's private life. Professor Dowden holds a brief for Shelley; he pleads for Shelley as an
advocate pleads for his client, and this strain of pleading, united with an attitude of adoration which in Mrs.
Shelley had its charm, but which Professor Dowden was
not bound to adopt from her, is unserviceable to Shelley,
nay, injurious to him, because it inevitably begets, in
many readers of the story which Professor Dowden has
to tell, impatience and revolt. Further, let me remark
that the biography before us is of prodigious length,
although its hero died before he was thirty years old,
and that it might have been considerably shortened if it
had been more plainly and simply written. I see that
one of Professor Dowden's critics, while praising his
style for "a certain poetic quality of fervour and pic-
turesqueness," laments that in some important passages
Professor Dowden "fritters away great opportunities for
sustained and impassioned narrative." I am inclined
much rather to lament that Professor Dowden has not
steadily kept his poetic quality of fervour and pictur-
esqueness more under control. Is it that the Home
Rulers have so loaded the language that even an Irishman who is not one of them catches something of their
full habit of style? No, it is rather, I believe, that Professor Dowden, of poetic nature himself, and dealing
with a poetic nature like Shelley, is so steeped in sentiment by his subject that in almost every page of the
biography the sentiment runs over. A curious note of his
style, suffused with sentiment, is that it seems incapable
of using the common word *child*. A great many births
are mentioned in the biography, but always it is a poetic

babe that is born, not a prosaic *child*. And so, again,
André Chénier is not guillotined, but "too foully done to
death." Again, Shelley after his runaway marriage with
Harriet Westbrook was in Edinburgh without money
and full of anxieties for the future, and complained of
his hard lot in being unable to get away, in being
"chained to the filth and commerce of Edinburgh." Natural enough; but why should Professor Dowden improve
the occasion as follows? "The most romantic of northern
cities could lay no spell upon his spirit. His eye was not
fascinated by the presences of mountains and the sea,
by the fantastic outlines of aërial piles seen amid the
wreathing smoke of Auld Reekie, by the gloom of the
Canongate illuminated with shafts of sunlight streaming
from its interesting wynds and alleys; nor was his imagination kindled by storied house or palace, and the
voices of old, forgotten, far-off things, which haunt their
walls." If Professor Dowden, writing a book in prose,
could have brought himself to eschew poetic excursions
of this kind and to tell his story in a plain way, lovers of
simplicity, of whom there are some still left in the world,
would have been gratified, and at the same time his book
would have been the shorter by scores of pages.

These reserves being made, I have little except praise
for the manner in which Professor Dowden has performed his task; whether it was a task which ought to be
performed at all, probably did not lie with him to decide.
His ample materials are used with order and judgment;
the history of Shelley's life develops itself clearly before
our eyes; the documents of importance for it are given
with sufficient fulness, nothing essential seems to have
been kept back, although I would gladly, I confess, have
seen more of Miss Clairmont's journal, whatever arrangement she may in her later life have chosen to exercise
upon it. In general all documents are so fairly and fully

cited, that Professor Dowden's pleadings for Shelley, though they may sometimes indispose and irritate the reader, produce no obscuring of the truth; the documents manifest it of themselves. Last but not least of Professor Dowden's merits, he has provided his book with an excellent index.

Undoubtedly this biography, with its full account of the occurrences of Shelley's private life, compels one to review one's former impression of him. Undoubtedly the brilliant and attaching rebel who in thinking for himself had of old our sympathy so passionately with him, when we come to read his full biography makes us often and often inclined to cry out: "My God! he had far better have thought like other people." There is a passage in Hogg's capitally written and most interesting account of Shelley which I wrote down when I first read it and have borne in mind ever since; so beautifully it seemed to render the true Shelley. Hogg has been speaking of the intellectual expression of Shelley's features, and he goes on: "Nor was the moral expression less beautiful than the intellectual; for there was a softness, a delicacy, a gentleness, and especially (though this will surprise many) that air of profound religious veneration that characterises the best works and chiefly the frescoes (and into these they infused their whole souls) of the great masters of Florence and of Rome." What we have of Shelley in poetry and prose suited with this charming picture of him; Mrs. Shelley's account suited with it; it was a possession which one would gladly have kept unimpaired. It still subsists, I must now add; it subsists even after one has read the present biography; it subsists, but so as by fire. It subsists with many a scar and stain; never again will it have the same pureness and beauty which it had formerly. I regret this, as I have said, and I confess I do not see what has been gained.

Our ideal Shelley was the true Shelley after all; what has been gained by making us at moments doubt it? What has been gained by forcing upon us much in him which is ridiculous and odious, by compelling any fair mind, if it is to retain with a good conscience its ideal Shelley, to do that which I propose to do now? I propose to mark firmly what is ridiculous and odious in the Shelley brought to our knowledge by the new materials, and then to show that our former beautiful and lovable Shelley nevertheless survives.

Almost everybody knows the main outline of the events of Shelley's life. It will be necessary for me, however, up to the date of his second marriage, to go through them here. Percy Bysshe Shelley was born at Field Place, near Horsham, in Sussex, on the 4th of August 1792. He was of an old family of country gentlemen, and the heir to a baronetcy. He had one brother and five sisters, but the brother so much younger than himself as to be no companion for him in his boyhood at home, and after he was separated from home and England he never saw him. Shelley was brought up at Field Place with his sisters. At ten years old he was sent to a private school at Isleworth, where he read Mrs. Radcliffe's romances and was fascinated by a popular scientific lecturer. After two years of private school he went in 1804 to Eton. Here he took no part in cricket or football, refused to fag, was known as "mad Shelley" and much tormented; when tormented beyond endurance he could be dangerous. Certainly he was not happy at Eton; but he had friends, he boated, he rambled about the country. His school lessons were easy to him, and his reading extended far beyond them; he read books on chemistry, he read Pliny's *Natural History*, Godwin's *Political Justice*, Lucretius, Franklin, Condorcet. It is said he was called "atheist Shelley" at Eton, but this is not so well established as his having been called "mad Shelley." He was full, at any rate, of new and revolutionary ideas, and he declared at a later time that he was twice expelled from the school but recalled through the interference of his father.

In the spring of 1810 Shelley, now in his eighteenth year, entered University College, Oxford, as an exhibitioner. He had already written novels and poems; a poem on the Wandering Jew, in seven or eight cantos, he sent to Campbell, and was told by Campbell that there were but two good lines in it. He had solicited the correspondence of Mrs. Hemans, then Felicia Browne and unmarried; he had fallen in love with a charming cousin, Harriet Grove. In the autumn of 1810 he found a publisher for his verse; he also found a friend in a very clever and free-minded commoner of his college, Thomas Jefferson Hogg, who has admirably described the Shelley of those Oxford days, with his chemistry, his eccentric habits, his charm of look and character, his conversation, his shrill discordant voice. Shelley read incessantly. Hume's *Essays* produced a powerful impression on him; his free speculation led him to what his father, and worse still his cousin Harriet, thought "detestable principles"; his cousin and his family became estranged from him. He, on his part, became more and more incensed against the "bigotry" and "intolerance" which produced such estrangement. "Here I swear, and as I break my oaths, may Infinity, Eternity, blast me—here I swear that never will I forgive intolerance." At the beginning of 1811 he prepared and published what he called a "leaflet for letters," having for its title *The Necessity of Atheism*. He sent copies to all the bishops, to the Vice-Chancellor of Oxford, and to the heads of houses. On Lady Day he was summoned before the authorities of his College, refused to answer the question whether he

had written *The Necessity of Atheism,* told the Master
and Fellows that "their proceedings would become a
court of inquisitors but not free men in a free country,"
and was expelled for contumacy. Hogg wrote a letter of
remonstrance to the authorities, was in his turn summoned before them and questioned as to his share in
the "leaflet," and, refusing to answer, he also was expelled.

Shelley settled with Hogg in lodgings in London. His
father, excusably indignant, was not a wise man and
managed his son ill. His plan of recommending Shelley
to read Paley's *Natural Theology,* and of *reading it with
him himself,* makes us smile. Shelley, who about this
time wrote of his younger sister, then at school at Clapham, "There are some hopes of this dear little girl, she
would be a divine little scion of infidelity if I could get
hold of her," was not to have been cured by Paley's
Natural Theology administered through Mr. Timothy
Shelley. But by the middle of May Shelley's father had
agreed to allow him two hundred pounds a year. Meanwhile in visiting his sisters at their school in Clapham,
Shelley made the acquaintance of a schoolfellow of
theirs, Harriet Westbrook. She was a beautiful and lively
girl, with a father who had kept a tavern in Mount
Street, but had now retired from business, and one sister
much older than herself, who encouraged in every possible way the acquaintance of her sister of sixteen with
the heir to a baronetcy and a great estate. Soon Shelley
heard that Harriet met with cold looks at her school for
associating with an atheist; his generosity and his ready
indignation against "intolerance" were roused. In the
summer Harriet wrote to him that she was persecuted
not at school only but at home also, that she was lonely
and miserable, and would gladly put an end to her life.
Shelley went to see her; she owned her love for him, and

he engaged himself to her. He told his cousin Charles Grove that his happiness had been blighted when the other Harriet, Charles's sister, cast him off; that now the cnly thing worth living for was self-sacrifice. Harriet's persecutors became yet more troublesome, and Shelley, at the end of August, went off with her to Edinburgh and they were married. The entry in the register is this:

August 28, 1811.—Percy Bysshe Shelley, farmer, Sussex, and Miss Harriet Westbrook, St. Andrew Church Parish, daughter of Mr. John Westbrook, London.

After five weeks in Edinburgh the young farmer and his wife came southwards and took lodgings at York, under the shadow of what Shelley calls that "gigantic pile of superstition," the Minster. But his friend Hogg was in a lawyer's office in York, and Hogg's society made the Minster endurable. Mr. Timothy Shelley's happiness in his son was naturally not increased by the runaway marriage; he stopped his allowance, and Shelley determined to visit "this thoughtless man," as he calls his parent, and to "try the force of truth" upon him. Nothing could be effected; Shelley's mother, too, was now against him. He returned to York to find that in his absence his friend Hogg had been making love to Harriet, who had indignantly repulsed him. Shelley was shocked, but after a "terrible day" of explanation from Hogg, he "fully, freely pardoned him," promised to retain him still as "his friend, his bosom friend," and "hoped soon to convince him how lovely virtue was." But for the present it seemed better to separate. In November he and Harriet, with her sister Eliza, took a cottage at Keswick. Shelley was now in great straits for money; the great Sussex neighbour of the Shelley's, the Duke of Norfolk, interposed in his favour, and his father and grandfather seem to have offered him at this time an income of

£ 2000 a year, if he would consent to entail the family estate. Shelley indignantly refused to "forswear his principles," by accepting "a proposal so insultingly hateful." But in December his father agreed, though with an ill grace, to grant him his allowance of £ 200 a year again, and Mr. Westbrook promised to allow a like sum to his daughter. So after four months of marriage the Shelleys began 1812 with an income of £ 400 a year.

Early in February they left Keswick and proceeded to Dublin, where Shelley, who had prepared an address to the Catholics, meant to "devote himself towards forwarding the great ends of virtue and happiness in Ireland." Before leaving Keswick he wrote to William Godwin, "the regulator and former of his mind," making profession of his mental obligations to him, of his respect and veneration, and soliciting Godwin's friendship. A correspondence followed; Godwin pronounced his young disciple's plans for "disseminating the doctrines of philanthropy and freedom" in Ireland to be unwise; Shelley bowed to his mentor's decision and gave up his Irish campaign, quitting Dublin on the 4th of April 1812. He and Harriet wandered first to Nant-Gwillt in South Wales, near the upper Wye, and from thence after a month or two to Lynmouth in North Devon, where he busied himself with his poem of *Queen Mab,* and with sending to sea boxes and bottles containing a "Declaration of Rights" by him, in the hope that the winds and waves might carry his doctrines where they would do good. But his Irish servant, bearing the prophetic name of Healy, posted the "Declaration" on the walls of Barnstaple and was taken up; Shelley found himself watched and no longer able to enjoy Lynmouth in peace. He moved in September 1812 to Tremadoc, in North Wales, where he threw himself ardently into an enterprise for recovering a great stretch of drowned land from the sea.

But at the beginning of October he and Harriet visited
London, and Shelley grasped Godwin by the hand at
last. At once an intimacy arose, but the future Mary
Shelley—Godwin's daughter by his first wife, Mary
Wollstonecraft—was absent on a visit in Scotland when
the Shelleys arrived in London. They became acquainted, however, with the second Mrs. Godwin, on
whom we have Charles Lamb's friendly comment: "A
very disgusting woman, and wears green spectacles!"
with the amiable Fanny, Mary Wollstonecraft's daughter
by Imlay, before her marriage with Godwin; and probably also with Jane Clairmont, the second Mrs. Godwin's
daughter by a first marriage, and herself afterwards the
mother of Byron's Allegra. Complicated relationships, as
in the Theban story! and there will be not wanting,
presently, something of the Theban horrors. During this
visit of six weeks to London Shelley renewed his intimacy with Hogg; in the middle of November he returned to Tremadoc. There he remained until the end of
February 1813, perfectly happy with Harriet, reading
widely, and working at his *Queen Mab* and at the notes
to that poem. On the 26th of February an attempt was
made, or so he fancied, to assassinate him, and in high
nervous excitement he hurriedly left Tremadoc and re-
paired with Harriet to Dublin again. On this visit to Ireland he saw Killarney, but early in April he and Harriet
were back again in London.

There in June 1813 their daughter Ianthe was born;
at the end of July they moved to Bracknell, in Berkshire.
They had for neighbours there a Mrs. Boinville and her
married daughter, whom Shelley found to be fascinating
women, with a culture which to his wife was altogether
wanting. Cornelia Turner, Mrs. Boinville's daughter, was
melancholy, required consolation, and found it, Hogg
tells us, in Petrarch's poetry; "Bysshe entered at once

fully into her views and caught the soft infection, breathing the tenderest and sweetest melancholy as every true poet ought." Peacock, a man of keen and cultivated mind, joined the circle at Bracknell. He and Harriet, not yet eighteen, used sometimes to laugh at the gushing sentiment and enthusiasm of the Bracknell circle; Harriet had also given offence to Shelley by getting a wet-nurse for her child; in Professor Dowden's words, "the beauty of Harriet's motherly relation to her babe was marred in Shelley's eyes by the introduction into his home of a hireling nurse to whom was delegated the mother's tenderest office." But in September Shelley wrote a sonnet to his child which expresses his deep love for the mother also, to whom in March 1814 he was remarried in London, lest the Scotch marriage should prove to have been in any point irregular. Harriet's sister Eliza, however, whom Shelley had at first treated with excessive deference, had now become hateful to him. And in the very month of the London marriage we find him writing to Hogg that he is staying with the Boinvilles, having "escaped, in the society of all that philosophy and friendship combine, from the dismaying solitude of myself." Cornelia Turner, he adds, whom he once thought cold and reserved, "is the reverse of this, as she is the reverse of everything bad; she inherits all the divinity of her mother." Then comes a stanza, beginning

> Thy dewy looks sink in my breast,
> Thy gentle words stir poison there.

It has no meaning, he says; it is only written in thought. "It is evident from this pathetic letter," says Professor Dowden, "that Shelley's happiness in his home had been fatally stricken." This is a curious way of putting the matter. To me what is evident is rather that Shelley had, to use Professor Dowden's words again—for in these

things of high sentiment I gladly let him speak for me—
"a too vivid sense that here (in the society of the Boinville family) were peace and joy and gentleness and
love." In April come some more verses to the Boinvilles,
which contain the first good stanza that Shelley wrote.
In May comes a poem to Harriet, of which Professor
Dowden's prose analysis is as poetic as the poem itself.
"If she has something to endure (from the Boinville attachment), it is not much, and all her husband's weal
hangs upon her loving endurance, for see how pale and
wildered anguish has made him!" Harriet, unconvinced,
seems to have gone off to Bath in resentment, from
whence, however, she kept up a constant correspondence with Shelley, who was now of age, and busy in
London raising money on post-obit bonds for his own
wants and those of the friend and former of his mind,
Godwin.

And now, indeed, it was to become true that if from
the inflammable Shelley's devotion to the Boinville
family poor Harriet had had "something to endure," yet
this was "not much" compared with what was to follow.
At Godwin's house Shelley met Mary Wollstonecraft
Godwin, his future wife, then in her seventeenth year.
She was a gifted person, but, as Professor Dowden says,
she "had breathed during her entire life an atmosphere
of free thought." On the 8th of June Hogg called at Godwin's with Shelley; Godwin was out, but "a door was
partially and softly opened, a thrilling voice called
'Shelley!' a thrilling voice answered 'Mary!'" Shelley's
summoner was "a very young female, fair and fair-
haired, pale indeed, and with a piercing look, wearing
a frock of tartan." Already they were "Shelley" and
"Mary" to one another; "before the close of June they
knew and felt," says Professor Dowden, "that each was

to the other inexpressibly dear." The churchyard of St. Pancras, where her mother was buried, became "a place now doubly sacred to Mary, since on one eventful day Bysshe here poured forth his griefs, his hopes, his love, and she, in sign of everlasting union, placed her hand in his." In July Shelley gave her a copy of *Queen Mab*, printed but not published, and under the tender dedication to Harriet he wrote: "Count Slobendorf was about to marry a woman who, attracted solely by his fortune, proved her selfishness by deserting him in prison." Mary added an inscription on her part: "I love the author beyond all powers of expression . . . by that love we have promised to each other, although I may not be yours I can never be another's,"—and a good deal more to the same effect.

Amid these excitements Shelley was for some days without writing to Harriet, who applied to Hookham the publisher to know what had happened. She was expecting her confinement; "I always fancy something dreadful has happened," she wrote, "if I do not hear from him . . . I cannot endure this dreadful state of suspense." Shelley then wrote to her, begging her to come to London; and when she arrived there, he told her the state of his feelings, and proposed separation. The shock made Harriet ill; and Shelley, says Peacock, "between his old feelings towards Harriet, and his new passion for Mary, showed in his looks, in his gestures, in his speech, the state of a mind 'suffering, like a little kingdom, the nature of an insurrection.'" Godwin grew uneasy about his daughter, and after a serious talk with her, wrote to Shelley. Under such circumstances, Professor Dowden tells us, "to youth, swift and decisive measures seem the best." In the early morning of the 28th of July 1814 "Mary Godwin stepped across her father's threshold into the summer air," she and Shelley went off together in a post-chaise to Dover, and from thence crossed to the Continent.

On the 14th of August the fugitives were at Troyes on their way to Switzerland. From Troyes Shelley addressed a letter to Harriet, of which the best description I can give is that it is precisely the letter which a man in the writer's circumstances should not have written.

My dearest Harriet [he begins]—I write to you from this detestable town; I write to show that I do not forget you; I write to urge you to come to Switzerland, where you will at last find one firm and constant friend to whom your interests will be always dear—by whom your feelings will never wilfully be injured. From none can you expect this but me—all else are either unfeeling or selfish, or have beloved friends of their own.

Then follows a description of his journey with Mary from Paris, "through a fertile country, neither interesting from the character of its inhabitants nor the beauty of the scenery, with a mule to carry our baggage, as Mary, who has not been sufficiently well to walk, fears the fatigue of walking." Like St. Paul to Timothy, he ends with commissions:

I wish you to bring with you the two deeds which Tahourdin has to prepare for you, as also a copy of the settlement. Do not part with any of your money. But what shall be done about the books? You can consult on the spot. With love to my sweet little Ianthe, ever most affectionately yours, S.
I write in great haste; we depart directly.

Professor Dowden's flow of sentiment is here so agitating, that I relieve myself by resorting to a drier world. Certainly my comment on this letter shall not be his, that it "assures Harriet that her interests were still dear to Shelley, though now their lives had moved apart." But neither will I call the letter an odious letter, a hideous letter. I prefer to call it, applying an untranslatable French word, a *bête* letter. And it is *bête* from what is the signal, the disastrous want and weakness of Shelley, with all his fine intellectual gifts—his utter deficiency in humour.

Harriet did not accept Shelley's invitation to join him and Mary in Switzerland. Money difficulties drove the travellers back to England in September. Godwin would not see Shelley, but he sorely needed, continually demanded, and eagerly accepted, pecuniary help from his erring "spiritual son." Between Godwin's wants and his own, Shelley was hard pressed. He got from Harriet, who still believed that he would return to her, twenty pounds which remained in her hands. In November she was confined; a son and heir was born to Shelley. He went to see Harriet, but "the interview left husband and wife each embittered against the other." Friends were severe; "when Mrs. Boinville wrote, her letter· seemed cold and even sarcastic," says Professor Dowden. "Solitude," he continues, "unharassed by debts and duns, with Mary's companionship, the society of a few friends, and the delights of study and authorship, would have made these winter months to Shelley months of unusual happiness and calm." But, alas! creditors were pestering, and even Harriet gave trouble. In January 1815 Mary had to write in her journal this entry: "Harriet sends her creditors here; nasty woman. Now we must change our lodgings."

One day about this time Shelley asked Peacock, "Do you think Wordsworth could have written such poetry if he ever had dealings with money-lenders?" Not only had Shelley dealings with money-lenders, he now had dealings with bailiffs also. But still he continued to read largely. In January 1815 his grandfather, Sir Bysshe Shelley, died. Shelley went down into Sussex; his father would not suffer him to enter the house, but he sat outside the door and read *Comus,* while the reading of his grandfather's will went on inside. In February was born Mary's first child, a girl, who lived but a few days. All the spring Shelley was ill and harassed, but by June it was settled that he should have an allowance from his father of £1000 a year, and that his debts (including £1200 promised by him to Godwin) should be paid. He on his part paid Harriet's debts and allowed her £200 a year. In August he took a house on the borders of Windsor Park, and made a boating excursion up the Thames as far as Lechlade, an excursion which produced his first entire poem of value, the beautiful *Stanzas in Lechlade Churchyard.* They were followed, later in the autumn, by *Alastor.* Henceforth, from this winter of 1815 until he was drowned between Leghorn and Spezzia in July 1822, Shelley's literary history is sufficiently given in the delightful introductions prefixed by Mrs. Shelley to the poems of each year. Much of the history of his life is there given also; but with some of those "occurrences of his private life" on which Mrs. Shelley forbore to touch, and which are now made known to us in Professor Dowden's book, we have still to deal.

Mary's first son, William, was born in January 1816, and in February we find Shelley declaring himself "strongly urged, by the perpetual experience of neglect or enmity from almost every one but those who are supported by my resources, to desert my native country, hiding myself and Mary from the contempt which we so unjustly endure." Early in May he left England with Mary and Miss Clairmont; they met Lord Byron at Geneva and passed the summer by the Lake of Geneva in his company. Miss Clairmont had already in London, without the knowledge of the Shelleys, made Byron's acquaintance and become his mistress. Shelley determined, in the course of the summer, to go back to England, and, after all, "to make that most excellent of nations my perpetual resting-place." In September he and his ladies returned; Miss Clairmont was then expecting her confinement. Of her being Byron's mistress the Shelleys were now aware; but "the moral indignation," says Professor Dowden, "which Byron's act might justly arouse, seems to have been felt by neither Shelley nor Mary." If Byron and Claire Clairmont, as she was now called, loved and were happy, all was well.

The eldest daughter of the Godwin household, the amiable Fanny, was unhappy at home and in deep dejection of spirits. Godwin was, as usual, in terrible straits for money. The Shelleys and Miss Clairmont settled themselves at Bath; early in October Fanny Godwin passed through Bath without their knowing it, travelled on to Swansea, took a bedroom at the hotel there, and was found in the morning dead, with a bottle of laudanum on the table beside her and these words in her handwriting:

I have long determined that the best thing I could do was to put an end to the existence of a being whose birth was unfortunate,[1] and whose life has only been a series of pain to those persons who have hurt their health in endeavouring to promote her welfare. Perhaps to hear of my death will give you pain, but you will soon have the blessing of forgetting that such a creature ever existed as . . .

There is no signature.

A sterner tragedy followed. On the 9th of November 1816 Harriet Shelley left the house in Brompton where

[1] She was Mary Wollstonecraft's natural daughter by Imlay. (Arnold's note.)

she was then living, and did not return. On the 10th
of December her body was found in the Serpentine; she
had drowned herself. In one respect Professor Dowden
resembles Providence: his ways are inscrutable. His
comment on Harriet's death is: "There is no doubt she
wandered from the ways of upright living." But, he
adds: "That no act of Shelley's, during the two years
which immediately preceded her death, tended to cause
the rash act which brought her life to its close, seems
certain." Shelley had been living with Mary all the
time; only that!

On the 30th of December 1816 Mary Godwin and
Shelley were married. I shall pursue "the occurrences
of Shelley's private life" no further. For the five years
and a half which remain, Professor Dowden's book adds
to our knowledge of Shelley's life much that is interesting; but what was chiefly important we knew already.
The new and grave matter which we did not know, or
knew in the vaguest way only, but which Shelley's
family and Professor Dowden have now thought it well
to give us in full, ends with Shelley's second marriage.

I regret, I say once more, that it has been given. It
is a sore trial for our love of Shelley. What a set! what a
world! is the exclamation that breaks from us as we come
to an end of this history of "the occurrences of Shelley's
private life." I used the French word *bête* for a letter of
Shelley's; for the world in which we find him I can only
use another French word, *sale*. Godwin's house of sordid
horror, and Godwin preaching and holding the hat, and
the green-spectacled Mrs. Godwin, and Hogg the faithful friend, and Hunt the Horace of this precious world,
and, to go up higher, Sir Timothy Shelley, a great
country gentleman, feeling himself safe while "the exalted mind of the Duke of Norfolk [the drinking Duke]
protects me with the world," and Lord Byron with his

deep grain of coarseness and commonness, his affectation, his brutal selfishness—what a set! The history carries us to Oxford, and I think of the clerical and respectable Oxford of those old times, the Oxford of Copleston and the Kebles and Hawkins, and a hundred more, with the relief Keble declares himself to experience from Izaak Walton,

> When, wearied with the tale thy times disclose,
> The eye first finds thee out in thy secure repose.

I am not only thinking of morals and the house of Godwin, I am thinking also of tone, bearing, dignity. I appeal to Cardinal Newman, if perchance he does me the honour to read these words, is it possible to imagine Copleston or Hawkins declaring himself safe "while the exalted mind of the Duke of Norfolk protects me with the world"?

Mrs. Shelley, after her marriage and during Shelley's closing years, becomes attractive; up to her marriage her letters and journal do not please. Her ability is manifest, but she is not attractive. In the world discovered to us by Professor Dowden as surrounding Shelley up to 1817, the most pleasing figure is poor Fanny Godwin; after Fanny Godwin, the most pleasing figure is Harriet Shelley herself.

Professor Dowden's treatment of Harriet is not worthy —so much he must allow me in all kindness, but also in all seriousness, to say—of either his taste or his judgment. His pleading for Shelley is constant, and he does more harm than good to Shelley by it. But here his championship of Shelley makes him very unjust to a cruelly used and unhappy girl. For several pages he balances the question whether or not Harriet was unfaithful to Shelley before he left her for Mary, and he leaves the question unsettled. As usual Professor Dowden (and it is his signal merit) supplies the evidence decisive against himself. Thornton Hunt, not well disposed to Harriet, Hogg, Peacock, Trelawny, Hookham, and a member of Godwin's own family, are all clear in their evidence that up to her parting from Shelley Harriet was perfectly innocent. But that precious witness, Godwin, wrote in 1817 that "she had proved herself unfaithful to her husband before their separation. . . . Peace be to her shade!" Why, Godwin was the father of Harriet's successor. But Mary believed the same thing. She was Harriet's successor. But Shelley believed it too. He had it from Godwin. But he was convinced of it earlier. The evidence for this is, that, in writing to Southey in 1820, Shelley declares that "the single passage of a life, otherwise not only spotless but spent in an impassioned pursuit of virtue, which looks like a blot," bears that appearance "merely because I regulated my domestic arrangements without deferring to the notions of the vulgar, although I might have done so quite as conveniently had I descended to their base thoughts." From this Professor Dowden concludes that Shelley believed he could have got a divorce from Harriet had he so wished. The conclusion is not clear. But even were the evidence perfectly clear that Shelley believed Harriet unfaithful when he parted from her, we should have to take into account Mrs. Shelley's most true sentence in her introduction to *Alastor*: "In all Shelley did, he, at the time of doing it, believed himself justified to his own conscience."

Shelley's asserting a thing vehemently does not prove more than that he chose to believe it and did believe it. His extreme and violent changes of opinion about people show this sufficiently. Eliza Westbrook is at one time "a diamond not so large" as her sister Harriet but "more highly polished"; and then: "I certainly hate her with

all my heart and soul. I sometimes feel faint with the
fatigue of checking the overflowings of my unbounded
abhorrence for this miserable wretch." The antipathy,
Hogg tells us, was as unreasonable as the former excess
of deference. To his friend Miss Hitchener he says:
"Never shall that intercourse cease, which has been the
day-dawn of my existence, the sun which has shed
warmth on the cold drear length of the anticipated prospect of life." A little later, and she has become "the
Brown Demon, a woman of desperate views and dreadful passions, but a cool and undeviating revenge." Even
Professor Dowden admits that this is absurd; that the
real Miss Hitchener was not seen by Shelley, either
when he adored or when he detested.

Shelley's power of persuading himself was equal to
any occasion; but would not his conscientiousness and
high feeling have prevented his exerting this power at
poor Harriet's expense? To abandon her as he did, must
he not have known her to be false? Professor Dowden
insists always on Shelley's "conscientiousness." Shelley
himself speaks of his "impassioned pursuit of virtue."
Leigh Hunt compared his life to that of "Plato himself,
or, still more, a Pythagorean," and added that he "never
met a being who came nearer, perhaps so near, to the
height of humanity," to being an "angel of charity." In
many respects Shelley really resembled both a Pythagorean and an angel of charity. He loved high thoughts,
he cared nothing for sumptuous lodging, fare, and rai-
ment, he was poignantly afflicted at the sight of misery,
he would have given away his last farthing, would
have suffered in his own person, to relieve it. But in one
important point he was like neither a Pythagorean nor
an angel: he was extremely inflammable. Professor Dowden leaves no doubt on the matter. After reading his
book, one feels sickened forever of the subject of irreg-

ular relations; God forbid that I should go into the scandals about Shelley's "Neapolitan charge," about Shelley and Emilia Viviani, about Shelley and Miss Clairmont, and the rest of it! I will say only that it is visible enough that when the passion of love was aroused in Shelley (and it was aroused easily) one could not be sure of him, his friends could not trust him. We have seen him with the Boinville family. With Emilia Viviani he is the same. If he is left much alone with Miss Clairmont, he evidently makes Mary uneasy; nay, he makes Professor Dowden himself uneasy. And I conclude that an entirely human inflammability, joined to an inhuman want of humour and a superhuman power of self-deception, are the causes which chiefly explain Shelley's abandonment of Harriet in the first place, and then his behaviour to her and his defence of himself afterwards.

His misconduct to Harriet, his want of humour, his self-deception, are fully brought before us for the first time by Professor Dowden's book. Good morals and good criticism alike forbid that when all this is laid bare to us we should deny, or hide, or extenuate it. Nevertheless I go back after all to what I said at the beginning; still our ideal Shelley, the angelic Shelley, subsists. Unhappily the data for this Shelley we had and knew long ago, while the data for the unattractive Shelley are fresh; and what is fresh is likely to fix our attention more than what is familiar. But Professor Dowden's volumes, which give so much, which give too much, also afford data for picturing anew the Shelley who delights, as well as for picturing for the first time a Shelley who, to speak plainly, disgusts; and with what may renew and restore our impression of the delightful Shelley I shall end.

The winter at Marlow, and the ophthalmia caught among the cottages of the poor, we knew, but we have from Professor Dowden more details of this winter and of Shelley's work among the poor; we have above all, for the first time I believe, a line of verse of Shelley's own which sums up truly and perfectly this most attractive side of him—

> I am the friend of the unfriended poor.

But that in Shelley on which I would especially dwell is that in him which contrasts most with the ignobleness of the world in which we have seen him living, and with the pernicious nonsense which we have found him talking. The Shelley of "marvellous gentleness," of feminine refinement, with gracious and considerate manners, "a perfect gentleman, entirely without arrogance or aggressive egotism," completely devoid of the proverbial and ferocious vanity of authors and poets, always disposed to make little of his own work and to prefer that of others, of reverent enthusiasm for the great and wise, of high and tender seriousness, of heroic generosity, and of a delicacy in rendering services which was equal to his generosity—the Shelley who was all this is the Shelley with whom I wish to end. He may talk nonsense about tyrants and priests, but what a high and noble ring in such a sentence as the following, written by a young man who is refusing £2000 a year rather than consent to entail a great property!

That I should entail £120,000 of command over labour, of power to remit this, to employ it for benevolent purposes, on one whom I know not—who might, instead of being the benefactor of mankind, be its bane, or use this for the worst purposes, which the real delegates of my chance-given property might convert into a most useful instrument of benevolence! No! this you will not suspect me of.

And again:

> I desire money because I think I know the use of it. It commands labour, it gives leisure; and to give leisure to those who will employ it in the forwarding of truth is the noblest present an individual can make to the whole.

If there is extravagance here, it is extravagance of a beautiful and rare sort, like Shelley's "underhand ways" also, which differed singularly, the cynic Hogg tells us, from the underhand ways of other people; "the latter were concealed because they were mean, selfish, sordid; Shelley's secrets, on the contrary (kindnesses done by stealth), were hidden through modesty, delicacy, generosity, refinement of soul."

His forbearance to Godwin, to Godwin lecturing and renouncing him and at the same time holding out, as I have said, his hat to him for alms, is wonderful; but the dignity with which he at last, in a letter perfect for propriety of tone, reads a lesson to his ignoble father-in-law, is in the best possible style:

> Perhaps it is well that you should be informed that I consider your last letter to be written in a style of haughtiness and encroachment which neither awes nor imposes on me; but I have no desire to transgress the limits which you place to our intercourse, nor in any future instance will I make any remarks but such as arise from the strict question in discussion.

And again:

> My astonishment, and, I will confess, when I have been treated with most harshness and cruelty by you, my indignation, has been extreme, that, knowing as you do my nature, any considerations should have prevailed on you to have been thus harsh and cruel. I lamented also over my ruined hopes of all that your genius once taught me to expect from your virtue, when I found that for yourself, your family, and

your creditors, you would submit to that communication with me which you once rejected and abhorred, and which no pity for my poverty or sufferings, assumed willingly for you, could avail to extort.

Moreover, though Shelley has no humour, he can show as quick and sharp a tact as the most practised man of the world. He has been with Byron and the Countess Guiccioli, and he writes of the latter:

La Guiccioli is a very pretty, sentimental, innocent Italian, who has sacrificed an immense future for the sake of Lord Byron, and who, if I know anything of my friend, of her, and of human nature, will hereafter have plenty of opportunity to repent her rashness.

Tact also, and something better than tact, he shows in his dealings, in order to befriend Leigh Hunt, with Lord Byron. He writes to Hunt:

Particular circumstances, or rather, I should say, particular dispositions in Lord Byron's character, render the close and exclusive intimacy with him, in which I find myself, intolerable to me; thus much, my best friend, I will confess and confide to you. No feelings of my own shall injure or interfere with what is now nearest to them—your interest; and I will take care to preserve the little influence I may have over this Proteus, in whom such strange extremes are reconciled, until we meet.

And so we have come back again, at last, to our original Shelley—to the Shelley of the lovely and well-known picture, to the Shelley with "flushed, feminine, artless face," the Shelley "blushing like a girl," of Trelawny. Professor Dowden gives us some further attempts at portraiture. One by a Miss Rose, of Shelley at Marlow:

He was the most interesting figure I ever saw; his eyes like a deer's, bright but rather wild; his white throat unfettered; his slender but to me almost faultless shape; his brown long coat with curling lambs' wool collar and cuffs—in fact, his whole appearance—are as fresh in my recollection as an occurrence of yesterday.

Feminine enthusiasm may be deemed suspicious, but a Captain Kennedy must surely be able to keep his head. Captain Kennedy was quartered at Horsham in 1813, and saw Shelley when he was on a stolen visit, in his father's absence, at Field Place:

He received me with frankness and kindliness, as if he had known me from childhood, and at once won my heart. I fancy I see him now as he sate by the window, and hear his voice, the tones of which impressed me with his sincerity and simplicity. His resemblance to his sister Elizabeth was as striking as if they had been twins. His eyes were most expressive; his complexion beautifully fair, his features exquisitely fine; his hair was dark, and no peculiar attention to its arrangement was manifest. In person he was slender and gentlemanlike, but inclined to stoop; his gait was decidedly not military. The general appearance indicated great delicacy of constitution. One would at once pronounce of him that he was different from other men. There was an earnestness in his manner and such perfect gentleness of breeding and freedom from everything artificial as charmed every one. I never met a man who so immediately won upon me.

Mrs. Gisborne's son, who knew Shelley well at Leghorn, declared Captain Kennedy's description of him to be "the best and most truthful I have ever seen."

To all this we have to add the charm of the man's writings—of Shelley's poetry. It is his poetry, above everything else, which for many people establishes that he is an angel. Of his poetry I have not space now to speak. But let no one suppose that a want of humour and a self-delusion such as Shelley's have no effect upon a man's poetry. The man Shelley, in very truth, is not entirely sane, and Shelley's poetry is not entirely sane either. The Shelley of actual life is a vision of beauty and radiance, indeed, but availing nothing, effecting nothing. And in poetry, no less than in life, he is "a beautiful *and ineffectual* angel, beating in the void his luminous wings in vain."

◐

LITERATURE AND SCIENCE

◐

PRACTICAL people talk with a smile of Plato and of his absolute ideas; and it is impossible to deny that Plato's ideas do often seem unpractical and impracticable, and especially when one views them in connection with the life of a great work-a-day world like the United States. The necessary staple of the life of such a world Plato regards with disdain; handicraft and trade and the working professions he regards with disdain; but what becomes of the life of an industrial modern community if you take handicraft and trade and the working professions out of it? The base mechanic arts and handicrafts, says Plato, bring about a natural weakness in the principle of excellence in a man, so that he cannot govern the ignoble growths in him, but nurses them, and cannot understand fostering any other. Those who exercise such arts and trades, as they have their bodies, he says, marred by their vulgar businesses, so they have their souls, too, bowed and broken by them. And if one of these uncomely people has a mind to seek self-culture and philosophy, Plato compares him to a bald little tinker, who has scraped together money, and has got his release from service, and has had a bath, and bought a new coat, and is rigged out like a bridegroom about to marry the daughter of his master who has fallen into poor and helpless estate.

Nor do the working professions fare any better than trade at the hands of Plato. He draws for us an inimitable picture of the working lawyer, and of his life of bondage; he shows how this bondage from his youth up has stunted and warped him, and made him small and crooked of soul, encompassing him with difficulties which he is not man enough to rely on justice and truth as means to encounter, but has recourse, for help out of them, to falsehood and wrong. And so, says Plato, this poor creature is bent and broken, and grows up from boy to man without a particle of soundness in him, although exceedingly smart and clever in his own esteem.

One cannot refuse to admire the artist who draws these pictures. But we say to ourselves that his ideas show the influence of a primitive and obsolete order of things, when the warrior caste and the priestly caste were alone in honour, and the humble work of the world was done by slaves. We have now changed all that; the modern majority consists in work, as Emerson declares; and in work, we may add, principally of such plain and dusty kind as the work of cultivators of the ground, handicraftsmen, men of trade and business, men of the working professions. Above all is this true in a great industrious community such as that of the United States.

Now education, many people go on to say, is still mainly governed by the ideas of men like Plato, who lived when the warrior caste and the priestly or philosophical class were alone in honour, and the really useful part of the community were slaves. It is an education fitted for persons of leisure in such a community. This education passed from Greece and Rome to the feudal communities of Europe, where also the warrior caste and the priestly caste were alone held in honour, and where the really useful and working part of the community, though not nominally slaves as in the pagan world, were practically not much better off than slaves, and not more seriously regarded. And how absurd it is, people end by saying, to inflict this education upon an industrious modern community, where very few indeed are persons of leisure, and the mass to be considered has not leisure, but is bound, for its own great good, and for the great good of the world at large, to plain labour and to industrial pursuits, and the education in question tends necessarily to make men dissatisfied with these pursuits and unfitted for them!

That is what is said. So far I must defend Plato, as to plead that his view of education and studies is in the general, as it seems to me, sound enough, and fitted for all sorts and conditions of men, whatever their pursuits may be. "An intelligent man," says Plato, "will prize those studies which result in his soul getting soberness, righteousness, and wisdom, and will less value the others." I cannot consider *that* a bad description of the aim of education, and of the motives which should govern us in the choice of studies, whether we are preparing ourselves for a hereditary seat in the English House of Lords or for the pork trade in Chicago.

Still I admit that Plato's world was not ours, that his scorn of trade and handicraft is fantastic, that he had no conception of a great industrial community such as that of the United States, and that such a community must and will shape its education to suit its own needs. If the usual education handed down to it from the past does not suit it, it will certainly before long drop this and try another. The usual education in the past has been mainly literary. The question is whether the studies which were long supposed to be the best for all of us are practically the best now; whether others are not better. The tyranny of the past, many think, weighs on us injuriously in the predominance given to letters in education. The question is raised whether, to meet the needs of our modern life, the predominance ought not now to pass from letters to science; and naturally the question is nowhere raised with more energy than here in the United States. The design of abasing what is called "mere literary instruction and education," and of exalting what is called "sound, extensive, and practical scientific knowledge," is, in this intensely modern world of the United States, even more perhaps than in Europe, a very popular design, and makes great and rapid progress.

I am going to ask whether the present movement for ousting letters from their old predominance in education, and for transferring the predominance in education to the natural sciences, whether this brisk and flourishing movement ought to prevail, and whether it is likely that in the end it really will prevail. An objection may be raised which I will anticipate. My own studies have been almost wholly in letters, and my visits to the field of the natural sciences have been very slight and inadequate, although those sciences have always strongly moved my curiosity. A man of letters, it will perhaps be said, is not competent to discuss the comparative merits of letters and natural science as means of education. To this objection I reply, first of all, that his incompetence, if he attempts the discussion but is really incompetent for it, will be abundantly visible; nobody will be taken in; he will have plenty of sharp observers and critics to save mankind from that danger. But the line I am going to follow is, as you will soon discover, so extremely simple, that perhaps it may be followed without failure even by one who for a more ambitious line of discussion would be quite incompetent.

Some of you may possibly remember a phrase of mine which has been the object of a good deal of comment; an observation to the effect that in our culture, the aim being *to know ourselves and the world,* we have, as the means to this end, *to know the best which has been thought and said in the world.* A man of science, who is also an excellent writer and the very prince of debaters, Professor Huxley, in a discourse at the opening of Sir Josiah Mason's college at Birmingham, laying hold of this phrase, expanded it by quoting some more words of mine, which are these: "The civilised world is to be regarded as now being, for intellectual and spiritual purposes, one great confederation, bound to a joint action and working to a common result; and whose members have for their proper outfit a knowledge of Greek, Roman, and Eastern antiquity, and of one another. Special local and temporary advantages being put out of account, that modern nation will in the intellectual and spiritual sphere make most progress, which most thoroughly carries out this programme."

Now on my phrase, thus enlarged, Professor Huxley remarks that when I speak of the above-mentioned knowledge as enabling us to know ourselves and the world, I assert *literature* to contain the materials which suffice for thus making us know ourselves and the world. But it is not by any means clear, says he, that after having learnt all which ancient and modern literatures have to tell us, we have laid a sufficiently broad and deep foundation for that criticism of life, that knowledge of ourselves and the world, which constitutes culture. On the contrary, Professor Huxley declares that he finds himself "wholly unable to admit that either nations or individuals will really advance, if their outfit draws nothing from the stores of physical science. An army without weapons of precision, and with no particular base of operations, might more hopefully enter upon a campaign on the Rhine, than a man, devoid of a knowledge of what physical science has done in the last century, upon a criticism of life."

This shows how needful it is for those who are to discuss any matter together, to have a common understanding as to the sense of the terms they employ,—how needful, and how difficult. What Professor Huxley says, implies just the reproach which is so often brought against the study of *belles lettres,* as they are called: that the study is an elegant one, but slight and ineffectual; a smattering of Greek and Latin and other ornamental things, of little use for any one whose object is to get at truth, and to be a practical man. So, too, M. Renan talks of the "superficial humanism" of a school-course which treats us as if we were all going to be poets, writers, preachers, orators, and he opposes this humanism to positive science, or the critical search after truth. And there is always a tendency in those who are remonstrating against the predominance of letters in education, to understand by letters *belles lettres,* and by *belles lettres* a superficial humanism, the opposite of science or true knowledge.

But when we talk of knowing Greek and Roman antiquity, for instance, which is the knowledge people have called the humanities, I for my part mean a knowledge which is something more than a superficial humanism, mainly decorative. "I call all teaching *scientific*," says Wolf, the critic of Homer, "which is systematically laid out and followed up to its original sources. For example: a knowledge of classical antiquity is scientific when the remains of classical antiquity are correctly studied in the original languages." There can be no doubt that Wolf is perfectly right; that all learning is scientific which is systematically laid out and followed up to its original sources, and that a genuine humanism is scientific.

When I speak of knowing Greek and Roman antiquity, therefore, as a help to knowing ourselves and the world, I mean more than a knowledge of so much vocabulary, so much grammar, so many portions of authors in the Greek and Latin languages. I mean knowing the Greeks and Romans, and their life and genius, and what they were and did in the world; what we get from them, and what is its value. That, at least, is the ideal; and when we talk of endeavouring to know Greek and Roman antiquity, as a help to knowing ourselves and the world, we mean endeavouring so to know them as to satisfy this ideal, however much we may still fall short of it.

The same also as to knowing our own and other modern nations, with the like aim of getting to understand ourselves and the world. To know the best that has been thought and said by the modern nations, is to know says Professor Huxley, "only what modern *literatures* have to tell us; it is the criticism of life contained in modern literature." And yet "the distinctive character of our times," he urges, "lies in the vast and constantly increasing part which is played by natural knowledge." And how, therefore, can a man, devoid of knowledge of what physical science has done in the last century, enter hopefully upon a criticism of modern life?

Let us, I say, be agreed about the meaning of the terms we are using. I talk of knowing the best which has been thought and uttered in the world; Professor Huxley says this means knowing *literature*. Literature is a large word; it may mean everything written with letters or printed in a book. Euclid's *Elements* and Newton's *Principia* are thus literature. All knowledge that reaches us through books is literature. But by literature Professor Huxley means *belles lettres*. He means to make me say, that knowing the best which has been thought and said by the modern nations is knowing their *belles lettres* and no more. And this is no sufficient equipment, he argues, for a criticism of modern life. But as I do not mean, by knowing ancient Rome, knowing merely more or less of Latin *belles lettres,* and taking no account of Rome's military, and political, and legal, and administrative work in the world; and as, by knowing ancient Greece, I understand knowing her as the giver of Greek art, and the guide to a free and right use of reason and to scientific method, and the founder of our mathematics and physics and astronomy and biology,—I understand knowing her as all this, and not merely knowing certain Greek poems, and histories, and treatises, and speeches,—so as to the knowledge of modern nations also. By knowing modern nations, I mean not merely knowing their *belles lettres*, but knowing also what has been done by such men as Copernicus, Galileo, Newton, Darwin. "Our ancestors learned," says Professor Huxley, "that the earth is the centre of the visible universe, and that man is the cynosure of things terrestrial; and more especially was it inculcated that the course of nature had no fixed order, but that it could be, and constantly was, altered." But for us now, continues Professor Huxley, "the notions of the beginning and the end of the world entertained by our forefathers are no longer credible. It is very certain that the earth is not the chief body in the material universe, and that the world is not subordinated to man's use. It is even more certain that nature is the expression of a definite order, with which nothing interferes." "And yet," he cries, "the purely classical education advocated by the representatives of the humanists in our day gives no inkling of all this!"

In due place and time I will just touch upon that vexed question of classical education; but at present the question is as to what is meant by knowing the best which modern nations have thought and said. It is not knowing their *belles lettres* merely which is meant. To know Italian *belles lettres* is not to know Italy, and to know English *belles lettres* is not to know England. Into knowing Italy and England there comes a great deal more, Galileo and Newton, amongst it. The reproach of being a superficial humanism, a tincture of *belles lettres*, may attach rightly enough to some other disciplines; but to the particular discipline recommended when I proposed knowing the best that has been thought and said in the world, it does not apply. In that best I certainly include what in modern times has been thought and said by the great observers and knowers of nature.

There is, therefore, really no question between Professor Huxley and me as to whether knowing the great results of the modern scientific study of nature is not required as a part of our culture, as well as knowing the products of literature and art. But to follow the processes by which those results are reached, ought, say the friends of physical science, to be made the staple of education for the bulk of mankind. And here there does arise a question between those whom Professor Huxley calls with playful sarcasm "the Levites of culture," and those whom the poor humanist is sometimes apt to regard as its Nebuchadnezzars.

The great results of the scientific investigation of nature we are agreed upon knowing, but how much of our study are we bound to give to the processes by which those results are reached? The results have their visible bearing on human life. But all the processes, too, all the items of fact, by which those results are reached and established, are interesting. All knowledge is interesting to a wise man, and the knowledge of nature is interesting to all men. It is very interesting to know, that, from the albuminous white of the egg, the chick in the egg gets the materials for its flesh, bones, blood, and feathers; while, from the fatty yolk of the egg, it gets the heat and energy which enable it at length to break its shell and begin the world. It is less interesting, perhaps, but still it is interesting, to know that when a taper burns, the wax is converted into carbonic acid and water. Moreover, it is quite true that the habit of dealing with facts, which is given by the study of nature, is, as the friends of physical science praise it for being, an excellent discipline. The appeal, in the study of nature, is constantly to observation and experiment; not only is it said that the thing is so, but we can be made to see that it is so. Not only does a man tell us that when a taper burns the wax is converted into carbonic acid and water, as a man may tell us, if he likes, that Charon is punting his ferry-boat on the river Styx, or that Victor Hugo is a sublime poet, or Mr. Gladstone the most admirable of statesmen; but we are made to see that the conversion into carbonic acid and water does actually happen. This reality of natural knowledge it is, which makes the friends of physical science contrast it, as a knowledge of things, with the humanist's knowledge, which is, say they, a knowledge of words. And hence Professor Huxley is moved to lay it down that, "for the purpose of attaining real culture, an exclusively scientific education is at least as effectual as an exclusively literary education." And a certain President of the Section for Mechanical Science in the British Association is, in Scripture phrase, "very bold," and declares that if a man, in his mental training, "has substituted literature and history for natural science, he has chosen the less useful alternative." But whether we go these lengths or not, we must all admit that in natural science the habit gained of dealing with facts is a most valuable discipline, and that every one should have some experience of it.

More than this, however, is demanded by the reformers. It is proposed to make the training in natural science the main part of education, for the great majority of mankind at any rate. And here, I confess, I part company with the friends of physical science, with whom up to this point I have been agreeing. In differing from them, however, I wish to proceed with the utmost caution and diffidence. The smallness of my own acquaintance with the disciplines of natural science is ever before my mind, and I am fearful of doing these disciplines an injustice. The ability and pugnacity of the partisans of natural science makes them formidable persons to contradict. The tone of tentative inquiry, which befits a being of dim faculties and bounded knowledge, is the tone I would wish to take and not to depart from. At present it seems to me, that those who are for giving to natural knowledge, as they call it, the chief place in the education of the majority of mankind, leave one important thing out of their account: the constitution of human nature. But I put this forward on the strength of some facts not at all recondite, very far from it; facts capable of being stated in the simplest possible fashion, and to which, if I so state them, the man of science will, I am sure, be willing to allow their due weight.

Deny the facts altogether, I think, he hardly can. He can hardly deny, that when we set ourselves to enumerate the powers which go to the building up of human life, and say that they are the power of conduct, the power of intellect and knowledge, the power of beauty, and the power of social life and manners,—he can hardly deny that this scheme, though drawn in rough

and plain lines enough, and not pretending to scientific
exactness, does yet give a fairly true representation of
the matter. Human nature is built up by these powers;
we have the need for them all. When we have rightly
met and adjusted the claims of them all, we shall then
be in a fair way for getting soberness and righteousness,
with wisdom. This is evident enough, and the friends
of physical science would admit it.

But perhaps they may not have sufficiently observed
another thing: namely, that the several powers just
mentioned are not isolated, but there is, in the generality of mankind, a perpetual tendency to relate them one
to another in divers ways. With one such way of relating
them I am particularly concerned now. Following our
instinct for intellect and knowledge, we acquire pieces
of knowledge; and presently, in the generality of men,
there arises the desire to relate these pieces of knowledge to our sense for conduct, to our sense for beauty,—
and there is weariness and dissatisfaction if the desire
is baulked. Now in this desire lies, I think, the strength
of that hold which letters have upon us.

All knowledge is, as I said just now, interesting; and
even items of knowledge which from the nature of the
case cannot well be related, but must stand isolated in
our thoughts, have their interest. Even lists of exceptions have their interest. If we are studying Greek accents, it is interesting to know that *pais* and *pas,* and
some other monosyllables of the same form of declen-
sion, do not take the circumflex upon the last syllable
of the genitive plural, but vary, in this respect, from the
common rule. If we are studying physiology, it is interesting to know that the pulmonary artery carries dark
blood and the pulmonary vein carries bright blood, de-
parting in this respect from the common rule for the division of labour between the veins and the arteries. But

every one knows how we seek naturally to combine the pieces of our knowledge together, to bring them under general rules, to relate them to principles; and how unsatisfactory and tiresome it would be to go on for ever learning lists of exceptions, or accumulating items of fact which must stand isolated.

Well, that same need of relating our knowledge, which operates here within the sphere of our knowledge itself, we shall find operating, also, outside that sphere. We experience, as we go on learning and knowing,—the vast majority of us experience,—the need of relating what we have learnt and known to the sense which we have in us for conduct, to the sense which we have in us for beauty.

A certain Greek prophetess of Mantineia in Arcadia, Diotima by name, once explained to the philosopher Socrates that love, and impulse, and bent of all kinds, is, in fact, nothing else but the desire in men that good should for ever be present to them. This desire for good, Diotima assured Socrates, is our fundamental desire, of which fundamental desire every impulse in us is only some one particular form. And therefore this fundamental desire it is, I suppose,—this desire in men that good should be for ever present to them,—which acts in us when we feel the impulse for relating our knowledge to our sense for conduct and to our sense for beauty. At any rate, with men in general the instinct exists. Such is human nature. And the instinct, it will be admitted, is innocent, and human nature is preserved by our following the lead of its innocent instincts. Therefore, in seeking to gratify this instinct in question, we are following the instinct of self-preservation in humanity.

But, no doubt, some kinds of knowledge cannot be made to directly serve the instinct in question, cannot be directly related to the sense for beauty, to the sense for conduct. These are instrument-knowledges; they lead on to other knowledges, which can. A man who passes his life in instrument-knowledges is a specialist. They may be invaluable as instruments to something beyond, for those who have the gift thus to employ them; and they may be disciplines in themselves wherein it is useful for every one to have some schooling. But it is inconceivable that the generality of men should pass all their mental life with Greek accents or with formal logic. My friend Professor Sylvester, who is one of the first mathematicians in the world, holds transcendental doctrines as to the virtue of mathematics, but those doctrines are not for common men. In the very Senate House and heart of our English Cambridge I once ventured, though not without an apology for my profaneness, to hazard the opinion that for the majority of mankind a little of mathematics, even, goes a long way. Of course this is quite consistent with their being of immense importance as an instrument to something else; but it is the few who have the aptitude for thus using them, not the bulk of mankind.

The natural sciences do not, however, stand on the same footing with these instrument-knowledges. Experience shows us that the generality of men will find more interest in learning that, when a taper burns, the wax is converted into carbonic acid and water, or in learning the explanation of the phenomenon of dew, or in learning how the circulation of the blood is carried on, than they find in learning that the genitive plural of *pais* and *pas* does not take the circumflex on the termination. And one piece of natural knowledge is added to another, and others are added to that, and at last we come to propositions so interesting as Mr. Darwin's famous proposition that "our ancestor was a hairy quadruped furnished with a tail and pointed ears, probably arboreal in his habits." Or we come to propositions of such reach and magnitude as those which Professor Huxley delivers, when he says that the notions of our forefathers about the beginning and the end of the world were all wrong, and that nature is the expression of a definite order with which nothing interferes.

Interesting, indeed, these results of science are, important they are, and we should all of us be acquainted with them. But what I now wish you to mark is, that we are still, when they are propounded to us and we receive them, we are still in the sphere of intellect and knowledge. And for the generality of men there will be found, I say, to arise, when they have duly taken in the proposition that their ancestor was "a hairy quadruped furnished with a tail and pointed ears, probably arboreal in his habits," there will be found to arise an invincible desire to relate this proposition to the sense in us for conduct, and to the sense in us for beauty. But this the men of science will not do for us, and will hardly even profess to do. They will give us other pieces of knowledge, other facts, about other animals and their ancestors, or about plants, or about stones, or about stars; and they may finally bring us to those great "general conceptions of the universe, which are forced upon us all," says Professor Huxley, "by the progress of physical science." But still it will be *knowledge* only which they give us; knowledge not put for us into relation with our sense for conduct, our sense for beauty, and touched with emotion by being so put; not thus put for us, and therefore, to the majority of mankind, after a certain while, unsatisfying, wearying.

Not to the born naturalist, I admit. But what do we mean by a born naturalist? We mean a man in whom the zeal for observing nature is so uncommonly strong and eminent, that it marks him off from the bulk of mankind. Such a man will pass his life happily in collecting natural knowledge and reasoning upon it, and will ask for nothing, or hardly anything, more. I have heard it said that the sagacious and admirable naturalist whom we lost not very long ago, Mr. Darwin, once owned to a friend that for his part he did not experience the necessity for two things which most men find so necessary to them,—religion and poetry; science and the domestic affections, he thought, were enough. To a born naturalist, I can well understand that this should seem so. So absorbing is his occupation with nature, so strong his love for his occupation, that he goes on acquiring natural knowledge and reasoning upon it, and has little time or inclination for thinking about getting it related to the desire in man for conduct, the desire in man for beauty. He relates it to them for himself as he goes along, so far as he feels the need; and he draws from the domestic affections all the additional solace necessary. But then Darwins are extremely rare. Another great and admirable master of natural knowledge, Faraday, was a Sandemanian. That is to say, he related his knowledge to his instinct for conduct and to his instinct for beauty, by the aid of that respectable Scottish sectary, Robert Sandeman. And so strong, in general, is the demand of religion and poetry to have their share in a man, to associate themselves with his knowing, and to relieve and rejoice it, that, probably, for one man amongst us with the disposition to do as Darwin did in this respect, there are at least fifty with the disposition to do as Faraday.

Education lays hold upon us, in fact, by satisfying this demand. Professor Huxley holds up to scorn mediæval education, with its neglect of the knowledge of nature, its poverty even of literary studies, its formal logic devoted to "showing how and why that which the Church said was true must be true." But the great mediæval Universities were not brought into being, we may be sure, by the zeal for giving a jejune and contemptible education. Kings have been their nursing fathers, and queens have been their nursing mothers, but not for this. The mediæval Universities came into being, because the supposed knowledge, delivered by Scripture and the Church, so deeply engaged men's hearts, by so simply, easily, and powerfully relating itself to their desire for conduct, their desire for beauty. All other knowledge was dominated by this supposed knowledge and was subordinated to it, because of the surpassing strength of the hold which it gained upon the affections of men, by allying itself profoundly with their sense for conduct, their sense for beauty.

But now, says Professor Huxley, conceptions of the universe fatal to the notions held by our forefathers have been forced upon us by physical science. Grant to him that they are thus fatal, that the new conceptions must and will soon become current everywhere, and that every one will finally perceive them to be fatal to the beliefs of our forefathers. The need of humane letters, as they are truly called, because they serve the paramount desire in men that good should be for ever present to them,—the need of humane letters, to establish a relation between the new conceptions, and our instinct for beauty, our instinct for conduct, is only the more visible. The Middle Age could do without humane letters, as it could do without the study of nature, because its supposed knowledge was made to engage its emotions so powerfully. Grant that the supposed knowledge disappears, its power of being made to engage the emotions will of course disappear along with it,—but the emotions themselves, and their claim to be engaged and satisfied, will remain. Now if we find by experience that humane letters have an undeniable power of engaging the emotions, the importance of humane letters in a man's training becomes not less, but greater, in proportion to the success of modern science in extirpating what it calls "mediæval thinking."

Have humane letters, then, have poetry and eloquence, the power here attributed to them of engaging the emotions, and do they exercise it? And if they have it and exercise it, *how* do they exercise it, so as to exert an influence upon man's sense for conduct, his sense for beauty? Finally, even if they both can and do exert an influence upon the senses in question, how are they to relate to them the results,—the modern results,—of natural science? All these questions may be asked. First, have poetry and eloquence the power of calling out the emotions? The appeal is to experience. Experience shows that for the vast majority of men, for mankind in general, they have the power. Next do they exercise it? They do. But then, *how* do they exercise it so as to affect man's sense for conduct, his sense for beauty? And this is perhaps a case for applying the Preacher's words: "Though a man labour to seek it out, yet he shall not find it; yea, farther, though a wise man think to know it, yet shall he not be able to find it." [1] Why should it be one thing, in its effect upon the emotions, to say, "Patience is a virtue," and quite another thing, in its effect upon the emotions, to say with Homer,

τλητὸν γὰρ Μοῖραι θυμὸν θέσαν ἀνθρώποισιν—[2]

"for an enduring heart have the destinies appointed to the children of men"? Why should it be one thing, in its effect upon the emotions, to say with the philosopher Spinoza, *Felicitas in eo consistit quod homo suum esse*

---

[1] *Ecclesiastes*, viii, 17. (Arnold's note.)
[2] *Iliad*, xxiv, 49. (Arnold's note.)

conservare potest—"Man's happiness consists in his being able to preserve his own essence," and quite another thing, in its effect upon the emotions, to say with the Gospel, "What is a man advantaged, if he gain the whole world, and lose himself, forfeit himself?" How does this difference of effect arise? I cannot tell, and I am not much concerned to know; the important thing is that it does arise, and that we can profit by it. But how, finally, are poetry and eloquence to exercise the power of relating the modern results of natural science to man's instinct for conduct, his instinct for beauty? And here again I answer that I do not know *how* they will exercise it, but that they can and will exercise it I am sure. I do not mean that modern philosophical poets and modern philosophical moralists are to come and relate for us, in express terms, the results of modern scientific research to our instinct for conduct, our instinct for beauty. But I mean that we shall find, as a matter of experience, if we know the best that has been thought and uttered in the world, we shall find that the art and poetry and eloquence of men who lived, perhaps, long ago, who had the most limited natural knowledge, who had the most erroneous conceptions about many important matters, we shall find that this art, and poetry, and eloquence, have in fact not only the power of refreshing and delighting us, they have also the power,—such is the strength and worth, in essentials, of their authors' criticism of life,—they have a fortifying, and elevating, and quickening, and suggestive power, capable of wonderfully helping us to relate the results of modern science to our need for conduct, our need for beauty. Homer's conceptions of the physical universe were, I imagine, grotesque; but really, under the shock of hearing from modern science that "the world is not subordinated to man's use, and that man is not the cynosure of things terrestrial," I could, for my own part, desire no better comfort than Homer's line which I quoted just now,

τλητὸν γὰρ Μοῖραι θυμὸν θέσαν ἀνθρώποισιν—

"for an enduring heart have the destinies appointed to the children of men!"

And the more that men's minds are cleared, the more that the results of science are frankly accepted, the more that poetry and eloquence come to be received and studied as what in truth they really are,—the criticism of life by gifted men, alive and active with extraordinary power at an unusual number of points;—so much the more will the value of humane letters, and of art also, which is an utterance having a like kind of power with theirs, be felt and acknowledged, and their place in education be secured.

Let us therefore, all of us, avoid indeed as much as possible any invidious comparison between the merits of humane letters, as means of education, and the merits of the natural sciences. But when some President of a Section for Mechanical Science insists on making the comparison, and tells us that "he who in his training has substituted literature and history for natural science has chosen the less useful alternative," let us make answer to him that the student of humane letters only, will, at least, know also the great general conceptions brought in by modern physical science; for science, as Professor Huxley says, forces them upon us all. But the student of the natural sciences only, will, by our very hypothesis, know nothing of humane letters; not to mention that in setting himself to be perpetually accumulating natural knowledge, he sets himself to do what only specialists have in general the gift for doing genially. And so he will probably be unsatisfied, or at any rate incomplete, and even more incomplete than the student of humane letters only.

I once mentioned in a school-report, how a young man in one of our English training colleges having to paraphrase the passage in *Macbeth* beginning,

> Can'st thou not minister to a mind diseased?

turned this line into, "Can you not wait upon the lunatic?" And I remarked what a curious state of things it would be, if every pupil of our national schools knew, let us say, that the moon is two thousand one hundred and sixty miles in diameter, and thought at the same time that a good paraphrase for

> Can'st thou not minister to a mind diseased?

was, "Can you not wait upon the lunatic?" If one is driven to choose, I think I would rather have a young person ignorant about the moon's diameter, but aware that "Can you not wait upon the lunatic?" is bad, than a young person whose education had been such as to manage things the other way.

Or to go higher than the pupils of our national schools. I have in my mind's eye a member of our British Parliament who comes to travel here in America, who afterwards relates his travels, and who shows a really masterly knowledge of the geology of this great country and of its mining capabilities, but who ends by gravely suggesting that the United States should borrow a prince from our Royal Family, and should make him their king, and should create a House of Lords of great landed proprietors after the pattern of ours; and then America, he thinks, would have her future happily and perfectly secured. Surely, in this case, the President of the Section for Mechanical Science would himself hardly say that our member of Parliament, by concentrating himself

upon geology and mineralogy, and so on, and not attending to literature and history, had "chosen the more
useful alternative."

If then there is to be separation and option between
humane letters on the one hand, and the natural sciences
on the other, the great majority of mankind, all who
have not exceptional and overpowering aptitudes for the
study of nature, would do well, I cannot but think, to
choose to be educated in humane letters rather than in
the natural sciences. Letters will call out their being at
more points, will make them live more.

I said that before I ended I would just touch on the
question of classical education, and I will keep my word.
Even if literature is to retain a large place in our education, yet Latin and Greek, say the friends of progress,
will certainly have to go. Greek is the grand offender in
the eyes of these gentlemen. The attackers of the established course of study think that against Greek, at any
rate, they have irresistible arguments. Literature may
perhaps be needed in education, they say; but why on
earth should it be Greek literature? Why not French or
German? Nay, "has not an Englishman models in his
own literature of every kind of excellence?" As before,
it is not on any weak pleadings of my own that I rely
for convincing the gainsayers; it is on the constitution of
human nature itself, and on the instinct of self-preservation in humanity. The instinct for beauty is set in human
nature, as surely as the instinct for knowledge is set
there, or the instinct for conduct. If the instinct for
beauty is served by Greek literature and art as it is
served by no other literature and art, we may trust to the
instinct of self-preservation in humanity for keeping
Greek as part of our culture. We may trust to it for
even making the study of Greek more prevalent than it
is now. Greek will come, I hope, some day to be studied

more rationally than at present; but it will be increasingly studied as men increasingly feel the need in them for beauty, and how powerfully Greek art and Greek literature can serve this need. Women will again study Greek, as Lady Jane Grey did; I believe that in that chain of forts, with which the fair host of the Amazons are now engirdling our English universities, I find that here in America, in colleges like Smith College in Massachusetts, and Vassar College in the State of New York, and in the happy families of the mixed universities out West, they are studying it already.

Defuit una mihi symmetria prisca,—"The antique symmetry was the one thing wanting to me," said Leonardo da Vinci; and he was an Italian. I will not presume to speak for the Americans, but I am sure that, in the Englishman, the want of this admirable symmetry of the Greeks is a thousand times more great and crying than in any Italian. The results of the want show themselves most glaringly, perhaps, in our architecture, but they show themselves, also, in all our art. *Fit details strictly combined, in view of a large general result nobly conceived;* that is just the beautiful *symmetria prisca* of the Greeks, and it is just where we English fail, where all our art fails. Striking ideas we have, and well-executed details we have; but that high symmetry which, with satisfying and delightful effect, combines them, we seldom or never have. The glorious beauty of the Acropolis at Athens did not come from single fine things stuck about on that hill, a statue here, a gateway there;—no, it arose from all things being perfectly combined for a supreme total effect. What must not an Englishman feel about our deficiencies in this respect, as the sense for beauty, whereof this symmetry is an essential element, awakens and strengthens within him! what will not one day be his respect and desire for Greece and its *sym-*

metria prisca, when the scales drop from his eyes as he
walks the London streets, and he sees such a lesson in
meanness as the Strand, for instance, in its true deform-
ity! But here we are coming to our friend Mr. Ruskin's
province, and I will not intrude upon it, for he is its very
sufficient guardian.

And so we at last find, it seems, we find flowing in
favour of the humanities the natural and necessary
stream of things, which seemed against them when we
started. The "hairy quadruped furnished with a tail and
pointed ears, probably arboreal in his habits," this good
fellow carried hidden in his nature, apparently, something destined to develop into a necessity for humane
letters. Nay, more; we seem finally to be even led to the
further conclusion that our hairy ancestor carried in his
nature, also, a necessity for Greek.

And therefore, to say the truth, I cannot really think
that humane letters are in much actual danger of being
thrust out from their leading place in education, in spite
of the array of authorities against them at this moment.
So long as human nature is what it is, their attractions
will remain irresistible. As with Greek, so with letters
generally: they will some day come, we may hope, to be
studied more rationally, but they will not lose their
place. What will happen will rather be that there will
be crowded into education other matters besides, far too
many; there will be, perhaps, a period of unsettlement
and confusion and false tendency; but letters will not in
the end lose their leading place. If they lose it for a
time, they will get it back again. We shall be brought
back to them by our wants and aspirations. And a poor
humanist may possess his soul in patience, neither strive
nor cry, admit the energy and brilliancy of the partisans
of physical science, and their present favour with the
public, to be far greater than his own, and still have a

happy faith that the nature of things works silently on behalf of the studies which he loves, and that, while we shall all have to acquaint ourselves with the great results reached by modern science, and to give ourselves as much training in its disciplines as we can conveniently carry, yet the majority of men will always require humane letters; and so much the more, as they have the more and the greater results of science to relate to the need in man for conduct, and to the need in him for beauty.

Politics

EDITOR'S NOTE

TWO words are central to English history and English political thought in the nineteenth century. They are "democracy" and "the state." The same two words are, of course, central to our own history and to our own political thought. But the contemporary reader is likely to become confused by these familiar words as they appear in their earlier context. This is in part to be accounted for by the difference of the two contexts, ours so much the grimmer. But there are other reasons for his possible confusion, of which the reader must be aware. One is that, in the nineteenth century, political thought, *as thought,* existed in a way of which we have now scarcely any contemporary examples. However much our lives may now be occupied by politics, what at present passes for political thought for the ordinary intelligent man is really nothing more than the academic statement of partisan slogans. Thus, for example, it is no longer possible to take seriously *as thought*—whatever we might want to say of their right feeling—the political utterances of our liberal weeklies. Things were different in the nineteenth century. Leaving out of account the massive revolutionary minds of the age, we see that the political thought of the middle class was of the greatest vigor. The position of liberalism was stated by the Philosophical Radicals, men of powerful intellect, of whom the best known is John Stuart Mill; and there then existed, to match the theory of liberalism and to be matched by it, what now no longer exists and now can scarcely be conceived, a powerful and intellectual defense of the conservative position, carried on not only by men like Carlyle and Herbert Spencer but also by subtler and more genial minds like Fitzjames Stephen and Walter Bagehot. To both groups, the liberal and the conservative, the two words "democracy" and "the state" were still relatively fresh and new, still available to explora-

433

tion by the critical intellect, still, as we say, open to question. This, and the attempt to answer the questions by means of the intelligence, are likely to lead the modern reader to feel that the words do not have the same meanings then and now. And then he is likely to become bewildered because, apparently, the wrong people are asking the questions. He finds the liberal philosophers aligned with the "liberal" manufacturers in the denunciation of laws regulating child labor, or that the chief opponents of compulsory state-aided education are the Utilitarians, Mill among them. Conversely, he will wonder how it comes about that the Tories are the proponents of the factory legislation of the period.

It is in the light of an awareness of this, to us, anomalous situation that Matthew Arnold's political writings must be read, and his essay "Democracy," which first appeared as the introduction to his report, *Popular Education in France* (1861), is a good statement of the anomalies. Arnold called himself "a liberal of the future." He wished to suggest by this phrase that he was in accord with all in the liberal ideal that was enlarging and liberating, and that he was yet not bound by the shibboleths of liberal thought, of which the most notable—a remnant of the origins of liberalism in a rising middle class which had had to make its way against the restrictions of an aristocratic state—was the certainty that a strong state must necessarily be repressive.

Culture and Anarchy, one of Arnold's most brilliant works, was occasioned by the Reform Bill of 1867. Arnold's purpose in writing it was to allay the hysterical fears of the upper classes now that the franchise had been given to a very large part of the working class, and also to suggest how a huge, untrained, unlettered class was rightly to be inducted into participation in the life of the nation. The gist of its argument is that England exists in a condition of "anarchy" which will grow worse unless the dictate of "culture" is heeded, which is that a state be conceived and formed which transcends the special interests of any class. The ultimate desire of "culture" is of course that class differences shall not exist, an idea which Arnold developed in the spirited essay "Equality."

The essential matter of *Culture and Anarchy* is to be found in the Introduction and first four chapters, which are printed here. I have omitted the Author's Preface, the last two chapters, and the Conclusion, which are largely topical and local.

DEMOCRACY

IN GIVING an account of education in certain
countries of the Continent, I have often spoken of
the State and its action in such a way as to offend, I
fear, some of my readers, and to surprise others. With
many Englishmen, perhaps with the majority, it is a
maxim that the State, the executive power, ought to be
entrusted with no more means of action than those
which it is impossible to withhold from it; that the State
neither would nor could make a safe use of any more
extended liberty; would not, because it has in itself a
natural instinct of despotism, which, if not jealously
checked, would become outrageous; could not, because
it is, in truth, not at all more enlightened, or fit to assume
a lead, than the mass of this enlightened community.

No sensible man will lightly go counter to an opinion
firmly held by a great body of his countrymen. He will
take for granted, that for any opinion which has struck
deep root among a people so powerful, so successful, and
so well worthy of respect as the people of this country,
there certainly either are, or have been, good and sound
reasons. He will venture to impugn such an opinion with
real hesitation, and only when he thinks he perceives
that the reasons which once supported it exist no longer,
or at any rate seem about to disappear very soon. For
undoubtedly there arrive periods, when, the circumstances and conditions of government having changed,
the guiding maxims of government ought to change also.

J'ai dit souvent, says Mirabeau,[1] admonishing the Court of France in 1790, *qu'on devait changer de manière de gouverner, lorsque le gouvernement n'est plus le même.* And these decisive changes in the political situation of a people happen gradually as well as violently. "In the silent lapse of events," says Burke,[2] writing in England twenty years before the French Revolution, "as material alterations have been insensibly brought about in the policy and character of governments and nations, as those which have been marked by the tumult of public revolutions."

I propose to submit to those who have been accustomed to regard all State-action with jealousy, some reasons for thinking that the circumstances which once made that jealousy prudent and natural have undergone an essential change. I desire to lead them to consider with me, whether, in the present altered conjuncture, that State-action, which was once dangerous, may not become, not only without danger in itself, but the means of helping us against dangers from another quarter. To combine and present the considerations upon which these two propositions are based, is a task of some difficulty and delicacy. My aim is to invite impartial reflection upon the subject, not to make a hostile attack against old opinions, still less to set on foot and fully equip a new theory. In offering, therefore, the thoughts which have suggested themselves to me, I shall studiously avoid all particular applications of them likely to give offence, and shall use no more illustration and development than may be indispensable to enable the reader to seize and appreciate them.

[1] *Correspondance entre le Comte de Mirabeau et le Comte de la Marck,* publiée par M. de Bacourt, Paris, 1851, vol. ii, p. 143. (Arnold's note.)

[2] Burke's Works (edit. of 1852), vol. iii, p. 115. (Arnold's note.)

The dissolution of the old political parties which have governed this country since the Revolution of 1688 has long been remarked. It was repeatedly declared to be happening long before it actually took place, while the vital energy of these parties still subsisted in full vigour, and was threatened only by some temporary obstruction. It has been eagerly deprecated long after it had actually begun to take place, when it was in full progress, and inevitable. These parties, differing in so much else, were yet alike in this, that they were both, in a certain broad sense, *aristocratical* parties. They were combinations of persons considerable, either by great family and estate, or by Court favour, or lastly, by eminent abilities and popularity; this last body, however, attaining participation in public affairs only through a conjunction with one or other of the former. These connections, though they contained men of very various degrees of birth and property, were still wholly leavened with the feelings and habits of the upper class of the nation. They had the bond of a common culture; and, however their political opinions and acts might differ, what they said and did had the stamp and style imparted by this culture, and by a common and elevated social condition.

Aristocratical bodies have no taste for a very imposing executive, or for a very active and penetrating domestic administration. They have a sense of equality among themselves, and of constituting in themselves what is greatest and most dignified in the realm, which makes their pride revolt against the overshadowing greatness and dignity of a commanding executive. They have a temper of independence, and a habit of uncontrolled action, which makes them impatient of encountering, in the management of the interior concerns of the country, the machinery and regulations of a superior and peremptory power. The different parties amongst them, as they

successively get possession of the government, respect
this jealous disposition in their opponents, because they
share it themselves. It is a disposition proper to them as
great personages, not as ministers; and as they are great
personages for their whole life, while they may probably
be ministers but for a very short time, the instinct of
their social condition avails more with them than the
instinct of their official function. To administer as little
as possible, to make its weight felt in foreign affairs
rather than in domestic, to see in ministerial station
rather the means of power and dignity than a means of
searching and useful administrative activity, is the natural tendency of an aristocratic executive. It is a tendency
which is creditable to the good sense of aristocracies,
honourable to their moderation, and at the same time
fortunate for their country, of whose internal development they are not fitted to have the full direction.

One strong and beneficial influence, however, the administration of a vigorous and high-minded aristocracy
is calculated to exert upon a robust and sound people. I
have had occasion, in speaking of Homer, to say very
often, and with much emphasis, that he is *in the grand
style*. It is the chief virtue of a healthy and uncorrupted
aristocracy, that it is, in general, in this grand style. That
elevation of character, that noble way of thinking and
behaving, which is an eminent gift of nature to some
individuals, is also often generated in whole classes of
men (at least when these come of a strong and good
race) by the possession of power, by the importance and
responsibility of high station, by habitual dealing with
great things, by being placed above the necessity of constantly struggling for little things. And it is the source
of great virtues. It may go along with a not very quick
or open intelligence; but it cannot well go along with a
conduct vulgar and ignoble. A governing class imbued

with it may not be capable of intelligently leading the masses of a people to the highest pitch of welfare for them; but it sets them an invaluable example of qualities without which no really high welfare can exist. This has been done for their nation by the best aristocracies. The Roman aristocracy did it; the English aristocracy has done it. They each fostered in the mass of the peoples they governed,—peoples of sturdy moral constitution and apt to learn such lessons,—a greatness of spirit, the natural growth of the condition of magnates and rulers, but not the natural growth of the condition of the common people. They made, the one of the Roman, the other of the English people, in spite of all the shortcomings of each, great peoples, peoples *in the grand style.* And this they did, while wielding the people according to their own notions, and in the direction which seemed good to them; not as servants and instruments of the people, but as its commanders and heads; solicitous for the good of their country, indeed, but taking for granted that of that good they themselves were the supreme judges, and were to fix the conditions.

The time has arrived, however, when it is becoming impossible for the aristocracy of England to conduct and wield the English nation any longer. It still, indeed, administers public affairs; and it is a great error to suppose, as many persons in England suppose, that it administers but does not govern. He who administers, governs,[1] because he infixes his own mark and stamps his own character on all public affairs as they pass through his hands; and, therefore, so long as the English aristocracy administers the commonwealth, it still governs it. But signs not to be mistaken show that its headship and leadership of the nation, by virtue of the substantial

---

[1] *Administrer, c'est gouverner,* says Mirabeau; *gouverner, c'est régner; tout se réduit là.* (Arnold's note.)

acquiescence of the body of the nation in its predominance and right to lead, is nearly over. That acquiescence was the tenure by which it held its power; and it is fast giving way. The superiority of the upper class over all others is no longer so great; the willingness of the others to recognise that superiority is no longer so ready.

This change has been brought about by natural and inevitable causes, and neither the great nor the multitude are to be blamed for it. The growing demands and audaciousness of the latter, the encroaching spirit of democracy, are, indeed, matters of loud complaint with some persons. But these persons are complaining of human nature itself, when they thus complain of a manifestation of its native and ineradicable impulse. Life itself consists, say the philosophers, in the effort *to affirm one's own essence*; meaning by this, to develop one's own existence fully and freely, to have ample light and air, to be neither cramped nor overshadowed. Democracy is trying to *affirm its own essence*; to live, to enjoy, to possess the world, as aristocracy has tried, and successfully tried, before it. Ever since Europe emerged from barbarism, ever since the condition of the common people began a little to improve, ever since their minds began to stir, this effort of democracy has been gaining strength; and the more their condition improves, the more strength this effort gains. So potent is the charm of life and expansion upon the living; the moment men are aware of them, they begin to desire them, and the more they have of them, the more they crave.

This movement of democracy, like other operations of nature, merits properly neither blame nor praise. Its partisans are apt to give it credit which it does not deserve, while its enemies are apt to upbraid it unjustly. Its friends celebrate it as the author of all freedom. But political freedom may very well be established by aristocratic founders; and, certainly, the political freedom of England owes more to the grasping English barons than to democracy. Social freedom,—equality,—that is rather the field of the conquests of democracy. And here what I must call the injustice of its enemies comes in. For its seeking after equality, democracy is often, in this country above all, vehemently and scornfully blamed; its temper contrasted with that worthier temper which can magnanimously endure social distinctions; its operations all referred, as of course, to the stirrings of a base and malignant envy. No doubt there is a gross and vulgar spirit of envy, prompting the hearts of many of those who cry for equality. No doubt there are ignoble natures which prefer equality to liberty. But what we have to ask is, when the life of democracy is admitted as something natural and inevitable, whether this or that product of democracy is a necessary growth from its parent stock, or merely an excrescence upon it. If it be the latter, certainly it may be due to the meanest and most culpable passions. But if it be the former, then this product, however base and blameworthy the passions which it may sometimes be made to serve, can in itself be no more reprehensible than the vital impulse of democracy is in itself reprehensible; and this impulse is, as has been shown, identical with the ceaseless vital effort of human nature itself.

Now, can it be denied, that a certain approach to equality, at any rate a certain reduction of signal inequalities, is a natural, instinctive demand of that impulse which drives society as a whole,—no longer individuals and limited classes only, but the mass of a community,—to develop itself with the utmost possible fulness and freedom? Can it be denied, that to live in a society of equals tends in general to make a man's spirits expand, and his faculties work easily and actively; while, to live in a society of superiors, although it may occasionally be a very good discipline, yet in general tends to tame the spirits and to make the play of the faculties less secure and active? Can it be denied, that to be heavily overshadowed, to be profoundly insignificant, has, on the whole, a depressing and benumbing effect on the character? I know that some individuals react against the strongest impediments, and owe success and greatness to the efforts which they are thus forced to make. But the question is not about individuals. The question is about the common bulk of mankind, persons without extraordinary gifts or exceptional energy, and who will ever require, in order to make the best of themselves, encouragement and directly favouring circumstances. Can any one deny, that for these the spectacle, when they would rise, of a condition of splendour, grandeur, and culture, which they cannot possibly reach, has the effect of making them flag in spirit, and of disposing them to sink despondingly back into their own condition? Can any one deny, that the knowledge how poor and insignificant the best condition of improvement and culture attainable by them must be esteemed by a class incomparably richer-endowed, tends to cheapen this modest possible amelioration in the account of those classes also for whom it would be relatively a real progress, and to disenchant their imaginations with it? It seems to me impossible to deny this. And therefore a philosophic observer,[1] with no love for democracy, but

---

[1] M. de Tocqueville. See his *Démocratie en Amérique* (edit. of 1835), vol. i, p. 11. "*Le peuple est plus grossier dans les pays aristocratiques que partout ailleurs. Dans ces lieux, où se recontrent des hommes si forts et si riches, les faibles et les pauvres se sentent comme accablés de leur bassesse; ne découvrant aucun point par lequel ils puissent regagner l'égalité, ils désespèrent entièrement d'eux-mêmes, et se laissent tomber au-dessous de la dignité humaine.*" (Arnold's note.)

rather with a terror of it, has been constrained to remark,
that "the common people is more uncivilised in aristocratic countries than in any others"; because there "the
lowly and the poor feel themselves, as it were, overwhelmed with the weight of their own inferiority." He
has been constrained to remark,[1] that "there is such a
thing as a manly and legitimate passion for equality,
prompting men to desire to be, *all* of them, in the enjoyment of power and consideration." And, in France, that
very equality, which is by us so impetuously decried,
while it has by no means improved (it is said) the upper
classes of French society, has undoubtedly given to the
lower classes, to the body of the common people, a self-
respect, an enlargement of spirit, a consciousness of
counting for something in their country's action, which
has raised them in the scale of humanity. The common
people, in France, seems to me the soundest part of the
French nation. They seem to me more free from the
two opposite degradations of multitudes, brutality and
servility, to have a more developed human life, more
of what distinguishes elsewhere the cultured classes from
the vulgar, than the common people in any other country with which I am acquainted.

I do not say that grandeur and prosperity may not be
attained by a nation divided into the most widely distinct classes, and presenting the most signal inequalities
of rank and fortune. I do not say that great national
virtues may not be developed in it. I do not even say
that a popular order, accepting this demarcation of
classes as an eternal providential arrangement, not ques-
tioning the natural right of a superior order to lead it,
content within its own sphere, admiring the grandeur
and high-mindedness of its ruling class, and catching on
its own spirit some reflex of what it thus admires, may

[1] *Démocratie en Amérique*, vol. i, p. 60. (Arnold's note.)

not be a happier body, as to the eye of the imagination it is certainly a more beautiful body, than a popular order, pushing, excited, and presumptuous; a popular order, jealous of recognising fixed superiorities, petulantly claiming to be as good as its betters, and tastelessly attiring itself with the fashions and designations which have become unalterably associated with a wealthy and refined class, and which, tricking out those who have neither wealth nor refinement, are ridiculous. But a popular order of that old-fashioned stamp exists now only for the imagination. It is not the force with which modern society has to reckon. Such a body may be a sturdy, honest, and sound-hearted lower class; but it is not a democratic people. It is not that power, which at the present day in all nations is to be found existing; in some, has obtained the mastery; in others, is yet in a state of expectation and preparation.

The power of France in Europe is at this day mainly owing to the completeness with which she has organised democratic institutions. The action of the French State is excessive; but it is too little understood in England that the French people has adopted this action for its own purposes, has in great measure attained those purposes by it, and owes to its having done so the chief part of its influence in Europe. The growing power in Europe is democracy; and France has organised democracy with a certain indisputable grandeur and success. The ideas of 1789 were working everywhere in the eighteenth century; but it was because in France the State adopted them that the French Revolution became an historic epoch for the world, and France the lode-star of Continental democracy. Her airs of superiority and her overweening pretensions come from her sense of the power which she derives from this cause. Every one knows how Frenchmen proclaim France to be at the head of civilisation, the French army to be the soldier of God, Paris to be the brain of Europe, and so on. All this is, no doubt, in a vein of sufficient fatuity and bad taste; but it means, at bottom, that France believes she has so organised herself as to facilitate for all members of her society full and free expansion; that she believes herself to have remodelled her institutions with an eye to reason rather than custom, and to right rather than fact; it means, that she believes the other peoples of Europe to be preparing themselves, more or less rapidly, for a like achievement, and that she is conscious of her power and influence upon them as an initiatress and example. In this belief there is a part of truth and a part of delusion. I think it is more profitable for a Frenchman to consider the part of delusion contained in it; for an Englishman, the part of truth.

It is because aristocracies almost inevitably fail to appreciate justly, or even to take into their mind, the instinct pushing the masses towards expansion and fuller life, that they lose their hold over them. It is the old story of the incapacity of aristocracies for ideas; the secret of their want of success in modern epochs. The people treats them with flagrant injustice, when it denies all obligation to them. They can, and often do, impart a high spirit, a fine ideal of grandeur, to the people; thus they lay the foundations of a great nation. But they leave the people still the multitude, the crowd; they have small belief in the power of the ideas which are its life. Themselves a power reposing on all which is most solid, material, and visible, they are slow to attach any great importance to influences impalpable, spiritual, and viewless. Although, therefore, a disinterested looker-on might often be disposed, seeing what has actually been achieved by aristocracies, to wish to retain or replace them in their preponderance, rather than commit a nation to the hazards of a new and untried future; yet the masses instinctively feel that they can never consent to this without renouncing the inmost impulse of their being; and that they should make such a renunciation cannot seriously be expected of them. Except on conditions which make its expansion, in the sense understood by itself, fully possible, democracy will never frankly ally itself with aristocracy; and on these conditions perhaps no aristocracy will ever frankly ally itself with it. Even the English aristocracy, so politic, so capable of compromises, has shown no signs of being able so to transform itself as to render such an alliance possible. The reception given by the Peers to the bill for establishing life-peerages was, in this respect, of ill omen. The separation between aristocracy and democracy will probably, therefore, go on still widening.

And it must in fairness be added, that as in one most important part of general human culture,—openness to ideas and ardour for them,—aristocracy is less advanced than democracy, to replace or keep the latter under the tutelage of the former would in some respects be actually unfavourable to the progress of the world. At epochs when new ideas are powerfully fermenting in a society, and profoundly changing its spirit, aristocracies, as they are in general not long suffered to guide it without question, so are they by nature not well fitted to guide it intelligently.

In England, democracy has been slow in developing itself, having met with much to withstand it, not only in the worth of the aristocracy, but also in the fine qualities of the common people. The aristocracy has been more in sympathy with the common people than perhaps any other aristocracy. It has rarely given them great umbrage; it has neither been frivolous, so as to provoke their contempt, nor impertinent, so as to provoke their irritation. Above all, it has in general meant to act with justice, according to its own notions of justice. Therefore the feeling of admiring deference to such a class was more deep-rooted in the people of this country, more cordial, and more persistent, than in any people of the Continent. But, besides this, the vigour and high spirit of the English common people bred in them a self-reliance which disposed each man to act individually and independently; and so long as this disposition prevails through a nation divided into classes, the predominance of an aristocracy, of the class containing the greatest and strongest individuals of the nation, is secure. Democracy is a force in which the concert of a great number of men makes up for the weakness of each man taken by himself; democracy accepts a certain relative rise in their condition, obtainable by this concert for a great number, as something desirable in itself, because though this is undoubtedly far below grandeur, it is yet a good deal above insignificance. A very strong, self-reliant people neither easily learns to act in concert, nor easily brings itself to regard any middling good, any good short of the best, as an object ardently to be coveted and striven for. It keeps its eye on the grand prizes, and these are to be won only by distancing competitors, by getting before one's comrades, by succeeding all by one's self; and so long as a people works thus individually, it does not work democratically. The English people has all the qualities which dispose a people to work individually; may it never lose them! A people without the salt of these qualities, relying wholly on mutual co-operation, and proposing to itself second-rate ideals, would arrive at the pettiness and stationariness of China. But the English people is no longer so entirely ruled by them as not to show visible beginnings of democratic action; it becomes more and more sensible to the irresistible seduction of democratic ideas, promising to each individual of the multitude increased self-respect, and expansion with the increased importance and authority of the multitude to which he belongs, with the diminished preponderance of the aristocratic class above him.

While the habit and disposition of deference are thus dying out among the lower classes of the English nation, it seems to me indisputable that the advantages which command deference, that eminent superiority in high feeling, dignity, and culture, tend to diminish among the highest class. I shall not be suspected of any inclination to underrate the aristocracy of this country. I regard it as the worthiest, as it certainly has been the most successful aristocracy, of which history makes record. If it has not been able to develop excellences which do not belong to the nature of an aristocracy, yet it has been able to avoid defects to which the nature of an aristocracy is peculiarly prone. But I cannot read the history of the flowering time of the English aristocracy, the eighteenth century, and then look at this aristocracy in our own century, without feeling that there has been a change. I am not now thinking of private and domestic virtues, of morality, of decorum. Perhaps with respect to these there has in this class, as in society at large, been a change for the better. I am thinking of those public and conspicuous virtues by which the multitude is captivated and led,—lofty spirit, commanding character, exquisite culture. It is true that the advance of all classes in culture and refinement may make the culture of one class, which, isolated, appeared remarkable, appear so no longer; but exquisite culture and great dignity are always something rare and striking, and it is the distinction of the English aristocracy, in the eighteenth century, that not only was their culture something rare by comparison with the rawness of the masses, it was something rare and admirable in itself. It is rather that this rare culture of the highest class has actually somewhat declined,[1] than that it has come to look less by juxtaposition with the augmented culture of other classes.

Probably democracy has something to answer for in this falling off of her rival. To feel itself raised on high, venerated, followed, no doubt stimulates a fine nature to keep itself worthy to be followed, venerated, raised on high; hence that lofty maxim, *noblesse oblige*. To feel its culture something precious and singular, makes such a nature zealous to retain and extend it. The elation and energy thus fostered by the sense of its advantages, certainly enhances the worth, strengthens the behaviour, and quickens all the active powers of the class enjoying it. *Possunt quia posse videntur*. The removal of the stimulus a little relaxes their energy. It is not so much that they sink to be somewhat less than themselves, as that they cease to be somewhat more than themselves. But, however this may be, whencesoever the change may proceed, I cannot doubt that in the aristocratic virtue, in the intrinsic commanding force of the English upper class, there is a diminution. Relics of a great generation are still, perhaps, to be seen amongst them, surviving exemplars of noble manners and consummate culture; but they disappear one after the other, and no one of their kind takes their place. At the very moment when democracy becomes less and less disposed to follow and

[1] This will appear doubtful to no one well acquainted with the literature and memoirs of the last century. To give but two illustrations out of a thousand. Let the reader refer to the anecdote told by Robert Wood in his *Essay on the Genius of Homer* (London, 1775), p. vii, and to Lord Chesterfield's *Letters* (edit. of 1845), vol. i, pp. 115, 143; vol. ii, p. 54; and then say, whether the culture there indicated as the culture of a *class* has maintained itself at that level. (*Arnold's note*.)

to admire, aristocracy becomes less and less qualified to command and to captivate.

On the one hand, then, the masses of the people in this country are preparing to take a much more active part than formerly in controlling its destinies; on the other hand, the aristocracy (using this word in the widest sense, to include not only the nobility and landed gentry, but also those reinforcements from the classes bordering upon itself, which this class constantly attracts and assimilates), while it is threatened with losing its hold on the rudder of government, its power to give to public affairs its own bias and direction, is losing also that influence on the spirit and character of the people which it long exercised.

I know that this will be warmly denied by some persons. Those who have grown up amidst a certain state of things, those whose habits, and interests, and affections, are closely concerned with its continuance, are slow to believe that it is not a part of the order of nature, or that it can ever come to an end. But I think that what I have here laid down will not appear doubtful either to the most competent and friendly foreign observers of this country, or to those Englishmen who, clear of all influences of class or party, have applied themselves steadily to see the tendencies of their nation as they really are. Assuming it to be true, a great number of considerations are suggested by it; but it is my purpose here to insist upon one only.

That one consideration is: On what action may we rely to replace, for some time at any rate, that action of the aristocracy upon the people of this country, which we have seen exercise an influence in many respects elevating and beneficial, but which is rapidly, and from inevitable causes, ceasing? In other words, and to use a short and significant modern expression which every one understands, what influence may help us to prevent the English people from becoming, with the growth of democracy, *Americanised*? I confess I am disposed to answer: On the action of the State.

I know what a chorus of objectors will be ready. One will say: Rather repair and restore the influence of aristocracy. Another will say: It is not a bad thing, but a good thing, that the English people should be Americanised. But the most formidable and the most widely entertained objection, by far, will be that which founds itself upon the present actual state of things in another country; which says: Look at France! there you have a signal example of the alliance of democracy with a powerful State-action, and see how it works.

This last and principal objection I will notice at once. I have had occasion to touch upon the first already, and upon the second I shall touch presently. It seems to me, then, that one may save one's self from much idle terror at names and shadows if one will be at the pains to remember what different conditions the different character of two nations must necessarily impose on the operation of any principle. That which operates noxiously in one, may operate wholesomely in the other; because the unsound part of the one's character may be yet further inflamed and enlarged by it, the unsound part of the other's may find in it a corrective and an abatement. This is the great use which two unlike characters may find in observing each other. Neither is likely to have the other's faults, so each may safely adopt as much as suits him of the other's qualities. If I were a Frenchman I should never be weary of admiring the independent, individual, local habits of action in England, of directing attention to the evils occasioned in France by the excessive action of the State; for I should be very sure that, say what I might, the part of the State would never be too small in France, nor that of the individual too large. Being an Englishman, I see nothing but good in freely recognising the coherence, rationality, and efficaciousness which characterise the strong State-action of France, of acknowledging the want of method, reason, and result which attend the feeble State-action of England; because I am very sure that, strengthen in England the action of the State as one may, it will always find itself sufficiently controlled. But when either the *Constitutionnel* sneers at the do-little talkativeness of parliamentary government, or when the *Morning Star* inveighs against the despotism of a centralised administration, it seems to me that they lose their labour, because they are hardening themselves against dangers to which they are neither of them liable. Both the one and the other, in plain truth,

> Compound for sins they are inclined to,
> By damning those they have no mind to.

They should rather exchange doctrines one with the other, and each might thus, perhaps, be profited.

So that the exaggeration of the action of the State, in France, furnishes no reason for absolutely refusing to enlarge the action of the State in England; because the genius and temper of the people of this country are such as to render impossible that exaggeration which the genius and temper of the French rendered easy. There is no danger at all that the native independence and individualism of the English character will ever belie itself, and become either weakly prone to lean on others, or blindly confiding in them.

English democracy runs no risk of being over-mastered by the State; it is almost certain that it will throw off the tutelage of aristocracy. Its real danger is, that it will have far too much its own way, and be left far too much to itself. "What harm will there be in that?" say some; "are we not a self-governing people?" I answer: "We have never yet been a *self-governing democracy,* or anything like it." The difficulty for democracy is, how to find and keep high ideals. The individuals who compose it are, the bulk of them, persons who need to follow an ideal, not to set one; and one ideal of greatness, high feeling, and fine culture, which an aristocracy once supplied to them, they lose by the very fact of ceasing to be a lower order and becoming a democracy. Nations are not truly great solely because the individuals composing them are numerous, free, and active; but they are great when these numbers, this freedom, and this activity are employed in the service of an ideal higher than that of an ordinary man, taken by himself. Our society is probably destined to become much more democratic; who or what will give a high tone to the nation then? That is the grave question.

The greatest men of America, her Washingtons, Hamiltons, Madisons, well understanding that aristocratical institutions are not in all times and places possible; well perceiving that in their Republic there was no place for these; comprehending, therefore, that from these that security for national dignity and greatness, an ideal commanding popular reverence, was not to be obtained, but knowing that this ideal was indispensable, would have been rejoiced to found a substitute for it in the dignity and authority of the State. They deplored the weakness and insignificance of the executive power as a calamity. When the inevitable course of events has made our self-government something really like that of America, when it has removed or weakened that security for national dignity, which we possessed in *aristocracy,* will the substitute of the *State* be equally wanting to us? If it is, then the dangers of America will really be ours; the dangers which come from the multitude being in power, with no adequate ideal to elevate or guide the multitude.

It would really be wasting time to contend at length, that to give more prominence to the idea of the State is now possible in this country, without endangering liberty. In other countries the habits and dispositions of the people may be such that the State, if once it acts, may be easily suffered to usurp exorbitantly; here they certainly are not. Here the people will always sufficiently keep in mind that any public authority is a trust delegated by themselves, for certain purposes, and with certain limits; and if that authority pretends to an absolute, independent character, they will soon enough (and very rightly) remind it of its error. Here there can be no question of a paternal government, of an irresponsible executive power, professing to act for the people's good, but without the people's consent, and, if necessary, against the people's wishes; here no one dreams of removing a single constitutional control, of abolishing a single safeguard for securing a correspondence between the acts of government and the will of the nation. The question is, whether, retaining all its power of control over a government which should abuse its trust, the nation may not now find advantage in voluntarily allowing to it purposes somewhat ampler, and limits somewhat wider within which to execute them, than formerly; whether the nation may not thus acquire in the State an ideal of high reason and right feeling, representing its best self, commanding general respect, and forming a rallying-point for the intelligence and for the worthiest instincts of the community, which will herein find a true bond of union.

I am convinced that if the worst mischiefs of democracy ever happen in England, it will be, not because a new condition of things has come upon us unforeseen, but because, though we all foresaw it, our efforts to deal with it were in the wrong direction. At the present time, almost every one believes in the growth of democracy, almost every one talks of it, almost every one laments it; but the last thing people can be brought to do is to make timely preparation for it. Many of those who, if they would, could do most to forward this work of preparation, are made slack and hesitating by the belief that, after all, in England, things may probably never go very far; that it will be possible to keep much more of the past than speculators say. Others, with a more robust faith, think that all democracy wants is vigorous putting-down; and that, with a good will and strong hand, it is perfectly possible to retain or restore the whole system of the Middle Ages. Others, free from the prejudices of class and position which warp the judgment of these, and who would, I believe, be the first and greatest gainers by strengthening the hands of the State, are averse from doing so by reason of suspicions and fears, once perfectly well-grounded, but, in this age and in the present circumstances, well-grounded no longer.

I speak of the middle classes. I have already shown how it is the natural disposition of an aristocratical class to view with jealousy the development of a considerable State-power. But this disposition has in England found extraordinary favour and support in regions not aristocratical,—from the middle classes; and, above all, from the kernel of these classes, the Protestant Dissenters. And for a very good reason. In times when passions ran high, even an aristocratical executive was easily stimulated into using, for the gratification of its friends and the abasement of its enemies, those administrative engines which, the moment it chose to stretch its hand forth, stood ready for its grasp. Matters of domestic concern, matters of religious profession and religious exercise, offered a peculiar field for an intervention gainful and agreeable to friends, injurious and irritating to enemies. Such an intervention was attempted and practised. Government lent its machinery and authority to the aristocratical and ecclesiastical party, which it regarded as its best support. The party which suffered comprised the flower and strength of that middle class of society, always very flourishing and robust in this country. That powerful class, from this specimen of the administrative activity of government, conceived a strong antipathy against all intervention of the State in certain spheres. An active, stringent administration in those spheres, meant at that time a High Church and Prelatic administration in them, an administration galling to the Puritan party and to the middle class; and this aggrieved class had naturally no proneness to draw nice philosophical distinctions between State-action in these spheres, as a thing for abstract consideration, and State-action in them as they practically felt it and supposed themselves likely long to feel it, guided by their adversaries. In the minds of the English middle class, therefore, State-action in social and domestic concerns became inextricably associated with the idea of a Conventicle Act, a Five-Mile Act, an Act of Uniformity. Their abhorrence of such a State-action as this they extended to State-action in general; and, having never known a beneficent and just State-power, they enlarged their hatred of a cruel and partial State-power, the only one they had ever known, into a maxim that no State-power was to be trusted, that the least action, in certain provinces, was rigorously to be denied to the State, whenever this denial was possible.

Thus that jealousy of an important, sedulous, energetic executive, natural to grandees unwilling to suffer their personal authority to be circumscribed, their individual grandeur to be eclipsed, by the authority and grandeur of the State, became reinforced in this country by a like sentiment among the middle classes, who had no such authority or grandeur to lose, but who, by a hasty reasoning, had theoretically condemned for ever an agency which they had practically found at times oppressive. *Leave us to ourselves!* magnates and middle classes alike cried to the State. Not only from those who were full and abounded went up this prayer, but also from those whose condition admitted of great amelioration. Not only did the whole repudiate the physician, but also those who were sick.

For it is evident, that the action of a diligent, an impartial, and a national government, while it can do little to better the condition, already fortunate enough, of the highest and richest class of its people, can really do much, by institution and regulation, to better that of the middle and lower classes. The State can bestow certain broad collective benefits, which are indeed not much if compared with the advantages already possessed by individual grandeur, but which are rich and valuable if compared with the make-shifts of mediocrity and poverty. A good thing meant for the many cannot well be so exquisite as the good things of the few; but it can easily, if it comes from a donor of great resources and wide power, be incomparably better than what the many could, unaided, provide for themselves.

In all the remarks which I have been making, I have hitherto abstained from any attempt to suggest a positive application of them. I have limited myself to simply pointing out in how changed a world of ideas we are living; I have not sought to go further, and to discuss in what particular manner the world of facts is to adapt itself to this changed world of ideas. This has been my rule so far; but from this rule I shall here venture to depart, in order to dwell for a moment on a matter of practical institution, designed to meet new social exigencies: on the intervention of the State in public education.

The public secondary schools of France, decreed by the Revolution and established under the Consulate, are said by many good judges to be inferior to the old colleges. By means of the old colleges and of private tutors, the French aristocracy could procure for its children (so it is said, and very likely with truth) a better training than that which is now given in the lyceums. Yes; but the boon conferred by the State, when it founded the lyceums, was not for the aristocracy; it was for the vast middle class of Frenchmen. This class, certainly, had not already the means of a better training for its children, before the State interfered. This class, certainly, would not have succeeded in procuring by its own efforts a better training for its children, if the State had not interfered. Through the intervention of the State this class enjoys better schools for its children, not than the great and rich enjoy (that is not the question), but than the same class enjoys in any country where the State has not interfered to found them. The lyceums may not be so good as Eton or Harrow; but they are a great deal better than a *Classical and Commercial Academy*.

The aristocratic classes in England may, perhaps, be well content to rest satisfied with their Eton and Harrow. The State is not likely to do better for them. Nay, the superior confidence, spirit, and style, engendered by a training in the great public schools, constitute for these classes a real privilege, a real engine of command, which they might, if they were selfish, be sorry to lose by the establishment of schools great enough to beget a like spirit in the classes below them. But the middle classes in England have every reason not to rest content with their private schools; the State can do a great deal better for them. By giving to schools for these classes a public character, it can bring the instruction in them under a criticism which the stock of knowledge and judgment in our middle classes is not of itself at present able to supply. By giving to them a national character, it can confer on them a greatness and a noble spirit, which the tone of these classes is not of itself at present adequate to impart. Such schools would soon prove notable competitors with the existing public schools; they would do these a great service by stimulating them, and making them look into their own weak points more closely. Economical, because with charges uniform and under severe revision, they would do a great service to that large body of persons who, at present, seeing that on the whole the best secondary instruction to be found is that of the existing public schools, obtain it for their children from a sense of duty, although they can ill afford it, and although its cost is certainly exorbitant. Thus the middle classes might, by the aid of the State, better their instruction, while still keeping its cost moderate. This in itself would be a gain; but this gain would be slight in comparison with that of acquiring the sense of belonging to great and honourable seats of learning, and of breathing in their youth the air of the best culture of their nation. This sense would be an educational influence for them of the highest value. It would really augment their self-respect and moral force; it would truly fuse them with the class above, and tend to bring about for them the equality which they are entitled to desire.

So it is not State-action in itself which the middle and lower classes of a nation ought to deprecate; it is State-action exercised by a hostile class, and for their oppression. From a State-action reasonably, equitably, and nationally exercised, they may derive great benefit;

greater, by the very nature and necessity of things, than
can be derived from this source by the class above them.
For the middle or lower classes to obstruct such a State-
action, to repel its benefits, is to play the game of their
enemies, and to prolong for themselves a condition of
real inferiority.

This, I know, is rather dangerous ground to tread
upon. The great middle classes of this country are conscious of no weakness, no inferiority; they do not want
any one to provide anything for them. Such as they are,
they believe that the freedom and prosperity of England
are their work, and that the future belongs to them. No
one esteems them more than I do; but those who esteem
them most, and who most believe in their capabilities,
can render them no better service than by pointing out
in what they underrate their deficiences, and how their
deficiencies, if unremedied, may impair their future.
They want culture and dignity; they want ideas. Aristocracy has culture and dignity; democracy has readiness for new ideas, and ardour for what ideas it
possesses. Of these, our middle class has the last only:
ardour for the ideas it already possesses. It believes
ardently in liberty, it believes ardently in industry; and,
by its zealous belief in these two ideas, it has accomplished great things. What it has accomplished by its
belief in industry is patent to all the world. The liberties
of England are less its exclusive work than it supposes;
for these, aristocracy has achieved nearly as much. Still,
of one inestimable part of liberty, liberty of thought, the
middle class has been (without precisely intending it)
the principal champion. The intellectual action of the
Church of England upon the nation has been insignificant; its social action has been great. The social
action of Protestant Dissent, that genuine product of
the English middle class, has not been civilising; its

positive intellectual action has been insignificant; its negative intellectual action,—in so far as by strenuously maintaining for itself, against persecution, liberty of conscience and the right of free opinion, it at the same time maintained and established this right as a universal principle,—has been invaluable. But the actual results of this negative intellectual service rendered by Protestant Dissent,—by the middle class,—to the whole community, great as they undoubtedly are, must not be taken for something which they are not. It is a very great thing to be able to think as you like; but, after all, an important question remains: *what* you think. It is a fine thing to secure a free stage and no favour; but, after all, the part which you play on that stage will have to be criticised. Now, all the liberty and industry in the world will not ensure these two things: a high reason and a fine culture. They may favour them, but they will not of themselves produce them; they may exist without them. But it is by the appearance of these two things, in some shape or other, in the life of a nation, that it becomes something more than an independent, an energetic, a successful nation,—that it becomes a *great* nation.

In modern epochs the part of a high reason, of ideas, acquires constantly increasing importance in the conduct of the world's affairs. A fine culture is the complement of a high reason, and it is in the conjunction of both with character, with energy, that the ideal for men and nations is to be placed. It is common to hear remarks on the frequent divorce between culture and character, and to infer from this that culture is a mere varnish, and that character only deserves any serious attention. No error can be more fatal. Culture without character is, no doubt, something frivolous, vain, and weak; but character without culture is, on the other hand, something raw, blind, and dangerous. The most interesting, the most truly glorious peoples, are those in which the alliance of the two has been effected most successfully, and its result spread most widely. This is why the spectacle of ancient Athens has such profound interest for a rational man; that it is the spectacle of the culture of a *people*. It is not an aristocracy, leavening with its own high spirit the multitude which it wields, but leaving it the unformed multitude still; it is not a democracy, acute and energetic, but tasteless, narrow-minded, and ignoble; it is the middle and lower classes in the highest development of their humanity that these classes have yet reached. It was the *many* who relished those arts who were not satisfied with less than those monuments. In the conversations recorded by Plato, or even by the matter-of-fact Xenophon, which for the free yet refined discussion of ideas have set the tone for the whole cultivated world, shopkeepers and tradesmen of Athens mingle as speakers. For any one but a pedant, this is why a handful of Athenians of two thousand years ago are more interesting than the millions of most nations our contemporaries. Surely, if they knew this, those friends of progress, who have confidently pronounced the remains of the ancient world to be so much lumber, and a classical education an aristocratic impertinence, might be inclined to reconsider their sentence.

The course taken in the next fifty years by the middle classes of this nation will probably give a decisive turn to its history. If they will not seek the alliance of the State for their own elevation, if they go on exaggerating their spirit of individualism, if they persist in their jealousy of all governmental action, if they cannot learn that the antipathies and the shibboleths of a past age are now an anachronism for them—that will not prevent them, probably, from getting the rule of their country for a season, but they will certainly *Americanise* it. They will rule it by their energy, but they will deteriorate it by their low ideals and want of culture. In the decline of the aristocratical element, which in some sort supplied an ideal to ennoble the spirit of the nation and to keep it together, there will be no other element present to perform this service. It is of itself a serious calamity for a nation that its tone of feeling and grandeur of spirit should be lowered or dulled. But the calamity appears far more serious still when we consider that the middle classes, remaining as they are now, with their narrow, harsh, unintelligent, and unattractive spirit and culture, will almost certainly fail to mould or assimilate the masses below them, whose sympathies are at the present moment actually wider and more liberal than theirs. They arrive, these masses, eager to enter into possession of the world, to gain a more vivid sense of their own life and activity. In this their irrepressible development, their natural educators and initiators are those immediately above them, the middle classes. If these classes cannot win their sympathy or give them their direction, society is in danger of falling into anarchy.

Therefore, with all the force I can, I wish to urge upon the middle classes of this country, both that they might be very greatly profited by the action of the State, and also that they are continuing their opposition to such action out of an unfounded fear. But at the same time I say that the middle classes have the right, in admitting the action of government, to make the condition that this government shall be one of their own adoption, one that they can trust. To ensure this is now in their own power. If they do not as yet ensure this, they ought to do so, they have the means of doing so. Two centuries ago they had not; now they have. Having this security, let them now show themselves jealous to keep the action of the State equitable and rational, rather than to exclude the action of the State altogether. If the State acts amiss, let them check it, but let them no longer take it for granted that the State cannot possibly act usefully.

The State—but what is the State? cry many. Speculations on the idea of a State abound, but these do not satisfy them; of that which is to have practical effect and power they require a plain account. The full force of the term, *the State,* as the full force of any other important term, no one will master without going a little deeply, without resolutely entering the world of ideas; but it is possible to give in very plain language an account of it sufficient for all practical purposes. The State is properly just what Burke called it—*the nation in its collective and corporate character.* The State is the representative acting-power of the nation; the action of the State is the representative action of the nation. Nominally emanating from the Crown, as the ideal unity in which the nation concentrates itself, this action, by the constitution of our country, really emanates from the ministers of the Crown. It is common to hear the depreciators of State-action run through a string of ministers' names, and then say: "Here is really your *State;* would you accept the action of these men as your own representative action? In what respect is their judgment on national affairs likely to be any better than that of the rest of the world?" In the first place I answer: Even supposing them to be originally no better or wiser than the rest of the world, they have two great advantages from their position: access to almost boundless means of information, and the enlargement of mind which the habit of dealing with great affairs tends to produce. Their position itself, therefore, if they are men of only average honesty and capacity, tends to give them a fitness for acting on behalf of the nation superior to that of other men of equal honesty and capacity who are not in the same position. This fitness may be yet further increased by treating them as persons on whom, indeed, a very grave responsibility has fallen, and from whom very much will be expected;—nothing less than the representing, each of them in his own department, under the control of Parliament, and aided by the suggestions of public opinion, the collective energy and intelligence of his nation. By treating them as men on whom all this devolves to do, to their honour if they do it well, to their shame if they do it ill, one probably augments their faculty of well-doing; as it is excellently said: "To treat men as if they were better than they are, is the surest way to *make* them better than they are." But to treat them as if they had been shuffled into their places by a lucky accident, were most likely soon to be shuffled out of them again, and meanwhile ought to magnify themselves and their office as little as possible; to treat them as if they and their functions could without much inconvenience be quite dispensed with, and they ought perpetually to be admiring their own inconceivable good fortune in being permitted to discharge them;—this is the way to paralyse all high effort in the executive government, to extinguish all lofty sense of responsibility; to make its members either merely solicitous for the gross advantages, the emolument, and self-importance, which they derive from their offices, or else timid, apologetic, and self-mistrustful in filling them; in either case, formal and inefficient.

But in the second place I answer: If the executive government is really in the hands of men no wiser than the bulk of mankind, of men whose action an intelligent man would be unwilling to accept as representative of his own action, whose fault is that? It is the fault of the nation itself, which, not being in the hands of a despot or an oligarchy, being free to control the choice of those who are to sum up and concentrate its action, controls it in such a manner that it allows to be chosen agents so little in its confidence, or so mediocre, or so incompetent, that it thinks the best thing to be done with them is to reduce their action as near as possible to a nullity. Hesitating, blundering, unintelligent, inefficacious, the action of the State may be; but, such as it is, it is the collective action of the nation itself, and the nation is responsible for it. It is our own action which we suffer to be thus unsatisfactory. Nothing can free us from this responsibility. The conduct of our affairs is in our own power. To carry on into its executive proceedings the indecision, conflict, and discordance of its parliamentary debates, may be a natural defect of a free nation, but it is certainly a defect; it is a dangerous error to call it, as some do, a perfection. The want of concert, reason, and organisation in the State, is the want of concert, reason, and organisation in the collective nation.

Inasmuch, therefore, as collective action is more efficacious than isolated individual efforts, a nation having great and complicated matters to deal with must greatly gain by employing the action of the State. Only, the State-power which it employs should be a power which really represents its best self, and whose action its intelligence and justice can heartily avow and adopt; not a power which reflects its inferior self, and of whose action, as of its own second-rate action, it has perpetually to be ashamed. To offer a worthy initiative, and to set a standard of rational and equitable action,—this is what the nation should expect of the State; and the more the State fulfils this expectation, the more will it be accepted in practice for what in idea it must always be. People will not then ask the State, what title it has to commend or reward genius and merit, since commendation and reward imply an attitude of superiority, for it will then be felt that the State truly acts for the English nation; and the genius of the English nation is greater than the genius of any individual, greater even than Shakespeare's genius, for it includes the genius of Newton also.

I will not deny that to give a more prominent part to the State would be a considerable change in this country; that maxims once very sound, and habits once very salutary, may be appealed to against it. The sole question is, whether those maxims and habits are sound and salutary at this moment. A yet graver and more difficult change,—to reduce the all-effacing prominence of the State, to give a more prominent part to the individual, —is imperiously presenting itself to other countries. Both are the suggestions of one irresistible force, which is gradually making its way everywhere, removing old conditions and imposing new, altering long-fixed habits, undermining venerable institutions, even modifying national character: *the modern spirit*.

Undoubtedly we are drawing on towards great changes; and for every nation the thing most needful is to discern clearly its own condition, in order to know in what particular way it may best meet them. Openness and flexibility of mind are at such a time the first of virtues. *Be ye perfect*, said the Founder of Christianity; *I count not myself to have apprehended*, said its greatest Apostle. Perfection will never be reached; but to recognize a period of transformation when it comes, and to adapt themselves honestly and rationally to its laws, is perhaps the nearest approach to perfection of which men and nations are capable. No habits or attachments should prevent their trying to do this; nor indeed, in the long run, can they. Human thought, which made all institutions, inevitably saps them, resting only in that which is absolute and eternal.

◑

CULTURE AND ANARCHY

◑

INTRODUCTION

IN ONE of his speeches a short time ago, that fine speaker and famous Liberal, Mr. Bright, took occasion to have a fling at the friends and preachers of culture. "People who talk about what they call *culture*!" said he, contemptuously; "by which they mean a smattering of the two dead languages of Greek and Latin." And he went on to remark, in a strain with which modern speakers and writers have made us very familiar, how poor a thing this culture is, how little good it can do to the world, and how absurd it is for its possessors to set much store by it. And the other day a younger Liberal than Mr. Bright, one of a school whose mission it is to bring into order and system that body of truth with which the earlier Liberals merely fumbled, a member of the University of Oxford, and a very clever writer, Mr. Frederic Harrison, developed, in the systematic and stringent manner of his school, the thesis which Mr. Bright had propounded in only general terms. "Perhaps the very silliest cant of the day," said Mr. Frederic Harrison, "is the cant about culture. Culture is a desirable

quality in a critic of new books, and sits well on a pos-
sessor of *belles lettres*; but as applied to politics, it means
simply a turn for small fault-finding, love of selfish ease,
and indecision in action. The man of culture is in politics one of the poorest mortals alive. For simple pedantry
and want of good sense no man is his equal. No assumption is too unreal, no end is too unpractical for him. But
the active exercise of politics requires common sense,
sympathy, trust, resolution, and enthusiasm, qualities
which your man of culture has carefully rooted up, lest
they damage the delicacy of his critical olfactories. Perhaps they are the only class of responsible beings in the
community who cannot with safety be entrusted with
power."

Now for my part I do not wish to see men of culture
asking to be entrusted with power; and, indeed, I have
freely said, that in my opinion the speech most proper,
at present, for a man of culture to make to a body of his
fellow-countrymen who get him into a committee-room,
is Socrates's: *Know thyself!* and this is not a speech to
be made by men wanting to be entrusted with power.
For this very indifference to direct political action I
have been taken to task by the *Daily Telegraph*, cou-
pled, by a strange perversity of fate, with just that very
one of the Hebrew prophets whose style I admire the
least, and called "an elegant Jeremiah." It is because I
say (to use the words which the *Daily Telegraph* puts
in my mouth):—"You mustn't make a fuss because you
have no vote,—that is vulgarity; you mustn't hold big
meetings to agitate for reform bills and to repeal corn
laws,—that is the very height of vulgarity,"—it is for
this reason that I am called sometimes an elegant Jeremiah, sometimes a spurious Jeremiah, a Jeremiah about
the reality of whose mission the writer in the *Daily Telegraph* has his doubts. It is evident, therefore, that I have

so taken my line as not to be exposed to the whole brunt
of Mr. Frederic Harrison's censure. Still, I have often
spoken in praise of culture, I have striven to make all
my works and ways serve the interests of culture. I take
culture to be something a great deal more than what
Mr. Frederic Harrison and others call it: "a desirable
quality in a critic of new books." Nay, even though to a
certain extent I am disposed to agree with Mr. Frederic
Harrison, that men of culture are just the class of responsible beings in this community of ours who cannot
properly, at present, be entrusted with power, I am not
sure that I do not think this the fault of our community
rather than of the men of culture. In short, although,
like Mr. Bright and Mr. Frederic Harrison, and the editor of the *Daily Telegraph,* and a large body of valued
friends of mine, I am a Liberal, yet I am a Liberal tempered by experience, reflection, and renouncement, and
I am, above all, a believer in culture. Therefore I propose now to try and inquire, in the simple unsystematic
way which best suits both my taste and my powers,
what culture really is, what good it can do, what is
our own special need of it; and I shall seek to find some
plain grounds on which a faith in culture,—both my
own faith in it and the faith of others,—may rest securely.

I. SWEETNESS AND LIGHT

The disparagers of culture make its motive curiosity;
sometimes, indeed, they make its motive mere exclu-
siveness and vanity. The culture which is supposed to
plume itself on a smattering of Greek and Latin is a
culture which is begotten by nothing so intellectual as
curiosity; it is valued either out of sheer vanity and ignorance or else as an engine of social and class distinc-

tion, separating its holder, like a badge or title, from other people who have not got it. No serious man would call this *culture*, or attach any value to it, as culture, at all. To find the real ground for the very different estimate which serious people will set upon culture, we must find some motive for culture in the terms of which may lie a real ambiguity; and such a motive the word *curiosity* gives us.

I have before now pointed out that we English do not, like the foreigners, use this word in a good sense as well as in a bad sense. With us the word is always used in a somewhat disapproving sense. A liberal and intelligent eagerness about the things of the mind may be meant by a foreigner when he speaks of curiosity, but with us the word always conveys a certain notion of frivolous and unedifying activity. In the *Quarterly Review*, some little time ago, was an estimate of the celebrated French critic, M. Sainte-Beuve, and a very inadequate estimate it in my judgment was. And its inadequacy consisted chiefly in this: that in our English way it left out of sight the double sense really involved in the word *curiosity*, thinking enough was said to stamp M. Sainte-Beuve with blame if it was said that he was impelled in his operations as a critic by curiosity, and omitting either to perceive that M. Sainte-Beuve himself, and many other people with him, would consider that this was praiseworthy and not blameworthy, or to point out why it ought really to be accounted worthy of blame and not of praise. For as there is a curiosity about intellectual matters which is futile, and merely a disease, so there is certainly a curiosity,—a desire after the things of the mind simply for their own sakes and for the pleasure of seeing them as they are,—which is, in an intelligent being, natural and laudable. Nay, and the very desire to see things as they are implies a balance and regulation

of mind which is not often attained without fruitful effort, and which is the very opposite of the blind and
diseased impulse of mind which is what we mean to
blame when we blame curiosity. Montesquieu says:
"The first motive which ought to impel us to study is
the desire to augment the excellence of our nature, and
to render an intelligent being yet more intelligent." This
is the true ground to assign for the genuine scientific
passion, however manifested, and for culture, viewed
simply as a fruit of this passion; and it is a worthy
ground, even though we let the term *curiosity* stand to
describe it.

But there is of culture another view, in which not
solely the scientific passion, the sheer desire to see things
as they are, natural and proper in an intelligent being,
appears as the ground of it. There is a view in which all
the love of our neighbour, the impulses towards action,
help, and beneficence, the desire for removing human
error, clearing human confusion, and diminishing human misery, the noble aspiration to leave the world better and happier than we found it,—motives eminently
such as are called social,—come in as part of the grounds
of culture, and the main and pre-eminent part. Culture
is then properly described not as having its origin in
curiosity, but as having its origin in the love of perfection; it is *a study of perfection*. It moves by the force,
not merely or primarily of the scientific passion for pure
knowledge, but also of the moral and social passion for
doing good. As, in the first view of it, we took for its
worthy motto Montesquieu's words: "To render an intelligent being yet more intelligent!" so, in the second
view of it, there is no better motto which it can have
than these words of Bishop Wilson: "To make reason
and the will of God prevail!"

Only, whereas the passion for doing good is apt to

be overhasty in determining what reason and the will of God say, because its turn is for acting rather than thinking and it wants to be beginning to act; and whereas it is apt to take its own conceptions, which proceed from its own state of development and share in all the imperfections and immaturities of this, for a basis of action; what distinguishes culture is, that it is possessed by the scientific passion as well as by the passion of doing good; that it demands worthy notions of reason and the will of God, and does not readily suffer its own crude conceptions to substitute themselves for them. And knowing that no action or institution can be salutary and stable which is not based on reason and the will of God, it is not so bent on acting and instituting, even with the great aim of diminishing human error and misery ever before its thoughts, but that it can remember that acting and instituting are of little use, unless we know how and what we ought to act and to institute.

This culture is more interesting and more far-reaching than that other, which is founded solely on the scientific passion for knowing. But it needs times of faith and ardour, times when the intellectual horizon is opening and widening all round us, to flourish in. And is not the close and bounded intellectual horizon within which we have long lived and moved now lifting up, and are not new lights finding free passage to shine in upon us? For a long time there was no passage for them to make their way in upon us, and then it was of no use to think of adapting the world's action to them. Where was the hope of making reason and the will of God prevail among people who had a routine which they had christened reason and the will of God, in which they were inextricably bound, and beyond which they had no power of looking? But now the iron force of adhesion

to the old routine,—social, political, religious,—has
wonderfully yielded; the iron force of exclusion of all
which is new has wonderfully yielded. The danger now
is, not that people should obstinately refuse to allow
anything but their old routine to pass for reason and the
will of God, but either that they should allow some novelty or other to pass for these too easily, or else that they
should underrate the importance of them altogether,
and think it enough to follow action for its own sake,
without troubling themselves to make reason and the
will of God prevail therein. Now, then, is the moment
for culture to be of service, culture which believes in
making reason and the will of God prevail, believes in
perfection, is the study and pursuit of perfection, and
is no longer debarred, by a rigid invincible exclusion of
whatever is new, from getting acceptance for its ideas,
simply because they are new.

The moment this view of culture is seized, the moment it is regarded not solely as the endeavour to see
things as they are, to draw towards a knowledge of the
universal order which seems to be intended and aimed
at in the world, and which it is a man's happiness to go
along with or his misery to go counter to,—to learn, in
short, the will of God,—the moment, I say, culture is considered not merely as the endeavour to *see* and *learn*
this, but as the endeavour, also, to make it *prevail,* the
moral, social, and beneficent character of culture becomes manifest. The mere endeavour to see and learn
the truth for our own personal satisfaction is indeed a
commencement for making it prevail, a preparing the
way for this, which always serves this, and is wrongly,
therefore, stamped with blame absolutely in itself and
not only in its caricature and degeneration. But perhaps
it has got stamped with blame, and disparaged with the

dubious title of curiosity, because in comparison with this wider endeavour of such great and plain utility it looks selfish, petty, and unprofitable.

And religion, the greatest and most important of the efforts by which the human race has manifested its impulse to perfect itself,—religion, that voice of the deepest human experience,—does not only enjoin and sanction the aim which is the great aim of culture, the aim of setting ourselves to ascertain what perfection is and to make it prevail; but also, in determining generally in what human perfection consists, religion comes to a conclusion identical with that which culture,—culture seeking the determination of this question through *all* the voices of human experience which have been heard upon it, of art, science, poetry, philosophy, history, as well as of religion, in order to give a greater fulness and certainty to its solution,—likewise reaches. Religion says: *The kingdom of God is within you;* and culture, in like manner, places human perfection in an *internal* condition, in the growth and predominance of our humanity proper, as distinguished from our animality. It places it in the ever-increasing efficacy and in the general harmonious expansion of those gifts of thought and feeling, which make the peculiar dignity, wealth, and happiness of human nature. As I have said on a former occasion: "It is in making endless additions to itself, in the endless expansion of its powers, in endless growth in wisdom and beauty, that the spirit of the human race finds its ideal. To reach this ideal, culture is an indispensable aid, and that is the true value of culture." Not a having and a resting, but a growing and a becoming, is the character of perfection as culture conceives it; and here, too, it coincides with religion.

And because men are all members of one great whole, and the sympathy which is in human nature will not allow one member to be indifferent to the rest or to have a perfect welfare independent of the rest, the expansion of our humanity, to suit the idea of perfection which culture forms, must be a *general* expansion. Perfection, as culture conceives it, is not possible while the individual remains isolated. The individual is required, under pain of being stunted and enfeebled in his own development if he disobeys, to carry others along with him in his march towards perfection, to be continually doing all he can to enlarge and increase the volume of the human stream sweeping thitherward. And here, once more, culture lays on us the same obligation as religion, which says, as Bishop Wilson has admirably put it, that "to promote the kingdom of God is to increase and hasten one's own happiness."

But, finally, perfection,—as culture from a thorough disinterested study of human nature and human experience learns to conceive it,—is a harmonious expansion of *all* the powers which make the beauty and worth of human nature, and is not consistent with the over-development of any one power at the expense of the rest. Here culture goes beyond religion, as religion is generally conceived by us.

If culture, then, is a study of perfection, and of harmonious perfection, general perfection, and perfection which consists in becoming something rather than in having something, in an inward condition of the mind and spirit, not in an outward set of circumstances,—it is clear that culture, instead of being the frivolous and useless thing which Mr. Bright, and Mr. Frederic Harrison, and many other Liberals are apt to call it, has a very important function to fulfil for mankind. And this function is particularly important in our modern world, of which the whole civilisation is, to a much greater degree than the civilisation of Greece and Rome, mechani-

cal and external, and tends constantly to become more
so. But above all in our own country has culture a
weighty part to perform, because here that mechanical
character, which civilisation tends to take everywhere,
is shown in the most eminent degree. Indeed nearly all
the characters of perfection, as culture teaches us to fix
them, meet in this country with some powerful tendency
which thwarts them and sets them at defiance. The idea
of perfection as an *inward* condition of the mind and
spirit is at variance with the mechanical and material
civilisation in esteem with us, and nowhere, as I have
said, so much in esteem as with us. The idea of perfection as a *general* expansion of the human family is at
variance with our strong individualism, our hatred of
all limits to the unrestrained swing of the individual's
personality, our maxim of "every man for himself."
Above all, the idea of perfection as a *harmonious* expansion of human nature is at variance with our want of
flexibility, with our inaptitude for seeing more than one
side of a thing, with our intense energetic absorption in
the particular pursuit we happen to be following. So
culture has a rough task to achieve in this country. Its
preachers have, and are likely long to have, a hard time
of it, and they will much oftener be regarded, for a
great while to come, as elegant or spurious Jeremiahs
than as friends and benefactors. That, however, will not
prevent their doing in the end good service if they per-
severe. And, meanwhile, the mode of action they have
to pursue, and the sort of habits they must fight against,
ought to be made quite clear for every one to see, who
may be willing to look at the matter attentively and dis-
passionately.

Faith in machinery is, I said, our besetting danger;
often in machinery most absurdly disproportioned to the
end which the machinery, if it is to do any good at all,

is to serve; but always in machinery, as if it had a value in and for itself. What is freedom but machinery? what is population but machinery? what is coal but machinery? what are railroads but machinery? what is wealth but machinery? what are, even, religious organisations but machinery? Now almost every voice in England is accustomed to speak of these things as if they were precious ends in themselves, and therefore had some of the characters of perfection indisputably joined to them. I have before now noticed Mr. Roebuck's stock argument for proving the greatness and happiness of England as she is, and for quite stopping the mouths of all gainsayers. Mr. Roebuck is never weary of reiterating this argument of his, so I do not know why I should be weary of noticing it. "May not every man in England say what he likes?"—Mr. Roebuck perpetually asks; and that, he thinks, is quite sufficient, and when every man may say what he likes, our aspirations ought to be satisfied. But the aspirations of culture, which is the study of perfection, are not satisfied, unless what men say, when they may say what they like, is worth saying,—has good in it, and more good than bad. In the same way the *Times*, replying to some foreign strictures on the dress, looks, and behaviour of the English abroad, urges that the English ideal is that every one should be free to do and to look just as he likes. But culture indefatigably tries, not to make what each raw person may like the rule by which he fashions himself; but to draw ever nearer to a sense of what is indeed beautiful, graceful, and becoming, and to get the raw person to like that.

And in the same way with respect to railroads and coal. Every one must have observed the strange language current during the late discussions as to the possible failures of our supplies of coal. Our coal, thousands of people were saying, is the real basis of our national greatness; if our coal runs short, there is an end of the greatness of England. But what *is* greatness?—culture makes us ask. Greatness is a spiritual condition worthy to excite love, interest, and admiration; and the outward proof of possessing greatness is that we excite love, interest, and admiration. If England were swallowed up by the sea to-morrow, which of the two, a hundred years hence, would most excite the love, interest, and admiration of mankind,—would most, therefore, show the evidences of having possessed greatness,—the England of the last twenty years, or the England of Elizabeth, of a time of splendid spiritual effort, but when our coal, and our industrial operations depending on coal, were very little developed? Well, then, what an unsound habit of mind it must be which makes us talk of things like coal or iron as constituting the greatness of England, and how salutary a friend is culture, bent on seeing things as they are, and thus dissipating delusions of this kind and fixing standards of perfection that are real!

Wealth, again, that end to which our prodigious works for material advantage are directed,—the commonest of commonplaces tells us how men are always apt to regard wealth as a precious end in itself; and certainly they have never been so apt thus to regard it as they are in England at the present time. Never did people believe anything more firmly than nine Englishmen out of ten at the present day believe that our greatness and welfare are proved by our being so very rich. Now, the use of culture is that it helps us, by means of its spiritual standard of perfection, to regard wealth as but machinery, and not only to say as a matter of words that we regard wealth as but machinery, but really to perceive and feel that it is so. If it were not for this purging effect wrought upon our minds by culture, the whole world, the future as well as the present, would inevitably belong to the

Philistines. The people who believe most that our greatness and welfare are proved by our being very rich, and
who most give their lives and thoughts to becoming
rich, are just the very people whom we call Philistines.
Culture says: "Consider these people, then, their way
of life, their habits, their manners, the very tones of
their voice; look at them attentively; observe the literature they read, the things which give them pleasure, the
words which come forth out of their mouths, the thoughts
which make the furniture of their minds; would any
amount of wealth be worth having with the condition
that one was to become just like these people by having
it?" And thus culture begets a dissatisfaction which is
of the highest possible value in stemming the common
tide of men's thoughts in a wealthy and industrial community, and which saves the future, as one may hope,
from being vulgarised, even if it cannot save the present.

Population, again, and bodily health and vigour, are
things which are nowhere treated in such an unintelligent, misleading, exaggerated way as in England. Both
are really machinery; yet how many people all around
us do we see rest in them and fail to look beyond them!
Why, one has heard people, fresh from reading certain
articles of the *Times* on the Registrar-General's returns
of marriages and births in this country, who would talk
of our large English families in quite a solemn strain, as
if they had something in itself beautiful, elevating, and
meritorious in them; as if the British Philistine would
have only to present himself before the Great Judge
with his twelve children, in order to be received among
the sheep as a matter of right!

But bodily health and vigour, it may be said, are not
to be classed with wealth and population as mere machinery; they have a more real and essential value. True;
but only as they are more intimately connected with a

perfect spiritual condition than wealth or population are. The moment we disjoin them from the idea of a perfect spiritual condition, and pursue them, as we do pursue them, for their own sake and as ends in themselves, our worship of them becomes as mere worship of machinery, as our worship of wealth or population, and as unintelligent and vulgarising a worship as that is. Every one with anything like an adequate idea of human perfection has distinctly marked this subordination to higher and spiritual ends of the cultivation of bodily vigour and activity. "Bodily exercise profiteth little; but godliness is profitable unto all things," says the author of the Epistle to Timothy. And the utilitarian Franklin says just as explicitly:—"Eat and drink such an exact quantity as suits the constitution of thy body, *in reference to the services of the mind.*" But the point of view of culture, keeping the mark of human perfection simply and broadly in view, and not assigning to this perfection, as religion or utilitarianism assigns to it, a special and limited character, this point of view, I say, of culture is best given by these words of Epictetus:—"It is a sign of ἀφυΐα," says he,—that is, of a nature not finely tempered, —"to give yourselves up to things which relate to the body; to make, for instance, a great fuss about exercise, a great fuss about eating, a great fuss about drinking, a great fuss about walking, a great fuss about riding. All these things ought to be done merely by the way: the formation of the spirit and character must be our real concern." This is admirable; and, indeed, the Greek word εὐφυΐα, a finely tempered nature, gives exactly the notion of perfection as culture brings us to conceive it: a harmonious perfection, a perfection in which the characters of beauty and intelligence are both present, which unites "the two noblest of things,"—as Swift, who of one of the two, at any rate, had himself all too little, most happily calls them in his *Battle of the Books*,—"the two noblest of things, *sweetness and light*." The εὐφυής is the man who tends towards sweetness and light; the ἀφυής, on the other hand, is our Philistine. The immense spiritual significance of the Greeks is due to their having been inspired with this central and happy idea of the essential character of human perfection; and Mr. Bright's misconception of culture, as a smattering of Greek and Latin, comes itself, after all, from this wonderful significance of the Greeks having affected the very machinery of our education, and is in itself a kind of homage to it.

In thus makng sweetness and light to be characters of perfection, culture is of like spirit with poetry, follows one law with poetry. Far more than on our freedom, our population, and our industrialism, many amongst us rely upon our religious organisations to save us. I have called religion a yet more important manifestation of human nature than poetry, because it has worked on a broader scale for perfection, and with greater masses of men. But the idea of beauty and of a human nature perfect on all its sides, which is the dominant idea of poetry, is a true and invaluable idea, though it has not yet had the success that the idea of conquering the obvious faults of our animality, and of a human nature perfect on the moral side,—which is the dominant idea of religion,— has been enabled to have; and it is destined, adding to itself the religious idea of a devout energy, to transform and govern the other.

The best art and poetry of the Greeks, in which religion and poetry are one, in which the idea of beauty and of a human nature perfect on all sides adds to itself a religious and devout energy, and works in the strength of that, is on this account of such surpassing interest and instructiveness for us, though it was,—as, having regard

to the human race in general, and, indeed, having regard
to the Greeks themselves, we must own,—a premature
attempt, an attempt which for success needed the moral
and religious fibre in humanity to be more braced and
developed than it had yet been. But Greece did not err
in having the idea of beauty, harmony, and complete
human perfection, so present and paramount. It is impossible to have this idea too present and paramount;
only, the moral fibre must be braced too. And we, because we have braced the moral fibre, are not on that
account in the right way, if at the same time the idea
of beauty, harmony, and complete human perfection, is
wanting or misapprehended amongst us; and evidently
it *is* wanting or misapprehended at present. And when
we rely as we do on our religious organisations, which
in themselves do not and cannot give us this idea, and
think we have done enough if we make them spread and
prevail, then, I say, we fall into our common fault of
overvaluing machinery.

Nothing is more common than for people to confound
the inward peace and satisfaction which follows the
subduing of the obvious faults of our animality with
what I may call absolute inward peace and satisfaction,
—the peace and satisfaction which are reached as we
draw near to complete spiritual perfection, and not
merely to moral perfection, or rather to relative moral
perfection. No people in the world have done more and
struggled more to attain this relative moral perfection
than our English race has. For no people in the world
has the command to *resist the devil, to overcome the
wicked one,* in the nearest and most obvious sense of
those words, had such a pressing force and reality. And
we have had our reward, not only in the great worldly
prosperity which our obedience to this command has
brought us, but also, and far more, in great inward peace

and satisfaction. But to me few things are more pathetic than to see people, on the strength of the inward peace and satisfaction which their rudimentary efforts towards perfection have brought them, employ, concerning their incomplete perfection and the religious organisations within which they have found it, language which properly applies only to complete perfection, and is a far-off echo of the human soul's prophecy of it. Religion itself, I need hardly say, supplies them in abundance with this grand language. And very freely do they use it; yet it is really the severest possible criticism of such an incomplete perfection as alone we have yet reached through our religious organisations.

The impulse of the English race towards moral development and self-conquest has nowhere so powerfully manifested itself as in Puritanism. Nowhere has Puritanism found so adequate an expression as in the religious organisation of the Independents. The modern Independents have a newspaper, the *Nonconformist*, written with great sincerity and ability. The motto, the standard, the profession of faith which this organ of theirs carries aloft, is: "The Dissidence of Dissent and the Protestantism of the Protestant religion." There is sweetness and light, and an ideal of complete harmonious human perfection! One need not go to culture and poetry to find language to judge it. Religion, with its instinct for perfection, supplies language to judge it, language, too, which is in our mouths every day. "Finally, be of one mind, united in feeling," says St. Peter. There is an ideal which judges the Puritan ideal: "The Dissidence of Dissent and the Protestantism of the Protestant religion!" And religious organisations like this are what people believe in, rest in, would give their lives for! Such, I say, is the wonderful virtue of even the beginnings of perfection, of having conquered even the plain faults of our animality, that the religious organisation which has helped us to do it can seem to us something precious, salutary, and to be propagated, even when it wears such a brand of imperfection on its forehead as this. And men have got such a habit of giving to the language of religion a special application, of making it a mere jargon, that for the condemnation which religion itself passes on the shortcomings of their religious organisations they have no ear; they are sure to cheat themselves and to explain this condemnation away. They can only be reached by the criticism which culture, like poetry, speaking a language not to be sophisticated, and resolutely testing these organisations by the ideal of a human perfection complete on all sides, applies to them.

But men of culture and poetry, it will be said, are again and again failing, and failing conspicuously, in the necessary first stage to a harmonious perfection, in the subduing of the great obvious faults of our animality, which it is the glory of these religious organisations to have helped us to subdue. True, they do often so fail. They have often been without the virtues as well as the faults of the Puritan; it has been one of their dangers that they so felt the Puritan's faults that they too much neglected the practice of his virtues. I will not, however, exculpate them at the Puritan's expense. They have often failed in morality, and morality is indispensable. And they have been punished for their failure, as the Puritan has been rewarded for his performance. They have been punished wherein they erred; but their ideal of beauty, of sweetness and light, and a human nature complete on all its sides, remains the true ideal of perfection still; just as the Puritan's ideal of perfection remains narrow and inadequate, although for what he did well he has been richly rewarded. Notwithstanding the mighty results of the Pilgrim Fathers' voyage, they and their

standard of perfection are rightly judged when we figure
to ourselves Shakespeare or Virgil,—souls in whom sweetness and light, and all that in human nature is most
humane, were eminent,—accompanying them on their
voyage, and think what intolerable company Shakespeare
and Virgil would have found them! In the same way let
us judge the religious organisations which we see all
around us. Do not let us deny the good and the happiness which they have accomplished; but do not let us fail
to see clearly that their idea of human perfection is narrow and inadequate, and that the Dissidence of Dissent
and the Protestantism of the Protestant religion will
never bring humanity to its true goal. As I said with
regard to wealth: Let us look at the life of those who
live in and for it,—so I say with regard to the religious
organisations. Look at the life imaged in such a newspaper as the *Nonconformist,*—a life of jealousy of the
Establishment, disputes, tea-meetings, openings of chapels, sermons; and then think of it as an ideal of a human
life completing itself on all sides, and aspiring with all
its organs after sweetness, light, and perfection!

Another newspaper, representing, like the *Nonconformist,* one of the religious organisations of this country,
was a short time ago giving an account of the crowd at
Epsom on the Derby day, and of all the vice and hideousness which was to be seen in that crowd; and then
the writer turned suddenly round upon Professor Huxley, and asked him how he proposed to cure all this
vice and hideousness without religion. I confess I felt
disposed to ask the asker this question: and how do you
propose to cure it with such a religion as yours? How is
the ideal of a life so unlovely, so unattractive, so incomplete, so narrow, so far removed from a true and satisfying ideal of human perfection, as is the life of your religious organisation as you yourself reflect it, to conquer

and transform all this vice and hideousness? Indeed, the strongest plea for the study of perfection as pursued by culture, the clearest proof of the actual inadequacy of the idea of perfection held by the religious organisations, —expressing, as I have said, the most widespread effort which the human race has yet made after perfection,— is to be found in the state of our life and society with these in possession of it, and having been in possession of it I know not how many hundred years. We are all of us included in some religious organisation or other; we all call ourselves, in the sublime and aspiring language of religion which I have before noticed, *children of God.* Children of God;—it is an immense pretension!—and how are we to justify it? By the works which we do, and the words which we speak. And the work which we collective children of God do, our grand centre of life, our *city* which we have builded for us to dwell in, is London! London, with its unutterable external hideousness, and with its internal canker of *publice egestas, privatim opulentia,*—to use the words which Sallust puts into Cato's mouth about Rome,—unequalled in the world! The word, again, which we children of God speak, the voice which most hits our collective thought, the newspaper with the largest circulation in England, nay, with the largest circulation in the whole world, is the *Daily Telegraph!* I say that when our religious organisations, —which I admit to express the most considerable effort after perfection that our race has yet made,—land us in no better result than this, it is high time to examine carefully their idea of perfection, to see whether it does not leave out of account sides and forces of human nature which we might turn to great use; whether it would not be more operative if it were more complete. And I say that the English reliance on our religious organisations and on their ideas of human perfection just as they stand, is like our reliance on freedom, on muscular Christianity, on population, on coal, on wealth,—mere belief in machinery, and unfruitful; and that it is wholesomely counteracted by culture, bent on seeing things as they are, and on drawing the human race onwards to a more complete, a harmonious perfection.

Culture, however, shows its single-minded love of perfection, its desire simply to make reason and the will of God prevail, its freedom from fanaticism, by its attitude towards all this machinery, even while it insists that it *is* machinery. Fanatics, seeing the mischief men do themselves by their blind belief in some machinery or other, —whether it is wealth and industrialism, or whether it is the cultivation of bodily strength and activity, or whether it is a political organisation,—or whether it is a religious organisation,—oppose with might and main the tendency to this or that political and religious organisation, or to games and athletic exercises, or to wealth and industrialism, and try violently to stop it. But the flexibility which sweetness and light give, and which is one of the rewards of culture pursued in good faith, enables a man to see that a tendency may be necessary, and even, as a preparation for something in the future, salutary, and yet that the generations or individuals who obey this tendency are sacrificed to it, that they fall short of the hope of perfection by following it; and that its mischiefs are to be criticised, lest it should take too firm a hold and last after it has served its purpose.

Mr. Gladstone well pointed out, in a speech at Paris, —and others have pointed out the same thing,—how necessary is the present great movement towards wealth and industrialism, in order to lay broad foundations of material well-being for the society of the future. The worst of these justifications is, that they are generally addressed to the very people engaged, body and soul, in the movement in question; at all events, that they are always seized with the greatest avidity by these people, and taken by them as quite justifying their life; and that thus they tend to harden them in their sins. Now, culture admits the necessity of the movement towards fortune-making and exaggerated industrialism, readily allows that the future may derive benefit from it; but insists, at the same time, that the passing generations of industrialists,—forming, for the most part, the stout main body of Philistinism,—are sacrificed to it. In the same way, the result of all the games and sports which occupy the passing generation of boys and young men may be the establishment of a better and sounder physical type for the future to work with. Culture does not set itself against the games and sports; it congratulates the future, and hopes it will make a good use of its improved physical basis; but it points out that our passing generation of boys and young men is, meantime, sacrificed. Puritanism was perhaps necessary to develop the moral fibre of the English race, Nonconformity to break the yoke of ecclesiastical domination over men's minds and to prepare the way for freedom of thought in the distant future; still, culture points out that the harmonious perfection of generations of Puritans and Nonconformists have been, in consequence, sacrificed. Freedom of speech may be necessary for the society of the future, but the young lions of the *Daily Telegraph* in the meanwhile are sacrificed. A voice for every man in his country's government may be necessary for the society of the future, but meanwhile Mr. Beales and Mr. Bradlaugh are sacrificed.

Oxford, the Oxford of the past, has many faults; and she has heavily paid for them in defeat, in isolation, in want of hold upon the modern world. Yet we in Oxford, brought up amidst the beauty and sweetness of that beautiful place, have not failed to seize one truth,—the truth that beauty and sweetness are essential characters of a complete human perfection. When I insist on this, I am all in the faith and tradition of Oxford. I say boldly that this our sentiment for beauty and sweetness, our sentiment against hideousness and rawness, has been at the bottom of our attachment to so many beaten causes, of our opposition to so many triumphant movements. And the sentiment is true, and has never been wholly defeated, and has shown its power even in its defeat. We have not won our political battles, we have not carried our main points, we have not stopped our adversaries' advance, we have not marched victoriously with the modern world; but we have told silently upon the mind of the country, we have prepared currents of feeling which sap our adversaries' position when it seems gained, we have kept up our own communications with the future. Look at the course of the great movement which shook Oxford to its centre some thirty years ago! It was directed, as any one who reads Dr. Newman's *Apology* may see, against what in one word may be called "Liberalism." Liberalism prevailed; it was the appointed force to do the work of the hour; it was necessary, it was inevitable that it should prevail. The Oxford movement was broken, it failed; our wrecks are scattered on every shore:

> Quæ regio in terris nostri non plena laboris?

But what was it, this liberalism, as Dr. Newman saw it, and as it really broke the Oxford movement? It was the great middle-class liberalism, which had for the cardinal points of its belief the Reform Bill of 1832, and local self-government, in politics; in the social sphere, free-trade, unrestricted competition, and the making of large industrial fortunes; in the religious sphere, the Dissidence of

Dissent and the Protestantism of the Protestant religion. I do not say that other and more intelligent forces than this were not opposed to the Oxford movement: but this was the force which really beat it; this was the force which Dr. Newman felt himself fighting with; this was the force which till only the other day seemed to be the paramount force in this country, and to be in possession of the future; this was the force whose achievements fill Mr. Lowe with such inexpressible admiration, and whose rule he was so horror-struck to see threatened. And where is this great force of Philistinism now? It is thrust into the second rank, it is become a power of yesterday, it has lost the future. A new power has suddenly appeared, a power which it is impossible yet to judge fully, but which is certainly a wholly different force from middle-class liberalism; different in its cardinal points of belief, different in its tendencies in every sphere. It loves and admires neither the legislation of middle-class Parliaments, nor the local self-government of middle-class vestries, nor the unrestricted competition of middle-class industrialists, nor the dissidence of middle-class Dissent and the Protestantism of middle-class Protestant religion. I am not now praising this new force, or saying that its own ideals are better; all I say is, that they are wholly different. And who will estimate how much the currents of feeling created by Dr. Newman's movements, the keen desire for beauty and sweetness which it nourished, the deep aversion it manifested to the hardness and vulgarity of middle-class liberalism, the strong light it turned on the hideous and grotesque illusions of middle-class Protestantism,—who will estimate how much all these contributed to swell the tide of secret dissatisfaction which has mined the ground under self-confident liberalism of the last thirty years, and has prepared the way for its sudden collapse and supersession? It is in this

manner that the sentiment of Oxford for beauty and
sweetness conquers, and in this manner long may it continue to conquer!

In this manner it works to the same end as culture,
and there is plenty of work for it yet to do. I have said
that the new and more democratic force which is now
superseding our old middle-class liberalism cannot yet be
rightly judged. It has its main tendencies still to form.
We hear promises of its giving us administrative reform,
law reform, reform of education, and I know not what;
but those promises come rather from its advocates, wishing to make a good plea for it and to justify it for superseding middle-class liberalism, than from clear tendencies which it has itself yet developed. But meanwhile it
has plenty of well-intentioned friends against whom culture may with advantage continue to uphold steadily its
ideal of human perfection; that this is *an inward spiritual
activity, having for its characters increased sweetness,
increased light, increased life, increased sympathy.* Mr.
Bright, who has a foot in both worlds, the world of
middle-class liberalism and the world of democracy, but
who brings most of his ideas from the world of middle-
class liberalism in which he was bred, always inclines to
inculcate that faith in machinery to which, as we have
seen, Englishmen are so prone, and which has been the
bane of middle-class liberalism. He complains with a
sorrowful indignation of people who "appear to have no
proper estimate of the value of the franchise"; he leads
his disciples to believe,—what the Englishman is always
too ready to believe,—that the having a vote, like the
having a large family, or a large business, or large mus-
cles, has in itself some edifying and perfecting effect
upon human nature. Or else he cries out to the democracy,—"the men," as he calls them, "upon whose shoulders the greatness of England rests,"—he cries out to

them: "See what you have done! I look over this country and see the cities you have built, the railroads you have made, the manufactures you have produced, the cargoes which freight the ships of the greatest mercantile navy the world has ever seen! I see that you have converted by your labours what was once a wilderness, these islands, into a fruitful garden; I know that you have created this wealth, and are a nation whose name is a word of power throughout all the world." Why, this is just the very style of laudation with which Mr. Roebuck or Mr. Lowe debauches the minds of the middle classes, and makes such Philistines of them. It is the same fashion of teaching a man to value himself not on what he *is*, not on his progress in sweetness and light, but on the number of the railroads he has constructed, or the bigness of the tabernacle he has built. Only the middle classes are told they have done it all with their energy, self-reliance, and capital, and the democracy are told they have done it all with their hands and sinews. But teaching the democracy to put its trust in achievements of this kind is merely training them to be Philistines to take the place of the Philistines whom they are superseding; and they too, like the middle class, will be encouraged to sit down at the banquet of the future without having on a wedding garment, and nothing excellent can then come from them. Those who know their besetting faults, those who have watched them and listened to them, or those who will read the instructive account recently given of them by one of themselves, the *Journeyman Engineer*, will agree that the idea which culture sets before us of perfection,—an increased spiritual activity, having for its characters increased sweetness, increased light, increased life, increased sympathy, —is an idea which the new democracy needs far more than the idea of the blessedness of the franchise, or the wonderfulness of its own industrial performances.

Other well-meaning friends of this new power are for leading it, not in the old ruts of middle-class Philistinism, but in ways which are naturally alluring to the feet of democracy, though in this country they are novel and untried ways. I may call them the ways of Jacobinism. Violent indignation with the past, abstract systems of renovation applied wholesale, a new doctrine drawn up in black and white for elaborating down to the very smallest details a rational society for the future,—these are the ways of Jacobinism. Mr. Frederic Harrison and other disciples of Comte,—one of them, Mr. Congreve, is an old friend of mine, and I am glad to have an opportunity of publicly expressing my respect for his talents and character,—are among the friends of democracy who are for leading it in paths of this kind. Mr. Frederic Harrison is very hostile to culture, and from a natural enough motive; for culture is the eternal opponent of the two things which are the signal marks of Jacobinism, —its fierceness, and its addiction to an abstract system. Culture is always assigning to system-makers and systems a smaller share in the bent of human destiny than their friends like. A current in people's minds sets towards new ideas; people are dissatisfied with their old narrow stock of Philistine ideas, Anglo-Saxon ideas, or any other; and some man, some Bentham or Comte, who has the real merit of having early and strongly felt and helped the new current, but who brings plenty of narrowness and mistakes of his own into his feeling and help of it, is credited with being the author of the whole current, the fit person to be entrusted with its regulation and to guide the human race.

The excellent German historian of the mythology of

Rome, Preller, relating the introduction at Rome under the Tarquins of the worship of Apollo, the god of light, healing, and reconciliation, will have us observe that it was not so much the Tarquins who brought to Rome the new worship of Apollo, as a current in the mind of the Roman people which set powerfully at that time towards a new worship of this kind, and away from the old run of Latin and Sabine religious ideas. In a similar way, culture directs our attention to the natural current there is in human affairs, and to its continual working, and will not let us rivet our faith upon any one man and his doings. It makes us see not only his good side, but also how much in him was of necessity limited and transient; nay, it even feels a pleasure, a sense of an increased freedom and of an ampler future, in so doing.

I remember, when I was under the influence of a mind to which I feel the greatest obligations, the mind of a man who was the very incarnation of sanity and clear sense, a man the most considerable, it seems to me, whom America has yet produced,—Benjamin Franklin,—I remember the relief with which, after long feeling the sway of Franklin's imperturbable common-sense, I came upon a project of his for a new version of the Book of Job, to replace the old version, the style of which, says Franklin, has become obsolete, and thence less agreeable. "I give," he continues, "a few verses, which may serve as a sample of the kind of version I would recommend." We all recollect the famous verse in our translation: "Then Satan answered the Lord and said: 'Doth Job fear God for nought?'" Franklin makes this: "Does your Majesty imagine that Job's good conduct is the effect of mere personal attachment and affection?" I well remember how, when first I read that, I drew a deep breath of relief, and said to myself: "After all, there is a stretch of humanity beyond Franklin's victorious good sense!" So, after hearing Bentham cried loudly up as the renovator of modern society, and Bentham's mind and ideas proposed as the rulers of our future, I open the *Deontology*. There I read: "While Xenophon was writing his history and Euclid teaching geometry, Socrates and Plato were talking nonsense under pretence of talking wisdom and morality. This morality of theirs consisted in words; this wisdom of theirs was the denial of matters known to every man's experience." From the moment of reading that, I am delivered from the bondage of Bentham! the fanaticism of his adherents can touch me no longer. I feel the inadequacy of his mind and ideas for supplying the rule of human society, for perfection.

Culture tends always thus to deal with the men of a system, of disciples, of a school; with men like Comte, or the late Mr. Buckle, or Mr. Mill. However much it may find to admire in these personages, or in some of them, it nevertheless remembers the text: "Be not ye called Rabbi!" and it soon passes on from any Rabbi. But Jacobinism loves a Rabbi; it does not want to pass on from its Rabbi in pursuit of a future and still unreached perfection; it wants its Rabbi and his ideas to stand for perfection, that they may with the more authority recast the world; and for Jacobinism, therefore, culture,—eternally passing onwards and seeking,—is an impertinence and an offence. But culture, just because it resists this tendency of Jacobinism to impose on us a man with limitations and errors of his own along with the true ideas of which he is the organ, really does the world and Jacobinism itself a service.

So, too, Jacobinism, in its fierce hatred of the past and of those whom it makes liable for the sins of the past, cannot away with the inexhaustible indulgence proper to culture, the consideration of circumstances, the severe judgment of actions joined to the merciful judgment of persons. "The man of culture is in politics," cries Mr. Frederic Harrison, "one of the poorest mortals alive!" Mr. Frederic Harrison wants to be doing business, and he complains that the man of culture stops him with a "turn for small fault-finding, love of selfish ease, and indecision in action." Of what use is culture, he asks, except for "a critic of new books or a professor of *belles lettres?*" Why, it is of use because, in presence of the fierce exasperation which breathes, or rather, I may say, hisses through the whole production in which Mr. Frederic Harrison asks that question, it reminds us that the perfection of human nature is sweetness and light. It is of use because, like religion,—that other effort after perfection,—it testifies that, where bitter envying and strife are, there is confusion and every evil work.

The pursuit of perfection, then, is the pursuit of sweetness and light. He who works for sweetness and light, works to make reason and the will of God prevail. He who works for machinery, he who works for hatred, works only for confusion. Culture looks beyond machinery, culture hates hatred; culture has one great passion, the passion for sweetness and light. It has one even yet greater!—the passion for making them *prevail*. It is not satisfied till we *all* come to a perfect man; it knows that the sweetness and light of the few must be imperfect until the raw and unkindled masses of humanity are touched with sweetness and light. If I have not shrunk from saying that we must work for sweetness and light, so neither have I shrunk from saying that we must have a broad basis, must have sweetness and light for as many as possible. Again and again I have insisted how those are the happy moments of humanity, how those are the marking epochs of a people's life, how those are the flowering times for literature and art and all the cre-

ative power of genius, when there is a *national* glow of
life and thought, when the whole of society is in the fullest measure permeated by thought, sensible to beauty,
intelligent and alive. Only it must be *real* thought and
real beauty; *real* sweetness and *real* light. Plenty of people will try to give the masses, as they call them, an intellectual food prepared and adapted in the way they
think proper for the actual condition of the masses. The
ordinary popular literature is an example of this way of
working on the masses. Plenty of people will try to in-
doctrinate the masses with the set of ideas and judgments constituting the creed of their own profession or
party. Our religious and political organisations give an
example of this way of working on the masses. I condemn neither way; but culture works differently. It does
not try to teach down to the level of inferior classes; it
does not try to win them for this or that sect of its own,
with ready-made judgments and watchwords. It seeks to
do away with classes; to make the best that has been
thought and known in the world current everywhere; to
make all men live in an atmosphere of sweetness and
light, where they may use ideas, as it uses them itself,
freely,—nourished, and not bound by them.

This is the *social idea*; and the men of culture are the
true apostles of equality. The great men of culture are
those who have had a passion for diffusing, for making
prevail, for carrying from one end of society to the
other, the best knowledge, the best ideas of their time;
who have laboured to divest knowledge of all that was
harsh, uncouth, difficult, abstract, professional, exclusive; to humanise it, to make it efficient outside the
clique of the cultivated and learned, yet still remaining
the *best* knowledge and thought of the time, and a true
source, therefore, of sweetness and light. Such a man
was Abelard in the Middle Ages, in spite of all his im-

perfections; and thence the boundless emotion and enthusiasm which Abelard excited. Such were Lessing and Herder in Germany, at the end of the last century; and their services to Germany were in this way inestimably precious. Generations will pass, and literary monuments will accumulate, and works far more perfect than the works of Lessing and Herder will be produced in Germany; and yet the names of these two men will fill a German with a reverence and enthusiasm such as the names of the most gifted masters will hardly awaken. And why? Because they *humanised* knowledge; because they broadened the basis of life and intelligence; because they worked powerfully to diffuse sweetness and light, to make reason and the will of God prevail. With Saint Augustine they said: "Let us not leave thee alone to make in the secret of thy knowledge, as thou didst before the creation of the firmament, the division of light from darkness; let the children of thy spirit, placed in their firmament, make their light shine upon the earth, mark the division of night and day, and announce the revolution of the times; for the old order is passed, and the new arises; the night is spent, the day is come forth; and thou shalt crown the year with thy blessing, when thou shalt send forth labourers into thy harvest sown by other hands than theirs; when thou shalt send forth new labourers to new seed-times, whereof the harvest shall be not yet."

II. DOING AS ONE LIKES

I have been trying to show that culture is, or ought to be, the study and pursuit of perfection; and that of perfection as pursued by culture, beauty and intelligence, or, in other words, sweetness and light, are the main characters. But hitherto I have been insisting chiefly on beauty, or sweetness, as a character of perfection. To complete rightly my design, it evidently remains to speak also of intelligence, or light, as a character of perfection.

First, however, I ought perhaps to notice that, both here and on the other side of the Atlantic, all sorts of objections are raised against the "religion of culture," as the objectors mockingly call it, which I am supposed to be promulgating. It is said to be a religion proposing parmaceti, or some scented salve or other, as a cure for human miseries; a religion breathing a spirit of cultivated inaction, making its believer refuse to lend a hand at uprooting the definite evils on all sides of us, and filling him with antipathy against the reforms and reformers which try to extirpate them. In general, it is summed up as being not practical, or,—as some critics familiarly put it,—all moonshine. That Alcibiades, the editor of the *Morning Star*, taunts me, as its promulgator, with living out of the world and knowing nothing of life and men. That great austere toiler, the editor of the *Daily Telegraph*, upbraids me,—but kindly, and more in sorrow than in anger,—for trifling with æsthetics and poetical fancies, while he himself, in that arsenal of his in Fleet Street, is bearing the burden and heat of the day. An intelligent American newspaper, the *Nation*, says that it is very easy to sit in one's study and find fault with the course of modern society, but the thing is to propose practical improvements for it. While, finally, Mr. Frederic Harrison, in a very good-tempered and witty satire, which makes me quite understand his having apparently achieved such a conquest of my young Prussian friend, Arminius, at last gets moved to an almost stern moral impatience, to behold, as he says,

"Death, sin, cruelty stalk among us, filling their maws with innocence and youth," and me, in the midst of the general tribulation, handing out my pouncet-box.

It is impossible that all these remonstrances and reproofs should not affect me, and I shall try my very best, in completing my design and in speaking of light as one of the characters of perfection, and of culture as giving us light, to profit by the objections I have heard and read, and to drive at practice as much as I can, by showing the communications and passages into practical life from the doctrine which I am inculcating.

It is said that a man with my theories of sweetness and light is full of antipathy against the rougher or coarser movements going on around him, that he will not lend a hand to the humble operation of uprooting evil by their means, and that therefore the believers in action grow impatient with him. But what if rough and coarse action, ill-calculated action, action with insufficient light, is, and has for a long time been, our bane? What if our urgent want now is, not to act at any price, but rather to lay in a stock of light for our difficulties? In that case, to refuse to lend a hand to the rougher and coarser movements going on round us, to make the primary need, both for oneself and others, to consist in enlightening ourselves and qualifying ourselves to act less at random, is surely the best and in real truth the most practical line our endeavours can take. So that if I can show what my opponents call rough or coarse action, but what I would rather call random and ill-regulated action,—action with insufficient light, action pursued because we like to be doing something and doing it as we please, and do not like the trouble of thinking and the severe constraint of any kind of rule,—if I can show this to be, at the present moment, a practical mischief and dangerous to us, then I have found a practical use for light in correcting this state of things, and have only to exemplify how, in cases which fall under everybody's observation, it may deal with it.

When I began to speak of culture, I insisted on our bondage to machinery, on our proneness to value machinery as an end in itself, without looking beyond it to the end for which alone, in truth, it is valuable. Freedom, I said, was one of those things which we thus worshipped in itself, without enough regarding the ends for which freedom is to be desired. In our common notions and talk about freedom, we eminently show our idolatry of machinery. Our prevalent notion is,—and I quoted a number of instances to prove it,—that it is a most happy and important thing for a man merely to be able to do as he likes. On what he is to do when he is thus free to do as he likes, we do not lay so much stress. Our familiar praise of the British Constitution under which we live, is that it is a system of checks,—a system which stops and paralyses any power in interfering with the free action of individuals. To this effect Mr. Bright, who loves to walk in the old ways of the Constitution, said forcibly in one of his great speeches, what many other people are every day saying less forcibly, that the central idea of English life and politics is *the assertion of personal liberty*. Evidently this is so; but evidently, also, as feudalism, which with its ideas and habits of subordination was for many centuries silently behind the British Constitution, dies out, and we are left with nothing but our system of checks, and our notion of its being the great right and happiness of an Englishman to do as far as possible what he likes, we are in danger of drifting towards anarchy. We have not the notion, so familiar on the Continent and to antiquity, of *the State*,—the nation in its collective and corporate character, entrusted with stringent powers for the general advantage, and controlling individual wills in the name of an interest wider than that of individuals. We say, what is very true, that this notion is often made instrumental to tyranny; we say that a State is in reality made up of the individuals who compose it, and that every individual is the best judge of his own interests. Our leading class is an aristocracy, and no aristocracy likes the notion of a State-authority greater than itself, with a stringent administrative machinery superseding the decorative inutilities of lord-lieutenancy, deputy-lieutenancy, and the *posse comitatus*, which are all in its own hands. Our middle class, the great representative of trade and Dissent, with its maxims of every man for himself in business, every man for himself in religion, dreads a powerful administration which might somehow interfere with it; and besides, it has its own decorative inutilities of vestrymanship and guardianship, which are to this class what lord-lieutenancy and the county magistracy are to the aristocratic class, and a stringent administration might either take these functions out of its hands, or prevent its exercising them in its own comfortable, independent manner, as at present.

Then as to our working class. This class, pressed constantly by the hard daily compulsion of material wants, is naturally the very centre and stronghold of our national idea, that it is man's ideal right and felicity to do as he likes. I think I have somewhere related how M. Michelet said to me of the people of France, that it was "a nation of barbarians civilised by the conscription." He meant that through their military service the idea of public duty and of discipline was brought to the mind of these masses, in other respects so raw and uncultivated. Our masses are quite as raw and uncultivated as the French; and so far from their having the idea of public duty and of discipline, superior to the individual's self-

will, brought to their mind by a universal obligation of
military service, such as that of the conscription,—so
far from their having this, the very idea of a conscription is so at variance with our English notion of the
prime right and blessedness of doing as one likes, that
I remember the manager of the Clay Cross works in
Derbyshire told me during the Crimean war, when our
want of soldiers was much felt and some people were
talking of a conscription, that sooner than submit to a
conscription the population of that district would flee to
the mines, and lead a sort of Robin Hood life under
ground.

For a long time, as I have said, the strong feudal
habits of subordination and deference continued to
tell upon the working class. The modern spirit has now
almost entirely dissolved those habits, and the anarchical
tendency of our worship of freedom in and for itself, of
our superstitious faith, as I say, in machinery, is becoming very manifest. More and more, because of this
our blind faith in machinery, because of our want of
light to enable us to look beyond machinery to the end
for which machinery is valuable, this and that man, and
this and that body of men, all over the country, are beginning to assert and put in practice an Englishman's
right to do what he likes; his right to march where he
likes, meet where he likes, enter where he likes, hoot
as he likes, threaten as he likes, smash as he likes. All
this, I say, tends to anarchy; and though a number
of excellent people, and particularly my friends of the
Liberal or progressive party, as they call themselves,
are kind enough to reassure us by saying that these
are trifles, that a few transient outbreaks of rowdyism
signify nothing, that our system of liberty is one which
itself cures all the evils which it works, that the educated and intelligent classes stand in overwhelming

strength and majestic repose, ready, like our military force in riots, to act at a moment's notice,—yet one finds that one's Liberal friends generally say this because they have such faith in themselves and their nostrums, when they shall return, as the public welfare requires, to place and power. But this faith of theirs one cannot exactly share, when one has so long had them and their nostrums at work, and sees that they have not prevented our coming to our present embarrassed condition. And one finds, also, that the outbreaks of rowdyism tend to become less and less of trifles, to become more frequent rather than less frequent; and that meanwhile our educated and intelligent classes remain in their majestic repose, and somehow or other, whatever happens, their overwhelming strength, like our military force in riots, never does act.

How, indeed, *should* their overwhelming strength act, when the man who gives an inflammatory lecture, or breaks down the park railings, or invades a Secretary of State's office, is only following an Englishman's impulse to do as he likes; and our own conscience tells us that we ourselves have always regarded this impulse as something primary and sacred? Mr. Murphy lectures at Birmingham, and showers on the Catholic population of that town "words," says the Home Secretary, "only fit to be addressed to thieves or murderers." What then? Mr. Murphy has his own reasons of several kinds. He suspects the Roman Catholic Church of designs upon Mrs. Murphy; and he says if mayors and magistrates do not care for their wives and daughters, he does. But, above all, he is doing as he likes; or, in worthier language, asserting his personal liberty. "I will carry out my lectures if they walk over my body as a dead corpse; and I say to the Mayor of Birmingham that he is my servant while I am in Birmingham, and as my servant he must do his duty and protect me." Touching and beautiful words, which find a sympathetic chord in every British bosom! The moment it is plainly put before us that a man is asserting his personal liberty, we are half disarmed; because we are believers in freedom, and not in some dream of a right reason to which the assertion of our freedom is to be subordinated. Accordingly, the Secretary of State had to say that although the lecturer's language was "only fit to be addressed to thieves or murderers," yet, "I do not think he is to be deprived, I do not think that anything I have said could justify the inference that he is to be deprived, of the right of protection in a place built by him for the purpose of these lectures; because the language was not language which afforded grounds for a criminal prosecution." No, nor to be silenced by Mayor, or Home Secretary, or any administrative authority on earth, simply on their notion of what is discreet and reasonable! This is in perfect consonance with our public opinion, and with our national love for the assertion of personal liberty.

In quite another department of affairs, an experienced and distinguished Chancery Judge relates an incident which is just to the same effect as this of Mr. Murphy. A testator bequeathed £300 a year, to be for ever applied as a pension to some person who had been unsuccessful in literature, and whose duty should be to support and diffuse, by his writings, the testator's own views, as enforced in the testator's publications. The views were not worth a straw, and the bequest was appealed against in the Court of Chancery on the ground of its absurdity; but, being only absurd, it was upheld, and the so-called charity was established. Having, I say, at the bottom of our English hearts a very strong belief in freedom, and a very weak belief in right reason, we are soon silenced when a man pleads the prime right to do as he likes, because this is the prime right for ourselves too; and even if we attempt now and then to mumble something about reason, yet we have ourselves thought so little about this and so much about liberty, that we are in conscience forced, when our brother Philistine with whom we are meddling turns boldly round upon us and asks: *Have you any light?*—to shake our heads ruefully, and to let him go his own way after all.

There are many things to be said on behalf of this exclusive attention of ours to liberty, and of the relaxed habits of government which it has engendered. It is very easy to mistake or to exaggerate the sort of anarchy from which we are in danger through them. We are not in danger from Fenianism, fierce and turbulent as it may show itself; for against this our conscience is free enough to let us act resolutely and put forth our overwhelming strength the moment there is any real need for it. In the first place, it never was any part of our creed that the great right and blessedness of an Irishman, or, indeed, of anybody on earth except an Englishman, is to do as he likes; and we can have no scruple at all about abridging, if necessary, a non-Englishman's assertion of personal liberty. The British Constitution, its checks, and its prime virtues, are for Englishmen. We may extend them to others out of love and kindness; but we find no real divine law written on our hearts constraining us so to extend them. And then the difference between an Irish Fenian and an English rough is so immense, and the case, in dealing with the Fenian, so much more clear! He is so evidently desperate and dangerous, a man of a conquered race, a Papist, with centuries of ill-usage to inflame him against us, with an alien religion established in his country by us at his expense, with no admiration of our institutions, no love of our virtues, no

talents for our business, no turn for our comfort! Show
him our symbolical Truss Manufactory on the finest site
in Europe, and tell him that British industrialism and
individualism can bring a man to that, and he remains
cold! Evidently, if we deal tenderly with a sentimental-
ist like this, it is out of pure philanthropy.

But with the Hyde Park rioter how different! He is
our own flesh and blood; he is a Protestant; he is framed
by nature to do as we do, hate what we hate, love what
we love; he is capable of feeling the symbolical force
of the Truss Manufactory; the question of questions,
for him, is a wages question. That beautiful sentence
Sir Daniel Gooch quoted to the Swindon workmen, and
which I treasure as Mrs. Gooch's Golden Rule, or the
Divine Injunction "Be ye Perfect" done into British,—
the sentence Sir Daniel Gooch's mother repeated to him
every morning when he was a boy going to work:—
*"Ever remember, my dear Dan, that you should look
forward to being some day manager of that concern!"*—
this truthful maxim is perfectly fitted to shine forth in
the heart of the Hyde Park rough also, and to be his
guiding-star through life. He has no visionary schemes
of revolution and transformation, though of course he
would like his class to rule, as the aristocratic class like
their class to rule, and the middle class theirs. But meanwhile our social machine is a little out of order; there
are a good many people in our paradisiacal centres of
industrialism and individualism taking the bread out
of one another's mouths. The rough has not yet quite
found his groove and settled down to his work, and so
he is just asserting his personal liberty a little, going
where he likes, assembling where he likes, bawling as
he likes, hustling as he likes. Just as the rest of us,—as
the country squires in the aristocratic class, as the political dissenters in the middle class,—he has no idea of a

State, of the nation in its collective and corporate character controlling, as government, the free swing of this or that one of its members in the name of the higher reason of all of them, his own as well as that of others. He sees the rich, the aristocratic class, in occupation of the executive government, and so if he is stopped from making Hyde Park a bear-garden or the streets impassable, he says he is being butchered by the aristocracy.

His apparition is somewhat embarrassing, because too many cooks spoil the broth; because, while the aristocratic and middle classes have long been doing as they like with great vigour, he has been too undeveloped and submissive hitherto to join in the game; and now, when he does come, he comes in immense numbers, and is rather raw and rough. But he does not break many laws, or not many at one time; and, as our laws were made for very different circumstances from our present (but always with an eye to Englishmen doing as they like), and as the clear letter of the law must be against our Englishman who does as he likes and not only the spirit of the law and public policy, and as Government must neither have any discretionary power nor act resolutely on its own interpretation of the law if any one disputes it, it is evident our laws give our playful giant, in doing as he likes, considerable advantage. Besides, even if he can be clearly proved to commit an illegality in doing as he likes, there is always the resource of not putting the law in force, or of abolishing it. So he has his way, and if he has his way he is soon satisfied for the time. However, he falls into the habit of taking it oftener and oftener, and at last begins to create by his operations a confusion of which mischievous people can take advantage, and which, at any rate, by troubling the common course of business throughout the country, tends to cause distress, and so to increase the sort of anarchy

and social disintegration which had previously commenced. And thus that profound sense of settled order
and security, without which a society like ours cannot
live and grow at all, sometimes seems to be beginning to
threaten us with taking its departure.

Now, if culture, which simply means trying to perfect oneself, and one's mind as part of oneself, brings
us light, and if light shows us that there is nothing so
very blessed in merely doing as one likes, that the worship of the mere freedom to do as one likes is worship
of machinery, that the really blessed thing is to like what
right reason ordains, and to follow her authority, then
we have got a practical benefit out of culture. We have
got a much wanted principle, a principle of authority,
to counteract the tendency to anarchy which seems to
be threatening us.

But how to organise this authority, or to what hands
to entrust the wielding of it? How to get your *State,*
summing up the right reason of the community, and
giving effect to it, as circumstances may require, with
vigour? And here I think I see my enemies waiting for
me with a hungry joy in their eyes. But I shall elude
them.

The *State,* the power most representing the right reason of the nation, and most worthy, therefore, of ruling,
—of exercising, when circumstances require it, authority
over us all,—is for Mr. Carlyle the aristocracy. For Mr.
Lowe, it is the middle class with its incomparable Parliament. For the Reform League, it is the working class,
the class with "the brightest powers of sympathy and
readiest powers of action." Now culture, with its disinterested pursuit of perfection, culture, simply trying to
see things as they are in order to seize on the best and to
make it prevail, is surely well fitted to help us to judge
rightly, by all the aids of observing, reading, and think-

ing, the qualifications and titles to our confidence of
these three candidates for authority, and can thus render
us a practical service of no mean value.

So when Mr. Carlyle, a man of genius to whom we
have all at one time or other been indebted for refresh-
ment and stimulus, says we should give rule to the aristocracy, mainly because of its dignity and politeness,
surely culture is useful in reminding us, that in our idea
of perfection the characters of beauty and intelligence
are both of them present, and sweetness and light, the
two noblest of things, are united. Allowing, therefore,
with Mr. Carlyle, the aristocratic class to possess sweetness, culture insists on the necessity of light also, and
shows us that aristocracies, being by the very nature of
things inaccessible to ideas, unapt to see how the world
is going, must be somewhat wanting in light, and must
therefore be, at a moment when light is our great requisite, inadequate to our needs. Aristocracies, those children of the established fact, are for epochs of concentration. In epochs of expansion, epochs such as that in
which we now live, epochs when always the warning
voice is again heard: *Now is the judgment of this world,*
—in such epochs aristocracies with their natural clinging to the established fact, their want of sense for the
flux of things, for the inevitable transitoriness of all
human institutions, are bewildered and helpless. Their
serenity, their high spirit, their power of haughty resistance,—the great qualities of an aristocracy, and the
secret of its distinguished manners and dignity,—these
very qualities, in an epoch of expansion, turn against
their possessors. Again and again I have said how the
refinement of an aristocracy may be precious and edu-
cative to a raw nation as a kind of shadow of true refinement; how its serenity and dignified freedom from
petty cares may serve as a useful foil to set off the vulgar-

ity and hideousness of that type of life which a hard middle class tends to establish, and to help people to see this vulgarity and hideousness in their true colours. But the true grace and serenity is that of which Greece and Greek art suggest the admirable ideals of perfection,— a serenity which comes from having made order among ideas and harmonised them; whereas the serenity of aristocracies, at least the peculiar serenity of aristocracies of Teutonic origin, appears to come from their never having had any ideas to trouble them. And so, in a time of expansion like the present, a time for ideas, one gets perhaps, in regarding an aristocracy, even more than the idea of serenity, the idea of futility and sterility.

One has often wondered whether upon the whole earth there is anything so unintelligent, so unapt to perceive how the world is really going, as an ordinary young Englishman of our upper class. Ideas he has not, and neither has he that seriousness of our middle class which is, as I have often said, the great strength of this class, and may become its salvation. Why, a man may hear a young Dives of the aristocratic class, when the whim takes him to sing the praises of wealth and material comfort, sing them with a cynicism from which the conscience of the veriest Philistine of our industrial middle class would recoil in affright. And when, with the natural sympathy of aristocracies for firm dealing with the multitude, and his uneasiness at our feeble dealing with it at home, an unvarnished young Englishman of our aristocratic class applauds the absolute rulers on the Continent, he in general manages completely to miss the grounds of reason and intelligence which alone can give any colour of justification, any possibility of existence, to those rulers, and applauds them on grounds which it would make their own hair stand on end to listen to.

And all this time we are in an epoch of expansion; and the essence of an epoch of expansion is a movement of ideas, and the one salvation of an epoch of expansion is a harmony of ideas. The very principle of the authority which we are seeking as a defence against anarchy is right reason, ideas, light. The more, therefore, an aristocracy calls to its aid its innate forces,—its impenetrability, its high spirit, its power of haughty resistance, —to deal with an epoch of expansion, the graver is the danger, the greater the certainty of explosion, the surer the aristocracy's defeat; for it is trying to do violence to nature instead of working along with it. The best powers shown by the best men of an aristocracy at such an epoch are, it will be observed, non-aristocratical powers, powers of industry, powers of intelligence; and these powers thus exhibited, tend really not to strengthen the aristocracy, but to take their owners out of it, to expose them to the dissolving agencies of thought and change, to make them men of the modern spirit and of the future. If, as sometimes happens, they add to their non-aristocratical qualities of labour and thought, a strong dose of aristocratical qualities also,—of pride, defiance, turn for resistance,—this truly aristocratical side of them, so far from adding any strength to them, really neutralises their force and makes them impracticable and ineffective.

Knowing myself to be indeed sadly to seek, as one of my many critics says, in "a philosophy with coherent, interdependent, subordinate, and derivative principles," I continually have recourse to a plain man's expedient of trying to make what few simple notions I have, clearer and more intelligible to myself by means of example and illustration. And having been brought up at Oxford in the bad old times, when we were stuffed with Greek and Aristotle, and thought nothing of preparing our-

selves by the study of modern languages,—as after Mr.
Lowe's great speech at Edinburgh we shall do,—to fight
the battle of life with the waiters in foreign hotels, my
head is still full of a lumber of phrases we learnt at Oxford from Aristotle, about virtue being in a mean, and
about excess and defect, and so on. Once when I had
had the advantage of listening to the Reform debates in
the House of Commons, having heard a number of interesting speakers, and among them a well-known lord
and a well-known baronet, I remember it struck me, applying Aristotle's machinery of the mean to my ideas
about our aristocracy, that the lord was exactly the perfection, or happy mean, or virtue, of aristocracy, and
the baronet the excess. And I fancied that by observing
these two we might see both the inadequacy of aristocracy to supply the principle of authority needful for our
present wants, and the danger of its trying to supply it
when it was not really competent for the business. On
the one hand, in the brilliant lord, showing plenty of
high spirit, but remarkable, far above and beyond his
gift of high spirit, for the fine tempering of his high
spirit, for ease, serenity, politeness,—the great virtues,
as Mr. Carlyle says, of aristocracy,—in this beautiful
and virtuous mean, there seemed evidently some insufficiency of light; while, on the other hand, the worthy
baronet, in whom the high spirit of aristocracy, its impenetrability, defiant courage, and pride of resistance,
were developed even in excess, was manifestly capable,
if he had his way given him, of causing us great danger,
and, indeed, of throwing the whole commonwealth into
confusion. Then I reverted to that old fundamental notion of mine about the grand merit of our race being
really our honesty. And the very helplessness of our
aristocratic or governing class in dealing with our per-
turbed social condition, their jealousy of entrusting too

much power to the State as it now actually exists—that is to themselves—gave me a sort of pride and satisfaction; because I saw they were, as a whole, too honest to try and manage a business for which they did not feel themselves capable.

Surely, now, it is no inconsiderable boon which culture confers upon us, if in embarrassed times like the present it enables us to look at the ins and the outs of things in this way, without hatred and without partiality, and with a disposition to see the good in everybody all round. And I try to follow just the same course with our middle class as with our aristocracy. Mr. Lowe talks to us of this strong middle part of the nation, of the unrivalled deeds of our Liberal middle-class Parliament, of the noble, the heroic work it has performed in the last thirty years; and I begin to ask myself if we shall not, then, find in our middle class the principle of authority we want, and if we had not better take administration as well as legislation away from the weak extreme which now administers for us, and commit both to the strong middle part. I observe, too, that the heroes of middle-class liberalism, such as we have hitherto known it, speak with a kind of prophetic anticipation of the great destiny which awaits them, and as if the future was clearly theirs. The advanced party, the progressive party, the party in alliance with the future, are the names they like to give themselves. "The principles which will obtain recognition in the future," says Mr. Miall, a personage of deserved eminence among the political Dissenters, as they are called, who have been the backbone of middle-class liberalism,—"the principles which will obtain recognition in the future are the principles for which I have long and zealously laboured. I qualified myself for joining in the work of harvest by doing to the best of my ability the duties of seedtime." These duties, if one is to gather them from the works of the great Liberal party in the last thirty years, are, as I have elsewhere summed them up, the advocacy of free trade, of Parliamentary reform, of abolition of church-rates, of voluntaryism in religion and education, of non-interference of the State between employers and employed, and of marriage with one's deceased wife's sister.

Now I know, when I object that all this is machinery, the great Liberal middle class has by this time grown cunning enough to answer that it always meant more by these things than meets the eye; that it has had that within which passes show, and that we are soon going to see, in a Free Church and all manner of good things, what it was. But I have learned from Bishop Wilson (if Mr. Frederic Harrison will forgive my again quoting that poor old hierophant of a decayed superstition): "If we would really know our heart let us impartially view our actions"; and I cannot help thinking that if our Liberals had had so much sweetness and light in their inner minds as they allege, more of it must have come out in their sayings and doings.

An American friend of the English Liberals says, indeed, that their Dissidence of Dissent has been a mere instrument of the political Dissenters for making reason and the will of God prevail (and no doubt he would say the same of marriage with one's deceased wife's sister); and that the abolition of a State Church is merely the Dissenter's means to this end, just as culture is mine. Another American defender of theirs says just the same of their industrialism and free trade; indeed, this gentleman, taking the bull by the horns, proposes that we should for the future call industrialism culture, and the industrialists the men of culture, and then of course there can be no longer any misapprehension about their true character; and besides the pleasure of being wealthy and comfortable, they will have authentic recognition as vessels of sweetness and light.

All this is undoubtedly specious; but I must remark that the culture of which I talked was an endeavour to come at reason and the will of God by means of reading, observing, and thinking; and that whoever calls anything else culture, may, indeed, call it so if he likes, but then he talks of something quite different from what I talked of. And, again, as culture's way of working for reason and the will of God is by directly trying to know more about them, while the Dissidence of Dissent is evidently in itself no effort of this kind, nor is its Free Church, in fact, a church with worthier conceptions of God and the ordering of the world than the State Church professes, but with mainly the same conceptions of these as the State Church has, only that every man is to comport himself as he likes in professing them,—this being so, I cannot at once accept the Nonconformity any more than the industrialism and the other great works of our Liberal middle class as proof positive that this class is in possession of light, and that here is the true seat of authority for which we are in search; but I must try a little further, and seek for other indications which may enable me to make up my mind.

Why should we not do with the middle class as we have done with the aristocratic class,—find in it some representative men who may stand for the virtuous mean of this class, for the perfection of its present qualities and mode of being, and also for the excess of them. Such men must clearly not be men of genius like Mr. Bright; for, as I have formerly said, so far as a man has genius he tends to take himself out of the category of class altogether, and to become simply a man. Some more ordinary man would be more to the purpose,— would sum up better in himself, without disturbing influences, the general liberal force of the middle class, the force by which it has done its great works of free trade, Parliamentary reform, voluntaryism, and so on, and the spirit in which it has done them. Now it happens that a typical middle-class man, the member for one of our chief industrial cities, has given us a famous sentence which bears directly on the resolution of our present question: whether there is light enough in our middle class to make it the proper seat of the authority we wish to establish. When there was a talk some little while ago about the state of middle-class education, our friend, as the representative of that class, spoke some memorable words:—"There had been a cry that middle-class education ought to receive more attention. He confessed himself very much surprised by the clamour that was raised. He did not think that class need excite the sympathy either of the legislature or the public." Now this satisfaction of our middle-class member of Parliament with the mental state of the middle class was truly representative, and makes good his claim to stand as the beautiful and virtuous mean of that class. But it is obviously at variance with our definition of culture, or the pursuit of light and perfection, which made light and perfection consist, not in resting and being, but in growing and becoming, in a perpetual advance in beauty and wisdom. So the middle class is by its essence, as one may say, by its incomparable self-satisfaction decisively expressed through its beautiful and virtuous mean, self-excluded from wielding an authority of which light is to be the very soul.

Clear as this is, it will be made clearer still if we take some representative man as the excess of the middle class, and remember that the middle class, in general, is to be conceived as a body swaying between the qualities of its mean and of its excess, and on the whole, of course, as human nature is constituted, inclining rather towards the excess than the mean. Of its excess no better representative can possibly be imagined than a Dissenting minister from Walsall, who came before the public in connection with the proceedings at Birmingham of Mr. Murphy, already mentioned. Speaking in the midst of an irritated population of Catholics, this Walsall gentleman exclaimed: "I say, then, away with the Mass! It is from the bottomless pit; and in the bottomless pit shall all liars have their part, in the lake that burneth with fire and brimstone." And again: "When all the praties were black in Ireland, why didn't the priests say the hocus-pocus over them, and make them all good again?" He shared, too, Mr. Murphy's fears of some invasion of his domestic happiness: "What I wish to say to you as Protestant husbands is, *Take care of your wives!*" And finally, in the true vein of an Englishman doing as he likes, a vein of which I have at some length pointed out the present dangers, he recommended for imitation the example of some churchwardens at Dublin, among whom, said he, "there was a Luther and also a Melanchthon," who had made very short work with some ritualist or other, hauled him down from his pulpit, and kicked him out of church. Now it is manifest, as I said in the case of our aristocratical baronet, that if we let this excess of the sturdy English middle class, this conscientious Protestant Dissenter, so strong, so self-reliant, so fully persuaded in his own mind, have his way, he would be capable, with his want of light,—or, to use the language of the religious world, with his zeal without knowledge, —of stirring up strife which neither he nor any one else could easily compose.

And then comes in, as it did also with the aristocracy, the honesty of our race, and by the voice of another middle-class man, Alderman of the City of London and

Colonel of the City of London Militia, proclaims that it has twinges of conscience, and that it will not attempt to cope with our social disorders, and to deal with a business which it feels to be too high for it. Every one remembers how this virtuous Alderman-Colonel, or Colonel-Alderman, led his militia through the London streets; how the bystanders gathered to see him pass; how the London roughs, asserting an Englishman's best and most blissful right of doing what he likes, robbed and beat the bystanders; and how the blameless warrior-magistrate refused to let his troops interfere. "The crowd," he touchingly said afterwards, "was mostly composed of fine healthy strong men, bent on mischief; if he had allowed his soldiers to interfere they might have been overpowered, their rifles taken from them and used against them by the mob; a riot, in fact, might have ensued, and been attended with bloodshed, compared with which the assaults and loss of property that actually occurred would have been as nothing." Honest and affecting testimony of the English middle class to its own inadequacy for the authoritative part one's admiration would sometimes incline one to assign to it! "Who are we," they say by the voice of their Alderman-Colonel, "that we should not be overpowered if we attempt to cope with social anarchy, our rifles taken from us and used against us by the mob, and we, perhaps, robbed and beaten ourselves? Or what light have we, beyond a free-born Englishman's impulse to do as he likes, which could justify us in preventing, at the cost of bloodshed, other free-born Englishmen from doing as they like, and robbing and beating us as much as they please?"

This distrust of themselves as an adequate centre of authority does not mark the working class, as was shown by their readiness the other day in Hyde Park to take upon themselves all the functions of government. But this comes from the working class being, as I have often said, still an embryo, of which no one can yet quite foresee the final development; and from its not having the same experience and self-knowledge as the aristocratic and middle classes. Honesty it no doubt has, just like the other classes of Englishmen, but honesty in an inchoate and untrained state; and meanwhile its powers of action, which are, as Mr. Frederic Harrison says, exceedingly ready, easily run away with it. That it cannot at present have a sufficiency of light which comes by culture,—that is, by reading, observing, and thinking,—is clear from the very nature of its condition; and, indeed, we saw that Mr. Frederic Harrison, in seeking to make a free stage for its bright powers of sympathy and ready powers of action, had to begin by throwing overboard culture, and flouting it as only fit for a professor of *belles-lettres*. Still, to make it perfectly manifest that no more in the working class than in the aristocratic and middle classes can one find an adequate centre of authority,—that is, as culture teaches us to conceive our required authority, of light,—let us again follow, with this class, the method we have followed with the aristocratic and middle classes, and try to bring before our minds representative men, who may figure to us its virtue and its excess.

We must not take, of course, men like the chiefs of the Hyde Park demonstration, Colonel Dickson or Mr. Beales; because Colonel Dickson, by his martial profession and dashing exterior, seems to belong properly, like Julius Cæsar and Mirabeau and other great popular leaders, to the aristocratic class, and to be carried into the popular ranks only by his ambition or his genius; while Mr. Beales belongs to our solid middle class, and, perhaps, if he had not been a great popular leader, would have been a Philistine. But Mr. Odger, whose speeches we have all read, and of whom his friends relate, besides, much that is favourable, may very well stand for the beautiful and virtuous mean of our present working class; and I think everybody will admit that in Mr. Odger there is manifestly, with all his good points, some insufficiency of light. The excess of the working class, in its present state of development, is perhaps best shown in Mr. Bradlaugh, the iconoclast, who seems to be almost for baptizing us all in blood and fire into his new social dispensation, and to whose reflections, now that I have once been set going on Bishop Wilson's track, I cannot forbear commending this maxim of the good old man: "Intemperance in talk makes a dreadful havoc in the heart." Mr. Bradlaugh, like our types of excess in the aristocratic and middle classes, is evidently capable, if he had his head given him, of running us all into great dangers and confusion. I conclude, therefore,—what indeed, few of those who do me the honour to read this disquisition are likely to dispute,— that we can as little find in the working class as in the aristocratic or in the middle class our much-wanted source of authority, as culture suggests it to us.

Well, then, what if we tried to rise above the idea of class to the idea of the whole community, *the State*, and to find our centre of light and authority there? Every one of us has the idea of country, as a sentiment; hardly any one of us has the idea of *the State*, as a working power. And why? Because we habitually live in our ordinary selves, which do not carry us beyond the ideas and wishes of the class to which we happen to belong. And we are all afraid of giving to the State too much power, because we only conceive of the State as something equivalent to the class in occupation of the executive government, and are afraid of that class abusing power to its own purposes. If we strengthen the State with the aristocratic class in occupation of the executive government, we imagine we are delivering ourselves up captive to the ideas and wishes of our fierce aristocratical baronet; if with the middle class in occupation of the executive government, to those of our truculent middle-class Dissenting minister; if with the working class, to those of its notorious tribune, Mr. Bradlaugh. And with much justice; owing to the exaggerated notion which we English, as I have said, entertain of the right and blessedness of the mere doing as one likes, of the affirming oneself, and oneself just as it is. People of the aristocratic class want to affirm their ordinary selves, their likings and dislikings; people of the middle class the same, people of the working class the same. By our every day selves, however, we are separate, personal, at war; we are only safe from one another's tyranny when no one has any power; and this safety, in its turn, cannot save us from anarchy. And when, therefore, anarchy presents itself as a danger to us, we know not where to turn.

But by our *best self* we are united, impersonal, at harmony. We are in no peril from giving authority to this, because it is the truest friend we all of us can have; and when anarchy is a danger to us, to this authority we may turn with sure trust. Well, and this is the very self which culture, or the study of perfection, seeks to develop in us; at the expense of our old untransformed self, taking pleasure only in doing what it likes or is used to do, and exposing us to the risk of clashing with every one else who is doing the same! So that our poor culture, which is flouted as so unpractical, leads us to the very ideas capable of meeting the great want of our present embarrassed times! We want an authority, and we find nothing but jealous classes, checks, and a deadlock; culture suggests the idea of *the State*. We find no basis for a firm State-power in our ordinary selves; culture suggests one to us in our *best self*.

It cannot but acutely try a tender conscience to be accused, in a practical country like ours, of keeping aloof from the work and hope of a multitude of earnest-hearted men, and of merely toying with poetry and æsthetics. So it is with no little sense of relief that I find myself thus in the position of one who makes a contribution in aid of the practical necessities of our times. The great thing, it will be observed, is to find our *best* self, and to seek to affirm nothing but that; not,—as we English with our over-value for merely being free and busy have been so accustomed to do,—resting satisfied with a self which comes uppermost long before our best self, and affirming that with blind energy. In short,—to go back yet once more to Bishop Wilson,—of these two excellent rules of Bishop Wilson's for a man's guidance: "Firstly, never go against the best light you have; secondly, take care that your light be not darkness," we English have followed with praiseworthy zeal the first rule, but we have not given so much heed to the second. We have gone manfully according to the best light we have; but we have not taken enough care that this should be really the best light possible for us, that it should not be darkness. And, our honesty being very great, conscience has whispered to us that the light we were following, our ordinary self, was, indeed, perhaps, only an inferior self, only darkness; and that it would not do to impose this seriously on all the world.

But our best self inspires faith, and is capable of affording a serious principle of authority. For example. We are on our way to what the late Duke of Wellington, with his strong sagacity, foresaw and admirably described as "a revolution by due course of law." This is undoubtedly,—if we are still to live and grow, and this famous nation is not to stagnate and dwindle away on the one hand, or, on the other, to perish miserably in mere anarchy and confusion,—what we are on the way to. Great changes there must be, for a revolution cannot accomplish itself without great changes; yet order there must be, for without order a revolution cannot accomplish itself by due course of law. So whatever brings risk of tumult and disorder, multitudinous processions in the streets of our crowded towns, multitudinous meetings in their public places and parks,—demonstrations perfectly unnecessary in the present course of our affairs,—our best self, or right reason, plainly enjoins us to set our faces against. It enjoins us to encourage and uphold the occupants of the executive power, whoever they may be, in firmly prohibiting them. But it does this clearly and resolutely, and is thus a real principle of authority, because it does it with a free conscience; because in thus provisionally strengthening the executive power, it knows that it is not doing this merely to enable our aristocratical baronet to affirm himself as against our working-men's tribune, or our middle-class Dissenter to affirm himself as against both. It knows that it is establishing *the State*, or organ of our collective best self, of our national right reason. And it has the testimony of conscience that it is stablishing the State on behalf of whatever great changes are needed, just as much as on behalf of order; stablishing it to deal just as stringently, when the time comes, with our baronet's aristocratical prejudices, or with the fanaticism of our middle-class Dissenter, as it deals with Mr. Bradlaugh's street-processions.

III. BARBARIANS, PHILISTINES, POPULACE

From a man without a philosophy no one can expect philosophical completeness. Therefore I may observe without shame, that in trying to get a distinct notion of our aristocratic, our middle, and our working class, with a view of testing the claims of each of these classes to become a centre of authority, I have omitted, I find, to complete the old-fashioned analysis which I had the fancy of applying, and have not shown in these classes, as well as the virtuous mean and the excess, the defect also. I do not know that the omission very much matters. Still, as clearness is the one merit which a plain, unsystematic writer, without a philosophy, can hope to have, and as our notion of the three great English classes may perhaps be made clearer if we see their distinctive qualities in the defect, as well as in the excess and in the mean, let us try, before proceeding further, to remedy this omission.

It is manifest, if the perfect and virtuous mean of that fine spirit which is the distinctive quality of aristocracies, is to be found in a high, chivalrous style, and its excess in a fierce turn for resistance, that its defect must lie in a spirit not bold and high enough, and in an excessive and pusillanimous unaptness for resistance. If, again, the perfect and virtuous mean of that force by which our middle class has done its great works, and of that self-reliance with which it contemplates itself and them, is to be seen in the performances and speeches of our commercial member of Parliament, and the excess of that force and of that self-reliance in the performances and speeches of our fanatical Dissenting minister, then it is manifest that their defect must lie in a helpless inaptitude for the great works of the middle class, and in a poor and despicable lack of its self-satisfaction.

To be chosen to exemplify the happy mean of a good quality, or set of good qualities, is evidently a praise to a man; nay, to be chosen to exemplify even their excess, is a kind of praise. Therefore I could have no hesitation in taking actual personages to exemplify, respectively, the mean and the excess of aristocratic and middle-class qualities. But perhaps there might be a want of urbanity in singling out this or that personage as the representative of defect. Therefore I shall leave the defect of aristocracy unillustrated by any representative man. But with oneself one may always, without impropriety, deal quite freely; and, indeed, this sort of plain-dealing with oneself has in it, as all the moralists tell us, something very wholesome. So I will venture to humbly offer myself as an illustration of defect in those forces and qualities which make our middle class what it is. The too well-founded reproaches of my opponents declare how little I have lent a hand to the great works of the middle class; for it is evidently these works, and my slackness at them, which are meant, when I am said to "refuse to lend a hand to the humble operation of uprooting certain definite evils" (such as church-rates and others), and that therefore "the believers in action grow impatient" with me. The line, again, of a still unsatisfied seeker which I have followed, the idea of self-transformation, of growing towards some measure of sweetness and light not yet reached, is evidently at clean variance with the perfect self-satisfaction current in my class, the middle class, and may serve to indicate in me, therefore, the extreme defect of this feeling. But these confessions, though salutary, are bitter and unpleasant.

To pass, then, to the working class. The defect of this class would be the falling short in what Mr. Frederic

Harrison calls those "bright powers of sympathy and ready powers of action," of which we saw in Mr. Odger the virtuous mean, and in Mr. Bradlaugh the excess. The working class is so fast growing and rising at the present time, that instances of this defect cannot well be now very common. Perhaps Canning's "Needy Knife-Grinder" (who is dead, and therefore cannot be pained at my taking him for an illustration) may serve to give us the notion of defect in the essential quality of a working class; or I might even cite (since, though he is alive in the flesh, he is dead to all heed of criticism) my poor old poaching friend, Zephaniah Diggs, who, between his hare-snaring and his gin-drinking, has got his powers of sympathy quite dulled and his powers of action in any great movement of his class hopelessly impaired. But examples of this defect belong, as I have said, to a bygone age rather than to the present.

The same desire for clearness, which has led me thus to extend a little my first analysis of the three great classes of English society, prompts me also to improve my nomenclature for them a little, with a view to making it thereby more manageable. It is awkward and tiresome to be always saying the aristocratic class, the middle class, the working class. For the middle class, for that great body which, as we know, "has done all the great things that have been done in all departments," and which is to be conceived as moving between its two cardinal points of our commercial member of Parliament and our fanatical Protestant Dissenter,—for this class we have a designation which now has become pretty well known, and which we may as well still keep for them, the designation of Philistines. What this term means I have so often explained that I need not repeat it here. For the aristocratic class, conceived mainly as a body moving between the two cardinal points of our chivalrous lord and our defiant baronet, we have as yet got no special designation. Almost all my attention has naturally been concentrated on my own class, the middle class, with which I am in closest sympathy, and which has been, besides, the great power of our day, and has had its praises sung by all speakers and newspapers.

Still the aristocratic class is so important in itself, and the weighty functions which Mr. Carlyle proposes at the present critical time to commit to it, must add so much to its importance, that it seems neglectful, and a strong instance of that want of coherent philosophic method for which Mr. Frederic Harrison blames me, to leave the aristocratic class so much without notice and denomination. It may be thought that the characteristic which I have occasionally mentioned as proper to aristocracies,—their natural inaccessibility, as children of the established fact, to ideas,—points to our extending to this class also the designation of Philistines; the Philistine being, as is well known, the enemy of the children of light or servants of the idea. Nevertheless, there seems to be an inconvenience in thus giving one and the same designation to two very different classes; and besides, if we look into the thing closely, we shall find that the term Philistine conveys a sense which makes it more peculiarly appropriate to our middle class than to our aristocratic. For *Philistine* gives the notion of something particularly stiff-necked and perverse in the resistance to light and its children; and therein it specially suits our middle class, who not only do not pursue sweetness and light, but who even prefer to them that sort of machinery of business, chapels, tea-meetings, and addresses from Mr. Murphy, which makes up the dismal and illiberal life on which I have so often touched. But the aristocratic class has actually, as we have seen, in its well-known politeness, a kind of image or shadow of sweetness; and as for light, if it does not pursue light, it is not that it perversely cherishes some dismal and illiberal existence in preference to light, but it is lured off from following light by those mighty and eternal seducers of our race which weave for this class their most irresistible charms,—by worldly splendour, security, power, and pleasure. These seducers are exterior goods, but in a way they are goods; and he who is hindered by them from caring for light and ideas, is not so much doing what is perverse as what is too natural.

Keeping this in view, I have in my own mind often indulged myself with the fancy of employing, in order to designate our aristocratic class, the name of *The Barbarians*. The Barbarians, to whom we all owe so much, and who reinvigorated and renewed our worn-out Europe, had, as is well known, eminent merits; and in this country, where we are for the most part sprung from the Barbarians, we have never had the prejudice against them which prevails among the races of Latin origin. The Barbarians brought with them that staunch individualism, as the modern phrase is, and that passion for doing as one likes, for the assertion of personal liberty, which appears to Mr. Bright the central idea of English life, and of which we have, at any rate, a very rich supply. The stronghold and natural seat of this passion was in the nobles of whom our aristocratic class are the inheritors; and this class, accordingly, have signally manifested it, and have done much by their example to recommend it to the body of the nation, who already, indeed, had it in their blood. The Barbarians, again, had the passion for field-sports; and they have handed it on to our aristocratic class, who of this passion too, as of the passion for asserting one's personal liberty, are the great natural stronghold. The care of the Barbarians for the body, and for all manly exercises; the vigour, good looks,

and fine complexion which they acquired and perpetu-
ated in their families by these means,—all this may be
observed still in our aristocratic class. The chivalry of
the Barbarians, with its characteristics of high spirit,
choice manners, and distinguished bearing,—what is
this but the attractive commencement of the politeness
of our aristocratic class? In some Barbarian noble, no
doubt, one would have admired, if one could have been
then alive to see it, the rudiments of our politest peer.
Only, all this culture (to call it by that name) of the
Barbarians was an exterior culture mainly. It consisted
principally in outward gifts and graces, in looks, manners, accomplishments, prowess. The chief inward gifts
which had part in it were the most exterior, so to speak,
of inward gifts, those which come nearest to outward
ones; they were courage, a high spirit, self-confidence.
Far within, and unawakened, lay a whole range of powers of thought and feeling, to which these interesting
productions of nature had, from the circumstances of
their life, no access. Making allowances for the difference of the times, surely we can observe precisely the
same thing now in our aristocratic class. In general its
culture is exterior chiefly; all the exterior graces and
accomplishments, and the more external of the inward
virtues, seem to be principally its portion. It now, of
course, cannot but be often in contact with those studies
by which, from the world of thought and feeling, true
culture teaches us to fetch sweetness and light; but its
hold upon these very studies appears remarkably external, and unable to exert any deep power upon its
spirit. Therefore the one insufficiency which we noted in
the perfect mean of this class was an insufficiency of
light. And owing to the same causes, does not a subtle
criticism lead us to make, even on the good looks and
politeness of our aristocratic class, and of even the most

fascinating half of that class, the feminine half, the one qualifying remark, that in these charming gifts there should perhaps be, for ideal perfection, a shade more *soul*?

I often, therefore, when I want to distinguish clearly the aristocratic class from the Philistines proper, or middle class, name the former, in my own mind, *the Barbarians*. And when I go through the country, and see this and that beautiful and imposing seat of theirs crowning the landscape, "There," I say to myself, "is a great fortified post of the Barbarians."

It is obvious that that part of the working class which, working diligently by the light of Mrs. Gooch's Golden Rule, looks forward to the happy day when it will sit on thrones with commercial members of Parliament and other middle-class potentates, to survey, as Mr. Bright beautifully says, "the cities it has built, the railroads it has made, the manufactures it has produced, the cargoes which freight the ships of the greatest mercantile navy the world has ever seen,"—it is obvious, I say, that this part of the working class is, or is in a fair way to be, one in spirit with the industrial middle class. It is notorious that our middle-class Liberals have long looked forward to this consummation, when the working class shall join forces with them, aid them heartily to carry forward their great works, go in a body to their tea-meetings, and, in short, enable them to bring about their millennium. That part of the working class, therefore, which does really seem to lend itself to these great aims, may, with propriety, be numbered by us among the Philistines. That part of it, again, which so much occupies the attention of philanthropists at present,—the part which gives all its energies to organising itself, through trades' unions and other means, so as to constitute, first, a great working-class power independent of the middle and aristocratic classes, and then, by dint of numbers, give the law to them and itself reign absolutely,—this lively and promising part must also, according to our definition, go with the Philistines; because it is its class and its class instinct which it seeks to affirm—its ordinary self, not its best self; and it is a machinery, an industrial machinery, and power and pre-eminence and other external goods, which fill its thoughts, and not an inward perfection. It is wholly occupied, according to Plato's subtle expression, with the things of itself and not its real self, with the things of the State and not the real State. But that vast portion, lastly, of the working class which, raw and half-developed, has long lain half-hidden amidst its poverty and squalor, and is now issuing from its hiding-place to assert an Englishman's heaven-born privilege of doing as he likes, and is beginning to perplex us by marching where it likes, meeting where it likes, bawling what it likes, breaking what it likes,— to this vast residuum we may with great propriety give the name of *Populace*.

Thus we have got three distinct terms, *Barbarians, Philistines, Populace,* to denote roughly the three great classes into which our society is divided; and though this humble attempt at a scientific nomenclature falls, no doubt, very far short in precision of what might be required from a writer equipped with a complete and coherent philosophy, yet, from a notoriously unsystematic and unpretending writer, it will, I trust, be accepted as sufficient.

But in using this new, and, I hope, convenient division of English society, two things are to be borne in mind. The first is, that since, under all our class divisions, there is a common basis of human nature, therefore, in every one of us, whether we be properly Barbarians, Philistines, or Populace, there exists, some-

times only in germ and potentially, sometimes more or
less developed, the same tendencies and passions which
have made our fellow-citizens of other classes what they
are. This consideration is very important, because it has
great influence in begetting that spirit of indulgence
which is a necessary part of sweetness, and which, indeed, when our culture is complete, is, as I have said,
inexhaustible. Thus, an English Barbarian who ex-
amines himself will, in general, find himself to be not so
entirely a Barbarian but that he has in him, also, something of the Philistine, and even something of the Populace as well. And the same with Englishmen of the two
other classes.

This is an experience which we may all verify every
day. For instance, I myself (I again take myself as a sort
of *corpus vile* to serve for illustration in a matter where
serving for illustration may not by every one be thought
agreeable), I myself am properly a Philistine,—Mr.
Swinburne would add, the son of a Philistine. And although, through circumstances which will perhaps one
day be known if ever the affecting history of my conversion comes to be written, I have, for the most part,
broken with the ideas and the tea-meetings of my own
class, yet I have not, on that account, been brought
much the nearer to the ideas and works of the Barbarians or of the Populace. Nevertheless, I never take a gun
or a fishing-rod in my hands without feeling that I have
in the ground of my nature the self-same seeds which,
fostered by circumstances, do so much to make the Barbarian; and that, with the Barbarian's advantages, I
might have rivalled him. Place me in one of his great
fortified posts, with these seeds of a love for field-sports
sown in my nature, with all the means of developing
them, with all pleasures at my command, with most
whom I met deferring to me, every one I met smiling on

me, and with every appearance of permanence and
security before me and behind me,—then I too might
have grown, I feel, into a very passable child of the
established fact, of commendable spirit and politeness,
and, at the same time, a little inaccessible to ideas and
light; not, of course, with either the eminent fine spirit
of our type of aristocratic perfection, or the eminent turn
for resistance of our type of aristocratic excess, but,
according to the measure of the common run of mankind, something between the two. And as to the Populace, who, whether he be Barbarian or Philistine, can
look at them without sympathy, when he remembers
how often,—every time that we snatch up a vehement
opinion in ignorance and passion, every time that we
long to crush an adversary by sheer violence, every time
that we are envious, every time that we are brutal, every
time that we adore mere power or success, every time
that we add our voice to swell a blind clamour against
some unpopular personage, every time that we trample
savagely on the fallen,—he has found in his own bosom
the eternal spirit of the Populace, and that there needs
only a little help from circumstances to make it triumph
in him untamably.

The second thing to be borne in mind I have indicated several times already. It is this. All of us, so far
as we are Barbarians, Philistines, or Populace, imagine
happiness to consist in doing what one's ordinary self
likes. What one's ordinary self likes differs according to
the class to which one belongs, and has its severer and its
lighter side; always, however, remaining machinery, and
nothing more. The graver self of the Barbarian likes
honours and consideration; his more relaxed self, field-
sports and pleasure. The graver self of one kind of Philistine likes fanaticism, business, and money-making; his
more relaxed self, comfort and tea-meetings. Of another

kind of Philistine, the graver self likes rattening; the relaxed self, deputations, or hearing Mr. Odger speak. The sterner self of the Populace likes bawling, hustling, and smashing; the lighter self, beer. But in each class there are born a certain number of natures with a curiosity about their best self, with a bent for seeing things as they are, for disentangling themselves from machinery, for simply concerning themselves with reason and the will of God, and doing their best to make these prevail;—for the pursuit, in a word, of perfection. To certain manifestations of this love for perfection mankind have accustomed themselves to give the name of genius; implying, by this name, something original and heaven-bestowed in the passion. But the passion is to be found far beyond those manifestations of it to which the world usually gives the name of genius, and in which there is, for the most part, a *talent* of some kind or other, a special and striking faculty of execution, informed by the heaven-bestowed ardour, or genius. It is to be found in many manifestations besides these, and may best be called, as we have called it, the love and pursuit of perfection; culture being the true nurse of the pursuing love, and sweetness and light the true character of the pursued perfection. Natures with this bent emerge in all classes,—among the Barbarians, among the Philistines, among the Populace. And this bent always tends to take them out of their class, and to make their distinguishing characteristic not their Barbarianism or their Philistinism, but their *humanity*. They have, in general, a rough time of it in their lives; but they are sown more abundantly than one might think, they appear where and when one least expects it, they set up a fire which enfilades, so to speak, the class with which they are ranked; and, in general, by the extrication of their best self as the self to develop, and by the simplicity of the

ends fixed by them as paramount, they hinder the unchecked predominance of that class-life which is the
affirmation of our ordinary self, and seasonably discon-
cert mankind in their worship of machinery.

Therefore, when we speak of ourselves as divided into
Barbarians, Philistines, and Populace, we must be understood always to imply that within each of these classes
there are a certain number of *aliens*, if we may so call
them,—persons who are mainly led, not by their class
spirit, but by a general *humane* spirit, by the love of human perfection; and that this number is capable of being
diminished or augmented. I mean, the number of those
who will succeed in developing this happy instinct will
be greater or smaller, in proportion both to the force of
the original instinct within them, and to the hindrance
or encouragement which it meets with from without. In
almost all who have it, it is mixed with some infusion
of the spirit of an ordinary self, some quantity of class-
instinct, and even, as has been shown, of more than one
class-instinct at the same time; so that, in general, the
extrication of the best self, the predominance of the *humane* instinct, will very much depend upon its meeting,
or not, with what is fitted to help and elicit it. At a moment, therefore, when it is agreed that we want a source
of authority, and when it seems probable that the right
source is our best self, it becomes of vast importance to
see whether or not the things around us are, in general,
such as to help and elicit our best self, and if they are
not, to see why they are not, and the most promising
way of mending them.

Now, it is clear that the very absence of any powerful
authority amongst us, and the prevalent doctrine of the
duty and happiness of doing as one likes, and asserting
our personal liberty, must tend to prevent the erection
of any very strict standard of excellence, the belief in

any very paramount authority of right reason, the recognition of our best self as anything very recondite and hard to come at. It may be, as I have said, a proof of our honesty that we do not attempt to give to our ordinary self, as we have it in action, predominant authority, and to impose its rule upon other people. But it is evident also, that it is not easy, with our style of proceeding, to get beyond the notion of an ordinary self at all, or to get the paramount authority of a commanding best self, or right reason, recognised. The learned Martinus Scriblerus well says:—"the taste of the bathos is implanted by nature itself in the soul of man; till, perverted by custom or example, he is taught, or rather compelled, to relish the sublime." But with us everything seems directed to prevent any such perversion of us by custom or example as might compel us to relish the sublime; by all means we are encouraged to keep our natural taste for the bathos unimpaired

I have formerly pointed out how in literature the absence of any authoritative centre, like an Academy, tends to do this. Each section of the public has its own literary organ, and the mass of the public is without any suspicion that the value of these organs is relative to their being nearer a certain ideal centre of correct information, taste, and intelligence, or farther away from it. I have said that within certain limits, which any one who is likely to read this will have no difficulty in drawing for himself, my old adversary, the *Saturday Review*, may, on matters of literature and taste, be fairly enough regarded, relatively to the mass of newspapers which treat these matters, as a kind of organ of reason. But I remember once conversing with a company of Nonconformist admirers of some lecturer who had let off a great firework, which the *Saturday Review* said was all noise and false lights, and feeling my way as tenderly as I could about the effect of this unfavourable judgment upon those with whom I was conversing. "Oh," said one who was their spokesman, with the most tranquil air of conviction, "it is true the *Saturday Review* abuses the lecture, but the *British Banner*" (I am not quite sure it was the *British Banner*, but it was some newspaper of that stamp) "says that the *Saturday Review* is quite wrong." The speaker had evidently no notion that there was a scale of value for judgments on these topics, and that the judgments of the *Saturday Review* ranked high on this scale, and those of the *British Banner* low; the taste of the bathos implanted by nature in the literary judgments of man had never, in my friend's case, encountered any let or hindrance.

Just the same in religion as in literature. We have most of us little idea of a high standard to choose our guides by, of a great and profound spirit which is an authority while inferior spirits are none. It is enough to give importance to things that this or that person says them decisively, and has a large following of some strong kind when he says them. This habit of ours is very well shown in that able and interesting work of Mr. Hepworth Dixon's, which we were all reading lately, *The Mormons, by One of Themselves*. Here, again, I am not quite sure that my memory serves me as to the exact title, but I mean the well-known book in which Mr. Hepworth Dixon described the Mormons, and other similar religious bodies in America, with so much detail and such warm sympathy. In this work it seems enough for Mr. Dixon that this or that doctrine has its Rabbi, who talks big to him, has a staunch body of disciples, and, above all, has plenty of rifles. That there are any further stricter tests to be applied to a doctrine, before it is pronounced important, never seems to occur to him. "It is easy to say," he writes of the Mormons, "that these saints are dupes and fanatics, to laugh at Joe Smith and his church, but what then? *The great facts remain.* Young and his people are at Utah; a church of 200,000 souls; an army of 20,000 rifles." But if the followers of a doctrine are really dupes, or worse, and its promulgators are really fanatics, or worse, it gives the doctrine no seriousness or authority the more that there should be found 200,000 souls,—200,000 of the innumerable multitude with a natural taste for the bathos,—to hold it, and 20,000 rifles to defend it. And again, of another religious organisation in America: "A fair and open field is not to be refused when hosts so mighty throw down wager of battle on behalf of what they hold to be true, however strange their faith may seem." A fair and open field is not to be refused to any speaker; but this solemn way of heralding him is quite out of place, unless he has, for the best reason and spirit of man, some significance. "Well, but," says Mr. Hepworth Dixon, "a theory which has been accepted by men like Judge Edmonds, Dr. Hare, Elder Frederick, and Professor Bush!" And again: "Such are, in brief, the bases of what Newman Weeks, Sarah Horton, Deborah Butler, and the associated brethren, proclaimed in Rolt's Hall as the new covenant!" If he was summing up an account of the doctrine of Plato, or of St. Paul, and of its followers, Mr. Hepworth Dixon could not be more earnestly reverential. But the question is, Have personages like Judge Edmonds, and Newman Weeks, and Elderess Polly, and Elderess Antoinette, and the rest of Mr. Hepworth Dixon's heroes and heroines, anything of the weight and significance for the best reason and spirit of man that Plato and St. Paul have? Evidently they, at present, have not; and a very small taste of them and their doctrines ought to have convinced Mr. Hepworth Dixon that they never could have. "But," says he, "the magnetic power which Shakerism is exercising on American thought would of itself compel us,"—and so on. Now, so far as real thought is concerned,—thought which affects the best reason and spirit of man, the scientific or the imaginative thought of the world, the only thought which deserves speaking of in this solemn way, —America has up to the present time been hardly more than a province of England, and even now would not herself claim to be more than abreast of England; and of this only real human thought, English thought itself is not just now, as we must all admit, the most significant factor. Neither, then, can American thought be; and the magnetic power which Shakerism exercises on American thought is about as important, for the best reason and spirit of man, as the magnetic power which Mr. Murphy exercises on Birmingham Protestantism. And as we shall never get rid of our natural taste for the bathos in religion,—never get access to a best self and right reason which may stand as a serious authority,—by treating Mr. Murphy as his own disciples treat him, seriously, and as if he was as much an authority as any one else: so we shall never get rid of it while our able and popular writers treat their Joe Smiths and Deborah Butlers, with their so many thousand souls and so many thousand rifles, in the like exaggerated and misleading manner, and so do their best to confirm us in a bad mental habit to which we are already too prone.

If our habits make it hard for us to come at the idea of a high best self, of a paramount authority, in literature or religion, how much more do they make this hard in the sphere of politics! In other countries the governors, not depending so immediately on the favour of the governed, have everything to urge them, if they know anything of right reason (and it is at least supposed that governors should know more of this than the mass of the governed), to set it authoritatively before the community. But our whole scheme of government being representative, every one of our governors has all possible temptation, instead of setting up before the governed who elect him, and on whose favour he depends, a high standard of right reason, to accommodate himself as much as possible to their natural taste for the bathos; and even if he tries to go counter to it, to proceed in this with so much flattering and coaxing, that they shall not suspect their ignorance and prejudices to be anything very unlike right reason, or their natural taste for the bathos to differ much from a relish for the sublime. Every one is thus in every possible way encouraged to trust in his own heart; but, "he that trusteth in his own heart," says the Wise Man, "is a fool"; and at any rate this, which Bishop Wilson says, is undeniably true: "The number of those who need to be awakened is far greater than that of those who need comfort."

But in our political system everybody is comforted. Our guides and governors who have to be elected by the influence of the Barbarians, and who depend on their favour, sing the praises of the Barbarians, and say all the smooth things that can be said of them. With Mr. Tennyson, they celebrate "the great broad-shouldered genial Englishman," with his "sense of duty," his "reverence for the laws," and his "patient force," who saves us from the "revolts, republics, revolutions, most no graver than a schoolboy's barring out," which upset other and less broad-shouldered nations. Our guides who are chosen by the Philistines and who have to look to their favour, tell the Philistines how "all the world knows that the great middle class of this country supplies the mind, the will, and the power requisite for all the great and good things that have to be done," and congratulate them on their "earnest good sense, which penetrates through sophisms, ignores commonplaces, and gives to conventional illusions their true value." Our guides who look to the favour of the Populace, tell them that "theirs are the brightest powers of sympathy, and the readiest powers of action."

Harsh things are said too, no doubt, against all the great classes of the community; but these things so evidently come from a hostile class, and are so manifestly dictated by the passions and prepossessions of a hostile class, and not by right reason, that they make no serious impression on those at whom they are launched, but slide easily off their minds. For instance, when the Reform League orators inveigh against our cruel and bloated aristocracy, these invectives so evidently show the passions and point of view of the Populace, that they do not sink into the minds of those at whom they are addressed, or awaken any thought or self-examination in them. Again, when our aristocratical baronet describes the Philistines and the Populace as influenced with a kind of hideous mania for emasculating the aristocracy, that reproach so clearly comes from the wrath and excited imagination of the Barbarians, that it does not much set the Philistines and the Populace thinking. Or when Mr. Lowe calls the Populace drunken and venal, he so evidently calls them this in an agony of apprehension for his Philistine or middle-class Parliament, which has done so many great and heroic works, and is now threatened with mixture and debasement, that the Populace do not lay his words seriously to heart.

So the voice which makes a permanent impression on each of our classes is the voice of its friends, and this is from the nature of things, as I have said, a comforting voice. The Barbarians remain in the belief that the great broad-shouldered genial Englishman may be well satisfied with himself; the Philistines remain in the belief that the great middle class of this country, with its earnest common-sense penetrating through sophisms and ignoring commonplaces, may be well satisfied with itself; the Populace, that the working man with his bright powers of sympathy and ready powers of action, may be well satisfied with himself. What hope, at this rate, of extinguishing the taste of the bathos implanted by nature itself in the soul of man, or of inculcating the belief that excellence dwells among high and steep rocks, and can only be reached by those who sweat blood to reach her?

But it will be said, perhaps, that candidates for political influence and leadership, who thus caress the self-love of those whose suffrages they desire, know quite well that they are not saying the sheer truth as reason sees it, but that they are using a sort of conventional language, or what we call clap-trap, which is essential to the working of representative institutions. And therefore, I suppose, we ought rather to say with Figaro: *Qui est-ce qu'on trompe ici?* Now, I admit that often, but not always, when our governors say smooth things to the self-love of the class whose political support they want, they know very well that they are overstepping, by a long stride, the bounds of truth and soberness; and while they talk, they in a manner, no doubt, put their tongue in their cheek. Not always; because, when a Barbarian appeals to his own class to make him their representative and give him political power, he, when he pleases their self-love by extolling broad-shouldered genial Englishmen with their sense of duty, reverence for the laws, and patient force, pleases his own self-love and extols himself, and is, therefore, himself ensnared by his own smooth words. And so, too, when a Philistine wants to be sent to Parliament by his brother Philistines, and extols the earnest good sense which characterises

Manchester and supplies the mind, the will, and the power, as the *Daily News* eloquently says, requisite for all the great and good things that have to be done, he intoxicates and deludes himself as well as his brother Philistines who hear him.

But it is true that a Barbarian often wants the political support of the Philistines; and he unquestionably, when he flatters the self-love of Philistinism, and extols, in the approved fashion, its energy, enterprise, and self-reliance, knows that he is talking clap-trap, and so to say, puts his tongue in his cheek. On all matters where Nonconformity and its catchwords are concerned, this insincerity of Barbarians needing Nonconformist support, and, therefore, flattering the self-love of Nonconformity and repeating its catchwords without the least real belief in them, is very noticeable. When the Nonconformists, in a transport of blind zeal, threw out Sir James Graham's useful Education Clauses in 1843, one-half of their Parliamentary advocates, no doubt, who cried aloud against "trampling on the religious liberty of the Dissenters by taking the money of Dissenters to teach the tenets of the Church of England," put their tongue in their cheek while they so cried out. And perhaps there is even a sort of motion of Mr. Frederic Harrison's tongue towards his cheek when he talks of "the shriek of superstition," and tells the working class that "theirs are the brightest powers of sympathy and the readiest powers of action." But the point on which I would insist is, that this involuntary tribute to truth and soberness on the part of certain of our governors and guides never reaches at all the mass of us governed, to serve as a lesson to us, to abate our self-love, and to awaken in us a suspicion that our favourite prejudices may be, to a higher reason, all nonsense. Whatever by-play goes on among the more intelligent of our leaders, we do not see it; and we are left to believe that, not only in our own eyes, but in the eyes of our representative and ruling men, there is nothing more admirable than our ordinary self, whatever our ordinary self happens to be, Barbarian, Philistine, or Populace.

Thus everything in our political life tends to hide from us that there is anything wiser than our ordinary selves, and to prevent our getting the notion of a paramount right reason. Royalty itself, in its idea the expression of the collective nation, and a sort of constituted witness to its best mind, we try to turn into a kind of grand advertising van, meant to give publicity and credit to the inventions, sound or unsound, of the ordinary self of individuals.

I remember, when I was in North Germany, having this very strongly brought to my mind in the matter of schools and their institution. In Prussia, the best schools are Crown patronage schools, as they are called; schools which have been established and endowed (and new ones are to this day being established and endowed) by the Sovereign himself out of his own revenues, to be under the direct control and management of him or of those representing him, and to serve as types of what schools should be. The Sovereign, as his position raises him above many prejudices and littlenesses, and as he can always have at his disposal the best advice, has evident advantages over private founders in well planning and directing a school; while at the same time his great means and his great influence secure, to a wellplanned school of his, credit and authority. This is what, in North Germany, the governors do in the matter of education for the governed; and one may say that they thus give the governed a lesson, and draw out in them the idea of a right reason higher than the suggestions of an ordinary man's ordinary self.

But in England how different is the part which in
this matter our governors are accustomed to play! The
Licensed Victuallers or the Commercial Travellers propose to make a school for their children; and I suppose,
in the matter of schools, one may call the Licensed Victuallers or the Commercial Travellers ordinary men,
with their natural taste for the bathos still strong; and
a Sovereign with the advice of men like Wilhelm von
Humboldt or Schleiermacher may, in this matter, be a
better judge, and nearer to right reason. And it will be
allowed, probably, that right reason would suggest that,
to have a sheer school of Licensed Victuallers' children,
or a sheer school of Commercial Travellers' children,
and to bring them all up, not only at home but at school
too, in a kind of odour of licensed victualism or of bag-
manism, is not a wise training to give to these children.
And in Germany, I have said, the action of the national
guides or governors is to suggest and provide a better.
But, in England, the action of the national guides or
governors is, for a Royal Prince or a great Minister to
go down to the opening of the Licensed Victuallers' or
of the Commercial Travellers' school, to take the chair,
to extol the energy and self-reliance of the Licensed
Victuallers or the Commercial Travellers, to be all of
their way of thinking, to predict full success to their
schools, and never so much as to hint to them that they
are probably doing a very foolish thing, and that the
right way to go to work with their children's education
is quite different. And it is the same in almost every
department of affairs. While, on the Continent, the idea
prevails that it is the business of the heads and representatives of the nation, by virtue of their superior means,
power, and information, to set an example and to
provide suggestions of right reason, among us the idea
is that the business of the heads and representatives of

the nation is to do nothing of the kind, but to applaud the natural taste for the bathos showing itself vigorously in any part of the community, and to encourage its works.

Now I do not say that the political system of foreign countries has not inconveniences which may outweigh the inconveniences of our own political system; nor am I the least proposing to get rid of our own political system and to adopt theirs. But a sound centre of authority being what, in this disquisition, we have been led to seek, and right reason, or our best self, appearing alone to offer such a sound centre of authority, it is necessary to take note of the chief impediments which hinder, in this country, the extrication or recognition of this right reason as a paramount authority, with a view to afterwards trying in what way they can best be removed.

This being borne in mind, I proceed to remark how not only do we get no suggestions of right reason, and no rebukes of our ordinary self, from our governors, but a kind of philosophical theory is widely spread among us to the effect that there is no such thing at all as a best self and a right reason having claim to paramount authority, or, at any rate, no such thing ascertainable and capable of being made use of; and that there is nothing but an infinite number of ideas and works of our ordinary selves, and suggestions of our natural taste for the bathos, pretty nearly equal in value, which are doomed either to an irreconcilable conflict, or else to a perpetual give and take; and that wisdom consists in choosing the give and take rather than the conflict, and in sticking to our choice with patience and good humour.

And, on the other hand, we have another philosophical theory rife among us, to the effect that without the labour of perverting ourselves by custom or example to relish right reason, but by continuing all of us to follow freely our natural taste for the bathos, we shall, by the mercy of Providence, and by a kind of natural tendency of things, come in due time to relish and follow right reason.

The great promoters of these philosophical theories are our newspapers, which, no less than our parliamentary representatives, may be said to act the part of guides and governors to us; and these favourite doctrines of theirs I call,—or should call, if the doctrines were not preached by authorities I so much respect,—the first, a peculiarly British form of Atheism, the second, a peculiarly British form of Quietism. The first-named melancholy doctrine is preached in the *Times* with great clearness and force of style; indeed, it is well known, from the example of the poet Lucretius and others, what great masters of style the atheistic doctrine has always counted among its promulgators. "It is of no use," says the *Times*, "for us to attempt to force upon our neighbours our several likings and dislikings. We must take things as they are. Everybody has his own little vision of religious or civil perfection. Under the evident impossibility of satisfying everybody, we agree to take our stand on equal laws and on a system as open and liberal as is possible. The result is that everybody has more liberty of action and of speaking here than anywhere else in the Old World." We come again here upon Mr. Roebuck's celebrated definition of happiness, on which I have so often commented: "I look around me and ask what is the state of England? Is not every man able to say what he likes? I ask you whether the world over, or in past history, there is anything like it? Nothing. I pray that our unrivalled happiness may last." This is the old story of our system of checks and every

Englishman doing as he likes, which we have already
seen to have been convenient enough so long as there
were only the Barbarians and the Philistines to do what
they liked, but to be getting inconvenient, and productive of anarchy, now that the Populace wants to do what
it likes too.

But for all that, I will not at once dismiss this famous
doctrine, but will first quote another passage from the
Times, applying the doctrine to a matter of which we
have just been speaking,—education. "The difficulty
here" (in providing a national system of education), says
the *Times*, "does not reside in any removable arrangements. It is inherent and native in the actual and invet-
erate state of things in this country. All these powers and
personages, all these conflicting influences and varieties
of character, exist, and have long existed among us;
they are fighting it out, and will long continue to fight
it out, without coming to that happy consummation
when some one element of the British character is to
destroy or to absorb all the rest." There it is! the various
promptings of the natural taste for the bathos in this
man and that amongst us are fighting it out; and the day
will never come (and, indeed, why should we wish it
to come?) when one man's particular sort of taste for
the bathos shall tyrannise over another man's; nor when
right reason (if that may be called an element of the
British character) shall absorb and rule them all. "The
whole system of this country, like the constitution we
boast to inherit, and are glad to uphold, is made up of
established facts, prescriptive authorities, existing usages,
powers that be, persons in possession, and communities
or classes that have won dominion for themselves, and
will hold it against all comers." Every force in the world,
evidently, except the one reconciling force, right reason!
Barbarian here, Philistine there, Mr. Bradlaugh and

Populace striking in!—pull devil, pull baker! Really, presented with the mastery of style of our leading journal, the sad picture, as one gazes upon it, assumes the iron and inexorable solemnity of tragic Destiny.

After this, the milder doctrine of our other philosophical teacher, the *Daily News,* has, at first, something very attractive and assuaging. The *Daily News* begins, indeed, in appearance, to weave the iron web of necessity round us like the *Times.* "The alternative is between a man's doing what he likes and his doing what some one else, probably not one whit wiser than himself, likes." This points to the tacit compact, mentioned in my last paper, between the Barbarians and the Philistines, and into which it is hoped that the Populace will one day enter; the compact, so creditable to English honesty, that since each class has only the ideas and aims of its ordinary self to give effect to, none of them shall, if it exercise power, treat its ordinary self too seriously, or attempt to impose it on others; but shall let these others, —the fanatical Protestant, for instance, in his Papist-baiting, and the popular tribune in his Hyde Park anarchy-mongering,—have their fling. But then the *Daily News* suddenly lights up the gloom of necessitarianism with bright beams of hope. "No doubt," it says, "the common reason of society ought to check the aberrations of individual eccentricity." This common reason of society looks very like our best self or right reason, to which we want to give authority, by making the action of the *State,* or nation in its collective character, the expression of it. But of this project of ours, the *Daily News,* with its subtle dialectics, makes havoc. "Make the State the organ of the common reason?"—it says. "You make it the organ of something or other, but how can you be certain that reason will be the quality which will be embodied in it?" You cannot be certain of it, undoubtedly, if you never try to bring the thing about; but the question is, the action of the State being the action of the collective nation, and the action of the collective nation carrying naturally great publicity, weight, and force of example with it, whether we should not try to put into the action of the State as much as possible of right reason or our best self, which may, in this manner, come back to us with new force and authority; may have visibility, form, and influence; and help to confirm us, in the many moments when we are tempted to be our ordinary selves merely, in resisting our natural taste of the bathos rather than in giving way to it?

But no! says our teacher: "It is better there should be an infinite variety of experiments in human action; the common reason of society will in the main check the aberrations of individual eccentricity well enough, if left to its natural operation." This is what I call the specially British form of Quietism, or a devout, but excessive reliance on an over-ruling Providence. Providence, as the moralists are careful to tell us, generally works in human affairs by human means; so, when we want to make right reason act on individual inclination, our best self on our ordinary self, we seek to give it more power of doing so by giving it public recognition and authority, and embodying it, so far as we can, in the State. It seems too much to ask of Providence, that while we, on our part, leave our congenital taste for the bathos to its natural operation and its infinite variety of experiments, Providence should mysteriously guide it into the true track, and compel it to relish the sublime. At any rate, great men and great institutions have hitherto seemed necessary for producing any considerable effect of this kind. No doubt we have an infinite variety of experiments and an ever-multiplying multitude of explorers. Even in these few chapters I have enumerated many:

the *British Banner,* Judge Edmonds, Newman Weeks,
Deborah Butler, Elderess Polly, Brother Noyes, Mr.
Murphy, the Licensed Victuallers, the Commercial
Travellers, and I know not how many more; and the
members of the noble army are swelling every day. But
what a depth of Quietism, or rather, what an over-
bold call on the direct interposition of Providence, to
believe that these interesting explorers will discover
the true track, or at any rate, "will do so in the main
well enough" (whatever that may mean) if left to
their natural operation; that is, by going on as they
are! Philosophers say, indeed, that we learn virtue by
performing acts of virtue; but to say that we shall learn
virtue by performing any acts to which our natural
taste for the bathos carries us, that the fanatical Protestant comes at his best self by Papist-baiting, or
Newman Weeks and Deborah Butler at right reason by
following their noses, this certainly does appear over-
sanguine.

It is true, what we want is to make right reason act
on individual reason, the reason of individuals; all our
search for authority has that for its end and aim. The
Daily News says, I observe, that all my argument for
authority "has a non-intellectual root"; and from what I
know of my own mind and its poverty I think this so
probable, that I should be inclined easily to admit it,
if it were not that, in the first place, nothing of this
kind, perhaps, should be admitted without examination;
and, in the second, a way of accounting for the charge being made, in this particular instance, without good
grounds, appears to present itself. What seems to me to
account here, perhaps, for the charge, is the want of flexibility of our race, on which I have so often remarked. I
mean, it being admitted that the conformity of the individual reason of the fanatical Protestant or the popular

rioter with right reason is our true object, and not the
mere restraining them, by the strong arm of the State,
from Papist-baiting, or railing-breaking,—admitting this,
we English have so little flexibility that we cannot readily
perceive that the State's restraining them from these indulgences may yet fix clearly in their minds that, to the
collective nation, these indulgences appear irrational
and unallowable, may make them pause and reflect, and
may contribute to bringing, with time, their individual
reason into harmony with right reason. But in no country, owing to the want of intellectual flexibility above
mentioned, is the leaning which is our natural one, and,
therefore, needs no recommending to us, so sedulously
recommended, and the leaning which is not our natural
one, and, therefore, does not need dispraising to us, so
sedulously dispraised, as in ours. To rely on the individual being, with us, the natural leaning, we will
hear of nothing but the good of relying on the individual; to act through the collective nation on the
individual being not our natural leaning, we will hear
nothing in recommendation of it. But the wise know
that we often need to hear most of that to which we are
least inclined, and even to learn to employ, in certain
circumstances, that which is capable, if employed amiss,
of being a danger to us.

Elsewhere this is certainly better understood than
here. In a recent number of the *Westminster Review,*
an able writer, but with precisely our national want of
flexibility of which I have been speaking, has unearthed,
I see, for our present needs, an English translation,
published some years ago, of Wilhelm von Humboldt's
book, *The Sphere and Duties of Government.* Humboldt's object in this book is to show that the operation
of government ought to be severely limited to what
directly and immediately relates to the security of per-

son and property. Wilhelm von Humboldt, one of the most beautiful souls that have ever existed, used to say that one's business in life was first to perfect one's self by all the means in one's power, and secondly, to try and create in the world around one an aristocracy, the most numerous that one possibly could, of talents and characters. He saw, of course, that, in the end, everything comes to this,—that the individual must act for himself, and must be perfect in himself; and he lived in a country, Germany, where people were disposed to act too little for themselves, and to rely too much on the Government. But even thus, such was his flexibility, so little was he in bondage to a mere abstract maxim, that he saw very well that for his purpose itself, of enabling the individual to stand perfect on his own foundations and to do without the State, the action of the State would for long, long years be necessary. And soon after he wrote his book on *The Sphere and Duties of Government,* Wilhelm von Humboldt became Minister of Education in Prussia; and from his ministry all the great reforms which give the control of Prussian education to the State,—the transference of the management of public schools from their old boards of trustees to the State, the obligatory State-examination for schoolmasters, and the foundation of the great State-University of Berlin,—take their origin. This his English reviewer says not a word of. But, writing for a people whose dangers lie, as we have seen, on the side of their unchecked and unguided individual action, whose dangers none of them lie on the side of an over-reliance on the State, he quotes just so much of Wilhelm von Humboldt's example as can flatter them in their propensities, and do them no good; and just what might make them think, and be of use to them, he leaves on one side. This precisely recalls the manner, it will be observed, in which we have seen that our royal and noble personages proceed with the Licensed Victuallers.

In France the action of the State on individuals is yet more preponderant than in Germany; and the need which friends of human perfection feel for what may enable the individual to stand perfect on his own foundations is all the stronger. But what says one of the staunchest of these friends, M. Renan, on State action; and even State action in that very sphere where in France it is most excessive, the sphere of education? Here are his words:—"A Liberal believes in liberty, and liberty signifies the non-intervention of the State. *But such an ideal is still a long way off from us, and the very means to remove it to an indefinite distance would be precisely the State's withdrawing its action too soon.*" And this, he adds, is even truer of education than of any other department of public affairs.

We see, then, how indispensable to that human perfection which we seek is, in the opinion of good judges, some public recognition and establishment of our best self, or right reason. We see how our habits and practice oppose themselves to such a recognition, and the many inconveniences which we therefore suffer. But now let us try to go a little deeper, and to find, beneath our actual habits and practice, the very ground and cause out of which they spring.

IV. HEBRAISM AND HELLENISM

This fundamental ground is our preference of doing to thinking. Now this preference is a main element in our nature, and as we study it we find ourselves opening up a number of large questions on every side.

Let me go back for a moment to Bishop Wilson, who says: "First, never go against the best light you have;

secondly, take care that your light be not darkness." We show, as a nation, laudable energy and persistence in walking according to the best light we have, but are not quite careful enough, perhaps, to see that our light be not darkness. This is only another version of the old story that energy is our strong point and favourable characteristic, rather than intelligence. But we may give to this idea a more general form still, in which it will have a yet larger range of application. We may regard this energy driving at practice, this paramount sense of the obligation of duty, self-control, and work, this earnestness in going manfully with the best light we have, as one force. And we may regard the intelligence driving at those ideas which are, after all, the basis of right practice, the ardent sense for all the new and changing combinations of them which man's development brings with it, the indomitable impulse to know and adjust them perfectly, as another force. And these two forces we may regard as in some sense rivals,—rivals not by the necessity of their own nature, but as exhibited in man and his history,—and rivals dividing the empire of the world between them. And to give these forces names from the two races of men who have supplied the most signal and splendid manifestations of them, we may call them respectively the forces of Hebraism and Hellenism. Hebraism and Hellenism,—between these two points of influence moves our world. At one time it feels more powerfully the attraction of one of them, at another time of the other; and it ought to be, though it never is, evenly and happily balanced between them.

The final aim of both Hellenism and Hebraism, as of all great spiritual disciplines, is no doubt the same: man's perfection or salvation. The very language which they both of them use in schooling us to reach this aim is often identical. Even when their language indicates by variation,—sometimes a broad variation, often a but slight and subtle variation,—the different courses of thought which are uppermost in each discipline, even then the unity of the final end and aim is still apparent. To employ the actual words of that discipline with which we ourselves are all of us most familiar, and the words of which, therefore, come most home to us, that final end and aim is "that we might be partakers of the divine nature." These are the words of a Hebrew apostle, but of Hellenism and Hebraism alike this is, I say, the aim. When the two are confronted, as they very often are confronted, it is nearly always with what I may call a rhetorical purpose; the speaker's whole design is to exalt and enthrone one of the two, and he uses the other only as a foil and to enable him the better to give effect to his purpose. Obviously, with us, it is usually Hellenism which is thus reduced to minister to the triumph of Hebraism. There is a sermon on Greece and the Greek spirit by a man never to be mentioned without interest and respect, Frederick Robertson, in which this rhetorical use of Greece and the Greek spirit, and the inadequate exhibition of them necessarily consequent upon this, is almost ludicrous, and would be censurable if it were not to be explained by the exigencies of a sermon. On the other hand, Heinrich Heine, and other writers of his sort, give us the spectacle of the tables completely turned, and of Hebraism brought in just as a foil and contrast to Hellenism, and to make the superiority of Hellenism more manifest. In both these cases there is injustice and misrepresentation. The aim and end of both Hebraism and Hellenism is, as I have said, one and the same, and this aim and end is august and admirable.

Still, they pursue this aim by very different courses. The uppermost idea with Hellenism is to see things as they really are; the uppermost idea with Hebraism is conduct and obedience. Nothing can do away with this ineffaceable difference. The Greek quarrel with the body and its desires is, that they hinder right thinking; the Hebrew quarrel with them is, that they hinder right acting. "He that keepeth the law, happy is he"; "Blessed is the man that feareth the Eternal, that delighteth greatly in his commandments";—that is the Hebrew notion of felicity; and, pursued with passion and tenacity, this notion would not let the Hebrew rest till, as is well known, he had at last got out of the law a network of prescriptions to enwrap his whole life, to govern every moment of it, every impulse, every action. The Greek notion of felicity, on the other hand, is perfectly conveyed in these words of a great French moralist: "*C'est le bonheur des hommes*,"—when? when they abhor that which is evil?—no; when they exercise themselves in the law of the Lord day and night?—no; when they die daily?—no; when they walk about the New Jerusalem with palms in their hands?—no; but when they think aright, when their thought hits: "*quand ils pensent juste.*" At the bottom of both the Greek and the Hebrew notion is the desire, native in man, for reason and the will of God, the feeling after the universal order,—in a word, the love of God. But, while Hebraism seizes upon certain plain, capital intimations of the universal order, and rivets itself, one may say, with unequalled grandeur of earnestness and intensity on the study and observance of them, the bent of Hellenism is to follow, with flexible activity, the whole play of the universal order, to be apprehensive of missing any part of it, of sacrificing one part to another, to slip away from resting in this or that intimation of it, however capital. An unclouded clearness of mind, an unimpeded play of thought, is what this bent drives at. The governing idea of Hellenism is *spontaneity of consciousness*; that of Hebraism, *strictness of conscience*.

Christianity changed nothing in this essential bent of Hebraism to set doing above knowing. Self-conquest, self-devotion, the following not our own individual will, but the will of God, *obedience*, is the fundamental idea of this form, also, of the discipline to which we have attached the general name of Hebraism. Only, as the old law and the network of prescriptions with which it enveloped human life were evidently a motive-power not driving and searching enough to produce the result aimed at,—patient continuance in well-doing, self-conquest,—Christianity substituted for them boundless devotion to that inspiring and affecting pattern of self-conquest offered by Jesus Christ; and by the new motive-power, of which the essence was this, though the love and admiration of Christian churches have for centuries been employed in varying, amplifying, and adorning the plain description of it, Christianity, as St. Paul truly says, "establishes the law," and in the strength of the ampler power which she has thus supplied to fulfil it, has accomplished the miracles, which we all see, of her history.

So long as we do not forget that both Hellenism and Hebraism are profound and admirable manifestations of man's life, tendencies, and powers, and that both of them aim at a like final result, we can hardly insist too strongly on the divergence of line and of operation with which they proceed. It is a divergence so great that it most truly, as the prophet Zechariah says, "has raised up thy sons, O Zion, against thy sons, O Greece!" The difference whether it is by doing or by knowing that we set most store, and the practical consequences which follow from this difference, leave their mark on all the history of our race and of its development. Language may be abundantly quoted from both Hellenism and Hebraism to make it seem that one follows the same current as the other towards the same goal. They are, truly, borne towards the same goal; but the currents which bear them are infinitely different. It is true, Solomon will praise knowing: "Understanding is a well-spring of life unto him that hath it." And in the New Testament, again, Jesus Christ is a "light," and "truth makes us free." It is true, Aristotle will undervalue knowing: "In what concerns virtue," says he, "three things are necessary—knowledge, deliberate will, and perseverance; but, whereas the two last are all-important, the first is a matter of little importance." It is true that with the same impatience with which St. James enjoins a man to be not a forgetful hearer, but a *doer of the work,* Epictetus exhorts us to *do* what we have demonstrated to ourselves we ought to do; or he taunts us with futility, for being armed at all points to prove that lying is wrong, yet all the time continuing to lie. It is true, Plato, in words which are almost the words of the New Testament or the Imitation, calls life a learning to die. But underneath the superficial agreement the fundamental divergence still subsists. The understanding of Solomon is "the walking in the way of the commandments"; this is "the way of peace," and it is of this that blessedness comes. In the New Testament, the truth which gives us the peace of God and makes us free, is the love of Christ constraining us to crucify, as he did, and with a like purpose of moral regeneration, the flesh with its affections and lusts, and thus establishing, as we have seen, the law. The moral virtues, on the other hand, are with Aristotle but the porch and access to the intellectual, and with these last is blessedness. That partaking of the divine life, which both Hellenism and

Hebraism, as we have said, fix as their crowning aim,
Plato expressly denies to the man of practical virtue
merely, of self-conquest with any other motive than that
of perfect intellectual vision. He reserves it for the lover
of pure knowledge, of seeing things as they really are,
—the φιλομαθής.

Both Hellenism and Hebraism arise out of the wants
of human nature, and address themselves to satisfying
those wants. But their methods are so different, they
lay stress on such different points, and call into being by
their respective disciplines such different activities, that
the face which human nature presents when it passes
from the hands of one of them to those of the other, is
no longer the same. To get rid of one's ignorance, to see
things as they are, and by seeing them as they are to
see them in their beauty, is the simple and attractive
ideal which Hellenism holds out before human nature;
and from the simplicity and charm of this ideal, Hellenism, and human life in the hands of Hellenism, is in-
vested with a kind of aërial ease, clearness, and radi-
ancy; they are full of what we call sweetness and light.
Difficulties are kept out of view, and the beauty and
rationalness of the ideal have all our thoughts. "The best
man is he who most tries to perfect himself, and the
happiest man is he who most feels that he *is* perfecting
himself,"—this account of the matter by Socrates, the
true Socrates of the *Memorabilia,* has something so simple, spontaneous, and unsophisticated about it, that it
seems to fill us with clearness and hope when we hear
it. But there is a saying which I have heard attributed
to Mr. Carlyle about Socrates,—a very happy saying,
whether it is really Mr. Carlyle's or not,—which excellently marks the essential point in which Hebraism differs from Hellenism. "Socrates," this saying goes, "is
terribly *at ease in Zion.*" Hebraism,—and here is the

source of its wonderful strength,—has always been severely preoccupied with an awful sense of the impossibility of being at ease in Zion; of the difficulties which oppose themselves to man's pursuit or attainment of that perfection of which Socrates talks so hopefully, and, as from this point of view one might almost say, so glibly. It is all very well to talk of getting rid of one's ignorance, of seeing things in their reality, seeing them in their beauty; but how is this to be done when there is something which thwarts and spoils all our efforts?

This something is *sin*; and the space which sin fills in Hebraism, as compared with Hellenism, is indeed prodigious. This obstacle to perfection fills the whole scene, and perfection appears remote and rising away from earth, in the background. Under the name of sin, the difficulties of knowing oneself and conquering oneself which impede man's passage to perfection, become, for Hebraism, a positive, active entity hostile to man, a mysterious power which I heard Dr. Pusey the other day, in one of his impressive sermons, compare to a hideous hunchback seated on our shoulders, and which it is the main business of our lives to hate and oppose. The discipline of the Old Testament may be summed up as a discipline teaching us to abhor and flee from sin; the discipline of the New Testament, as a discipline teaching us to die to it. As Hellenism speaks of thinking clearly, seeing things in their essence and beauty, as a grand and precious feat for man to achieve, so Hebraism speaks of becoming conscious of sin, of awakening to a sense of sin, as a feat of this kind. It is obvious to what wide divergence these differing tendencies, actively followed, must lead. As one passes and repasses from Hellenism to Hebraism, from Plato to St. Paul, one feels inclined to rub one's eyes and ask oneself whether man is indeed a gentle and simple being, showing the traces of a noble and divine nature; or an unhappy chained captive, labouring with groanings that cannot be uttered to free himself from the body of this death.

Apparently it was the Hellenic conception of human nature which was unsound, for the world could not live by it. Absolutely to call it unsound, however, is to fall into the common error of its Hebraising enemies; but it was unsound at that particular moment of man's development, it was premature. The indispensable basis of conduct and self-control, the platform upon which alone the perfection aimed at by Greece can come into bloom, was not to be reached by our race so easily; centuries of probation and discipline were needed to bring us to it. Therefore the bright promise of Hellenism faded, and Hebraism ruled the world. Then was seen that astonishing spectacle, so well marked by the often-quoted words of the prophet Zechariah, when men of all languages and nations took hold of the skirt of him that was a Jew, saying:—*"We will go with you, for we have heard that God is with you."* And the Hebraism which thus received and ruled a world all gone out of the way and altogether become unprofitable, was, and could not but be, the later, the more spiritual, the more attractive development of Hebraism. It was Christianity; that is to say, Hebraism aiming at self-conquest and rescue from the thrall of vile affections, not by obedience to the letter of a law, but by conformity to the image of a self-sacrificing example. To a world stricken with moral enervation Christianity offered its spectacle of an inspired self-sacrifice; to men who refused themselves nothing, it showed one who refused himself everything;—*"my Saviour banished joy!"* says George Herbert. When the *alma Venus*, the life-giving and joy-giving power of nature, so fondly cherished by the Pagan world, could not save her followers from self-dissatisfaction and ennui, the severe words of the apostle came bracingly and refreshingly: "Let no man deceive you with vain words, for because of these things cometh the wrath of God upon the children of disobedience." Through age after age and generation after generation, our race, or all that part of our race which was most living and progressive, was *baptized into a death*; and endeavoured, by suffering in the flesh, to cease from sin. Of this endeavour, the animating labours and afflictions of early Christianity, the touching asceticism of mediæval Christianity, are the great historical manifestations. Literary monuments of it, each in its own way incomparable, remain in the Epistles of St. Paul, in St. Augustine's *Confessions*, and in the two original and simplest books of the *Imitation*.[1]

Of two disciplines laying their main stress, the one, on clear intelligence, the other, on firm obedience; the one, on comprehensively knowing the grounds of one's duty, the other, on diligently practising it; the one, on taking all possible care (to use Bishop Wilson's words again) that the light we have be not darkness, the other, that according to the best light we have we diligently walk,—the priority naturally belongs to that discipline which braces all man's moral powers, and founds for him an indispensable basis of character. And, therefore, it is justly said of the Jewish people, who were charged with setting powerfully forth that side of the divine order to which the words *conscience* and *self-conquest* point, that they were "entrusted with the oracles of God"; as it is justly said of Christianity, which followed Judaism and which set forth this side with a much deeper effectiveness and a much wider influence, that the wisdom of the old Pagan world was foolishness compared to it. No words of devotion and admiration can

---

[1] The two first books. (*Arnold's note.*)

be too strong to render thanks to these beneficent forces
which have so borne forward humanity in its appointed
work of coming to the knowledge and possession of itself; above all, in those great moments when their action
was the wholesomest and the most necessary.

But the evolution of these forces, separately and in
themselves, is not the whole evolution of humanity,—
their single history is not the whole history of man;
whereas their admirers are always apt to make it stand
for the whole history. Hebraism and Hellenism are,
neither of them, the *law* of human development, as their
admirers are prone to make them; they are, each of
them, *contributions* to human development,—august
contributions, invaluable contributions; and each showing itself to us more august, more invaluable, more preponderant over the other, according to the moment in
which we take them, and the relation in which we stand
to them. The nations of our modern world, children of
that immense and salutary movement which broke up
the Pagan world, inevitably stand to Hellenism in a relation which dwarfs it, and to Hebraism in a relation
which magnifies it. They are inevitably prone to take
Hebraism as the law of human development, and not as
simply a contribution to it, however precious. And yet
the lesson must perforce be learned, that the human
spirit is wider than the most priceless of the forces which
bear it onward, and that to the whole development of
man Hebraism itself is, like Hellenism, but a contribution.

Perhaps we may help ourselves to see this clearer
by an illustration drawn from the treatment of a single
great idea which has profoundly engaged the human
spirit, and has given it eminent opportunities for showing its nobleness and energy. It surely must be perceived
that the idea of immortality, as this idea rises in its gen-

erality before the human spirit, is something grander,
truer, and more satisfying, than it is in the particular
forms by which St. Paul, in the famous fifteenth chapter
of the Epistle to the Corinthians, and Plato, in the
Phædo, endeavour to develop and establish it. Surely
we cannot but feel, that the argumentation with which
the Hebrew apostle goes about to expound this great
idea is, after all, confused and inconclusive; and that
the reasoning, drawn from analogies of likeness and
equality, which is employed upon it by the Greek philosopher, is over-subtle and sterile. Above and beyond
the inadequate solutions which Hebraism and Hellenism here attempt, extends the immense and august
problem itself, and the human spirit which gave birth
to it. And this single illustration may suggest to us how
the same thing happens in other cases also.

But meanwhile, by alternations of Hebraism and
Hellenism, of a man's intellectual and moral impulses,
of the effort to see things as they really are, and the effort to win peace by self-conquest, the human spirit proceeds; and each of these two forces has its appointed
hours of culmination and seasons of rule. As the great
movement of Christianity was a triumph of Hebraism
and man's moral impulses, so the great movement which
goes by the name of the Renascence[1] was an uprising
and re-instatement of man's intellectual impulses and
of Hellenism. We in England, the devoted children of
Protestantism, chiefly know the Renascence by its subordinate and secondary side of the Reformation. The
Reformation has been often called a Hebraising revival,
a return to the ardour and sincereness of primitive Christianity. No one, however, can study the development of

---

[1] I have ventured to give to the foreign word *Renaissance,*—
destined to become of more common use amongst us as the movement which it denotes comes, as it will come, increasingly to interest
us,—an English form. (*Arnold's note.*)

Protestantism and of Protestant churches without feeling that into the Reformation too,—Hebraising child
of the Renascence and offspring of its fervour, rather
than its intelligence, as it undoubtedly was,—the subtle
Hellenic leaven of the Renascence found its way, and
that the exact respective parts, in the Reformation, of
Hebraism and of Hellenism, are not easy to separate.
But what we may with truth say is, that all which Protestantism was to itself clearly conscious of, all which it
succeeded in clearly setting forth in words, had the
characters of Hebraism rather than of Hellenism. The
Reformation was strong, in that it was an earnest return
to the Bible and to doing from the heart the will of God
as there written. It was weak, in that it never consciously
grasped or applied the central idea of the Renascence,
—the Hellenic idea of pursuing, in all lines of activity,
the law and science, to use Plato's words, of things as
they really are. Whatever direct superiority, therefore,
Protestantism had over Catholicism was a moral superiority, a superiority arising out of its greater sincerity
and earnestness,—at the moment of its apparition at
any rate,—in dealing with the heart and conscience. Its
pretensions to an intellectual superiority are in general
quite illusory. For Hellenism, for the thinking side in
man as distinguished from the acting side, the attitude
of mind of Protestantism towards the Bible in no respect
differs from the attitude of mind of Catholicism towards
the Church. The mental habit of him who imagines that
Balaam's ass spoke, in no respect differs from the mental habit of him who imagines that a Madonna of wood
or stone winked; and the one, who says that God's
Church makes him believe what he believes, and the
other, who says that God's Word makes him believe
what he believes, are for the philosopher perfectly alike
in not really and truly knowing, when they say *God's*

Church and *God's Word,* what it is they say, or whereof they affirm.

In the sixteenth century, therefore, Hellenism re-entered the world, and again stood in presence of Hebraism,—a Hebraism renewed and purged. Now, it has not been enough observed, how, in the seventeenth century, a fate befell Hellenism in some respects analogous to that which befell it at the commencement of our era. The Renascence, that great re-awakening of Hellenism, that irresistible return of humanity to nature and to seeing things as they are, which in art, in literature, and in physics, produced such splendid fruits, had, like the anterior Hellenism of the Pagan world, a side of moral weakness and of relaxation or insensibility of the moral fibre, which in Italy showed itself with the most startling plainness, but which in France, England, and other countries was very apparent too. Again this loss of spiritual balance, this exclusive preponderance given to man's perceiving and knowing side, this unnatural defect of his feeling and acting side, provoked a reaction. Let us trace that reaction where it most nearly concerns us.

Science has now made visible to everybody the great and pregnant elements of difference which lie in race, and in how signal a manner they make the genius and history of an Indo-European people vary from those of a Semitic people. Hellenism is of Indo-European growth, Hebraism is of Semitic growth; and we English, a nation of Indo-European stock, seem to belong naturally to the movement of Hellenism. But nothing more strongly marks the essential unity of man, than the affinities we can perceive, in this point or that, between members of one family of peoples and members of another. And no affinity of this kind is more strongly marked than that likeness in the strength and prominence of the moral fibre, which, notwithstanding immense elements of difference, knits in some special sort the genius and history of us English, and our American descendants across the Atlantic, to the genius and history of the Hebrew people. Puritanism, which has been so great a power in the English nation, and in the strongest part of the English nation, was originally the reaction in the seventeenth century of the conscience and moral sense of our race, against the moral indifference and lax rule of conduct which in the sixteenth century came in with the Renascence. It was a reaction of Hebraism against Hellenism; and it powerfully manifested itself, as was natural, in a people with much of what we call a Hebraising turn, with a signal affinity for the bent which was the master-bent of Hebrew life. Eminently Indo-European by its *humour*, by the power it shows, through this gift, of imaginatively acknowledging the multiform aspects of the problem of life, and of thus getting itself unfixed from its own over-certainty, of smiling at its own over-tenacity, our race has yet (and a great part of its strength lies here), in matters of practical life and moral conduct, a strong share of the assuredness, the tenacity, the intensity of the Hebrews. This turn manifested itself in Puritanism, and has had a great part in shaping our history for the last two hundred years. Undoubtedly it checked and changed amongst us that movement of the Renascence which we see producing in the reign of Elizabeth such wonderful fruits. Undoubtedly it stopped the prominent rule and direct development of that order of ideas which we call by the name of Hellenism, and gave the first rank to a different order of ideas. Apparently, too, as we said of the former defeat of Hellenism, if Hellenism was defeated, this shows that Hellenism was imperfect, and that its ascendency at that moment would not have been for the world's good.

Yet there is a very important difference between the defeat inflicted on Hellenism by Christianity eighteen hundred years ago, and the check given to the Renascence by Puritanism. The greatness of the difference is well measured by the difference in force, beauty, significance, and usefulness, between primitive Christianity and Protestantism. Eighteen hundred years ago it was altogether the hour of Hebraism. Primitive Christianity was legitimately and truly the ascendant force in the world at that time, and the way of mankind's progress lay through its full development. Another hour in man's development began in the fifteenth century, and the main road of his progress then lay for a time through Hellenism. Puritanism was no longer the central current of the world's progress, it was a side stream crossing the central current and checking it. The cross and the check may have been necessary and salutary, but that does not do away with the essential difference between the main stream of man's advance and a cross or side stream. For more than two hundred years the main stream of man's advance has moved towards knowing himself and the world, seeing things as they are, spontaneity of consciousness; the main impulse of a great part, and that the strongest part, of our nation has been towards strictness of conscience. They have made the secondary the principal at the wrong moment, and the principal they have at the wrong moment treated as secondary. This contravention of the natural order has produced, as such contravention always must produce, a certain confusion and false movement, of which we are now beginning to feel, in almost every direction, the inconvenience. In all directions our habitual causes of action seem to be losing efficaciousness, credit, and control, both with others and even with ourselves. Everywhere we see the beginnings of confusion, and we want a clue to some sound order and authority. This we can only get by going back upon the actual instincts and forces which rule our life, seeing them as they really are, connecting them with other instincts and forces, and enlarging our whole view and rule of life.

◌

EQUALITY

◌

THERE is a maxim which we all know, which occurs in our copy-books, which occurs in that solemn and beautiful formulary against which the Nonconformist genius is just now so angrily chafing,—the Burial Service. The maxim is this: "Evil communications corrupt good manners." It is taken from a chapter of the First Epistle to the Corinthians; but originally it is a line of poetry, of Greek poetry. *Quid Athenis et Hierosolymis?* asks a Father; what have Athens and Jerusalem to do with one another? Well, at any rate, the Jerusalemite Paul, exhorting his converts, enforces what he is saying by a verse of Athenian comedy,—a verse, probably, from the great master of that comedy, a man unsurpassed for fine and just observation of human life, Menander. Φθείρουσιν ἤθη χρήσθ' ὁμιλίαι κακαί—"Evil communications corrupt good manners."

In that collection of single, sententious lines, printed at the end of Menander's fragments, where we now find the maxim quoted by St. Paul, there is another striking maxim, not alien certainly to the language of the Christian religion, but which has not passed into our copy-books: "Choose equality and flee greed." The same profound observer, who laid down the maxim so universally accepted by us that it has become commonplace, the maxim that evil communications corrupt good manners, laid down also, as a no less sure result of the accurate study of human life, this other maxim as well: "Choose equality and flee greed"—Ἰσότητα δ᾽ αἱροῦ καὶ πλεονεξίαν φύγε.

Pleonexia, or greed, the wishing and trying for the bigger share, we know under the name of covetousness. We understand by covetousness something different from what *pleonexia* really means: we understand by it the longing for other people's goods: and covetousness, so understood, it is a commonplace of morals and of religion with us that we should shun. As to the duty of pursuing equality, there is no such consent amongst us. Indeed, the consent is the other way, the consent is against equality. Equality before the law we all take as a matter of course; that is not the equality which we mean when we talk of equality. When we talk of equality, we understand social equality; and for equality in this Frenchified sense of the term almost everybody in England has a hard word. About four years ago Lord Beaconsfield held it up to reprobation in a speech to the students at Glasgow;—a speech so interesting, that being asked soon afterwards to hold a discourse at Glasgow, I said that if one spoke there at all at that time it would be impossible to speak on any other subject but equality. However, it is a great way to Glasgow, and I never yet have been able to go and speak there.

But the testimonies against equality have been steadily accumulating from the date of Lord Beaconsfield's Glasgow speech down to the present hour. Sir Erskine May winds up his new and important *History of Democ-*

racy by saying: "France has aimed at social equality. The fearful troubles through which she has passed have checked her prosperity, demoralised her society, and arrested the intellectual growth of her people." Mr. Froude, again, who is more his own master than I am, has been able to go to Edinburgh and to speak there upon equality. Mr. Froude told his hearers that equality splits a nation into a "multitude of disconnected units," that "the masses require leaders whom they can trust," and that "the natural leaders in a healthy country are the gentry." And only just before the *History of Democracy* came out, we had that exciting passage of arms between Mr. Lowe and Mr. Gladstone, where equality, poor thing, received blows from them both. Mr. Lowe declared that "no concession should be made to the cry for equality, unless it appears that the State is menaced with more danger by its refusal than by its admission. No such case exists now or ever has existed in this country." And Mr. Gladstone replied that equality was so utterly unattractive to the people of this country, inequality was so dear to their hearts, that to talk of concessions being made to the cry for equality was absurd. "There is no broad political idea," says Mr. Gladstone quite truly, "which has entered less into the formation of the political system of this country than the love of equality." And he adds: "It is not the love of equality which has carried into every corner of the country the distinct undeniable popular preference, wherever other things are equal, for a man who is a lord over a man who is not. The love of freedom itself is hardly stronger in England than the love of aristocracy." Mr. Gladstone goes on to quote a saying of Sir William Molesworth, that with our people the love of aristocracy "is a religion." And he concludes in his copious and eloquent way: "Call this love of inequality by what name you please,—the complement of the love of freedom, or its negative pole, or the shadow which the love of freedom casts, or the reverberation of its voice in the halls of the constitution,—it is an active, living, and life-giving power, which forms an inseparable essential element in our political habits of mind, and asserts itself at every step in the processes of our system."

And yet, on the other side, we have a consummate critic of life like Menander, delivering, as if there were no doubt at all about the matter, the maxim: "Choose equality!" An Englishman with any curiosity must surely be inclined to ask himself how such a maxim can ever have got established, and taken rank along with "Evil communications corrupt good manners." Moreover, we see that among the French, who have suffered so grievously, as we hear, from choosing equality, the most gifted spirits continue to believe passionately in it nevertheless. "The human ideal, as well as the social ideal, is," says George Sand, "to achieve equality." She calls equality "the goal of man and the law of the future." She asserts that France is the most civilised of nations, and that its pre-eminence in civilisation it owes to equality.

But Menander lived a long while ago, and George Sand was an enthusiast. Perhaps their differing from us about equality need not trouble us much. France, too, counts for but one nation, as England counts for one also. Equality may be a religion with the people of France, as inequality, we are told, is a religion with the people of England. But what do other nations seem to think about the matter?

Now, my discourse to-night is most certainly not meant to be a disquisition on law, and on the rules of bequest. But it is evident that in the societies of Europe, with a constitution of property such as that which the

feudal Middle Age left them with,—a constitution of
property full of inequality,—the state of the law of bequest shows us how far each society wishes the inequality to continue. The families in possession of great
estates will not break them up if they can help it. Such
owners will do all they can, by entail and settlement,
to prevent their successors from breaking them up. They
will preserve inequality. Freedom of bequest, then, the
power of making entails and settlements, is sure, in an
old European country like ours, to maintain inequality.
And with us, who have the religion of inequality, the
power of entailing and settling, and of willing property
as one likes, exists, as is well known, in singular fulness,
—greater fulness than in any country of the Continent.
The proposal of a measure such as the Real Estates In-
testacy Bill is, in a country like ours, perfectly puerile.
A European country like ours, wishing not to preserve
inequality but to abate it, can only do so by interfering
with the freedom of bequest. This is what Turgot, the
wisest of French statesmen, pronounced before the Revolution to be necessary, and what was done in France
at the great Revolution. The *Code Napoléon,* the actual
law of France, forbids entails altogether, and leaves a
man free to dispose of but one-fourth of his property, of
whatever kind, if he have three children or more, of
one-third if he have two children, of one-half if he have
but one child. Only in the rare case, therefore, of a
man's having but one child, can that child take the whole
of his father's property. If there are two children, two-
thirds of the property must be equally divided between
them; if there are more than two, three-fourths. In this
way has France, desiring equality, sought to bring
equality about.

Now the interesting point for us is, I say, to know
how far other European communities, left in the same

situation with us and with France, having immense inequalities of class and property created for them by
the Middle Age, have dealt with these inequalities by
means of the law of bequest. Do they leave bequest
free, as we do? then, like us, they are for inequality.
Do they interfere with the freedom of bequest, as
France does? then, like France, they are for equality.
And we shall be most interested, surely, by what the
most civilised European communities do in this matter,
—communities such as those of Germany, Italy, Belgium, Holland, Switzerland. And among those communities we are most concerned, I think, with such as, in
the conditions of freedom and of self-government which
they demand for their life, are most like ourselves. Germany, for instance, we shall less regard, because the
conditions which the Germans seem to accept for their
life are so unlike what we demand for ours; there is so
much personal government there, so much *junkerism,*
militarism, officialism; the community is so much more
trained to submission than we could bear, so much more
used to be, as the popular phrase is, sat upon. Countries
where the community has more a will of its own, or
can more show it, are the most important for our present
purpose,—such countries as Belgium, Holland, Italy,
Switzerland. Well, Belgium adopts purely and simply,
as to bequest and inheritance, the provisions of the
Code Napoléon. Holland adopts them purely and simply. Italy has adopted them substantially. Switzerland
is a republic, where the general feeling against inequality is strong, and where it might seem less necessary,
therefore, to guard against inequality by interfering with
the power of bequest. Each Swiss canton has its own
law of bequest. In Geneva, Vaud, and Zurich,—perhaps
the three most distinguished cantons,—the law is identical with that of France. In Berne, one-third is the fixed

proportion which a man is free to dispose of by will; the rest of his property must go among his children equally. In all the other cantons there are regulations of a like kind. Germany, I was saying, will interest us less than these freer countries. In Germany,—though there is not the English freedom of bequest, but the rule of the Roman law prevails, the rule obliging the parent to assign a certain portion to each child,—in Germany entails and settlements in favour of an eldest son are generally permitted. But there is a remarkable exception. The Rhine countries, which in the early part of this century were under French rule, and which then received the *Code Napoléon,* these countries refused to part with it when they were restored to Germany; and to this day Rhenish Prussia, Rhenish Hesse, and Baden, have the French law of bequest, forbidding entails, and dividing property in the way we have seen.

The United States of America have the English liberty of bequest. But the United States are, like Switzerland, a republic, with the republican sentiment for equality. Theirs is, besides, a new society; it did not inherit the system of classes and property which feudalism established in Europe. The class by which the United States were settled was not a class with feudal habits and ideas. It is notorious that to acquire great landed estates and to entail them upon an eldest son, is neither the practice nor the desire of any class in America. I remember hearing it said to an American in England: "But, after all, you have the same freedom of bequest and inheritance as we have, and if a man to-morrow chose in your country to entail a great landed estate rigorously, what could you do?" The American answered: "Set aside the will on the ground of insanity."

You see we are in a manner taking the votes for and against equality. We ought not to leave out our own colonies. In general they are, of course, like the United States of America, new societies. They have the English liberty of bequest. But they have no feudal past, and were not settled by a class with feudal habits and ideas. Nevertheless it happens that there have arisen, in Australia, exceedingly large estates, and that the proprietors seek to keep them together. And what have we seen happen lately? An Act has been passed which in effect inflicts a fine upon every proprietor who holds a landed estate of more than a certain value. The measure has been severely blamed in England; to Mr. Lowe such a "concession to the cry for equality" appears, as we might expect, pregnant with warnings. At present I neither praise it nor blame it; I simply count it as one of the votes for equality. And is it not a singular thing, I ask you, that while we have the religion of inequality, and can hardly bear to hear equality spoken of, there should be, among the nations of Europe which have politically most in common with us, and in the United States of America, and in our own colonies, this diseased appetite, as we must think it, for equality? Perhaps Lord Beaconsfield may not have turned your minds to this subject as he turned mine, and what Menander or George Sand happens to have said may not interest you much; yet surely, when you think of it, when you see what a practical revolt against inequality there is amongst so many people not so very unlike to ourselves, you must feel some curiosity to sift the matter a little further, and may be not ill-disposed to follow me while I try to do so.

I have received a letter from Clerkenwell, in which the writer reproaches me for lecturing about equality at this which he calls "the most aristocratic and exclusive place out." I am here because your secretary invited me. But I am glad to treat the subject of equality before such an audience as this. Some of you may remember that I have roughly divided our English society into Barbarians, Philistines, Populace, each of them with their prepossessions, and loving to hear what gratifies them. But I remarked at the same time, that scattered throughout all these classes were a certain number of generous and humane souls, lovers of man's perfection, detached from the prepossessions of the class to which they might naturally belong, and desirous that he who speaks to them should, as Plato says, not try to please his fellow-servants, but his true and legitimate master—the heavenly Gods. I feel sure that among the members and frequenters of an institution like this, such humane souls are apt to congregate in numbers. Even from the reproach which my Clerkenwell friend brings against you of being too aristocratic, I derive some comfort. Only I give to the term *aristocratic* a rather wide extension. An accomplished American, much known and much esteemed in this country, the late Mr. Charles Sumner, says that what particularly struck him in England was the large class of gentlemen as distinct from the nobility, and the abundance amongst them of serious knowledge, high accomplishment, and refined taste,—taste fastidious perhaps, says Mr. Sumner, to excess, but erring on virtue's side. And he goes on: "I do not know that there is much difference between the manners and social observances of the highest classes of England and those of the corresponding classes of France and Germany; but in the rank immediately below the highest,—as among the professions, or military men, or literary men,—there you will find that the Englishmen have the advantage. They are better educated and better bred, more careful in their personal habits and in social conventions, more refined." Mr. Sumner's remark is just and important; this large class of gentlemen in the professions, the services, literature, politics,—and a good contingent is now added from business also,—this large class, not of the nobility, but with the accomplishments and taste of an upper class, is something peculiar to England. Of this class I may probably assume that my present audience is in large measure composed. It is aristocratic in this sense, that it has the tastes of a cultivated class, a certain high standard of civilisation. Well, it is in its effects upon *civilisation* that equality interests me. And I speak to an audience with a high standard of civilisation. If I say that certain things in certain classes do not come up to a high standard of civilisation, I need not prove how and why they do not; you will feel instinctively whether they do or no. If they do not, I need not prove that this is a bad thing, that a high standard of civilisation is desirable; you will instinctively feel that it is. Instead of calling this "the most aristocratic and exclusive place out," I conceive of it as a *civilised* place; and in speaking about civilisation half one's labour is saved when one speaks about it among those who are civilised.

Politics are forbidden here; but equality is not a question of English politics. The abstract right to equality may, indeed, be a question of speculative politics. French equality appeals to this abstract natural right as its support. It goes back to a state of nature where all were equal, and supposes that "the poor consented," as Rousseau says, "to the existence of rich people," reserving always a natural right to return to the state of nature. It supposes that a child has a natural right to his equal share in his father's goods. The principle of abstract right, says Mr. Lowe, has never been admitted in England, and is false. I so entirely agree with him, that I run no risk of offending by discussing equality upon the basis of this principle. So far as I can sound human

consciousness, I cannot, as I have often said, perceive
that man is really conscious of any abstract natural rights
at all. The natural right to have work found for one to
do, the natural right to have food found for one to eat—
rights sometimes so confidently and so indignantly asserted—seem to me quite baseless. It cannot be too
often repeated: peasants and workmen have no natural
rights, not one. Only we ought instantly to add, that
kings and nobles have none either. If it is the sound English doctrine that all rights are created by law and are
based on expediency, and are alterable as the public
advantage may require, certainly that orthodox doctrine
is mine. Property is created and maintained by law. It
would disappear in that state of private war and scram-
ble which legal society supersedes. Legal society creates,
for the common good, the right of property; and for the
common good that right is by legal society limitable.
That property should exist, and that it should be held
with a sense of security and with a power of disposal,
may be taken, by us here at any rate, as a settled matter
of expediency. With these conditions a good deal of inequality is inevitable. But that the power of disposal
should be practically *unlimited,* that the inequality
should be *enormous,* or that the degree of inequality admitted at one time should be admitted *always,*—this is
by no means so certain. The right of bequest was in
early times, as Sir Henry Maine and Mr. Mill have
pointed out, seldom recognised. In later times it has
been limited in many countries in the way that we have
seen; even in England itself it is not formally quite unlimited. The question is one of expediency. It is assumed, I grant, with great unanimity amongst us, that
our signal inequality of classes and property is expedient
for our civilisation and welfare. But this assumption, of

which the distinguished personages who adopt it seem
so sure that they think it needless to produce grounds
for it, is just what we have to examine.

Now, there is a sentence of Sir Erskine May, whom
I have already quoted, which will bring us straight to
the very point that I wish to raise. Sir Erskine May, after
saying, as you have heard, that France has pursued
social equality, and has come to fearful troubles, demoralisation, and intellectual stoppage by doing so, continues thus: "Yet is she high, if not the first, in the·scale
of civilised nations." Why, here is a curious thing, surely!
A nation pursues social equality, supposed to be an
utterly false and baneful ideal; it arrives, as might have
been expected, at fearful misery and deterioration by
doing so; and yet, at the same time, it is high, if not
the first, in the scale of civilised nations. What do we
mean by *civilised*? Sir Erskine May does not seem to
have asked himself the question, so we will try to answer
it for ourselves. Civilisation is the humanisation of man
in society. To be humanised is to comply with the true
law of our human nature: *servare modum, finemque
tenere, Naturamque sequi,* says Lucan; "to keep our
measure, and to hold fast our end, and to follow Nature." To be humanised is to make progress towards this,
our true and full humanity. And to be civilised is to
make progress towards this in civil society; in that civil
society "without which," says Burke, "man could not by
any possibility arrive at the perfection of which his nature is capable, nor even make a remote and faint approach to it." To be the most civilised of nations, therefore, is to be the nation which comes nearest to human
perfection, in the state which that perfection essentially
demands. And a nation which has been brought by the
pursuit of social equality to moral deterioration, intel-

lectual stoppage, and fearful troubles, is perhaps the nation which has come nearest to human perfection in
that state which such perfection essentially demands!
Michelet himself, who would deny the demoralisation
and the stoppage, and call the fearful troubles a sublime expiation for the sins of the whole world, could
hardly say more for France than this. Certainly Sir
Erskine May never intended to say so much. But into
what a difficulty has he somehow run himself, and what
a good action would it be to extricate him from it! Let
us see whether the performance of that good action may
not also be a way of clearing our minds as to the uses
of equality.

When we talk of man's advance towards his full humanity, we think of an advance, not along one line only,
but several. Certain races and nations, as we know, are
on certain lines pre-eminent and representative. The
Hebrew nation was pre-eminent on one great line.
"What nation," it was justly asked by their lawgiver,
"hath statutes and judgments so righteous as the law
which I set before you this day? Keep therefore and do
them; for this is your wisdom and your understanding
in the sight of the nations which shall hear all these
statutes and say: Surely this great nation is a wise and
understanding people!" The Hellenic race was pre-
eminent on other lines. Isocrates could say of Athens:
"Our city has left the rest of the world so far behind
in philosophy and eloquence, that those educated by
Athens have become the teachers of the rest of mankind;
and so well has she done her part, that the name of
Greeks seems no longer to stand for a race but to stand
for intelligence itself, and they who share in our culture
are called Greeks even before those who are merely of
our own blood." The power of intellect and science, the
power of beauty, the power of social life and manners,

—these are what Greece so felt, and fixed, and may stand for. They are great elements in our humanisation. The power of conduct is another great element; and this was so felt and fixed by Israel that we can never with justice refuse to permit Israel, in spite of all his shortcomings, to stand for it.

So you see that in being humanised we have to move along several lines, and that on certain lines certain nations find their strength and take a lead. We may elucidate the thing yet further. Nations now existing may be said to feel or to have felt the power of this or that element in our humanisation so signally that they are characterised by it. No one who knows this country would deny that it is characterised, in a remarkable degree, by a sense of the power of conduct. Our feeling for religion is one part of this; our industry is another. What foreigners so much remark in us,—our public spirit, our love, amidst all our liberty, for public order and for stability, —are parts of it too. Then the power of beauty was so felt by the Italians that their art revived, as we know, the almost lost idea of beauty, and the serious and successful pursuit of it. Cardinal Antonelli, speaking to me about the education of the common people in Rome, said that they were illiterate indeed, but whoever mingled with them at any public show, and heard them pass judgment on the beauty or ugliness of what came before them,—"è brutto," "è bello,"—would find that their judgment agreed admirably, in general, with just what the most cultivated people would say. Even at the present time, then, the Italians are pre-eminent in feeling the power of beauty. The power of knowledge, in the same way, is eminently an influence with the Germans. This by no means implies, as is sometimes supposed, a high and fine general culture. What it implies is a strong sense of the necessity of knowing scien-

tifically, as the expression is, the things which have to be known by us; of knowing them systematically, by the regular and right process, and in the only real way. And this sense the Germans especially have. Finally, there is the power of social life and manners. And even the Athenians themselves, perhaps, have hardly felt this power so much as the French.

Voltaire, in a famous passage where he extols the age of Louis the Fourteenth and ranks it with the chief epochs in the civilisation of our race, has to specify the gift bestowed on us by the age of Louis the Fourteenth, as the age of Pericles, for instance, bestowed on us its art and literature, and the Italian Renascence its revival of art and literature. And Voltaire shows all his acuteness in fixing on the gift to name. It is not the sort of gift which we expect to see named. The great gift of the age of Louis the Fourteenth to the world, says Voltaire, was this: *l'esprit de société,* the spirit of society, the social spirit. And another French writer, looking for the good points in the old French nobility, remarks that this at any rate is to be said in their favour: they established a high and charming ideal of social intercourse and manners, for a nation formed to profit by such an ideal, and which has profited by it ever since. And in America, perhaps, we see the disadvantages of having social equality before there has been any such high standard of social life and manners formed.

We are not disposed in England, most of us, to attach all this importance to social intercourse and manners. Yet Burke says: "There ought to be a system of manners in every nation which a well-formed mind would be disposed to relish." And the power of social life and manners is truly, as we have seen, one of the great elements in our humanisation. Unless we have cultivated it, we are incomplete. The impulse for cultivating it is not, indeed, a moral impulse. It is by no means identical with the moral impulse to help our neighbour and to do him good. Yet in many ways it works to a like end. It brings men together, makes them feel the need of one another, be considerate of one another, understand one another. But, above all things, it is a promoter of equality. It is by the humanity of their manners that men are made equal. "A man thinks to show himself my equal," says Goethe, "by being *grob*,—that is to say, coarse and rude; he does not show himself my equal, he shows himself *grob*." But a community having humane manners is a community of equals, and in such a community great social inequalities have really no meaning, while they are at the same time a menace and an embarrassment to perfect ease of social intercourse. A community with the spirit of society is eminently, therefore, a community with the spirit of equality. A nation with a genius for society, like the French or the Athenians, is irresistibly drawn towards equality. From the first moment when the French people, with its congenital sense for the power of social intercourse and manners, came into existence, it was on the road to equality. When it had once got a high standard of social manners abundantly established, and at the same time the natural, material necessity for the feudal inequality of classes and property pressed upon it no longer, the French people introduced equality and made the French Revolution. It was not the spirit of philanthropy which mainly impelled the French to that Revolution, neither was it the spirit of envy, neither was it the love of abstract ideas, though all these did something towards it; but what did most was the spirit of society.

The well-being of the many comes out more and more distinctly, in proportion as time goes on, as the object we must pursue. An individual or a class, concentrating their efforts upon their own well-being exclusively, do but beget troubles both for others and for themselves also. No individual life can be truly prosperous, passed, as Obermann says, in the midst of men who suffer; *passée au milieu des générations qui souffrent*. To the noble soul, it cannot be happy; to the ignoble, it cannot be secure. Socialistic and communistic schemes have generally, however, a fatal defect; they are content with too low and material a standard of well-being. That instinct of perfection, which is the master-power in humanity, always rebels at this, and frustrates the work. Many are to be made partakers of well-being, true; but the ideal of well-being is not to be, on that account, lowered and coarsened. M. de Laveleye, the political economist, who is a Belgian and a Protestant, and whose testimony therefore we may the more readily take about France, says that France, being the country of Europe where the soil is more divided than anywhere except in Switzerland and Norway, is at the same time the country where material well-being is most widely spread, where wealth has of late years increased most, and where population is least outrunning the limits which, for the comfort and progress of the working classes themselves, seem necessary. This may go for a good deal. It supplies an answer to what Sir Erskine May says about the bad effects of equality upon French prosperity. But I will quote to you from Mr. Hamerton what goes, I think, for yet more. Mr. Hamerton is an excellent observer and reporter, and has lived for many years in France. He says of the French peasantry that they are exceedingly ignorant. So they are. But he adds: "They. are at the same time full of intelligence; their manners are excellent, they have delicate perceptions, they have tact, they have a certain refinement which a brutalised peasantry could not possibly have. If you talk to one of them at his own home, or in his field, he will enter into conversation with you quite easily, and sustain his part in a perfectly becoming way, with a pleasant combination of dignity and quiet humour. The interval between him and a Kentish labourer is enormous."

This is indeed worth your attention. Of course all mankind are, as Mr. Gladstone says, of our own flesh and blood. But you know how often it happens in England that a cultivated person, a person of the sort that Mr. Charles Sumner describes, talking to one of the lower class, or even of the middle class, feels, and cannot but feel, that there is somehow a wall of partition between himself and the other, that they seem to belong to two different worlds. Thoughts, feelings, perceptions, susceptibilities, language, manners,—everything is different. Whereas, with a French peasant, the most cultivated man may find himself in sympathy, may feel that he is talking to an equal. This is an experience which has been made a thousand times, and which may be made again any day. And it may be carried beyond the range of mere conversation, it may be extended to things like pleasures, recreations, eating and drinking, and so on. In general the pleasures, recreations, ·eating and drinking of English people, when once you get below that class which Mr. Charles Sumner calls the class of gentlemen, are to one of that class unpalatable and impossible. In France there is not this incompatibility. Whether he mix with high or low, the gentleman feels himself in a world not alien or repulsive, but a world where people make the same sort of demands upon life, ·in things of this sort, which he himself does. In all these respects France is the country where the people, as distinguished from a wealthy refined class, most lives what we call a humane life, the life of civilised man.

Of course, fastidious persons can and do pick holes

in it. There is just now, in France, a *noblesse* newly revived, full of pretension, full of airs and graces and disdains; but its sphere is narrow, and out of its own sphere no one cares very much for it. There is a general equality in a humane kind of life. This is the secret of the passionate attachment with which France inspires all Frenchmen, in spite of her fearful troubles, her checked prosperity, her disconnected units, and the rest of it. There is so much of the goodness and agreeableness of life there, and for so many. It is the secret of her having been able to attach so ardently to her the German and Protestant people of Alsace, while we have been so little able to attach the Celtic and Catholic people of Ireland. France brings the Alsatians into a social system so full of the goodness and agreeableness of life; we offer to the Irish no such attraction. It is the secret, finally, of the prevalence which we have remarked in other continental countries of a legislation tending, like that of France, to social equality. The social system which equality creates in France is, in the eyes of others, such a giver of the goodness and agreeableness of life, that they seek to get the goodness by getting the equality.

Yet France has had her fearful troubles, as Sir Erskine May justly says. She suffers too, he adds, from demoralisation and intellectual stoppage. Let us admit, if he likes, this to be true also. His error is that he attributes all this to equality. Equality, as we have seen, has brought France to a really admirable and enviable pitch of humanisation in one important line. And this, the work of equality, is so much a good in Sir Erskine May's eyes, that he has mistaken it for the whole of which it is a part, frankly identifies it with civilisation, and is inclined to pronounce France the most civilised of nations.

But we have seen how much goes to full humanisation, to true civilisation, besides the power of social life and manners. There is the power of conduct, the power of intellect and knowledge, the power of beauty. The power of conduct is the greatest of all. And without in the least wishing to preach, I must observe, as a mere matter of natural fact and experience, that for the power of conduct France has never had anything like the same sense which she has had for the power of social life and manners. Michelet, himself a Frenchman, gives us the reason why the Reformation did not succeed in France. It did not succeed, he says, because *la France ne voulait pas de réforme morale*—moral reform France would not have; and the Reformation was above all a moral movement. The sense in France for the power of conduct has not greatly deepened, I think, since. The sense for the power of intellect and knowledge has not been adequate either. The sense for beauty has not been adequate. Intelligence and beauty have been, in general, but so far reached, as they can be and are reached by men who, of the elements of perfect humanisation, lay thorough hold upon one only,—the power of social intercourse and manners. I speak of France in general; she has had, and she has, individuals who stand out and who form exceptions. Well then, if a nation laying no sufficient hold upon the powers of beauty and knowledge, and a most failing and feeble hold upon the power of conduct, comes to demoralisation and intellectual stoppage and fearful troubles, we need not be inordinately surprised. What we should rather marvel at is the healing and bountiful operation of Nature, whereby the laying firm hold on one real element in our humanisation has had for France results so beneficent.

And thus, when Sir Erskine May gets bewildered between France's equality and fearful troubles on the one hand, and the civilisation of France on the other, let us suggest to him that perhaps he is bewildered by his data because he combines them ill. France has not exemplary disaster and ruin as the fruits of equality, and at the same time, and independently of this, an exemplary civilisation. She has a large measure of happiness and success as the fruits of equality, and she has a very large measure of dangers and troubles as the fruits of something else.

We have more to do, however, than to help Sir Erskine May out of his scrape about France. We have to see whether the considerations which we have been employing may not be of use to us about England.

We shall not have much difficulty in admitting whatever good is to be said of ourselves, and we will try not to be unfair by excluding all that is not so favourable. Indeed, our less favourable side is the one which we should be the most anxious to note, in order that we may mend it. But we will begin with the good. Our people has energy and honesty as its good characteristics. We have a strong sense for the chief power in the life and progress of man,—the power of conduct. So far we speak of the English people as a whole. Then we have a rich, refined, and splendid aristocracy. And we have, according to Mr. Charles Sumner's acute and true remark, a class of gentlemen, not of the nobility, but well-bred, cultivated, and refined, larger than is to be found in any other country. For these last we have Mr. Sumner's testimony. As to the splendour of our aristocracy, all the world is agreed. Then we have a middle class and a lower class; and they, after all, are the immense bulk of the nation.

Let us see how the civilisation of these classes appears to a Frenchman, who has witnessd, in his own country, the considerable humanisation of these classes by equality. To such an observer our middle class divides itself into a serious portion and a gay or rowdy portion; both are a marvel to him. With the gay or rowdy portion we need not much concern ourselves; we shall figure it to our minds sufficiently if we conceive it as the source of that war-song produced in these recent days of excitement:

> We don't want to fight, but by jingo, if we do,
> We've got the ships, we've got the men, and we've got
> the money too.

We may also partly judge its standard of life, and the needs of its nature, by the modern English theatre, perhaps the most contemptible in Europe. But the real strength of the English middle class is in its serious portion. And of this a Frenchman, who was here some little time ago as the correspondent, I think, of the *Siècle* newspaper, and whose letters were afterwards published in a volume, writes as follows. He had been attending some of the Moody and Sankey meetings, and he says: "To understand the success of Messrs. Moody and Sankey, one must be familiar with English manners, one must know the mind-deadening influence of a narrow Biblism, one must have experienced the sense of acute ennui, which the aspect and the frequentation of this great division of English society produce in others, the want of elasticity and the chronic ennui which characterise this class itself, petrified in a narrow Protestantism and in a perpetual reading of the Bible."

You know the French;—a little more Biblism, one may take leave to say, would do them no harm. But an audience like this,—and here, as I said, is the advantage of an audience like this,—will have no difficulty in admitting the amount of truth which there is in the Frenchman's picture. It is the picture of a class which, driven by its sense for the power of conduct, in the beginning of the seventeenth century entered,—as I have more than once said, and as I may more than once have occasion in future to say,—*entered the prison of Puritanism, and had the key turned upon its spirit there for two hundred years.* They did not know, good and earnest people as they were, that to the building up of human life there belong all those other powers also,— the power of intellect and knowledge, the power of beauty, the power of social life and manners. And something, by what they became, they gained, and the whole nation with them; they deepened and fixed for this nation the sense of conduct. But they created a type of life and manners, of which they themselves indeed are slow to recognise the faults, but which is fatally condemned by its hideousness, its immense ennui, and against which the instinct of self-preservation in humanity rebels.

Partisans fight against facts in vain. Mr. Goldwin Smith, a writer of eloquence and power, although too prone to acerbity, is a partisan of the Puritans, and of the Noncomformists who are the special inheritors of the Puritan tradition. He angrily resents the imputation upon that Puritan type of life, by which the life of our serious middle class has been formed, that it was doomed to hideousness, to immense ennui. He protests that it had beauty, amenity, accomplishment. Let us go to facts. Charles the First, who, with all his faults, had the just idea that art and letters are great civilisers, made, as you know, a famous collection of pictures,—our first National Gallery. It was, I suppose, the best collection at that time north of the Alps. It contained nine Raphaels, eleven Correggios, twenty-eight Titians. What became of that collection? The journals of the House of Commons will tell you. There you may see the Puritan Parliament disposing of this Whitehall or York House collection as follows: "Ordered, that all such pictures and statues there as are without any superstition, shall be forthwith sold. . . . Ordered, that all such pictures there as have the representation of the Second Person in Trinity upon them, shall be forthwith burnt. Ordered, that all such pictures there as have the representation of the Virgin Mary upon them, shall be forthwith burnt." There we have the weak side of our parliamentary government and our serious middle class. We are incapable of sending Mr. Gladstone to be tried at the Old Bailey because he proclaims his antipathy to Lord Beaconsfield. A majority in our House of Commons is incapable of hailing, with frantic laughter and applause, a string of indecent jests against Christianity and its Founder. But we are not, or were not, incapable of producing a Parliament which burns or sells the masterpieces of Italian art. And one may surely say of such a Puritan Parliament, and of those who determine its line for it, that they had not the spirit of beauty.

What shall we say of amenity? Milton was born a humanist, but the Puritan temper, as we know, mastered him. There is nothing more unlovely and unamiable than Milton the Puritan disputant. Some one answers his *Doctrine and Discipline of Divorce*. "I mean not," rejoins Milton, "to dispute philosophy with this pork, who never read any." However, he does reply to him, and throughout the reply Milton's great joke is, that his adversary, who was anonymous, is a serving-man. "Finally, he winds up his text with much doubt and trepidation; for it may be his trenchers were not scraped, and that which never yet afforded corn of favour to his noddle,—the salt-cellar,—was not rubbed; and therefore, in this haste, easily granting that his answers fall foul upon each other, and praying you would not think he writes as a prophet, but as a man, he runs to the black jack, fills his flagon, spreads the table, and serves up dinner." There you have the same spirit of urbanity and amenity, as much of it, and as little, as generally informs the religious controversies of our Puritan middle class to this day.

But Mr. Goldwin Smith insists, and picks out his own exemplar of the Puritan type of life and manners; and even here let us follow him. He picks out the most favourable specimen he can find,—Colonel Hutchinson, whose well-known memoirs, written by his widow, we have all read with interest. "Lucy Hutchinson," says Mr. Goldwin Smith, "is painting what she thought a perfect Puritan would be; and her picture presents to us not a coarse, crop-eared, and snuffling fanatic, but a highly accomplished, refined, gallant, and most amiable, though religious and seriously minded, gentleman." Let us, I say, in this example of Mr. Goldwin Smith's own choosing, lay our finger upon the points where this type deflects from the truly humane ideal.

Mrs. Hutchinson relates a story which gives us a good notion of what the amiable and accomplished social intercourse, even of a picked Puritan family, was. Her husband was governor of Nottingham. He had occasion, she says, "to go and break up a private meeting in the cannoneer's chamber"; and in the cannoneer's chamber "were found some notes concerning pædobaptism, which, being brought into the governor's lodgings, his wife having perused them and compared them with the Scriptures, found not what to say against the truths they asserted concerning the misapplication of that ordinance to infants." Soon afterwards she expects her confinement, and communicates the cannoneer's doubts about pædobaptism to her husband. The fatal cannoneer makes a breach in him too. "Then he bought and read all the eminent treatises on both sides, which at that time came thick from the presses, and still was cleared in the error of the pædobaptists." Finally, Mrs. Hutchinson is confined. Then the governor "invited all the ministers to dinner, and propounded his doubt and the ground thereof to them. None of them could defend their practice with any satisfactory reason, but the tradition of the Church from the primitive times, and their main buckler of federal holiness, which Tombs and Denne had excellently overthrown. He and his wife then, professing themselves unsatisfied, desired their opinions." With the opinions I will not trouble you, but hasten to the result: "Whereupon that infant was not baptized."

No doubt to a large division of English society at this very day, that sort of dinner and discussion, and, indeed, the whole manner of life and conversation here suggested by Mrs. Hutchinson's narrative, will seem both natural and amiable, and such as to meet the needs of man as a religious and social creature. You know the conversation which reigns in thousands of middle-class families at this hour, about nunneries, teetotalism, the confessional, eternal punishment, ritualism, disestablishment. It goes wherever the class goes which is moulded on the Puritan type of life. In the long winter evenings of Toronto Mr. Goldwin Smith has had, probably, abundant experience of it. What is its enemy? The instinct of self-preservation in humanity. Men make crude types and try to impose them, but to no purpose. "*L'homme s'agite, Dieu le mène*," says Bossuet. "There are many devices in a man's heart; nevertheless the counsel of the Eternal, that shall stand." Those who offer us the Puritan type of life offer us a religion not true, the claims of intellect and knowledge not satisfied, the claim of beauty not satisfied, the claim of manners not satisfied. In its strong sense for conduct that life touches truth; but its other imperfections hinder it from employing even this sense aright. The type mastered our nation for a time. Then came the reaction. The nation said: "This type, at any rate, is amiss; we are not going to be all like *that!*" The type retired into our middle class, and fortified itself there. It seeks to endure, to emerge, to deny its own imperfections, to impose itself again;—impossible! If we continue to live, we must outgrow it. The very class in which it is rooted, our middle class, will have to acknowledge the type's inadequacy, will have to acknowledge the hideousness, the immense ennui of the life which this type has created, will have to transform itself thoroughly. It will have to admit the large part of truth which there is in the criticisms of our Frenchman, whom we have too long forgotten.

After our middle class he turns his attention to our lower class. And of the lower and larger portion of this, the portion not bordering on the middle class and sharing its faults, he says: "I consider this multitude to be absolutely devoid, not only of political principles, but even of the most simple notions of good and evil. Certainly it does not appeal, this mob, to the principles of '89, which you English make game of; it does not insist on the rights of man; what it wants is beer, gin, and *fun.*" [1]

That is a description of what Mr. Bright would call the residuum, only our author seems to think the residuum a very large body. And its condition strikes him with amazement and horror. And surely well it may. Let us recall Mr. Hamerton's account of the most illiterate class in France; what an amount of civilisation they have notwithstanding! And this is always to be understood, in hearing or reading a Frenchman's praise of England. He envies our liberty, our public spirit, our trade, our stability. But there is always a reserve in his mind. He never

[1] So in the original. (Arnold's note.)

means for a moment that he would like to change with us. Life seems to him so much better a thing in France for so many more people, that, in spite of the fearful troubles of France, it is best to be a Frenchman. A Frenchman might agree with Mr. Cobden, that life is good in England for those people who have at least £5000 a year. But the civilisation of that immense majority who have not £5000 a year, or £500, or even £100,—of our middle and lower class,—seems to him too deplorable.

And now what has this condition of our middle and lower class to tell us about equality? How is it, must we not ask, how is it that, being without fearful troubles, having so many achievements to show and so much success, having as a nation a deep sense for conduct, having signal energy and honesty, having a splendid aristocracy, having an exceptionally large class of gentlemen, we are yet so little civilised? How is it that our middle and lower classes, in spite of the individuals among them who are raised by happy gifts of nature to a more humane life, in spite of the seriousness of the middle class, in spite of the honesty and power of true work, the *virtus verusque labor,* which are to be found in abundance throughout the lower, do yet present, as a whole, the characters which we have seen?

And really it seems as if the current of our discourse carried us of itself to but one conclusion. It seems as if we could not avoid concluding, that just as France owes her fearful troubles to other things and her civilisedness to equality, so we owe our immunity from fearful troubles to other things, and our uncivilisedness to inequality. "Knowledge is easy," says the wise man, "to him that understandeth"; easy, he means, to him who will use his mind simply and rationally, and not to make him think he can know what he cannot, or to maintain, *per fas et nefas,* a false thesis with which he fancies his interests to be bound up. And to him who will use his mind as the wise man recommends, surely it is easy to see that our shortcomings in civilisation are due to our inequality; or in other words, that the great inequality of classes and property, which came to us from the Middle Age and which we maintain because we have the religion of inequality, that this constitution of things, I say, has the natural and necessary effect, under present circumstances, of materialising our upper class, vulgarising our middle class, and brutalising our lower class. And this is to fail in civilisation.

For only just look how the facts combine themselves. I have said little as yet about our aristocratic class, except that it is splendid. Yet these, "our often very unhappy brethren," as Burke calls them, are by no means matter for nothing but ecstasy. Our charity ought certainly, Burke says, to "extend a due and anxious sensation of pity to the distresses of the miserable great." Burke's extremely strong language about their miseries and defects I will not quote. For my part, I am always disposed to marvel that human beings, in a position so false, should be so good as these are. Their reason for existing was to serve as a number of centres in a world disintegrated after the ruin of the Roman Empire, and slowly re-constituting itself. Numerous centres of material force were needed, and these a feudal aristocracy supplied. Their large and hereditary estates served this public end. The owners had a positive function, for which their estates were essential. In our modern world the function is gone; and the great estates, with an infinitely multiplied power of ministering to mere pleasure and indulgence, remain. The energy and honesty of our race does not leave itself without witness in this class, and nowhere are there more conspicuous examples of

individuals raised by happy gifts of nature far above
their fellows and their circumstances. For distinction
of all kinds this class has an esteem. Everything which
succeeds they tend to welcome, to win over, to put on
their side; genius may generally make, if it will, not bad
terms for itself with them. But the total result of the
class, its effect on society at large and on national progress, are what we must regard. And on the whole, with
no necessary function to fulfil, never conversant with
life as it really is, tempted, flattered, and spoiled from
childhood to old age, our aristocratic class is inevitably
materialised, and the more so the more the development
of industry and ingenuity augments the means of luxury. Every one can see how bad is the action of such
an aristocracy upon the class of newly enriched people,
whose great danger is a materialistic ideal, just because
it is the ideal they can easiest comprehend. Nor is the
mischief of this action now compensated by signal services of a public kind. Turn even to that sphere which
aristocracies think specially their own, and where they
have under other circumstances been really effective,—
the sphere of politics. When there is need, as now, for
any large forecast of the course of human affairs, for an
acquaintance with the ideas which in the end sway mankind, and for an estimate of their power, aristocracies
are out of their element, and materialised aristocracies
most of all. In the immense spiritual movement of our
day, the English aristocracy, as I have elsewhere said,
always reminds me of Pilate confronting the phenomenon of Christianity. Nor can a materialised class have
any serious and fruitful sense for the power of beauty.
They may imagine themselves to be in pursuit of
beauty; but how often, alas, does the pursuit come to
little more than dabbling a little in what they are

pleased to call art, and making a great deal of what
they are pleased to call love!

Let us return to their merits. For the power of manners an aristocratic class, whether materialised or not,
will always, from its circumstances, have a strong sense.
And although for this power of social life and manners,
so important to civilisation, our English race has no special natural turn, in our aristocracy this power emerges
and marks them. When the day of general humanisation
comes, they will have fixed the standard of manners.
The English simplicity, too, makes the best of the English aristocracy more frank and natural than the best of
the like class anywhere else, and even the worst of them
it makes free from the incredible fatuities and absurd-
ities of the worst. Then the sense of conduct they share
with their countrymen at large. In no class has it such
trials to undergo; in none is it more often and more
grievously overborne. But really the right comment on
this is the comment of Pepys upon the evil courses of
Charles the Second and the Duke of York and the court
of that day: "At all which I am sorry; but it is the effect
of idleness, and having nothing else to employ their
great spirits upon."

Heaven forbid that I should speak in dispraise of that
unique and most English class which Mr. Charles
Sumner extols—the large class of gentlemen, not of the
landed class or of the nobility, but cultivated and refined.
They are a seemly product of the energy and of the
power to rise in our race. Without, in general, rank and
splendour and wealth and luxury to polish them, they
have made their own the high standard of life and manners of an aristocratic and refined class. Not having all
the dissipations and distractions of this class, they are
much more seriously alive to the power of intellect and

knowledge, to the power of beauty. The sense of conduct, too, meets with fewer trials in this class. To some extent, however, their contiguousness to the aristocratic class has now the effect of materialising them, as it does the class of newly enriched people. The most palpable action is on the young amongst them, and on their standard of life and enjoyment. But in general, for this whole class, established facts, the materialism which they see regnant, too much block their mental horizon, and limit the possibilities of things to them. They are deficient in openness and flexibility of mind, in free play of ideas, in faith and ardour. Civilised they are, but they are not much of a civilising force; they are somehow bounded and ineffective.

So on the middle class they produce singularly little effect. What the middle class sees is that splendid piece of materialism, the aristocratic class, with a wealth and luxury utterly out of their reach, with a standard of social life and manners, the offspring of that wealth and luxury, seeming utterly out of their reach also. And thus they are thrown back upon themselves—upon a defective type of religion, a narrow range of intellect and knowledge, a stunted sense of beauty, a low standard of manners. And the lower class see before them the aristocratic class, and its civilisation, such as it is, even infinitely more out of *their* reach than out of that of the middle class; while the life of the middle class, with its unlovely types of religion, thought, beauty, and manners, has naturally, in general, no great attractions for them either. And so they too are thrown back upon themselves; upon their beer, their gin, and their *fun*. Now, then, you will understand what I meant by saying that our inequality materialises our upper class, vulgarises our middle class, brutalises our lower.

And the greater the inequality the more marked is

its bad action upon the middle and lower classes. In Scotland the landed aristocracy fills the scene, as is well known, still more than in England; the other classes are more squeezed back and effaced. And the social civilisation of the lower middle class and of the poorest class, in Scotland, is an example of the consequences. Compared with the same class even in England, the Scottish lower middle class is most visibly, to vary Mr. Charles Sumner's phrase, *less* well-bred, *less* careful in personal habits and in social conventions, *less* refined. Let any one who doubts it go, after issuing from the aristocratic solitudes which possess Loch Lomond, let him go and observe the shopkeepers and the middle class in Dumbarton, and Greenock, and Gourock, and the places along the mouth of the Clyde. And for the poorest class, who that has seen it can ever forget the hardly human horror, the abjection and uncivilisedness of Glasgow?

What a strange religion, then, is our religion of inequality! Romance often helps a religion to hold its ground, and romance is good in its way; but ours is not even a romantic religion. No doubt our aristocracy is an object of very strong public interest. The *Times* itself bestows a leading article by way of epithalamium on the Duke of Norfolk's marriage. And those journals of a new type, full of talent, and which interest me particularly because they seem as if they were written by the young lion of our youth,—the young lion grown mellow and, as the French say, *viveur,* arrived at his full and ripe knowledge of the world, and minded to enjoy the smooth evening of his days,—those journals, in the main a sort of social gazette of the aristocracy, are apparently not read by that class only which they most concern, but are read with great avidity by other classes also. And the common people too have undoubtedly, as Mr. Gladstone says, a wonderful preference for a lord. Yet our aristocracy, from the action upon it of the Wars of the Roses, the Tudors, and the political necessities of George the Third, is for the imagination a singularly modern and uninteresting one. Its splendour of station, its wealth, show, and luxury, is then what the other classes really admire in it; and this is not an elevating admiration. Such an admiration will never lift us out of our vulgarity and brutality, if we chance to be vulgar and brutal to start with; it will rather feed them and be fed by them. So that when Mr. Gladstone invites us to call our love of inequality "the complement of the love of freedom or its negative pole, or the shadow which the love of freedom casts, or the reverberation of its voice in the halls of the constitution," we must surely answer that all this mystical eloquence is not in the least necessary to explain so simple a matter; that our love of inequality is really the vulgarity in us, and the brutality, admiring and worshipping the splendid materiality.

Our present social organisation, however, will and must endure until our middle class is provided with some better ideal of life than it has now. Our present organisation has been an appointed stage in our growth; it has been of good use, and has enabled us to do great things. But the use is at an end, and the stage is over. Ask yourselves if you do not sometimes feel in yourselves a sense, that in spite of the strenuous efforts for good of so many excellent persons amongst us, we begin somehow to flounder and to beat the air; that we seem to be finding ourselves stopped on this line of advance and on that, and to be threatened with a sort of standstill. It is that we are trying to live on with a social organisation of which the day is over. Certainly equality will never of itself alone give us a perfect civilisation. But, with such inequality as ours, a perfect civilisation is impossible.

To that conclusion, facts, and the stream itself of this discourse, do seem, I think, to carry us irresistibly. We arrive at it because they so choose, not because we so choose. Our tendencies are all the other way. We are all of us politicians, and in one of two camps, the Liberal or the Conservative. Liberals tend to accept the middle class as it is, and to praise the nonconformists; while Conservatives tend to accept the upper class as it is, and to praise the aristocracy. And yet here we are at the conclusion, that whereas one of the great obstacles to our civilisation is, as I have often said, British nonconformity, another main obstacle to our civilisation is British aristocracy! And this while we are yet forced to recognise excellent special qualities as well as the general English energy and honesty, and a number of emergent humane individuals, in both nonconformists and aristocracy. Clearly such a conclusion can be none of our own seeking.

Then again, to remedy our inequality, there must be a change in the law of bequest, as there has been in France; and the faults and inconveniences of the present French law of bequest are obvious. It tends to overdivide property; it is unequal in operation, and can be eluded by people limiting their families; it makes the children, however ill they may behave, independent of the parent. To be sure, Mr. Mill and others have shown that a law of bequest fixing the maximum, whether of land or money, which any one individual may take by bequest or inheritance, but in other respects leaving the testator quite free, has none of the inconveniences of the French law, and is in every way preferable. But evidently these are not questions of practical politics. Just imagine Lord Hartington going down to Glasgow, and meeting his Scotch Liberals there, and saying to them: "You are ill at ease, and you are calling for change, and very justly. But the cause of your being ill at ease is not what you suppose. The cause of your being ill at ease is the profound imperfectness of your social civilisation. Your social civilisation is indeed such as I forbear to characterise. But the remedy is not disestablishment. The remedy is social equality. Let me direct your attention to a reform in the law of bequest and entail." One can hardly speak of such a thing without laughing. No, the matter is at present one for the thoughts of those who think. It is a thing to be turned over in the minds of those who, on the one hand, have the spirit of scientific inquirers, bent on seeing things as they really are; and, on the other hand, the spirit of friends of the humane life, lovers of perfection. To your thoughts I commit it. And perhaps, the more you think of it, the more you will be persuaded that Menander showed his wisdom quite as much when he said *Choose equality,* as when he assured us that *Evil communications corrupt good manners.*

Letters

EDITOR'S NOTE

FOR some time the only considerable collection of Arnold's letters—and, really, the only memorial of his personal life—was the two volumes first published in 1895 under the editorship of G. W. E. Russell. The greater number of these letters were written to members of Arnold's own family, and while it is true that Arnold could speak quite freely to his mother of certain near concerns and that on occasion he could open his heart in weariness and despair to his favorite sister Jane (he calls her "K"; she became Mrs. W. E. Forster), yet men do limit the confidences which they address to their families. Then too, these letters largely date from Arnold's later years, from a time when his character and career were formed; most men at this period of their lives do not write intimately of themselves and we ought not expect them to do so. And then we can scarcely help entertaining the belief that the letters of Russell's two volumes were selected and edited in the interests of reticence, and this belief was in some sense confirmed when in 1932 the Oxford University Press published Dr. Howard Foster Lowry's admirable edition of *The Letters of Matthew Arnold to Arthur Hugh Clough*. To many modern readers these letters were a revelation, for they showed an Arnold who was grainier, livelier, more irritably passionate than the twentieth century had supposed, an Arnold who could be ribald and headlong and willful. If we compare the two collections in their entirety, there can be no doubt that Dr. Lowry's is far superior in interest to Russell's; nevertheless the Russell collection contains many letters which are very interesting indeed, richly suggestive of Arnold's life situation, or amusing, or deeply pathetic; and it is these which I have tried to select.

I have kept separate and placed first the letters to Clough because they make in themselves a coherent story of friendship and of the literary life as it becomes the spiritual life. Dr. Lowry has been more than generous in giving me permission to use his edition of these letters, for he has allowed me to reprint not only the letters themselves but also, and at my discretion, his very full explanatory notes. I have availed myself of his kindness and have drawn upon his scholarship wherever I thought a reader who was not a scholar would stand in need of help. Some of his footnotes I have omitted entirely and have renumbered the remaining notes accordingly. Wherever I have omitted part of a note, I have indicated the omission by four dots, but I have not indicated the omission of cross references. A very few footnotes I have supplied myself from Dr. Lowry's information; these are indicated by square brackets. The introductory notes in square brackets are all Dr. Lowry's. The letters which I have selected are numbered in the original text as follows: 5, 6, 7, 22, 24, 25, 32, 40, 42, 58.

TO ARTHUR HUGH CLOUGH[1]

[London]
[shortly after December 6, 1847]

My dear Clough

I sent you a beastly vile note the other day: but I was all rasped by influenza and a thousand other bodily discomforts. Upon this came all the exacerbation produced by your apostrophes to duty: and put me quite wrong: so that I did not at all do justice to the great precision and force you have attained in those inward ways. I do think however that rare as individuality is you have to be on your guard against it—you particularly:—tho: indeed I do not really know that I think so. Shakspeare says that if imagination would apprehend some joy it comprehends some bringer of that joy: and this latter operation which makes palatable the bitterest or most arbitrary original apprehension you seem to me to despise. Yet to *solve* the Universe as you try to do is as irritating as Tennyson's dawdling with its painted shell is fatiguing to me to witness: and yet I own that to *re-construct* the Universe is not a satisfactory attempt either—I keep saying, Shakspeare, Shakspeare, you are as obscure as life is:[2] yet this unsatisfactoriness goes against the poetic office in general: for this must I think certainly be its end. But have I been inside you, or Shakspeare? Never. Therefore heed me not, but come to what you can. Still my first note was cynical and beastly-vile. To compensate it, I have got you the Paris diamond edition of Beranger, like mine. Tell me when you are com-

[1] From *The Letters of Matthew Arnold to Arthur Hugh Clough.* Edited with an introductory study by Howard F. Lowry. Used by permission of Oxford University Press, Inc.

[2] This passage is interesting because it is really Arnold's own paraphrase of his sonnet on Shakespeare.

ing up hither. I think it possible Tom may have trotted into Arthur's Bosom in some of the late storms; which would have been a pity as he meant to enjoy himself in New Zealand. It is like your noble abstemiousness not to have shown him the Calf Poem: he would have worshipped like the children of Israel. Farewell.

yours most truly

M. ARNOLD

[There is a question whether the two letters that follow are separate fragments or parts of the same letter. The break in the first manuscript without a period to end the concluding sentence, and the differences in the paper and the handwriting between the two sheets suggest that they were written at different times and with different pens.

On the other hand, the first sheet, by its tearing shows that it was never part of a folder. And the numbering at the top of the second sheet, the only instance of its kind in the whole correspondence, could well imply that it goes with a first and somewhat different looking piece of paper.

For lack of positive evidence to the contrary, the letters are here printed as two fragments. They both are closely related in subject-matter, following logically the discussion of Clough's poems in the previous letters. Arnold apparently acknowledges Clough's reply to the letter of apology written about the middle of December.]

London. Tuesday.

[December 1847; or early part of 1848]

My dearest Clough

My heart warms to the kindness of your letter: it is necessity not inclination indeed that ever repels me from you.

I forget what I said to provoke your explosion about Burbidge:[1] au reste, I have formed my opinion of him, as Nelson said of Mack. One does not always remember that one of the signs of the Decadence of a literature, one of the factors of its decadent condition indeed, is this—that new authors attach themselves to the poetic expression the founders of a literature have flowered into, which may be *learned* by a sensitive person, to the neglect of an inward poetic life. The strength of the German literature consists in this—that having no national models from whence to get an idea of *style* as half the work, they were thrown upon themselves, and driven to make the fulness of the content of a work atone for deficiencies of form. Even Goethe at the end of his life has not the inversions, the taking tourmenté style we admire in the Latins, in some of the Greeks, and in the great French and English authors. And had Shakspeare and Milton lived in the atmosphere of modern feeling, had they had the multitude of new thoughts and feelings to deal with a modern has, I think it likely the style of each would have been far less *curious* and exquisite. For in a *man* style is the saying in the best way *what you have to say*. The *what you have to say* depends on your age. In the 17th century it was *a smaller harvest than now,* and sooner to be reaped: and therefore to its reaper was left time to stow it more finely and curiously. Still more was this the case in the ancient world. The poet's matter being *the hitherto experience of the world, and his own,* increases with every century. Burbidge lives quite beside the true poetical life, under a little gourd. So much for him. For me you may often hear my sinews cracking under the effort to unite matter. . . .

[Thomas Burbidge, a poet in a small way, was a friend of Clough's. In 1849 they published together a volume of their verse, *Ambarvalia,* which was to call forth Arnold's strictures.]

[London, about February 24, 1848]

A growing sense of the deficiency of the *beautiful* in your poems, and of this alone being properly *poetical* as distinguished from rhetorical, devotional or metaphysical, made me speak as I did. But your line is a line: and you have most of the promising English versewriters with you now: Festus[1] for instance. Still, problem as the production of the beautiful remains still to me, I will die protesting against the world that the other is false and JARRING.

No—I doubt your being an artist: but have you read Novalis? He certainly is not one either: but in the way of direct communication, insight, and report, his tendency has often reminded me of yours, though tenderer and less systematic than you. And there are the sciences: in which I think the passion for truth, not special curiosities about birds and beasts, makes the great professor.—

—Later news than any of the papers have, is, that the National Guard have declared against a Republic, and were on the brink of a collision with the people when the express came away.

—I trust in God that feudal industrial class as the French call it, you worship, will be clean trodden under. Have you seen Michelet's characterisation (superb) of your brothers[2]—"La dure inintelligence des Anglo-Americains."—Tell Edward I shall be ready to take flight with him the very moment the French land, and have engaged a Hansom to convey us both from the possible scene of carnage.

—yours

M. A.

---

[1] *Festus*, the twenty-thousand line poem by Philip James Bailey, appeared in 1839, and had a wide sale. It is based upon the Faust legend.

[2] Clough's early boyhood had been spent in Charleston, South Carolina.

Baths of Leuk. Sept^{ber} 29, 1848.

My dear Clough

A woodfire is burning in the grate and I have been
forced to drink champagne to guard against the cold
and the café noir is about to arrive, to enable me to
write a little. For I am all alone in this vast hotel: and
the weather having been furious rain for the last few
days, has tonight turned itself towards frost. Tomorrow
I repass the Gemmi and get to Thun: linger one day at
the Hotel Bellevue for the sake of the blue eyes of one
of its inmates: and then proceed by slow stages down
the Rhine to Cologne, thence to Amiens and Boulogne
and England.

The day before yesterday I passed the Simplon—and
yesterday I repassed it. The day before yesterday I lay
at Domo d'Ossola and yesterday morning the old man
within me and the guide were strong for proceeding to
the Lago Maggiore: but no, I said, first impressions must
not be trifled with: I have but 3 days and they, according to the public voice will be days of rain: coupons
court à notre voyage—revenons en Suisse—So I ordered
a char yesterday morning to remount the Simplon. It
rained still . . . here and there was something un-
blurred by rain. Précisions: I have noticed in Italy—the
chestnuts: the vines: the courtliness and kingliness of
buildings and people as opposed to this land of a republican peasantry: and one or two things more: but
d——n description. My guide assures me he saw one
or two "superbes filles" in Domo d'Ossola (nothing improper): but I rose late and disheartened by the furious
rain, and saw nothing but what I saw from the carriage.
So Italy remains for a second entry. From Isella to
Simplon the road is glory to God. In these rains maps
and guides have suffered more or less: but your Keller

very little: I travel with a live guide as well as Murray:
an expensive luxury: but if he is a good Xtian and a
family man like mine, a true comfort. I gave him today
a foulard for his daughter who is learning French at
Neufchatel to qualify her first for the place of fille de
chambre in a hotel and afterwards for that of soubrette
in a private family. I love gossip and the small-wood of
humanity generally among these raw mammoth-belched
half-delightful objects the Swiss Alps. The lime stone is
terribly gingerbready: the pines terribly larchy: and
above all the grand views being ungifted with self-
controul almost invariably desinunt in piscem. And the
curse of the dirty water—the real pain it occasions to
one who looks upon water as the Mediator between the
inanimate and man is not to be described.—I have seen
clean water in parts of the lake of Geneva (w[hi]ch
whole locality is spoiled by the omnipresence there of
that furiously flaring bethiefed rushlight, the vulgar
Byron): in the Aar at the exit of the Lac de Thoune:
and in the little stream's beginnings on the Italian side
of the Simplon. I have however done very little, having
been baffled in two main wishes—the Tschingel Glacier
and the Monte Moro, by the weather. My golies, how
jealous you would have been of the first: "we fools accounted his calves meagre, and his legs to be without
honor." All I have done however is to ascend the Faul-
horn—8300 above the sea, my duck.

This people, the Swiss, are on the whole what they
should be; so I am satisfied.—L'homme sage ne cherche
point le sentiment parmi les habitans des montagnes: ils
ont quelque chose de mieux—le bonheur. That is but
indifferent French though. For their extortion, it is all
right I think—as the wise man pumpeth the fool, who is
made for to be pumped.

I have with me only Béranger and Epictetus: the

latter tho: familiar to me, yet being Greek, when tired I
am, is not much read by me: of the former I am getting
tired. Horace whom he resembles had to write only
for a circle of highly cultivated desillusionés roués, in
a sceptical age: we have the sceptical age, but a far
different and wider audience: voilà pourquoi, with all
his genius, there is something "fade" about Beranger's
Epicureanism. Perhaps you don't see the pourquoi, but
I think my love does and the paper draws to an end.
In the reste, I am glad to be tired of an author: one
link in the immense series of cognoscenda et indagenda
despatched. More particularly is this my feeling with
regard to (I hate the word) women. We know beforehand all they can teach us: yet we are obliged to learn it
directly from them. Why here is a marvellous thing. The
following is curious—

> "Say this of her:
> The day was, thou wert not: the day will be,
> Thou wilt be most unlovely: shall I chuse
> Thy little moment life of loveliness
> Betwixt blank nothing and abhorred decay
> To glue my fruitless gaze on, and to pine,
> Sooner than those twin reaches of great time,
> When thou art either nought, and so not loved,
> Or somewhat, but that most unloveable,
> That preface and post-scribe thee?"—[1]

Farewell, my love, to meet I hope at Oxford: not alas in
Heaven: tho: thus much I cannot but think: that our
spirits retain their conquests: that from the height they
succeed in raising themselves to, they can never fall.
Tho: this uti possedetes principle may be compatible

[1] The "curious" thing is unquestionably Arnold's own. I was interested to find it scribbled, with one minor change, in the back of
his copy of Burnett's *Life of Matthew Hale*. The thought is very
close to that of the last part of the "Horatian Echo."

with entire loss of individuality and of the power to recognize one another. Therefore, my well-known love, accept my heartiest greeting and farewell, while it is called today.

Yours,

M. ARNOLD.

[This letter has nothing in it that fixes a definite date. The handwriting suggests strongly that it is of the 1848-49 period. The edition of Keats's life and letters by Monckton Milnes appeared in 1848. See review in *The Times,* September 19, p. 3. Milnes had been communicating with Clough about this work before it was published. I assume the publication date roughly fixes the time of this letter.]

London. Monday. [after September 1848-49]
My dearest Clough

What a brute you were to tell me to read Keats' Letters. However it is over now: and reflexion resumes her power over agitation.

What harm he has done in English Poetry. As Browning is a man with a moderate gift passionately desiring movement and fulness, and obtaining but a confused multitudinousness, so Keats with a very high gift, is yet also consumed by this desire: and cannot produce the truly living and moving, as his conscience keeps telling him. They will not be patient neither understand that they must begin with an Idea of the world in order not to be prevailed over by the world's multitudinousness: or if they cannot get that, at least with isolated ideas: and all other things shall (perhaps) be added unto them.

—I recommend you to follow up these letters with the

Laocoön of Lessing: it is not quite satisfactory, and a little mare's nesty—but very searching.

—I have had that desire of fulness without respect of the means, which may become almost maniacal: but nature had placed a bar thereto not only in the conscience (as with all men) but in a great numbness in that direction. But what perplexity Keats Tennyson et id genus omne must occasion to young writers of the ὁπλίτης[1] sort: yes and those d——d Elizabethan poets generally. Those who cannot read G[ree]k sh[ou]ld read nothing but Milton and parts of Wordsworth: the state should see to it: for the failures of the σταθμοί[2] may leave them good citizens enough, as Trench: but the others go to the dogs failing or succeeding.

So much for this inspired "cheeper" as they are saying on the moon.

My own good man farewell.

M. A.

L[ansdowne] H[ouse]
Friday [early part of February 1849]

My dear Clough—

If I were to say the real truth as to your poems in general, as they impress me—it would be this—that they are not *natural*.

Many persons with far lower gifts than yours yet seem to find their natural mode of expression in poetry, and tho: the contents may not be very valuable they appeal with justice from the judgement of the mere thinker to the world's general appreciation of naturalness—i.e.— an absolute propriety—of form, as the sole *necessary* of Poetry as such: whereas the greatest wealth and depth of matter is merely a superfluity in the Poet *as such*.

[1] "heavy-armed foot soldier."
[2] "march of the day"; in plural here it means "stages along the royal road."

—Form of Conception comes by nature certainly, but is generally developed late: but this lower form, of expression, is found from the beginning amongst all born poets, even feeble thinkers, and in an unpoetical age: as Collins, Green[e] and fifty more, in England only.

The question is not of congruity between conception and expression: which when both are poetical, is the poet's highest result:—you say what you mean to say: but in such a way as to leave it doubtful whether your mode of expression is not quite arbitrarily adopted.

I often think that even a slight gift of poetical expression which in a common person might have developed itself easily and naturally, is overlaid and crushed in a profound thinker so as to be of no use to him to help him to express himself.—The trying to go into and to the bottom of an object instead of grouping *objects* is as fatal to the sensuousness of poetry as the mere painting, (for, *in Poetry,* this is not *grouping*) is to its airy and rapidly moving life.

"Not deep the Poet sees, but wide":[1]—think of this as you gaze from the Cumner Hill toward Cirencester and Cheltenham.

—You succeed best you see, in fact, in the hymn, where man, his deepest personal feelings being in play, finds poetical expression as *man* only, not as artist:—but consider whether you attain the *beautiful,* and whether your product gives PLEASURE, not excites curiosity and reflexion. Forgive me all this: but I am always prepared myself to give up the attempt, on conviction: and so, I know, are you: and I only urge you to reflect whether you are advancing. Reflect too, as I cannot but do here more and more, in spite of all the nonsense some people talk, how deeply *unpoetical* the age and all one's sur-

[1] The line is quoted from Arnold's own "Resignation." . . .

roundings are. Not unprofound, not ungrand, not un-
moving:—but *unpoetical*.

Ever yrs
M. A.

Thun. Sunday. Sept^{ber} 23 [1849]

My dear Clough

I wrote to you from this place last year. It is long since
I have communicated with you and I often think of you
among the untoward generation with whom I live and of
whom all I read testifies. With me it is curious at present: I am getting to feel more independent and un-
affectible as to all intellectual and poetical performance
the impatience at being faussé in which drove me some
time since so strongly into myself, and more snuffing
after a moral atmosphere to respire in than ever before
in my life. Marvel not that I say unto you, ye must be
born again. While I will not much talk of these things,
yet the considering of them has led me constantly to
you the only living one almost that I know of of

> The children of the second birth
> Whom the world could not tame—[1]

for my dear Tom has not sufficient besonnenheit for it to
be any *rest* to think of him any more than it is a *rest* to
think of mystics and such cattle—not that Tom is in any
sense cattle or even a mystic but he has not a "still, considerate mind." [2]

[1] From his own "Stanzas in Memory of the Author of Obermann,"
which he was then writing:
> For thou art gone away from earth,
> And place with those dost claim,
> The Children of the Second Birth,
> Whom the world could not tame; . . .

[2] Although there was always a deep and real affection between
Arnold and his brother Tom, their intellectual differences were no-

What I must tell you is that I have never yet succeeded in any one great occasion in consciously mastering myself: I can go thro: the imaginary process of mastering myself and see the whole affair as it would then stand, but at the critical point I am too apt to hoist up the mainsail to the wind and let her drive. However as I get more awake to this it will I hope mend for I find that with me a clear almost palpable intuition (damn the logical senses of the word) is necessary before I get into prayer: unlike many people who set to work at their duty self-denial etc. like furies in the dark hoping to be gradually illuminated as they persist in this course. Who also perhaps may be sheep but not of my fold, whose one natural craving is not for profound thoughts, mighty spiritual workings etc. etc. but a distinct seeing of my way as far as my own nature is concerned: which I believe to be the reason why the mathematics were ever foolishness to me.[1]

—I am here in a curious and not altogether comfortable state: however tomorrow I carry my aching head to the mountains and to my cousin the Blümlis Alp.

torious in the family. One can hardly imagine the author of *Literature and Dogma* ever following Newman into the Catholic Church, although the power and attraction of that church he saw strongly. The depth of religious feeling this letter reveals is genuine, but of another sort. It belongs to him who wrote sometime later: "I think, as Goethe thought, that the right thing is . . . to keep pushing on one's posts into the darkness, and to establish no post that is not perfectly in light and firm."

[1] Recalling one of their early tutors, Tom Arnold wrote, "Euclid he taught us also; but here the natural bent of my brother's mind showed itself. Ratiocination did not at that time charm him; and the demonstration of what he did not care to know found him languid" (*Passages in a Wandering Life*, p. 10). One of Matthew Arnold's worst hardships as inspector of schools was concocting the dull problems in arithmetic with which he would have to sweep down upon a class. His note-books are inked with entries from six great literatures; and scribbled over them in pencil are sums and problems painfully stored up against an evil hour.

Fast, fast by my window   4½
The rushing winds go
Towards the ice-cumber'd gorges,
The vast fields of snow.
There the torrents drive upward
Their rock strangled hum,
And the avalanche thunders
The hoarse torrent dumb.
I come, O ye mountains—
Ye torrents, I come.[1]

Yes, I come, but in three or four days I shall be back here, and then I must try how soon I can ferociously turn towards England.

My dearest Clough these are damned times—everything is against one—the height to which knowledge is come, the spread of luxury, our physical enervation, the absence of great *natures*, the unavoidable contact with millions of small ones, newspapers, cities, light profligate friends, moral desperadoes like Carlyle, our own selves, and the sickening consciousness of our difficulties: but for God's sake let us neither be fanatics nor yet chalf blown by the wind but let us be ὡς ο φρονιμος διαρισειεν and not as any one else διαρισειεν.[2] When I come to town I tell you beforehand I will have a real effort at managing myself as to newspapers and the talk of the

---

[1] This passage is incorporated into "Parting," the second poem of the "Switzerland" group [see p. 107].

[2] In his Greek phrases, Arnold is trying to suggest Aristotle's *Nicomachæan Ethics*, Book II, vi, 15: Ἔστιν ἄρα ἡ ἀρετὴ ἕξις προαιρετική, ἐν μεσότητι οὖσα τῇ πρὸς ἡμᾶς, ὡρισμένη λόγῳ καὶ ὡς ἂν ὁ φρόνιμος ὁρίσειε. "Virtue, therefore, is a habit, accompanied with deliberate preference, in the relative mean, defined by reason, and as the prudent man would define it." Arnold means, therefore: "but let us be 'as the prudent man would define,' and not as any one else would 'define.'"

day. Why the devil do I read about L^d. Grey's sending convicts to the Cape, and excite myself thereby, when I can thereby produce no possible good. But public opinion consists in a multitude of such excitements. Thou fool—that which is morally worthless remains so, and undesired by Heaven, whatever results flow from it. And which of the units which has felt the excitement caused by reading of Lord Grey's conduct has been made one iota a better man thereby, or can honestly call his excitement a *moral* feeling.

You will not I know forget me. You cannot answer this letter for I know not how I come home.

Yours faithfully,
M. A.

[Clough was now more than ever eager to get some employment whereby he might marry. On June 17, 1852, he wrote Emerson asking if there were any chance of "earning bread and water, if not bread and flesh, anywhere between the Atlantic and the Mississippi, by teaching Latin, Greek, or English." When Emerson encouraged him, Clough decided to go, sailing from Liverpool for Boston on the *Canada*, October 30 of the same year. This is a ship letter. . . .]

Milford B.[oys] S.[chool] Oct^ber 28 [18]52
My dear Clough

I have got your note: Shairp I hope will come to me for a day, and then he can bring the money.

As to that article.[1] I am anxious to say that so long as I am prosperous, nothing would please me more than for you to make use of me, at any time, as if I were your brother.

And now what shall I say? First as to the poems.

[1] [By "that article" Arnold means money.]

Write me from America concerning them, but do not read them in the hurry of this week. Keep them, as the Solitary did his Bible, for the silent deep.[1]

More and more I feel that the difference between a mature and a youthful age of the world compels the poetry of the former to use great plainness of speech as compared with that of the latter: and that Keats and Shelley were on a false track when they set themselves to reproduce the exuberance of expression, the charm, the richness of images, and the felicity, of the Elizabethan poets. Yet critics cannot get to learn this, because the Elizabethan poets are our greatest, and our canons of poetry are founded on their works. They still think that the object of poetry is to produce exquisite bits and images—such as Shelley's *clouds shepherded by the slow unwilling wind,* and Keats passim: whereas modern poetry can only subsist by its *contents*: by becoming a complete magister vitae as the poetry of the ancients did: by including, as theirs did, religion with poetry, instead of existing as poetry only, and leaving religious wants to be supplied by the Christian religion, as a power existing independent of the poetical power. But the language, style and general proceedings of a poetry which has such an immense task to perform, must be very plain direct and severe: and it must not lose itself in parts and episodes and ornamental work, but must press forwards to the whole.

A new sheet will cut short my discourse: however, let us, as far as we can, continue to exchange our thoughts, as with all our differences we agree more with one another than with the rest of the world, I think. What do you say to a bi-monthly mail?

It was perhaps as well that the Rugby meeting was a Bacchic rout, for after all on those occasions there is

[1] See Wordsworth, *The Excursion*, III, 861-4.

nothing to be said.—God bless you wherever you go—with all my scepticism I can still say that. I shall go over and see Miss Smith from Hampton in December, and perhaps take Fanny Lucy with me. I am not very well or in very good spirits, but I subsist:—what a difference there is between reading in poetry and morals of the loss of youth, and experiencing it! And after all there is so much to be done, if one could but do it.—Goodbye again and again, my dear Clough—

your ever affectionate
M. ARNOLD.

[Long before his departure for America, Clough had formed the notion that Arnold was growing somewhat cold toward him. From Boston he has apparently written a frank account of his feeling. This letter is Arnold's answer. It fully explains itself and the situation out of which Clough's impression arose.]

Edgbaston. February 12th, 1853

My dear Clough

I received your letter ten days since—just as I was leaving London—but I have since that time had too much to do to attempt answering it, or indeed to attempt any thing else that needed any thing of "recueillement." I do not like to put off writing any longer, but to say the truth I do not feel in the vein to write even now, nor do I feel certain that I can write as I should wish. I am past thirty, and three parts iced over—and my pen, it seems to me is even stiffer and more cramped than my feeling.

But I will write historically, as I can write naturally in no other way. I did not really think you had been hurt at anything I did or left undone while we were together in town: that is, I did not think any impression of hurt you

might have had for a moment, had lasted. I remember
your being annoyed once or twice, and that I was vexed
with myself: but at that time I was absorbed in my speculations and plans and agitations respecting Fanny
Lucy, and was as egoistic and anti-social as possible.
People in the condition in which I then was always are.
I thought I had said this and explained one or two
pieces of apparent carelessness in this way: and that
you had quite understood it. So entirely indeed am I
convinced that being in love generally unfits a man for
the society of his friends, that I remember often smiling
to myself at my own selfishness in half compelling you
several times to meet me in the last few months before
you left England, and thinking that it was only I who
could make such unreasonable demands or find pleasure
in meeting and being with a person, for the mere sake
of meeting and being with them, without regarding
whether they would be absent and preoccupied or not.
I never, while we were both in London, had any feeling
towards you but one of attachment and affection: if
I did not enter into much explanation when you expressed annoyance, it was really because I thought the
mention of my circumstances accounted for all and
more than all that had annoyed you. I remember Walrond telling me you were vexed one day that on a return to town after a longish absence I let him stop in
Gordon Square without me: I was then expecting to find
a letter—or something of that sort—it all seems trivial
now, but it was enough at the time to be the cause of
heedlessness selfishness and heartlessness—in all directions but one—without number. It ought not to have
been so perhaps—but it was so—and I quite thought
you had understood that it was so.

There was one time indeed—shortly after you had
published the Bothie—that I felt a strong disposition to

intellectual seclusion, and to the barring out all influences that I felt troubled without advancing me: but I soon found that it was needless to secure myself against a danger from which my own weakness even more than my strength—my coldness and want of intellectual robustness—sufficiently exempted me—and besides your company and mode of being always had a charm and a salutary effect for me, and I could not have foregone these on a mere theory of intellectual dietetics.

In short, my dear Clough, I cannot say more than that I really have clung to you in spirit more than to any other man—and have never been seriously estranged from you at any time—for the estrangement I have just spoken of was merely a contemplated one and it never took place: I remember saying something about it to you at the time—and your answer, which struck me for the genuineness and faith it exhibited as compared with my own—not want of faith exactly—but invincible languor of spirit, and fickleness and insincerity even in the gravest matters. All this is dreary work—and I cannot go on with it now: but tomorrow night I will try again—for I have one or two things more to say. Goodnight now.—

Sunday, 6 P.M.
I will not look at what I wrote last night—one endeavours to write deliberately out what is in one's mind, without any veils of flippancy levity metaphor or demimot, and one succeeds only in putting upon the paper a string of dreary dead sentences that correspond to nothing in one's inmost heart or mind, and only represent themselves. It was your own fault partly for forcing me to it. I will not go on with it: only remember, *pray* remember that I am and always shall be, whatever I do

or say, powerfully attracted towards you, and vitally
connected with you: this I am sure of: the period of my
development (God forgive me the d——d expression!)
coincides with that of my friendship with you so exactly
that I am for ever linked with you by intellectual bonds
—the strongest of all: more than you are with me: for
your development was really over before you knew me,
and you had properly speaking come to your *assiette* for
life. You ask me in what I think or have thought you
going wrong: in this: that you would never take your
assiette as something determined final and unchangeable
for you and proceed to work away on the basis of that:
but were always poking and patching and cobbling at
the assiette itself—could never finally, as it seemed—
"resolve to be thyself" [1]—but were looking for this and
that experience, and doubting whether you ought not
to adopt this or that mode of being of persons qui ne
vous valaient pas because it might possibly be nearer the
truth than your own: you had no reason for thinking it
was, but it *might* be—and so you would try to adapt
yourself to it. You have I am convinced lost infinite time
in this way: it is what I call your morbid conscientiousness—you are the most conscientious man I ever knew:
but on some lines morbidly so, and it spoils your action.

There—but now we will have done with this: we are
each very near to the other—write and tell me that you
feel this: as to my behaviour in London I have told you
the simple truth: it is I fear too simple than that (excuse
the idiom) you with your raffinements should believe
and appreciate it.

There is a power of truth in your letter and in what

[1] *Resolve to be thyself*; and know that he,
Who finds himself, loses his misery!
is the conclusion of Arnold's *Self-Dependence* [see p. 120].

you say about America and this country: yes—*congestion of the brain* is what we suffer from—I always feel it and say it—and cry for air like my own Empedocles. But this letter shall be what it is. I have a number of things I want to talk to you about—they shall wait till I have heard again from you. Pardon me, but we *will* exchange intellectual aperçus—we shall both be the better for it. Only let us pray all the time—God keep us both from aridity! *Arid*—that is what the times are.— Write soon and tell me you are well—I was sure you were not well. God bless you. Flu sends her kindest remembrances. ever yours

M. A.

We called the other day at Combe Hurst[1] but found vacuas sedes et inania arcana. But we shall meet in town. What does Emerson say to my poems—or is he gone crazy as Miss Martineau says. But this is probably one of her d——d lies.[2] Once more fare*well*, in every sense.

---

[1] The home of Miss Blanche Smith [Clough's fiancée.].

[2] Harriet Martineau (1802-76), the writer, was a neighbour of the Arnold family at Fox How. Arnold's opinions of her are varied from time to time. He was glad enough to have a chance to "speak of her with respect" in his "Haworth Churchyard": "I cannot but praise a person whose one effort seems to have been to deal perfectly honestly with herself, although for the speculations into which this effort has led her I have not the slightest sympathy." In 1869, he recalls, "Miss Martineau has always been a good friend to me." But in 1877 he informs an acquaintance, "I had forgotten the poem about Charlotte Brontë and Harriet Martineau, but I will look it up. I think there were things not bad in it, but I do not want to overpraise a personage so antipathetic to me as H. M. My first impression of her is, in spite of her undeniable talent, energy, and merit— what an unpleasant life and unpleasant nature!"

TO MRS. ARTHUR HUGH CLOUGH [1]

2, Chester Square [London]
Dec^ber 2nd, 1861

My dear Mrs. Clough

This will not reach you till your return home, for, from some delay, I received Miss Clough's letter only a day or two ago, and was afraid, if I wrote to Florence, that my letter might not get there until after you had left it.

Slight as your acquaintance with me has been, and much as circumstances have in the last few years separated me from him, you will not doubt that few can have received such a shock in hearing of his death as I did. Probably you hardly know how very intimate we once were; our friendship was, from my age at the time when it was closest, more important to me than it was to him, and no one will ever again be to me what he was. I shall always think—although I am not sure that he would have thought this himself,—that no one ever appreciated him—no one of his men friends, that is—so thoroughly as I did; with no one of them was the conviction of his truly great and profound qualities so entirely independent of any visible success in life which he might achieve. I had accustomed myself to think that no success of this kind, at all worthy of his great powers, would he now achieve—and, after all, this would only have been common to him with one or two other men the influence of whose works is most precious to me—but now his early death seems to have reopened all the possibilities for him, and I think of him again as my father thought of him and as we all thought of him in the extraordinary opening of his youth, as not only able but

[1] Lourcy, op. cit.

likely to have been as profoundly impressive and interesting to the world as he was to us. Alas, who else of us had freshness and depth enough left for his friends to have been able to feel thus of him, dying at 42?

You will let me know when I may come and see you: believe me that I shall always have the strongest interest in you and in his children.

Most sincerely yours
Matthew Arnold

I shall be most anxious to know what is done about the unpublished things he has left. I could not yet write about him for the newspapers: but I said a few words in a lecture at Oxford on Saturday.

TO HIS SISTER JANE[1]

Lansdowne House, Tuesday [May 1848].

My own dearest K.

I am writing here (6¼ P.M.), till Lord L. comes back from the House; but if he does not arrive by 6½ he begged me to go. I have not opened my great table to write to you, but I have set my paper on an account of Scinde, and hold this on my knee. It is beginning to grow dusk, but it has been a sweet day, with sun and a playing wind and a softly broken sky. The crocusses, which have long starred the lawn in front of the windows, growing like daisies out of the turf, have nearly vanished—but the lilacs that border the court are thrusting their leaves out to make amends.

> "The clouds of sickness cast no stain upon
> Her vallies and blue hills:

[1] This and all the following letters are taken from *Letters of Matthew Arnold, 1848-1888*, collected and arranged by George W. Russell (New York: Macmillan, 1900).

> The Doubt, that assails all things, never won
> This faithful impulse of unfaithful wills."

It gets more and more gray and indistinct, and the musical clock behind me is quickening its pace in preparation for its half-hour peal—I shut this up and go.

TO HIS MOTHER

London, May 7 [1848].

My dearest Mamma

Though I believe the balance of correspondence is in my favour at present, I will write to you a few lines instead of sitting idle till Lord L. summons me. I have just finished a German book I brought with me here: a mixture of poems and travelling journal by Heinrich Heine, the most famous of the young German literary set. He has a good deal of power, though more trick; however, he has thoroughly disgusted me. The Byronism of a German, of a man trying to be gloomy, cynical, impassioned, moqueur, etc., all à la fois, with their honest bonhommistic language and total want of experience of the kind that Lord Byron, an English peer with access everywhere, possessed, is the most ridiculous thing in the world. Goethe wisely said the Germans could not have a national comedy because they had no social life; he meant the social life of highly civilised corrupt communities like Athens, Paris, or London; and for the same reason they cannot have a Byronic-poetry. I see the French call this Heine a "Voltaire au clair de lune," which is very happy.

I have been returning to Goethe's Life, and think higher of him than ever. His thorough sincerity—writing about nothing that he had not experienced—is in modern literature almost unrivalled. Wordsworth resembles him in this respect; but the difference between the range of their two experiences is immense, and not in the Englishman's favour. I have also been again reading Las Cases, and been penetrated with admiration for Napoleon, though his southern recklessness of assertion is sometimes staggering. But the astonishing clearness and width of his views on almost all subjects, and when he comes to practice his energy and precision in arranging details, never struck me so much as now. His contest with England is in the highest degree tragic. The inability of the English of that time in any way to comprehend him, and yet their triumph over him—and the sense of this contrast in his own mind—there lies the point of the tragedy. The number of ideas in his head which "were not dreamed of in their philosophy," on government and the *future of Europe,* and yet their crushing him, really *with the best intentions,* but a total ignorance of him—what a subject! But it is too near at hand to be treated, I am afraid. To one who knew the English, his fate must have seemed inevitable; and therefore his plans must have seemed imperfect; but what foreigner could divine the union of invincibility and speculative dulness in England?

Ever yours,

M. A.

TO HIS SISTER JANE

London, January 25, 1851.

My dearest K.

Since you do not write to me I must be the first. So long as I was at Fox How I heard your letters, but in town, unless we write to each other, I shall almost lose sight of you, which must not be.

How strong the tendency is, though, as characters take their bent, and lives their separate course, to submit oneself gradually to the silent influence that attaches us more and more to those whose characters are like ours, and whose lives are running the same way with our own, and that detaches us from everything besides, as if we could only acquire any solidity of shape and power of acting by narrowing and narrowing our sphere, and diminishing the number of affections and interests which continually distract us while young, and hold us unfixed and without energy to mark our place in the world; which we thus succeed in marking only by making it a very confined and joyless one. The aimless and unsettled, but also open and liberal state of our youth we *must* perhaps all leave and take refuge in our morality and character; but with most of us it is a melancholy passage from which we emerge shorn of so many beams that we are almost tempted to quarrel with the law of nature which imposes it on us.

I feel this in my own case, and in no respect more strongly than in my relations to all of you. I am by nature so very different from you, the worldly element enters so much more largely into my composition, that as I become *formed* there seems to grow a gulf between us, which tends to widen till we can hardly hold any intercourse across it. But as Thomas à Kempis recommended, frequenter tibi ipsi violentiam fac, and as some philosopher advised to consort with our enemies because by them we were most surely apprised of our faults, so I intend not to give myself the rein in following my natural tendency, but to make war against it till it ceases to isolate me from you, and leaves me with the power to discern and adopt the good which you have, and I have not.

This is a general preface to saying that I mean to write about the end of every month, as I can at the time, and I hope you, my dearest K., will do the same.

I have not now left room for more than to say I was grieved to hear of you at the water cure. Kindest regards to William.

Ever, dearest K., your most affectionate

M. A.

TO HIS WIFE

Oldham Road Lancasterian School,
Manchester, October 15, 1851.

I think I shall get interested in the schools after a little time; their effects on the children are so immense, and their future effects in civilising the next generation of the lower classes, who, as things are going, will have most of the political power of the country in their hands, may be so important. It is really a fine sight in Manchester to see the anxiety felt about them, and the time and money the heads of their cotton-manufacturing population are willing to give to them. In arithmetic, geography, and history the excellence of the schools I have seen is quite wonderful, and almost all the children have an equal amount of information; it is not confined, as in schools of the richer classes, to the one or two cleverest boys. We shall certainly have a good deal of moving about; but we both like that well enough, and we can always look forward to retiring to Italy on £200 a year. I intend seriously to see what I can do in such a case in the literary way that might increase our income. But for the next three or four years I think we shall both like it well enough.

Sudbury, Tuesday, 6 P.M. [1853].

I got here a little before two, had a sandwich, and then went to the school. I don't know why, but I certainly find inspecting peculiarly oppressive just now; but I must tackle to, as it would not do to let this feeling get too strong. All this afternoon I have been haunted by a vision of living with you at Berne, on a diplomatic appointment, and how different that would be from this incessant grind in schools; but I could laugh at myself, too, for the way in which I went on drawing out our life in my mind. After five I took a short walk, got back to dinner at a quarter to six, dined, and started the pupil teachers, and am just writing this to catch the post. Direct to me, P. O., Ipswich.

TO HIS MOTHER

London, Wednesday [May 1855].

As to the poem in Fraser, I hope K. sent you a letter I wrote to her on that subject, in which I told her that I knew absolutely nothing of Harriet Martineau's works nor debated matters—had not even seen them, that I know of, nor do I ever mention her creed with the slightest applause, but only her boldness in avowing it. The want of independence of mind, the shutting their eyes and professing to believe what they do not, the running blindly together in herds, for fear of some obscure danger and horror if they go alone, is so eminently a vice of the English, I think, of the last hundred years—has led them, and is leading them into such scrapes and bewilderment, that I cannot but praise a person whose one effort seems to have been to deal perfectly honestly and sincerely with herself, although for the speculations into which this effort has led her I have not the slightest sympathy. I shall never be found to identify myself with her and her people, but neither shall I join, nor have I the least community of feeling with, her attackers. And I think a perfectly impartial person may say all in her praise that I have said.[1]

M. A.

TO HIS SISTER JANE

Martigny, August 6, 1858.

My dearest K.

Here is a pouring wet day, to give me an opportunity of paying my long-standing debt to you. I have never thanked you for sending me Kingsley's remarks on my poems, which you rightly judged I should like to hear. They reached me when I was worried with an accumulation of all sorts of business, and I kept putting off and putting off writing to thank you for them; at last, when I had fairly made up my mind to write, I heard you were gone to Holland. What on earth did you go to do there?

Kingsley's remarks were very *handsome,* especially coming from a brother in the craft. I should like to send you a letter which I had from Froude about Merope, just at the same time that your record of Kingsley's criticisms reached me. If I can find it when I return to England I will send it to you. It was to beg me to discontinue the Merope line, but entered into very interesting developments, as the French say, in doing so. Indeed, if the opinion of the general public about my poems were the same as that of the leading literary men, I should make more money by them than I do. But, more than this, I should gain the stimulus necessary to enable me to produce my best—all that I have in me, whatever that may be,—to produce which is no light matter with an existence so hampered as mine is. People do not understand what a temptation there is, if you

[1] In "Haworth Churchyard." (*G. W. E. Russell's note.*)

cannot bear anything not *very good*, to transfer your operations to a region where form is everything. Perfection of a certain kind may there be attained, or at least approached, without knocking yourself to pieces, but to attain or approach perfection in the region of thought and feeling, and to unite this with perfection of form, demands not merely an effort and a labour, but an actual tearing of oneself to pieces, which one does not readily consent to (although one is sometimes forced to it) unless one can devote one's whole life to poetry. Wordsworth could give his whole life to it, Shelley and Byron both could, and were besides driven by their demon to do so. Tennyson, a far inferior natural power to either of the three, can; but of the moderns Goethe is the only one, I think, of those who have had an existence assujettie, who has thrown himself with a great result into poetry. And even he felt what I say, for he could, no doubt, have done more, *poetically*, had he been freer; but it is not so light a matter, when you have other grave claims on your powers, to submit voluntarily to the exhaustion of the best poetical production in a time like this. Goethe speaks somewhere of the endless matters on which he had employed himself, and says that with the labour he had given to them he might have produced half a dozen more good tragedies; but to produce these, he says, I must have been sehr zerrissen. It is only in the best poetical epochs (such as the Elizabethan) that you can descend into yourself and produce the best of your thought and feeling naturally, and without an overwhelming and in some degree morbid effort; for then all the people around you are more or less doing the same thing. It is natural, it is the bent of the time to do it; its being the bent of the time, indeed, is what makes the time a *poetical* one. But enough of this.

It is nearly a fortnight since Walrond and I started,

and in ten days I hope to be at home again. They will have kept you more or less informed from Fox How, I daresay, of our travelling proceedings. We have hitherto done just what we intended: Geneva, Bex and the Diablerets, Zermatt, and the Grand St. Bernard. The fates are against us today for the first time, for at this moment we ought to be on the Col de Balme, and we are here kept to the house by good heavy Westmorland rain. It will be curious if I again miss Chamouni, which I have missed so often; but we are resolutely staying over the day here, not to miss it if the weather will give us a chance. If it rains tomorrow, however, we shall go on to Geneva. I am glad to have been here again, and Walrond has admirable qualities for a travelling companion; but I have found two things: one, that I am not sure but I have begun to feel with papa about the time lost of mere mountain and lake hunting (though every one should see the Alps once to know what they are), and to desire to bestow my travelling solely on eventful countries and cities; the other that I miss Flu as a travelling companion more than I could have believed possible, and will certainly never travel again for *mere pleasure* without her. To go to Rome or Greece would not be travelling for mere pleasure, I consider; but to Rome I would not easily go without her. I shall conclude with one anecdote of dear old Budge. Just before we left Dover, the Judge, who was staying with us, took us all in a carriage to St. Radigund's Abbey, a beautiful ruin near Dover. We entered the precinct, and there were the beautiful ruins, and capitals and fragments of arches lying about the grass, as you see them at such places. We all said how beautiful, etc., etc.; but Budge, surveying the litter with the greatest contempt, exclaimed at last these words—"What a nasty, *beastly* place this is!" You have no notion what a comic effect the child and his speech produced.

God bless you, my dear old K. Suppose you write me a line to reach me at the *Hotel Windsor, Paris,* on or before this day week; if not that, write to me soon at Fox How. My love to William.

Your ever affectionate

M. A.

TO HIS MOTHER

Folkestone, August 15, 1861.

. . . Budge very nearly wheedled me into bringing him all by himself, but, as I told him, I should have found him, when I came back from my schools, making mud-pies in the harbour with all the dirty little ragamuffins of Folkestone. I meet here and at Dover a vast number of people I know; that, too, is a sign one *is* getting old. I came here at twenty-four without meeting a soul I knew, and that was the best time, too. Tell Fan I must finish off for the present my critical writings between this and forty, and give the next ten years earnestly to poetry. It is my last chance. It is not a bad ten years of one's life for poetry if one resolutely uses it, but it is a time in which, if one does not use it, one dries up and becomes prosaic altogether. Thackeray is here with his daughters. I see a good deal of him. He is much interested in me just now because of the Saturday Review's attack, he also being an object of that newspaper's dislike. *Their* calling *anybody conceited* is, he says, the most amusing piece of audacity he ever knew. Lady de Rothschild [1] is at Dover; the Balguys too,

[1] *Née* Louisa Montefiore; wife of Sir Anthony de Rothschild. (*G. W. E. Russell's* note.) [See page 650.]

and a number of other people I know, and whom I stumbled on one after the other. Next week I sleep on Monday at Faversham, at a friend's house, on Tuesday at Tunbridge Wells, at another friend's; then I have a day or two to wind up my affairs in London, and on Friday I think we shall all come to you, if that day suits you—the 23rd.

October 29, 1863.

My dearest Mother

I have today inspected a school, and read some things here which I wanted to read. I am having a delightful spell of reading without writing before I begin my Joubert article. I must begin that in a week's time, however. I have left at home an interesting letter (in German) which I have had lately from a German in England on the subject of my Heine article; Fan will translate it to you, unless all the money paid to Eber was quite thrown away. Papa is mentioned in it. I was in poor force and low spirits for the first ten days after I returned; now I am all right again, and hope to have a busy year. It is very animating to think that one at last has a chance of *getting at* the English public. Such a public as it is, and such a work as one wants to do with it! Partly nature, partly time and study have also by this time taught me thoroughly the precious truth that everything turns upon one's exercising the power of *persuasion, of charm;* that without this all fury, energy, reasoning power, acquirement, are thrown away and only render their owner more miserable. Even in one's ridicule one must preserve a sweetness and good-humour. I had a pleasant visit at Aston Clinton, but the life of these country houses (as I now neither shoot nor hunt, both of which I should have done to excess had I not been so torn away from them) wearies me more and more, with its endless talking and radical want of occupation. But Lady de Rothschild I am very fond of, and she has given me the prettiest little gold pencil in the world. I made acquaintance with two more Rothschilds, Clementine de Rothschild of Frankfort, and Alice de Rothschild of Vienna—the first exquisitely beautiful, the second with a most striking character. What women these Jewesses are! with a *force* which seems to triple that of the women of our Western and Northern races.

Your ever affectionate

M. A.

The Athenæum, London,
December 24, 1863.

My dearest Mother

Business first. I am delighted with the wooden platter and bread knife, for which articles I have long had a fancy, the platter too I like all the better for not having an inscription, only a border of corn ears. Dear Rowland's book has not yet come. Thank her for it all the same, and tell her I will write to her when I receive it. And thank dear K. for her letter, and dear Fan for her note, and receive all my thanks for your own, my dearest mother.

While writing these last words I have heard the startling news of the sudden death of Thackeray. He was found dead in his bed this morning. If you have not seen it in the newspaper before you read this, you will all be greatly startled and shocked, as I am. I have heard no particulars. I cannot say that I thoroughly liked him, though we were on friendly terms; and he is not, to my thinking, a great writer. Still, this sudden cessation of an existence so lately before one's eyes, so vigorous and full of life, and so considerable a power in the country, is very sobering, if, indeed, after the shock of a fort-night ago, one still needs sobering. Today I am forty-one, the middle of life, in any case, and for me, perhaps, much more than the middle. I have ripened, and am ripening so slowly that I should be glad of as much time as possible, yet I can feel, I rejoice to say, an inward spring which seems more and more to gain strength, and to promise to resist outward shocks, if they must come, however rough. But of this inward spring one must not talk, for it does not like being talked about, and threatens to depart if one will not leave it in mystery.

Budge's letter which you sent us was a great pleasure to me, far the longest of his I have seen, and the naïveté of his reason for its length was charming. We are very well pleased with him, and with Matt Buckland's ac-count of him; and that school does not harden his heart is a great peril surmounted. He cried bitterly at his grandpapa's funeral, and Matt Buckland writes me word that he could not sleep the night after. This was not his grief perhaps so much as his imagination, which had been strongly moved by the service, the hearse, the plumes, the coffin; but in a healthy boy like Budge one is pleased that the imagination too should be alive. Flu tells me that his account to her of the funeral was quite beautiful, and most affecting. He was a great favourite of his grandpapa's, and what one likes is that he should now feel this with tenderness, and not, with the hideous levity of our nature, instantly forget it.

We dine to-morrow in Eaton Place, where I have dined on so many Christmas Days. The first Christmas Day after our marriage we spent at Fox How; every one since that I have passed with the Judge.

My love to all at Fox How on Christmas Day.

Your ever most affectionate

M. A.

Aston Clinton Park, Tring,
January 28, 1864.

My dearest Mother

It will take at least this sheet added to the one I
wrote the other night to make my proper weekly letter.
I have so often refused to come here, alleging my inspecting duties, that I thought this time I would come,
and I am glad I have. I inspected yesterday in Bethnal
Green, got home to a late luncheon, and a little before
five left home again in a hansom for Euston Square.
When I got to Tring I found the court outside the station full of carriages bound for Aston Clinton and no
means of getting a fly; but Count d'Apponyi, the Aus-
trian Ambassador, took me with him. We got here
just after the Bishop, at half-past seven, just in time to
dress, and a little after eight we dined. The house was
quite full last night. Count d'Apponyi, the Bishop of
Oxford, the Disraelis, Sir Edward and Lady Filmer,
Lord John Hay, the young Lord Huntly, the young
Nathaniel Rothschild, Mr. Dawson Damer, Mr. Raikes
Currie, Mr. John Abel Smith, Archdeacon Bickersteth,
and one or two other clergy were the party at dinner,
almost all of them staying in the house. I took Constance
Rothschild in to dinner, and was placed between her
and Mrs. Disraeli; on Mrs. Disraeli's other side was the
Bishop of Oxford. I thought the Bishop a little subdued
and guarded, though he talked incessantly. Mrs. Disraeli
is not much to my taste, though she is a clever woman,
and told me some amusing stories. Dizzy sat opposite,
looking moody, black, and silent, but his head and face,
when you see him near and for some time, are very
striking. After the ladies went he was called over by the
Bishop to take Mrs. Disraeli's vacant place. After a
little talk to the Bishop he turned to me and asked me

very politely if this was my first visit to Buckingham-
shire, how I liked the country, etc.; then he said he
thought he had seen me somewhere, and I said Lord
Houghton had introduced me to him eight or nine years
ago at a literary dinner among a crowd of other people.
"Ah yes, I remember," he said, and then he went on:
"At that time I had a great respect for the name you
bore, but you yourself were little known. Now you are
well known. You have made a reputation, but you will
go further yet. You have a great future before you, and
you deserve it." I bowed profoundly, and said something
about his having given up literature. "Yes," he said,
"one does not settle these things for oneself, and politics
and literature both are very attractive; still, in the one
one's work lasts, and in the other it doesn't." He
went on to say that he had given up literature because
he was not one of those people who can do two things
at once, but that he admired most the men like Cicero,
who could. Then we talked of Cicero, Bolingbroke, and
Burke. Later in the evening, in the drawing-room, we
talked again. I mentioned William Forster's name,
telling him my connexion with him, and he spoke most
highly of him and of his prospects, saying, just as I
always say, how his culture and ideas distinguished him
from the mob of Radicals. He spoke strongly of the
harm he and Stansfeld and such men suffered in letting
themselves be "appropriated," as he called it, by Palmerston, with whom they really had not the least agreement. Of Bright's powers as a speaker he spoke very
highly, but thought his cultivation defective and his
powers of mind not much; for Cobden's powers of mind
he professed the highest admiration. "He was born a
Statesman," he said, "and his reasoning is always like
a Statesman's, and striking." He ended by asking if I
lived in London, and begging me to come and see him.

I daresay this will not go beyond my leaving a card, but at all events what I have already seen of him is very interesting. I daresay the chief of what he said about me myself was said in consequence of Lady de Rothschild, for whom he has a great admiration, having told him she had a high opinion of me; but it is only from politicians who have themselves felt the spell of literature that one gets these charming speeches. Imagine Palmerston or Lord Granville making them; or again, Lowe or Cardwell. The Disraelis went this morning. Of the Bishop and his sermon I must tell you in my next. I had hardly any talk with him. He too is now gone, but there is a large party tonight again; early tomorrow morning I return to London. My love to Fan.

Your ever affectionate

M. A.

TO HIS SISTER JANE

January 4, 1868.

My dearest K.

Poor little Basil died this afternoon, a few minutes before one o'clock. I sat up with him till four this morning, looking over my papers, that Flu and Mrs. Tuffin might get some sleep, and at the end of every second paper I went to him, stroked his poor twitching hand and kissed his soft warm cheek, and though he never slept he seemed easy, and hardly moaned at all. This morning, about six, after I had gone to bed, he became more restless; about eleven he had another convulsion; from that time he sank. Flu, Mrs. Tuffin, and I were all round him as his breathing gradually ceased, then the spasm of death passed over his face; after that the eyes closed, all the features relaxed, and now as he lies with his hands folded, and a white camellia Georgina Wightman brought him lying on his breast, he is the sweetest and most beautiful sight possible.

And so this loss comes to me just after my forty-fifth birthday, with so much other "suffering in the flesh,"—the departure of youth, cares of many kinds, an almost painful anxiety about public matters,—to remind me that *the time past of our life may suffice us!*—words which have haunted me for the last year or two, and that we "should no longer live the rest of our time in the flesh to the lusts of men, but to the will of God." However different the interpretation we put on much of the facts and history of Christianity, we may unite in the bond of this call, which is true for all of us, and for me, above all, how full of meaning and warning.

Ever, my dearest K., your most affectionate

M. A.

TO LADY DE ROTHSCHILD

Harrow, November 30, 1868.

My dear Lady de Rothschild

I was sure you would be touched by the death of my poor little boy, to whom you have so often showed kindness. I imagine every one here thought he could not get through the winter, though they could give no special name to his complaint except to call it, with the doctors, "failure in vital power" following upon the slight shock given to him by his fall from a pony in Westmorland. But his mother and I had watched him through so many ebbings and flowings of his scanty stock of vital power that we had always hopes for him, and till I went into his room last Monday morning an hour before the end I did not really think he would die. The astonishing self-control which he had acquired in suffering was never shown more than in the last words he said to me, when his breath grew shorter and shorter, and from this, and the grieved face of the doctor as he entered the room, he knew, I am sure, that the end was come; and he turned to me, and—his mamma, who was always with him, and whom he adored, having gone into the next room for a moment—he whispered to me, in his poor labouring voice, "Don't let mamma come in." At his age that seems to me heroic self-control; and it was this patience and fortitude in him, joined to his great fragility and his exquisite turn for music, which interested so many people in him, and which brings us a sort of comfort now in all the kind and tender things that are said to us of him. But to Mrs. Arnold the loss of the occupation of her life—for so the care of him really was—will for some time to come be terrible.

Many thanks and kindest regards to Sir Anthony and your daughters, and believe me always, dear Lady de Rothschild, sincerely yours,

MATTHEW ARNOLD.

TO HIS MOTHER

Harrow, December 24,[1] 1868.

My dearest Mother

I have been doing papers till the last moment, but I must put them aside to write to you and thank you and Edward, Susy and Fan for your letters and good wishes. Now I am within one year of papa's age when he ended his life; and how much he seems to have put into it, and to what ripeness of character he had attained! Everything has seemed to come together to make this year the beginning of a new time to me: the gradual settle-

---

[1] His birthday. (G. W. E. Russell's note.)

ment of my own thought, little Basil's death, and then my dear, dear Tommy's. And Tommy's death in particular was associated with several awakening and epoch-marking things. The chapter for the day of his death was that great chapter, the 1st of Isaiah; the first Sunday after his death was Advent Sunday, with its glorious collect, and in the Epistle the passage[1] which converted St. Augustine. All these things point to a new beginning, yet it may well be that I am near my end, as papa was at my age, but without papa's ripeness, and that there will be little time to carry far the new beginning. But that is all the more reason for carrying it as far as one can, and as earnestly as one can, while one lives.

The weather is wonderful—so mild, and such storms of wind and rain. Yesterday it was beautiful, and in the evening it seemed going to freeze, but to-day is stormier than ever, with the barometer lower than I have ever seen it—down to 28.10. How low has yours been? Our three or four hundred feet above the sea always makes our barometer readings lower than those of most people, but I shall be curious to hear what yours are. Tell Edward I divide my papers (second year Grammar) through every day, taking in Christmas Day, Saturdays, and Sundays. In this way I bring them down to twenty-five a day, which I can do without the strain on my head and eyes which forty a day, or—as I used often to make it in old times by delaying at first—eighty or ninety a day would be. I am up at six, and work at the preface to my Culture and Anarchy Essays, work again at this, and read, between breakfast and luncheon. Play racquets and walk between luncheon and four; from four to seven look over my twenty-five papers, and then after dinner write my letters and read a little. My dream

[1] Romans 13:13. (*G. W. E. Russell's note.*)

is some day to take Rydal Lodge for three weeks at Christmas, and to come down to the old Christmas country of my early years once again. My love all round.

I am always, my dearest mother, your most affectionate

M. A.

Harrow, December 4, 1870.

My dearest Mother

Tomorrow I dine with the Literary Club and sleep in Waterloo Place, as Mr. George Smith kindly puts at my disposal his rooms over Smith and Elder's. The rooms are delightful, and the situation most convenient—at the bottom of Waterloo Place, and quite close to the Athenæum. My interview with the Income Tax Commissioners at Edgware the other day, who had assessed my profits at £1000 a year, on the plea that I was a most distinguished literary man, my works were mentioned everywhere and must have a wide circulation, would have amused you. "You see before you, gentlemen," I said, "what you have often heard of, *an unpopular author*." It was great fun, though going to Edgware was a bore. The assessment was finally cut down to £200 a year, and I told them I should have to write more articles to prevent my being a loser by submitting to even that assessment, upon which the Chairman politely said, "Then the public will have reason to be much obliged to us." I wrote to dear old Tom on his birthday, and I saw K. on Friday. The week after next I hope to dine with her. My love to Fan. I hope Rowland's cold is better.

Your ever most affectionate

M. A.

Harrow, February 18, 1872.

My dearest Mother

I do not know that I shall write much, but I must tell you what pleasure it gave us to have your letter and Fan's this morning. When I wrote last Sunday there was not even a trace of illness to be seen in Budge, though I hear now he had been much knocked up by running a mile very fast the day before; but he was entirely himself all Saturday and Sunday, and indeed particularly gay. When I came home on Monday evening Flu told me that Budge had gone to bed with a bad cold and toothache. I saw him three times that evening and found him very sick and miserable. I concluded he had a bilious attack, such as I often used to have when a boy, and that he had a cold with it. So it went on, headache taking the place of toothache, and I cannot say I was the least uneasy. But, when Victorine called to us on Friday morning and I found him light-headed wandering about the room, I was very uneasy; he knew me, however, and said, "ah! papa!" but I went off at once for Dr. Tonge, the doctor who lives nearest. When I came back he seemed dropping into a heavy doze. I had to go very early to London, and he seemed in the same heavy doze when I left him. The rest you have heard; when I saw him again at 2 P.M. all the doctors were there, besides Hutton, who had come down with me; and it was clear there was no hope. He never showed the least spark of consciousness, till his breathing ceased with a sort of deep sigh. How fond you were of him, and how I like to recall this! He looks beautiful, and my main feeling about him is, I am glad to say, what I have put in one of my poems, the "Fragment of a Dejaneira." [1] William Forster has just come. Walter has written a very feeling and kind letter. Love to Fan and to Rowland.

Your ever affectionate

M. A.

TO JOHN MORLEY, M.P.

Fox How, Ambleside, August 10, 1883.

My dear Morley

To my surprise, I have just had a letter from your great leader offering me a pension of £250 "as a public recognition of service to the poetry and literature of England." To my further surprise, those about me think I ought to accept it, and I am told that —— thinks the same. I have written to him, but have not yet got his answer.

I write to you, that, whatever his answer may be, I may be fortified by your opinion also, for I have an instinct which tells me that in matters of feeling you and I are apt to be in sympathy.

It seems to me that, the fund available for literary pensions being small, and literary men being numerous and needy, it would not look well if a man drawing already from the public purse an income of nearly £1000 a year took £250 a year more from the small public fund available for pensions to letters, science, and art.

---

[1] But him, on whom, in the prime
Of life, with vigour undimm'd,
With unspent mind, and a soul
Unworn, undebased, undecay'd,
Mournfully grating, the gates
Of the city of death have for ever closed—
Him, I count *him* well-starr'd. (*G. W. E. Russell's note.*)

[See p. 107.]

I feel this so strongly that I should have at once re-fused, if it were not for those about me. Of course, I should be glad of an addition of £250, and if I find everybody thinking that my scruple is a vain one, I shall at least consider the matter very carefully, though really I do not feel at present as if I *could* accept the offer.

Let me have a line here as soon as possible, as I must send an answer to your Pericles.

Ever affectionately yours,

MATTHEW ARNOLD.

Fox How, August 16, 1883.

My dear Morley

I relied on a dissuader from you; when you failed me I wrote to Lingen, but he too advised me to look at the daughters of the horse-leech, and govern myself accord-ingly. I have done so. I have written to your great leader, who has this morning read my acceptance. . . .

Lingen tells me, however, that Professor Owen has for some forty years held a pension along with his offi-cial salary as a Superintendent at the British Museum. This is a real precedent, but I still think there will be murmurs, and that I shall lose something of the "bene-volentia civium," of which I have not too large a stock to begin with. "Magnum telum ad res gerendas existi-mare oportet benevolentiam civium," says Cicero, and how true it is, and what a pedant is Mommsen, who runs this charming personage down!

Ever yours affectionately,

M. A.

TO HIS SISTER JANE

Hartford, Connecticut,
November 15, 1883.

My dearest K.

I am hard driven, but there is no one at home who so often comes into my mind, I think, over here as your dear, dear self, and I must scratch you a line at any rate. We are here with a nice old couple called Clark. We met their daughter in New York. This is said to be, for its size, the richest town in New England, and Mr. Clark was the richest merchant in it. He has retired from business, is seventy-seven years old, and occupies himself in good works. It is exactly like the wealthy Quaker families I have stayed in when inspecting in England; only Mr. Clark is much more free in his religious ideas than they were, and the whole family have, compared with our middle class at home, that buoyancy, enjoyment, and freedom from constraint which are everywhere in America, and which confirmed me in all I have said about the way in which the aristocratic class acts as an *incubus* upon our middle class at home. This universal enjoyment and good nature are what strike one most here. On the other hand, some of the best English qualities are clean gone; the love of quiet and dislike of a crowd is gone out of the American entirely. They say Washington had it, as our Lord Althorp had it, and as so many of us have it still in England; but I have seen no American yet, except Norton at Cambridge, who does not seem to desire constant publicity and to be on the go all the day long. It is very fatiguing. I thank God it only confirms me in the desire to "hide my life," as the Greek philosopher recommended, as much as possible. They are very kind, inconceivably kind, and one must have been accustomed to the total want of real popular interest among the English at home in anything but politics to feel the full difference of things here. The newspapers report all one's goings about and sayings—the Commodore at Newport sends to put his launch at my disposal, Blaine telegraphs to the New York press his regrets that he cannot come up on purpose to hear me lecture, General Grant thanks the Tribune for reporting me so fully—and so on. It is perfectly astounding, but there is not much real depth in it all. I have liked best a visit to Dartmouth College in New Hampshire. You remember how papa talked of New Hampshire and said he would emigrate there if he emigrated to the States at all. I stayed with a professor, a widower, in a small way of life, and saw what this small way was—it is better than with us. Still, what we call a gentleman has a tremendous pull in the old world —or at any rate in England—over the gentleman here. What it is in the towns, to have practically no cabs and to be obliged to use trams, you cannot imagine. It is as if in our Stockwell expedition we had had to get there by the tram, with two or three changes, and a walk at each end, and the chance of bad weather. And every one has to use these who has not a carriage. It is the best country for a Rothschild I ever knew, his superior pull is so manifest. We stayed with a sort of Rothschild on the Hudson—a Delano married to an Astor; but he grumbled, ungrateful man, because every one took a right of way through his grounds just as they pleased. But what made me think of you was the living power which papa's memory was still in that New Hampshire community at Dartmouth College. All through New England, however, he has had a prodigious effect, and perhaps he, like Luther, has been less pushed out by new men and new things than in the old world. Flu and

Lucy enjoy it all, I think, though they get very tired. We had an immense reception here last night—the Governor and Senator for this sterling little old State of Connecticut, and every one thence downwards. The night before last I dined and slept at Barnum's. He said my lecture[1] was "grand," and that he was determined to belong to *the remnant*; that term is going the round of the United States, and I understand what Dizzy meant when he said that I performed "a great achievement" by launching phrases. My love to William. Tell him it is curious to find how one is driven here to study the "technique" of speaking, and how one finds it may be learnt like other things. I could not half make myself heard at first, but I am improving. A Professor Churchill, said to be "the best elocutionist in the United States," came twice from Andover to Boston on purpose to try and be of use to me, because, he said, he had got more pleasure from F. Robertson, Ruskin, and me than from any other men. This will give you a good notion of their kindness. Now I must stop. We go to Boston tomorrow, then on Monday back to New York. Love to all your dear party.

Your most affectionate brother,

M. A.

---

[1] "Numbers: or the Majority and the Remnant." (G. W. E. Russell's note.)